RUNNING LINES

Jeris Jean

Copyright © 2021 Jeris Jean

All rights reserved

The characters and events portrayed in this book are fictitious. Any similarity to real persons, living or dead, is coincidental and not intended by the author.

No part of this book may be reproduced, or stored in a retrieval system, or transmitted in any form or by any means, electronic, mechanical, photocopying, recording, or otherwise, without express written permission of the publisher.

ISBN-13: 9798579722331

*For Eric, Lora, and Sara for your
unwavering support.*

CONTENTS

CHAPTER 1
CHAPTER 2
CHAPTER 3
CHAPTER 4
CHAPTER 5
CHAPTER 6
CHAPTER 7
CHAPTER 8
CHAPTER 9
CHAPTER 10
CHAPTER 11
CHAPTER 12
CHAPTER 13
CHAPTER 14
CHAPTER 15
CHAPTER 16
CHAPTER 17
EPILOGUE
8 Months Later
ACKNOWLEDGEMENTS
ABOUT THE AUTHOR
LETTER FROM JERIS

CHAPTER 1

Finn stepped out of the black limo's back seat to a frenzy of flashing cameras, a sea of evening-gown and tuxedo-clad bodies, and frantic screams as he took his first few steps out onto the red carpet. He took in a deep breath of the warm Los Angeles air and then flashed his boyish, swoon-worthy grin toward the crowd. This wasn't his first time on a red carpet. In fact, even at the age of 22, he was an old pro, having walked them for the last three years due to his success as the lead on the hit teen soap *Luna's Cove*. It was, however, his first time on the red carpet as a cast member of the biggest period drama in television history. *Frost Manor* was a worldwide phenomenon, and this premiere of its second season was a star-studded event of much larger magnitude than even Finn was used to. Silently taking in the pandemonium for a few seconds, Finn braced himself to make it through the carpet's media gauntlet and, more importantly, make a good impression on his new *Frost Manor* colleagues.

Sensing Finn's slight hesitation, his agent, Kayla Hudson, ushered him along as she whispered, "You're the hottest star on this carpet, Finny. You belong here. Just look at all the screaming teenagers here tonight. Who do you think they're here to see?" She nodded at the stands of fans behind the fences that kept spectators away from the media members lining the edges of the red carpet. She gave him a quick wink, and he smiled at her in thanks as he made his way to the first designated photography stop. He stood tall in his custom designer suit, which fit his trim frame closely. The black suit was covered with a grey velvet floral print, a nod to Finn's whimsical style while still looking elegant and displaying his runner's body to full effect. He turned his brilliant smile at the shouts of "Finn, over here," "We love you Finn!" and "Who are you wearing?" He didn't mind the attention one bit.

Falling into the rhythm of the carpet wasn't difficult, and he was soon smoothly maneuvering from photo ops to the fences to sign autographs for fans during back-ups on the carpet. One of the leads on *Frost Manor*, Lydia Mason, was directly in front of Finn on the carpet. She was arguably an even bigger star than Finn, so she stopped longer at some spots, showing off all angles of her slinky silver dress. She was full of personality, giggling, blowing kisses over her shoulder at the crowd, and charming anyone in her vicinity. Finn grinned at her antics, amused. He suspected he'd get along well with Lydia, and he looked forward to getting to know her.

About half-way down the carpet, as Finn waited for the next entertainment news anchor to finish interviewing Lydia, Kayla put a hand on his arm and said, "This next one is for Major TV, and you'll need to answer a few questions, but you'll do great. You know the drill."

She moved a few strands of his blonde hair around, no doubt ensuring his artfully tousled look was still intact. Then she was wandering off chatting with another agent, presumably, because the woman was dressed similarly to Kayla in a no-nonsense black pantsuit, distinguishing them from the starlets in organza and silk dresses. When Lydia finished her interview with the Marjor TV anchor, she passed by Finn where he was waiting for his turn. When she saw him, her eyes got big and bright, and she launched herself at him, drawing him into a tight hug. "Finn Everett! I'm so happy to meet you," she practically squealed. "We are going to be best friends. Seriously. You have no choice. I insisted that your trailer be next to mine. I am a HUGE fan of *Luna's Cove*. I *cannot* believe you are on our show." At this point she was giggling as she squeezed Finn one last time. Her own agent was dragging her away along the carpet before Finn could even respond.

Finn stepped up to the waiting Major TV anchor, whose name was Bennett Orion. Finn gave a winning grin as Bennett said, "Finn Everett, Great to see you buddy."

After a quick handshake, and a "Happy to be here" from Finn, Bennett was firing questions.

"So, Finn, how does it feel to have wrapped *Luna's Cove*? Your fans are sure sad to see the series end," Bennett said.

"It was a great run and I'm so thankful for the years I spent on *Luna's Cove*. It was an excellent experience, and now I'm ready to take on new challenges," Finn answered.

"Indeed, you are," Bennett said, smiling a little wickedly and taking a minute to look Finn over from head to toe and back up again before continuing. "You've certainly entered the big leagues by joining the cast of *Frost Manor*. This is the biggest, most popular show on television right now. Are you nervous to be the new guy on set of such a beloved show?"

Finn fidgeted just the slightest bit with his cuff link and chuckled slightly, going for good-humored, before responding, "Not nervous, exactly. I'd say I'm more excited than anything." Finn tried for his most self-assured smile. From the corner of his eye, he saw that Kayla was back now, listening to the interview and giving him a thumbs-up.

Bennett smiled back at him, but didn't seem satisfied with this response from Finn, so he dug a little deeper, "But aren't you worried about how your image as a teen heartthrob might impact viewers' ability to see you in this role? *Frost Manor* is so much different from *Luna's Cove*. Do you feel that you have something to prove joining this cast on an established drama?"

Well *fuck*. That was exactly the kind of question Finn was hoping to avoid tonight. He did not need Bennett-freaking-Orion reminding him of all the doubts he had swirling around in his brain about his ability to pull this off and be taken seriously as an actor. Kayla was now staring daggers at Bennett in Finn's peripheral vision. Finn controlled his facial expression, keeping his smile in place as he responded.

"I know I have a lot to prove by joining this fantastic cast, but I am more than up to the challenge." He even gave Bennett a flirty wink to really sell it. He was not going to let on how much self-doubt he really had about this role.

With humor sparkling in his eyes, Bennett said, "In that case, what are you most excited about with joining this show?"

Finn's brain immediately said, *the chance to be in the same vicinity as Grayson Winter*, but of course, he wasn't going to say that. Sure, he'd jumped up and down in the middle of the airport when he got the call from Kayla that he'd won the part. But that excitement wasn't solely because it meant getting to work with his biggest celebrity crush, Grayson Winter. That wasn't the whole reason.

He was happy to get a chance to try to expand his horizons and transition into more challenging roles. But he would be lying if he said he wasn't at least equally thrilled at the chance to meet Grayson. Finn also wasn't going to admit that he was staring at the cover of *ActorLife*, admiring the extremely hot Grayson Winter in all his tight v-neck sweater and glasses-wearing glory at the very moment that call came in. That was something no one needed to know.

Instead of the truth in response to Bennett's question, Finn recited the soundbite Kayla had provided while coaching him in the limo on the ride over. "I'm just excited to be part of such a fantastic cast and crew. I'm a huge fan of the show, so being here is just surreal." With another flash of his boy-next-door smile, Finn shook Bennett's hand and moved along the carpet with Kayla.

Damn, L.A. is hot. Grayson silently cursed whoever thought it was a good idea to put people in tuxedos outside in 85-degree weather to pose for photographs and answer ridiculous questions for hours. It's not that he wasn't extremely grateful for his job as an actor. He was able to do what he loved, and playing James Beechworth on *Frost Manor* was the most rewarding role he'd ever had. So, even if he was uncomfortable, sweating, and annoyed, he was able to paste a smile on his face and go through this red carpet bullshit a couple times a year. But that didn't mean he had to particularly like it.

Muttering to himself about *Goddamn contractual obligations*, Grayson strode over to the last photography stop where he was to pose with his co-star, Astrid Hayes, yet again. This was the fifth or sixth time on this carpet that he put an arm around Astrid's supermodel-thin waist and smiled for the cameras. Grayson's agent, Kayla Hudson, had threatened him with more interviews and appearances if he didn't make nice with Astrid on the carpet, appearing to love every minute of it.

Kayla was on the carpet somewhere with her other client, Finn Everett, and she made Grayson swear up and down that he could handle the interviews and photos with Astrid. He agreed because Kayla knew her shit. She was the best agent in the business, so he did what she told him. But it wasn't remotely easy. Astrid, his love interest on *Frost Manor*, was not a pleasant person. She was opportunistic, and she didn't give a shit about anyone but herself. And so, because it was good for their show's ratings, and their "personal brands," whatever the hell that meant, Astrid was cozying up to Grayson in a much-too-familiar manner. Her hand was practically on his ass as she contorted to show off even more cleavage than was already present in her low-cut, emerald green mermaid-style dress.

The illusion or speculation that they were a couple was good for the show, or so said Astrid. Kayla agreed. So here was Grayson, Astrid hanging off him shamelessly, dying to get to the end of this nightmare of a red carpet. Frankly, he thought it was complete bullshit to use gossip sites and tabloids to generate buzz for their show. It's not like the show couldn't get viewers on merit alone. But what the fuck did he know? If Kayla said romance rumors between him and Astrid equaled ratings, he had no way of refuting that. Kayla had said something like "Just let the fans imagine you two having sex so they'll watch the show." So, even if it turned his stomach to pretend they were an item, he could do it for the good of the show.

Once he was able to extricate himself from Astrid and her overly-friendly hands, he was ready to hit the last media stop on the carpet before he could go inside, get a drink, and enjoy the air conditioned theatre. Grayson had already answered some variation of the same three questions at each interview along the carpet: "Grayson, you look fabulous, as always. Who are you wearing?" and "You and Astrid look fantastic together on the carpet tonight! Is there something going on there?" and "What do you think of Finn Everett joining the cast?" Grayson was more than a little annoyed that these were the things he had to discuss all night. Every time he tried to mention his charity work or talk about his character's arc this season, the hosts lost interest and went back to asking about his suit, Astrid, or Finn Everett. And Grayson did not particularly want to discuss any of those topics.

This last interview was no different. After answering the required questions about his classic black tux, the answers to which Kayla had made him memorize over the phone this morning, the interviewer moved on to Astrid. The interviewer was a thirty-something woman with a lot of makeup on her face, and she smiled so widely it was almost scary. Grayson held back a cringe when she said, "And speaking of gorgeous creatures, you looked mighty cozy with Astrid Hayes back there. Are the dating rumors true?"

Grayson gave his standard, Kayla-approved answer, working to keep his tone light as he said, "You know I don't discuss my dating life. I like to keep my private life private." He gave a tolerant smile, and the woman seemed to accept that answer, thankfully. She moved on swiftly to the other of his least-favorite questions of the night: "So, how do you feel about Finn Everett joining the cast? I know I'm thrilled, along with his 10 million Instagram followers!" She was beaming and had a dreamy look in her eyes. *Here we go again*.

It seemed like everyone he knew was enamored with Finn Everett. Even Grayson's best friend, Felix, had about lost it when he saw the news on twitter. Felix had been in the middle of putting Grayson through grueling reps in the gym while scrolling through his phone, the bastard. Felix wasn't just Grayson's oldest, best friend and roommate, he was his personal trainer. And he loved nothing more than to torture Grayson with workouts. Without warning, Felix had squealed like a little child, nearly causing Grayson to drop the bar mid bench press. Grayson had not been amused. "What the fuck man?"

"You know that super-hot blond guy from *Luna's Cove*?"

"You are well aware I don't know anyone from that shitty teen soap," Grayson had said, letting his annoyance show in his words as he righted the bar and placed it on the rack. He had sat up on the bench and glared at Felix.

"Well you better get to know him because he's the new Wesley Crown on *Frost Manor*. And you are *so* going to introduce me once he gets to set, because he is damn tasty. Look," Felix had said, as he shoved his phone in front of Grayson.

Grayson had automatically glanced at the phone that was thrust in his face, and *holy shit*. The guy was crazy attractive. He had messy blonde hair, twisted around with some kind of product, wide blue eyes, a deep ocean color, and a few freckles along the tops of his cheeks and nose. His smile was almost shy, contrasting with the worn leather jacket open over an extremely bare, lithe chest. The photo cut off right above his abs. And then Grayson had been thinking about what his abs might look like. *Shit.*

"I told you, dude," Felix had said. "Total hottie."

Grayson had just rolled his eyes and said, "he looks barely old enough to drive." He didn't need Felix getting the satisfaction of knowing Grayson agreed with him about Finn Everett's hotness. No way.

"He's 22, jackass," Felix had said. "Now dips – we can't have you slacking on your workouts. Your status as the hottest guy on *Frost Manor* is in serious jeopardy now," Felix had teased. Grayson had been more than happy to get back to his workout, loving the sweat and ache of a good gym visit. He had decided he could worry about his new castmate later.

And, it turned out, this red carpet was that "later." Not a single interviewer had failed to mention Finn Everett, and it was getting really damn old. He didn't want to talk about Finn Everett. He didn't even want to *think* about Finn Everett. That just led to Grayson thinking about sexy blue eyes and lean muscles and *no. No*. Nothing good would come of that line of thought. It was going to be hard enough to work with him everyday on the show and maintain his standards of professionalism.

As Grayson clung to his last shred of patience for this interview, he answered the question the same way he had all night. "I trust our showrunners and casting director. But I haven't personally met Finn Everett yet, so I don't have an opinion of my own." The words sounded colder, more robotic than he'd intended.

As if on cue, his agent Kayla's familiar voice broke into the conversation, interrupting the interview. "We can fix that, Grayson! You can meet right now." She was tugging someone by the hand and then shoving him into the interview right next to Grayson. The interviewer was clapping her hands in thrilled excitement, her smile widening to an even more frightening degree. Before he knew what was happening, he was shaking hands with Finn Everett, looking right into those dark blue eyes. There were only two words Grayson's brain could manage at that moment: *Holy. Fuck.* Finn Everett was gorgeous.

Gaining his composure was difficult, but Grayson was a professional actor, so he knew how to pull himself together before anyone noticed how dumbstruck he was at the sight of Finn Everett. He hoped. The interviewer was now asking Finn how it felt to meet Grayson. Finn was staring at Grayson with the oddest expression – it was almost like...admiration? Grayson felt himself hold his breath, waiting to hear Finn's answer.

Finn turned back to the interviewer, and he

said smoothly, "It is an absolute pleasure. I can't wait to work with him. I'm sure there's a lot he can teach me." Finn smiled shyly, his eyes dipping to the carpet and then back up to glance cautiously at Grayson through his lashes. Grayson met his eyes briefly, and he felt a tingle in his belly. His lips automatically quirked up at the corners without his permission. What was happening? Why was he acting like a total fool all of a sudden? It had to be that this red carpet media circus had finally wore him down completely. He was exhausted and too warm. That would make anyone's head spin. That was totally it.

Thankfully, Kayla came to his rescue, grabbing both him and Finn by the hands and dragging them away from the interviewer, barking something about needing to get inside to take their seats. Grayson's head was dizzy as he finally stepped into the cool air conditioning of the theatre.

"Look at this, my two favorite clients making friends," Kayla said, smiling at Grayson and then Finn. "I had a hunch you'd hit it off," she added as she let go of Grayson's hand and dragged Finn further into the building.

Grayson was left in the entryway of the theatre, finally alone for the moment. He leaned against the marble wall behind him. He closed his eyes and took a deep breath to steady himself.

He was in trouble.

CHAPTER 2

The golf cart came to a stop in front of a trailer with a sign on the door that read "Wesley Crown/Finn Everett." Ethan, the PA, who was the personal assistant to both *Frost Manor*'s showrunners, pocketed the keys and hopped down from the cart, motioning for Finn to follow. "Here we are. Welcome home," Ethan said as he opened the trailer door wide and stepped aside so Finn could enter.

Before Finn could take more than two steps into his new home-away-from-home, Ethan was rattling off information a mile-a-minute. The PA was fairly young, maybe 25, Finn thought. Ethan had the whole adorable thing going for him: black hair spilling over his forehead, thick-framed glasses, tight jeans and a Minecraft t-shirt. He was also crazy organized and schedule-driven, which must be why he was the "PA Extraordinaire," as the showrunners described him in their brief meeting with Finn that morning before passing him off into Ethan's capable hands.

"Then, after hair and makeup, you have a photoshoot in full costume for some network promos," Ethan was saying. "But first, Jasper and Gwen really wanted me to bring you over to editing before anything else to watch some footage from yesterday. It'll be essential to understanding the tone of your big scene tomorrow," Ethan continued. "They seemed really adamant that getting you there was priority number one, so we should really get going."

Jasper and Gwen were the co-creators and showrunners of *Frost Manor*. They were extremely hands-on in all decision making, including casting, and Finn knew that what they said was followed to the letter by everyone on set, without question or complaint. They were basically geniuses, and Finn was forever grateful to them for taking this huge chance on him, so he was eager to show them they'd made the right decision. He had been told that Ethan is essentially their right-hand man, as well as their eyes and ears on set. So, what Ethan said, Finn would do, too. With that in mind, he followed Ethan back out to the golf cart and over to editing.

The editing department on the set of *Frost Manor* was a larger trailer, dim and stuffy, with a bank of computers along one wall. The woman working at one of the computers slipped headphones off her ears when she saw Ethan and Finn, and she had a warm smile and greeting for Ethan.

Not only was he essential on set, he was clearly beloved by all.

"Hey Thelma, could you cue up that footage from yesterday for Finn? We are kinda tight for time this morning," Ethan said, a sincere smile on his face.

"I've got it right here," she said as she slid over to the computer to her right, tapping and clicking around a bit. "Here you go, honey," Thelma said to Finn, pulling a chair close to the monitor and handing him a pair of headphones. Ethan was now absorbed by his phone, typing like the wind, so Finn simply accepted the chair and slid the headphones over his ears.

On the screen was what appeared to be a rough cut of a scene between James Beechworth and his younger sister, Elizabeth Beechworth, portrayed by Grayson Winter and Lydia Mason, respectively. Finn recognized Lydia right away, even though her period skirts and petticoats were a far cry from her slinky silver dress from the premiere. And, of course, he would know Grayson Winter anywhere.

Grayson and Lydia played brother and sister on *Frost Manor*, and this scene was a private conversation between the two siblings just after the death of their mother. The camera was alternating between closeups of Lydia and Grayson's faces as their characters comforted one another in their grief.

They discussed how difficult it would be to go on without their mother, who was dear to them both, and James Beechworth tried to reassure Elizabeth that they would make it through this together. "But it's only been a year since we lost Papa," Elizabeth whispered. "How can we possibly go on now that we've lost them both?" Her lower lip quivered on this last line.

Elizabeth then broke down into uncontrollable tears, and James's devastated face fought visibly to hold it together for his little sister. His eyes were glassy, his jaw was clenched, and he reached out to enfold Elizabeth in a tight hug before his own tears could fall. As James embraced his weeping sister and attempted to soothe her, the tone of his voice was ravaged and raw. His posture was stiff, like he had to keep each muscle tense in order not to fall apart himself. "We shall survive this," James choked out, the tears slipping down his cheeks now, too. He tightened his arms around Elizabeth, and she nuzzled her face against his chest, her small back shaking with the power of her sobs.

Blinking back his own tears, Finn jolted back to reality as Thelma hit a button, pausing the screen on that last image of James Beechworth's grief-stricken face as his sister clung to him.

Finn slid the headphones back over his head, letting them rest around his neck, feeling dazed. *Well, damn.* For a minute there, Finn had forgotten where he was. Instead of Lydia Mason and Grayson Winter, he had been watching Elizabeth and James Beechworth grieve their mother. He felt their pain and the depth of their loss, and he was completely absorbed in the scene. He turned to Thelma's amused face. "You've got your work cut out for ya, Sweetheart," was all Thelma said before slipping her own headphones back over her ears and returning to her own screen.

Ethan came over to Finn then, and said, "She's right, you know. Grayson and Lydia are really raising the bar this season. The whole crew was in tears yesterday after they filmed this scene. I heard Gwen tell Jasper that Grayson's performance is Portrayer-material this year. Anyway, you see the tone they are looking for now, right?"

Fuck. Finn was in over his head. That scene had him shook. It was only two minutes long, but he felt like he was put through the emotional ringer. And that was *rough footage*. No sad music and dramatic lighting. Just pure, raw emotion and acting chops that Finn feared he could never match.

Ethan rushed Finn off in the golf cart once again, this time to get to costume, hair, and makeup to get him ready for his in-character photoshoot for the new network promos. On the way there, Ethan slapped a thick packet of papers in Finn's lap. His script. "You better get started looking that over now. The scene tomorrow is a doozy, even by *Frost Manor* standards." *Frost Manor* was notorious for its intense, emotional scenes, Finn knew, and the scripts were at least a third longer than a regular show's, fitting in so much complicated dialogue.

Flipping through his script, Finn saw that the scene he was shooting tomorrow was an outdoor scene in which his character confronts Grayson Winter's character, and they have a heated disagreement. Turns out Finn's character's family owns the neighboring estate to the Beechworth's. And it also turns out that Finn's character has no scruples arguing with a grieving James Beechworth about property. The scene consisted of pages and pages of dialogue with very few action lines or notes. He would have to work his ass off to have this memorized in time, let alone know it well enough to pull off the emotional nuance.

"Oh, and Finn," Ethan said as he left Finn in a makeup chair a few minutes later, "no scripts on set while filming. Gwen and Jasper have a strict off-book policy when it comes to shooting days." Ethan was on his way out, apparently needed for an Astrid Hayes-related emergency elsewhere on set.

"Ethan! Wait!" Finn's voice sounded frantic. He was in panic mode now. "Can you help me run these lines after the photoshoot? I am out of my depth here, man," Finn confessed.

"No can do, sorry. I have class. But tell you

what, I'll see if I can find someone else to run lines with you. I'll send someone by your trailer around 2:00," Ethan offered, giving Finn a wave as he disappeared out of the hair and makeup trailer. What had Finn gotten himself into? He was going to make an absolute fool of himself in front of Grayson Winter tomorrow. *Fuck, fuck, fuck.*

◆ ◆ ◆

"Are you fucking kidding me, right now, Kayla?" Grayson was incredulous, and he was angry. "You're telling me that I am *banned* from the runway show you *begged* me to attend under threat of bodily harm?" He was pacing the short expanse of his trailer, dragging his fingers through his wavy, dark hair, a venomous gaze shooting out toward his agent.

"Come on now, Grayson, you didn't want to go to that thing, anyway," Kayla said, her tone much calmer than his. "You hate fashion shows and red carpet appearances. You're the one always telling me a serious actor (she used finger quotes around the term) doesn't mingle with socialites and reality tv stars. Look at this as Thomas doing you a favor."

"Right, Kayla. My ex banning me from a runway show is a favor to me. It doesn't make me look like an asshole or loser at all. Shit. I can only imagine what he's saying about me to every person in L.A. right now. What a fucking joke." Grayson stopped pacing long enough to shoot Kayla a severe look. At 6'2" with a muscled build, Grayson was an imposing figure in general, and in his cramped trailer, he towered over the petite woman. Grayson wasn't one to use his size to intimidate anyone, though, so it showed how rattled he was that he was looming over her, fists clenched at his sides. But Kayla was no pushover. She had dealt with no shortage of alpha male prima donnas in her rise to her position as power agent to the stars. So, she just stared him down right back before responding, her tone still much more even than Grayson's.

"Thomas Logan is a bratty supermodel. He is trying to save face because you dumped him. No one, and I mean *no one*, takes him seriously. But there's no reason to even fuck around with his drama; just don't go to the show," Kayla said, tone matter-of-fact, emphasizing her point with a crisp nod of her head, her sleek, angled bob not even mussed in the process. "Wash your hands of him and his bullshit." She left no room for Grayson to argue further.

Grayson knew she was right. He didn't want to go sit in the front row of a runway show, anyway, posing for cameras with a bunch of attention-hungry celebutantes. But damn if it wasn't embarrassing that Thomas was dragging Grayson through the mud after their breakup. Grayson knew going out with Thomas was a bad idea from the start. Grayson wasn't exactly vocal about his bisexuality, but he wasn't in the closet, either. So, when Thomas Logan had sauntered up to him at a record-producer friend's party one night, Grayson had been prepared for the pick-up line from the exceedingly confident model. And Thomas had cut right to the chase.

"I've been asking around about you, Grayson Winter, and rumor has it you're single," Thomas had said by way of greeting. He had been wearing a pair of black dress slacks with a crisp white shirt unbuttoned just a little farther than was decent. His cocky grin and sparkling eyes had been intoxicating, even if they had screamed "bad idea."

"If that's the case," he'd went on, "you should know I'm interested." He had winked at Grayson and then introduced himself. Grayson wasn't much of a fashion guy, but he had heard of the male supermodel who was the face (and body) of some major designer campaigns. From that first meeting, Thomas had pursued Grayson doggedly, and Grayson had been flattered by the attention. And it hadn't hurt that Thomas was...well...a supermodel.

But their relationship had fizzled fast when it became clear that Thomas was more interested in showing Grayson off at parties and practically posing for the paparazzi all around L.A. Grayson wasn't into the club scene, and Thomas had always been annoyed by Grayson's desire to stay in and focus on work, spending his evenings reading scripts and hitting the gym with Felix.

Grayson and Thomas had a knock-down, drag-out fight one night when Grayson didn't want to "make an appearance" at a party for a pop diva's birthday. Grayson had been chafing a bit at the way the press was portraying him as a partier, and his relationship with Thomas was constant tabloid fodder. While Thomas seemed to relish having their pictures plastered on every magazine and gossip blog, Grayson did not. It was not the image Grayson wanted for himself. He was trying to be a serious actor, and Thomas just didn't respect that.

Still, Thomas had seemed blindsided when Grayson had broken up with him. He had been furious, hurt, and clearly, he was still not over it. *Wonderful.* This was exactly why dating anyone in Hollywood was a bad idea. Maybe someday, Grayson would find a nice barista or lawyer or preschool teacher and settle down. But no more models or celebrities. Grayson could not afford that drama.

Kayla, for once, seemed to agree with Grayson on this point. "Look. Just let this blow over. Focus on kicking ass on this show. I've heard a lot of chatter about you as a real Portrayer contender this year, and honestly, Thomas Logan is the last person you need to be associated with in any way. We want the voters to see you for who you are – a serious actor. Not a Hollywood fuckboy like Thomas Logan." Kayla walked over and placed a hand on Grayson's arm and squeezed gently, "You are an amazing actor, Grayson. You'll get the recognition you deserve. Just hit it out of the park on these next few episodes, and you'll have your pick of quality film scripts headed your way." She knew how much Grayson wanted to break into films, and she had the confidence he could get there if he focused and brought his A-game.

Grayson really did appreciate Kayla's support. She was one hell of an agent. And it wasn't her fault his ex was a self-centered asshole. "Thanks, Kayla. Sorry I took my frustration out on you," he said, genuine apology in his expression.

"No problem, big guy. Now get your gorgeous ass in gear and kill that scene tomorrow." Kayla gave him a quick salute and exited the trailer.

The scene tomorrow. Son of a bitch. Grayson had to film about a dozen pages of dialogue with Finn Everett the next day. He had still only met the guy in passing on the red carpet at the premiere, and now he had to have an emotional confrontation scene with him on camera tomorrow. And he needed the scene to go well. He had a lot riding on this.

There was only one thing to do, and that was to run his lines until he knew them back and forth. He had to be so comfortable with all the dialogue that he could focus on connecting with the scene on an emotional level. And the only way he was going to get to that point was by running through the scene. Grayson picked up his phone and called Ethan. The PA was a real lifesaver and one of Grayson's closest friends on set.

"Hey, Grayson," Ethan said, a bit breathlessly, when he answered. "Can't really talk right now. I'm just heading into class. But what's up?"

Shit. Grayson forgot Ethan would be off set today. Ethan was finishing up his degree in communications. He was an amazing screenwriter, but his focus was on the business side of things, hoping to become a talent agent. Grayson wasn't sure why Ethan didn't pursue screenwriting. Ethan had let Grayson read some of his scripts for classes, and Grayson though he had real talent.

"Sorry, man. I forgot you had class. I was just hoping to run through the scene for tomorrow, but no worries." Grayson tried to keep the disappointment and anxiety from his voice.

"Oh! I have a solution for that!" Ethan seemed to perk up and spoke quickly, "Head over to Finn's trailer at 2:00 pm. You guys can run through the scene together. He needs to go through it, and since it is a scene between the two of you, it only makes sense to rehearse together." Ethan said this as if it were only logical and a perfect solution. Grayson couldn't think of a good reason to refuse, even if his stomach flopped around at the thought of seeking out Finn Everett to rehearse.

"Uh. Sure. Okay," Grayson said, already feeling slightly panicked at the thought. "Thanks, E. Talk to you later." Grayson hung up, checking the time on his phone. It was 1:30 pm. He had exactly half an hour to mentally prepare himself to walk over to Finn Everett's trailer and knock on the door. He would not focus on how out-of-this-world gorgeous Finn was. He wouldn't stare at those deep-sea eyes or count the adorable freckles on the bridge of his nose. He would be all business. The perfect professional. He could do that. No big deal. They were co-stars, now, after all, and Finn Everett's ridiculous cuteness was irrelevant. There was no reason for this to make Grayson nervous. Or excited to see Finn. To talk to Finn. *Damn it.* Grayson really needed to get his head on straight.

CHAPTER 3

Finn was toweling off his hair after showing off the makeup and hair product from the photo shoot. He had made two discoveries in the last fifteen minutes. First, his tiny trailer shower didn't have much hot water – like maybe three minutes' worth. Second, he needed to ask Ethan for some normal-sized towels. He struggled to dry his hair with one hand as he used his other one to keep the seemingly child-sized towel around his hips from falling off completely.

A brisk knock at his trailer door had Finn cursing and stumbling around for his clothing, which he had placed...somewhere. *Shit.* He was so disorganized. The day had been a whirlwind so far, and he wasn't sure where he'd put that stack of clean clothes. Before he could find something to throw on, the knocking resumed, this time even more insistently. "Jesus, impatient much," Finn mumbled as he gave up on finding clothes and ambled over to open the door, his grip tight around the barely-closed towel at his lean waist.

Instead of Ethan or Kayla or some other assistant, Grayson Winter stood there, eyes huge as he took in Finn's state of undress. And *oh my God*, he was even hotter than Finn remembered from the premiere. He had a foot on the bottom step leading up to the trailer door, one hand on a narrow hip and the other wrapped around a rolled-up script at his side. He was wearing a fitted pair of jeans and a plain back t-shirt that stretched across his muscled chest and shoulders.

"Oh, hey, sorry," Finn said, a bit too loudly. He was very aware of his near-nakedness, and he felt immediately flustered at having forgotten that someone was dropping by at 2:00 pm to run lines with him. "Let me just…um…I was just getting out of the shower. Hang on. Just one second. Sorry." Words were falling out of Finn's mouth in a nervous jumble as he twirled around and went back into the trailer, leaving Grayson in the open doorway.

Finn disappeared back into the tiny trailer bathroom where he quickly found some joggers to pull on his still damp body. They would have to do. Judging by Grayson's expression, he was in no mood to wait around while Finn sorted through his mess of a trailer to find an outfit. When Finn emerged from the bathroom, he motioned Grayson into the trailer.

"Maybe I got the time wrong? I thought Ethan said 2:00," Grayson said as he stepped into the space, gently closing the door behind him. On closer inspection, Grayson looked less annoyed and a bit...startled? Confused? Finn wasn't exactly sure how to read the expression on Grayson's handsome face. All Finn knew for sure at that moment was his own feeling of utter mortification. He knew he'd make a fool of himself in front of Grayson Winter his very first day on set. He just knew it. And here he was, proving himself right about that.

"No, you're right about the time. Sorry about that again. I'm still adjusting to the pace of this show, I guess," Finn apologized. "I wasn't exactly expecting *you* when Ethan said he'd find someone to run lines with me." Grayson was still hovering near the trailer door, but he met Finn's gaze then. And, *damn*. Finn felt a little breathless at a real-life Grayson Winter up close. He was perfection. Tall, broad-shouldered, chocolate wavy hair, and the most intense hazel eyes Finn had ever seen. *And that stubbled jawline. And those sexy, tortoise-shell framed glasses.* And Finn was staring. *Fuck.* He hoped he wasn't literally drooling.

"Who were you expecting?" Grayson had an amused smirk on his face.

"I...I don't know. Someone less...*you*." Finn said, gesturing at Grayson in all his Grayson-ness. *Ugh*. He knew he sounded like such an idiot.

"Well, I will be the one filming the scene with you tomorrow, so it only makes sense we run through it together, right?" Grayson said, still seeming slightly amused with Finn's flustered behavior. "Want to head out to the location to get the full feel of it?"

"Uh, sure, let's do it," Finn agreed, gaining some much-needed composure as he took a deep breath and pulled a t-shirt on over his head. He grabbed his script on his way out of the trailer behind Grayson.

Thankfully, Finn was able to act semi-normal on their walk out to the filming location, which was just a field north of where the trailers were parked. The only reason he was able to do so, however, was by not speaking or looking directly at Grayson. If he didn't speak, he couldn't make more of an ass of himself. They made their way silently across the field, film scripts in hand. They reached their designated spot and stopped, both looking around a bit, taking in their surroundings.

The location was an expanse of grass with a fence running through it. The fence was to represent the border of land between the estates of Finn's character, Wesley Crown, and Grayson's character, James Beechworth. The two men were to happen upon one another while walking their respective properties and end up in a confrontation about how to best utilize the land. The scene included lines upon lines of emotionally charged dialogue and subtle animosity between characters.

The sun was beating down on them when they took their places facing one another and opened their scripts, flipping to the beginning of the scene. Finn could feel the sweat starting to form on the small of his back, and he was way too jittery to focus on running lines. Before they could start, Finn had to clear some of the awkwardness. It was hard enough to try to run through his first scene on a new show – a drama, no less, but it was nearly impossible to do it when the air was charged with uncomfortable tension and nervous energy. Surely, Finn though, Grayson wasn't nervous in the least. He was the picture of composed professionalism. But that didn't matter. Finn was more than nervous enough for them both. He needed to say something to break the tension so they could just run the damn lines.

"Hey, uh, Grayson?"

"Yes?" Grayson looked up at him.

Finn felt Grayson's eyes on him like laser beams, so intent that Finn felt sure they could see right inside him. He summoned up as much courage as he could and continued.

"Let me just get this out of the way, and then I swear I'll be able to rehearse like a functional human." He made a strangled giggling sound before clearing his throat and continuing. "Truth is, I am a huge fan of yours, and this is totally surreal. That is why I'm acting like such a spazz right now. I'm pretty much obsessed with you. I have seen everything you've ever been in – even that episode of *Middle School Mayhem* when you were like 12." Finn continued, the words flooding out without his permission, "I think you are amazing, Grayson, and I am essentially feeling like a full-on fanboy right now."

Finn felt his face flush and his hands shake a bit. He squeezed his eyes shut in annoyance with himself for letting those embarrassing comments come out of his mouth. *God.* Why did he have to be such a freak? He was probably just turning up the awkward dial, not setting it back like he'd hoped.

Finn's eyes flew open when he felt a gentle touch on his shoulder. "Hey, Finn," Grayson said, his deep voice soothing and his eyes focused on Finn's face. He was taller than Finn by just an inch or two, so he barely had to tilt his head down to catch Finn's eyes with his. "Thank you. Really, that means a lot. And if anyone should feel embarrassed right now, it's me. I'm the one who was on *Middle School Mayhem*." Grayson smiled broadly and squeezed Finn's shoulder before dropping his arm, his gaze returning to his script. Then he said, in a surprisingly quiet voice, "I'm looking forward to working with you, too." His eyes were on the pages in his hands, not on Finn. There was something so earnest and almost shy in the way he said that last bit, it caused Finn's stomach to flutter and his cheeks to heat once again.

Finn just stared at Grayson for a second, feeling like his shoulder was on fire where Grayson had touched it. Had his dream guy, the celebrity crush of his fantasies, just said he was looking forward to working with *him* too? Finn knew Grayson was probably just being polite, but damn if it didn't feel good to hear just the same. He blinked a few times and shook his head a little, attempting to clear it and focus. Finn couldn't help but smile to himself a little, though, as he turned his attention to his own script. "Okay. Take it from the top?"

◆ ◆ ◆

"Was that too angry?" Finn asked Grayson, his face serious, brows slightly pulled in and tilted downward as he waited for Grayson's response. It was clear that Finn genuinely wanted to hear Grayson's notes on his delivery of the lines. It had been going this way for the better part of the afternoon. They'd run the lines of the scene, and then Finn would insist upon a debriefing of sorts, asking Grayson's thoughts and coming up with tweaks to his delivery. Finn was energetic and clearly a hard worker.

"Not at all. It was perfect," Grayson said, making eye contact with Finn only briefly before turning away. And, it really had been perfect. Grayson was blown away by Finn's ability to slip into character. He was off book by the third run-through, adding in mannerisms and body language to really bring the performance alive. Grayson was more than a little surprised to see Mr. Teen Soap bringing such intensity and determination to the scene. And if Grayson was being completely honest, he was pretty damn impressed, too. He'd never seen anyone adapt so naturally to a character and tackle a scene with such capability. All the tension the scene required was vibrating between them as they ran the lines. They had crazy-good chemistry. *But that is just good acting*, Grayson told himself, quickly burying the thought about whether or not they'd have good chemistry in other situations, as well.

"I think we've got it," Grayson said. He bent to pick up his long-since discarded script from the ground and shifted awkwardly from one foot to the other as he straightened up. He waited for Finn to pick up his own script so they could walk back toward their trailers. Why was Grayson suddenly so uncomfortable? They had just spent hours rehearsing together, and that had gone unbelievably smoothly – much better than Grayson could have ever anticipated. They worked together with ease, building upon one another's performances until Grayson was confident that this scene would be his best of the season so far. But as soon as they dropped character, a jittery feeling overtook Grayson's entire body. He felt suddenly awkward in his skin, which was not something that happened to him very often.

Actually, it *never* happened to him. Grayson didn't lack in the confidence department. He knew he was attractive, which was evident by the number of people – both men and women, who had made that quite clear to him. He could hold his own in just about any conversation, and he was a successful actor. What did he have to be self-conscious about? It's not like he had an out-of-control ego, or anything, though. He just wasn't one for bullshit, and false modesty was most certainly bullshit.

But there was just something about running those lines with Finn, though, that caused Grayson to feel bizarrely off-kilter. He was more aware than ever of his physical attraction to Finn. Finn was obviously hot. That fact had been hammered home when Finn answered his trailer door in nothing but a tiny towel. All that smooth skin over lean muscle had had Grayson's heart pounding double-time and had left him feeling a little dizzy. But there was also something sweet about Finn. The way he had bumbled through that admission of being a fan of Grayson's was so freaking adorable Grayson could barely stand it. Finn was such an appealing mix of cute and sexy, Grayson had difficulty focusing on the job when they first started running through the scene.

And then Finn had to go and shock the hell out of Grayson with his ability to actually act. Grayson was not expecting that. He assumed Finn was going to go all teen idol on him and have no emotional depth. Quite the opposite was the case. Grayson found himself trying to step up his own game to match Finn's delivery of the lines. He felt a strange need to prove that he was worthy of the praise Finn had given him. He wanted to live up to every expectation Finn had of him, though he didn't really want to focus on why that was the case.

Finn had memorized the scene quickly and had discarded his script so fast Grayson wasn't sure he could keep up. But he had tossed his script away, too, and they ran the lines over and over, each time fine-tuning until the scene was just right. Way more than in his rehearsals with Astrid, and maybe even more than in those with Lydia, Grayson had felt like he was being pushed to do his best work during that rehearsal with Finn. That fact added another layer to his growing fascination with his new co-star. His interest was something beyond the physical attraction he'd initially felt when meeting Finn, and that was something Grayson definitely hadn't anticipated.

Grayson and Finn made their way back to the trailers in silence, but Grayson felt reluctant for their time together to come to an end. Before he could think better of it, Grayson said, "Do you have dinner plans tonight? I got banned from this fashion show I was supposed to attend. I was dreading it, though, so I plan to celebrate being off the hook by ordering some Thai food." He tried to keep his tone as casual as possible. He was just trying to be nice to his new co-star. *You aren't asking him on a date,* Grayson told himself. No matter how much he had to work to convince himself he didn't wish it were otherwise. *Finn would not be interested in anything like that. Hell, he's probably straight.*

Finn stopped and looked at Grayson, his eyes wide with surprise. "What, like at your place?"

"Yeah. I live like eight miles from here, and there's a great Thai place that delivers. Felix and I order from there once a week, at least."

Finn studied him then, curiosity in his eyes, "And, Felix is your...?"

"Roomate!" Grayson replied a little too quickly. "He's my roommate," he said more calmly this time. "And my best friend since we were like 9. And my trainer," he explained. "He'll be there, too. At the house, I mean," he added lamely, as if that would convince Finn to accept the invite.

Finn's mouth twitched up at the corners. *God, he has a nice smile*, Grayson thought. *All white teeth and pink lips that are just the right fullness. No. No, no, no. Quit looking at his mouth, for fuck's sake.*

"So, we'd have a chaperone, then," Finn said in a teasing tone. He raised a dark blonde eyebrow, his smile turning sly. "In that case, it should be safe for me to go to your place." Finn's eyes lingered on Grayson's for a minute before he turned his face downward and looked at his feet, almost like he was embarrassed for making the chaperone comment.

Yep. He is so damn adorable.

After a few seconds, in a much less flirty voice, Finn said, "Seriously, though, that sounds cool."

"Cool," Grayson echoed. "I'll text you the address. I'm done here after a quick meeting, so I'm thinking around 7." He turned to go then, but Finn called him back.

"Don't you want my number? You know, so you can text me the address?"

"Oh, yeah. Guess I'll need that," Grayson said, grabbing his phone from his pocket. He pushed his glasses up the bridge of his nose before he clicked around a bit and then passed the phone to Finn.

Finn entered his contact information and gave the phone back to Grayson. "There you go." Their hands brushed then, and tingles spread up Grayson's fingers and through his entire arm. *Jesus.* What was going on here? Why was he having this reaction to a 22-year-old teen soap actor that he barely knew? This was bad. So very bad.

"So...I'll see you later, then," Finn said, flashing one more of those adorable grins before turning and heading toward his trailer.

"See you later," Grayson called after him, waving awkwardly at Finn's back.

As Grayson headed toward his trailer, he couldn't hold back his own grin. Finn was coming over later. To his house. He felt a bit lightheaded at the thought. *This is NOT a date, dumbass. It is not a date.*

"Making friends, I see." Grayson turned his head toward the voice and groaned to himself.

"Hello, Astrid."

"You didn't waste any time cozying up to Finn Everett, did you?" Astrid Hayes strode over to where Grayson stood a few feet from his trailer's door. She was dressed in full costume, likely having just come from shooting a scene, a cigarette dangling from one hand. "Don't get me wrong, I don't blame you. Not one bit." Her gaze drifted in the direction Finn had gone.

"It's called being welcoming to the new guy," Grayson said coldly. "Believe it or not, it can be helpful to get along with the people you have to work with every day."

Astrid's smile was sickly-sweet. "Well, he's totally yummy. You shouldn't have blown your chance with me when you had it," she said, invading Grayson's space and placing her non-cigarette-holding hand on his chest. She patted his chest a few times as she continued, "because with him around, you are *so* old news." She took a long drag of her cigarette and blew the smoke in Grayson's direction. Grayson rolled his eyes and stepped back from her.

She narrowed her eyes at Grayson, her look spiteful. "I bet Finn will know a good thing when he sees it." Then, as she turned and slipped back toward her own trailer, she said, "Nighty-night, Grayson," her voice an exaggerated singsong.

CHAPTER 4

"And then you'll go to the riding lesson after you meet with the dialect coach." Ethan had rattled off the multitude of tasks crowding Finn's schedule that day in rapid succession. "But you can't wear that," Ethan said, pointing at Finn's track pants, faded Arcade Fire t-shirt and Jordans. "They'll want you in full hunting costume to get accustomed to it on horseback."

"On what, now?" Finn couldn't have heard him right.

"On horseback. What did you think I meant by riding lesson? You shoot a hunting scene Friday." Ethan was quickly growing exasperated, though he did his best to hide it. It actually amazed Finn how calm Ethan was most of the time, especially since he seemed to single-handedly manage all the show's cast members and their insane schedules on set.

"I was under the impression that's what the stunt crew was for. My agent told me that I wouldn't do my own riding," Finn said, more confused than defiant.

Ethan chuckled. "Sounds like something Kayla Hudson would say." He shook his head, amused. "Kayla also told Jasper and Gwen that you were an accomplished equestrian, and riding would be, and I quote, 'absolutely no problem' for you. The riding lesson today was just supposed to get you used to wearing the period costume and familiarize you with the horse." Ethan chuckled again, head still shaking, "This should be good." Ethan said this with good humor, but that didn't stop Finn from rapidly starting to panic.

"I can't ride a horse! I grew up in L.A. and I worked on a teen soap. My biggest 'stunt work' was playing beer pong and occasionally kicking around a soccer ball." Finn's eyes were wild, and he grabbed Ethan by both arms. "You gotta help me, man. What am I going to do?"

Ethan looked him in the eye, his tone soothing, "You'll catch on quick, don't worry. You're an athletic dude. Maybe we can grab Lydia to work with you a little more after the lesson. She and Grayson both ride for fun. I think she used to compete at some point," Ethan said. "Though her shooting schedule is pretty packed today," he continued as he scrolled through something on his phone.

Just then, Finn's own phone beeped with an incoming text. Immediately, a big, stupid grin covered his face, and his heart thumped at the hope that it was Grayson. Ever since the Thai food night, when he'd gone to Grayson's house, they'd texted back and forth semi-regularly. It had started with a simple text early the morning after they'd hung out.

Grayson: *Sorry about Felix. I knew he was a fan of yours, but I didn't think he'd go full on creeper on you.*

Finn: *No need to apologize. I had fun. Felix seems really nice, and I didn't mind signing the autograph. Although I could have done without his rundown of his Top 10 Luna's Cove Episodes. That was a little intense. Laughing emoji.*

Grayson: *Oh God, I forgot that he asked you for your autograph. Sorry. Probably scared you off hanging out at our place ever again.*

Finn: *Not scared off. Winky-face emoji.*

Finn really had enjoyed hanging out at Grayson's that night, and he thought Felix was fun. It was a little strange that Grayson's freakishly-fit, personal trainer-to-the-stars roommate was such a big fan of *Luna's Cove*, though. Finn was used to his fans being more...high school aged. And often more female. But, he had been flattered.

The Thai food was awesome, and he had had a blast talking with Grayson about his acting career and getting the inside scoop on everything about *Frost Manor*, from the best place to find coffee on set to knowing to avoid doing anything Ethan said would take "just a quick minute." That was sure to be an undesirable task Ethan had been charged with, and he was not above trying to enlist the actors to help him out.

Apparently, Grayson was really into history, and the house was crowded with bookshelves full of biographies of the founding fathers, and there were vintage maps framed on many of the walls. Finn asked him about it, and Grayson spoke for long stretches about why it was important to understand the people and their motivations, not just the events that took place in the past. He'd said that the people were the real history. Grayson's eyes lit up when he spoke about the idealism and bravery of various historical figures, from Alexander Hamilton to Martin Luther King, Jr. Finn was enthralled, mainly because he was getting a peek at how Grayson's brain worked.

They'd discussed their favorite movies and tv shows, Grayson swearing that the best movie ever made was *Saving Private Ryan* and Finn expressing his undying love for *Schitt's Creek*. They had laughed and talked until past midnight, and Finn left feeling a little light-headed from happiness.

That happiness faded slightly when Finn reminded himself that it hadn't been a date. Of course it hadn't. There had been just a moment when Finn had this silly hope that when Grayson had asked him about his dinner plans that night, he was asking him *out*-out. But that hadn't been the case at all. It had been more of a casual hang between co-workers, at best. At worst, it was Grayson setting him up with his fanboy roommate Felix.

Finn hadn't missed the eager curiosity in Felix's eyes when he had bluntly asked Finn, "So what's your deal, anyway? I follow you on Insta, and I've never seen you post about a girlfriend...or anything. Don't tell me you're single."

"Totally single. Kinda hard to make time for a boyfriend," Finn had said, shrugging. He knew he was giving away a lot more than usual with the "boyfriend" clarification, but he really wanted Grayson to have that information, so Felix would have to be trusted with it, too. Finn had made sure to look at Grayson then and smile, wanting it to be clear that his interest was not in Felix. Grayson hadn't met his eye contact, and that had been discouraging.

But then the texting had started, and Finn had felt a tiny flicker of hope that Grayson might be interested, after all. After that initial exchange about Felix, Finn and Grayson had continued to text off and on for the last week. Finn often initiated the conversations by asking something about the shooting schedule or where to find something on set. But Grayson always responded and continued to chat beyond the basic answers to the questions. Up until this morning, however, Grayson had only initiated the texting once, and that was that first time. So, Finn couldn't help but feel a little giddy at the prospect of Grayson reaching out to him first today.

Finn looked at his phone. The text was from Grayson.

Grayson: *Running lines with Astrid this morning. Is it wrong to kill oneself on set? I don't remember seeing anything prohibiting that in the contract.*

Finn laughed out loud and quickly typed a response.

Finn: *She's not that bad, is she?*

Grayson: *Worse than you could imagine. And I get to propose marriage to her all morning...with a kiss. She is the last person I want to make out with right now. #smokerbreath*

The thought of Grayson kissing Astrid, or anyone for that matter, made Finn ridiculously jealous. And when Finn was jealous, he was also apparently reckless.

Finn: *So... who is the first person?*

Grayson: *What?*

Finn: *If Astrid is the last person you want to kiss right now, who is the first?*

When Grayson didn't respond, Finn cursed himself for asking the stupid question. Why couldn't he leave well-enough alone? He had to go and ruin the little progress he'd felt at Grayson initiating the texting today by being too flirty. *Damn it.* Finn had made it weird and now Grayson was probably spooked. He waited another few minutes before typing out, *Wish me luck. I'm off to learn to ride a horse, apparently. If anyone is dying on set today, it's going to be me.*

It turned out that Finn did take to riding quickly. The horses were beautiful, and he made the most of his brief lesson with the riding instructor, mounting the horse fluidly and learning how to control the movement of the horse with the reigns. They trotted along a small corral at the far east side of the set, Finn loving the feel of the sun on his face and the gentle sway of the horse's steps. His horse, Sherlock, was a seasoned pro, docile and responsive to the slightest tug of the reigns or cluck of the tongue from Finn. Too soon, the instructor had to go, leaving Ethan to help Finn return Sherlock to the animal handler.

Before they were out of the corral, Lydia Mason jogged over. "Got your text, E. Still need someone to help with riding?" Her smile was warm and friendly as she greeted Ethan and Finn. Lydia was a petite girl, maybe 5'3" with curly dark hair and big brown eyes. She was in costume, complete with petticoats and corset, but riding boots peeked out from her heap of skirts.

"That'd be great, Lyd, thank you," Ethan

said, already handing off Sherlock's lead to her, Finn still in the saddle. "Apparently Gwen and Jasper need me to wrangle Astrid. Some sort of emergency...again." Ethan and Lydia exchanged knowing looks, Lydia's full of sympathy.

"You go. I've got this," Lydia said, smiling up at Finn as Ethan jogged away, face glued to his phone as he left.

Soon, Lydia had saddled and mounted Watson, a beautiful dappled horse with just as serene a temperament as Sherlock. "Okay, ready to really ride?" she asked Finn, her eyes sparkling. She and Watson exited the corral in the direction of an open field.

"Lead the way," Finn said, him and Sherlock trotting right behind her.

Lydia tapped Watson's flanks with her boot heels, clicked her tongue, and she was off, brown curls streaming behind her from beneath her riding helmet. She shouted over her shoulder, "Keep up, Everett!"

Finn grinned and tapped Sherlock's flanks, laughing as they galloped after Lydia.

◆ ◆ ◆

Grayson reread the text from Finn for the hundredth time that day. *If Astrid is the last person you want to kiss right now, who is the first?*

When Grayson first read that text, he had

felt his cheeks go bright red, and he nearly choked on his swig of bottled water. *Holy shit.* While Grayson had certainly picked up on some flirty energy from Finn the night he'd come over, this was the bluntest he'd been about it. Grayson had wanted to flirt back, saying something coy like, *wouldn't you like to know*, but he just wasn't that kind of guy. He didn't do playful.

There was something about Finn's easy smile and open conversation that made Grayson wish he could be more carefree, though. The night they'd ordered in the Thai food, Grayson had found himself laughing a lot. Part of it was his amusement at Felix's fawning over Finn, but mostly it had just been Finn. He had a self-deprecating humor and dry wit that Grayson found ridiculously appealing. That night had been one of the best Grayson had had in a long time. Finn had continued to surprise him with his intelligence, curiosity, and overall positive energy. There was much more to Finn than Grayson had expected, and the more he found out about him, the more he liked him.

They'd kept up casual contact via text since, and Grayson found himself far too eager for the next chime of his phone, keeping it glued to his hand as much as possible. He'd even broken down and texted Finn first today. He really needed to chill. *Don't get all obsessed over Finn Everett.* He was *so* not that guy.

Even as Grayson tried to tell himself that, he found himself taking the long way back from the interior manor house set, skirting past the corral on his way back to his trailer. Finn was probably already done with his riding lesson, and Grayson didn't need to act like some ridiculous stalker anyway, but he couldn't help but feel a pang of disappointment to see the corral empty of any horses or riders.

Just when Grayson was about to give up on this little detour and go back to his trailer, he heard laughter coming from the field beyond the corral. The rich laughs mingled with the sound of hoofbeats as two horses trotted over a nearby hill. It was Lydia and Finn, grinning as they bantered happily, faces flushed from the ride in the warm midday sun. The horses, Watson and Sherlock, slowed to a clop as they approached the corral. Grayson made his way over to the corral as well, and he stood leaning against the fence as Lydia and Finn reached him. The three of them exchanged friendly greetings, both riders dismounting and petting the horses gently as they made small talk.

"Are you going to ride?" Lydia asked Grayson, a curious look on her face. She knew he didn't randomly take the horses for rides in the middle of the day, and Grayson avoided meeting her eyes.

"No, I was just taking a walk. Needed some fresh air after filming that proposal scene all morning."

"I see." Lydia smiled, her eyes darting quickly between Grayson and Finn. "In that case, I'm going to get these boys some carrots and bring them over to the handler. I bet they are thirsty, too," she said as she took Sherlock's lead from Finn, Watson's in her other hand. "Thanks for the race, Finn. See ya, Grayson." Lydia gave them both one last grin before walking away with the horses.

That left Grayson alone with Finn, and Grayson was very, very aware of the way his body was reacting to that situation. He was conscious of his breathing speeding up along with his heartbeat. He could also feel heat prickling through his chest and neck as he looked over at Finn. *Holy hell*, Finn was a sight. His hair was all disheveled from the ride, blonde locks flopping over his forehead haphazardly. His cheeks were pink, his eyes bright. And *damn*, did he look good in his snug beige breeches and tall black riding boots. The fitted waistcoat and jacket were cut to perfectly hug his shoulders and slim waist. Grayson had never once considered their hunting costumes as anything other than a pain in the ass to wear while filming, but he was starting to appreciate them in a whole new light.

"Walk with me?" Grayson asked, not able to take his eyes off Finn and hoping the walking would distract him from staring.

Finn nodded, his smile bright when he met Grayson's eyes for the briefest moment. "Sure."

As they made their way toward the trailers, walking at a leisurely pace, Grayson couldn't help but sneak glances at Finn. The way he looked striding along in his costume was giving Grayson all kinds of crazy thoughts. *What would it feel like to unbutton that jacket and slip it off Finn's shoulders? What would his skin feel like under that prim waistcoat and shirt? How would the muscles of those thighs feel under my palms? Wrapped around me?* That line of thinking sent a jolt straight to Grayson's groin, so he cleared his throat and forced himself to pull his eyes away from Finn.

Worried that all of his embarrassing thoughts would somehow be visible on his face if he didn't start talking, Grayson asked Finn about the riding lesson. From there, they continued in easy conversation about their mornings. Finn shared how much he enjoyed his first experience with horses, and he mentioned how much he liked Lydia. Grayson told Finn about the seemingly endless takes they'd had to do of the proposal scene with Astrid. "In all seriousness, I believe she was botching her lines repeatedly just to annoy me," Grayson confided. "It's like she gets drunk off my misery."

Finn laughed out loud at that, seemingly amused by Grayson's ire for Astrid. They reached Grayson's trailer first and stopped there. Grayson's trailer was parked near the edge of the location's property line, and it was fairly secluded due to the palms and foliage that separated the trailers from the parking lot. It wasn't far away from Finn's, but it definitely had more privacy, likely due to Grayson's A-list status and seniority on set. While Finn's trailer was only a few minutes' walk further, Finn didn't immediately move to go.

Uncertain silence fell between them once they had stopped walking. "Um. Do you want to come in quick and grab a water?" Grayson asked, needing to fill the silence.

Finn accepted, they stepped inside, and Grayson grabbed two waters from his mini fridge. He handed one to Finn, and then he leaned against the small counter, watching as Finn took a long drink from the bottle. Grayson should have invited him to sit down, but instead, the two of them just stood there for a minute, tension rising. Grayson sipped his water, too, and then they both sat the bottles down on the counter. Finn leaned against the wall opposite Grayson, looking up at him with a guarded expression that Grayson couldn't read. The air between them felt charged, like it was alive with a current of some kind pulsing between them. Finally, when Grayson met his gaze, Finn said quietly, "You never answered my question."

"What question?" Grayson's voice came out low and a bit raspy.

Finn held eye contact with Grayson, but his voice was still soft, with a slight nervous tremble to the words when he said, "You never told me who your first choice would be...to kiss."

Grayson swallowed loudly, his palms starting to sweat. Finn's dark blue eyes looked so vulnerable, but they also seemed to hold a bit of a challenge in them. Almost like they were begging Grayson to tell the truth. Daring him.

Grayson felt himself take a step closer to Finn, closing the gap between them to mere inches. "I think you know that answer," Grayson said, his voice sounding much more composed than he felt.

Finn took a shaky breath before he said in an almost whisper, "I'm not entirely sure that I do." He broke eye contact and looked down at his feet.

Before Finn could step away from him, Grayson moved even closer, placing his hands gently on Finn's hips. Grayson couldn't tell if the trembling he felt was coming from Finn's body or his own. Finn looked up at him then, and Grayson answered the question definitively by tilting his head down to press his lips to Finn's. He kissed him carefully at first, nerves and uncertainty holding him back, but then Finn responded to the kiss, bringing his hands to rest on Grayson's chest and parting his lips under Grayson's.

Grayson tightened his hold on Finn, one hand sliding to the small of Finn's back, deepening the kiss as he did so. His tongue slid into Finn's mouth, slowly caressing the tip of Finn's tongue before retreating, giving Grayson just enough of a taste to have his head spinning. This was not Grayson's first kiss by any stretch of the imagination, but it was the first one where he literally felt breathless. He was lightheaded and tingly all over. He had never experienced any of the clichés about magical kisses – time stopping, world tilting, fireworks exploding. But he felt every single one of them and then some when his lips had touched Finn Everett's.

CHAPTER 5

"Cut!" the director's shout cut through the crowded room, jarring Finn out of character. This was his first time filming a scene with most of the cast members at once, and it was overwhelming, to put it mildly. The scene was a formal dinner party, a Frost Manor staple, where the Beechworths of Frost Manor were to dine with Wesley Crown, Finn's character, and Rose Danbury, Astrid's character. There were a few other minor characters seated at the lavishly set dining table, as well, mainly serving as props and seat fillers.

James Beechworth was announcing his engagement to Rose Danbury to their friends and neighbors. So, Finn had spent the last hour watching Grayson clasp Astrid's hand and present her as his bride-to-be. Lucky for Finn, the characters' marriage would be one of convenience, not love, and his character got to scoff and judge them for it, which Finn enjoyed immensely.

"Again, from the top of Wesley's speech,"

the director said, and when he hollered, "Action!" Finn snapped back into character.

"Let me express my congratulations to the both of you, truly, on the strategic partnership," Wesley/Finn said, his eyes cold and dull, voice uninterested.

"Strategic partnership – what an odd thing to say," Elizabeth/Lydia said, followed by a nervous giggle.

Rose/Astrid glared at him, eyes narrowed, chin tilted up in disdain.

"Not odd at all, really," Wesley/Finn replied. "They are certainly not a love match, so the only explanation can be that James sees the merits in Rose's fortune, and she sees the value of rising up in society with the Beechworth name. If that's not strategic, I don't know what to call it."

At this, James/Grayson leaned back in his chair, drank leisurely from his wine glass, then turned his gaze to Wesley/Finn. Eyes hard as stone, he chuckled darkly, no humor in it, and said, "Wesley, you speak as if you object to marrying for rational reasons. Don't tell us you're a *romantic*." He said the word "romantic" like it was a festering wound.

"Actually," Wesley/Finn responded, his tone developing a defiant edge in place of his earlier disinterest, "I am saying that the only truly rational reason to marry is for love." His blue eyes were livelier now, laser focused on James/Grayson as he said this.

Rather than laugh at that, as was written in the script, James/Grayson met Wesley/Finn's stare with a shadow of sadness in his eyes, and delivered his next line, "I'm sorry that I cannot agree with you on that point." He shook his head ruefully, looking down into his wine glass.

"As am I," Wesley/Finn responded, his stare also dropping, his shoulders curling inward ever-so-slightly.

"Cut!" the director called. "We got it, people."

Finn was still sitting at the table, trying to shake himself out of Wesley's head and back into his own, when he noticed that the showrunners, Gwen and Jasper, had come into the room. They didn't come around often during filming, but they checked in from time-to-time. They were crowding around the camera, presumably watching the playback with the director. The rest of the cast was milling around, hesitant to go too far lest the director need a few more shots of them in full dinner party dress.

Finn could just hear the director speaking to Gwen and Jasper over the chatter of his castmates and the crewmembers. "I tell you what, I about lost my shit when Grayson ignored the script's notes here, but damn, the boy is a genius. Watch this part...right here...we got in extra tight on his expression, and when he was supposed to laugh, he changed it up. He looked so regretful. His jaw tight, his eyes mournful." The director was clearly enthused. "He is a freaking rock star; it is such a better approach for his character."

Both Jasper and Gwen were nodding, and they said something too quiet for Finn to catch. Suddenly, Gwen lifted her head and was calling out to him. "Finn, would you come here a sec," she motioned him over to where they were leaning over the camera. Finn joined them and stared at his own face on the screen. The shot was so close he could see the freckles on his cheeks, and he immediately felt self-conscious. *They could warn a guy that they were going to zoom in like that.*

"I'm not sure how you did it, but that look on your face is tearing my freakin' heart out, Finn," Jasper said to him, placing a hand on his shoulder and leaning in a bit closer to the camera's screen. He pointed in the direction of Finn's furrowed eyebrows and intent gaze. "You look like you really mean what you're saying and that you're devastated, deep down, though you're trying not to show it. I didn't even know it was possible for someone to say all that with a facial expression, but you did. Nice work, kid."

"What did I say?" Gwen said with an "I-told-you-so" smirk on her face.

"Really, the two of them ramped each other

up like I've never seen before," the director interjected, gesturing to onscreen Finn and Grayson as the camera continued the playback. "It's like one of them would make a tweak to the delivery of a line, and the other would pick it up and run with it. The tension was so thick in here…"

Before the director could finish that thought, Astrid had wedged her way into the little crowd and interrupted. "Jasper," she addressed the showrunner as she placed a hand on his forearm. "You wouldn't mind if I steal you away for a minute," she said, lips curled into a smile. *What is this, The Bachelorette*, Finn thought to himself, mentally rolling his eyes at her.

"Astrid, sweetie, check out this footage," Jasper said, apparently oblivious to her request to speak in private. As she dutifully turned her attention to the camera, a scowl on her pretty face, Finn took the opportunity to sneak away. No way did he want to spend any unnecessary time around Astrid, and he still felt weird about the showrunners watching his performance with him right there. It was unnerving, though he could admit to himself that he was proud of his work on the scene.

In the chaos following the scene's wrapping, Finn hadn't seen Grayson. He must have gone back to his trailer already. And just the thought of Grayson's trailer had Finn's blood heating. He thought back to the previous day, him and Grayson, alone in the trailer. Grayson's big hands on his hips. His hands on Grayson's hard chest, the quick, steady rhythm of Grayson's heartbeat below Finn's fingers. The confident slide of Grayson's mouth across his, the feel of a warm tongue teasing his own. Finn was embarrassingly turned on just remembering that moment, which was why he couldn't wait for another chance to be alone with Grayson.

The whole day filming the dinner party scene had been torture. Grayson was right there across the table from him, looking so elegant in the tailcoat, his wavy hair combed back from his face, hazel eyes gleaming in the light from the flickering taper candles. All he could think about was that kiss and the way Grayson had smiled at him afterward. It had made Finn so damn hopeful. Like maybe there was a small chance that the kiss had been as mind-melting for Grayson as it had been for Finn, like maybe Grayson was feeling as intensely attracted to him as he was to Grayson. And Finn couldn't wait for a chance to find out.

Those thoughts had added to the substantial ball of nerves Finn already felt in his gut about shooting this scene. He didn't want to make an ass out of himself in front of the whole cast, especially not Grayson. He wanted to bring his A-game, and he willed himself to slip into character the second the director called "action," delivering a solid performance through an incredible amount of concentration and will.

And, if he was honest, Grayson ended up being a help, not a hindrance. When the camera was rolling, Grayson was enthralling. He *became* James Beechworth completely, even his posture straightening as he morphed into the 19th Century aristocrat. Grayson's absolute commitment to the scene made Finn want to stretch to meet the bar he set. And, like the director had been saying to Jasper and Gwen, the two played off each other in a way that was truly special. There was a palpable chemistry between them, and they were both somehow able to channel that into the animosity their characters felt for one another.

Finn had just entered his trailer and flung himself onto his small mattress when his phone dinged.

Grayson: *You were amazing today.*

Finn: *Thanks to you.*

Grayson: *Me?*

Finn: *Yes. You pushed me today. I was so nervous for filming that scene, and then it went better than I thought it would.*

Grayson: *It was awesome. The director was practically giddy with the footage. You should be proud of yourself.*

Finn: *I guess I am. You should be proud, too.*

Grayson: *You're right. We should both be*

proud. Want to celebrate?

Finn: *Celebrate? What did you have in mind?*

There were three quick knocks on Finn's trailer door. When he opened it, Grayson was there, holding up a Thai food takeout bag, a grin on his face. "Can I come in?"

◆ ◆ ◆

"Like I'm saying no to the world's hottest Thai food delivery guy," Finn said, laughing as he opened the door wide for Grayson to step into the trailer. Grayson hadn't allowed himself time to second-guess the impulse to send Ethan out for the Thai food immediately after wrapping the scene. Grayson had literally never planned a surprise for anyone in his life. He wasn't that type of guy. *For Finn you are*, he thought to himself, still baffled at his intense reaction to Finn. He wanted to be around him all the time, like he was being pulled in his direction against his will. His infatuation was intense in a way he didn't fully understand. He'd never been someone to go all moony over someone else, but there was just something about Finn that was different.

Grayson was still riding high on the buzz of the back-and-forth with Finn on camera, the way the whole set seemed to hum with their chemistry. Of course, he had hoped that the vibes he was sending Finn's way had seemed more "I find you rude and annoying, Wesley Crown" and less "I want to jump your bones, Finn Everett" when they were filming. He figured he had pulled it off when he saw how pleased the director had been. And now, he wanted to celebrate a job well done, and he wasn't going to think about how stupid he was for crushing so hard on his co-star.

"World's hottest delivery guy, huh?" Grayson asked, smirking at Finn as he passed him a container from the takeout bag. They sat opposite one another at the tiny table in the middle of the trailer, Grayson laying out the napkins and utensils between them. Finn was quick to take a large bite of noodles just then, a slight blush creeping over his cheeks. *So damn cute.*

They ate, Finn thanked Grayson for the food, and then the two of them slipped into easy conversation. They rehashed some of the details from the day's filming, like Lydia dinging her knife on the crystal in Grayson and Astrid's direction each time the director yelled "cut" at the end of the scene, like she was at a wedding reception prompting the newlyweds to kiss. Astrid's answering scowls had been hilarious.

Talking with Finn was easy, and Grayson was continually amazed at how much he was laughing. He couldn't remember ever laughing so much with another person. Sure, he laughed with Felix, but they'd know each other for two decades. This ease and comfort with someone he barely knew was not typical for him. But Grayson didn't feel like Finn was someone he barely knew. They actually had a lot in common, both essentially growing up on tv sets and in the public eye. It was liked they'd know each other for years, and Grayson was grateful to have someone who understood the pressures he faced.

When the food was gone Finn stood and busied himself with clearing the trash away. A charged silence overtook the space. "So...I should maybe go," Grayson said, moving to stand from the wooden dining chair.

But Finn stopped him by stepping into his space, a hand on his shoulder urging him to stay seated. "Or you could stay," Finn said, his deep blue eyes urging Grayson to accept what he was offering. Grayson's body was already reacting to Finn's proximity and the thoughts of what might happen if he stayed. He gave Finn a careful once-over. While Grayson had changed into worn jeans and a t-shirt after filming wrapped for the day, Finn was still in his tux from the dinner party scene, though he'd discarded the tailcoat and waistcoat at some point. He was still in a crisp white shirt, a few buttons undone at the neck now, tucked in to tailored black tuxedo pants. Grayson thought he looked sexy as hell.

And *damn*, just the slight pressure of Finn's hand on his shoulder and the weight of his intent gaze staring him down had Grayson's dick screaming at him to keep his ass in that chair. Who was he kidding? There was no universe in which he turned down any kind of offer from Finn, especially one that could lead to kissing him again. Truth be told, he had thought of little else in the last 24 hours.

"Come here," Grayson said, reaching up to wrap a hand around the back of Finn's neck and pulling him down into a needy kiss.

He tried to convey just how much he wanted Finn with the eagerness of his mouth. Unlike the kiss the day before, which had been careful and tentative, this one was all heat and urgency. Grayson slipped his tongue into Finn's mouth, an arm curling around his back to pull him even closer as he slid his tongue deeper. Finn moaned and leaned into the kiss. Grayson pulled back from him long enough to catch his breath and tugged Finn down into his lap. "You are so hot," Grayson whispered into Finn's ear as he settled him on his thighs. "Been thinking about this all day. You're making me crazy."

Finn laughed and snaked his arms around Grayson's neck, and *oh man*, Grayson loved Finn's laugh. It had so much joy in it, not like the false laughs he was used to in this business. Finn leaned in, turning his head so he could nip at Grayson's lower lip before resuming the kiss with smooth strokes of his tongue against Grayson's. Grayson felt drunk, all euphoric and a bit out of control.

Finn was stirring up things within Grayson he had never felt before, and all he really knew what that he needed *more*.

Grayson's hands found the buttons of Finn's shirt, and he went to work on them carefully. He undid them efficiently before tugging the bottom of the shirt free from Finn's pants. Finn wiggled his shoulders a little to help Grayson shuck the shirt off him, and soon there was a whole lot of smooth, warm skin under Grayson's hands. Grayson's mouth drifted down to Finn's jaw, then neck, tasting his soft skin, hands gliding along Finn's bare sides. Finn's eyes were closed, and he tilted his head to the side, allowing Grayson the room he needed to continue his mouth's exploration. Finn's skin tasted salty and perfect under Grayson's tongue, and he was certain Finn could feel how hard he was, his erection pressing up into Finn's thigh.

Finn sucked in a sharp breath when Grayson bit down gently at the juncture of his neck and shoulder. "I want to feel your skin, too," Finn said then, voice urgent, fingers grasping for the hem of Grayson's t-shirt. Finn had to lean back out of the way for Grayson to pull the shirt up and over his head, and rather than return to his position nestled on Grayson's lap, he sank down to his knees on the floor in front of Grayson.

"Oh hell yes," Grayson said as he looked down at Finn. Seeing Finn kneeling in front of him, big blue eyes looking up at him with hunger, Grayson felt like he might lose it right then. It wasn't like he hadn't done this before, but he'd never felt so much need, so much delicious anticipation threatening to cause his heart to combust.

Finn slowly ran his hands up Grayson's abs and chest and back down again. Grayson's muscles contracted at the touch, and he felt a shudder move through his entire body. Finn smiled at Grayson's reaction to his touch, and then he dropped a few soft kisses on the ridges of Grayson's abs. Finn was so much more attentive than Grayson was used to, like he was truly enjoying Grayson, not just running toward a finish line. With Thomas, it had often felt like the kissing and touching was something to get out of the way quickly, more of a chore than anything. Finn's exploring hands and gentle kisses, however, weren't rushed, and he was attuned to the way Grayson responded to his thorough attention. Grayson's hands balled into fists at his sides as he felt his cock straining at his zipper. "You're going to kill me," he muttered as Finn's tongue slowly traced the line of dark hair below Grayson's navel down to where it disappeared below the waist of his jeans.

Finn laughed as he popped the button of Grayson's fly and pulled down the zipper. "You better not die on me yet," he said, winking up at Grayson as he wrapped his fingers under the waistband of Grayson's boxers. "Help me out here," Finn said, urging Grayson to lift his hips enough for Finn to slide his boxers and jeans off him and toss them out of the way.

"Mmm," Finn hummed in appreciation as he looked over Grayson's naked body. Then he licked his lower lip, making Grayson's cock twitch in anticipation. Maybe he really was going to die. "You have no idea how many of my fantasies have started exactly like this," Finn said, his hands sliding up Grayson's thighs. Their eyes locked, and Finn leisurely licked up the underside of Grayson's shaft before tracing the head with the tip of his tongue.

"Fuuuck," Grayson muttered. He was trying to keep his eyes open to watch Finn, but when Finn wrapped his hand around the base and swallowed him down, Grayson's eyes snapped shut, his head thrown back. His hands landed gently in Finn's hair, just resting there in the soft strands. Finn began to bob his head in a steady rhythm, working his fist along with his mouth's movements. Grayson was desperately close already, and he worked to keep himself under control, not wanting this to end.

Leaning back in the chair, he lifted his head enough to see Finn when he cracked his eyes open. He watched as Finn worked his way up and down, tongue lapping at the head on his upstrokes before dipping down, gradually taking more and more of

Grayson's cock. "Finn. Fuck. Finn, I'm not gonna last," Grayson choked out. The sight of Finn's lips wrapped around him, cheeks hollowing with the suction, was the hottest thing Grayson had ever seen.

Finn hummed in encouragement at that, increasing his speed and sucking harder, and that was all it took. "Finn..." was all the warning Grayson could manage before he was coming, Finn swallowing around him through his climax. Grayson slumped back in the chair, utterly spent.

"That was fucking amazing," he managed to say, extending his hand to Finn to help him up.

Rather than let go of his hand, Grayson tugged Finn close and undid his fly. "Let me, okay? I need to touch you, too."

Finn didn't stop him from stripping off his remaining clothing, and Grayson was happy to direct his attention to Finn's hard cock. *God, he's perfect everywhere*, Grayson thought to himself. Finn chuckled when Grayson began smooth strokes, "It's not going to take much. Having you come in my mouth was the hottest thing ever." Grayson felt no small amount of pride at the compliment and increased his rhythm. He swiped the moisture leaking from the tip around Finn's length, which aided the slide of his fist. Finn's hips lifted into Grayson's hand, and Grayson tightened his grip a bit. He felt Finn's body tense up and cock harden even further under his touch.

Finn's voice was a strangled, moan-like sound, "Yes, that...feels so good. Gray..." Finn convulsed, eyes squeezed tight, legs wobbling. Then he was coming into Grayson's fist. Grayson stroked him through the orgasm, steadying his body with his free arm. When Finn stilled, Grayson drew him back down into his lap and sought out his mouth for a tired kiss, both of them exhausted, sticky, and completely blissed out.

"Is this a terrible idea?" Finn asked, head resting against Grayson's shoulder.

"Probably." *But so worth it.* Grayson kept that last part to himself as he tightened his arms around Finn. Holding him like that felt way better than it should.

CHAPTER 6

A light breeze tempered the midday heat, and Finn leaned his head back against the chaise, closing his eyes and soaking in the warmth of the sun on his face. The familiar voice of Bon Iver drifted through his AirPods at a low volume, and Finn allowed the sun and the music to lull him into almost dozing while he waited for Grayson. Grayson was busy on a phone call – something work-related, no doubt, and Finn was more than happy to relax while he waited for him.

"Fancy meeting you here...again," said a booming voice, jolting Finn out of his restfulness. Felix laughed loudly as he walked up to where Finn was lounging by Grayson and Felix's backyard pool. Felix bumped Finn's fist and plopped down into the chaise next to him.

Alert now, Finn flashed him a grin, "Don't tell me you are finally sick of having your favorite *Luna's Cove* star hanging out by your pool." Finn closed the script he'd left open on his stomach and sat up straighter to give his attention to chatting with Felix.

Over the last three weeks, Finn had been spending a lot of time at Grayson and Felix's, mainly due to the privacy and considerable comforts of Grayson's bedroom versus one of their trailers on set. It was surreal to Finn that he and Grayson were, for all intents and purposes, kind of dating. They stole secret touches and quick kisses while on set, texted constantly, and Finn was spending most nights at Grayson's. It felt like a dream.

Over the course of the last few weeks, Finn had gotten to know Felix, as well, and the two became fast friends. Felix was loud, cheerful, and extremely social. As Grayson's best friend and personal trainer, not to mention roommate, Felix was almost always around when Finn and Grayson hung out, and Finn didn't mind at all. It was nice seeing Grayson interact with Felix, the two of them so comfortable with one another. It brought out an ease in Grayson that wasn't typically there, and Finn really liked seeing that. Finn also loved hearing all of Felix's Grayson stories. He couldn't get enough of hearing how Grayson was a nerdy high schooler always talking about the Civil War or Alexander Hamilton. He'd also learned that Grayson had always been an over-achiever, never accepting second best at anything from soccer to chess. It was adorable to hear about younger Grayson, and Finn couldn't get enough. He was fascinated to learn anything he could about what made the serious, guarded man the way he was.

"Course I'm not sick of you," Felix said. "Grayson hasn't bitched about me leaving dirty dishes around or made me watch the History Channel since you've been in the picture. His grumpy ass could be a real downer, always so damn serious. Definitely keeping you around."

Finn felt warmth spread through his chest at those words, tiny embers of hope trying to catch fire. Was he really making Grayson happy? Finn knew he was full-on obsessed with Grayson at this point, but he still had a hard time believing Grayson was as into him, too.

They'd been spending a lot of time together, and Grayson did seem to enjoy hanging out with him, but he couldn't help but feel it was just a way for Grayson to pass the time. He was here, and he was convenient. That seemed to be the extent of his appeal as far as Grayson was concerned. Finn had heard rumors that Grayson had been in a relationship with Thomas Logan, and Finn knew he was nowhere near as successful or as good looking as Thomas. So, if that was Grayson's type, all muscular and high-fashion, Finn was an idiot for hoping Grayson would want him for anything more than casual hookups while they were working together.

This point had become even more evident whenever Finn tried to have a conversation of any substance with Grayson. If he ever tried to ask Grayson about his dating history, or his family, or anything personal at all, Grayson shut it down fast. He got quiet and distant, and switched into strictly "co-worker" mode. And, if Finn was honest, that really stung. The chill of Grayson's retreat and refusal to get to know one another better was getting harsher each time it happened.

"I'm not saying he's all sunshine and cotton candy now, but at least he doesn't stomp around with a perma-scowl anymore." Felix chuckled. "I told him he was going to ruin his perfect face if he kept that up, and then we'd both be out of work, seeing as he's my best advertisement." As Grayson's personal trainer, Felix's work spoke for itself in the form of Grayson's ridged abs, big arms, muscled calves, and defined shoulders. Grayson was able to spread the word to enough other actors that Felix was always booked solid with A-list clients now, a minor celebrity in his own right.

"Speaking of work, did Gray tell you about the charity run?"

Finn shook his head. "No. He hasn't said anything about it to me."

"Well, we are doing this celebrity 5K to raise funds for Grayson's charity," Felix explained. "We're hoping to top last year, and the goal is to raise enough to expand the program into 10 additional communities, but that'll be a stretch. Gotta dream big, though, right? We could really use your help – your 10 million followers couldn't hurt in the donation department. You know they'd shell out if you posted a shirtless pic on race day and asked them nicely with those swoony eyes of yours," Felix said, winking at him for emphasis.

Finn knew that Grayson had some type of youth charity, but he didn't know that much about it. He couldn't help but feel a little hurt that Grayson hadn't mentioned any of this to him. But to be fair, he hadn't asked, either. There had been plenty of making out and getting off, but not many deep conversations. But damn it, Finn wanted that to change. He wanted Grayson to tell him about his life, to let him in a little. *Don't be stupid*, he told himself. It's not like Grayson was ever going to be his boyfriend or anything. They were in two completely different leagues, no matter how much Finn wished it were otherwise. He should just be happy with the little pieces of himself that Grayson was willing to share and not go wanting things that he could never have.

"You ready?" Grayson's voice called to Finn from the French doors behind where he and Felix were sitting. When Finn stood and turned to face him, Grayson gave him a wide smile, eyes bright and crinkled a little at the corners when he saw Finn and Felix chatting. When Grayson looked at him like that, like the sight of him brightened his whole day, Finn felt those stupid hopes come rushing back, plowing over all the doubts and logical reasons not to invest his feelings in Grayson Winter.

Grayson and Finn had to be at the studio location today for a meeting with Gwen and Jasper to hammer out some details about their upcoming press engagements. Kayla would be there, too, of course, as she was both Finn and Grayson's agent. They only had a couple of episodes left of the season to film, and while the episodes were in post-production, Finn and Grayson would be making the rounds doing interviews and making appearances with the press.

This meeting was to "strategize," which basically meant they were going to be told what to wear, do, and say, and they were to agree to all of it. Luckily, it seemed like the showrunners had agreed to Kayla's proposal that Finn and Grayson do joint press. Her reasoning was that it would be a bigger draw for fans if they were both there – diehard *Frost Manor* fans for Grayson and new fans tuning in for Finn. It made sense, but Finn didn't care so much about the logical marketing strategy and was just happy to spend that much more time with Grayson.

After flashing his I.D. and pulling into a designated *Frost Manor* spot on the lot, Grayson hopped out of the car and tilted his head in the opposite direction of the offices. "This way, we need to make a quick stop."

"We do?"

"Yes, we do," Grayson assured him, leading the way down the lot.

He stopped in front of a coffee cart where a college-aged guy, Finn thought his name was Matt, was passing a coffee cup to a harried looking assistant with a headset dangling from his neck. When Grayson stepped up to the cart, he ordered a caramel macchiato. The barista was working alone, so she made Grayson's drink before taking Finn's order.

When it was Finn's turn, before he could place his order, Grayson handed him the cup he was holding. "Uh, this one's for you," he said, cheeks turning slightly pink. "I noticed you drifting off at the house when I was on the phone, and I figured you could use some caffeine." He shrugged and gave a shy smile. Finn took the cup from him, dumbfounded. Not only had Grayson been thoughtful enough to stop for him, but he'd somehow known Finn's coffee order.

Matt the Barista gave them a curious look and then a wide, knowing smile as they walked toward their meeting. Finn took a sip of the delicious caramel goodness and couldn't keep from grinning like a complete fool.

❖ ❖ ❖

If a simple espresso drink would make Finn

look at him like that, Grayson wanted to buy him the whole damn coffee cart. Grayson had felt a bit guilty for keeping Finn up so late the previous night – not too guilty, of course, because he was not a bit sorry about the stroking each other off part, but the poor guy had almost fallen asleep in a lounge chair in the yard. The least he could do was buy him a coffee. And it wasn't that big of a deal, honesty. Grayson realized he maybe should have asked him what he wanted rather than revealing that he'd paid attention to the scribbles on his paper cups. That seemed stalker-ish, but it was too late now. And Finn didn't seem put off by it. He seemed to practically burst with glee when Grayson handed him the cup, and why that made Grayson feel like his insides were melting, he didn't want to think about too much.

They spent the next hour listening to Kayla battle with Gwen and Jasper about the "talking points" and the "styling" they were going to employ on the upcoming press junket. Grayson's attention may have drifted to Finn a time or two, though he did try his best to listen. But every few minutes, he'd realize he was staring again.

There was something magnetic about Finn. He smiled so easily and laughed so often, always taking things in such good humor. Grayson envied that a bit. Finn just seemed so relaxed. His blonde hair hung messily across his forehead as he talked to Gwen about something, tan forearms rested on the table, elegant fingers hugging the coffee cup. There was absolutely nothing about him that wasn't appealing to Grayson. His long, lean torso in a relaxed posture, the crazy blue of his eyes, the dusting of freckles Grayson could just make out from across the table. He had never felt so drawn to anyone, and the more time he spent with Finn, the more it never seemed like enough.

What in the actual fuck is happening? He truly didn't know. He'd never felt like this, and it was scary as hell. Finn kept trying to get to know him, but Grayson knew that was a bad idea. Grayson didn't want to go getting in any deeper than he already was. Plus, once Finn knew how messed up he was, there was no way he'd want to be bogged down with all Grayson's baggage. Plus, Finn was 22. He would tire of Grayson's moody ass and end up with someone more fun, more carefree. Thomas had been sure to let Grayson know just how much of a downer he could be when they were dating. No, he wasn't going to bring Finn down. Finn was all cheerful lightness, and Grayson was anything but that. But he couldn't seem to keep his distance completely, and Finn chipped away at his resolve to keep him at arm's length a little more every day.

"Grayson. Hellloooo, Grayson!" Kayla swatted him with a manicured hand, pulling him out of his Finn-filled haze.

"Sorry. What was that?"

"I was just saying that we have one last thing to discuss, and I need everyone's full focus," Gwen was the one speaking now, her tone much more serious that it had been previously throughout the meeting. This couldn't be good.

Jasper cleared his throat and continued on behalf of them both. "It's really none of our business, and I wish we didn't have to even address this, but there are rumors on set."

"Rumors?" Grayson asked, gut suddenly churning. He did not look at Finn.

"Yes," Gwen said. "Basically, the rumor is that the two of you are *extremely* close. Beyond just costars or friends." She looked cautiously at Grayson, then at Finn, and then back to Grayson, her expression sympathetic.

"I guess I don't really understand what we're talking about here," Finn said carefully. His face was pale, and his posture had straightened with tension.

Kayla groaned and rolled her eyes, exasperation dripping from her voice. "People on set think you're fucking."

Grayson's eyes went wide, and he felt heat warming his neck and face. He took a few deep breaths to calm himself. He spoke in as steady a tone as he could manage, "I'm not sure why that is something we need to discuss in a meeting."

"The thing is," Jasper said, "we have a lot riding on this season, as you know. We don't want to have anything...detract from the show's success."

Kayla tagged on with, "We just want to protect you and do what's in the show's best interest. We aren't saying 'no fucking,' we're just saying to keep it out of the press." She, too, had sympathy in her eyes when she met Grayson's gaze despite her brash words.

"Your chemistry is undeniable, so we won't be able to pass the two of you off as indifferent to one another," Gwen added. "And I hate to ask this, but it is likely our best option from a marketing standpoint."

Grayson gritted his teeth. "Just spit it out. What do you need me to do?"

"We thought we could keep the buzz alive for the show, as well as make it easy for the two of you to spend time together doing press if we controlled the narrative," Jasper said.

Finn's brows were bunched together, his eyes skeptical. "What, exactly, does 'control the narrative' mean? You want us to hide? To lie?"

"No, no, not at all," Gwen said. "Well, not exactly."

Grayson rolled his eyes, his patience long gone.

Kayla was the one to finally spit it out. "We want you two to play up all of the tension between the two of you when you're on the press tour, but we want to make sure you play it off as animosity, not lust," she said, face completely serious as she stared at Grayson.

"What? Why? I don't see what that accomplishes," Finn said, though it was clear that Kayla, Gwen, and Jasper were here to convince Grayson, not Finn. They must have known Grayson was their ticket to success in this crazy plot.

"It's like this," Gwen said. "There was a viral post on a gossip blog. You know the one by that angry nerdy dude? Anyway, the post said there were rumors on the *Frost Manor* set about bad blood between the two of you. Grayson, you're supposedly threatened by Finn being the shiny new addition to the show, and Finn, you apparently think Grayson has been unwelcoming and arrogant on set."

Grayson was silent, and Kayla chimed in. "When I say viral, I mean *really fucking viral*. While we don't have all the data yet, there was a massive surge in the viewership of the episode that aired immediately after that post. The article claims to have an 'insider source,' and we've had a shitload of requests for comments. This is good buzz for us, and we're going to just keep it going."

Jasper spoke again, "You're actors. Just consider this as part of your role. It's only for press appearances, and it will pay off for all of us. I have no doubt. The network actually spoke to Gwen and I about the article, and they *suggested* we make the most of this story."

"Unbelievable," Grayson said. "So they're blackmailing us into this bullshit by implying renewal is contingent on it? We have the biggest show on tv. They're not going to cancel it."

"Grayson," Gwen said. "Can you just please do this for us?"

As much as it twisted his guts, he knew he'd agree. He couldn't burn bridges with the network or damage his relationship with Gwen and Jasper. He needed to keep these working relationships strong if he wanted to have longevity in this fickle industry, and he's spent his entire life working for this position in the business. If he remained on this trajectory, he'd be able to have his choice of roles and projects for life. He couldn't risk damaging his position.

Finn was silent now, head down, eyes firmly on the coffee cup he clenched in his hands.

Grayson was pissed. "For the record, this is complete bullshit, but apparently my opinion is fucking irrelevant."

Gwen was the one to respond, voice even, "We know how much we're asking, Grayson. We just wanted you to be aware that there could be severe consequences for the show and your careers if you aren't careful on this press tour. We still believe that having the two of you appear jointly for interviews and features is the best route. Just pretend not to like each other. For all our sake's."

Kayla got the last word in, "You know I love you both. And I don't give two fucks if you're dating or whatever. I just don't want you to lose this opportunity in the spotlight to your advantage. For you, Grayson, you've got a real shot at a Portrayer nomination this year, and all press is good press. And of course we don't want ratings to tank and the network to pass on renewing. Those are the stakes."

"Understood," Grayson gritted out. He stood and left the room, using all his strength to avoid looking at Finn when he walked away.

"Hey, wait up." Finn was jogging after him down the hall, following him out the door and into the bright sunlight. "Grayson, just hang on a minute."

Turning and running a hand through his hair, Grayson faced Finn. "What?" It came out harsher than he had intended, and Finn flinched and backed up a step.

"I don't know how the rumors started. I'm sorry, Grayson."

"Yeah. Me, too." He ran a hand through his hair in frustration. "I knew something like this would happen."

Finn looked like Grayson had punched him. "Wait, are you mad at me?"

Grayson looked at him then, the hurt in his eyes apparent. He did not like seeing that there. No matter how frustrated Grayson felt, he knew he couldn't stomach upsetting Finn.

"No, I'm not mad at you. I'm just mad at myself. I should never have started something with you. I knew it was a bad idea to get involved with a costar. You'd really think I'd have learned my lesson about hooking up with other people in the business by now."

"I see." Finn's eyes shuttered then, his expression no longer revealing any emotion. He nodded a few times, stepping further away from Grayson. "This 'hooking up' was a mistake. Got it." Finn turned to walk away from him then, and Grayson knew he'd said the absolute wrong thing.

This was turning into a complete nightmare. Grayson's head was throbbing at this point, the drumming in his temples and the twisting of his gut made him feel like he might vomit right there. It always amazed him how much physical pain could come from mental anguish.

He was not going to be able to let Finn walk away from him angry and hurt. That was the absolute last thing Grayson wanted. No matter how ill-advised, he acted on instinct and desperation. He stepped toward Finn and reached for his hand. When Finn didn't immediately pull away, Grayson laced their fingers together.

"Look, Finn," he pulled Finn over to lean against the brick wall of the building they'd exited, the two of them shoulder to shoulder, fingers intertwined, "I'm sorry. That really didn't come out right. I am not good with...this stuff." Because they were side by side, Grayson didn't have to look at Finn as he continued. "I am frustrated with myself, but not in the way you think. I'm frustrated that I wasn't able to stay away from you, even when I tried. I was in a relationship with another celebrity before, and it ended badly. He had wanted to be more public, almost like he liked being photographed and showing up in the gossip blogs. That is so not the way I am."

Grayson paused and chanced a glance at Finn. Finn was just listening, waiting for Grayson to continue. "So, I told myself that I wasn't going to get involved with anyone else in the business. That way, I might stay out of the media for anything other than my work. I put so much of myself into this role, and I guess I want to be recognized for that, not my dating life." Finn squeezed his hand, and he squeezed it back. "I hate that my talent as an actor is always being undercut by my personal life, and I just thought it wasn't worth the trouble. My plan was to keep all my focus on work, and to let that work speak for itself. And now..."

"And now you're afraid it's all happening again. All your hard work is going to be overshadowed by some juicy gossip or scandal about a teen soap star causing drama," Finn said, his voice filled with bitter-tinged sadness.

Grayson wasn't entirely sure he was making himself clear yet, but Finn's hand was still there in his, so it couldn't be going as poorly as he had thought. "Yes. To some extent, that's what's got me so angry. But I'm even angrier that our showrunners are somehow involved now, coaching me to play a stupid role in public, and I feel like a big fucking joke."

"You're not a joke. You're one of the best actors in the business, and everyone on this set respects the hell out of you, including me. I get it now. You don't want to mess up your career for the sake of a convenient hookup situation. I really do understand. I'm not thrilled about having to act like I hate you in order for viewers to accept me on this show. If I play the villain to your golden boy, they can make their peace with me being cast on the show. Like there's no way I belong here otherwise. If I'm making waves and stirring shit up, I can be here. It just sucks." Finn sounded so dejected Grayson's heart ached.

"Hey. No one who watches your performance this season will have any doubt that you earned this role. You are so talented, Finn. I don't want that taken away from you, either." Grayson shifted a little, sliding a little closer to Finn and turning his body to face him. "But you are wrong about something."

"I'm wrong about what?" Finn asked.

"It's not just a 'convenient hookup situation' to me. If that were the case, I would have been able to stop myself from pursuing you."

"It's not for me, either," Finn said, turning to face Grayson, their hands still threaded together tightly. "So, what now?"

"I guess we have to put on a good show on the press tour, but I don't want to stop seeing you." Grayson hesitated before adding, "Unless that's what you want."

"*You* are what I want," Finn said, and he tilted his face up to Grayson's for a kiss. Grayson felt a huge weight slide off his shoulders then. Sure, he was not pleased about the rumors or the talking-to they'd gotten from the showrunners and Kayla, but at least he hadn't lost what he had with Finn, too. That was something he would not have been able to handle.

CHAPTER 7

The knocking on Finn's door was so loud and forceful it rattled the whole trailer. "Finn! Finn! Open the door! It's here! It's here, and it is fucking awesome!" Lydia was hollering through the closed door. Finn opened the door to let her in, smiling in amusement at her hopping up and down and waving something around in front of her face.

She barreled passed him into the trailer and flopped down into a chair, thrusting a magazine at him. She stared at him expectantly, clearly eager for him to react to whatever it was she was showing him. "We look hot, right?" Her big brown eyes were bright, and she oozed excitement.

Finn looked at the magazine she'd given him, staring down at the two familiar figures gracing the cover. "Holy shit."

"I know, right? So badass. I cannot believe how great it turned out. And the interview is stellar, too." Lydia was beaming.

Finn could hardly believe what he was seeing. At the photoshoot last month, he and Lydia had posed together in a variety of different outfits and posed in innumerable ridiculous positions, including playing around with a wind machine. They'd had so much fun that day, goofing around and blasting Dua Lipa. He thought the images would turn out playful or silly, showing off the close friendship he and Lydia had developed over the course of his now four months working on *Frost Manor*, reflecting their goofiness that day in front of the camera. What he was looking at now was nothing like what he'd expected.

The image they'd selected for the cover was a close up of Finn and Lydia from the torso up, Finn's bare chest front-and-center, Lydia's palm pressed against him. Lydia's back and shoulders were the only parts of her body in the shot, and they showed only the hint of the black strapless gown she had been wearing. From the angle of the camera, it looked like she was wearing some type of lingerie corset, and Finn could have been naked for all the image showed. Lydia's back was to the camera, her face turned upward so that only her facial profile showed, and it was hard to read her expression from the limited view. It could have been a seductive stare.

Finn couldn't imagine how this had happened. He'd been clothed for all the shots. He was insistent upon that. He wanted to be taken seriously, and the last thing he needed was to go back to playing up the teen heartthrob angle. So, how? Unless...yes, he remembered this moment now. Lydia had been wearing the black gown, and he had been changing into a different tuxedo shirt because he had dribbled his latte all over the one he'd been wearing. Lydia had been razzing him while they waited for the stylists to produce a new shirt, and at one point she had swatted at his chest as she teased him. And somehow, it was just his luck that the photographer caught him topless, seemingly in a compromising position with his friend. *Fuck.*

Lydia was still chattering away about how amazing the cover looked, and that's when Finn noticed the headline and text copy accompanying the photograph. *Fuck, fuck, fuckity-fuck.* It read:

Hot, Young & Stripped Down: Finn Everett and Lydia Mason bring the sexy to Frost Manor Season 3.

Great, just wonderful. This was the last thing Finn needed, especially since that awful meeting with the showrunners about him and Grayson. This was the exact thing he'd been hoping to avoid. He didn't want the sex symbol image. He wanted to be taken seriously. And covers like this weren't going to make that happen. Not by a longshot.

"Lydia, this sucks. They took all those shots of us looking all elegant in formalwear, and this is what they printed. That doesn't bother you?"

"Hell no. I look hot as hell, as do you, my friend. This is a good thing. I have the whole good-girl-gone-bad vibe going for me here. I think it is fantastic," Lydia said. "And besides, the interview does actually discuss the show and not just your abs." She laughed at this.

Finn tried not to take this too much to heart. If Lydia was happy, it wasn't all bad, he supposed. *What will Grayson think when he sees this?* He couldn't help but worry about Grayson's reaction, but there was nothing he could do about any of that now. They needed to run if they wanted to get to the table read on time. The entire cast was meeting to read through the season finale episode, and Finn sure as hell didn't want to be late. He was careful to leave the magazine in the trailer. No way did he want Lydia parading it around in front of the whole cast.

Finn entered the room where the tables were pushed into a giant rectangle to accommodate the entire cast to sit facing one another. His gaze instinctively sought out Grayson. He spotted him sitting in the center of one of the tables, Ethan the PA next to him, both of them hunched over the script.

Grayson had a pencil in his hand, jotting down notes quickly in the margins of his script.

With his dark waves drifting down over his glasses, his brows slightly furrowed in concentration as he listened to Ethan, he looked like a sexy academic. Very Clark Kent, Finn thought as he looked on fondly. His big, burly guy all buttoned up and studious never failed to stir up Finn's libido. No doubt Grayson was correcting some miniscule historical inaccuracy in the script. He was always doing that. "But that watch wasn't made until the 1920s," Grayson would say, and everyone would grumble. Finn didn't grumble, though. He found it adorable. But it was more than that, too. Finn wanted so badly to know what Grayson was discussing with Ethan. He wanted to know what Grayson was thinking, what he was writing in those margins. Finn found him so fascinating, and he was always curious to know what was churning around in that gorgeous head of Grayson's.

Finn must have really been staring when Grayson and Ethan looked up and saw him there because they both cracked smiles, Grayson's warm and intimate, Ethan's amused and knowing. Ethan stood, saying, "I better get outta the way. Looks like it's about time for you guys to start." He motioned at the chair he'd just vacated, and Finn slid into it, taking his place beside Grayson.

"Hey," Grayson said quietly, scooting his chair ever-so-slightly closer to Finn's.

"Hey," Finn replied, grinning like a loon, he

was sure.

Finn felt Grayson's thigh slide up against his under the table, and the heat from Grayson soaked into Finn's body, lighting him up like a struck match. They both kept their eyes dutifully focused on the scripts in front of them, not risking too much eye contact with one another. They were not good with low-key, and Finn knew they really weren't fooling anyone, but they had to at least pretend to be professionals.

"Alright, people," Gwen said in an authoritative voice as she and Jasper strode into the room, "let's do this." She was such a small woman that Finn was often taken aback by her no-nonsense attitude and ability to make everyone fall in line. You'd never know by looking at her, her short blonde hair streaked with pink and her checkered Vans, that she was one of the most intelligent and successful players in the whole television industry. She suffered absolutely no fools, and she got shit done. The combination of her grit and Jasper's smooth and savvy charisma and interpersonal skills made them an unstoppable duo. Finn was exceedingly thankful they'd picked him to join their show. He was determined to do them proud.

"Before we start," Jasper said once he and Gwen took their places at the center of one of the tables, "we have a couple of updates." Everyone around the tables stilled and focused on Gwen and Jasper. "First, we want to congratulate our dynamic duo, our very own media darlings, Lydia and Finn, on making the cover of *Watcher* magazine. This is a big deal, and you two have done a great job of stirring up buzz for this season." He then held up a copy of the magazine Lydia had shown Finn earlier, and Finn slumped down in his seat a little.

"Yeah. Way to nakedly represent our show, Finn," Astrid sneered. "Typical." She glowered at him from her seat across the room.

"Anyway, we also wanted to share that The Portrayer Shortlist had been released, and our very own Grayson Winter is included there," Gwen said, pride clear in her voice as she looked over to Grayson. "That means he is expected to receive a nomination this year, according to various Hollywood insiders. We wanted to recognize his work thus far and really urge you all to do your best on the finale. A Portrayer nomination for anyone in the cast is huge for the whole show," she said.

"And while we're talking about the importance of the finale, we want to be transparent with you all," Jasper said. "The network has decided that the ratings of the next episode will determine whether or not they renew us. So, it goes without saying that this is make-or-break time, and we need you all to really bring it."

"Now," Gwen said, "we get to work."

◆ ◆ ◆

When Grayson walked into his kitchen that evening, Felix was standing at the counter, grinding something vaguely greenish in the blender. Not only was Felix a beast about burpees and deadlifts, he took his protein and antioxidants seriously. Stopping the blender, Felix looked up at Grayson, a wicked gleam in his eye. Bypassing a "hello," or "how was your day," he said, "Guess what I came across on a table at the gym today? A little light reading material."

"You saw Finn's cover, I take it?" Grayson knew he should be annoyed with Felix's teasing, but he couldn't help but be a little proud of Finn. That was his guy on the front of that magazine, looking gorgeous as hell.

"Oh, I saw it, alright," Felix said, not even attempting to mask his glee. "And I may or may not have brought it home with me. You know, to show you in case you missed it."

"Dude."

"You can't blame me for checking him out, Grayson. He's naked on the cover, looking all Leo-circa-1999 but with better abs," Felix said.

"He wasn't naked." Grayson shot Felix a warning look. "And did you even read the article? He talked a lot about how he's approaching his character on the show and the challenges of escaping the stereotype he faced after *Luna's Cove*." Grayson's voice was fond, and he knew he was bordering on gushing at this point, but Finn really was amazing in that interview. He'd clearly charmed the reporter, coming off as the perfect mix of confidence and vulnerability. That was Finn. "It's a great piece."

"Yeah, he is a great piece," Felix said, not able to help himself when Grayson made it so easy to push his buttons. Felix quickly scurried away as Grayson made a playful attempt at swatting his friend.

Grayson knew Felix was over his one-time crush on Finn, especially since Finn and Grayson were a thing now. Felix was nothing if not a loyal best friend, and Grayson knew he would never do anything to hurt him. Felix just liked to give him shit, and that's part of why they got along so well. He kept Grayson laughing, tempering his intensity and broodiness. Finn did the same thing, Grayson thought, though in a very, *very* different way. Grayson could recognize that he was drawn to good-natured people that brightened up his dark moods.

At the buzz of the intercom signaling there was someone at their driveway's gate, Grayson said, "And speak of the devil," as he walked over to the intercom to buzz Finn in. Finn and Ethan were coming over to work through a few more details of the press engagements they were starting as soon as filming wrapped, which was some time next week. *Man, filming flew by this season.*

Finn didn't like to drive, so he was riding along in Ethan's blue Honda Civic. The PA was nothing if not unassuming, even in his choice of vehicle. Grayson had assured Ethan that he could handle getting Finn home after their meeting. While they never explicitly disclosed their relationship to Ethan, both Finn and Grayson knew the sharp PA was aware of their situation, but neither of them was bothered by this. Ethan was a total ally on set, and he was truly a great friend to have.

After about 45 minutes of hammering out schedules, travel arrangements, and talking points, the "meeting," portion of the evening was over, leaving the guys to just hang out the rest of the night. Grayson had asked Finn and Ethan to stay for pizza, which he and Felix had planned to order in.

Three pizzas and a few beers later, the group moved out to the chairs along the pool, cracking open more beers and settling in. Grayson sat in one of the chaises, Finn tucked in front of him, leaning his shoulder blades up against Grayson's chest. He rested his head back on Grayson's shoulder, and Grayson tilted the side of his head to rest against Finn's. Felix and Ethan took to loungers side-by-side, chatting intently about Grayson's charity run. Ethan had been willing to help with the administrative tasks, including marketing and the logistics of collecting donations. Felix was kind of the "master of ceremonies" of the event, as he was Grayson's trainer and bbf, and this was exactly the kind of thing he thrived on doing.

The pool's surface was smooth as glass, the moonlight reflecting off it in a white-gold slash. The warm California air smelled sweet with the scent of the flowering shrubs along the fence, mixed with the scent of Finn's shampoo. Grayson tuned out Ethan and Felix's conversation and just allowed himself to relax, reveling in how good it felt to sit there with Finn wrapped in his arms, the darkening sky blanketing them.

Grayson had the overwhelming feeling that this moment was momentous. This was something he'd never done or had the slightest inkling to ever do. He was letting his guard down and getting comfortable with someone. He knew he'd never forget how this felt, sitting under the stars with Finn tucked against him. Nothing in his whole life had ever seemed so perfectly *right*. He was a contradiction of emotions; his stomach fluttered with his growing feelings for Finn, so all-consuming and intense, but he also felt a deep sense of soothing calm, like everything was just as it should be. It was so strange and so undeniably amazing.

Keeping his voice low so that the others couldn't hear him, he whispered into Finn's neck,

"Do you feel this, too?"

It took Finn much longer than Grayson would have liked to reply, though it was likely only the length of time it took to take a deep breath. "Do you want the truth?" Finn said this so carefully that Grayson could read nothing in his tone.

"Yes," Grayson whispered. "I want the truth." Then he held his breath for long seconds.

Finn's whispered breath was warm on Grayson's cheek, "I feel it, too."

The jolt of elation and terror that immediately surged through Grayson at those words was tamped down by a somewhat slurred, rowdy shout of, "Get a goddamn room already!" from a laughing Felix. Felix then turned to Ethan and stage whispered, drunkenly, "They are *always* like this. It's too fucking adorable for me to even stand it." Then, his tipsy friend gave Grayson a fond grin, clearly happy for him.

"Well, I guess that's my cue," Ethan said as he rose to go. "Thanks for letting me hang. With the semester wrapping and the show's schedule, I've been so swamped. I probably would have eaten a protein bar in the car for dinner if it weren't for you guys, so thanks for the pizza." When Ethan started to make his way across the lawn to go, Felix wobbled to standing calling, "Hey! I'll walk you out," as he trailed after Ethan.

Now it was just Grayson and Finn sitting out by the moonlight pool, the night air chilling slightly, but neither of them made any attempt to move from their cozy position on the chaise. Grayson just wrapped his arms tighter around Finn's stomach and breathed in the citrus scent of his hair. *He even smells amazing. Is it possible that Finn has no actual flaws to speak of?*

Grayson was contemplating Finn's utter perfection when he felt Finn sink back further into his chest, a heavy sigh escaping as he snuggled in closer.

"What's wrong?" Grayson asked.

Another sigh. "Nothing, really."

Grayson was not letting him off that easy.

"Come on, babe. Out with it."

"I'm just embarrassed about that stupid magazine thing. They didn't need to bring it up during the table read. I just don't need the constant reminder that I'm not a serious enough actor to appear on a magazine cover with actual clothes on." He added, "It was way worse that everyone kept talking about it in front of you."

"Are you crazy? Why would you be embarrassed? The article was great. You sounded thoughtful and intelligent. You came off as a dedicated actor with aspirations of proving stereotypes wrong. You should be proud of yourself," Grayson said.

"I could maybe be proud if anyone actually read the interview. But it's all about the shirtless pose and that Lydia had her hands on me. I just hate the way the media spins everything." Finn continued, sounding resigned, "Besides the embarrassment of the shirtless photograph, I really don't like people speculating that I'm dating Lydia. It seems like living a lie for publicity, but apparently that's my reality now. I just feel gross about it, I guess."

"Hey. What I took away from the cover photo was that my boyfriend is hot as hell and that his co-star looks as enamored with him as everyone who ever meets him is. People will speculate, but fuck 'em. The people who matter know the truth."

Finn didn't respond to this, and Grayson suddenly realized exactly what he'd just said. He'd called Finn his boyfriend. *Boyfriend.* They'd never had the "are we boyfriends?" conversation. Hell, they'd never even discussed if they were dating exclusively. Grayson knew he wasn't sleeping with anyone else, and he assumed the same was true of Finn. He hoped it was. The tricky part was the "boyfriend" of it all. If they were just hooking up while they were filming, the boyfriend label surely wouldn't apply. As the moments ticked by, Finn's silence felt more and more like a sledgehammer of disappointment slamming into Grayson's gut.

Grayson couldn't take it anymore. "Finn?" he asked, voice wary.

Grayson felt Finn's head nodding gently in acknowledgement that he'd heard Grayson. Finally, his voice terribly quiet, Finn asked, "You want me to be your boyfriend?"

Grayson thought about the question. He could try to backpedal here, somehow taking back the words that had landed him in this delicate conversation. But, he didn't want to do that. Finn deserved honesty. "Yeah. I do." Grayson waited. One breath. Two. Three. "Finn! Say something. You're killing me here."

Finn spun around to face Grayson, eyes so dark they matched the night sky above them. He looked at Grayson for a long moment, searching his face for something, and Grayson hoped to God he found what he was looking for.

"Hell, yes, I want to be boyfriends," Finn finally said, his gorgeous face lighting up.

When Grayson kissed him then, he felt like he was flying, soaring up out of his body, dizzy and disoriented. He had never felt this much joy in any single previous moment of his life.

CHAPTER 8

"Alright, people," the angry fedora-clad man standing at the front of the large room said, "this is not goddamn rocket science. You'd think a group of such pretty people wouldn't be such utterly hideous dancers." The man cupped his forehead with his hand, taking an exasperated breath, before letting it out loudly and saying, "From the top. 1, 2, 3..."

The music started up again, a traditional waltz, and Finn began a few tentative movements, guiding Lydia in a haphazard attempt at ballroom dancing. Out of the blue, Gwen and Jasper had decided that the final episode of *Frost Manor*, Season 3 was going to take place at a ball, rather than at a regular parlor/dining room gathering as originally written. They'd said something about the cinematic effect and the romance of a candle-lit ballroom. Everyone would be decked out in elaborate ball costumes, and it would be the perfect backdrop for the dramatic season finale.

Gwen and Jasper clearly underestimated

the amount of work it was going to take to shape up a pack of millennials into convincing 19th century aristocrats at a ball. Finn and Lydia constantly found themselves stepping on one another's feet, bonking heads, and dissolving into fits of giggles. That may have had something to do with why the dance instructor had his fedora in a twist. Finn didn't want to piss him off, and he really did need to figure this out quickly, but he also couldn't help but enjoy twirling around with Lydia, discovering that she was the only person on earth less cut out for formal dancing than he was.

Once Finn and Lydia managed to find a rhythm, moving somewhat competently to the 1-2-3, 1-2-3 beat of the waltz, he chanced a look over her shoulder and across the room. And his breath caught. Grayson looked ridiculously gorgeous as he danced. He twirled Astrid around so smoothly, his movements self-assured and elegant. Finn wondered if Grayson had done this before or if he was just naturally good at everything. He couldn't help but stare. Grayson's broad shoulders were squared, his posture tall and straight, but he still moved with an ease, as if waltzing was second nature to him, as if he belonged at an 1890s high-society ball.

What would it feel like to dance with Grayson? To be led effortlessly across the floor in smooth glides, Grayson's strong hand at his waist, his hazel eyes locking with Finn's, as they moved together through the crowd? *It would be a dream,* Finn thought.

And just like that, Finn felt less mesmerized by Grayson's competent movement on the dance floor and more consumed with gnawing, potent jealousy as his vision expanded beyond the Grayson-sized bubble it had been zoned in on and took in Grayson's dance partner. Astrid was there, looking up at Grayson with goo-goo eyes, her hand clutching his shoulder possessively. Finn examined the way Grayson's hand cradled Astrid's side, his other hand clasped with hers. He felt his guts roiling, and the rage boiling up in him was shocking in its unfamiliar intensity. Jealousy was something new for Finn, who'd never really been in a relationship before. He knew he had nothing to worry about with Grayson and Astrid, but he still didn't like seeing his boyfriend so close to someone else who clearly wanted him.

"Ouch! Shit, Finn!" Lydia smacked Finn in the chest and glared at him. He realized he'd just brutally trampled on her tiny foot in his fit of stupid jealousy.

"Sorry, Lyd. You okay?"

"I'm fine. Not like I haven't stepped on you about ten times today. Just took me by surprise because I thought we'd finally got the hang of it. Turns out we're tragically hopeless, I guess." She smiled at him, but it faded fast when she saw his sour expression. "Hey, are *you* okay?"

Finn did a quick mental pro/con list to decide how much to share with Lydia. Screw it. He needed someone to talk to, and Lydia had proven herself to be a kind and trustworthy friend to him. Sighing, Finn said, "I'm just a little distracted, I guess."

Lydia followed Finn's gaze across the room to where Astrid was tilting her head back and laughing exaggeratedly at something Grayson had said, the two of them looking ready to make their *Dancing with the Stars* debut. When Lydia looked back up at Finn, her face had softened into sympathy. "I thought you might have a thing for him. I was just waiting for you to tell me. I didn't want to pry." She smiled kindly.

"Yeah. You could say I have *a thing* for him, alright."

"Are you guys...? I mean, have you...?" Lydia's eyes widened, curiosity practically bubbling out of her.

"Yes. As unbelievable as it still is to me, we're...together...I guess." Finn felt himself blush.

"No. Way. That is awesome! You are basically the two most perfect humans alive. I don't know who I'm more jealous of, you for getting to fuck him or him for getting to fuck you." Lydia made a show of tapping her chin like she was seriously trying to puzzle out which of them she'd rather be.

"God, Lyd. No one's fucking anyone," he hiss-whispered, clearly embarrassed. "Not yet, at least. I mean, we've done *stuff*, but...Nevermind. That's not the point," Finn could feel his frustration rising as he fumbled over his words. He stopped attempting to dance and ran his fingers through his hair. "I need to take a break," he said, and he and Lydia made their way off the dance floor and over to a side table, which was stocked with bottled water and snacks for the cast. They each took a bottle and leaned up against the wall. They sipped the water and watched the other dancers in silence for a few minutes before Lydia spoke again.

"Okay. Sorry. But I'm confused. You're dating Grayson, but you're unhappy for some reason? You can't be jealous of him dancing with Astrid. She's a garbage human, and he has no interest in her." Lydia said this so matter-of-factly that it calmed Finn marginally.

"I guess I'm more jealous that she gets to dance with him. She gets to play the love interest. She gets to be on his arm on red carpets. It just... sucks, you know?"

"Aw, Finn. You want him to be more public with your relationship? He's not open to that?"

"No. Yes. Maybe? We haven't really talked about it, but we have been warned on threat of our careers and possibly death that us being together is bad for the show. We are supposed to play up the on-set-enemies angle to keep the buzz going after that stupid article.."

"No shit," Lydia said, "Jasper and Gwen asked you to do that?"

"I don't think it's that they, personally, want us to fuel those rumors, but they agreed with Kayla that it could be really good for the show if we did. Oh, and it sounds like the network actually proposed that we act like we hate each other. So, there's that. They said it could fuck up our chances at renewal if we didn't go along with the network on this.

And beyond that, I don't think Grayson's really the 'hey-look-at-me-with-my-boyfriend' kind of guy. I think he and Thomas Logan broke up when Thomas wanted to be more public than he did. I mean, he agreed to go along with this plan, so he must be okay with keeping our relationship quiet." Finn shrugged and focused on peeling the label from his water bottle.

"Sorry, Finn. That really sucks." Lydia wrapped an arm around his waist, giving him a comforting side-hug. Finn leaned down and kissed the top of her head. She really was a good friend.

As he stood at the side of the dance floor with Lydia, Finn stole another look at Grayson. Grayson had maneuvered Astrid so that her back was to them, and Grayson could see Finn over her shoulder. He had a look of concern on his face when he met Finn's eyes, clearly having noticed

Finn's abrupt retreat from the dance floor. Grayson mouthed, "You okay?"

Finn felt his chest warm and his body relax slightly. He smiled at Grayson and nodded, silently reassuring him that yes, he was okay. Lydia, apparently, hadn't missed this little exchange, and she grinned widely at Finn, squeezing him closer. "You have it so bad for him," she teased. "I am *so* going to be your maid of honor."

"Shut up." Finn knew he was now smiling like a fool, too.

That was when Furious Fedora Man approached them, one hand on his hip and the other waving a finger in their direction. "Oh no. Absolutely not. No, no, no. You two need more practice than anyone. Water break's over, kiddies!" Finn knew better than to look at Lydia, who was doing an even worse job of stifling her laugh than he was as the Furious Fedora waved his finger back and forth vigorously in their faces before pushing them back out onto the dance floor.

They ended up more in the middle of the action this time, and as they got into proper waltz position, Grayson and Astrid whirled by. Grayson shot Finn an amused smile and sidled up close enough to him to whisper, "Quit your slacking." He gave Finn a quick, flirty wink and a heated look as he brushed past him and back into the crowd of dancers. Not even Astrid's scowl could dampen the warm feeling Finn got from that tiny acknowledgement from Grayson. It was a miracle that the nearby dancers didn't feel the zing from the electricity that jittered between the two of them when Grayson had come near him.

Apparently, at least one person had felt it. "I'll be damned," Lydia said quietly once Grayson and Astrid were out of earshot. "He's totally in love with you, you lucky bastard."

Of course, that was crazy, Finn knew. No way was Grayson in love with him. Finn didn't even want to let himself hope that Grayson could love him some day. This was too complicated, and it was temporary. Of that, Finn was sure. Grayson was not the kind of guy to settle down with someone like Finn. He'd want someone more serious, someone more accomplished, someone older and with more experience. Finn was just happy to take what Grayson was willing to give him right now. No, he didn't need Grayson to love him. His rational brain told him that what they had now was more than enough. Now he just needed to convince his stupid heart of that fact.

◆ ◆ ◆

It was a cloudless, warm California Sunday, and Grayson, Finn, Lydia, and Ethan were heading off to brunch after another ballroom dancing lesson early that morning. Grayson had promised Felix he'd meet him at their favorite brunch spot downtown, and when he'd asked Finn if he'd like to join them, Lydia and Ethan happened to be in the vicinity, and he'd felt obligated to extend the invite to them, too. It's not that he minded; Grayson and Ethan were tight, and Lydia and Finn were bffs, so this might be fun. It also wouldn't hurt to be seen going to brunch with a crowd of friends, rather than arriving at the restaurant with just Finn, who he was supposed to despise. Less chance of the gossip blogs getting ideas about his and Finn's relationship if the paparazzi photographed them.

So, there they were, hopping out of an uber at the popular brunch place, making their way over to where Felix was sitting at an outdoor table along the sidewalk of the restaurant. By the looks of it, he was well into his mimosa already when he waved them over. The group found seats around the table, Grayson managing to strategically place himself next to Finn, and they settled in to peruse the menu. Grayson didn't really need to look; he knew what he was ordering. Eggs benedict, his usual.

Grayson loved this restaurant because it catered to celebs. Their staff never gushed over famous people, they discouraged all patrons from taking photos or asking for autographs, and Grayson had never been photographed by the paparazzi here. So, he and Felix came here just about every Sunday. The food was awesome, and it felt so good to get out somewhere where he could relax.

When the group had settled in, coffees and mimosas and chatter flowing freely, Grayson took a second to appreciatively look at Finn. His boyfriend. Grayson didn't think he would ever get tired of calling him that, even if he only ever called him that in his own head. Finn was leaning back in his chair, one ankle laying casually over one knee. He wore mirrored aviator sunglasses and a worn t-shirt that said, "The 1975." Grayson knew by now that 90 percent of Finn's wardrobe was fitted indie rock band shirts. He was such a cute hipster with his concert tees and constant chattering about Arctic Monkeys. Finn laughed at something Lydia had said, his eyes crinkling at the corners. Grayson's chest tightened a little bit, and he felt the increasingly familiar melting sensation that happened to his insides around Finn. He really loved that laugh.

It had been so hard to focus on the ballroom dancing this morning when he could see Finn and Lydia, twirling around in a blur of carefree giggles. They had looked like they were having so much fun. It was almost like Finn's happiness was a magnet, pulling Grayson's focus away from the drudgery of dancing with Astrid. He felt that same pull now, and he couldn't help himself from sliding his arm across the back of Finn's chair. He knew he shouldn't, it was clearly *not* the way one mortal enemy would sit next to another, but he just needed to be close to him. And now that Lydia knew that they were a couple, everyone here was privy to their relationship, so what would it really hurt?

That was when a familiar voice dragged Grayson's attention from Finn. "I thought I might find you here."

And there was Thomas Logan, swaggering up to their table. He was dressed in tight jeans and a sleeveless shirt, his tattooed arms on display. He slid his sunglasses up onto his bleached platinum hair as he stopped next to their table, eyes zeroed in on Grayson, a cocky smirk on his face. "Hi, Grayson."

"What the fuck do you want, Logan?" This came from Felix before Grayson could react to his ex's unexpected presence.

"Always great to see you, too, Felix," Thomas said, not even bothering to look away from Grayson.

Before Felix could get too riled up, Grayson knew he needed to deal with the situation. "What are you doing here, Thomas?"

"I just wanted to talk. I figured you still came here on Sundays, and I thought I might catch you."

"I don't think we have anything to say to one another," Grayson said flatly. He was well aware that Finn's shoulders had tensed, he could feel it under his arm, which was still slung along the back of Finn's chair. He gave Finn's shoulder a gentle squeeze that he hoped was reassuring.

"So, it is true," Thomas said, his eyes flitting to Grayson's hand on Finn's shoulder and quickly back to Grayson. "I told Astrid she was batshit crazy if she thought *you'd* hook up with *him*." Thomas was sure to use extra emphasis on that last word. "When I ran into her at the Versace show, she filled me in on the little rumor she'd heard on set, and I told her flat out that she was insane. I guess not, though." He made a face of feigned disbelief as he tilted his head to the side and continued to stare at Grayson in disappointment.

Lydia stepped in then. "You're an asshole and just jealous that you got dumped. Now, you can leave," she said to Thomas, her voice full of indignation on Finn's behalf, her pretty face hard as stone as she stared him down.

Thomas put his hands up in a "don't shoot" gesture, and he backed a couple of steps away from the table. Then, he said to Grayson, "I mean, if you're finally willing to go public with someone, I'm more than willing to take you back. Just saying. I know I said I was done with your secretive bullshit, but if you're over it, you should know you have…options." That was when Thomas leveled a glare at Finn, and said to Grayson, "Just think about it," and then turned and sauntered away.

"What a dick," Felix said.

"No kidding," Lydia agreed.

Ethan, who had been silent during the whole incident, turned to Finn then, and asked, "You okay?"

Finn nodded and looked down at his half-eaten veggie omelet. "Fine," he said.

Finn didn't go home with Grayson that night. He told Grayson he needed to work on his dance choreography with Lydia and promised to call him later. It was likely true that they could use the practice, but Grayson knew a brush-off when he saw it. That asshole Thomas had gotten under Finn's skin, which was exactly what he'd set out to do when he showed up at the restaurant. *Fuck that guy.*

Grayson hated that he'd just sat there like a dumbass and let Lydia and Felix be the ones to stand up to Thomas. What was his problem? He could have said something more, done something more to put a stop to that absolute shitshow of a display from his ex. He felt like such an idiot. But Grayson knew himself. He would replay that brunch incident and come up with plenty to say now that it was too late. Sometimes he hated himself for overthinking things. Sometimes it got in the way of just following his gut. Or his heart. And then he was in situations like this one, where he felt like he had fallen short when he should have stepped up.

He needed to talk to Finn, but he wasn't going to force a conversation Finn clearly didn't want to have right now. He'd give him his space and wait for him to call. But that was much easier said than done. Grayson felt a sick churning in his gut every time he thought about that shit-eating smirk on Thomas's face or the tension in Finn's body when Thomas had spoken to Grayson. Grayson hated that he was at least partially responsible for killing Finn's good mood and making him feel uncomfortable. This was exactly the kind of shit Grayson had been afraid of. He was going to bring Finn down.

Grayson had to do something. He couldn't just sit here stewing on this. Then, he got an idea. He went over to his laptop, pulled up google, and got to work. He needed to show Finn that he cared, even if he was too stupid to show it earlier. After a few hours of intense research, Grayson was ready. He pulled out his phone and shot out a quick text to Finn.

Grayson: *Not to be a pest, but I just wanted to give you a heads-up. I sent you an email. Hope you're having a good night.*

Grayson set his phone down on his nightstand, nerves swimming through his bloodstream as he lay in bed, waiting for Finn's reaction to his gesture.

Email from @grayson.winter to @finn.everett:

Finn,

I know it's no caramel macchiato, but I felt like a dick for not saying more when Thomas showed up at brunch. So, this is me doing the whole gesture thing, I guess. I think I've seen you wear all of these bands' shirts at some point. So, here goes.

> *How Grayson feels about Finn, confessions in hipster music. A playlist:*

1. *"Do I Wanna Know?" by Arctic Monkeys,*
2. *"Tear in My Heart" by Twenty One Pilots*
3. *"Electric Blue" by Arcade Fire*
4. *"To Be Alone with You" by Sufjan Stevens*
5. *"Read My Mind" by The Killers*
6. *"Blood Bank" by Bon Iver*
7. *"Part One" by Band of Horses*
8. *"Slide Away" by Oasis*
9. *"Chasing Cars" by Snow Patrol*

Bonus Track (Grayson's non-hipster choice):

10. *"Everlong" by Foo Fighters*

I actually listened to all these songs, too. They weren't bad. I think I mainly liked them because you like them. Anyway, feel free to laugh at this and how incredibly

lame I am. But I wanted to... you know, put it out there.
-Grayson

CHAPTER 9

Filming the season finale episode was bittersweet for Finn. On the one hand, he knew it would be an amazing episode. He even got competent enough at waltzing to get by. On the other hand, this was the end of his time on set for the season, and the future, the show's and Finn's, was still very much uncertain. And then there was his relationship with Grayson. That was the most uncertain piece of the whole puzzle. What would happen now? He knew they'd be going on the press tour together, but if this was the end of Frost Manor, would it also be the end of them?

Finn thought about the email Grayson had sent him. It had been so incredibly thoughtful. Grayson really did pay attention to him and what he liked, and he had put so much effort into finding those songs and creating that playlist. It had been pretty damn romantic. In the days since he received the email, Finn and Grayson hadn't had much chance to see one another, aside from on set. The filming schedule had been crazy as the season finale barreled down at them. But now, it seemed, they would have some time to be together. Too bad it was going to be on a press tour where they had to be cold co-workers at best, sworn enemies at worst, and absolutely nothing more than that. Kayla had reiterated to him just that morning the need for discretion about their real relationship and the importance of playing along. *This should be interesting.*

Finn was sitting in the semi-secluded courtyard of the hotel where he'd been staying during filming, sipping an iced coffee at a small bistro-style table as he waited for Grayson to pick him up. *Luna's Cove* had been filmed on the east coast, so he didn't have his own place in L.A. yet. He'd sort out his living situation when he knew whether or not the show would be renewed and, more importantly, if his own contract would be extended to future seasons. He was flipping through a stack of film scripts, listening to The Killers on his AirPods. Kayla had sent off a bunch of scripts, mainly offers of film roles in teen rom-coms. He wasn't really seeing anything that jumped out at him in this pile, so he slid it into his messenger bag and closed his eyes, soaking in the sun on his face, the scent of the flowering shrubs, and appreciating the lyrics Brandon Flowers was belting out.

He was startled by the sound of a chair scraping on the cobblestone of the courtyard's patio. "Hey there," Grayson said, taking a seat across from Finn at the small table. Finn pocketed his ear buds and grinned at his boyfriend. Grayson was wearing a pair of khaki shorts, a blue polo shirt, and his tortoiseshell-framed glasses, looking every bit the J Crew model, as usual. "You ready?"

"Where are we going again?" Finn remembered Grayson dodging that question when they were texting that morning.

"The studio, actually, but that's all you're getting out of me." Grayson stood and reached for Finn's hand, pulling him across the courtyard and toward Grayson's car. Grayson drove a silver Lexus, a nice car, but not too flashy. It suited him. Finn nodded his chin in the direction of the black Land Rover parked behind it which was driven by Grayson's personal security. Grayson's team was really cool, and they always gave them as much privacy as they could safely provide, for which Finn was thankful.

As soon as Finn slid into the passenger seat, he plugged his phone in and pulled up a playlist. Grayson wasn't really into music, at least not the way Finn was, so Finn always provided the tunes. Lately, Finn had a handful of certain songs on constant repeat. "So, you really aren't going to tell me why we're going in to work on a day off?" Finn asked, more curious than frustrated.

"Nope."

"You realize you don't have to keep springing surprises and gestures on me, right? I've wanted you since I was about 16. You've got me. No wooing required." Finn laughed as he said this, and Grayson's smiling response made Finn's insides wobble.

"Maybe I like surprising you. And you're crazy if you think this is a one-sided thing."

Finn was ridiculously happy at those words. A few minutes later, they pulled up to a parking spot in front of the studio building they'd been in yesterday to shoot the last of the ball scenes. Finn raised a questioning brow at Grayson as they got out of the car and started walking toward the entrance.

When they walked in, Finn was surprised to see that the set was almost completely preserved. The crew hadn't pulled down any of the chandeliers, removed any of the candles, or thrown out any of the elaborate floral arrangements. Weirder yet, the musicians they'd hired to play the music onscreen for the episode were seated in the corner of the room in full formal dress. The conductor of the quartet looked over his shoulder and Grayson gave him a nod. Then they started to play. That must have been the signal to some unseen accomplice, because the lights in the studio dimmed, leaving just the candles and chandeliers, a warm yellow glow illuminating the white roses and glinting off the golden candelabras. It was like they'd stepped back in time, and it did *not* feel the way it did when they were filming. Now, there was no camera, crew, or director to cut in. There weren't PAs running around, and there weren't any other cast members there, either. It was just him and Grayson.

Grayson stepped close to Finn then, taking one of his hands and sliding the other to his waist. They were a little too close, Grayson's touch a little too familiar, to be considered proper waltz form, but to Finn it felt absolutely perfect. He leaned in even closer, Grayson's hand snaking around to the small of his back.

"You know what I thought about while filming the dance sequences?" Grayson asked, his voice quiet despite them being alone in the room apart from the musicians.

"What?" Finn's voice was a soft whisper in reply.

"I thought about how much better it would be if you were the one dancing with me. I wanted you to be the one in my arms, and I wanted to be looking into those unbelievable blue eyes," he said as he led Finn in a flawless waltz. "It was probably the most difficult scene I'd ever had to film because I had to watch you from across the room as we each danced with other people, and I had to pretend that I was happy where I was and not like I was dying to be where you were."

Finn didn't trust himself to say anything just then, his heartbeat hammering away in his chest. He just looked up at Grayson's face, and was struck when he saw Grayson's hazel eyes reflecting what seemed like his own feelings back at him. They were overwhelmed with affection and wanting, just as he knew his were. Finn distantly wondered if Grayson's heartbeat was as wild as his own, or if Grayson was also finding it unusually hard to breathe.

Knowing that he needed to say something, he couldn't just leave Grayson hanging after he'd said all that, Finn managed a "Me, too" before he moved even closer to Grayson, his face nuzzling into Grayson's neck. Then Finn spoke, his mouth against Grayson's skin, "So is dancing with me everything you'd hoped?"

Grayson tightened his grip on Finn, unclasping their hands so he could wrap both his arms around Finn's back, bringing them chest to chest as their steps became a languid sway rather than a waltz. Grayson said, "It is even better," before taking Finn's mouth in a slow, deep kiss that turned Finn into a puddle of mush in Grayson's arms.

"Grayson," he said, pulling back just enough to speak, "take me back to my hotel?" It was phrased as a question, the invitation clear.

"Right now?" Grayson asked, searching Finn's face for something, though Finn wasn't entirely sure what.

"Yes. Right now," Finn said, dragging him by the hand toward the exit.

◆ ◆ ◆

Grayson woke up the next morning curled up around Finn, who was still breathing deep and even in a peaceful sleep. Grayson pulled him in even closer to his body and silently thanked the universe for bringing him Finn. It felt so nice to wake up together, feeling Finn's warm body and the cadence of his breathing against his chest.

They hadn't fucked the night before, although Finn had implied that he would have been up for that. Grayson wasn't sure that it was a good idea. He assumed Finn hadn't actually been with a lot of other guys, and Grayson didn't want to push him into anything that he wasn't ready for. There is plenty they can do without actually fucking, Grayson had told Finn, saying that he was more than happy to keep doing the things they were doing. Finn had been mock pouty, but then seemed pretty damn enthusiastic about engaging in their usual bedroom activities. Grayson certainly wasn't complaining. Not a bit. Finn blew his damn mind every time they were together.

"Hey," a sleepy Finn said, twisting around to face Grayson and give him a gentle kiss. "Good morning."

"Hi," Grayson said, sliding a hand through

Finn's messy bedhead. Looking at Finn all sleepy-eyed and disheveled, Grayson felt a tightness in his chest. "You're so beautiful. You know that?"

Finn smiled at him. "You're one to talk." Finn made a point of casting his eyes down to Grayson's bare chest and abs before trailing them slowly back up to Grayson's face. "This stubble is pretty hot," Finn said, stretching to place tiny, soft kisses along Grayson's jaw before nuzzling his own cheek against Grayson's.

Right as Grayson was ready to pounce on his way-too-enticing boyfriend, both of their phones started buzzing. Grayson dropped one more quick kiss on Finn's mouth before groaning and rolling over to the nightstand to check his phone.

"It's Ethan," he said, just as Finn was looking down at his own phone.

"It's Lydia."

They both took a second to read their messages, and then looked at one another. "I guess we better get dressed," Grayson said, resigned.

"Damn it," Finn whined exaggeratedly. "I wanted to have time for us to shower. I really wanted to suds up all those muscles." He winked as he made the teasing comment. "Do I at least get a raincheck?"

Grayson chuckled as he pulled on his pants and hunted for his discarded shirt. "Absolutely, you do."

The messages from Ethan and Lydia said essentially the same thing: Gwen and Jasper were calling an emergency meeting at the studio offices. Everyone needed to be there ASAP. While they weren't sure who "everyone," meant, exactly, Grayson knew it would likely include all the series regulars if Lydia had been the one to text Finn.

So, when Grayson and Finn walked into the studio's conference room, Grayson wasn't too surprised to see Gwen and Jasper at the head of the table, surrounded by Ethan, Lydia, and Astrid. Ethan was holding a stack of papers out for Gwen to look at, the two of them talking in hushed tones. Jasper was on his phone, typing rapidly.

Grayson took the empty seat next to Astrid, while Finn took the spot next to Lydia on the other side of the table. Abruptly, Jasper set his phone down and said, "Good. You're all here." Grayson hated surprise meetings and not knowing what to expect. He felt his nerves looping around in his stomach, and he was really wishing he would have snagged a banana from that fruit bowl in Finn's hotel room after all. Maybe that would have calmed his roiling gut.

Gwen took over then, crossing her legs underneath her in the chair and sliding her cat-eye reading glasses up onto her pink-blonde head. "We hate to do this to you all on short notice, but we really have no choice. All four of you are booked solid with press engagements for the next two weeks, but we need to rearrange some things." Grayson glanced over to Ethan, who he noticed looked frazzled and like he hadn't slept in days. Clearly, by "we need to rearrange some things," Gwen meant that Ethan was busting his ass to accommodate whatever new wrench was being tossed into the mix.

Astrid interrupted before Gwen could continue. "I cannot be expected to rearrange everything at the last minute. I'm already missing so many events, and I've passed on three high-end modeling campaigns because of all these press engagements. You're going to need to deal with my agent because I cannot handle this stress." She tilted her chin defiantly, crossing her arms in front of her like armor.

"Too bad you signed a contract agreeing to do the promotional obligations," Grayson said to her, feeling the need to defend Gwen and Jasper here. He knew that they weren't just changing things for the fun of it.

Astrid leveled her icy glare on Grayson then, her tone just as cold. "You're just happy because you get to do press with your little boy toy. Not all of us get to bring a fuck buddy along for all this shit."

Grayson clenched his fists where they rested atop his thighs. He knew better than to react to her. Stooping to her level was just what she'd want him to do, and he wasn't about to take the bait.

"Enough." Gwen was annoyed now, and she looked directly at Astrid as she continued. "The network is insisting on throwing a big viewing party for the season finale, and you will all be there. That means we need to move around some other press, but Ethan will handle that and give you all your updated schedules. We are optimistic that this party is a "congratulations" and means the network will be renewing us, but we don't know that for sure. In the meantime, we need you to be upbeat – I'm talking unicorns and rainbows-level upbeat – any time you speak about the network or the possibility of more seasons. These upcoming interviews must go well and paint the network and our future in the best possible light."

Jasper spoke then. "We know you guys are up for the challenge. And we wanted to make sure you were aware that this network viewing party is mandatory. You will be there and represent the show in a way that will make us proud."

After the group gave their assurances to Gwen and Jasper that they could handle that, the four actors and Ethan left the room, leaving Gwen and Jasper in hushed conversation. Lydia and Finn had walked out ahead of the others, Ethan trailing a few steps behind them. That left Grayson next to Astrid as they made their way down the hall.

"That meeting was useless," she said, not even looking at Grayson as she spoke. "I cannot believe they called me down here to tell me the most common-sense bullshit, like 'don't badmouth the network in charge of our renewal.' What do they think I am, some kind of fucking idiot?" Her high heels clicked loudly with each of her vigorous footfalls.

Grayson didn't respond, keeping his steps quick and his face forward.

"Oh, wait," Astrid said in an exaggeratedly dramatic voice, making a point to turn and look directly at Grayson. "They *do* think we are morons because *some people* are dumb enough to fuck their costars, therefore jeopardizing the reputation of the entire cast.

Lucky for you, the world believes you two can't stand each other, and that's for the best. Wouldn't want to alienate the millions of girls who want to believe that Finn Everett is straight, available, and that they'd have a snowball's chance in hell with him. We can really use those girls for ratings, Grayson, so keep your shit together at those interviews." The look she gave him was not simply angry. It almost looked like there was hurt there, too.

"That is really rich coming from you, Astrid," Grayson replied, somehow managing to keep himself under control. "You're the one who is always trying to make it look like we're together. You drape yourself over me on red carpets and constantly make flirty comments in front of reporters. If I can manage to go along with *that*, I can manage just about anything. Don't talk to me about 'jeopardizing' the cast's reputation. That is such bullshit."

"Fuck you, Grayson," she said, exiting the building through a door along the side of the hall.

Grayson continued on toward the exit near the parking lot where he'd left his car. He assumed Finn was waiting for him outside, probably still chatting with Lydia. Before Grayson could make it out to the parking lot, however, Ethan stopped him.

Ethan had been lurking by the door to the parking lot, slowly pacing the hall.

"What's up, E?"

"Hey, man. I just wanted to talk to you quickly." Ethan looked around as if to ensure there were no eavesdroppers in their vicinity.

"Okay..." Grayson was getting those nervous twinges in his gut again.

"It's about what Astrid said," Ethan looked up at Grayson with serious eyes, "you know, back in the meeting?"

"Yes, I recall," Grayson said.

"Anyway, I know it's not really my business or whatever, but I think you need to just ignore her. Don't take any of what she says to heart."

Grayson wasn't entirely sure where this was coming from or why Ethan was bringing this up. "I don't. I couldn't care less what she says."

Ethan nodded. "Good. That's good."

"E, why are we having this conversation? You know I don't listen to Astrid."

Ethan shifted his weight from foot-to-foot. "It's not really fair of me to get involved because I work with all of you, and I shouldn't use my position to eavesdrop or pass along anyone's personal information." He looked guiltily at his feet. "But you and I are friends, yeah? And I guess I just wanted to make sure that you don't mess up a good thing with Finn because of other people's bullshit. The guy's really into you. I had my doubts at first because he seemed a little flighty or something, but he has real, serious feelings for you. And I just…I think you deserve to be happy."

Grayson looked at his friend, carefully reading his expression. Had Ethan overheard Finn say something about him? And if so, what had he said? He knew better than to put Ethan on the spot by prying further. Instead, he simply said, "I am happy. Thanks, man."

Ethan smiled, then, and he looked like a weight was lifted from his droopy, tired shoulders. "I was just worried that what went down with Thomas would make you hesitant or distrustful or something. I know he was kind of a tool."

"That he is. But Finn is different. And all my

hesitation to be public with Thomas, I'm realizing now, was less about not wanting to be public and more about not wanting to be public *with him*. He just wasn't it for me, and I think I was looking for an excuse to tank things."

Ethan nodded again, seemingly satisfied by that response. "Finn's a good dude, G. You both are."

Grayson smiled. Ethan was a good friend. With that last thought in mind, Grayson decided he needed to step up his friend game, too.

"Hey, E?"

"Yeah?"

They pushed open the door to the parking lot now, stepping out into the sunlit afternoon and slowly heading toward Grayson's Lexus. "You look like death, dude. Jasper and Gwen running you too hard?"

"Nah. Not entirely their doing. I had finals this week, in addition to all this scheduling shit. But I passed, and I'm done with school now, so I should finally be able to get some sleep. At least a little, anyway." Ethan chuckled at the unlikeliness of him sleeping for more than a few hours at a time.

"That's awesome. Must be nice to be done. Any ideas about what comes next?"

"Actually, I've committed to the Wollstone Agency. I signed with them yesterday." Ethan grinned at Grayson. "Doesn't seem real yet. Probably won't until I stop fetching Jasper's dry cleaning and Gwen's lattes."

"Congratulations. That's a big-name outfit. You'll be great. Anyone would be lucky to have you for an agent. We should celebrate."

Ethan took the compliment graciously, and they discussed getting a group together to celebrate as they wandered up to where Finn was leaning against the passenger side of Grayson's car, clicking away on his phone. He looked up with a warm smile for Grayson and Ethan.

"Hey guys, what's up?"

"Ethan was just telling me that he's already signed with an agency," Grayson said. "And I want to take him out to celebrate."

"Oh no shit? That's awesome! We're totally going to celebrate. I bet Felix would be down, too."

"Cool," Ethan said, backing away briskly. "I'll see you guys later, though. I need to run if I'm going to handle this scheduling clusterfuck."

Ethan took a few steps away before turning around and walking back over to them abruptly. "And, guys? For the record, even though I haven't officially started as an agent, it's my professional opinion that you being out and open with your relationship would have no negative consequences for your careers or your projects. Your talent and work ethic speaks for itself. And if you are happy and confident about your personal life, that can only be a good thing when people consider working with you. Just saying." With that he turned and ambled off back toward the studio.

Grayson and Finn looked at one another, not saying anything, before climbing into the car and driving away.

CHAPTER 10

"The blue one. For sure," Lydia said decisively, nodding her head toward one of the shirts Finn held up in front of him. "Brings out your eyes." She went back to scrolling through Instagram while Finn slipped the shirt on and began buttoning it.

It was the night of the viewing party for the *Frost Manor* Season 3 Finale. Lydia was already dressed, looking gorgeous in a red tulle-skirted dress. Finn thought it made her look like a Disney princess gone bad. Finn put the finishing touches on his hair and asked for Lydia's final assessment. "Well, how do I look?" He had a wide grin that said he knew he looked good.

Lydia put her phone into her small black sequined clutch and gave Finn a thorough once-over. She whistled her approval. "You look hot. Grayson is one lucky man," she said, laughing lightly as they made their way out to the waiting limo. The network spared no expense on this soiree, sending fancy rides and booking a ballroom in a swanky downtown hotel. Finn told himself that all this extravagance was a good sign that the network was celebrating the show. He remained hopeful that they'd announce the show's renewal that night.

By the time Finn entered the party with Lydia on his arm, the celebration was in full swing. There were servers passing around trays of champagne and finger foods through a thick crowd of various people associated with *Frost Manor* and the network. There were also various other celebrities mingling in small groups around the room. Finn scanned the room for Grayson, who planned to meet Finn there to keep up their appearance of chilliness toward one another. They didn't actually know who the gossip site's "insider" was, or even if they really had one, but they didn't want to take their chances looking too friendly in such a big crowd, especially not in front of network execs and the showrunningers. Lydia had said that she *needed* a date and Finn *had* to take her to save her from going alone. Lydia could have easily found a more-than-willing date, but she wasn't seeing anyone at the time and it was clear she wanted to support Finn when he couldn't arrive with Grayson.

Grayson and Ethan were sitting at a table, deep in conversation, half-empty champagne flutes in front of them. Lydia and Finn snagged their own drinks and joined them. Gwen and Jasper were at the next table, seated with the network bigwigs. "How's the vibe?" Finn asked Grayson as he slid into the seat next to him.

"Seems good, but they are still keeping pretty tight-lipped. I think they're just waiting for the whole cast to arrive," Grayson said. He gave Finn an appreciative look before finally averting his eyes and rejoining the conversation with the rest of the table.

Apparently, Astrid still hadn't made her grand entrance, so no announcements yet. Finn downed his champagne and tried to banish the thoughts that this might be a "farewell" party rather than a renewal celebration. He reached for Grayson's hand under the table and they laced their fingers together, resting them on Grayson's knee.

"You've got to be fucking kidding me," Lydia's voice was incredulous. She was staring at the entrance to the ballroom, so Finn followed her gaze.

There was Astrid, dressed in a predictably revealing black minidress and sky-high heels, striding in on the arm of Grayson's ex, Thomas Logan. Finn knew the second Grayson saw him because of the way his grip tightened on Finn's hand, though he didn't react outwardly in any other way. Of course, Thomas looked like a goddamn walking fragrance ad. His supermodel physique was displayed in a form-fitting navy-blue suit, his bleached blonde hair was tousled artfully, and he had a self-satisfied grin on his stupid, flawless face. "Thanks for saving us seats," Astrid said sweetly, as she and Thomas claimed the last two open places at their table.

For a second, no one said anything. Finn felt physically ill. Not only did he hate being in the same room with Grayson's ex, he didn't understand why Astrid seemed so deadest on screwing with his life. He wondered what he'd done to make her hate him so much. Maybe it was Grayson she hated? Finn couldn't imagine that anyone would hate Grayson, though, so he couldn't help but feel this was somehow directed at him.

"Nice to see all of you," Thomas said, his eyes only on Grayson. "You're all looking well."

Astrid beamed at them from her seat next to Thomas. Lydia scowled right back. Ethan cleared his throat and became especially interested in his champagne glass. Grayson and Finn squeezed their hands together under the table.

Before the awkwardness of the situation could actually kill Finn, there was a dinging at the next table that drew everyone's attention to a now standing Jasper, a knife tinging into the side of a champagne flute he held in front of him. When everyone quieted, Jasper took a microphone from an assistant who had one at the ready.

"Welcome, everyone, and thanks so much

for being here tonight. We are thrilled to celebrate the completion of another fantastic season of *Frost Manor* with all of you, our beloved cast, amazing crew, and fans of the show. We have some big news to share, and for that, I'll pass the mic to my lovely partner in crime, Gwen Giles." Jasper handed her the mic, the crowd applauded, and Gwen stood to address the room.

"Hey there, everyone. As Jasper said, we are thrilled to have you all here tonight and to have had the opportunity to work with so many of you fabulous people." She took a beat before continuing, "Our wonderful network has shared with Jasper and me that the season ended with the highest ratings in the show's history." Loud whoops and applause halted Gwen for a minute, and she smiled at the room. "They've also let us know that *Frost Manor* will not be renewed for another season."

Dead silence. Disbelief.

Gwen took a deep breath, then said, "They've not renewed us for another season, but they have renewed us for *two more seasons!*" The crowd erupted into roars of relief and happiness at the news. Finn and Lydia jumped out of their seats and gripped one another in a hug while bouncing up and down with glee. Ethan and Grayson high-fived.

When the fervor died down enough for Gwen to speak again, she said, "We could not have done this without the amazing efforts of our incredibly talented cast and crew. Astrid, Lydia, you ladies are both so vibrant and commanding on camera. You draw people in, and you make people root for the success of your strong, female characters. I am proud to write for you and always so amazed by what you bring to the roles." Gwen gave them each a broad, fond smile before turning to Finn.

"Finn Everett, you magical little miracle, you!" Gwen beamed at him, her voice wavering a little. "We took a risk when we cast you," but I have never been happier with a decision in my entire career. "You blew us away. You turned all those stereotypes on their heads, and you brought such a raw, nuanced performance to this character. You are nothing short of magic on screen. And we love the positivity and light you carry with you around the set. You are the best, most wonderful addition to this team." Finn felt his eyes burning a little at this. He was not used to getting this type of recognition, and he wondered if it was possible to actually burst with pride.

Gwen turned to Grayson then, tears welling in her own eyes. "Grayson. Thank you. You are a showrunner's absolute dream. No matter what is written on the page, you make it come alive in ways that we could never have dreamt up on our own. You set the tone for any scene you're in, and you're the one everyone on set looks to as our steady, reliable, inspiring anchor. The bar that you set makes everyone else work harder and strive to be better. That is a rare gift. And this season, with the challenge of working with a new cast member, you welcomed the challenge and did what you do best – you were the emotional heart of the show." Gwens eyes shone and she paused for a few beats before she continued.

"And, Grayson and Finn, your scenes together exceeded our wildest expectations. They elevated the show to new heights, and we credit that electric chemistry with securing us these ratings and this two season renewal. Thank you, thank you, thank you. We cannot wait to see what you bring to Seasons Four and Five."

The champagne was flowing freely from that point on, everyone's mood buoyant and giddy. Finn thoroughly enjoyed his evening of dancing and partying. He twirled Lydia around a dance floor to Lizzo, all drunk and giggly and really, really happy. Sweat dripped down his forehead as he blamed it on his juice, Lydia shimmying seductively, if not a little wobbly, next to him. Finn was so happily buzzed, he almost forgot about Thomas Logan. He almost didn't secretly seethe when he noticed Thomas Logan drag Grayson away from the table and out of sight.

◆ ◆ ◆

Grayson followed Thomas through the crowd reluctantly, casting a glance behind him toward where Finn was working the dance floor. "This better be good," he said darkly as he and Thomas stepped in the hallway, far enough away from the party to be overheard.

Thomas stared at Grayson, eyes intense and pleading. "I'm sorry. I know I shouldn't have just showed up here with Astrid. Springing myself on you at a work party was not my best decision, I'll admit." He gave an uncertain half smile before continuing. "I just need you to know that I really miss you, Grayson. We were good together, and I know that if you gave it a chance – a real chance, we'd be so happy."

Grayson couldn't believe what he was hearing. He took in a deep breath and released it slowly before responding. "I don't know why you think we were so good together. We were a train wreck. That's why we broke up, remember? And I seem to remember you thinking we were so bad together that you had me *banned* from a runway show." Grayson laughed coldly, no humor in his expression. "You're out of your mind."

"I was hurt. I wanted to make you feel as badly as I did. It was so infuriating that you hated being seen with me in public. It was like you were embarrassed of me, and I felt like I was something you were ashamed of. That was a feeling I did not enjoy, so I thought breaking up with you would help you see how much you cared and wanted to be with me. I thought it would be the push to get you to go public so we could be together like a real couple." Thomas's eyes searched Grayson's. "And I know you just weren't ready, but clearly, you're ready to show the public who you really are now. I mean, you aren't exactly hiding that you're hooking up with Finn Everett. So, I guess what I'm saying is that if you are ready now, I've been waiting." Thomas looked expectantly at Grayson, hope clear in his eyes.

Grayson felt himself soften a little toward Thomas, and he said, carefully, "It's not that I wasn't ready. It was that we weren't right for each other. I'm sorry."

Thomas recoiled, looking truly shocked. "What? You cannot be serious right now." He started pacing. "I mean, you're willing to be public with *him* and not *me*?"

"First of all, we're not 'public.' Astrid should really keep her mouth shut. This is something that we are keeping quiet for now because of the show, and if you really do care about me, you'll respect that." Grayson's voice was even, and he hoped he conveyed how much it meant to him for Thomas to comply.

"But you're with him? Not just fucking around?"

"Yes. I'm serious about him."

"Jesus Christ. Unbelievable." Thomas threw his hands up in the air at this.

"Thomas, this has nothing to do with you. We just weren't good together."

"And you and *Finn Everett* are?" Thomas was nearly yelling now.

"Yeah, we are," Grayson said honestly.

Thomas's face scrunched up in a pained expression, saying "Fine. Got it. Later, Grayson," before stalking off.

Grayson scrubbed his hand over his face, took a few deep breaths, and turned to go back to the party. He found Finn standing a few feet away, leaning against the wall, waiting for him. Grayson walked over to him, wrapping him up in a hug.

"How much of that did you hear?" he asked.

Finn hugged him back and said, "Enough," with a sweet smile.

"You weren't worried, were you? That I went off with Thomas?" Grayson asked.

"Nah." Finn rested his cheek against Grayson's shoulder. "I didn't love him clearly trying to flirt with you, but I trust you." He added, "But would it be too much to ask for him to contract an unsightly skin condition or something?"

Grayson chuckled and rubbed his hands up and down Finn's back, soaking in his warmth and familiar scent. He always smelled like the beach, a mix of fresh air and sunscreen. He breathed him in, and he knew for certain that he would never regret turning Thomas Logan away. The choice had been one of the easiest he'd ever made.

"I've been thinking," Finn said, looking up at Grayson with a wicked gleam in his eyes. "You've been making all these wonderful declarations and gestures – the coffee, the playlist, the dancing. I've loved every single bit of it, but I'm starting to worry that I'm not pulling my weight here. I feel like I need to make some declarations and gestures of my own."

Finn's hands made their way to Grayson's chest as he continued, eyes cast downward now, almost shy. "As for the declaration, I think you already know this, but I'm completely crazy about you."

Grayson felt himself grin like a loon. He felt warmth swirl through his insides and he wanted to kiss his boyfriend senseless right there in the hallway. But Finn was still speaking. "And as for the gesture...my hotel's only a few blocks from here." He looked back up, his eyes locking with Grayson's. Finn's gaze was full of heat and a little trepidation. Grayson felt his breath hitch.

"Let's go," Grayson said, grabbing Finn's hand and heading for the exit.

CHAPTER 11

So, there they were, stumbling into Finn's hotel suite, attacking one another with lips and hands, clothes trailing along the floor behind them as they made their way to the bed. Finn backed onto the bed, scooting toward the middle, leaning back on his elbows. His eyes were fixed on Grayson's, and Grayson was overwhelmed by what he saw there. Their stunning blue color had darkened to a deep, almost indigo shade, and they held as much tenderness as heat, and that made Grayson's chest hurt.

"You make me crazy," Grayson said, before following him to the bed and climbing up after him. Grayson hovered over Finn, his mouth eager on Finn's, desire ramping up more and more with each stroke of their tongues. They were down to just boxers now, and Finn's warm skin felt like heaven against Grayson's, each place their bodies touched creating a zing of heat straight through him. When Grayson settled himself more fully between Finn's thighs, Grayson could tell Finn was just as turned on as he was, and Grayson groaned in pleasure as he ground his aching cock down into Finn's hard length, nothing between them but thin layers of cotton.

Finn made a small whimpering sound and reached for the waistband of Grayson's boxers. Grayson was more turned on than he thought physically possible, but he felt something nagging at the back of his consciousness that made him hesitate. Despite the serious protests of his dick, Grayson stopped Finn's hands, pulling back from the kiss to look Finn in the eye and put a bit of space between them.

"You know I didn't do any of that stuff to get you into bed, right? I don't want you to feel obligated to do...anything." His face was serious, and he tried his best to convey that he would be more than cool with slowing down and that they didn't have to do anything Finn didn't want to do. "The gestures are just easier for me than coming out and saying how I feel with words," Grayson said, his cheeks flushing. "But I don't expect anything in return. I need you to know that."

Grayson rolled to his side next to Finn and placed a hand on Finn's chest, fingers moving absently over the smooth, tan skin as he continued. "In the past, the people I've dated have said I'm not open enough. With my feelings. With taking the relationship public," his gaze was on his hand gently caressing Finn's chest and sides, his eyes not meeting Finn's. Grayson knew he needed to say this, and he didn't want to lose his nerve by looking at Finn, which always made it hard for him to concentrate. "I guess I want to make sure that I'm not holding back too much from you. I want you to know how I feel because this is different from those other relationships for me." Grayson met Finn's eyes then, his hand stilling, indicating that it was Finn's turn to speak. Grayson held his breath, his heart hanging out there, exposed, waiting to see what Finn would do with it.

◆ ◆ ◆

Finn felt his chest clench at the vulnerability in Grayson's words. Grayson really cared about him, and he wanted to make sure Finn was doing this for the right reasons. And that just made Finn want him even more. Finn knew that sex wasn't necessarily the best way to express feelings – that it could be complicated and messy, but he knew that he wanted to be with Grayson. He knew it would mean something with him. Finn didn't have a lot of experience with this particular act, but he was ready. If he had any nerves, it was only because he wanted it to be good for Grayson. Finn took a minute to consider his words before speaking.

"First," he began, reaching up to stroke Grayson's arm as he spoke, "you have been nothing but open with me, and I can tell you care." He continued, his tone serious, "Second, I don't feel pressured by you in any way." Finn turned to face Grayson now, the two of them on their sides, faces inches apart on the pillow. Finn took Grayson's hand in his, lacing their fingers together as he spoke. "I want to be with you because I *want to*," he said, his eyes focused on Grayson's face, willing him to really believe what he was saying. "This is different for me, too. I've never had a boyfriend before, but I've dated plenty. Nothing has ever stuck, I guess, and it's probably because I can't do anything that I'm not really feeling 100 percent. I pretend for a living, but I can't fake anything in real life, and I don't want to try." He took a deep breath then, calming himself and gathering his courage. He shifted from the vulnerable, confessional demeanor he had been using to one of certainty and confidence. "So, when I say that I want to *be* with you, I mean it, and it's not because I feel like I owe you anything. It's because I care about you, and it's what I want."

Grayson's lips curved up into a smile then, clearly believing Finn's words. "Thank Christ, because I want you so damn bad it hurts." Finn let out a relieved breath, and laughing, he pounced on Grayson, shoving Grayson's shoulder into the mattress and climbing atop him, straddling his hips. Finn shivered at the feel of Grayson's big hands sliding up and down his sides before they grasped Finn's hips roughly. Finn trailed open-mouthed kisses down Grayson's neck, reveling in the salty taste of his skin. Grayson slid his hands around Finn's hips until he was palming his ass and pulling their bodies even tighter against one another. Grayson moaned when Finn's teeth grazed his collarbone before he slid his mouth to Grayson's chest, sucking a nipple into his mouth. "Jesus," Grayson hissed as Finn released the nipple only to nip it with his teeth, then soothe the bite with a flick of his tongue.

Grayson's fingers kneaded into his ass as he pulled him to his mouth and kissed him again. The want was almost more than Finn could take. Emboldened by lust and need like he'd never felt before, Finn ghosted his mouth over Grayson's ear as their bodies rubbed together, and whispered, "I want you to fuck me." Finn could feel Grayson's shudder at his words, and Grayson's made a half-moan, half-growl sound in response.

"I have supplies," Finn said before dipping his head down and trailing his tongue over to Grayson's other nipple. "This is something I've been thinking about a lot lately. I wanted to be prepared in case you...agreed."

Grayson barked a strangled laugh at that. "Agreed? Like you'd have to convince me to want to fuck you?" His whole body shook with the force of his laughter. The sound and vibration of Grayson's laugh had Finn laughing, too, and soon they were alternating kisses and giggles, tongues wandering over bare flesh, hands exploring urgently.

Finn loved that they could laugh like this. It took away some of the nerves he'd had about taking this step. He didn't have doubts that he wanted to be with Grayson this way, he just didn't want to be bad at it. He assumed Grayson had plenty of experience with his supermodel ex, and likely others, as well. He didn't want him to be disappointed. Grayson seemed to be enjoying himself just fine so far, though, if the ragged breath and unbelievably hard cock were any indication.

Eventually, the giggles died down, and their mouths and bodies became more intent, straining into one another. Finn reached over and grabbed the lube and condoms from the nightstand drawer, dropping them on the mattress. Then he was in Grayson's arms again, Grayson taking control, rolling them so that Finn was pinned underneath his larger body. It felt so damn good to be there, encased in Grayson's arms, the weight of his muscular form a delicious pressure along Finn's whole body. Finn pulled Grayson's boxers down off his hips and Grayson kicked them off, making quick work of Finn's boxers, his glazed eyes devouring Finn's naked body stretched beneath him before he climbed back on top of him.

Grayson's kisses became deep, rhythmic strokes of his tongue as his body ground into Finn's. Finn was already way too close to the edge just from the feel of Grayson's thick erection sliding over his own hard length and Grayson's warm breath against his neck, whispering words like "so fucking hot," and "wanted this for so long," and "need you."

It was that last one that had Finn's insides fluttering as rapidly as his lust-fueled pulse. Finn reached blindly for the bottle of lube, thrusting it at Grayson. "Need you to touch me," Finn said.

Grayson eyed him wickedly before he slid down Finn's body, kneeling between his legs. Grayson dragged his hands down Finn's thighs and then grabbed the back of his knees, urging Finn to lift and bend them, allowing Grayson unimpeded access. Grayson gently kissed the inside of one trembling thigh, then the other, his hands gently coaxing Finn's knees to spread wider as he worked his mouth up one thigh. Finn was completely exposed to Grayson, fully vulnerable, but he also felt a surge of power. When he looked down the length of his body, he saw Grayson kneeling between his legs, muscled thighs brushing up against him, broad shoulders wedged between Finn's knees. That gorgeous man was kneeling there for *him*. He wanted *him*. It was the sexiest sight Finn had ever seen, and he felt his cock strain, drops of precum landing onto his abs. Grayson's eyes locked with Finn's. "You are so fucking beautiful, Finn," he said, maintaining eye contact as he slid his tongue over the wetness on the ridges of Finn's stomach, which contracted at the contact.

"Holy fuck," Finn whimpered, his fists

clenching in the sheets at his sides and his heels digging into the mattress as Grayson dipped his head and took Finn's cock deep into his mouth. He sucked hard, taking Finn in all the way to the back of his throat, one hand cupping and stroking Finn's balls. When Finn's hips bucked up in response, Grayson made a low humming noise in approval, which made Finn's spine tingle and balls tighten. "Gray. Fuck, Gray. I'm too close already. Don't wanna come this way." He knew his voice sounded desperate, but he was too turned on to care. He'd never wanted anything as badly as he wanted Grayson that instant.

Grayson pulled his mouth away from Finn's cock, and he slid up to kiss Finn on the mouth before grabbing a pillow. He slid the pillow under Finn's hips, and adjusted himself so that he was kneeling between Finn's legs again. Grayson gently pushed Finn's knees up closer to Finn's chest, folding Finn's flexible body enough so that Grayson could kiss his mouth while he fingered him. Finn heard the pop of the lube bottle, and then two slick fingers were sliding along the crack of ass, delving a bit further between his cheeks with each sweep. Finn's shivered with anticipation at the touch, and he felt himself pressing down to eagerly meet the gentle strokes. Soon, the two fingers were drawing lazy circles around Finn's opening, causing him to lose his ever-loving-mind. He felt tingling all over, in places that he didn't even know could tingle. As Grayson continued his torturously slow, teasing strokes, getting so close but never going exactly where Finn needed him to, Finn's composure completely snapped. He was writhing, mauling Grayson with sloppy kisses, and he heard himself say, "More. Need more."

Finn pushed harder into Grayson's touch, and when the tip of one of Grayson's fingers entered him, he hissed out a harsh breath. The slick finger was just inside the ring of tight muscle at his opening, and Grayson made no move to push it in further. "This okay?" Grayson asked, voice cautious.

"Oh fuck yes," Finn said, rocking into the touch, drawing Grayson's finger in deeper. He writhed under the gentle movements Grayson made, his finger slipping out and sliding back in, swirling around his rim before pushing in again and again, stretching Finn's tight muscles little by little. It felt like absolute heaven, and Finn thought he would die if he didn't get more. "Yes. Feels so good. More," Finn pleaded, urging Grayson to slide another finger in.

Grayson worked a second slick finger in with the first, and Finn moaned his approval. The stretch was delicious. He began shamelessly riding Grayson's fingers. "You like that?" Grayson asked cockily, "You getting off on my fingers inside you?"

"Yes. So much. Don't stop," Finn babbled.

Grayson had him worked up into a quivering mess of raw need with his clever fingers thrusting into him and dragging back slowly, almost completely out before pushing back in. Finn was vaguely aware of Grayson groaning into their kisses, too, his mouth becoming more frantic. The thought of Grayson getting turned on by touching him made Finn lose his last shred of control. He couldn't wait any longer. "Now, Gray. Please. Need you inside me."

Grayson was more than ready to comply, pulling back and finding the condom in the sheets. He rolled it on and slicked himself with a generous amount of lube. He positioned himself at Finn's opening, and Finn felt crazed at the rub of Grayson's cockhead against his rim. "I'll try to go slow," Grayson said shakily. "Ready?"

The care and concern in his words caused something to shift. The tone had changed from dirty talk and desperation to get off to something more intense and yet somehow gentler. Finn felt a swell of emotion as he nodded. "Ready," he said.

Finn pushed back at the same time Grayson slid forward, and when the tip of Grayson's cock edged past that tight ring of muscle, they both hissed in large breaths. Finn felt a stinging, followed by a fullness that was so much more than Grayson's fingers had been. Grayson's cock was thick and heavy, straining to fit inside Finn's body. Finn could feel Grayson trembling with restraint, muscles stiff with the effort of holding back. Finn willed his body to relax. After a few deep breaths, the pressure eased. Grayson was bracing himself with his quivering arms, clearly straining every muscle in his body with the effort to keep still. Finn slid a hand up to Grayson's cheek, running his thumb across the prominent cheekbone then sliding the hand down to rest on Grayson's stubbled jaw. "Baby, you can move," Finn told him, his voice thick with emotion.

Grayson's body relaxed a little, and he rocked cautiously forward, inching in further, a little at a time. All the while, Grayson's eyes stayed locked on Finn's as if to gauge his reaction for pain or discomfort. With one more careful thrust, which Finn pressed into, Grayson was fully inside him. "Oh my God," Grayson groaned, "you feel so amazing. So fucking perfect," he said, his body starting to find a slow rhythm of sliding out and thrusting smoothly back in. Finn's hands clutched Grayson's strong shoulders, digging into the thick muscle there as he rocked his hips up to meet Grayson's thrusts.

Sweat was beading along Grayson's hairline, likely from the work of restraint more than exertion, Finn thought, his dark hair disheveled, his eyes closing as he let more and more of the pleasure take over. Finn was mesmerized by how gorgeous he was like this, all power and graceful movements, muscles straining in his arms and veins standing out in his neck as he drove deeper and deeper into Finn.

Feelings overwhelmed Finn's entire being. The sensory overload of feeling Grayson moving deep inside him while his own cock slid along the ridges of Grayson's abs, Grayson's hot breath against his neck, the scratch of Grayson's stubble against his own cheek. The smooth way their bodies were moving together, Grayson's hazel eyes dark and full of flames, emotion brimming up in them as they locked with Finn's. It was almost too much; the emotion threatened to burn him to ashes.

"I don't know if I can hold back much longer," Grayson said in a strangled voice. "Can I go faster?"

"Yes," Finn urged, wrapping his legs around Grayson's waist and locking his ankles around Grayson's lower back. Grayson's thrusts came fast and hard now, and Finn felt a jolt of intense pleasure when Grayson's cock brushed against a bundle of nerves deep inside him. Finn's hips jerked up off the bed at the contact. "Right there. Holy shit. Grayson." He panted the words, desperate need taking over him completely. "I'm so close." Finn felt Grayson's big hand slide between them and wrap around his leaking cock, Grayson's grip firm as he began stroking him to the same rhythm as his thrusts. It didn't take much. "I'm gonna come. Gray." And Finn came hard, muscles clenching down around Grayson as he shuddered over and over again, hot spurts coating Grayson's fist and his own stomach.

The sight of Finn coming apart and the way Finn's inner muscles locked down around Grayson when he came had Grayson following him over the edge after two more thrusts. His hips stuttered and Finn could feel Grayson's cock pulsing deep inside of him as Grayson muttered Finn's name over and over again until the shudders subsided.

Grayson collapsed onto Finn, and they lay there taking deep breaths for long minutes. Grayson was careful when he pulled out of Finn, but it still stung, though Finn was too blissed out to care. Grayson took care of the condom and went to the bathroom to grab a towel. He flopped back down on the bed beside Finn, and after cleaning them both up with the damp towel, he gathered Finn up in his arms and placed sweet kisses to his shoulder and the top of his head.

Finn snuggled into him and sighed, deeply content and utterly spent. Grayson drew him in even closer, Finn's back to Grayson's chest, Grayson's arm tight around Finn's waist. "That was unbelievable," Grayson said softly. "Like really fucking amazing," he said as he nuzzled his face into Finn's neck. When Finn didn't immediately respond, Grayson asked, "You good?" his voice drowsy but tinged with concern.

Finn smiled, though he knew Grayson

couldn't see it, and said, "That was better than front row tickets to Arcade Fire," and closed his eyes to sleep.

CHAPTER 12

"You cannot seriously be upset about this?" Felix stared at Finn in utter disbelief as they slowed their pace to a cool-down speed jog. Grayson had invited Finn along for his run with Felix that morning, and Finn was happy to tag along. Felix was getting annoyed at Grayson flaking out on their training sessions to be with Finn, and Finn didn't want to make waves. But, he still wanted to spend every moment he could with Grayson, so here he was, dripping sweat and panting along in an attempt to keep up with Felix and Grayson's longer strides. Finn was a runner, too, but he may have underestimated the intensity level of the run Felix and Grayson were used to. Finn was hoping to join them for Grayson's charity run next month, if he could somehow do so without exposing the fact that he did not, in fact, hate Grayson Winter, so he probably needed to step it up if he didn't want to make a fool of himself.

If he was honest, Finn was starting to get really tired of keeping up the charade of a feud with Grayson. Really, he didn't think they were fooling anyone anymore, and he certainly didn't want to miss out on important parts of Grayson's life because of it. He promised himself he'd brainstorm ways to attend that charity run without messing everything up.

"It's embarrassing," Finn replied, slowing his steps to a walk as they neared the gate to Felix and Grayson's house.

"I don't get you, man," Felix shook his head and wiped his sweating face with the bottom of his t-shirt. "What dude doesn't want to be voted 'Hottest Male TV Star' at the Youth Picks Awards? That's like, being upset that you have perfect bone structure and a tight ass. That's nothing to be pissed about."

Finn sighed, and Grayson gave him a sympathetic look. "Yeah, it's every actor's dream to win a Youth Picks 'Hottie' Award. Screw the Oscars, I want that big surfboard." Finn was a little surprised at how bitter he sounded and tried to soften it with a smile, but it didn't reach his eyes. "It's a big fucking joke, is what it is."

Grayson punched in the gate's code and the trio trekked up the driveway. Grayson finally spoke, coming to Finn's rescue. "It's nothing to be embarrassed about, but I get your point. Don't worry – this isn't going to be the last award you ever win. You should just look at it as a nice ego boost and have fun at the event. I know Lydia is chomping at the bit to get another chance to strut her stuff down a red carpet."

Grayson wasn't wrong about that. Lydia was pleased as punch that she was voted "Hottest Female TV Star." Apparently, she did not take the news with reserved grace, either. Ethan had been at a press engagement with Lydia and Astrid when the news came in, and he said Astrid was downright fuming. Astrid did not take being overlooked or upstaged well, and Lydia was not above rubbing it in her face a little.

"Ugh. Why did you have to remind me that I need to walk a red carpet? I don't even want to go to the damn event. I highly doubt 'fun' is in the cards," Finn said.

"Aren't you going with him?" Felix asked Grayson. He said it so casually, like he just assumed Grayson would be Finn's date. Finn felt his cheeks heat and his insides wobble at the innocent question.

"Uh. Um." Grayson stammered a little bit, and Finn thought he would take his shot while he had it. What was the worst that could happen?

"You should come with me," he said to Grayson, a hopeful smile on his lips. "It would be a hell of a lot more fun with you there. And I don't think we still have to act like we hate each other. The show's been renewed already, so what's the harm, really?" Finn was aiming for casual, trying not to let on how much of his heart he was dangling out in front of Grayson with the suggestion.

Finn's heart plummeted with each second of Grayson's silence. He wasn't looking Finn in the eye, and when they entered the house, Grayson headed to the kitchen, leaving Finn and Felix to follow behind him. Grayson bent down to grab three bottles of water from the fridge and placed them on the kitchen island, opening his bottle and taking a drink. He was clearly stalling for time, and the awkwardness that filled the room was palpable. Felix glanced between Grayson and Finn, clearly catching on to something being amiss. Felix tactfully took his water to go, saying he needed to hit the shower.

"Look," Finn was the one to break the silence. "It was just a suggestion. No pressure. I know you aren't big on making appearances, and we haven't...you know...gone public with our relationship. But I was just thinking it's only a big deal if we make it one. Everyone who works on the show already knows we're together, so it's only a matter of time before the whole world knows anyway. I just thought we could just skip to the part where we just own that we're a couple and have it out there." Finn shrugged then, his voice becoming quieter by the end of his rambling. Grayson still wasn't looking at him, and Finn began to fidget, peeling at the label of his water bottle and shifting his feet around as the silence drew on.

"Finn." Grayson did look at him now, and

Finn wasn't sure how to read his expression. It was guarded, maybe a bit sad. "I can't go with you to the awards show. You know that."

Finn felt a surprising wave of anger come over him. The way Grayson tacked on the "You know that" pissed him off. He felt his shoulders tighten and he stood up straighter to look his boyfriend in the eye.

"Like I said," Finn replied, voice sharper now, "it was just a suggestion. No need to get all condescending with me."

Grayson's eyebrows raised in surprise. "Condescending?" His voice was growing louder and angrier, too. "How is it condescending to remind you of something you've clearly forgotten, which is that we cannot be a public couple. Not if we want to keep our jobs. Jesus."

Finn's hands balled into tight fists at his sides and he was downright shouting now. "The show got picked up for two more fucking seasons! No one will give a shit, Grayson. Our careers are secure for two more years. And if you haven't noticed, I'm already a goddamn joke, so I've got nothing to lose." He threw up his hands in disgust.

"Well maybe I do," Grayson said then, his eyes every bit as cold as his tone. Grayson began to pace back and forth in front of the island, and he raised his arms, lacing his fingers together behind his head, his expression full of agitated disbelief.

He mumbled something under his breath as he paced, and Finn couldn't quite catch it.

"What was that?" Finn demanded.

Grayson stopped pacing and faced Finn. "I said, I can't believe this is happening to me again."

Finn felt like Grayson had punched him in the stomach. He couldn't breathe, he was suddenly dizzy, and he felt his eyes start to sting. Was Grayson seriously just comparing him to Thomas Logan? Is that what he really thought of Finn? Wow, he had been delusional if that were the case. He was falling hard for Grayson, and he thought Grayson was starting to feel the same way about him. *Guess not.*

Finn was able to pull himself together enough to nod his head a couple of times in devastated resignation. When he looked at Grayson, he knew his eyes were glassy with unshed tears, and he was sure his face showed how gutted he felt, but he was beyond caring.

"Go to hell," he said, walking away from Grayson on trembling legs, leaving Grayson alone in his kitchen.

◆ ◆ ◆

Grayson was sitting at the counter of the gym's juice bar, waiting for Felix to finish flirting with the smoothie guy so they could go home. The TV mounted to the wall in the juice bar's seating area was tuned in to some entertainment "news" show, which was the last thing Grayson felt like listening to at the moment. He took a deep pull from his Strawberry Sunrise protein shake and mentally cursed himself again for fucking up so badly with Finn. It had been three weeks since their fight, and Grayson missed Finn a little more each day they were apart. He hated that he messed up one of the best things he'd had going for himself.

Grayson couldn't even understand why he'd overreacted so badly to Finn's invitation to accompany him to that awards show. If he were any kind of real boyfriend, he would have supported Finn. The real bitch of it was that Grayson was ridiculously proud that his guy won that award. Even if it wasn't an Oscar or Portrayer Award, it was still an honor and it meant Finn had legions of loyal fans. That was nothing to be ashamed of. But what had he done? He'd insulted Finn by comparing him to his jackass of an ex, rejected him, and let him walk away. *Fuck me.*

Felix took the stool next to Grayson then, sipping on some awful greenish juice concoction, a smug look on his face telling Grayson he'd gotten the smoothie guy's number. Felix's smile faded when he stared over Grayson's shoulder, though, and he said urgently, "time to go, big guy," and stood up from the stool.

Grayson whirled around to see what caused

Felix's abrupt mood shift, and his stomach dropped to the floor. On the tv, the entertainment show was recapping the Youth Picks Awards from the previous night, and a grinning, gorgeous Finn Everett was staring out at him from the screen. He had his arm wrapped around Lydia, who was kissing him on the cheek. They both looked happy, like they didn't have a care in the world. Grayson felt like he'd been kicked in the ribs. *Could have been you he had his arm around, you jackass.* Just when he thought his entire heart had been ripped up with regret, he saw the headline below the photo.

We Ship It! TVs winners for Hottest TV Male and Female Star Cozy Up Backstage.

And, like the absolute fucking moron he was, Grayson walked over to the TV to hear what the show's host was saying. He caught the tail end of it, which was "and our sources confirm that Everett and Mason were inseparable for the duration of the evening, looking quite close. It's nice to see that it's not all drama over at *Frost Manor*. Those sources also confirm that they are both single and 'having fun' together. Well, we ship it!"

Grayson was aware that Felix had stepped up beside him when he felt a strong hand squeeze his shoulder. "Why don't you just call him? You obviously miss him, and you know you acted like an asshole. So, call and apologize so I don't have to deal with your mopey ass. It's depressing," Felix said in his supportive, yet no bullshit way. Grayson knew he was right. It was a low blow to even insinuate that Finn was anything like Thomas or that their relationships were even in the same category, and he'd spent every day of the last three weeks regretting his words.

"I doubt he'll want to hear from me. It's been three weeks of us ignoring each other during press interviews and him fleeing the second they're over. It's ironic that we don't have to fake the rift between us anymore. He won't even look at me."

"You won't know unless you try. And I'm not saying it's a sure thing – you are going to have to grovel, dude. Lay it all out there. That's really your only play at this point," Felix patted him on the back a few times, and they walked out of the gym.

They were silent for several minutes as Grayson weaved through traffic on his way back to their house. Finally, Grayson spoke. "I miss him so much."

"I know," Felix said. "So do something about it. You're Grayson-fucking-Winter. You got this."

Grayson wasn't so sure, but he knew he had to try. It was the only chance he had at patching up the jagged gouge through his chest.

Grayson resolved to change and just show up at Finn's hotel and beg him for forgiveness. He didn't want to risk Finn not answering his phone, so he would just turn up, apologize, and hope like hell it was enough. He dropped his gym bag in his closet, and he dug around for a decent shirt to wear. His phone vibrated on his nightstand, and he felt his heart leap at the thought it could be Finn. Rushing over to answer it, he was hit by brutal disappointment when he saw the name "Kayla Hudson" on the display. While it wasn't who he was hoping to talk to, he needed to answer his agent's call.

"Hi, Kayla. How are you?"

"Not too fucking great, Grayson, but probably a shitload better than you."

Grayson groaned and rubbed a hand over his face. "Is this the 'I told you so,' talk? Because I am not in the mood right now."

"Well I did tell you so, but I don't care about being right. I care about you not fucking up your career. So listen up," she said. "You have looked like absolute shit on the last two tv spots. You grumble your way through those interviews, and you act like you are in physical pain just sitting there."

Well, that was true, Grayson thought. "I know. Kayla, I do, and I'm sorry. I've just been dealing with some shit."

"It stops now, Grayson. Right fucking now. You hear me? You are being overshadowed by your co-star. Finn wins the Youth Picks hottie award, you show up to an interview like a sad puppy. I don't care what's going on in your personal life – no one wants to see a gorgeous, rich famous person act ungrateful. And producers are not going to send any quality film scripts your way if you don't knock that shit off. You're always going on and on about wanting to be a leading man in films. Let me tell ya, this is not going to get you there, cupcake."

Grayson felt a mix of shame and frustration at her words. Yes, he was acting unprofessional, but he was heartbroken, damnit. There wasn't much he could do about that. He was showing up to the press engagements he'd agreed to. He'd never agreed to be happy about it. And what was this bullshit about Finn overshadowing him? Since when were they in competition? There was room for more than one star on *Frost Manor*.

Grayson struggled to stay calm as he responded. "I thought you said not to date Finn because looking too friendly would be bad for my career. Now it's bad for my career that we aren't dating anymore." He could feel his anger bubbling up as he continued, "Maybe *my agent* should be less concerned with my relationship and comparing me to my co-star and more concerned with my acting. Just a thought." Then he hung up.

There was no way Grayson could have gone to talk to Finn after that awful conversation with Kayla. Instead, he spent the night on the couch with Felix, re-watching *The Office* for the 17th time. As if the universe was getting enjoyment from his misery, another bomb dropped somewhere in the middle of the CPR Training episode. Felix was scrolling through his phone absently as they watched, but he suddenly froze and sat up straight. "Oh shit," he said.

"What?" Grayson didn't bother looking up from the show. He just didn't have the energy.

"Shit. Grayson. You are not going to like this."

Grayson took in Felix's suddenly pale face, and his gut twisted. This couldn't be good. Felix passed the phone over to Grayson. It was an Instagram post. The image was Finn, shirtless with low-slung jeans, the button undone. It was clearly an old photo, taken when Finn was still on *Luna's Cove*, judging by his shorter hair. Grayson felt a pang of anger that the entertainment site would use this old photo, which was clearly undercutting Finn's efforts to be considered more than a sex symbol. That anger was nothing compared to the all-out fury Grayson felt when he got to the caption.

Breaking News: Enemies to Lovers? Scandal at Frost Manor – A show insider exposes Finn Everett's secret relationship with Grayson Winter. Did Grayson pull strings to land Finn the role? Read on for what we know about the sexy co-stars' hookups.

Grayson felt ill. *Shit, Finn will be so upset about this.* It was as if Finn's worst nightmare was playing out exactly the way he'd feared it would. Grayson wanted to support Finn. He wanted to tell him that the article was bullshit, and that Finn was so much more than the stupid fucking gossip sites made him out to be. He wanted to hold him and promise him it would be okay, and he wanted to tell Finn exactly how awesome and talented and amazing he is. But Grayson couldn't do any of that, and that was killing him.

CHAPTER 13

Finn waited in the lobby of Gwen and Jasper's L.A. offices, Vampire Weekend drifting through his headphones, bouncing his knee nervously. He was on edge, like it was too hot in the room, his clothes itchy against his skin. He'd felt uneasy ever since that goddamn viral Instagram post about him sleeping his way onto Frost Manor. It was exactly the kind of thing he feared when he started up with Grayson, that people would never see him as an actor. Just a celebrity and a piece of gossip. First he was feuding with Grayson, now he fucked Grayson to get on the show? They couldn't even make up their minds. Finn was over it. He really didn't care what gossip was out there. People would clearly say whatever they wanted anyway, so why let it control his life?

Now that the theoretical worst had happened, it turned out it wasn't as devastating as he feared. If he were honest, it didn't compare to the sickness in his stomach over that awful blowout with Grayson. It had taken more strength than he knew he had to show up to those interviews and press engagements with Grayson. He'd struggled to keep his expression carefully shuttered, and he pretended it didn't tear him up inside just to be near Grayson when things were so messed up between them. It has been a long and brutal three weeks.

Now here he was, waiting to negotiate his new contract on the show that would keep him in close proximity to Grayson Winter for the foreseeable future. At the time of the show's renewal, Finn had been nothing but thrilled at the prospect of a future for himself with this show, with Grayson. But things had changed, and he cursed himself for being so naive about it all. He didn't have long to dwell on those depressing thoughts because his agent, Kayla, was bustling into the lobby, enormous sunglasses shading her eyes, clicking heels announcing her arrival.

Kayla wasted no time badgering the receptionist into letting them back to see Gwen and Jasper right away, though they were still ten minutes early. Finn just followed her into the room, taking a deep, steadying breath before he entered the office to shake Gwen's hand and then Jasper's. Once they were all seated, Jasper shuffled some papers around and handed Finn a heavy, silver pen for signing the contract. Gwen was grinning at him from ear-to-ear when she passed the contract to Finn for perusal.

Kayla hovered over Finn's shoulder to read

the documents carefully. Finn had already heard and agreed to the contract verbally through Kayla's mediation with Gwen and Jasper, but he wanted to read the fine print anyway. A few lines in, his finger slid over a particular line of text as he reread the words there one and then once more. He stopped and looked up at Gwen. Then he looked at Jasper. They were both beaming at him.

"This says I'm a 'series regular' for the next two seasons? Am I being promoted from 'recurring character'?"

Gwen and Jasper nodded simultaneously.

"Really?"

"Really," Gwen said, "you deserve it, Finn. Your work this season was beyond our wildest expectations. We see you as a core character now, and you are essential to this show's development going forward."

Jasper piggybacked on her words by saying, "We aren't the only ones impressed, either. We've heard buzz that you're a dark horse for a Supporting Actor Portrayer nomination. You've earned this, Finn."

Finn was shocked. He had not even imagined this was a possibility. This would mean more screen time in more episodes. It would mean a bigger per episode salary. It would mean a major opportunity to really stretch himself as an actor.

"I don't know what to say," he said, emotion

overwhelming him.

"Sign the damn papers before they change their minds," Kayla said, nudging him with her elbow.

Finn felt a small laugh escape him, and he signed the contract.

Still dazed from the meeting, Finn made his way back to his hotel. He felt wired and restless from the news. This was huge – it was more than he could have hoped for. So why didn't he feel elated? He felt shock, sure. Gratitude, too. But he didn't feel the rush of euphoria he knew he should, and he had a decent suspicion about why that was. The first thought that had run through his mind when he walked out of that meeting was that he wanted to tell Grayson. He couldn't wait to share the news with him, to tell him he had been right, and that Finn was being taken seriously, at least by some people in this business.

But he couldn't do that. Not now. It had been three awful weeks of awkward, uncomfortable, heart-shredding avoidance of Grayson. He'd been more miserable than he thought he could be, and he didn't know what to do to make it stop. Part of him wanted to call Grayson and just apologize for overreacting that day and tell him that he wanted to get back together. But why would Grayson want to get back together with him? Grayson thought Finn had pushed too far, had treated him the way Thomas Logan had. Finn's stomach churned at the memory of that conversation any time it surfaced in his thoughts, which was almost more often than Finn could stand.

Frustrated, Finn flung himself down onto his bed, not bothering to kick off his shoes as he lay back atop the comforter. He missed Grayson terribly. Looking back on their breakup, Finn still thought he had a right to be upset with Grayson's words, but he also knew he overreacted. He should have been able to see that Grayson was just having a bad moment, and they should have been able to talk through it. But Finn had been stubborn. Deep down, he knew he had been secretly waiting for the relationship to implode. He never felt that he was good enough for Grayson, and rather than wait for Grayson to realize that and leave, he bailed at the first sign of trouble.

Finn's phone chimed with an incoming text, stirring him from his self-pity. And *holy shit*. The display showed the text was from Grayson.

Grayson: *Saw that Instagram post. You okay?*

Finn felt his heart speed up, his head go swirly inside. Grayson reached out. Grayson wanted to know if he was okay. Grayson still cared about him. Maybe? He was already drowning in ridiculous hope.

Finn: *I'm okay. Nothing I was surprised to hear. I hate that you got dragged into it, though. You okay?*

Finn's phone rang then.

"Hello?"

"Hey," Grayson said.

It felt so good to hear his deep voice on the other end of the phone. Finn's chest tightened and warmth started to spread through it.

Grayson spoke again, "You know that article was complete bullshit, right?"

"I know," Finn said.

"They just want to get clicks. They don't care if they lie and hurt people. I just want you to know that you are more than what they made you out to be. You're really good at what you do, Finn, and I don't want that kind of press to get you down."

Finn sighed, "Thanks. I'm actually handling it better than I expected to. I mean, it had been my worst case scenario before – that people would gossip about us and that I'd be written off as a joke and a slut, but it turns out that isn't really the worst thing that could happen to me. And I surprisingly don't care that much about that type of press anymore. It's not what matters."

Grayson was silent for a minute. Then said, "That's good. Glad to hear you aren't upset."

"Grayson?"

"Yeah?"

"Why are you checking up on me?"

Grayson blew out a large breath. "Just... making sure you were okay. I spoke to Kayla yesterday, and she mentioned you had a big meeting with Gwen and Jasper today. I was hoping it didn't have anything to do with that stupid Instagram thing. Thought you might need to talk."

"It was actually my contract signing." Finn hesitated a minute and then just spit it out. "They promoted me to 'series regular' for the upcoming seasons."

"Really? That's so awesome, Finn! You earned it." Grayson sounded genuinely happy for him.

Finn smiled, and his eyes stung as he said, "Thanks, Gray. I don't know that it would have happened if I hadn't been working with you. You make a hell of a scene partner."

Silence fell over the line. Finn finally broke the silence with, "Well, thanks for checking on me. I'm really fine. About the Instagram thing at least." He was sure Grayson would catch the meaning of his last comment.

"Okay. Um...have a good night, I guess," was all Grayson said.

"Goodnight."

Finn ended the call and flung himself back on the bed. He buried his face in a pillow and tried to stop the increasingly intense stinging in his eyes.

♦ ♦ ♦

Grayson felt unsettled by the phone call with Finn the previous night. He had bitten the bullet and made the first move toward making peace. He had called to check in on Finn, and it hadn't gone too badly. It was uncomfortable, and Grayson felt awkward as hell, but Finn seemed to be taking the bad press in stride, which was a huge relief. And hell, Grayson was just relieved Finn had responded to his text in the first place. He counted that in the "win" column, though he didn't want to give himself false hope. The main thing was that Finn seemed to finally believe in himself. And Grayson was genuinely happy for Finn making "series regular." That was a big deal, and Finn deserved it. Now Grayson just had to figure out how to work with Finn without feeling like his heart was being freshly torn out each day.

Grayson had allowed himself only a moment of desperate hope that it wasn't too late to patch things up between him and Finn when Finn had made that comment about being okay with the "Instagram thing at least." Grayson wanted to believe that Finn was implying that he was shaken up about the breakup, too. But that was stupid. Of course he wasn't. Grayson had been a complete asshole, and Finn had broken up with him. Finn didn't need Grayson, and Grayson knew full well that Finn could take his pick of guys. Why would he put up with Grayson's moods? But maybe there was still a chance that they could at least get along while working together. Grayson hoped so.

Grayson was thinking about all of this when he should have been preparing for his audition, which took place in about four hours. He was up for a film role that he was desperate to land. It was to play a Navy SEAL, and Grayson had been dying to work with the director attached to the project. His dream had always been to have a steady run on *Frost Manor* and then transition into films. This was one step in that direction, and he wanted the part badly.

When Kayla had called that she'd booked him the audition, she'd cautioned him not to get his hopes up. Those Finn rumors weren't just bad for Finn, she'd said, they also took away some of Grayson's credibility. She'd said that the casting director would take the audition because she was a *Frost Manor* fan, and she liked Grayson, but Kayla wanted him to know his "tabloid exploits don't exactly scream 'leading man' or 'badass SEAL.' " Sometimes Grayson questioned whether Kayla employed tough love or if she was just callous. Kayla did assure him, however, that if he did manage a Best Actor in a Drama Series Portrayer nomination, he'd repair any damage his reputation currently suffered.

Tabloids and nominations aside, Grayson was determined to nail this audition. He fit the role, physically, which already placed him in a small pool of actors who'd be serious contenders for the part. SEALs were in insanely good shape, and most actors didn't have the right build. Grayson also knew he could bring the right nuance to the character. The script was solid and had emotional depth. The character wasn't just the standard "tough guy," all gruff reserve. The character went through the emotional ups and downs of bonding with his team, enduring long deployments away from loved ones, and surviving missions gone wrong and coping with their aftermath.

Ethan had actually been the one to encourage Grayson to read the script and audition. He thought Grayson would be the perfect actor to tackle the complex role. Grayson had loved the script, and he was surprised Kayla hadn't suggested he read for the part, but he was thankful Ethan had. Grayson knew he needed to provide a layered performance at the audition, and he could do that. He just needed to show the casting director what he was capable of in a 10-minute audition in order to make it to the next callback.

As he tried to run through his lines again, he was distracted by his phone's text alert. He was surprised to see Finn's name on the screen.

Finn: *Hey.*

Grayson's hands shook a bit as he typed

Grayson: *Hey.*

Finn: *You busy?*

Grayson's pulse was immediately racing. That goddamn false hope was flaring up like wildfire.

Grayson: *Sort of. Prepping for an audition. What's up?*

Finn: *I'm at your gate. Buzz me in?*

Grayson all but ran to the security panel and buzzed him in and made his way to the front door, eagerly flinging it open. *You have no, chill, Grayson Winter.* He didn't care. Finn must have been dropped off by an uber at the gate. He came walking up the driveway looking like an absolute dream. Wild blonde hair, Ray Bans, fitted concert t-shirt, snug black jeans, and a smile that essentially rendered Grayson stupid. The fluttering in Grayson's stomach intensified with each of Finn's long-legged strides closer.

Not able to hold back a wide grin, Grayson asked, "What are you doing here?" with a little chuckle as Finn stopped a couple of feet in front of him.

Finn slid his sunglasses up to his forehead and looked right at Grayson with those deep blue eyes, and up this close, Grayson could see a nervousness to his smile. He was so adorable, Grayson thought he might melt right there.

"Um. I don't want to interrupt if you're

busy, but I wanted to...um..." Finn trailed off, looking down at his feet and fidgeting a little. He seemed to make up his mind about something and his gaze slid back up to lock with Grayson's. "When you called yesterday, I guess I just wondered what it meant. I couldn't see your face over the phone, so I didn't know if it was a friendly olive-branch and you were checking in on me as a courteous co-worker, or if it was an 'I still care about you,' and you were checking in on me as a... you know." Finn shrugged, his cheeks going red. "So, I came to see in person."

Grayson stopped breathing for a second. He was cautious with his reply. "Which are you hoping for?"

"I am assuming it was the first one, but I am hoping like hell it's the second." Finn swallowed visibly, waiting.

"It is," Grayson said.

"It is what?"

"The second one," Grayson said. "I still care about you, and I was checking in on you as someone who misses you like crazy."

Finn's shoulders relaxed, and he seemed instantly lighter. "I miss you, too, Gray. I'm sorry I left like that. I was being a drama queen."

"I am so sorry for the shit I said, Finn. I didn't mean it at all. I should never have made that comparison. What we have is nothing like my messed up old relationship, and suggesting it was the worst thing I've ever done. I think I was just pushing you away. I never really thought you'd want to be with me long term, so maybe I was just kind of...trying to beat you to the punch. Making you leave before you chose to."

Finn took a step closer, and he reached for Grayson's hands, holding them in his.

Grayson's skin tingled from the contact, his breath quickening at Finn's nearness.

"So, where does that put us?" Grayson asked. "Am I forgiven?"

Finn laughed, "Am I?"

"Absolutely, you are," Grayson said, tugging on Finn's hands until they were chest to chest.

"You, too." Finn said quietly. "I missed you so much. You have no idea."

"I think I have a pretty good idea," Grayson said as he leaned in and brushed his lips over Finn's. Finn responded with a firmer kiss and then smiled against Grayson's lips.

"Now," Grayson said, "come help me run lines. I need to nail this audition," and he tugged Finn into the house.

CHAPTER 14

"Finally, Grinn lives again!" Felix said, and Finn winced at the "ship" name. "Grinn," which twitter had coined as his and Grayson's couple name, was almost as bad as Brangelina, but Finn was just happy that he and Grayson were a couple again, so he let it slide. "Well I'm glad you both got your heads out of your asses in time for the run tomorrow," Felix said to Finn. "You're gonna be there, right?"

"Uh...I guess I'll let Grayson decide if he wants me there, but I'd be up for it." Finn was lounging with Felix on the enormous sectional sofa of Grayson and Felix's living room. They were watching some sort of home renovation show on HGTV and waiting for Grayson to return from his big audition.

"Cool. It would be awesome if you could even just post something on your Insta stories, man. What do you have, like 11 million followers or something now?"

Finn felt uncomfortable talking about numbers of followers, but Felix was Grayson's best friend and a good guy. "Happy to post something. Want to do a selfie together? I'll tag you and we can link to your donation page."

Felix was enthusiastically in favor of the selfie, and while Finn shot down the idea of doing it shirtless, he gave a genuine smile when Felix sidled up next to him and snapped the shot. Finn passed his phone over to Felix to let him add the link and upload the photo for him. When he was done, Felix huddled next to Finn to show him the post, and he started to freak out about the flurry of likes and comments immediately flowing in. "You beautiful man, you! I'm happy to use your perfect face for my personal gain," Felix said, bumping his shoulder into Finn's.

Just then, Grayson walked into the room and took in the scene of Finn and Felix cozying up, hunched over the phone, Felix spouting off at the mouth about Finn's physical perfection.

"Hey now, I just got him back. I'm going to need you to take a few steps away from my boyfriend," Grayson said, shooting Felix a mock dirty look. Finn felt Grayson come up behind him, and Grayson wrapped his arms around Finn's waist in a tight hug. Grayson rested his chin on Finn's shoulder to peek at the phone. "What are we looking at?"

Finn leaned back into Grayson's body, grateful to have him this close again.

"Finn just posted about the run, and people are loving it. It's been three minutes, and there are already 2,048 likes and about 300 comments." Felix grinned over at Grayson, "And a ton of the comments are asking about Finn's hot friend," so it's a win-win situation. Felix was clearly pleased with himself.

"That's awesome," Grayson said, directing his words to Finn, "not the comments about Felix, but that you posted about the run. Thank you. Sharing the link to the donation page is huge." Grayson gave Finn a squeeze and a kiss on the cheek then released him and spoke to Felix.

"So, I'm going to skip out on the pre-run dinner tonight. You can handle it without me, right?" Grayson gave Felix a meaningful look, and Felix gave him a knowing smile. "I can manage without you." Felix made a show of looking at his non-existent wristwatch and added, "Would you look at that, I better be going. Don't want to be late." He winked at Grayson, slapped Finn on the shoulder and walked out of the room.

Finn immediately closed the space between him and Grayson, wrapping his arms around Grayson's neck and grinning up at him. He looked into Grayson's stunning hazel eyes, which were more gold than brown or green at the moment. Finn loved how they switched colors based on what Grayson was wearing or his mood. He wondered if gold meant he was happy. He hoped so. Grayson tilted his face down and rested his forehead against Finn's. It was like neither of them could stand to be separated from one another, even a little bit.

"How was the audition?" Finn whispered, "You killed it, right?"

"I think it went well. Thanks for running lines with me." Grayson touched his lips to Finn's in a soft, quick kiss.

"Anytime," Finn said, repeating the soft kiss, but holding it a second longer.

Grayson pulled Finn in a bit tighter so that his face was in Finn's neck, and Grayson spoke in a voice so low Finn could barely make out the words, "I was afraid you might not be here when I got back. Thought you might have changed your mind."

Finn pulled back so he could see Grayson's face. He saw a vulnerability in his expression that matched that of his words. "I'm not going to change my mind," Finn said, his gaze locked steadily with Grayson's. Finn hoped he was conveying just how much he meant that. He raised up on his toes to claim Grayson's lips with his own, this kiss firmer, trying to emphasize his point.

Grayson leaned into it, strong hands gripping Finn's hips tightly as he responded by delving his tongue into Finn's mouth in a deep, possessive kiss. Finn heard himself moan softly as he slid his hands into Grayson's thick, wavy hair, luxuriating in the way it curled around his fingers. He breathed in Grayson's scent, a mingling of woodsy and minty smells that drove Finn crazy. It was somehow clean and sophisticated, just like everything else about Grayson. Finn was overwhelmed by all the sensations bombarding him as he gave himself over fully to the embrace, loving the way Grayson took control. When they pulled apart, their breathing ragged, Finn said, "I missed this. Missed you."

Grayson slid his hands gently up and down Finn's sides, something relieved and warm shining in his expression as he looked at him thoughtfully. "I missed you, too. God, I was such a wreck. I have never felt like that after a breakup before."

"I've never really *had* a breakup before, so I have nothing to compare it to, but it sucked," Finn agreed, running his fingers gently along the nape of Grayson's neck, right at the spot where his hair met his skin. He loved the way the hair curled up slightly right there when Grayson was overdue for a haircut.

"That's how I knew for sure that this was different from every other relationship. How I felt about you was truly different. I hate that it took us breaking up for me to really see it, but now I have no doubts," Grayson said. "It wouldn't have hurt like that if I..." he trailed off, shaking his head a bit before planting a kiss on Finn's temple. "Anyway, want to order some food? Maybe watch a movie?"

Finn knew Grayson was clearly trying to backtrack away from the direction the conversation had been going with that abrupt change of topic, but he let it slide. Grayson had already opened up so much today. He wasn't going to push it. "Did you just ask me to Netflix and Chill?" Finn's eyes sparkled with humor.

Grayson nodded. "Absolutely, I did."

"Can we order the Thai food?" Finn asked, "And more importantly, can I pick the movie?"

Grayson's lips quirked, and he said, "Anything you want."

They didn't over-do it on the takeout because they had the charity run in the morning. Turns out Grayson did want Finn to go, and he readily agreed. They ended up watching *The Prestige* because Grayson had a thing for Hugh Jackman, Finn had a thing for Christian Bale, and Finn insisted that Grayson was going to land the part he auditioned for, and he wanted to get better acquainted with the director's earlier films. Grayson told Finn that the role wasn't his yet, but Finn could tell Grayson was pleased at Finn's confidence in him.

They cuddled on the couch as they watched, Finn tucked cozily into Grayson's side, Grayson's arm wrapped around him. Finn couldn't ever remember feeling this comfortable or this content. Before, he'd always felt a little bit uncertain with Grayson. Like Grayson was still a celebrity that Finn crushed on from afar and would never actually have. Now, though, things had changed. Especially after their short time apart, Finn came to realize that Grayson was in this just as much as he was. That they were equals in the relationship. Grayson had always shown Finn he was important to him, treating Finn in an almost reverent manner, but Finn had been slow to see or believe it. He thought he was seeing it clearly now, though. Maybe he did deserve Grayson. Maybe someday Grayson's feelings for him could even match the depth of his own feelings toward Grayson. Finn couldn't help but hope for that, but he knew without a doubt that he would love Grayson regardless.

◆ ◆ ◆

When Grayson woke up to a sleeping Finn next to him in bed, he once again thanked the universe for kicking him in the ass and bringing him to his senses. Reaching out to Finn with that text message, making the first move toward reconciliation, had scared the shit out of Grayson, but he knew now he made the right choice. He felt his chest tighten as he watched Finn's torso rise and fall with the deep, even breaths of sleep. Finn was on his stomach, one arm tucked under a pillow, one knee bent, a mess of tangled sheets gathered at his waist. Grayson wasn't sure that he'd ever seen anything as beautiful as Finn, relaxed and peaceful in his bed. *God, I love him.*

The thought just popped into Grayson's mind, startling him.

Did he love Finn?

Grayson had never been in love before. He loved his family, of course, but that was different. He'd never felt this way about someone he was dating. He thought about it rationally, as was his way. He knew that he found Finn insanely attractive, that he wanted to spend as much time with him as possible, and that he admired his talent and dedication. Finn was a good person, so fun and generous and all-around amazing. He loved the way Finn laughed and joked around with everyone. He loved the way he concentrated and worked so hard to do his best. He loved that he was a great listener and that he could make friends easily with anyone. He loved that he struggled through his self-doubt but fought it every step of the way and never gave up on himself. Grayson thought about the searing, blinding rage that filled him at the thought of Finn moving on with someone else when they had been apart. He recalled the emptiness that filled him when he had to see Finn at work but couldn't touch him or even have a real conversation with him. He remembered the overwhelming fear that Finn would never want to get back together. He also thought about how he would have accepted it, though, if Finn had rejected him. He knew he'd want Finn to be happy and successful, even if he never took Grayson back. That would have hurt like hell, but Grayson truly wanted Finn to have everything he dreamed of having, whether it included Grayson or not.

Well, that settles that, Grayson concluded. Who was he trying to kid? He was crazy in love with Finn Everett and had been for some time.

With that realization swirling in his head, Grayson slid over to Finn and pressed his lips to Finn's spine, just above the small of his back. Then he moved up his spine in a series of soft kisses, ending at the nape of his neck. Finn grumbled a little, but quickly got on board with Grayson's plans, rolling into Grayson's body, wiggling close to him, his ass resting right up against Grayson's fully hard cock. Grayson groaned at the contact, pressing in even closer and moving his mouth to nibble and lightly suck on Finn's neck.

Things heated up quickly then, Finn becoming fully alert and rocking back into Grayson. Grayson's hand curved over Finn's side and slid down his stomach, thumb swiping gently back and forth over his hip bone on the way down. Finn arched into him, urging his hand lower.

They were interrupted by four intense thumps on the door. "Yo Grinn! You bastards better save your strength for the run! Put your dicks away, and let's get a move on!" Felix yelled in his best trainer voice, effectively extinguishing the mood. Grayson and Finn both groaned, but after a few kisses, they regretfully rolled out of bed with the promise of picking up where they left off later.

The run went off without a hitch, and they ended up exceeding their fundraising goals. It didn't hurt that thousands of dollars in donations came in after Finn's Instagram post, and Grayson felt so much gratitude for his guy. While he kind of hated the idea of millions of random strangers creeping on photos of Finn, he had to admit there were benefits to Finn having hordes of obsessed fans, and this was certainly one of them. Grayson would be able to fund the new shelters, and he couldn't wait to get started.

Felix was also thrilled because a few other celebrities who had participated in the run wanted to hire him as their trainer once they saw how he'd kept Grayson in shape. It didn't hurt that Finn had let people assume he was his trainer, as well. Felix wasn't technically Finn's trainer, but the paparazzi had snapped a few shots of Finn running with him in the past, and Finn was cool with people jumping to that conclusion. It really was a win-win kind of situation, at least where Grayson and Felix were concerned. Grayson felt a surge of gratitude for his boyfriend as he considered the many selfless ways he helped other people, Grayson included.

The event was winding down. Volunteers were cleaning up the park where the run had taken place, and some photographers and reporters were still lurking, but most of the crowd had cleared out. Grayson spied Finn splayed in the grass under a tree next to Felix and Ethan. They were chatting casually, clearly waiting for Grayson to wrap up his duties so they could take off. Grayson felt warm and fuzzy at the sight of Finn fitting in so seamlessly with his friends. Sure, Ethan was a colleague, and Finn worked with him, too, but he and Grayson were close, not just work acquaintances. And Felix was Grayson's best friend, so it really mattered that Felix liked Finn and vice versa.

When Grayson made his way over to the group, he dropped in the grass next to Finn, so close their shoulders and thighs were touching. It was like there was an invisible pull drawing him in, and he just had to be as close to Finn as he could get. Ethan and Felix exchanged a look. "So glad we're over the heartbroken moping and depression phase," Ethan said.

"Tell me about it," Felix agreed. "Thought I was gonna have to put Grayson in therapy or some shit. Dude did not handle getting dumped well."

"Finn was no picnic, either," Ethan said. "Looked like someone stole his puppy."

"Hey, we're sitting right here," Grayson said, trying to sound offended.

Finn and Ethan both replied, "We know" in perfect unison.

Grayson rolled his eyes at his friends, but he wasn't really bothered by their comments. He had been miserable, and it gave him some satisfaction to know Finn had been miserable, too. He wondered briefly if that made him a bad person, but quickly dismissed the thought. It just felt good to know Finn had missed him.

Felix insisted on taking a group selfie before they left. Ethan had tried to talk his way out of being in the photo by offering to take the picture, but Felix was having none of that. So, they all crowded in together right there on the grass and grinned for the photo. It would be good press for the charity, and Grayson was happy to show his gratitude and appreciation to the fans that supported the event.

He and Finn had discussed it, and they decided that a few public appearances together, as long as they were never alone and there was no blatant PDA, would have to be permissible. Kayal wouldn't like it, nor would Jasper and Gwen, but they had to live their lives, at least in small, quiet ways until they were no longer obligated to listen to their showrunners and network. It sucked not being able to fully claim Finn publicly, which Grayson desperately wanted to do. He was surprised by just how much he'd wanted that. But he and Finn had had enough gossip about them in recent weeks that it was threatening to undercut their performances and respectability, at least according to Kayla. So, Finn came to the run, but he'd mostly kept his distance. Grayson figured that was better than nothing.

"Alright, lovebirds," Felix said as he stood up and pocketed his phone. "Let's go get some food." Felix reached a hand down to Ethan to help pull him to his feet. "You coming, too?"

Ethan hesitated a second, like he didn't know whether he should come along or not, so Grayson decided for him.

"Of course you are, E. Let's go."

The four of them headed back to Grayson and Felix's for quick showers and then they were off to the brunch spot. Grayson only had a slight flutter of nerves as he remembered their last brunch and his ex's ambush. He shook it off, though, because he wasn't going to let Thomas Logan ruin anything for him anymore. He assured himself that he would enjoy eating at his favorite restaurant, hanging out with his friends, and spending time with his guy. Grayson knew he was a lucky man, and he wasn't going to take it for granted.

CHAPTER 15

The morning after the charity run, Finn woke up in Grayson's bed, a deep contentment settling over him as he looked over to see Grayson beside him. Grayson's was on his side, already awake, head resting on one arm as he looked over at Finn. He had clearly been watching Finn sleep, and rather than crack a joke about how creepy that was, which was what Finn would normally do, something stopped him. He looked up into Grayson's still drowsy eyes and saw such warmth and affection radiating from them that Finn's heart actually stuttered.

"Morning," Grayson said, lips quirked up into a sexy smile.

"Morning," Finn replied, sliding over to Grayson and slipping an arm over his waist. Finn instantly snuggled into Grayson's warm, solid chest. A happy sigh escaped him, and he wasn't even sorry. There was no denying the pure bliss he felt when he was this close to Grayson.

"What's your plan for the day," Finn asked,

making no move to pull away from his cozy spot against Grayson's body. "Do you have anything scheduled? I don't think there's anywhere I need to be today – for once."

Grayson wrapped an arm around Finn, and he traced gentle lines up and down his arm and back. Grayson seemed just as content as Finn was to cuddle, and he didn't stop his light touches along Finn's skin when he spoke.

"I told Felix I was taking the day off from training, and that audition is over, so my day is wide open." He paused for dramatic effect, then added, "Do you have any ideas of what we could do with all this free time?" He slid his hand to the small of Finn's back and tugged him slightly closer, emphasizing the suggestive nature of the question.

"Hm." Finn pretended to think, then said, "I might be able to think of something," and trailed a few teasing kisses along Grayson's neck before pulling back to look at him, flashing him a wicked smile, "but I'm going to need coffee before I have the energy to execute them properly."

Grayson laughed and nipped Finn's shoulder. That's when both of their phones started blowing up. "This is starting to get old," Grayson grumbled as he rolled over to check what all the fuss was about. Getting interrupted while he was in bed with Finn was quickly becoming his least favorite thing ever.

Finn had to agree. It felt like the universe knew when he and Grayson were naked together and decided to interrupt at the worst times. It came with the job, though. Finn reached over to the nightstand to see who kept calling and texting. He had four missed calls and eight texts. What the hell?

Three of the missed calls were from Lydia. The fourth was from Ethan. All eight texts were from Lydia. Finn glanced over to where Grayson was swiping around on his phone on the other side of the bed.

"Lydia's freaking out about something," Finn said over his shoulder to Grayson as he opened up the first text.

Lydia: *Holy shit, Finn! Congratulations!*

Lydia: *Are you freaking the fuck out right now? I am!*

Lydia: *Gahhhh! And Grayson, too!*

Lydia: *Oh my god, you guys are like the new Brangelina!*

Lydia: *Finn! Finn, Finn, Finn!!!*

Lydia: *Damnit, Finn Everett, say something!*

Lydia: *Finn, are you passed out from the shock? Do you need me to call an ambulance or something?*

Lydia: *Will you take me as your date?*

Finn had no idea what she was talking

about. Before he bothered to listen to the voicemail message from Ethan – who the fuck left an actual voicemail these days? – he glanced back at Grayson. "Who was texting you?"

Grayson's voice was a little shaky. "It's Ethan. And Lydia. And Ethan again." Grayson turned to look at Finn over his shoulder. "I think..."

He couldn't finish that thought because both their phones started ringing again. Grayson said, "Gwen," and then answered the call.

Finn's screen said, "Jasper." He picked it up. He was vaguely aware of Grayson's murmured conversation with Gwen going on at the same time, but he was curious why Jasper was calling him directly.

"Hello?"

"Finn, great, glad I caught you," Jasper sounded a little out of breath.

"What's up," Finn asked.

"Didn't you see the announcement?"

"What announcement?"

"Finn. You are nominated for a Portrayer Award. Best Supporting Actor in a Drama Series!"

Finn couldn't have heard that correctly. He was suddenly lightheaded. "What?"

"Congratulations! You were a dark horse for the nomination, but I just had a feeling you'd get it. This is an enormous honor, Finn. Absolutely huge. I'm so glad we snagged you for two more seasons before you go off and become too big a star for us." Jasper laughed lightly, his tone swimming in pride.

"Holy shit. I mean...thanks, Jasper. I'm really grateful that you and Gwen took a chance on me and gave me this opportunity. It means more to me than you'll ever know." Finn felt a lump form in his throat and knew he needed to get off the phone before he made a blubbering fool out of himself.

"It's well-deserved, Finn. Congrats again. We'll talk soon."

"Thanks. Talk soon."

Jasper hung up, and Finn ended the call. He sat still then, dazed and frozen in disbelief. "Holy. Shit." He whispered the words to no one in particular, trying to process this news.

He was a Portrayer Nominee. He'd never in his wildest dreams expected this to happen.

He was jolted out of his daze by Grayson coming up behind him, wrapping his arms around him in a tight embrace and kissing him on the side of his head. "Congratulations," he whispered in Finn's ear. "I'm proud of you."

Finn was back on earth now, head finally spinning less frantically. "Thank you," he said, feeling warmth from not only the embrace but also Grayson's words. Finn thought back to Lydia's text messages. She'd said, "Grayson too," hadn't she? Finn didn't want to assume anything and be wrong, though, so he asked instead, "What did Gwen have to say?"

Grayson was still holding on to Finn, strong arms grounding him and warming him inside and out. "Well," Grayson said, "I may have news of my own..."

"You're nominated for Best Actor in a Drama Series?" Finn's voice verged on hysterical in it's hopefulness.

"Mmhmm," Grayson acknowledged, nuzzling into Finn's neck rather than bothering with words.

Finn wasn't going to let it go without fully acknowledging how awesome this was for Grayson, too, so he pulled away from him and stood. "Grayson Winter," he said with authority. Grayson looked up at him dutifully. "I am so freaking proud of you. I'm not surprised in the least, but I'm so glad you are getting the recognition you deserve."

Grayson smiled at him. "Thank you." Grayson stood and reached for Finn's hands, lacing them with his.

"Can I tell you a secret," Grayson asked, voice just above a whisper as he looked down at their joined hands.

"Of course," Finn said.

"It's because of you. The nomination, I mean. You make me better. As an actor, I'm always inspired by the way you play a scene, and it pushes me to do better."

Finn felt that damn lump forming in his throat again, and he struggled to keep his emotions in check. It was unreal to hear Grayson saying these things. They were so similar to the way Finn felt about him. Finn had always admired Grayson, and he knew that the desire to impress Grayson was at least some of the reason he'd worked so hard this season.

Finn pulled their joined hands up so they rested against his chest. He leaned in and brushed his lips over Grayson's in a quick, sweet kiss. "Hey. I think those are my lines," he said, a half-smile tugging his lips.

Grayson laughed softly and leaned down to rest his forehead against Finn's. Finn felt his chest clench again. He loved when Grayson did this. It felt so intimate, almost more than kissing, because there was no lust involved. It was just closeness. Finn took a deep, shaky breath, then said, "Can I tell *you* a secret now?"

"Absolutely, you can," Grayson said.

Finn's legs felt wobbly, and he had to take another deep breath in and out before he could speak. His silence must have alerted Grayson to the fact that this was something difficult for Finn to say, and Grayson searched Finn's face thoughtfully. When Finn met Grayson's stare and locked eyes with him, he suddenly felt calmer.

"I love you, Grayson," he said.

Grayson's mouth was on his the second after the words left him. The kiss was intense but also tender somehow. Finn imagined that he could literally feel the adrenaline as it pumped through his body from speaking those words, and this kiss only increased the rush. Finn thought his heart might actually explode right there in his chest.

Grayson was the one to break the kiss, and he looked directly at Finn, his voice steady and sure. "I love you, too. So much."

Finn laughed and attacked Grayson with more kisses.

◆ ◆ ◆

A week after Finn had told Grayson that he loved him, Grayson still felt giddy just thinking about it. He had never been happier in his life. Sure, he was thrilled about his Portrayer nomination, but that had not been the biggest thing that had happened to him that day. Not by a long shot.

When Finn had said those words to him, he felt like he was floating. He knew he had been in love with Finn for some time now, but he didn't know Finn felt the same way. Damn, it felt good. So did the sex they'd been having every night (and some mornings) for the last week. Everything was intensified now, which was hard to believe because it was already off-the-charts before they'd shared how they felt.

Grayson was lost in thoughts of a certain smoking-hot co-star when he heard a throat clearing. Right. He was in line at the studio coffee cart. And it was his turn to order. The barista, Matt, Grayson now knew due to many stops here to grab Finn's lattes, looked at him with an amused smirk on his face. "What can I get you?"

"Caramel macchiato, please," Grayson said.

"Anything for *you* this time?" Barista Matt asked.

Grayson looked at the guy. He was tall, maybe an inch or so shorter than Grayson, and he was cute in a punk kind of way. He had a small silver hoop through his bottom lip, the hint of a tattoo peeking out from under his rolled-up shirtsleeve. Grayish eyes and black hair, spiking out wildly on top but close-shaved on the sides and back. It seemed like Barista Matt might have been trying to flirt with him, Grayson thought. *Too bad, dude. I'm so taken.* As cute as he might be, he didn't have anything on Finn.

"Huh?" Grayson asked him, not really knowing how this guy knew the drink wasn't for him.

"This is you guy's drink, right?" Matt asked, his mouth still curling up at the corners. "Don't you want anything? We have things besides coffee."

"Uh. Right. Sure. I'll take a green tea."

Grayson paid him and gave him a good tip. Turns out he wasn't so much flirting with Grayson but trying to sell him more beverages. That was just good business, Grayson thought, as he waited for the drinks.

He was waiting for Finn. They were meeting with Kayla today, though he wasn't entirely sure why. It was convenient that she was both his and Finn's agent because they could get by with one meeting that way. Kayla had an appointment at the studio that day for another client, so they were all meeting here. Finn had an appointment with a stylist to settle on a tux for the Portrayer awards, so he hadn't ridden with Grayson that morning, and as pathetic as it was, Grayson already missed him after only a few hours apart. *Yep, I'm that guy now.* Grayson smiled to himself as he grabbed the drinks and found a small table near the coffee cart to wait.

Finn showed up just a few minutes later, greeted Grayson with a thorough kiss that was clearly a "fuck off" to anyone who wanted to say shit about them being together, and took a seat. *He is the hottest guy on earth*, Grayson thought, not for the first time, as Finn sipped his coffee. Finn closed his eyes and sighed as he drank, and Grayson couldn't help thinking about Finn closing his eyes and sighing in other situations, and he had to adjust himself in his seat.

"Oh for fuck's sake, Grayson, do I need to hose you down?" Kayla had arrived. Grayson shot her a glare as she slid into the empty seat at the table. "Yes, he's a goddamn perfect male specimen, we get it," Kayla said to Grayson. "But pull yourself together." She was shaking her head as she dug through her enormous purse and pulled out her wallet. She strode up to the coffee cart to order her extra hot nonfat vanilla latte.

At their table, Finn was chuckling, clearly delighted by Grayson being caught with a boner over Finn sipping a latte. Grayson had to admit, it was kinda funny. He was so far gone for Finn that there was nothing to do but laugh at his level of obsession.

Finn had a wicked gleam in his eye as he flicked his gaze over to where Kayla was waiting for Matt to finish her drink, then looked back at Grayson. "Thanks for the latte," Finn said in an exaggeratedly seductive tone. "It is soooo hot," Finn said, teasing him. "I want to take a long, slow swallow..." Finn was biting back a laugh as he made fun of Grayson.

"You're an asshole," Grayson said, grinning back at him.

Kayla was back then, and she rolled her eyes. "You guys are embarrassing yourselves." She plopped back down in the seat and arranged her purse on the ground beside her.

Finn and Grayson grinned at one another.

"So," Kayla said, her voice taking on her all-business tone. "We need to talk Portrayer Awards."

Grayson had expected she'd have things to say about the red carpet interviews and probably some warnings not to get too drunk during the ceremony, blah, blah, blah.

Kayla continued, her eyes drifting between him and Finn equally as she spoke, "You're both nominees, which, of course, is fantastic, but we need to discuss how to play this. Obviously, you aren't going to walk the carpet together. I don't even want you arriving within a half hour of one another. Finn, I assume you're bringing Lydia as your date, which will be perfect. Grayson, I know what you're going to say, but you need to listen to me. You are taking Astrid as your date and walking the carpet with her."

Kayla said this as a statement of fact. Grayson's eyes widened. "What?"

Kayla ignored him and went on with her game plan. "Now, about inside the ceremony. You'll have to be seated at the same table, of course, but you will need to use those acting skills to not make googly eyes at each other across the table. In fact, don't even look at each other. You guys have the subtlety of a Kardashian Christmas card. We want people to see you as leading-men types. If you want these next two seasons to be a success, and you want those film roles to come, you will keep your eyes and hands off each other whenever you're in public, and the Portrayer awards are fucking televised."

Grayson felt his fists clenching and his shoulders tightening. Kayla wasn't done, though.

"The Portrayers are only a few weeks out. You guys will stay the fuck out of the tabloids and gossip sites until then. The last thing Portrayer voters need to see is the two of you making out all over L.A. We don't want anything undermining your chances. You both killed it this season, and you deserve these awards. Bad press could tank your chances completely."

Kayla took a long swig of her latte, set it back on the table, and folded her manicured hands in front of her. "Any questions?"

Grayson felt sick. He glanced at Finn, who was staring at Kayla, eyes wide. Grayson couldn't tell exactly what Finn was thinking, but he didn't look happy.

Finn spoke then. "I don't get why we can't be together in the public. The story came out, and everyone knows we aren't really enemies. I just don't understand why there'd be blowback about us being together. The show's already renewed."

He shook his head in disbelief, clearly not about to understand Kayla's insistence on this.

Kayla looked like she was ready to snap Finn's head off, so Grayson jumped in before she could pounce.

"Let me get this straight," Grayson said to Kayla, losing the battle to keep his voice under control, "you want us to arrive to the awards with Lydia and *Astrid* as our dates, avoid one another on the carpet completely, don't look at one another during the ceremony, and stop seeing each other for the next three weeks so we don't sabotage our chances to get votes? Is that all?"

Finn fidgeted with his coffee cup and still didn't say anything.

Kayla turned her gaze on Finn, then on Grayson, and it was pure ice. "Grayson. I am your agent for a reason. I'm the best at what I do. You and Finn both got *Portrayer nominations*. Finn is one of the youngest actors to ever be nominated. And you are so cold and stoic it was nothing short of me working a miracle to get anyone to even *think* about nominating you, let alone securing it. I am sick of you fucking second-guessing me. Like what is this bullshit about auditioning for a role you aren't ready for? Oh, right, your *PA* suggested it, and he must know better than me. Fuck, Grayson. I thought you were supposed to be smart. If you're smart, you'll do exactly as I say. You can find another fuck buddy while voting is going on. You two can hook up again after you win."

She snatched her purse and stormed off then, shaking her head like she couldn't handle how exasperating it was to deal with them.

Once she was gone, Grayson let out a slow breath and unclenched his fists. He looked at Finn, who seemed decidedly downtrodden by the conversation. "Hey, Babe," Grayson said, "look at me."

Finn did, his eyes anxious and sad. Grayson wanted to punch something. He didn't ever want Finn to look that way. Who the fuck did Kayla think she was, anyway? She worked for him, not the other way around. He could take her horseshit attitude, but he was not going to stand for her pulling that with Finn.

"She was out of line, Finn. She shouldn't have dumped all that on us like that. She's out of her goddamn mind if she thinks I'm following those rules," Grayson said.

Finn shook his head morosely. "She does know what she's talking about, though. I don't understand it *at all*, but she is the best agent there is, so maybe she has a point?"

"What are you saying? We should listen to her crazy rules?"

Finn shrugged. "I don't want to mess with your chances at votes."

Grayson felt his throat tightening. "You think I really care about that?"

"*I* care about it. You deserve that award," Finn said.

Grayson didn't know how to feel. It was sweet of Finn to want to help Grayson win, but he didn't like the idea of putting their relationship on hold, or even hiding it for weeks. That didn't seem fair to Finn. Hell, it didn't seem fair to him. He didn't want to walk another red carpet with Astrid. He didn't want to ignore his boyfriend on the biggest night of both of their careers. He didn't want to do anything that contributed to that miserable look in Finn's eyes.

Grayson didn't know how, but he had to believe he was telling Finn the truth when he reached across the table for his hand and said, "It'll be okay. We'll figure it out."

CHAPTER 16

Finn adjusted his bow tie in the full-length mirror in the dressing area of his hotel suite. He was not too modest to admit that he looked good. His ensemble for that night's Portrayer Awards was a custom tuxedo, and Finn was nothing if not a risk taker when it came to his red carpet fashion, so he was decked out in fitted black pants, a white shirt, black silk bow tie and a vibrant, deep sangria red tuxedo jacket with satin lapels and an overall sheen that caught the light as he moved. Kayla had tried to talk him into something more "classic," but he told her "classic" was another word for "boring," and he wasn't having it. Not when he was headed to the Portrayer Awards for the very first time, not to mention that he was a nominee. He was going all out, damn it.

He tousled the front of his expertly styled hair so that the blond locks had a bit more of a messy look. He didn't want to be too polished; he'd leave that to Grayson. As if the thought summoned him, Grayson came up behind Finn and wrapped his arms around his waist, resting his chin on Finn's shoulder.

"*Damn*," Grayson said as he slowly checked him out in the mirror. His gaze drifted slowly from Finn's face all the way down his body to his shiny black shoes and back. Finn thought Grayson's eyes lingered longer in some areas than others, and those specific areas had taken notice. Grayson looked up at their reflections, met Finn's eyes, and gave him a sexy grin. Finn knew that look. It was not just appreciation. It was hunger.

Sure enough, Grayson dipped his head and brought his mouth to Finn's neck. Tingles ran up Finn's spine at the feel of Grayson's warm lips and flicking tongue. Finn tilted his head to the side, allowing Grayson better access, and he leaned back into Grayson's solid body. Finn heard himself make a "mmm" sound as he felt Grayson's cock rapidly thickening against him. He pushed his ass into it, and then Grayson was the one groaning.

"Do you have any idea what you do to me?" Grayson's voice was breathy as he spoke between kisses and nips at the exposed skin of Finn's neck. Grayson's hands were splayed wide now, kneading into Finn's abs and hips. Finn rocked into him again. "Jesus. Finn." Grayson's voice was rougher now, choking the words out. Grayson getting turned on was unbelievably hot, and Finn felt drunk with the power of causing that arousal. He couldn't take it anymore. He wanted *more*.

Finn spun around, slid his arms to the back

of Grayson's neck, tangled his hands in his hair, and pulled him down for a frantic kiss. Grayson chuckled against Finn's lips, "Whoa there," he said, pulling back from Finn's greedy mouth. "We have maybe 20 minutes before we have to leave. You sure you want to be starting something now?" Grayson's words had a hint of deviousness in them. Finn took that as a challenge.

"If you really think I need more than 20 minutes to get you off, I might be offended," Finn said. He ran his hand over Grayson's erection through his smooth tuxedo pants.

Finn looked Grayson up and down. He hadn't seen him in his tux until now, and *wow*. Finn always thought Grayson was hot, but him in a tux was next-level smoking. He was elegant but cool, the picture of a classic Hollywood leading man. His black tuxedo pants had a satin vertical stripe up the outside of each leg, the white shirt fit snugly under a perfectly tailored white tux jacket. The one deviation from classic was the deep crimson bow tie. It was nearly the same shade as Finn's jacket, and that made Finn smile. It was like their little rebellion at not being able to arrive together. All that was topped off with Grayson's thick hair slicked back showing off his sharp cheekbones and those killer eyes, all vibrant greenish-brown and flecked with gold.

Finn didn't care what time it was or where they were going. He tugged Grayson back into a deep kiss and his hands flew to the button of Grayson's pants. Grayson didn't try to stop him, so Finn dropped down to his knees, and he proved to Grayson that 20 minutes was more than enough time.

The whole experience of having Grayson's dick in his mouth while they were dressed up in tuxes that cost more than most peoples' cars was ridiculously hot, and Finn was so turned on that Grayson was able to return the favor, and they still had five minutes to spare.

They were busy righting their clothing and fixing their hair when Kayla banged on the door and said it was time to head out. When they emerged from the suite, Kayla gave them a quick once-over, and threw up her hands in frustration. "You gotta be fucking kidding me! You two look like you're doing the walk of shame, not heading to the red carpet." She started pushing buttons on her phone and then barking orders to someone about having hair and makeup brought back. "Hopefully they can salvage the two of you in the limos on the way over."

They made their way to the exit, followed closely by their personal security. "Grayson, you're in the second car with me," Kayla said, indicating one of the limos along the curb. "Finny, you're in the first car," she said. "Lydia's already waiting in there." Just then, the back window of the closest limo slid down and Lydia's face popped out.

"Get your hot ass in here, Everett! We're going to the Portrayer Awards! Woohoo!" She continued to whoop with glee as he made his way over to the limo. Finn couldn't help grinning at Lydia's enthusiasm, and he wondered if she'd already been popping bottles. Even though he wished he'd be going with Grayson as his date and walking the red carpet with him, he knew he'd have fun with Lydia. He always did.

"So, I'll see you there," Finn said to Grayson, who was stepping toward the other limo. Finn tried to communicate the unspoken *I love you* with his eyes.

"See you there," Grayson said, giving Finn a look that Finn could only imagine indicated the message was received and reciprocated.

They got into their separate limos.

This red carpet was so much more chaotic than the one from the season premiere. Finn was thankful to have Lydia on his arm to help him navigate the mass of press and stars and entourages and cameras. He didn't know where to look, where to go, how to move through the crowd. It was complete insanity.

Luckily, there was more posing for photos on this carpet and far fewer interviews with the press. There were too many A-listers there for Finn to be too much of a draw on this carpet. He still heard his name shouted out frequently, however, so he wasn't exactly flying under the radar. It just gave him a little more freedom to relax, somehow, when the attention was spread out among so many other celebrities.

There were occasional shouts of "Are you two dating?" or "You're such a gorgeous couple," as he and Lydia made their way along the crowded carpet. He doubted he'd ever be able to wrap his mind around the press's ability to create their own narratives out of thin air. They seemed to assume being within arm's reach of someone meant they were a couple. Hadn't they just "outed" his relationship with Grayson? Now they think he's with Lydia. Again? He was really just over it.

He simply smiled and pretended not to hear any of that, but he felt the knot in the pit of his stomach tighten up a little more each time someone assumed that Lydia was his girlfriend. It felt somehow wrong to have to deny his real relationship, like it was disloyal to Grayson or disrespectful of what they were to one another. Part of Finn stung each time he felt Lydia's arm wrap around his back to pose for the cameras. He wished it could be Grayson's arm there. He wished he could claim Grayson publicly. He loved him, and he wanted to share nights like this with him. He wanted the world to know Grayson was his boyfriend. Why was that too much to ask?

Finn couldn't help but think about what

Ethan had said to them all those weeks ago. He'd said that Finn and Grayson's relationship wouldn't be bad for their images, and it wouldn't ruin their careers. Ethan seemed to think that being authentic would only help them as actors, and that the parts would still come their way.

Finn didn't know if that was true, of course. Kayla seemed sure the opposite was the case. But it was a nice thought. Finn liked imagining a world in which he and Grayson's relationship status wasn't up for discussion with their bosses, for Christ's sake. That it was just something they were able to be open about, or not, depending on what the two of them wanted. That they didn't have to pretend to hate each other, or downplay their actual relationship, or who-knows-what else.

He longed for the day they made their decisions for *them*. Not for the network or their agent. Not because their personal lives were commodities that could impact their show and their careers. He liked to think that someday they could just be a couple, deciding on how much to share on their own terms. But tonight, he was keeping those wishes tucked away under a confident, if not entirely genuine, smile.

◆ ◆ ◆

To say Kayla's attitude toward Grayson was chilly would be putting it lightly. The limo ride was downright frigid. Grayson had flat-out refused to walk the carpet with Astrid, so he was going it alone. Kayla didn't like her suggestions ignored. They had barely spoken since Kayla laid down her "rules" for the Portrayer Awards. They had a few brief phone calls to discuss his still un-finalized contract negotiations for the next two seasons of *Frost Manor*, but even those conversations had been decidedly unpleasant.

Grayson just wanted to sign the contracts and be done with it. He had verbally agreed to the next two seasons, and Grayson considered himself fully committed. He wasn't about to back out on Jasper and Gwen or the show he'd been with since the beginning – especially not when he was gaining recognition for his performance. Why Kayla was dragging her heels on settling the contracts, he didn't know. She said something about Grayson deserving more, but he was more than happy to accept the salary they'd offered. In any case, he needed to focus on the here and now. He was going to the Portrayer Awards as a Best Actor in a Drama Series nominee. This was living the dream.

But when Grayson stepped out onto the red carpet alone, it felt much less like a dream than it should have. This was the biggest night of his career, and he wished he could have Finn by his side. He wanted his boyfriend's support, and he wanted to support and celebrate Finn's accomplishment, too. A fresh wave of annoyance caused Grayson's shoulders to tighten and made it difficult to exude the pleasant demeanor he'd hoped to pull off on the carpet. Somehow, the significance of the night was dampened by the absence of the person he loved. Worse, even, was that the person he loved was also somewhere on this carpet, arm-in-arm with someone who wasn't Grayson. Annoyance was giving way to anger.

The trip through the cameras and fake smiles and hollow wishes of "good luck tonight," went by in a blur. Grayson was able to zone out, plaster a smile on his face, and make it through the madness. Near the entrance to the theatre, Grayson found himself mere yards behind Finn and Lydia.

His heart soared and sank in quick succession at the sight of Finn. He was stunning in his tux, tall, lean, and so confident in his shining red jacket. Grayson was a little awestruck seeing him in this context. He fully understood why Finn had such rabid fans. There was just something about him that was so sexy, but at the same time so sweet. *He is everything I could ever want*, Grayson thought.

He was jolted out of that thought and hit in the gut with a blast of jealous anger so sharp he thought he might actually bleed. Finn was grinning for the photos, Lydia tucked close by his side, and she was pressing a kiss to his cheek. They looked so happy and so good together. After a few seconds, Lydia pulled away and took Finn by the hand. They were both laughing then, wide, open grins lighting up their faces. And it hurt like hell to watch from just yards away.

Grayson felt his eyes start to sting and mentally slapped himself out of it. He needed to pull it together. And really, he wasn't jealous of Lydia. He knew there was nothing going on between them beyond friendship, but he was jealous that they got to walk down the red carpet together, so openly affectionate. It stung much more than Grayson thought it would to follow Kayla's advice to hide their relationship. It just felt...wrong.

Kayla came up and took Grayson's elbow as he waited in a backup of celebrities to enter the theatre. Kayla wouldn't be entering the theatre, so she'd be leaving after he went in, but she had wanted to keep her eye on him on the carpet to make sure he didn't do anything to fuck up his image. *What the hell ever*. Grayson fought the urge to pull away from her as she leaned in to speak to him.

"You did well on the carpet. I knew you would. Now just get through the ceremony. Accept the award you know you deserve, and *for the love of God*, keep as far away from Finn as possible. You fuck this up, I'm not responsible for the fallout. You know what's at stake here; your contract hasn't been signed yet." She gave Grayson a meaningful look, then continued. "Just focus on what's important." She patted his arm and gave him a syrupy smile before they parted ways at the theatre's entrance.

With Kayla gone, Grayson took a deep, calming breath and entered the theatre. Some kind of assistant showed him where his table was located, and he found his place card at the round table, right between Gwen and Astrid. *Great.* Grayson needed a drink. Thankfully, the Portrayer Awards had booze. He made his way to the bar.

Grayson got in the line for the bar and caught sight of Jasper a few people ahead of him. Grayson was about to say hello when he noticed who Jasper was talking to. Clinging to Jasper's arm was a Vera Wang-clad Astrid, leaning in much too close as she listened to something he was saying to her. *She really is shameless*, Grayson thought, shaking his head.

Ever since Astrid seemed to accept that it was never going to happen with Grayson, she'd leeched on to Jasper. Grayson didn't fully understand why she was so desperate to latch on to a man. Astrid was gorgeous and a truly talented actress. Her personality could use some work, but she had what it took to make it in this business, with or without strategically attaching herself to a man. Grayson wondered if he'd ever get a chance to ask her about it, or if she'd always be conniving and vindictive. It was sad, really.

Astrid was laughing too loudly at something Jasper said as they accepted their drinks from the bartender and disappeared into the crowd. When it was Grayson's turn at the bar, he ordered a gin and tonic, and heard someone say, "Make that two."

When Grayson turned his head, he saw Finn next to him, keeping a safe distance away, drumming his fingers anxiously on the bar as he waited for the bartender to pour the drinks. Finn gave Grayson a half-smile and quickly turned his face forward, clearly not wanting to violate the "stay away from each other" rule too much. Grayson was thankful that he'd bent the rules a little, though, because it felt good just to be near him.

"How are you holding up?" Finn asked, his voice casual, his eyes still forward and not looking at Grayson.

"It could be better," Grayson said, chancing a quick glance at Finn.

Finn was still drumming his fingers on the bar when he nodded. "You got that right."

"Looked like you were having fun out there, at least," Grayson said.

Finn did turn to face Grayson then, his blue eyes sad as he said, "I'm a good actor." Finn gave a rueful shrug.

Grayson offered him a dismal attempt at a smile. He took note of Finn's fidgeting and restless fingers on the bar top. "You nervous?"

"A bit," Finn admitted.

Grayson wanted so badly to be able to take his hand in his or wrap a comforting arm around him.

The bartender was back and handed their drinks over.

"I guess we should find our seats," Finn said.

"Yeah."

Grayson followed Finn toward the table at a safe, respectable distance, using all the self-control he possessed to keep from reaching out and touching him.

CHAPTER 17

The group sitting around the Frost Manor table was cheerful, if not a bit tipsy. Finn was sitting next to Lydia, and the two of them were enjoying a conversation with Jasper when someone tapped Finn's shoulder. He turned to see Eileen Dunphey, one of the executive producers from his former show, Luna's Cove.

Finn smiled warmly and stood to hug Eileen. "Finn, it's so great to see you. Congratulations!" Eileen said as she squeezed him and kissed his cheek.

"Thanks. It's great to see you, too, Eileen. I miss everyone from the show so much. It's weird to go from spending 50 plus hours a week with people for years and then not seeing them at all," Finn said.

"I know what you mean," Eileen said. "But I have a new project in the works, so I guess I'll be getting a new work family. It sure looks like you've found that with *Frost Manor*," she said, glancing at the faces around the table.

Finn nodded. "Yeah, it's been great. Everyone's been really welcoming. I love it," he said, grinning.

"Well I'm glad to hear it. I knew there were big things in your future, and I couldn't be prouder that you started out with us at *Luna's Cove*."

Finn hugged her again and Eileen said her goodbyes to Finn and the rest of the table.

"So what's her new project," Jasper asked.

"Oh, it's this amazing dark comedy," Lydia said with clear enthusiasm. Finn shot her a look. How did she know about it when he didn't? Finn just shrugged it off. It wasn't like he kept up with many projects aside from *Frost Manor* at the moment.

The next few minutes passed in companionable chatter about industry gossip and what everyone had been binging on Netflix. Sitting there in that room, surrounded by the industry's finest talents, Finn really did feel like the old cliché about how it's great just to be nominated was true. The nomination itself was more than he'd ever hoped for, and it felt good to be a part of a show that was recognized at the Portrayer Awards, his work singled out. In a way, Finn dreaded the longshot possibility of winning. He didn't want to go up on stage and make a speech. He didn't want to hear his name called and not be able to hug Grayson or even look at him. He didn't want to give a speech thanking everyone besides the person that had truly helped him the most with his performance this year. So, if he was crossing his fingers that he *wouldn't* win, he had his reasons.

From across the table, Finn could make out snippets of Grayson's conversation with Gwen. They were talking about Ethan leaving the *Frost Manor* team to start with the talent agency.

"I'm happy for him, but I'm not going to lie, I'm going to miss that guy on set," Grayson was saying.

"Oh, don't I know it. I'm not even sure Jasper and I can function without Ethan Rhys as our eyes and ears and hands. Someone who can deal with the likes of all of you is one in a million," she teased, though it was clear she was sincerely sad to see Ethan go.

Jasper chimed in from across the table. "He is going to be one hell of an agent, though. Kid is one of the smartest people I've ever met, and he knows this business. He's the hardest worker and the nicest guy. But, yeah, we're basically fucked without him." Jasper laughed then and said, "It's one of many big changes we'll face in Season 4, but change can be good." Jasper didn't seem to be speaking to anyone in particular, but the whole table took note of his words.

Finn felt a little chill at the offhand mention of "many big changes." What did that mean? The loss of Ethan as a PA was a change, sure, but what else was Jasper talking about? Finn glanced around the table, which was suddenly very silent except for a few cleared throats and the sound of champagne glasses being drained and returned to the table. Finn looked at his co-stars. Lydia looked uncomfortable, Astrid was grinning wickedly, and Grayson seemed to be deep in thought.

They turned their attention to the stage when Finn's category was announced. He'd known it would be early in the ceremony, and he was happy to get it over with.

"And the nominees for Best Supporting Actor in a Drama Series are..."

Finn felt his heart hammering in his chest, and Lydia took his hand in hers and squeezed. As the nominees were read, clips of their work flashed across the huge screen on the stage. When the presenter said, "Finn Everett, *Frost Manor*," the clip they showed was from the dinner party scene where Finn and Grayson's characters had debated love and marriage.

"And the winner is..."

He squeezed Lydia's hand, and he met Grayson's eyes across the table. Grayson gave him an encouraging smile, full of love and pride. Finn breathed in, out, in again, and out again. "Madden Ames..." Finn exhaled in relief. He was off the hook.

Finn applauded along with the rest of the crowd. He looked at Grayson then, and Finn gave him a smile, trying to communicate that he was okay with losing. He truly was more relieved than anything. Now he could focus all his energy on nerves for Grayson's category. He knew Grayson was a real contender, and Grayson deserved this win.

Gwen and Jasper excused themselves to mingle during the commercial break. That left Finn with Lydia, Astrid, and Grayson. Astrid looked at Finn, and said, "Awww, that really is too bad, Finn. Tough break."

He simply shrugged.

"It could be worse, you know," Astrid continued, voice loud enough to address everyone remaining at the table. Lydia looked at Astrid with narrowed eyes.

"Just shut up, Astrid," she said. "It's really not the time." Finn loved her for her unflinching support.

Astrid had a sly quirk to her lips, and she had no intention of shutting up. "All I'm saying is that those 'big changes' coming next season mean bad news for someone. That's all I'm saying."

"What are you talking about?" Grayson asked.

"Oh, I thought you knew. Jasper and Gwen

got the two-season renewal on the promise that a series regular would be killed off next season. You know, a whole Red Wedding situation to keep viewers' attention and generate buzz for the show." Astrid took a swig of champagne and leaned back in her chair, smugness oozing off of her.

"And how would you know this?" Grayson asked, his expression schooled into casual indifference. Finn knew better, though, and could see the tension in Grayson's jaw, the rigidness of his posture.

Astrid gave a Cheshire Cat smile and looked at Grayson. "You know Jasper and I are...close," she said coyly. "I may have overheard some things."

Grayson rolled his eyes at her. "Sure. Okay, Astrid."

Astrid turned her attention to Finn then. "You signed a contract for the next two seasons, right Finn? So, you don't have anything to worry about," she said pleasantly. "And of course, I signed mine, too."

Lydia stepped in then. "Astrid. This is not only unprofessional, but inappropriate and insensitive to discuss here," she gritted out. "You're a great actress, but your people skills are absolutely for shit."

Finn squeezed Lydia's shoulder to soothe her while trying to stifle a giggle at the fact she had just called someone out as unprofessional and then used the phrase "absolutely for shit," in the exact same sentence.

The table was silent again, and Finn looked at Grayson. Grayson appeared shaken. He was restless, picking up his glass, remembering it was empty, setting it down again, and then picking it up once more a few seconds later. Grayson was normally so composed that this fidgeting startled Finn. Finn recalled that Grayson hadn't settled his contract negotiations yet, and he felt a knot form in his gut. They wouldn't kill off Grayson's character, would they?

◆ ◆ ◆

Grayson didn't know if there was a single scrap of truth to Astrid's words, but he had to admit they threw him for a loop. The whole Red Wedding strategy did sound like something Jasper would pitch to the network, and Grayson wouldn't put it past him to promise something like that to secure a renewal. But he wasn't the one on the chopping block. Right?

Sure, he hadn't finalized his contract yet, but it was verbally agreed upon. He trusted Jasper and Gwen. He had no reason not to. Kayla was the one dragging her feet in the negotiations, and it was probably due to the tension between them that the contracts weren't settled and signed by now.

Grayson looked across the table at Finn. He felt bad that Finn had lost his category, but he could see that Finn was okay with it. He was the kind of person that was really happy just to be nominated. Finn was looking at him thoughtfully, and Grayson knew he was sensing Grayson's discomfort with Astrid's supposed revelation.

Grayson smiled at his boyfriend in reassurance that he was not worried, and Finn smiled back. When Finn smiled at him like that, Grayson truly wasn't worried about anything. *God, I love that man.* Mixed emotions flooded Grayson. He was overcome with appreciation for Finn, and at the same time he was irate all over again at having to keep his distance from him. He hated not being the one to hold Finn's hand when his category was called, and he longed for Finn to be by his side now.

Jasper and Gwen returned to the table just as Grayson's category was announced.

"The nominees for Best Actor in a Drama Series are…"

Blood rushed in Grayson's ears. Everything was moving in slow motion. Grayson watched the screen at the stage flash through clips of all the nominees. He recognized the scene where his and Finn's characters argued in the field. It was Finn's first scene. Grayson's chest fluttered at the memory of that first day with Finn, running lines for that very scene. He looked over at Finn, who was flashing him that boyish smile, radiating pride. Grayson's insides melted a little every time Finn looked at him that way.

Wait. This is it. Grayson was aware of the clips stopping, and all five nominees' names were on the big screen. He heard the presenter say, "And the winner is..."

Deep breath in, and out.

"...Grayson Winter, *Frost Manor*!"

Time stopped for a second. Grayson saw Finn leap up out of his seat, fist pumping and screaming like a loon. *I won? I won.* Grayson's whole body trembled violently as it sank in. He won a Portrayer award. This was a once-in-a-lifetime achievement, and he knew he'd remember this night for the rest of his life.

Gwen was patting Grayson on the back, and the crowd surrounding them was applauding loudly. Grayson's eyes were still on Finn, who was beaming, clapping wildly, and hooting.

Fuck it. This is my moment.

He strode over to Finn, cupped his face in both his hands, and kissed him firmly on the mouth. Startled, Finn took a fraction of a second before kissing him back and then wrapping him in a tight hug.

"Congratulations, Baby. I knew you'd win," Finn whispered.

Grayson grinned at Finn and made his way to the stage.

Grayson took the statue from the presenter and stood at the podium. He hadn't prepared a speech. He hated when people read from pre-penned speeches like they'd expected to win. He was winging it.

Grayson's hands still shook as he held the statue and adjusted the mic. He felt the heat of the stage lights on his face, and he was vaguely aware of voices quieting and claps tapering off. Looking out at the crowd of his peers, mentors, and people he'd looked up to his whole life, he was overwhelmed with gratitude and pride in this accomplishment. *This is unreal.* He cleared his throat, took a steadying breath, and began to speak.

"Wow." His voice was shaky but clear in the microphone. "Thank you so much. This is a surprise, and I'm honored." Grayson looked out over the crowd and continued.

"For as long as I can remember, I've wanted to be an actor. When I got the part on *Frost Manor*, it felt like the universe had given me a gift, and I knew I'd work hard every day trying to deserve it. I feel like I hit the jackpot with the role of James Beechworth. He's a complex man, and I've spent the last three years trying to do this character justice." Grayson paused here, attempting to gather himself and keep his emotions in check.

"So, first, I'd like to thank Gwen Giles and Jasper Vincent, our showrunners, for taking a chance on me and believing that I could pull this off." He looked at Gwen and Jasper, and he felt the tears welling in his eyes.

"I'd like to thank Felix Lincoln, my best friend and chosen family. And Ethan Rhys, you've always gone above and beyond, and I'm proud to call you a friend. Thank you to the whole *Frost Manor* team. Lydia, you're the best fake sister a guy could have. I am thankful for the whole wonderful cast and crew every day I come to work. You're the absolute best."

Grayson cleared his throat again, and he made eye contact with Finn. "Lastly, I wouldn't be up here today if I hadn't been inspired this season to dig deeper in each and every scene, to pour more of myself into my performances, to be my best." Grayson locked eyes with Finn. "So, Finn Everett, thank you." Grayson saw Finn's eyes widen and that gorgeous grin spread across his face.

"You challenged me and pushed me, and you set the bar so high I couldn't help but strive and stretch to try to reach it." Grayson's voice wobbled a little as he continued. When he looked out at the crowd now, he could only see Finn.

"You are the best scene partner I could hope for. You made everything better when you joined the show, including me. So, thank you for everything. I love you more than you love Arcade Fire, Finn."

Grayson raised the trophy in the air and exited the stage to uproarious applause.

As soon as he stepped backstage, Grayson was nearly knocked over by the impact of Finn's body flinging into him. Grayson wrapped the arm that wasn't holding his Portrayer statue around Finn's waist as he crushed him into an embrace.

"I cannot *believe* you just did that," Finn said, glassy eyes searching Grayson's.

"Are you mad?" Grayson asked.

"Are you kidding me?" Finn claimed his mouth in a wild kiss.

Grayson kissed him back, the mix of adrenaline from the speech and the high from kissing Finn combining to render him lightheaded. He pulled back and laughed, his whole body coursing with euphoria. This was right. He took Finn's hand and they made their way back to their table, where Gwen and Lydia had rearranged people so that they could sit side by side.

Once they were seated, Grayson put a hand on Finn's knee and leaned in close to him. "I meant what I said up there. Thank you. For everything."

Finn smiled softly. "You're welcome."

Grayson laughed quietly. "I love you so much."

Finn's eyes sparkled. "I love you, too. More than all the hipster bands in the world combined."

EPILOGUE

8 Months Later

Finn stepped out of the back of the limo to an onslaught of flashing bulbs and voices shouting his name. No matter how many times he did this, there were always jitters, and Finn needed to stop to take a few calming breaths.

A hand slid in to hold his own, and Finn felt the gentle squeeze of familiar fingers. "You good?" Grayson's deep voice was tinged with concern, but just the sound of it and the feel of his hand holding Finn's was enough to ground Finn. They had this.

"All good," Finn said, smiling at his gorgeous boyfriend.

Hand in hand, they made their way down the red carpet for the film *No Win Outcome*. The film was about a Navy SEAL team's precarious mission, and it starred Grayson Winter. It was no surprise that their arrival on the carpet caused quite the stir among the press and fans. Everyone wanted a photo of Grinn, Hollywood's favorite "it" couple.

Finn and Grayson stopped for photographs and made their way through a couple of press interviews that had been arranged in advance by Ethan. Ever since Ethan had taken over as Grayson and Finn's agent, there were fewer, more strategic press engagements. Ethan had a knack for choosing the least painful interviews and media spots while still delivering plenty of great press for their projects.

It had been a no brainer to switch agents once Kayla threw a fit over Grayson's Portrayer speech. Both Finn and Grayson agreed that it was worth switching agents if it meant they could be themselves without any hiding. Ethan had said their relationship wouldn't hurt their careers, and it truly hadn't. Grayson had starred in this film, and both Finn and Grayson were constantly bombarded by offers of film and television roles for when they were not filming *Frost Manor*.

Frost Manor had also seen a major ratings bump after Grayson's Portrayer win and the show killing-off Lydia's character in Season 4. It turned out that Lydia felt constricted by the Regency-era show, and she was ready to move on to other opportunities. She was much happier starring in a contemporary dark comedy on a popular streaming service. The project was actually the one created by Finn's former boss, Eileen Dunphey, and it was amazing. Lydia was in her element, and Finn was thrilled for her.

Finn and Grayson stopped to chat with Bennet Orion, who greeted them with his cheesy megawatt smile.

"Hey there, guys," Bennett said, "what a treat to have both Grayson Winter and Finn Everett stop by. Or should I call you Grinn?" He absolutely beamed. "How are you both?"

Grayson was fielding the questions, as this was his carpet, but Finn had promised to chime in here and there to share the burden of doing press.

"Doing really well." Grayson said, smiling.

Bennett was happy to jump into the real questions. "You are both so great on *Frost Manor* this season. We've had word that the fifth season will be the last. How do you feel about that, and what's next for the two of you?"

Grayson was the first to respond again. "I couldn't be prouder to be a part of *Frost Manor*, and I am pleased to have been able to see it through to the end. Season 5 brings the show to a natural conclusion, and we all agree that it's best to quit while we're ahead."

Bennett turned to Finn then. "So, Finn, what's next for you once *Frost Manor* is over?"

Finn glanced at Grayson, and Grayson gave a small nod.

"Actually, Grayson and I have a new project in the works. We are executive producing and writing a new series about a young person coming to Hollywood and learning to make his way under the weight of the public eye, professional expectations, and falling in love."

"That sounds amazing," Bennett said. "Am I sensing a little autobiography in there?"

Finn and Grayson smirked at one another before Finn said, "Maybe a little."

They parted from Bennett and moved down the red carpet to screams of "We love you guys" and "Grayson, Finn, over here." At one such shout, Grayson stopped, wrapped an arm around Finn's waist, and turned to look at him. Grayson smiled at him with such genuine affection that Finn thought his heart might explode right there on the red carpet. Finn smiled back at him, leaned in a little closer, and then they both turned to face the cameras, wide grins on their faces, their happiness unmistakable.

◆ ◆ ◆

Want to find out what happens between Felix and Ethan? Read their story in *Drawing Lines*, the next book in the *Hollywood Hopefuls* series. Available on Amazon.

Acknowledgement

While the COVID-19 pandemic brought about some of the most challenging times in my life, there was a silver lining, for me, at least. I learned to let go of caring what people thought about me, and that simple alteration in my mindset unleashed a new urge to really pursue the things that make me happy. I read more in the last year than I have in the last ve, probably. I've jigsaw puzzled, and I've knit plenty. I also decided to change up my career, shifting to what brings me the most happiness, which is being creative.

So, I decided to write a novel, and here we are. I would never have had the confidence to make this change and pursue any of this without my partner in all things, my husband Eric. Eric, I know that you put up with a hell of a lot when it comes to me. You listen to all of my incessant talking about things you don't have any interest in, and you always reassure me when I'm anxious or uncertain or fearful. You carry me when I need it, and you keep the kids and I on track. I love you.

My kids will presumably never read this book, but it's worth begin said that their positivity and loving spirits help me in all ways, including as a writer.

To my mom, Lora. I have never had a bigger cheerleader in life than you. You have always made me feel like I was exceptional and could do anything. I know that if I ever need anything at all, you will help me. No matter what. I love you so much, mom.

To Sara. I am forever grateful that I met you. I didn't think I'd find a friend that understood me and supported me and made me laugh as much as you do. Thank you for being my person.

A huge thanks to Diana Peterfreund for being a willing listener and helper with my publication questions and for putting me in touch with Lucy. Lucy Lennox, thank you for being so exceedingly generous with your knowledge. I am beyond grateful for all you've shared to help me get started.

To the rest of my support system. Chelsea and Chris. Joe and Krysten. Phyllis and Darrel. Cassie Fournier. Thank you for always listening, making time, and inspiring me to just be myself. I am lucky to have you all in my life.

ABOUT THE AUTHOR

Jeris Jean

Jeris Jean is a life-long Minnesotan with an obsessive love of books. She has a master's degree in English Literature but didn't write her first novel until she was in her mid-thirties. Something just "clicked," and all fell into its rightful place.

Jeris is a lover of cats, coffee, binge-watching tv shows, her bff, puzzles, knitting, white sunglasses, black nail polish, and reading and writing like it's going out of style, especially lgbtq romance.

She lives with her husband, two sons and their cat, Fluffy Cat Love, in a lovely little suburb of Minneapolis.

LETTER FROM JERIS

Dear Reader,

Thank you so much for reading *Running Lines*! This is my first novel, and your support means a lot to me. I'd love it if you'd take a few minutes to review *Running Lines* on Amazon. Reader reviews really make a difference, and I sincerely appreciate every single one of them.

I wrote this book during the COVID-19 pandemic. The general idea and the characters came to me, and I was unable to not write it all down. I had a vision for a three-book series when I started *Running Lines*.

Up next is a novel featuring two characters that I fell in love with while writing the first book, Felix and Ethan. *Drawing Lines*, which you can get on Amazon.

Let's Connect!

Be sure to follow me on Amazon to be notified of new releases and look for me on Instagram and Facebook for updates on upcoming stories.

Newsletter: Sign up at www.jerisjean.com
Facebook Group: Team Jeris Jean
Instagram: @jeris.jean

Pinterest: Jeris Jean - Author
(See an inspo board for *Running Lines*)

Read on, Friends!

-Jeris

Made in the USA
Monee, IL
04 March 2021

HEALTH PSYCHOLOGY

This book provides a holistic understanding of the state of health psychology in the Indian context and the types of psychological and social support and welfare that are offered and required within treatment processes for various illnesses.

The book discusses why health care should be the prerogative of both the biomedical profession and health psychologists and how they work together with medical professionals to augment public health. It emphasises the shift from biomedical to biopsychosocial approach in strengthening health care outcomes. The book highlights the substantial contribution of health psychology to the Indian health care system through simple, cost-effective, indigenous, and standardised techniques that worked efficiently in the context of various diseases. It projects the emerging trends and innovative techniques in health psychology in handling challenging health care needs.

This book will be of interest to students, teachers, and researchers of psychology, psychiatry, social psychology, sociology, social work, and South Asian studies.

Meena Hariharan is a Professor and the Founder Director of the Centre for Health Psychology. She joined the University of Hyderabad in 1992. She has published extensively in the field of health psychology covering behavioural cardiology, ICU trauma, coping with non-communicable diseases, and resilience studies. She is the Founder President of the Association of Health Psychologists and the Chief Editor of *Indian Journal of Health Studies*.

Meera Padhy has been associated with the Centre for Health Psychology, University of Hyderabad, India, since 2007. She has published extensively on health psychology, developmental psychology, and occupational psychology. Her research interests include behavioural diabetology, occupational health, social support, leisure, and well-being.

Usha Chivukula is working as a faculty member at the Centre for Health Psychology, University of Hyderabad, and has extended her research into the areas of behavioural cardiology, community health psychology, and child and adolescent health.

HEALTH PSYCHOLOGY

Contributions to the Indian
Health System

*Edited by Meena Hariharan,
Meera Padhy, and Usha Chivukula*

Routledge
Taylor & Francis Group
LONDON AND NEW YORK

Designed cover image: Getty Images

First published 2023
by Routledge
4 Park Square, Milton Park, Abingdon, Oxon OX14 4RN

and by Routledge
605 Third Avenue, New York, NY 10158

Routledge is an imprint of the Taylor & Francis Group, an informa business

© 2023 selection and editorial matter, Meena Hariharan, Meera Padhy and Usha Chivukula; individual chapters, the contributors

The right of Meena Hariharan, Meera Padhy and Usha Chivukula to be identified as the authors of the editorial material, and of the authors for their individual chapters, has been asserted in accordance with sections 77 and 78 of the Copyright, Designs and Patents Act 1988.

All rights reserved. No part of this book may be reprinted or reproduced or utilised in any form or by any electronic, mechanical, or other means, now known or hereafter invented, including photocopying and recording, or in any information storage or retrieval system, without permission in writing from the publishers.

Trademark notice: Product or corporate names may be trademarks or registered trademarks, and are used only for identification and explanation without intent to infringe.

British Library Cataloguing-in-Publication Data
A catalogue record for this book is available from the British Library

ISBN: 978-1-032-28751-5 (hbk)
ISBN: 978-1-032-42105-6 (pbk)
ISBN: 978-1-003-36085-8 (ebk)

DOI: 10.4324/9781003360858

Typeset in Bembo
by KnowledgeWorks Global Ltd.

Dedicated to

Professor I. Ramabrahmam

The Inspiration Behind This Volume

CONTENTS

List of Figures x
List of Tables xi
Contributors xiii
Foreword xix
Preface xxi
Acknowledgements xxv

PART I
Holistic Approach to Health 1

1 Evidence-Based Health Care: Contributions of Health Psychology 3
   Meena Hariharan

2 Health Communication as a Preface to Management of Non-Communicable Diseases 25
   Sunayana Swain

3 Health and Well-Being for All: Policy Perspectives in the Indian Context 41
   Ramya Chitrapu

4 Implementation Research for Public Health and Preventive Health Care in India 54
   B. R. Shamanna

PART II
Health and Well-Being of Individuals in Society   71

5 Residential Crowding and Subjective Well-Being:
Mediating Role of Helplessness   73
Surendra Kumar Sia and P. S. Neethu

6 Health in the Culturally Changing Underdeveloped Adivasi
Communities   86
Purnima Awasthi, Madhurima Mukherjee, and R. C. Mishra

7 Smoking and Alcohol Consumption Among Type 2
Diabetics: Health Behaviour Models–Based Investigation   98
*Eslavath Rajkumar, J. Romate, R. Lakshmi,
and G. T. Kruthika*

PART III
Psychosocial Factors in Cardiovascular Diseases   113

8 Psychological Necessities of Patients Electing Cardiac
Bypass Surgery: A Review and Roadmap   115
Marlyn Thomas Savio

9 Illness Perception and Adherence Behaviour in Patients
with Coronary Artery Disease   127
Arti Singh and Shikha Dixit

10 Optimizing Hypertension Management: Children as
Adherence Monitors for Adult Patients   143
Sandra Roshni Monteiro

PART IV
Psychosocial Factors in Diabetes Management   157

11 Illness Perceptions and Quality of Life of Diabetic Patients:
Role of Perceived Control of Internal States   159
Meera Padhy and A. Sheila Kumari Valli

12 Illness Perceptions and Diabetes Self-Management:
A Mixed-Method Approach   177
Chelli Kavya

PART V
Critical Care Needs and Psychological Support   191

13 The Intensive Care Unit Experiences and Repercussions:
    Need for Psychosocial Care   193
    Usha Chivukula

14 An Interpretative Phenomenological Analysis: The Unmet
    Information and Supportive Care Needs of Cancer Patients   206
    *Mahati Chittem, Matsungshila Pongener, Sravannthi Maya,
    and Shweta Chawak*

Index   222

FIGURES

2.1	Public Health Care System in India.	33
4.1	What Is Implementation Research?	56
5.1	Proposed Model for the Mediating Role of Helplessness on the Relationship Between Crowding and Well-Being.	77
5.2	Structural Model for Crowding and Subjective Well-Being Mediated by Learned Helplessness.	79
8.1	Elements of the Biomedical Approach (left) and the Biopsychosocial Approach (right) to CABG care.	123
10.1	Bar Graph Representation of Percentage of Successful and Unsuccessful Reminders of Hypertension Management Record Booklet Documented by Children for Parameters of Medicine, Exercise, and Diet.	153
14.1	Interpretative Phenomenological Analysis Process.	209
14.2	Flow Chart of the Themes.	210

TABLES

1.1	Top ten causes of death in children in the age group of 5–14 years in India between 2010 and 2013	5
3.1	Total budgetary expenditure vis-à-vis health expenditure and percentage of gross domestic product (GDP) at the central level in India – a glimpse	47
3.2	Health infrastructure in India – an overview (as of March 2021)	48
5.1	Descriptive statistics, validity measures and correlation coefficients of the constructs	79
5.2	Standardized regression coefficient and bootstrap analysis of the indirect model crowding and subjective well-being through helplessness	80
7.1	Association of the HBM, TPB, and SET domains with smoking behaviour	103
7.2	Association of the HBM, TPB, and SET domains with alcohol use behaviour	105
9.1	Demographic details of participants	131
9.2	Multiple regression to identify predictors of various dimensions of Adherence Behaviour Scale	133
9.3	Identified themes, subthemes, and codes	134
10.1	Mean (M), standard deviation (SD), and t values of hypertension knowledge and its subscales among children participants ($N = 181$)	150
10.2	Mean (M), standard deviation (SD), and t values of hypertension knowledge and its subscale among adult participants ($N = 181$)	151
10.3	Mean (M), standard deviation (SD) and t values of hypertension compliance and its subscales among adult participants ($N = 181$)	151

10.4	Mean (*M*), standard deviation (*SD*), and *t* values of mean arterial pressure of adult participants (*N* = 181)	152
11.1	Correlation between demographic variables, dimensions of illness perception, perceived control of internal states, and dimensions of QoL (*N* = 150)	166
11.2	Multiple hierarchical regression analysis for demographic variables, subscales of illness perception, and perceived control of internal states predicting QoL (satisfaction)	167
11.3	Multiple hierarchical regression analysis for demographic variables, subscales of illness perception, and perceived control of internal states predicting QoL (impact)	168
11.4	Multiple hierarchical regression analysis for demographic variables, subscales of illness perception, and perceived control of internal states predicting QoL (social and vocational worries)	169
11.5	Multiple hierarchical regression analysis for demographic variables, subscales of illness perception, and perceived control of internal states predicting QoL (diabetes related worries)	170
11.6	Multiple hierarchical regression analysis for demographic variables, subscales of illness perception, and perceived control of internal states predicting QoL (total)	171
12.1	Demographic characteristics of participants phase II	179
12.2	Summary of simultaneous multiple regression for illness perceptions predicting diabetes self-management	182
12.3	Themes and their sub-themes	183
12.4	Themes and their sub-themes with illustrative quotation	184
13.1	Frequencies and percentages of stressors in the ICU	197
14.1	Demographic and medical information	208
14.2	Interview topics and sample questions	209

CONTRIBUTORS

Purnima Awasthi is Professor of Psychology at the Department of Psychology, Faculty of Social Sciences, Banaras Hindu University, Varanasi (UP), India. Her research interest includes health psychology, cross-cultural health psychology, social psychology, rehabilitation psychology, and positive psychology. She is primarily interested in the study of health beliefs and practices of people from different sections of Indian society, and their application to community development. She has contributed scientific research papers to various journals of national and international repute and also chapters in edited books in the areas of health psychology and Community Development. She carried out an Indian Council of Social Science Research project entitled 'Understanding and Management of Some Critical Health Problems in an Underdeveloped Kharwar Tribal Community'. She also published books on 'Leadership' (2009) with PHI, New Delhi, 'Write Your Script: The Scientific Way' with White Falcon Publishing, Chandigarh, and 'Power of Emotional Intelligence: Incredible Tool to Become Healthy and Wealthy' with Walnut Publications, Bhubaneswar, India.

Shweta Chawak, PhD, received her doctoral degree from the Indian Institute of Technology Hyderabad, India. Through her PhD, she developed and tested the feasibility of an intervention which introduced the *question prompt list* to Indian cancer patients undergoing radiation therapy and their primary family caregivers. Her research interests lie in health and medical psychology, with a special focus on understanding and improving communication in health care settings using a multistakeholder perspective.

Ramya Chitrapu was formerly Junior Research Fellow, Administrative Staff College of India (ASCI), Hyderabad, India. Ms. Chitrapu is presently a doctoral research scholar with the Department of Political Science, University of Hyderabad, India. Her research interests include policymaking, public service delivery, governance, and innovations in governance.

Mahati Chittem, PhD, is Associate Professor of Health and Medical Psychology with the Department of Liberal Arts, Indian Institute of Technology Hyderabad (IITH), India. Her research interests lie in chronic disease management (with a special focus on cancer, endocrinology, and chronic kidney disease) and health behaviour change (diet, exercise, and safe sex).

Usha Chivukula received a doctorate degree in Psychology from the Centre for Health Psychology, University of Hyderabad, for her research in the area of psychosocial care in intensive care units. Currently, she is working as a faculty at the Centre for Health Psychology, University of Hyderabad, and has extended her research into the areas of behavioural cardiology, community health psychology, and child and adolescent health.

Prof. Shikha Dixit is Professor of Psychology with the Department of Humanities and Social Sciences, Indian Institute of Technology, Kanpur, India. She has been in the profession for the last 28 years and has contributed significantly to areas such as health psychology and social representations.

Kruthika G.T. has completed a master's degree in Clinical and Counselling Psychology from the Central University of Karnataka during the 2017–2019 academic year. She worked on a thesis titled 'An association of social cognitive domains, self-care behaviour, and glucose control' as part of her curriculum.

Meena Hariharan is a Professor and the Founder Director of the Centre for Health Psychology. She joined the University of Hyderabad in 1992. She has published about 100 articles in peer-reviewed journals and four books. Her research work in the field of health psychology covers behavioural cardiology, ICU trauma, coping with non-communicable diseases, and resilience studies. She has supervised five PhDs in the last 10 years and five are presently working under her. She is the Founder President of the Association of Health Psychologists and the Chief Editor of Indian Journal of Health Studies. She is on the editorial boards of some peer-reviewed journals and is a member of the Board of Studies in several Universities.

Romate J. has 25 years of experience in teaching, researching, training, and managing various administrative positions at the university level. He was instrumental in the establishment of the Centre for Psychological Counselling at Bangalore University (1994), the MSc Holistic Psychological Counselling in the Department of Psychology (2000) at Bangalore University. He has also established and been heading the Department of Psychology at the Central University of Karnataka. He has more than 50 research papers published in reputed journals, has attended 56 conferences and presented scientific papers, and completed twenty research projects and eighteen academic consultancy assignments.

Chelli Kavya is currently working as Assistant Professor with the Department of Banaras Hindu University. She has completed PhD in Psychology from Centre for Health Psychology, University of Hyderabad. She has published articles in various national and international journals. Her research interest is health psychology.

R Lakshmi is a doctoral research scholar with the Department of Psychology, Central University of Karnataka. Her doctoral research is in the field of health psychology and focuses on health risk behaviours. She holds an ICSSR doctoral fellowship and has worked as a Research Associate on an ICSSR sanctioned major project. Her work has appeared in Bentham Science, Health Psychology Research, Springer Nature, and Elsevier, among others.

Sravannthi Maya, PhD, is a psycho-oncologist and a health and counselling psychologist. An alumnus of the Indian Institute of Technology Hyderabad (IITH), her areas of focus are Oncology (with a specific focus on adult and geriatric patients), Endocrinology (PCOD/PCOS and diabetes), End-of-life care, developing coping tools for an Indian population, and death and bereavement support. Her aim is to develop, test, and implement mental health interventions so as to improve the overall quality of life among Indian patient populations.

Ramesh C. Mishra (DPhil, University of Allahabad) is Professor Emeritus of Psychology at Banaras Hindu University, India. He has been a post-doctoral Research Fellow and Shastri Research Fellow at Queen's University, Canada, and a visiting Professor at the Universities of Konstanz (Germany) and Geneva (Switzerland). He has also been a Fellow-in-Residence of the Netherlands Institute of Advanced Study, Wassenaar (The Netherlands) and a Fulbright Scholar-in-Residence at Wittenberg University, Springfield (USA). He is the Past President and Fellow of the National Academy of Psychology (India). His research is focused on understanding ecological and cultural influences on human development. He is the co-author of Ecology, Acculturation and Psychological Adaptation: A Study of Adivasis in Bihar (SAGE) and Development of Geocentric Spatial Language and Cognition: An Ecocultural Perspective and co-editor of Psychology in Human and Social Development: Lessons from Diverse Cultures.

Sandra Roshni Monteiro is an Assistant Professor with the Department of Applied Psychology, GITAM School of Humanities and Social Sciences, GITAM (Deemed to be University), India. She was a recipient of Senior Research Fellowship from the Indian Council of Medical Research and had qualified for ICSSR Centrally Administered Doctoral Fellowship and UGC NET. She also received the Gold Medal in M.Sc. (specialisation in health psychology) from the University of Hyderabad. Her PhD research is about finding a sustainable biopsychosocial health care solution for optimising hypertension management by tapping onto children's role and value as family members. Other than the area of behavioural cardiology, she has published papers and is working in the areas concerning childhood stress, adolescent health, positive psychology, and occupational health.

Madhurima Mukherjee is a research scholar with the Department of Psychology, Faculty of Social Sciences, Banaras Hindu University, Varanasi (UP), India. Her interest lies in studying the cross-cultural adaptation and health of ethnic minorities.

Neethu P. S. is currently working as an Assistant Professor with the Department of Sports Psychology, Central University of Rajasthan. She has completed PhD in Applied Psychology from Pondicherry University. Her core areas of research include environmental psychology, sports psychology, and health and well-being. She has published articles in various national and international journals and also edited a book published by an international publisher. She is the recipient of Prof. Deepak Bhatt Award and Dr. Barbara Hanfstingal Inspa award.

Meera Padhy received her PhD from Utkal University in 1996. She was a recipient of UGC JRF fellowship during her PhD. She has been associated with the Centre for Health Psychology, University of Hyderabad, India, since 2007. She has published extensively on health psychology, developmental psychology, and occupational psychology in national and international journals of repute as well as presented in many conferences. Her work has been recognised with awards like the best Health Psychologist, IPERA, in 2013 and the best paper presenter award in the 52nd and 21st International Conference of the Indian Academy of Applied Psychology in 2017. Her research interests include behavioural diabetology, occupational health, social support, leisure, and well-being.

Matsungshila Pongener, MSc, is a PhD scholar with the Department of Liberal Arts, Indian Institute of Technology Hyderabad (IITH), India. Her PhD is focused on cervical cancer related lay understandings with interdisciplinary approaches from medical anthropology and public health. Her interests also lie in bringing together a confluence of making mental health more accessible to the general population with widespread awareness and affordability.

Eslavath Rajkumar is an Assistant Professor with the Central University of Karnataka's Department of Psychology in India. Currently, he is also Affiliate Assistant Professor with the University of Washington's School of Social Work, USA. Since 2014, he has been working in the field of health psychology, health risk behaviours among tribal and rural population, behaviour change interventions, social cognition, and rural health education. His notable works have been published in prestigious journals such as Nature Portfolio, Sage, Elsevier, Springer Nature, Frontiers, Hindawi, Taylor and Francis, and Bentham Science publishers. He is also a project director and co-director for DST-Satyam, ICSSR-funded, major projects.

Marlyn Thomas Savio currently works as a Behavioural Scientist for wellness & resiliency in TaskUs, a multinational business service provider and digital innovation company. Previously, she worked in clinical and teaching roles in health care and academia. Her research interests include interventions for chronic and terminal illnesses, occupational well-being, and phenomenology. She received the Prof. Anima Sen award for excellence in research (2017), Gold Medal in PhD (2017), and Prof. Deepak Bhat award for best paper presentation (2013). Her contribution to the peer review process of journals was appreciated by Elsevier (2018). She is a chartered psychologist (CPsychol), registered with the British Psychological Society.

B. R. Shamanna is a medical doctor by training with postgraduate degrees in community medicine, maternal & child health, social & preventive medicine, community eye health, and medical law & ethics. He served as a PHC Medical Officer at the beginning of his career and then was instrumental in setting up two WHO Collaborative Centres for Prevention of Blindness in Madurai, Tamil Nadu, and Hyderabad, Telangana. He has been Visiting Faculty in the Master's program at the London School of Hygiene and Tropical Medicine since 2002 and also has been certified as a Public Health Leader by the NIH supported project of Emory University, Atlanta, Georgia, USA. He has developed the Public Health portfolio at the University of Hyderabad.

Surendra Kumar Sia is presently working as a Professor with the Department of Applied Psychology, Pondicherry University. He has done his MA, MPhil, and PhD in Psychology from the University of Delhi. Prof. Sia has more than 17 years of teaching and research experience and successfully supervised nine PhD scholars and two MPhil students. To his credit he has more than 30 research publications in journals of national and international repute like South Asian Journal of Human Resource Management, Benchmarking: An International Journal, Asia-Pacific Journal of Management Research and Innovation, Global Business Review, Management and Labour Studies, Vision: The Journal of Business Perspectives, Journal of Indian Academy of Applied Psychology, Indian Journal of Industrial Relations, and Social Science International. His areas of interest include organisational behaviour, environmental psychology, and psychology of the elderly.

Dr. Arti Singh is Assistant Professor of Psychology with the Jindal School of Psychology and Counselling, O. P. Jindal Global University, Sonipat, Haryana,

India. Her research interest includes health psychology, social psychology, and media psychology.

Dr. Sunayana Swain, with an academic foundation in psychology, the author went on to earn a doctorate degree in the same discipline from Centre for Health Psychology, University of Hyderabad. Acknowledging the growing recognition of the role of effective communication in a clinical setting, the author's doctorate work focused on the impact of doctor-patient communication on the adherence among people living with hypertension. Various aspects of her work have been published in journals of international and national repute.

Currently working as a faculty with School of Gender Studies, Tata Institute of Social Sciences, the author is keen to expand her doctoral work by incorporating gender into the context of health communication and focus on the lived experiences of women living with chronic illnesses. Apart from that, the author has varied interests and collaborates on multiple projects with experts from different fields like gender, rural development, public policy, and education and has worked with organisations like State Resource Centre for Women (Department of Women Development and Child Welfare, Government of Telangana), Telangana State Prison Department, Telangana Social Welfare Residential Educational Institutions, and others.

A. Sheila Kumari Valli is a health psychologist pursuing her PhD (final year) from McMaster University, Canada. Her PhD thesis is focused on understanding the implementation and evaluation of workplace mental health resources for health care workers. Her research interests are implementation science, m-health (mobile health) apps, and advocating and promoting mental health literacy among a wide range of participant groups in the real-world context (young adults, college students, and workplace contexts). She has over 3 years of clinical experience and is also passionate about education and empowerment of young adults.

FOREWORD

'Human health' so far has largely been viewed as an issue related to improving the functions of the 'human body parts'. This area of research has been entirely dominated by the reductionist science which ushered in the branch of 'Biomedical sciences' where a human being is construed as a coordinated machine sustained by the integrated functions of various body parts, the psychological well-being of the 'human individual' being conveniently relegated to the footnotes of the discourses on human health. The reductionism-centric biomedical approach has now come under severe criticism, especially in the recent past and in the post-COVID era.

Human health is now being increasingly recognised as an area that needs to integrate the well-being of the human body with that of its mind harmoniously in a contextual manner, a realisation that calls for the active participation of health psychology as a robust ingredient contributing towards human health care. It is here that the current book, edited by Prof. Meena Hariharan, Dr. Meera Padhy, and Dr. Usha Chivukula, fills in the void elegantly, as summarised below. The diverse, but interrelated contents of various chapters in the book capture the role of health psychology in integrating biomedical care practices with methods that augment the psychological well-being of the patients. The book brings home the takeaway that the body-mind aspects are interwoven contextually, largely driven by sociocultural belief systems, within the framework of patient's awareness and resource levels.

This book largely focusses on non-communicable diseases (NCD) as a model system for uncovering various aspects of patient health psychology needs. The book makes an interesting and insightful reading on several aspects of human health care issues on how the Indian mental health ecosystem is beset with several implementational challenges. At the same time, some new hopeful scenarios are also discussed such as the processes of acculturation and learned helplessness among patients that facilitates subjective well beingness in them. I strongly believe that the area of 'the perception of illness' needs a special mention here. This is a fascinating future area of research, especially in the Indian biopsychosocial context. Finally, it is important to emphasise the areas covered in the book related to caregiver stresses experienced in ICU settings and how the unmet needs of the patients are to be realised and addressed. All in all, the book is a treasure-trove of insightful thoughts that are succinctly presented to a general audience in a highly readable form. I commend the authors as well as the editors who have done a superb job in bringing out this book, which is the need of the hour.

Prof. BJ Rao
Vice-Chancellor
University of Hyderabad

PREFACE

Between the years 1992 and 2006, alongside my responsibilities as a faculty in the Academic Staff College, University of Hyderabad (now called Human Resource Development Centre/HRDC), I continued my endeavour to convince the University to start a department of Psychology in the University. Finally, with the commitment of Prof. S. E. Hasnain and the support of UGC, the Centre for Health Psychology was launched in the year 2007. In the year 2012, Prof. T. S. Saraswathi said that while I concentrate on building the Centre, I should also plan my publication. The Centre still taking shape, I thought my undivided attention should be on building the place by starting new courses, developing laboratories, and organising seminars. By 2014, the Centre could complete a good number of studies and publish them in good journals. It was then that Prof. I. Ramabrahmam, my good colleague, planted the seed in my mind that we should plan to bring an edited book where the contributions of health psychologists in India should be projected. His conviction about the need for such a book was so strong that he would remind me about it at every opportunity. He left for his heavenly abode on 28 July 2021. His departure created a vacuum. His words of advice that we should come with a book on health psychology kept echoing in my ears. I discussed this with my two colleagues Dr. Meera and Dr. Usha, who have significantly contributed to the development of the Centre for Health Psychology. They too felt that it would be a great tribute to our friend to bring a book on Indian contributions to the field of health psychology. This book is the outcome.

We organised the book by carefully identifying the five significant areas where research contributions are relevant to Indian sociocultural needs. The book thus is organised into five sections. Section I is on the holistic approach to health care. Though the biopsychosocial approach is emphasised, the mindset of the health care professionals appears to be stuck on the biomedical path when it comes to implementation. The change in practice is possible with an appropriate thrust at the policy level. This can materialise with adequate evidence-based research findings supporting the need for a biopsychosocial approach to health care as a replacement for the biomedical approach. Public health measures through appropriate awareness campaigns and health literacy enhancing programmes are also the need of the hour where the participation of health psychologists is essential. A move towards holistic health will be complete by bringing about changes in health communication patterns and quality. Thus, the first section on the holistic approach to health care has taken into consideration the health policies of the country, the role of research contributions, and the communication practices that directly impact the patient. The first chapter titled 'Evidence-Based Health Care: Contributions of Health Psychology' is the lead chapter that covers a wide range of contributions from health psychology on samples ranging from paediatrics to geriatrics, encompassing Behavioural Cardiology, Behavioural Diabetology, Psycho-oncology, and other non-communicable diseases. It highlights the psychosocial interventions for chronic diseases and research contributions of health psychology in enhancing well-being of the individuals in society. This lead chapter takes an overview of the topics dealt with in the other chapters of this book. The second chapter titled 'Health Communication as a Preface to Management of Non-Communicable Diseases' delineates the importance of communication in enhancing knowledge, cognition, motivation, and health adherence behaviour so as to optimise the prognosis of non-communicable diseases. The third chapter titled 'Health and Wellbeing for All: Policy Perspectives in the Indian Context' critically analyses the health policies of the Government of India and identifies the lacunae, and suggests the steps for strengthening the health care system in the country. The fourth chapter in this section titled 'Implementation Research for Public Health and Preventive Health Care in India' discusses the multidisciplinary approach to complex health problems in the context of low- and middle-income countries. It highlights the need for translating knowledge to implementation.

Section II of the book related to the health and well-being of individuals in society has three chapters. The first chapter is titled 'Residential Crowding and Subjective Well-Being: Mediating Role of Helplessness'. It throws light on the mediating role played by the individual's helpless disposition in sustaining well-being in crowded living. This chapter assumes relevance in the context of the realities of living of middle-class and lower class populations in urban and semi-urban areas of low- and middle-income countries like India. The empirical study that the chapter enumerates was conducted in Kerala, Southern India. The second chapter in this section titled 'Health in the Culturally Changing Underdeveloped Adivasi Communities' throws light on the concept of health in a diverse country like India where the cultural health practices are unique. It refutes the concept of 'one-size-fits-all' in the context of India. The contents of this chapter make one ponder the feasibility of a national health policy in a country with cultural diversity. The third chapter in the section 'Smoking and Alcohol Consumption Among Type 2 Diabetics: Health Behaviour Model-Based

Investigation' is an empirical study based on a theoretical model. It examines the factors contributing to alcohol and tobacco consumption among patients with diabetes. These health risk behaviours, though are covered by the physician during the medical advice, tend to be received by the patients with a certain complacency. The results of the study provide an insight into the factors associated with it and help plan preventive and remedial steps to wean the individuals from these behaviours.

Section III of the book brings three chapters related to Psychosocial Factors in Cardiovascular Diseases. The three chapters in this section are: 'Psychological Necessities of Patients Electing Cardiac Bypass Surgery: A Review and Roadmap', 'Illness Perception and Adherence Behaviour in Patients with Coronary Artery Disease', and 'Optimizing Hypertension Management: Children as Adherence Monitors for Adult Patients'. The first chapter consolidates research evidence to support the need for assessment and intervention for the psychological state of the patient before and after coronary artery bypass grafting. The second chapter presents an empirical study on the way patients with coronary artery disease perceive their condition and its impact on the patient's adherence behaviour. The study, by highlighting the barriers to adherence, helps in conceptualising a foolproof intervention for enhancing adherence in patients with coronary artery diseases. The third chapter brings in innovative research that used children as health monitors for adult hypertension patients in the family after orienting them to gain adequate knowledge about hypertension. This study has a promise for cost-effective approaches to minimise the adversities arising out of non-compliance among the hypertensives and also prepare the younger generation to design a lifestyle that keeps hypertension at bay. The research design can be considered a double-edged sword that not only helps the contemporary hypertensives enhance their adherence and thereby reap a better prognosis but also take proactive preventive steps to arrest the future prevalence of the disease by training the youngsters in a healthy lifestyle.

Section IV of the book, Psychosocial Factors in Diabetes Management, presents two chapters related to Behavioural Diabetology. The first chapter titled 'Illness Perceptions and Quality of Life of Diabetic Patients: Role of Perceived Control of Internal States' is an empirical study on diabetic patients. It brings to light the impact of the patient's perceived control and self-efficacy on their quality of life. The chapter brings home the fact that the quality of life is just not impacted by the disease condition alone but also by the functional psychological aspects. This provides the logic for the biopsychosocial approach to the management of diabetes. The second chapter titled 'Illness Perceptions and Diabetes Self-Management: A Mixed Method Approach' is an empirical study. The qualitative analysis identifies the barriers that contribute to suboptimal management of the disease. Identification of barriers helps in building a preventive model to sustain adherence behaviour.

Section V of the book is Critical Care Needs and Psychological Support. Two chapters in the section with a specific focus on the experiences of Intensive

Care Units (ICUs) and the experiences of patients diagnosed with cancer constitute strong evidence for a psychosocial approach to critical care. The first chapter 'The Intensive Care Unit Experiences and Repercussions: Need for Psychosocial Care' reiterates the need for psychosocial care in ICU units in hospitals. It provides ample evidence of the environmental and system-induced stress among the patients that add to their critical physical health condition. The chapter argues for a shift from treating the disease to treating the patients in ICU by enumerating the short- and long-term adverse impacts on the cognition and emotion of the patient during and aftermath of the ICU stay. The second chapter titled 'An Interpretative Phenomenological Analysis: The Unmet Information and Supportive Care Needs of Cancer Patients' presented a thematic analysis of the cancer patients' experience of their unmet needs. The patient wishes to be apprised of the information on the disease, treatment course, impact, and prognosis.

Overall, the book covers the essentials of conceptual and clinical aspects to highlight the significance of health psychology in the field of health care by maintaining a good balance between the review articles and empirical studies. The authors of the chapters are from reputed apex academic institutions like central universities, IITs, private universities, international organisations, freelance consultants, and students in their Master's or Research Programmes. While the chapters discuss the contributions of health psychology to the Indian Health System, they also inadvertently expose the readers to a versatile approach to research in health psychology. The readers should focus on both aspects. We expect the book to be useful for the students in their Master's and Research Programmes. The researchers and academics from other nations interested in the unique contribution of the field of health psychology would benefit from this book.

Meena Hariharan

ACKNOWLEDGEMENTS

The idea originates in the mind. Between the thought and the action, there are many propellers. Between the idea of this book and seeing it in print, we had many such propellers – in the form of circumstances and situations and the in the form of well-wishers and supporters. This section of the book is an opportunity to express our gratitude to all those who constituted this support group.

Our first thoughts go to our good friend, well-wisher, and colleague Prof. I. Ramabrahmam. Though not from the discipline of Psychology, palpitating the need for a volume like this book, he kept reminding us to initiate the work. Unfortunately, he is not amidst us in his physical form, though his words of wisdom and the vision he created for us keep guiding us. Gratitude to him from the bottom of our hearts.

Our Vice-Chancellor, Prof. BJ Rao, who readily consented to write the foreword for this book, as a nurturing leader gave us that essential nudge to initiate further work in the related field with his valuable suggestions.

Many of our colleagues from the field of Psychology and other disciplines supported us in many ways. Some of our students who extended their technical support need a special mention. They are Adarsh K Varma and Vishnu V.

While mentioning those who supported us, we normally mention our families last. True, during the period of working for this book, we kept our families last in our priority. They understood extended total support and helped in many ways.

So, they were the people who played a significant role between the thought and the form of this book. Gratitude to one and all. And yes, 'Thank you' is too short an expression to communicate our real feelings.

Meena Hariharan
Meera Padhy
Usha Chivukula

PART I
Holistic Approach to Health

1
EVIDENCE-BASED HEALTH CARE
Contributions of Health Psychology

Meena Hariharan

The definition of health care is holistic, while the popular understanding is reductionist. Health care is defined as 'efforts made to maintain or restore physical, mental, or emotional well-being especially by trained and licensed professionals' (Merriam-Webster Dictionary 2022). It refers to not only the physical but also the mental and emotional well-being. Health care is extended to the population through well-organised structures. Extending health care to organisations and people, with a primary intention to promote, restore, or maintain the health of the population, is the responsibility of the health care system in a country. The ancient health care practice in India was built on the robust pillars of biological, psychological, social, spiritual, and environmental factors contributing to an individual's well-being. The *Ayurveda* model of the ancient Indian health practice associates health with multiple causes such as biological, psychological, environmental (including physical and social environment), and spiritual aspects related to the individual's life. This holistic approach was based on the individual's constitution, personality disposition, behavioural practices, and the individual's ecological connection with the environment. Since it was tailored to an individual's unique characteristics, no clinical studies could be carried out for bringing in gross generalisations. Nevertheless, it took the path of the biopsychosocial approach to health that concentrated on the individual but not the disease or the physical organ of the person that manifested abnormality and pathology. This practice perfectly suited the sociocultural needs of the nation. However, in the 18th century, on the direction of Macaulay the practice of *Ayurveda* was replaced with allopathy medicine, with which the biopsychosocial approach got replaced with the biomedical approach. Even after attaining independence, there have not been any concerted efforts to revert to the biopsychosocial approach that suited the Indian psyche.

DOI: 10.4324/9781003360858-2

For more than a decade, India has become a country for medical tourism. It can be strengthened further with a shift to a biopsychosocial approach which has been proved to be highly beneficial. Research findings in various aspects related to health care have proved the advantages of the biopsychosocial approach. There has been ample research evidence to argue for strengthening health care by taking a holistic approach. The findings related to preventive care as a public health measure, diagnostics as an approach to guide the treatment regimen, the treatment regimen itself that includes anxiety and depression management, psychoeducation influencing the health belief system, cognitive intervention for enhancing the health literacy, educating on the identification of alarm signs, inducing optimism, reducing hostility, strengthening health self-efficacy, or incentivising positive health behaviour. While assessing the health care system, the parameters normally taken into consideration are quantitative in nature, which identify the factors such as infrastructure, human resources (in terms of doctors and nurses), finances, administrative set-up, and so on. While these aspects do account for the quality of health care, the important aspect that is normally excluded is the patient well-being factor, which should take into account the psychological state of the target individual/group as part of the prognosis.

'Evidence-based medicine' is what seems to be the guiding force behind the contemporary health care practice. The term evidence-based medicine is a generic term to cover its reference to various fields of medical and paramedical disciplines such as 'evidence-based psychiatry, or evidence-based nursing'. Evidence-based health care (EBHC) refers to the use of evidence for making policy and management decisions (Bhargava & Bhargava, 2007). The term 'evidence' here refers to evidence in the form of research findings based on large, randomised samples at multinational, national, and single centre studies. When the findings of such studies are supported by the experience of experts (in practice) and the patients' need satisfaction, it is time that evidence-based health care should get into policy and large-scale implementation. In this context, discussing the contributions of research in Health Psychology assumes relevance. Based on its research findings, the discipline of Health Psychology has been advocating a biopsychosocial approach to optimise health care. The branches of Behavioural Cardiology, Behavioural Diabetology, and Psycho-Oncology gaining demand across the globe is evidence of the need for a holistic approach to patient care. Research in Health Psychology established a bidirectional relationship between psychological and physiological factors on the one hand and the symbiotic function of psychological, social, environmental, and physiological factors in determining the health and well-being of the individual and communities on the other. Thus, the contributions of Health Psychology extended not only to patient care and treatment but also to the areas of prevention and prediction of health. This is done through designing interventions like psychoeducation and public health awareness campaigns at community levels as well as need-based cognitive affective therapies and behaviour change modules at an individual level. The efficacy of these interventions has been proved across the various age groups covering the lifespan and across the sociocultural groups covering a wide range of the population. Such preliminary evidence should pave the path for large-scale randomised studies at national and multinational levels to warrant scientific evidence.

Studies on Paediatric and Geriatric Sample

Children are not miniature adults. Being in the process of development, they are not yet equipped cognitively, emotionally, or behaviourally to face life's adversities. Timely attainment of developmental milestones to a large extent contributes to the health and well-being of the individual. The major factors that take the child through the milestones and ensure health and well-being are family structure (Block et al., 1988; Dawson, 1991), school environment, and neighbourhood. The parameters to measure children's health and well-being are physical health, emotional state, and academic performance. The individual who encounters a setback in any one of these dimensions irrespective of the age is likely to show symptoms in the other dimensions too as per the body-mind integration model (Hariharan, 2020). It may appear more pronounced in the children due to a lack of competence in applying coping mechanisms. A number of studies have established the relationship between physical health and general well-being in children.

Children (below 18 years) in India constitute 36.7% of the total population (Census of India, 2011). This constitutes a little over one-third of the total population. According to the reports of the Census Commissioner's office, 0.6% of children between the age group of 5 and 14 years die every year due to various causes. The top ten causes of death for children in the age group of 5–14 years are presented in Table 1.1.

TABLE 1.1 Top ten causes of death in children in the age group of 5–14 years in India between 2010 and 2013

Rank	Causes of death	Death percentage
1	Unintentional injuries (other than motor vehicle accidents)	20.5
2	Diarrhoeal diseases	11.6
3	Other infectious and parasitic diseases	10.6
4	Malnutrition	7.7
5	Respiratory infections	6.5
6	Digestive diseases	6.4
7	Motor vehicle accidents	6.1
8	Fever of unknown origin	5.1
9	Neuropsychiatric conditions	3.7
10	Other non-communicable diseases	3.7
	All other remaining causes	18.0

Source: Census of India (2011). Table C-13. Office of the Registrar General & Census Commissioner, India, Ministry of Home Affairs, Govt. of India, New Delhi.

It can be observed from Table 1.1 that 3.7% of children die of non-communicable diseases while 28.7% die of diarrhoea and other infectious diseases. Infections are contacted by the children due to health inappropriate behaviour and lack of preventive measures. Stress causes immunosuppression in children. Further, chronic stress in childhood has been found to cause architectural and functional changes in the brain of the child (Hariharan et al., 2014; Hariharan, 2020). In view of these findings, there is a need to investigate the high death rates due to infections from this angle and contemplate intervention measures to minimise childhood stress.

Non-communicable diseases such as hypertension, diabetes, and cancer are found to be common among children. A systematic review and meta-analysis revealed that 7% of school-going children in India suffered from hypertension. Among them, a higher percentage was from an urban area and 29% of them were obese children (Meena et al., 2021). Prevalence of diabetes among the 10–19 years age group of Indian children was found to be 12.3% (pre-diabetes) and 8.4% (diabetes) (Kumar et al., 2021). As per the population-based cancer registry (PBCR), the incidence of cancer among Indian children below 15 years of age accounts for 0.7% to 4.4% of the total cancer diagnoses (National Centre for Disease Informatics and Research, 2012–2014).

In view of the increasing incidence and prevalence of non-communicable diseases among children, it is desirable that children have an adequate knowledge base about these chronic illnesses and their association with lifestyle so that preventive measures are likely to be adopted in case they have the disease, and they acquire the skills for effective management of these illnesses. A series of studies were conducted in this line by a team of researchers from the Centre for Health Psychology, University of Hyderabad in an attempt to measure the children's knowledge of causes, symptoms, timeline, treatment, and management of four non-communicable diseases. Children from the 6th to 10th/12th class constituted the sample. Results revealed a very low level of knowledge about hypertension (Hariharan et al., 2018), diabetes (Padhy et al., 2018), cancer (Kopparty et al., 2018), and HIV/AIDS (Nagpal et al., 2018). Almost all these studies, while endorsing a dismally low knowledge level, did observe a developmental trend in cognition of the concerned illness and a decrease in the misconceptions about the diseases among children. The studies recommended the inclusion of topics related to non-communicable diseases in the school curriculum. A knowledge base is very important because of the close connection between knowledge, affect, motivation, and behaviour.

Illness, particularly terminal illness, and chronic diseases induce considerable stress in the patient because of the pain, suffering, uncertainty, restrictions, and dependence that accompany the condition. Medications and invasive procedures address the physical pain, deformity, or pathology of the organ functioning. When the psychological state is left unattended, it impacts the physical healing by not responding or by the slow response. Law et al. (2019) in their meta-analysis of 44 studies on interventions for parents with children suffering from chronic illnesses came up with encouraging findings. The study included interventions for the parents of children suffering from asthma, diabetes, cancer, chronic pain, inflammatory bowel disease, skin diseases, and traumatic brain injury. They found cognitive behaviour therapy (CBT) and problem-solving therapy to be effective. The results revealed the positive impact of interventions on parental behaviour of children with cancer, diabetes, chronic pain, and traumatic brain injury. The therapeutic intervention was found useful in post-treatment follow-up of children with cancer and chronic pain, but not the others. However, the authors endorsed the limitation of insufficient data to interpret many variables. Rohan and Verma (2020) through the four case studies on children with chronic illnesses recommend a combination of interventions such as cognitive behaviour therapy, behaviour therapy, medical coping, parent training, and motivational interviewing for optimum outcome. There are other innovative therapies used to minimise the illness trauma of children. They include pet therapy, art therapy, and play therapy, to name a few.

According to the Census Report 2011, geriatric population in India totals 103 million constituting 8.5% of the population (Singh & Misra, 2018). Characterised by degenerative diseases, the elderly are in need of greater psychosocial support than any other age group through developmental stages. Most of the age-related problems at this stage of life do not promise a permanent cure, but the well-being can be optimised by inducing the feelings of being loved, being important, and being wanted in the family and society. The elderly population constitutes the native wisdom of a nation and hence needs to be protected and treated with care. Depression, somatisation, insomnia, pains and aches, problems related to the gastrointestinal system, cognitive degeneration, and sensory function degeneration are some of the common problems. Social support intervention either by family or non-family members is found to enhance the feelings of social security, well-being, and functional competence and alleviate stress (Rao, 2001; Umadevi, 1991). Meditation helped improve intellectual functioning and mental health (Ramamurti & Jamuna, 1999). Yoga was found to be beneficial by contributing to alertness and positive affect and disseminating negative feelings, anxiety, and depression. Researchers from the West and East have proved the positive contributions of spirituality, religion, prayers, chanting, and meditation (Kakar, 2003; Newport, 2006; Yoon & Lee, 2006). Thus, there is sufficient research evidence to suggest the dire need for psychosocial interventions for the geriatric population across the globe. This need is on the increase in Indian society given the transition from joint family to nuclear family structures and the large-scale migration of the educated urban youth to other countries and the rural youth's preference for urban life in pursuit of a career.

While psychosocial interventions for paediatric and geriatric populations have to carve their niche, the health psychological interventions in the field of non-communicable diseases have advanced fast to make an argument for a paradigm shift from the biomedical to biopsychosocial path.

Psychosocial Factors in Non-Communicable Diseases

Non-communicable diseases are also known as lifestyle diseases, having a close association with the health behaviour of the individual besides the genetic and congenital factors. Given this fact, apart from the medications, the individual diagnosed with the non-communicable disease has to adopt changes in lifestyle involving sometimes drastic changes in health behaviour by minimising health-compromising behaviour and enhancing health-promoting behaviour appropriate to the diagnosis. The gist of various theories of health behaviour brings the following salient points. Behavioural change is something that has an association with cognition, affect, motivation, and the incentives that ensure the sustenance of the changed behaviour. The individual is likely to contemplate behavioural change only if the self-efficacy, control, and benefits of the change are perceived as adequate and barriers to the change are perceived as low. At the same time, the assessed threat based on the severity and susceptibility should trigger the right proportion of fear, and the perceived benefits should be viewed as incentives. The combination of the fear of the severity and susceptibility of the illness and the potential benefits of behaviour change trigger motivation to contemplate behaviour change in the prescribed lines of lifestyle modifications. Further, for the intent of behaviour change to take a shape, one's attitudes towards the change, approval of significant others to the intended change, and the magnitude of disapproval for the existing health-compromising behaviour also contribute. What contributes to the beliefs is the information, awareness, and communication about the illness. Thus, broadly, what the theories of health behaviour suggest is that the change in health behaviour can be initiated through building a new cognitive base or replacing the existing one with facts put forth candidly to drive the seriousness and the individual's stakes, enhance the self-efficacy related to the initiation and sustenance of the behavioural change, help the person identify the benefits and barriers associated with changed behaviour along with a realistic assessment of the degree of control over them, and influence the person through the significant others. All the above can constitute the ingredients of interventions planned for enhancing health-optimising behaviour. Only when this forms a part of the treatment option can one optimise the prognosis. Health Psychology research on non-communicable diseases is adequate to prove the efficacy of psychosocial interventions.

Psychosocial Factors Associated with Cardiovascular Diseases (CVD)

The basis for the association between psychological factors and cardiovascular health is the physiological response to the individual's affect state. The physiological response to stress is marked by hypothalamic pituitary axis (HPA) response and sympathetic nervous system (SNS) activation, both of which result in accelerated cardiovascular activity, which, if prolonged, casts a burden on the cardiac muscle and cardiovascular system.

The close connection between the neurophysiological and cardiovascular systems runs parallel to the cardiovascular health and the psychological state of the individual. One of the factors related to the aetiology of cardiovascular diseases is traced to type A (Friedman, 1974) and type D personalities (Pedersen & Denollet, 2006). Studies have identified anger and hostility as the major affect factors related to cardiovascular diseases (CVD). Everson-Rose and Lewis (2005) investigated the association between psychosocial factors and cardiovascular diseases. They found that cardiovascular diseases have a significant relationship with psychological factors such as depression, anger, hostility and acute or chronic psychosocial stress and social factors such as social support and social conflict. The relationship between the affect state like depression and CVD has been confirmed both by research and clinical practice (Mulle & Vaccarino, 2013). The editorial in the Journal of American Heart Association by Peterson (2020) made an observation on the close association between psychosocial factors and health in general and cardiac health in particular. Psychological factors such as stress, depression, and anxiety and social factors such as socio-economic status and adversity were the identified factors. Santosa et al. (2021) conducted an 18-year longitudinal study on participants between the age group of 35–70 years old from 21 low-, middle-, and high-income countries spread over five continents to investigate the relationship between cardiovascular risks and psychosocial factors. The findings indicated a positive association. High levels of perceived stress were found to be associated with cardiovascular diseases, coronary heart diseases (CHD), strokes, and mortality. Thus, there are adequate studies that established the relationship between psychosocial factors and cardiac health. Based on these findings, treatment, care, and preventive interventions for cardiac health should include psychosocial aspects. The inclusion of psychosocial interventions changes the approach from 'treatment' to 'healing', where the focus on psychological factors supplements the biomedical treatment. Studies in these lines have shown encouraging results. Research on Indian samples has contributed immensely to the field of Behavioural Cardiology in particular and cardiac care in general. Some of these studies are briefly discussed below.

CVD and CHD are labelled lifestyle diseases. Hypertension is one of the conditions which if not managed effectively can lead to adversities, some of which may be irreversible. Ragupathy et al. (2014) presented significant statistics related to hypertension in India. They found that 33% of urban and 25% of rural Indians above 18 years suffer from hypertension. Not all of them are aware of their hypertension condition. Only 42% of urban and 25% of rural Indians are aware of their hypertension status. What is more alarming is that only 38% of urban and 25% of rural Indian hypertensive patients undergo treatment for the condition. These findings suggest that there is ample scope for work to be initiated by researchers and practitioners from the field of Behavioural Cardiology. Awareness and knowledge constitute the basis for cognition, motivation, and lifestyle (behavioural) change. The treating doctor has a major role in creating awareness about the disease. Hence, the quality of communication between the doctor and the patient is considered to contribute significantly to the patient's understanding of the role of self-management of the disease. Swain et al. (2015) studied the impact of quality of communication between doctors and their hypertensive patients. A total of 30 doctors and 300 hypertensive patients constituted the sample. The quality of communication that included the content communicated by the doctors and the comprehension of the same by the patients was measured using the similarity index. The blood pressure (BP) readings were taken at the baseline and after six weeks. In addition, the patients' clinical adherence was measured. Results revealed that the patients who had a high quality of communication with their doctors showed enhanced adherence with regard to medication, diet, and self-monitoring and significantly differed from those who had low quality of communication. Further, the patients with high quality of communication showed a significant drop in the systolic and diastolic measures of blood pressure as shown in the six-week follow-up. The pathway was traced from quality of communication to the effective management of BP readings through adherence behaviour. This indicated that when the patients have adequate information about the condition in a simple, comprehensible language, they tend to comply with the medical advice in letter and spirit culminating in good hypertension management. Another study (Thomas et al., 2014) that investigated the level of patient comprehension of doctor's communication found that less than 5% of patients understood the jargon used by cardiologists in their communication. The time cardiologists give their patients ranged from 2 to 22 minutes as per an unpublished study by the author reported in a newspaper article. This may happen because of the paucity of time for the doctor. It is time that the medical jargon of 'cardiac treatment' is replaced with 'comprehensive cardiac rehabilitation programme' and 'comprehensive intervention for cardiac disease prevention'.

In an attempt to study the differential impact of form and frequency of exposure to hypertension knowledge on patients diagnosed with hypertension, Andrew (2019) used group intervention on 256 participants divided into five groups. The first group was exposed to face-to-face knowledge intervention about hypertension by a qualified physician twice with a gap of two weeks. The second group also received the same intervention, but only once. The third group received the same knowledge intervention by the same physician but through video clipping which was played twice with a gap of two weeks. The fourth group received the intervention through video clipping but only once. The fifth group was a controlled group that received only standard medical care which was common as primary treatment for all the groups. All the participants were administered a number of psychological tests such as self-efficacy, perceived social support, and adherence behaviour. In addition, the BP levels were recorded for all prior to the exposure to the intervention. A six-week follow-up and post-test revealed that the four intervention groups significantly scored high on knowledge and adherence levels and scored low on the BP readings. This indicated that the knowledge intervention had a positive impact on the adherence behaviour. The group that received two face-to-face interventions reaped the optimum benefit, followed by the one that received a single face-to-face intervention and a single video intervention. The group that received repeated video interventions ranked fourth in terms of benefits and was more comparable with the control group. This indicated that direct interaction with the expert for the transfer of knowledge is highly beneficial in group interventions. The path analysis identified the benefit of knowledge intervention influencing the self-efficacy, which influenced adherence behaviour that finally culminated in the outcome benefit in terms of declined BP readings. In addition, self-efficacy also directly contributed to prognosis. The findings indicated that knowledge interventions in groups of hypertensives helped in creating a cognitive base that enhanced the confidence in the patients to manage their hypertension through behavioural changes and finally resulted in bringing down the BP levels.

The high prevalence and asymptomatic nature of hypertension may not have the potential to invoke negative emotions on being diagnosed with the condition, but the other cardiac conditions calling for invasive procedures may cause psychological distress to the patients. There should be a way to manage the distress through interventions. However, in view of the proven role it plays in adherence and prognosis, it is imperative to design alternative approaches to knowledge enhancement among hypertensive patients.

Savio and Hariharan (2020) studied the impact of the cognitive and affective intervention on the prognosis of patients who underwent coronary artery bypass surgery (CABG). The study developed an indigenous intervention package called Programme for Affective and Cognitive Education (PACE). The study compared the impact of this indigenous intervention with that of the standardised relaxation therapy called Guided Imagery. The sample consisted of 300 patients going for elective cardiac bypass surgery, divided into three groups. The first group received PACE intervention. The second group received Guided Imagery and the third was a controlled group. All the groups were administered a series of psychological tests prior to the surgery. They were exposed to the 30 minutes intervention session a day prior to the surgery and a repeated exposure the day before their discharge from the hospital. The audio/video CDs of the intervention modules were handed over to the patients to be used as and when needed after their discharge from the hospital. They were administered the tests to measure anxiety and depression the day before the surgery and a day before the discharge and at the time of the review visit after a month. Results indicated a significant positive impact of both interventions on prognosis compared to the control group. PACE group had the highest impact. The interventions were found to reduce the psychological distress, which in turn positively contributed to prognosis. Guided Imagery is an intervention that administered relaxation to the patients. PACE intervention is aimed at enhancing the patients' cognition simultaneously with addressing the negative affect of fear and apprehension about the surgery through knowledge intervention. Thus, the intervention that reduced distress through enhancing knowledge was found to be most effective. The patients in this group were ready to resume normal routine several weeks earlier than the other groups. There are a number of studies that proved that anxiety and depression caused a delay in recovery from surgical wounds (Bosch et al., 2007; Cole-King & Harding, 2001; Doering et al., 2005). This study in a way confirmed the findings in these lines because the patients in the PACE group were ready for normal routine and obviously recovered from surgical wounds earlier because the intervention could reduce their anxiety and depression.

Indian society being affiliation oriented, the natural social support is a strong built-in intervention for patients undergoing a cardiac procedure. It is unfortunate that the Indian health care system is not making attempts to integrate into the healing process to hasten the recovery. Chivukula et al. (2013) studied the modifier role of perceived social support on anxiety and depression in patients undergoing cardiac procedures. The results found that patients with high social support and awaiting CABG experienced lower anxiety and depression compared to those awaiting the angiogram procedure. CABG is considered major surgery with longer hospitalisation requirements and higher risk while angiogram is a relatively simple invasive diagnostic procedure requiring only a day care facility in the hospital. Yet, the patients of CABG experienced lower anxiety because of high perceived support compared to the group awaiting angiogram. This lower anxiety is advantageous for a faster pace of recovery.

Anxiety and depression were found to be comorbid conditions in a large percentage of cardiac patients. However, they remain unnoticed, undiagnosed, and untreated almost in all cases (Hariharan et al., 2014). These psychological states are not congenial for adherence behaviour. Hence, when the treatment regimen confines cardiac rehabilitation alone, ignoring the psychological state, the outcome is likely to be suboptimal. Psychological assessments and interventions are desirable inclusions in the treatment approach to cardiac problems in view of the long-established mind-body coordination. Wells et al. (2021) in a study on 332 cardiac patients attempted to combine psychological intervention alongside cardiac intervention with an objective to bring down the anxiety and depression in patients. The participants were divided into two groups. One group received Meta Cognition Therapy (MCT) alongside cardiac rehabilitation while the other group received only cardiac rehabilitation. After exposure to six sessions, the group that received MCT showed a significant reduction in depression, anxiety, and metacognitive beliefs with negative thoughts compared to the one that received only cardiac rehabilitation. This impact was found to have been sustained for 12 months. Psychological interventions are of use as an integral part of treatment or constitute a part of preventive measures through stress management programmes.

Psychosocial Factors in Diabetes

According to the International Diabetes Federation (Sun et al., 2021), more than 74 million Indians have diabetes, which is the second largest number (China has 141 million diabetics). Age-adjusted comparative prevalence of diabetes as of

2021 is reported to be 9.6%. This is expected to rise to 10.8% by the year 2045. Diabetes is classified as a lifestyle disease that demands changes in health behaviour. As discussed in the context of cardiovascular diseases, a strong cognitive base helps in bringing in behaviour change to suit the diabetic lifestyle. A study by Sandhu et al. (2015) revealed that only 23.8% of those diagnosed with the disease had good knowledge about the condition while 19.2% manifested poor knowledge. This suggests public health measures through effective campaigns to enhance awareness.

Research findings have confirmed the association between diabetes and stress (Jiang et al., 2008; Kelly & Ismail, 2015). Stressful situations in life are inevitable and are almost constantly present in an individual's life with some wide variations in degrees at different points in life. The individual who manages life stress well is the one who contributes to the effective management of any chronic illness, including diabetes.

Change in diet, maintenance of body weight and glycaemic levels, and maintenance of emotional equilibrium are aspects that call for cultivating certain habits and discipline in lifestyle. To bring this change in the behaviour, there is a need for certain psychological interventions to enhance awareness and induce motivation to initiate changes in lifestyle.

Illness cognition (Leventhal et al., 2012) and symptom perception (Broadbent, 2010) were found to have an impact on an individual's health behaviour. When the symptoms are extreme, they are perceived accurately and the health behaviour accordingly changes to compliance. Perceptions and beliefs about health are also influenced by the individual's personality. Chelli et al. (2017) in their study of Type 2 diabetes patients found that health hardiness explained significant variance in illness perception among the participants. Health hardiness measures the individual's ability to adapt to the real or potential health problem by use of control, commitment, and challenge. The involvement of the patients in disease management plays a crucial role in determining the prognosis. The patients who have an understanding of the significance of their participation in disease management and have the confidence in their ability to effectively control their diabetic conditions are likely to show a better prognosis. Lalnuntluangi et al. (2017) found that self-efficacy played a significant role in diabetes management in patients. Patients who had high self-efficacy were also found to show higher levels of well-being (Padhy et al., 2017). The patients if trained in the skill of self-management in addition to just knowledge intervention may show effective outcomes. Abraham et al. (2020) trained Type 2 diabetes patients in self-management skills and found a positive impact of it on HbA_{1c} levels, diabetes quality of life, diet, exercise care, medication, glucose testing, belief in treatment effectiveness, understanding of the disease, anxiety, and depression.

Harvey (2015) reported the effectiveness of motivational interviewing in improved self-efficacy, quality of life and reduced HbA1c, among Type 1 diabetes patients. Among Type 2 diabetes patients an improvement was observed in adherence, weight loss, diet, exercise, family support, and HbA1c. Cognitive behaviour therapy (CBT) was found to be an effective intervention in improving the self-monitoring behaviour of blood glucose level and well-being and lowering the stress, anxiety, and depression in Type 2 diabetes patients. Their HbA$_{1c}$ levels also showed improvement (Amsberg et al., 2009).

Diabetes management requires resolve and restraint in the patients to adhere to diet and exercise regimens. In a family set-up where the other non-diabetic members follow a normal routine and diet menu, adherence and its sustenance are possible with family support. Many a time, though the family is inclined to extend the support, they may not know how to go about it. Family support can bring effective outcomes with some intervention in the form of family counselling and therapy. Family interventions have been found to improve family relationships as well as blood sugar levels (Wysocki et al., 2008).

There is a need for more studies on the Indian sample because given the nature of the prescribed lifestyle for diabetes, and the dynamics of cultural requirements in India, the interventions and the approach to handling the patient may have to be different from that of Western countries.

Psychosocial Factors in Other Common Non-Communicable Diseases

Few other common non-communicable diseases associated with psychological and social factors are diseases such as arthritis, an autoimmune disease, asthma associated with the respiratory system, and renal disorders. A brief discussion on these diseases will strengthen the mind-body association.

Arthritis: Arthritis is a disease associated with inflammation of joints in the body with the symptoms of pain, redness, stiffness, heat in the location, fever, weight loss, breathing trouble, rash, or itching. It interferes with physical movements and hence the activities of the patient. There are several types of arthritis. The symptoms and treatment vary depending upon the type. Though it is normally known as a disease affecting the elderly, people of all ages are prone to it.

Rheumatoid arthritis is a type caused by the faulty reactions of the body's immune system. In this case, the body's immune system attacks the healthy cells in the lining of the joints causing inflammation, pain, and other symptoms. Though the causes of the disease are not yet conclusively proved, the research inputs suggest that a combination of genetic predisposition, hormonal factors, and triggering environmental factors such as smoking, infection, or encountering severe stress have their contributions. Stress is one of the factors contributing to the cause, and symptom aggravation opens a wide scope for psychosocial research in the field.

Harris et al. (2012) conducted a longitudinal study on a sample of 10,509 Australian women of the 1946–1951 cohort. The results revealed a number of psychosocial factors associated with the disease. Women reporting moderate to high stress levels showed a 2.5 times increase in the diagnosis of arthritis. Interpersonal conflict and illness in the family or close friends showed 1.4-fold increase in the presence of arthritis problems. Besides this, optimism and perceived social support were found to have been significantly reduced in the women reporting arthritis. Further analysis revealed that anxiety was the only psychological factor associated with the disease. The patient will have to live with the pain, stiffness, and limitations in mobility. This contributes to compromising the quality of life and psychosocial well-being (Tsai et al., 2003). Patients with higher levels of pain were found to have higher levels of psychological distress, reported higher unemployment, and had lower self-efficacy (James et al., 2005). Briani et al. (2018) based on the meta-analyses of the review articles concluded that cognitive behaviour therapy with or without combination with physical exercise had no significant effect in positively influencing depression, distress, or self-efficacy. Sharpe (2016) stated that cognitive behaviour therapy at the early stages is effective in pain management while mindfulness meditation is effective in handling depression in rheumatoid arthritis patients. Chavare and Natu (2020) conducted a qualitative study on a sample of eight Indian patients with arthritis to understand the resilience process in the management of the disease. The thematic analysis identified seven aspects contributing to their resilience leading to health outcomes. They referred to an internal locus of control, optimism, inventing pragmatic practices for pain management, engaging oneself in meaningful activities, seeking social support, accepting of buffering effect of pain, and leaning on spiritual support. They suggested a biopsychosocial approach to pain management for optimising the prognosis.

Asthma: This is a condition related to the respiratory system marked by attacks of spasms in the bronchi of the lungs leading to breathing difficulties in the patient. Of the many causes, allergic reactions and hypersensitivity are the major ones. A total of 300 million people across the globe suffer from asthma. Of this, 6% of children and 2% of adults are Indians.

Psychosocial causes are found to be closely associated with asthma. In a European population-based study by Wainwright et al. (2007), on a sample of 20,888, a total of 8.1% reported a diagnosis of asthma. The results showed a significant association of asthma with psychosocial factors. After adjusting for demographic factors like age, gender, and social class, health-related factors like myocardial infarction, diabetes, and cancer, and health risks behaviours like smoking, the psychosocial factors that showed a strong association with asthma were depression, adversities in childhood, life event-related stress in adulthood, negative aspects of support of confidant, and prolonged stress during adulthood. Rajhans et al. (2021) found that children and adolescents with asthma had psychiatric conditions as comorbidities and behavioural problems too.

Apart from psychological factors, asthma is also found to be associated with a number of social variables. Rashmi et al. (2021) came up with significant findings based on the data of the 75th round of the National Survey Sample (NSS) collected in the year 2017-18. The survey was on a sample of 555,289 Indians. Analysis of the data revealed that demographic factors such as age, gender, and residential location and factors such as the type of fuel used for cooking, drinking water source, size of the house, and facilities for garbage disposal showed significant association with asthma in the Indian population. People from high socio-economic status and those in the age group of 45–65 years were found to have higher vulnerability.

Van Lieshout and MacQueen (2008) portrayed a relatively complex relationship between asthma and depression. They argued that asthma and depression share a number of risk factors. They also showed similar patterns of dysregulation in major biological systems such as cytokines, neuroendocrine stress response, and neuropeptides. Costa et al. (2015) based on their review study suggested that there is no scientific evidence on the connection between asthma and psychological factors such as subjective perception, alexithymia, coping style, depression, and anxiety. Based on this evidence and the assumption that the relationship between the asthma and the psychological state could be bidirectional, the authors feel that it is about time that the treatment plan for asthma should include targeting the psychological states.

Renal diseases: Renal diseases are marked by problems in kidney functioning. When kidney functioning gets disrupted, there is a problem in separating the toxins from the blood and expulsion of the same from the body. Certain problems associated with renal functioning are treated and cured while some others are chronic and some may be fatal.

Chronic kidney disease (CKD) refers to long-standing kidney disease leading to failure of kidney functioning. Failure of kidney functioning leads to the accumulation of toxic matter and water retention in the body associated with a number of complications. Since the expulsion of waste matter and water is a continuous process, the failure necessitates an artificially induced function of this activity involving rigorous monitoring and treatment that interferes with the normal routine and effective living in the patients. It is but natural that disruption of normal activities, loss of autonomy, and dependence on others have psychosocial repercussions. CKD is found to be closely associated with high stress levels and depressive disorders. Ahlawat et al. (2018) identified a number of psychosocial factors contributing to depression in CKD patients. They are the age and gender of patients, body mass index, availability of funding for treatment, education, income, duration of the disease, comorbid conditions, and the need for haemodialysis. Persistent fatigue, restrictions in activities and diet, and rigorous treatment regimens associated with CKD induce psychological distress in the patients (Tong et al., 2009). This in turn activates the HPA axis which is associated with enhanced stress levels. According to the meta-analysis of Palmer et al. (2013), the lifetime prevalence of depression among CKD stage 5D patients is 22.8% as against 10.8% in the general population. Khan et al. (2019) opined that patients of CKD have a depressive burden hidden behind the poor quality of life irrespective of whether the treatment regimen involves dialysis or medical management. Depression in CKD patients is the consequence of illness burden, lowered quality of life, social support deficit, abnormality in hormonal secretion changes in autonomic activities, and comorbid conditions (Shirazian, 2018). Muthukumaran et al. (2021) in their study of haemodialysis patients found that depression was associated with lower educational level, high pill burden, low quality of life, and perception of a burden on the caregiver. The above findings clearly suggest that it is desirable to include professional psychologists in the team of nephrologists treating the patients.

Psychosocial Interventions for Cancer

Unlike cardiovascular diseases and diabetes, cancer cannot be described with a common group of symptoms. The symptoms, treatment, and prognosis vary with the location, grade, and stage of the disease. However, the common physical characteristics are fatigue, weight loss, appetite loss, and pain. Psychological characteristics are anxiety, depression, apprehension, fear of death, hopelessness, helplessness, anger, and guilt, to name a few. The advancement in treatment and the ageing population are two factors responsible for increasing incidence and a large number of cancer survivors needing interventions for optimising quality of life. Given its characteristic of aggressive treatment, moderate to poor prognosis, the severity of pain, lowered quality of life, and late diagnosis and palliation, the disease of cancer is associated with deep emotions not only for the patient but also for the family and the loved ones. There are research findings indicating the outcome effectiveness of medical treatment on patients with lower levels of anxiety and depression (Papakostas et al., 2008). In view of this, psychological interventions for cancer patients gain importance. The objectives of psychosocial interventions for cancer patients are to help the patients adapt to the disease and the treatment as well as optimise their state of well-being. A high stress level in the patient and the family is normally the common denominator. The first important step of psychosocial intervention is to address and aim at minimising stress levels. The common approach has been the application of psychoeducation, cognitive behaviour therapy, and building social support for the patient (Ranchor et al., 2017). Endorsing the significance of it, the International Psycho-Oncology Society and WHO have been working on integrating psychological interventions for patients and their families into cancer care across the globe (Alexander & Murthy, 2020). Anxiety and depression are the common affect states of the patients with cancer. Management of depression through appropriate interventions was found to be effective in improving the quality of life among patients (Sharpe et al., 2014). Agarwal and Maroko-Afek (2018) discussed the use of Yoga as a therapeutic intervention for cancer.

For optimising the care of cancer patients, caregiver health care constitutes an important factor. Considering the intensity duration and emergencies involved in cancer care, the primary caregiver often endures what is called the 'caregiver burden' characterised by extreme fatigue, depression, anxiety, exhaustion, and stress. This adversely impacts the quality of caregiving. In the interest of the patient, there is a need to sustain the quality of care. For this reason, appropriate interventions are designed for the caregiver with the objective of minimising the caregiver's burden.

Kedia et al. (2020) conducted a systematic review of literature on studies related to interventions for informal caregivers of lung cancer patients. They identified four categories of interventions, that is, communication-based interventions, interventions aimed at stress reduction, for enhancing coping skills, and multi-component interventions. They found that most of the interventions and specifically communication-based and multicomponent interventions proved effective in reducing caregiver burden and negative affects such as anxiety, depression, and distress and could enhance the self-efficacy, quality of life, and coping skills of caregivers. Zhang et al. (2020) found that psychosocial interventions could significantly reduce anxiety and depression but not general distress in caregivers of cancer patients. Psychosocial interventions may vary with the needs of the caregiver. Various intervention models that include cognitive behaviour therapy, emotion-focused intervention, existential behaviour therapy, Comprehensive Health Enhancement Support System (CHESS), and problem-solving therapy are a few tested methods. A systematic review on this found that interventions that had the patient-caregiver dyad with an objective of enhancing the interpersonal connection between them, self-care, and symptom management of patients helped in reducing the caregiver depression and quality of life, and music therapy helped in alleviating the anxiety in caregivers (Fu et al., 2017).

A wide range of interventions targeting cognition, affect, and behaviour have been used on patients of great diversities. They included the standard CBT, behavioural interventions, relaxation, music therapy, play therapy, and so on. The common conclusion different authors arrived at was to increase the trials on Indian patients and caregivers and evolve modules based on randomised control trials (Lee et al., 2021; Peddireddy, 2019; Satapathy et al., 2018).

Enhancing Health and Well-Being for Individuals and Society

Health care is not limited to clinical settings. It includes the well-being of the individual in society. American Psychological Association in its dictionary defines well-being as 'a state of happiness and contentment, with low levels of distress, overall good physical and mental health and outlook, or good quality of life'. Ensuring and sustaining this in the common citizen of any country depends on the economic, social, and spiritual environment backed by a strong political will. Discussion on that is beyond the scope of this chapter. However, a brief discussion on community health is within the purview of Health Psychology. Major aspects of community health include the following:

- Identification of public health concerns typical to certain geographic areas, which may even cover social and environmental factors related to a healthy life
- Identification of resource gaps in community health services
- Identification of resources within the community to be utilised in health services

- Community Health Education and counselling to optimise a healthy lifestyle
- Advocating for improved care for the population at risk

The points mentioned above are in addition to the basic health care provisions in the community. Research inputs in these aspects are multidisciplinary, with the involvement of Public Health, Health Psychology, Social Work, Clinical Psychology, Nursing Science, and so on. There is a dire need for research in the field of Community Health Psychology in the Indian context. However, since the discipline of Health Psychology is still in its infancy in the country, the specialised branch of Community Health Psychology is yet to take off. But it is about time that the researchers in the field of Health Psychology focus on community health, which is a contemporary need. Sporadic studies in this area deserve attention, dissemination, and encouragement.

Evidence-based medicine is a systematic spiral process. It involves steps such as posing the question and exploring and investigating an answer which constitutes the evidence. It is not sufficient to gather single evidence or pieces of evidence in a specific context. The power of the evidence calls for an appropriate assessment in terms of multi-centre randomised control trials. Even though such trials establish the evidence, the acceptance of identified practice depends on its matching with the target population's values and preferences. However, such a rigorous process necessary for clinical trials of medicines and devices may not be needed in the case of Health Psychology interventions. Study results based on robust research designs, quasi-experiments, and control group trials on an acceptable sample size with scope for replication can be considered strong evidence.

Contributions of Health Psychology to the field of health care have now stood the test of scientific evidence. Large control group studies on large samples consisting of all age ranges, covering paediatric to geriatric health, and covering all fields ranging from cardiovascular health to cancer research have provided sufficient evidence on the bidirectional relationship between the psychological states and physical health status and the effectiveness of the psychosocial interventions in healing the chronic diseases, acute diseases, recovery from surgical procedures, and softening the trauma in terminal illnesses. Hence, the established intervention models that have passed the test of 'evidence-based treatment model' need to be widely disseminated, matched with user values, and integrated into the regular treatment protocols. This is possible with radical changes in national health policies emphasising a holistic approach to diagnosis, care treatment, and rehabilitation that has wellness as the focus.

References

Abraham, A. M., Sudhir, P. M., Philip, M., & Bantwal, G. (2020). Efficacy of a brief self-management intervention in type 2 diabetes mellitus: A randomized controlled trial from India. *Indian Journal of Psychological Medicine, 42*(6), 540–548.

Agarwal, R. P., & Maroko-Afek, A. (2018). Yoga into cancer care: A review of the evidence-based research. *International Journal of Yoga, 11*(1), 3.

Ahlawat, R., Tiwari, P., & D'Cruz, S. (2018). Prevalence of depression and its associated factors among patients of chronic kidney disease in a public tertiary care hospital in India: A cross-sectional study. *Saudi Journal of Kidney Diseases and Transplantation: An Official Publication of the Saudi Center for Organ Transplantation, Saudi Arabia, 29*(5), 1165–1173. https://doi.org/10.4103/1319-2442.243972

Alexander, A., & Murthy, R. S. (2020). Living with cancer: Urgent need for emotional health support. *Indian Journal of Cancer, 57*(3), 360.

Amsberg, S., Anderbro, T., Wredling, R., Lisspers, J., Lins, P. E., Adamson, U., & Johansson, U. B. (2009). A cognitive behavior therapy-based intervention among poorly controlled adult type 1 diabetes patients: A randomized controlled trial. *Patient Education and Counseling, 77*(1), 72–80.

Andrew, A., (2019). Form and frequency of cognitive intervention: Impact on adherance and managament of primary hypertension. PhD thesis submitted to University of Hyderabad.

Bhargava, K., & Bhargava, D. (2007). Evidence based health care a scientific approach to health care. *Sultan Qaboos University Medical Journal [SQUMJ], 7*(2), 105–107.

Block, J., Block, J. H., & Gjerde, P. F. (1988). Parental functioning and the home environment in families of divorce: Prospective and concurrent analyses. *Journal of the American Academy of Child & Adolescent Psychiatry, 27*(2), 207–213.

Bosch, J. A., Engeland, C. G., Cacioppo, J. T., & Marucha, P. T. (2007). Depressive symptoms predict mucosal wound healing. *Psychosomatic Medicine, 69*(7), 597–605.

Briani, R. V., Ferreira, A. S., Pazzinatto, M. F., Pappas, E., De Oliveira Silva, D., & Azevedo, F. M. (2018). What interventions can improve quality of life or psychosocial factors of individuals with knee osteoarthritis? A systematic review with meta-analysis of primary outcomes from randomised controlled trials. *British Journal of Sports Medicine, 52*(16), 1031–1038.

Broadbent, E. (2010). Illness perceptions and health: Innovations and clinical applications. *Social and Personality Psychology Compass, 4*(4), 256–266.

Census of India. (2011). Table C-13. Office of the Registrar General & Census Commissioner, India, Ministry of Home Affairs, Govt. of India, New Delhi.

Chavare, S., & Natu, S. (2020). Exploring resilience in Indian women with rheumatoid arthritis: A qualitative approach. *Journal of Psychosocial Research, 15*(1), 305–316.

Chelli, K., Lalnuntluangi, R., & Padhy, M. (2017). Health hardiness and illness perceptions in Type 2 Diabetes Patients. *Journal of Indian Health Psychology, 12*(1), 24–35.

Chivukula, U., Swain, S., Rana, S., & Hariharan, M. (2013). Perceived social support and type of cardiac procedures as modifiers of hospital anxiety and depression. *Psychological Studies, 58*(3), 242–247.

Cole-King, A., & Harding, K. G. (2001). Psychological factors and delayed healing in chronic wounds. *Psychosomatic Medicine, 63*(2), 216–220.

Costa, E., Giardini, A., Savin, M., Menditto, E., Lehane, E., Laosa, O., Pecorelli, S., Monaco, A., & Marengoni, A. (2015). Interventional tools to improve medication adherence: Review of literature. *Patient Preference and Adherence, 9*, 1303–1314. https://doi.org/10.2147/PPA.S87551

Dawson, D. A. (1991). Family structure and children's health and well-being: Data from the 1988 National Health Interview Survey on Child Health. *Journal of Marriage and the Family, 53*(3), 573–584.

Doering, L. V., Moser, D. K., Lemankiewicz, W., Luper, C., & Khan, S. (2005). Depression, healing, and recovery from coronary artery bypass surgery. *American Journal of Critical Care, 14*(4), 316–324.

Everson-Rose, S. A., & Lewis, T. T. (2005). Psychosocial factors and cardiovascular diseases. *Annual Review Public Health, 26*, 469–500.

Friedman, M. (1974). *Treating Type A Behavior and Your Heart*. Fawcett Crest.
Fu, F., Zhao, H., Tong, F., & Chi, I. (2017). A systematic review of psychosocial interventions to cancer caregivers. *Frontiers in Psychology, 8*, 834.
Harvey, J. N. (2015). Psychosocial interventions for the diabetic patient. *Diabetes, Metabolic Syndrome and Obesity: Targets and therapy, 8*, 29.
Hariharan, M. (2020). *Health Psychology: Theory, Practice and Research*. Sage Publications.
Hariharan, M., Andrew, A., Kallevarapu, V., Rao, C. R., & Chivukula, U. (2018). Conceptualizing hypertension: A developmental trend in school children. *International Journal of Health & Allied Sciences, 7*(3), 177.
Hariharan, M., Swain, S., & Chivukula, U. (2014). Childhood stress and its impact on learning and academic performance. In Holliman, A. J. (ed.), *Educational Psychology* (pp. 127–139). Routledge.
Hariharan, M., Thomas, M. T., Gadiraju, P., Vemuganti, G. (2014). *Prevalence of Depression in Patients Reporting Cardiac, Gastro-intestinal, Pulmonary and Skin Problems: Implications for Health Policy (Unpublished Project Report)*. University of Hyderabad, Hyderabad, India.
Harris, M. L., Loxton, D., Sibbritt, D. W., & Byles J. E. (2012). The relative importance of psychosocial factors in arthritis: Findings from 10,509 Australian women. *Journal of Psychosomatic Research, 73*(4), 251–256.
James, N. T., Miller, C. W., Brown, K. C., & Weaver, M. (2005). Pain disability among older adults with arthritis. *Journal of Aging and Health, 17*(1), 56–69. https://doi.org/10.1177/0898264304272783
Jiang, L., Beals, J., Whitesell, N. R., Roubideaux, Y., Manson, S. M., & AI-SUPERPFP Team. (2008). Stress burden and diabetes in two American Indian reservation communities. *Diabetes Care, 31*(3), 427–429.
Kakar, S. (2003). Psychoanalysis and eastern spiritual healing traditions. *Journal of Analytical Psychology, 48*(5), 659–678.
Kedia, S. K., Collins, A., Dillon, P. J., Akkus, C., Ward, K. D., & Jackson, B. M. (2020). Psychosocial interventions for informal caregivers of lung cancer patients: A systematic review. *Psycho-Oncology, 29*(2), 251–262.
Kelly, S. J., & Ismail, M. (2015). Stress and type 2 diabetes: A review of how stress contributes to the development of type 2 diabetes. *Annual Review of Public Health, 36*, 441–462.
Khan, W. A., Ali, S. K., Prasad, S., Deshpande, A., Khanam, S., & Ray, D. S. (2019). A comparative study of psychosocial determinants and mental well-being in chronic kidney disease patients: A closer look. *Industrial Psychiatry Journal, 28*(1), 63–67. https://doi.org/10.4103/ipj.ipj_23_19
Kopparty, S., Vanlalhruaii, C., Hariharan, M., Gadiraju, P., & Rao, C. R. (2018). Children's understanding of cancer: Developmental trend in their conceptual complexity. *Indian Journal of Public Health Research & Development, 9*(10).
Kumar, P., Srivastava, S., Mishra, P. S., & Mooss, E. K. (2021). Prevalence of pre-diabetes/type 2 diabetes among adolescents (10–19 years) and its association with different measures of overweight/obesity in India: A gendered perspective. *BMC Endocrine Disorders, 21*(1), 1–12.
Lalnuntluangi, R., Chelli, K., & Padhy, M. (2017). Self-efficacy, outcome expectancy and self-management of type 2 diabetes patients. *Indian Journal of Health & Wellbeing, 8*(9), 1040–1043.
Law, E., Fisher, E., Eccleston, C., & Palermo, T. M. (2019). Psychological interventions for parents of children and adolescents with chronic illness. *Cochrane Database of Systematic Reviews, 18*(3), CD009660. https://doi.org/10.1002/14651858.CD009660.pub4

Lee, J. Z. J., Chen, H. C., Lee, J. X., & Klainin-Yobas, P. (2021). Effects of psychosocial interventions on psychological outcomes among caregivers of advanced cancer patients: A systematic review and meta-analysis. *Supportive Care in Cancer, 29*(12), 7237–7248.

Leventhal, H., Bodnar-Deren, S., Breland, J. Y., Hash-Converse, J., Phillips, L. A., Leventhal, E. A., & Cameron, L. D. (2012). *Modeling Health and Illness Behavior: The Approach of the Commonsense Model*. Psychology Press, New York (NY).

Meena, J., Singh, M., Agarwal, A., Chauhan, A., & Jaiswal, N. (2021). Prevalence of hypertension among children and adolescents in India: A systematic review and meta-analysis. *Indian Journal of Pediatrics, 88*(11), 1107–1114.

Mulle, J. G., & Vaccarino, V. (2013). Cardiovascular disease, psychosocial factors, and genetics: The case of depression. *Progress in Cardiovascular Diseases, 55*(6), 557–562.

Muthukumaran, A., Natarajan, G., Thanigachalam, D., Sultan, S. A., Jeyachandran, D., & Ramanathan, S. (2021). The role of psychosocial factors in depression and mortality among urban hemodialysis patients. *Kidney International Reports, 6*(5), 1437–1443. https://doi.org/10.1016/j.ekir.2021.02.004

Nagpal, N. A., Aarthi, R., Hariharan, M., Naga Seema, N. D. S., & Rao, C. R. (2018). Conceptualizing HIV/AIDS: Developmental trends in school children. *IOSR Journal of Nursing and Health Science (IOSR-JNHS), 6*, 74–81.

National Centre for Disease Informatics and Research. (2012–2014). *Three-Year Report of Population Based Cancer Registries. Report of 27 PBCRs in India*

Newport, F. (2006). Religion most important to Blacks, Women and Older Americans. https://news.gallup.com/poll/25585/religion-most-important-blacks-women-older-americans.aspx

Padhy, M., Krishnakumar, N., Lalnuntluangi, R., Chelli, K. (2017). Relationship between self-efficacy and health locus of control in primary hypertensive patients. *Recent Advances in Psychology: An International Journal, 4*(1), 18–29.

Padhy, M., Lalnuntluangi, R., Chelli, K., & Hariharan, M. (2018). Conceptual complexity in children's understanding of diabetes. *Indian Journal of Health & Wellbeing, 9*(3).

Palmer, S., Vecchio, M., Craig, J. C., Tonelli, M., Johnson, D. W., Nicolucci, A., Pellegrini, F., Saglimbene, V., Logroscino, G., Fishbane, S., & Strippoli, G. F. (2013). Prevalence of depression in chronic kidney disease: Systematic review and meta-analysis of observational studies. *Kidney International, 84*(1), 179–191. https://doi.org/10.1038/ki.2013.77

Papakostas, G. I., Stahl, S. M., Krishen, A., Seifert, C. A., Tucker, V. L., Goodale, E. P., & Fava, M. (2008). Efficacy of bupropion and the selective serotonin reuptake inhibitors in the treatment of major depressive disorder with high levels of anxiety (anxious depression): A pooled analysis of 10 studies. *The Journal of Clinical Psychiatry, 69*(8), 5993.

Peddireddy, V. (2019). Psychological interventions to improve the quality of life in Indian lung cancer patients: A neglected area. *Journal of Health Psychology, 24*(1), 100–112.

Pedersen, S., & Denollet, J. (2006). Is type D personality here to stay? Emerging evidence across cardiovascular disease patient groups. *Current Cardiology Reviews, 2*, 205–213.

Peterson, P. N. (2020). JAHA spotlight on psychosocial factors and cardiovascular disease. *Journal of the American Heart Association, 9*(9), e017112.

Ragupathy, A., Nanda, K. K., Hira, P., Hassan, K., Oscar, H. F., Angelantonio, E. D., & Prabhakaran, D. (2014). Hypertension in India: A systematic review and meta-analysis of prevalence, awareness, and control of hypertension. *Journal of Hypertension, 32*(6), 1170–1177.

Rajhans, P., Sagar, R., Patra, B. N., Bhargava, R., & Kabra, S. K. (2021). Psychiatric morbidity and behavioral problems in children and adolescents with bronchial asthma. *Indian Journal of Pediatrics, 88*(10), 968–973. https://doi.org/10.1007/s12098-021-03661-4

Ramamurti, P. V., & Jamuna, D. (1999). Perspectives on geropsychology in India: A review. *Indian Psychological Abstracts and Reviews, 2*, 207–267.

Ranchor, A. V., Fleer, J., Sanderman, R., Van der Ploeg, K. M., Coyne, J. C., & Schroevers, M. (2017). Psychological interventions for cancer survivors and cancer patients in the palliative phase. *The Cochrane Database of Systematic Reviews, 30*(5), CD009511. https://doi.org/10.1002/14651858.CD009511.pub2

Rao, V. A. (2001). The world of the elderlies (preventive geriatrics). *Annals of the National Academy of Medical Sciences (India), 37*(1&2), 11–17.

Rashmi, R., Kumar, P., Srivastava, S., & Muhammad, T. (2021). Understanding socio-economic inequalities in the prevalence of asthma in India: An evidence from national sample survey 2017-18. *BMC Pulmonary Medicine, 21*(1), 372. https://doi.org/10.1186/s12890-021-01742-w

Rohan, J. M., & Verma, T. (2020). Psychological considerations in pediatric chronic illness: Case examples. *International Journal of Environmental Research and Public Health, 17*(5), 1644.

Sandhu, S., Chauhan, R., & Mazta, S. R. (2015). Prevalence of risk factors for noncommunicable diseases in working population. *MAMC Journal of Medical Science, 1*(2), 101–104.

Santosa, A., Rosengren, A., Ramasundarahettige, C., Rangarajan, S., Chifamba, J., Lear, S. A., Poirier, P., Yeates, K. E., Yusuf, R., Orlandini, A., Weida, L., Sidong, L., Yibing, Z., Mohan, V., Kaur, M., Zatonska, K., Ismail, N., Lopez-Jaramillo, P., Iqbal, R., ... & Yusuf, S. (2021). Psychosocial risk factors and cardiovascular disease and death in a population-based cohort from 21 low-, middle-, and high-income countries. *JAMA Network Open, 4*(12), e2138920.

Satapathy, S., Kaushal, T., Bakhshi, S., & Chadda, R. K. (2018). Non-pharmacological interventions for pediatric cancer patients: A comparative review and emerging needs in India. *Indian Pediatrics, 55*(3), 225–232.

Savio, M. T., & Hariharan, M. (2020). Impact of psychosocial intervention on prognosis of cardiac surgery patients. *Health Psychology Research, 8*(3).

Sharpe, L. (2016). Psychosocial management of chronic pain in patients with rheumatoid arthritis: Challenges and solutions. *Journal of Pain Research, 9*(3), 137–146. https://doi.org/10.2147/JPR.S83653

Sharpe, M., Walker, J., Holm Hansen, C., Martin, P., Symeonides, S., Gourley, C., Wall, L., Weller, D., Murray, G., & SMaRT (Symptom Management Research Trials) Oncology-2 Team. (2014). Integrated collaborative care for comorbid major depression in patients with cancer (SMaRT Oncology-2): A multicentre randomised controlled effectiveness trial. *Lancet, 384*(9948), 1099–1108. https://doi.org/10.1016/S0140-6736(14)61231-9

Shirazian, S. (2018). Depression in CKD: Understanding the mechanisms of disease. *Kidney International Reports, 4*(2), 189–190. https://doi.org/10.1016/j.ekir.2018.11.013

Singh, S., & Misra, I. (2018). Alternative interventions for fortifying health of the Indian elderly. In *Psychosocial Interventions for Health and Well-Being* (pp. 175–189). Springer.

Sun, H., Saeedi, P., Karuranga, S., Pinkepank, M., Ogurtsova, K., Duncan, B. B., & Magliano, D. J. (2021). IDF diabetes atlas: Global, regional and country-level diabetes prevalence estimates for 2021 and projections for 2045. *Diabetes Research and Clinical Practice*, 2022 Jan, *183*, 109119. https://doi.org/10.1016/j.diabres.2021.109119. Epub 2021 Dec 6.

Swain, S., Hariharan, M., Rana, S., Chivukula, U., & Thomas, M. (2015). Doctor-patient communication: Impact on adherence and prognosis among patients with primary hypertension. *Psychological Studies*, *60*, 25–32.

Thomas, M., Hariharan, M., Rana, S., Swain, S., & Andrew, A. (2014). Medical jargons as hindrance in doctor–patient communication. *Psychological Studies*, *59*(4), 394–400.

Tong, A., Sainsbury, P., Chadban, S., Walker, R. G., Harris, D. C., Carter, S. M., Hall, B., Hawley, C., & Craig, J. C. (2009). Patients' experiences and perspectives of living with CKD. *American journal of kidney diseases* *53*(4), 689–700. https://doi.org/10.1053/j.ajkd.2008.10.050

Tsai, P., Tak, S., Moore, C., & Palencia, I. (2003). Testing a theory of chronic pain. *Journal of Advanced Nursing*, *43*(2), 158–169.

Umadevi, A. (1991). *Study of disability in old age and perception of social support*. Master's Dissertation, S. V. University, Tirupati.

Van Lieshout, R. J., & MacQueen, G. (2008). Psychological factors in asthma. *Allergy, Asthma & Clinical Immunology*, *4*(12). https://doi.org/10.1186/1710-1492-4-1-12

Wainwright, N. W., Surtees, P. G., Wareham, N. J., & Harrison, B. D. (2007). Psychosocial factors and asthma in a community sample of older adults. *Journal of Psychosomatic Research*, *62*(3), 357–361. https://doi.org/10.1016/j.jpsychores.2006.10.013

Wells, A., Reeves, D., Capobianco, L., Heal, C., Davies, L., Heagerty, A., Dohert, P., & Fisher, P. (2021). Improving the effectiveness of psychological interventions for depression and anxiety in cardiac rehabilitation: PATHWAY—a single-blind, parallel, randomized, controlled trial of group metacognitive therapy. *Circulation*, *144*(1), 23–33.

Wysocki, T., Harris, M. A., Buckloh, L. M., Mertlich, D., Lochrie, A. S., Taylor, A., Sadler, M., & White, N. H. (2008). Randomized, controlled trial of behavioral family systems therapy for diabetes: Maintenance and generalization of effects on parent-adolescent communication. *Behavior Therapy*, *39*(1), 33–46.

Yoon, D. P., & Lee, E. K. O. (2006). The impact of religiousness, spirituality, and social support on psychological well-being among older adults in rural areas. *Journal of Gerontological Social Work*, *48*(3–4), 281–298.

Zhang, Z., Wang, S., Liu, Z., & Li, Z. (2020). Psychosocial interventions to improve psychological distress of informal caregivers of cancer patients: A meta-analysis of randomized controlled trial. *American Journal of Nursing*, *9*(6), 459–465.

2
HEALTH COMMUNICATION AS A PREFACE TO MANAGEMENT OF NON-COMMUNICABLE DISEASES

Sunayana Swain

From the slogans used in mass campaigns in public health settings to dyadic conversations between a doctor and a patient of interpersonal nature, effective communication holds the key to delivering the macro and micro aspects of health care services. Communication in the context of health care has three-pronged goals. First is the curative facet, focusing on the alleviation of the health condition of the individual seeking treatment, that is, health seeker or patients, and the second is the preventive objective to reduce the disease burden on the individual as well as the health care system, while health promotion constitutes the third aspect. For instance, the policy regulations around the messages delivered by the public health agencies on COVID-19 protocols constitute the macro aspects of health care, with a preventive goal. The doctor's medical advice to individual patients relates more to the micro aspects with a curative goal. Initiatives to create awareness for disease prevention and control, among the rural and urban populations like India's National Rural Health Mission and National Urban Health Mission (National Health Mission, Government of India, 2017) majorly through the strengthening of the health systems, constitute the promotive aspect. Health communication strategies vary according to type of the disease, the targeted audience, and the intended outcomes. Realisation of these goals rests on effective exchange of health-related knowledge between the health seekers and the health care providers, including the nurses, and paramedical personnel, especially in the context of one-to-one communication. In a typical clinical setting, the health seekers share their medical history with the health provider, that is, the doctor, mainly through probing, and that conversation becomes the fulcrum of the consultation process. In other words, the communication between the patient and their doctor determines the accuracy of the diagnosis, efficacy of the treatment plan, and consequently the prognosis. However, limitations like low doctor-patient ratio, abysmal health literacy, and poor communication skills punctuate

DOI: 10.4324/9781003360858-3

the health care services that invariably affect the quality of such clinical communication. As a result, the constraints arising due to ineffective health communication in a clinical setting risk reducing the health seeker to their 'diseased body'.

From Biomedical to Biopsychosocial Paradigms of Diseases

The permutation of diseases from communicable to largely non-communicable calls for a revisit to the notions that inform our understanding of human bodies. Going back in history, the proposition of dualism of mind and body by René Descartes in the 17th century led to the belief that the mind or soul is independent of the body, a radical conceptual departure from the church's mythological view of human bodies that attributed diseases to religious deviances. The mind-body dualism challenged the existing religious notion and laid the foundation of the biomedical model that viewed human beings as biological organisms, with diseases resulting from malfunctioning of the biological systems (Mehta, 2011). The following 18th century witnessed the emergence of hospitals that became central to medical care. A more profound understanding of the role of microbes in illnesses changed the clinical process, with the doctors assuming the role of an expert who could diagnose and cure the patient. This systematic approach to understanding diseases, labelled as the biomedical paradigm, resulted in a reductionist view of the human body that considered symptoms as indicators of abnormalities and the clinical conversation as a means to collect 'medically relevant information' to treat the symptoms. As the field of medicine advanced, in the 19th century doctors came to be seen as specialists with the know-how to treat disease-ridden bodies and legitimized the practice that discounted the individual's subjective experience of the disease, further reinforcing the biomedical paradigm.

Consequently, the individual seeking medical help assumed the status of a passive recipient. Simultaneously the doctors inherited the power granted by the expert clinical and anatomical knowledge of the human body that allowed for the 'medical gaze' (Foucault, 1989) to dominate the consultation process. The imposed passivity absolved the patient of any health-related responsibility and allowed them to adapt and perform the 'sick' role until the doctor cured them of their ailment (Parsons, 1951). Criticising the paternalistic tone of the biomedical model, George Engel reviewed the doctor-patient relationship in the context of psychiatry, wherein he proposed a new medical care model that juxtaposed the biomedical symptoms against the psychosocial and cultural factors (Engel, 1977), known as the Biopsychosocial Model (BPS). The BPS model re-imagined the relationship between the doctor and the patient as one of collaborative nature, characterised by mutual participation and respect and transparent communication that were crucial to the healing process. The 'medical gaze' (Foucault, 1989) that had dominated the medical discourse via the biomedical model was rendered ineffective. The BPS model emerged to be a good fit for the medical care discourse, especially in the backdrop of the inclusive definition of health given by the Constitution of the World Health Organization (WHO) that described health as 'a state of complete physical, mental and social well-being and not merely the absence of disease or infirmity' (WHO, 1948). Understanding health in its entirety required recognising the role of the psychosocial context of the disease and acknowledging the importance of the 'life world' (Mishler, 1984) of the patient in the clinical relationship. The BPS model proved to be a pragmatic framework to negate the limitations of the reductionist-dualist biomedical model by moving away from biomedicine to a 'patient-centred medicine' that aided the doctors in understanding the uniqueness of their patients (Balint, 1957) and the accompanying illness. Although conceived in the realm of psychiatry practice (Engel, 1977), the BPS model's implications were observed in varied categories of diseases, both communicable and non-communicable. In the case of non-communicable diseases notably, the BPS model, through its patient-centred approach, extended its impact on symptom management and behaviour modification, enhancing the management of the disease.

Management of Non-Communicable Diseases

Due to the global prevalence, non-communicable diseases (NCDs) have reached an epidemic status. WHO Fact Sheet (2021) reports that 41 million people die each year due to NCDs, accounting for 71% of global deaths, projected to increase to 55 million by 2030. Among those, almost 37% are between the ages of 30 and 69 years, that is, more than 15 million premature deaths, the majority of which are preventable. A large percentage, around 77%, of the population from low- and middle-income countries figure in the cases of premature deaths. Global Burden of Disease Study 2017 (2019) data includes NCDs like ischemic heart disease as the leading cause of death worldwide and stroke being ranked third, with both being cardiovascular diseases (CVDs). The WHO fact sheet (2021) confirms that CVDs, cancer, respiratory diseases, and diabetes lead the statistics on deaths due to NCDs.

While NCDs are not fatal, the death risk from such diseases increases because of their chronic nature, which gets compounded because of risky behaviours like sedentary lifestyle, alcohol abuse, unhealthy diet, and high levels of stress (Ghosh & Kumar, 2019). Although the aetiology of NCDs is mainly unknown, a mélange of genetic, physiological, environmental, and behavioural factors (WHO Fact sheet, 2021) tends to be responsible, which reinforces the need for the BPS model. When viewed from the BPS framework, diseases are understood as the result of a complex interaction of biological, psychological, and cultural factors, impacting the health behaviour of the individual and the course of the disease itself (Hatala, 2012). Co-morbidities further complicate the health condition in the case of NCDs.

Diabetes and hypertension (commonly known as high blood pressure) exemplify the criticality of NCDs. Diabetes is medically explained as the inability of the body to break down carbohydrates (from food) into glucose due to insufficient production of the hormone insulin secreted by the pancreas or because of insulin resistance which means failure to uptake the good insulin despite its availability (Diabetes Atlas, International Diabetes Federation, 2020). The most common symptoms of diabetes are excessive thirst and dry mouth, sudden weight loss, frequent urination, and tiredness. Usually, people living with diabetes are required to take medication for the rest of their lives, and in severe cases, patients are advised to inject insulin into their bodies to compensate for its deficiency, without which the disease can turn fatal. The chronic nature of the disease affects various organs like the kidneys, eyes, and lower extremities.

Similarly, hypertension is characterised by elevated levels (above the normal 120/80 mm Hg) of systolic and diastolic blood pressure readings consistently (NCD Risk Factor Collaboration, 2021). Due to its asymptomatic nature, hypertension is often referred to as a 'silent killer'. It can remain undetected unless a health issue (like renal failure, blindness, cognitive impairment) reveals the condition or the individual suffers a stroke necessitating a thorough diagnosis. In several cases, the stroke due to the uncontrolled hypertension turns fatal by restricting blood supply to the brain and can also lead to haemorrhage and stroke (ibid.).

An estimated 77 million diabetics live in India as per the Diabetes Atlas (2019) report of the International Diabetes Federation, occupying the second spot globally after China. By 2045, India will have over a staggering 134 million people living with diabetes. In the case of hypertension, secondary data analysis from the National Family Health Survey (NFHS 4) showed the overall prevalence to be 16.32% among men and 11.56% in women (Kumar & Misra, 2021), having trebled between 2004-05 and 2011-12 (Patel et al., 2019). The underreported figures in India are attributed to a lack of awareness about the disease itself that manifests in poor treatment rates, exposing a large population to the risks of hypertension (Zhou et al., 2021), which increases with a high incidence of pre-hypertensive condition that is estimated to be around 45.3% among males and 32.7% for females (Rai et al., 2020).

Medically there are no cures for NCDs, and hence management of the disease is central to the process of health-seeking behaviour of the patient and the clinical guidance by health care professionals. Adherence (compliance to the treatment regimen), regular monitoring of body vitals (routine health check-ups), and behaviour modification (increased physical activity, improved diet, stress management) form the crux of such disease management approaches. In NCDs, disease management is understood as a strategy or collection of strategies developed to provide crucial support to individuals living with a chronic medical condition while promoting positive health behaviour that improves health outcomes. Ideally, it involves a gamut of services offered by physicians, specialists, health psychologists, and other paramedical personnel. Described from the rationale of health care economics, Epstein and Sherwood (1996) define it as 'efforts based on systematic population-based approaches to identifying persons at risk, intervening with specific programmes of care, and measuring clinical and other outcomes'. Similarly, Dellby (1996) defines it as the amalgamation of knowledge base quantifying the economics of the entire treatment, a non-traditional health care delivery model, and an information loop that feeds into improving the first two components. Offering the most far-reaching meaning, the Disease Management Association of America (DMMA, n.d), a non-profit trade association, described disease management as 'a system of coordinated health care interventions and communications for populations with conditions in which patient self-care efforts are significant'(ibid). The elements of such programmes range from creating a collaborative relationship between the different stakeholders in health care, aspects of the process, outcomes, evaluation and management of the intervention, and regular reporting and self-management strategies.

The heterogeneous nature of the causality of NCDs, the associated risk factors, the chronicity, and the high prevalence underscore the importance of a robust base for disease management that includes the employment of multidimensional strategies aimed at prevention and health promotion. The efficacy of any such approach is dependent on the integration of practices that reflect the biopsychosocial context and nature of such diseases, foregrounding the necessity of adopting a patient-centred approach, a hallmark of the BPS model. Patient-centred care in medicine not only relies on the clinical evidence but also considers the needs, goals, and preferences of the patient (Epstein & Street, 2007). Such a philosophy underscores the collaborative nature of the doctor-patient relationship. The salient features of such an approach are to regard the patients as human beings, go beyond the disease, acknowledge the psychosocial context of the illness, recognise the patients' agency (viz. shared power and responsibility), and establish a therapeutic relationship and concerted decision-making. In the context of patient-centred care, patient-centred communication becomes the *mantra* for the attainment and maintenance of health goals.

Communication in Health Care

Communication in health care or health communication plays a decisive role in the ultimate objective of behaviour change, whether at the individual or community level. Centers for Disease Control and Prevention and National Cancer Institute (n.d.) have defined health communication as 'the study and use of communication strategies to inform and influence individual decisions that enhance health'. Health communication is an umbrella term used for communication in the health care context, which encompasses all aspects of health care of public and private nature for community and global health. Its scope includes disease prevention, health promotion, health care policy, and enhancement of the quality of life and health of individuals within the community (Ratzan et al., 1994). Based on various definitions of health communication, critical phrases like 'to inform and influence', 'to motivate', 'behaviour change', 'improve knowledge and understanding', 'empowering', 'exchange of information, on different aspects of health have been developed (Schiavo, 2007). Theories from the disciplines of Psychology, Sociology, Public health, Demography, and Communication encapsulate the expanse of these types of interactions. As a multidisciplinary field of theory, research, and practice, it studies and uses communication strategies, methods, programmes, and interventions to inform and influence community health and the health of individual patients, leading to positive health behaviour (Swain, 2013).

As communication takes place at many levels, health communication was initially envisaged as a form of health education, promotion, and disease prevention, reflecting the organisational and intrapersonal communication in health care settings (Malikhao, 2020). Interpersonal health communication describes person-to-person communication about health (e.g., communication between a doctor and a patient). In comparison, organisational health communication refers to interactions within complex organisations to coordinate programmes/actions among diverse groups, for example, WHO or various governmental ministries. Intrapersonal health communication depicts the internal psychological processes that influence an individual's health-related decisions (e.g., perceptions, expectations, memory, resilience, and locus of control). Research in health communication relies on models to explain, plan, and propose strategies for health behaviour that largely borrow from disciplines of Psychology and Social Psychology (Malikhao, 2020). For instance, the Theory of Planned Behavior (Ajzen, 1991) can explain intrapersonal health communication, Bandura's (2004) Social Cognitive Theory focusses on the interpersonal aspect, and the Diffusion of Innovation model (Rogers, 2003) describe organisational health communication.

Depending on the characteristics of interactions, health communication serves three functions – 1. Communal (to build community support for an intended health outcome), 2. Informational (to create awareness at an individual or community level about a health issue), and 3. Social control (to emphasise prevalent social norms). In recent times, the dissemination of the COVID-19 pandemic-related information (such as wearing masks, following social distance, washing hands, testing, avoidance of public gatherings) by WHO, union government, state governments, and medical communities via different channels (one-to-one communication, phone, text messages, billboards, TV advertisements, radio programmes) clearly showcases the instrumental aspects of health communication via different media. Health communication approaches include a range of contexts that utilise communication tools to maximise the health gains of individuals and communities. Techniques of interpersonal nature (like patient-centred communication), public relations and advocacy, community mobilisation, professional medical communication, and constituency relations are fundamental to health communication. Optimal health communication has been hailed as the master key to unlock the health challenges like the NCDs affecting the global population, and, importantly, the re-emergence of communicable diseases like COVID-19 has made it vital to health care services.

Doctor-Patient Communication and Its Role in Disease Management of NCDs

The relationship between the patients and their doctors operates with curative, preventive, and promotive goals that constitute the range of health interventions. The therapeutic relationship supports the doctors in engaging with the patient closely, effectively conveying empathy, genuineness, concern, trust, and respect, working on the principles of a patient-centred approach. Makoul (2001) spells out seven essential elements: relationship building, discussion, collecting information, understanding patients' perspectives, information sharing, collaboration on problems and plans, and providing closure. Effective communication is the cornerstone of doctor-patient relationships (Zolneirek et al., 2009; Chichirez & Purcărea, 2018) which entails using appropriate communication skills to build a therapeutic relationship, rather than a partnership, and encourage the patients' commitment to their own health goals through high adherence to the recommended treatment regimen.

In the evolving landscape of health care services, primarily due to globalisation and the paradigmatic shift from communicable to non-communicable diseases (NCDs), effective communication is essential to delivering the objectives of any health care intervention. In this context, health communication performs a critical role in disease management. Referring to DMAA (2006), one of the core elements of disease management is creating a knowledge base for the self-management of the disease that dictates the need for provision of vital information regarding the diagnosis, symptoms, medication, side effects, physical activity, diet, and related information to the patient, which is the essence of the doctor-patient communication.

Doctor-patient communication serves three primary purposes: creation and maintenance of the therapeutic relationship, exchange of relevant information, and decision-making pertaining to the health conditions (Ong et al., 1995), which are complimentary to each other. A closer look reveals the necessity of specific skills that lead to the fulfillment of the purposes which Silverman et al. (2013) describe as core skills such as respectfulness, acceptance, empathy, acknowledgement, sensitivity, supportiveness, attentive listening, facilitation skills, open-ended questioning, addressing concerns about risks and errors, and usage of language that is jargon-free and non-technical. Apart from their cross-cutting nature, these 'core skills' support and guide the doctors in establishing effective communication with the patients to achieve the ultimate goal of the best treatment outcome and patient satisfaction (Brinkman et al., 2007; Herndon & Pollick, 2002). It is important to note that the clinical communication takes place in a complex environment with elements of anxiety, vulnerability, apprehension, confusion, fear, concerns, and even thoughts of death, present in considerable amounts with the inherent power dynamics playing in the background of the clinical relationship. Hence, the core skills are especially crucial in clinical communication and ordinary communication skills will not suffice when it comes to disease management.

The impact of effective communication is expansive and can be witnessed across various aspects of the therapeutic relationship, particularly in many direct and indirect ways that ultimately feed into the efficacy of the intervention.

- Patient's Trust: Gaining the trust of the patient is fundamental to the clinical process. Admittedly, the patient approaching the doctor is itself an act of trust though with a great degree of vulnerability and dependence. However, to build a therapeutic relationship, the doctors need to convey their patience, attentiveness, and respect for the patient's preferences, all of which contribute to trust-building in the clinical relationship. Consequently, the patients are encouraged to share the distress, symptoms, and other medically relevant information, necessary for accurate diagnosis (Chandra et al., 2018) that translates into strengthening the clinical relationship.

- Accuracy of Diagnosis: As the patients' trust in the doctors is established, they are more likely to share details of their illness, their medical history that brought them to the hospital/clinic initially. This information gathered in the medical interview guides the doctors to arrive at a diagnosis (Berman & Chutka, 2016). The accuracy of this component is crucial in deciding on the therapeutic intervention to be proposed for the patient.
- Therapeutic Adherence: Identified as one of the most important health outcomes in a clinical setting, adherence to the treatment regimen is integral to the therapeutic intervention. The doctor's ability to effectively communicate the necessity of following the recommended treatment modalities (viz. medical tests, medications, diet, exercise) impacts the adherence in patients that in turn affects health outcomes (Swain et al., 2015; Zolneirek et al., 2009).
- Disease Prognosis: Medically, the result of any treatment regimen is in terms of prognosis (the likely course of a disease) which is largely determined by the patient's adherence to the treatment regimen. That way, effective doctor-patient communication indirectly influences the prognosis of the disease. Subsequently, the management mechanisms may be modified depending on the direction of progression of the disease (Swain et al., 2015).
- Patient Satisfaction: Patient's perception of the outcomes of the clinical consultation is determined by the quality of the communication that leads to patient satisfaction (Ha & Longnecker, 2010). Patient's satisfaction with the quality of health care is associated with the clinical communication. The predictors of patient satisfaction, like explaining the symptoms, possible causes behind them, and likely duration, are the aspects of the clinical communication. Patient satisfaction also contributes to increased adherence to the recommended treatment regimen, facilitating the disease management.

Other benefits like job satisfaction for the doctors, lower levels of work-related stress, and decreased burnout (Ha & Longnecker, 2010) are also accrued. The clarity in communication also lower the chances of malpractice claims (Huntington & Kuhn, 2003) by reducing the scope for misinterpretations of the medical directives. While various factors influence the patient's experience with the health care system, effective doctor-patient communication serves as the master key that can unlock the complications that are ubiquitous in the health care context.

NCDs and Disease Management in the Indian Health Care System

The Indian health care system is mainly public and is categorised at different levels, with each of the centres operating based on the total population, geographical location, and medical concerns that it can handle. Located in the most

```
                    Medical Colleges and Research
                    Institutions (8 in the country)

                  District Hospitals (1 per district)

                  Community Health Centres
                  (80,000–120,000 population)

                Primary Health Centres (20,000–
                       30,000 population)

              Sub Centres (<5000 population)
```

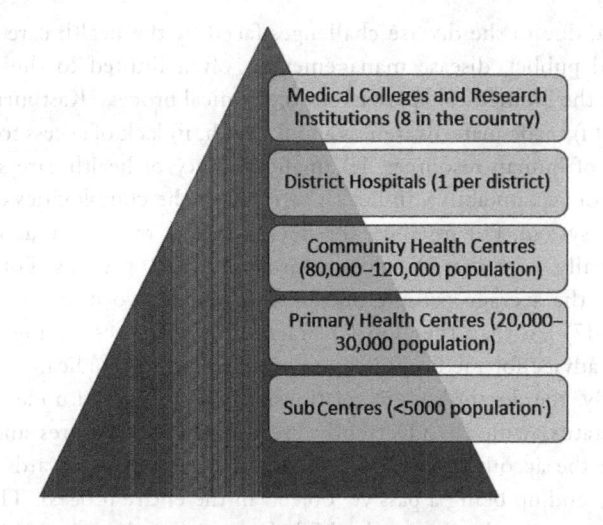

FIGURE 2.1 Public Health Care System in India.

rural regions are the Sub Centres, followed by Primary Health Centres (PHCs), Community Health Centres (CHCs), District Hospitals, and at the apex are the Medical Colleges and Research Institutions (Figure 2.1). While the Sub Centres cater primarily to the rural communities, the others serve both rural and urban populations, emphasizing on the curative, preventive, and promotive health care services starting at the District Hospital level.

Each of the District Hospitals is required to have an NCD Cell, established under the National Program for Prevention and Control of Cancer, Diabetes, Cardiovascular Diseases and Stroke (NPCDCS, 2010), which is the largest initiative launched for NCDs, under the aegis of the Ministry of Health and Family Welfare (MoHFW), Government of India. The Program lists numerous ambitious plans, frameworks, guidelines, and training manuals (for community level functionaries) for common NCDs. Many of those emphasise the need for patient education, counselling, training of medical officers at PHC and CHC level for prevention, and control of NCDs and promotion of positive health behaviours through screening, detection, and treatment. Together this sums up the disease management approaches by the public health system of the country.

These approaches align with WHO's (WHO Fact sheet, 2021) rationale that emphasises detection, screening, and treatment as critical components to the management of NCDs that can be imagined as the parameters of the response of the public health care system to NCDs. Early detection of a chronic condition can alter the course of the disease by identifying the symptoms and emerging co-morbidities and contribute to a good prognosis. Screening of the population can reveal the prevalence of the disease in the communities and help the health care systems design appropriate preventive interventions to tackle it. Post diagnosis, medication adherence, and behaviour modification constitute the 'treatment' of the condition.

In India, due to the diverse challenges faced by the health care sector (both private and public), disease management is often limited to the consultation room with the biomedical approach to the clinical process. Kasthuri (2018) postulated that i) inadequate awareness about health, ii) lack of access to health care, iii) dearth of human resources, iv) unaffordability of health care services, and v) absence of accountability in health care reflect the complexities of the Indian health care system. For instance, the doctor-patient ratio in India is one of the lowest globally, with that of 1 doctor for almost 2000 patients (Potnuru, 2017), which puts the average consultation time to under two minutes (Times Now Report, 2017) less than the global average of five minutes (Irving et al., 2017), before the advice for medical tests and prescription for medication is provided. Additionally, the doctor-patient relationship gets subsumed under the doctors' demigod status, which inadvertently creates power structures and effectively takes away the accountability on the part of the patients towards their health where they end up being a passive 'object' in the entire process. The low levels of health literacy further impact health behaviour (Singh et al., 2018) and inhibit the patient's clinical consultation participation. The accessibility to health care is another major detriment to the health care process. In India, health insurance covers about 37.4% of the health expenditure, while the remaining 62.6% amounts as out-of-pocket expenses (Sriram & Khan, 2020), which leads to a certain degree of lassitude in health behaviour like seeking medical attention at the right time, routine check-ups, and adhering to medication. In 2016, India ranked 154th among 195 nations worldwide in quality and accessibility to health care (Global Burden of Disease Study, 2018), which reflects the country's inadequacies in health care services. Besides the structural challenges, non-adherence or non-compliance is a significant impediment to the management of NCDs. Non-adherence rates for NCDs range from 33% to 55% (Yuvraj et al., 2019) and are associated with therapeutic failures (Swain et al., 2018). Against the backdrop of a large percentage of the burgeoning population living with multiple chronic conditions (increasingly in the rural areas), the drawbacks mentioned above engender ad hoc health interventions, adding to the woes of an already burdened health care system.

The role of health communication is integral to every component of the management of NCDs, be it of organisational, interpersonal, or intrapersonal type. The Indian public health care context utilises a mix of health communication strategies to respond to the challenges posed by the NCDs. For instance, the NPCDCS (2010) operational guidelines reflect strategies under the organisational and interpersonal type of health communication, leading to intrapersonal changes. It is right on the part of the Indian health sector to recognise NCDs as a public health issue and adopt multisectoral strategies (involving different governmental ministries, civil society organizations, media) and to involve the frontline community health workers (known as *ASHAs*, the acronym for Accredited Social Health Activists) at the very basic levels of detection and screening. However, the efforts fall short as the guidelines lack emphasis on health communication at the intrapersonal level that can bring changes at the behavioural level. In order to maximise the impact of such efforts, interventions have to be designed that incorporate the influence of interpersonal elements on intrapersonal (health-seeking behaviour, adherence, positive health behaviour) within the overarching organisational health communication frameworks. That would drive home the criticality of the message. That can also contribute to developing a sense of active participation and personal responsibility in the people towards their own health in collaboration with the health agencies and personnel. Another significant approach can be to develop measurement techniques to assess the quality of health communication using multiple variables (e.g., gender, socio-economic status, education, caste, and language) and including the role of each of the stakeholders in the communication process.

Conclusion

In India, one in four individuals is susceptible to die from an NCD (heart and lung diseases, stroke, cancer, and diabetes) before 70 years of age, which translates into 5.8 million deaths (WHO, 2015). The disease burden due to NCDs in terms of 'disability-adjusted life years' (DALYs) increased from 30% in 1990 to 55% in 2016, displaying an epidemiological shift in the disease burden pattern. Urbanisation and the growing proportion of the aged population will further add to the disease burden and challenge the country's health system in the future (Global Burden of Disease Study, 2018). The increasing prevalence of NCDs among the rural population in the last ten years, attributable to the changing lifestyle, poverty, and stress, is an added cause of worry. The psychosocial vulnerabilities leave the marginalised population at a greater risk. The out-of-pocket expenditures rising due to the prohibitive costs of the private health care facilities might prevent the patients from approaching such health care facilities, and the lack of facilities at PHCs is also discouraging. Thus forcing them to suffer through the distress until it reaches a critical stage requiring multispecialty care, making it a costly affair. Disease management programmes need to stress holistic approaches taking the patient-centred approach while accounting for the constraints plaguing public health (e.g., high non-adherence, low health literacy, and poor human resources). Health communication strategies that include the interpersonal, organisational, and intrapersonal elements can work in tandem to deliver favourable health outcomes by confronting the challenges of structural and psychosocial nature.

India witnessed an expenditure of around 2.6 trillion rupees in the health sector or 1.29% of GDP in the financial year of 2020, a considerable jump from 1.58 trillion rupees in 2018. The action plan to address the NCDs as a public health issue need to consider the biopsychosocial nature of the diseases. Because of the multidimensional aetiology, any interventions to manage the NCDs need to embody the psychosocial nature of the diseases and focus on alleviation of physiological distress also. There has to be an effective transmission of the NCD-related information from the health care providers to the individual, leading to changes at the intrapersonal level (cognitive, affective, and behavioural) that can address the high non-adherence rates. Hence, there is a strong case for the inclusion of robust and cost-effective patient-centred communication skills training for all the stakeholders to plug the leak in the transmission of knowledge from the health care systems to the population. The urgency of addressing the prevalence and impact of NCDs is further ingeminated as they appear in the list of Sustainable Development Goals (SDGs) with a target 'to reduce by one third [relative to 2015 levels] premature mortality from NCDs through prevention and treatment and promote mental health and well-being by 2030' (SDG target 3.4) (United Nations, 2020). Controlling the prevalence of an NCD like hypertension can have a substantial impact on SDGs (Kontis et al., 2014; NCD Countdown 2030 Collaborators, 2020). The epidemic proportions witnessed in NCDs call for a multipronged approach that must be prefaced by cogent health communication strategies at all levels of disease management.

Recommendations

Recognition of the active role that the health consumers play can recalibrate the skewed power dynamics in the health care services. Outcomes such as positive health behaviour, increased patient satisfaction, less burnout in the medical personnel, and effective utilization of health care services can then be possible. Supplementary to a patient-centred approach, the following ideas are articulated:

- Creating a cadre of professionally trained health psychologists that can work in tandem with doctors and paramedical personnel within the hospital setting and contribute to building a more patient-centred environment in hospitals
- Placing a multidisciplinary team with professionals from the field of Medicine, Health Psychology and Counselling Psychology, and nutritionists to design, monitor, and evaluate disease management programmes (to propose and develop health interventions based on the integration of various models of health communication, respecting the transdisciplinary nature of the field)
- Designing appropriate evidence-based health communication strategies to create changes at the intrapersonal level, along with interpersonal elements in health interventions, including the psychosocial context of the patients (to increase the impact of the interventions)
- Conducting health awareness camps routinely at community levels (to improve health literacy)
- Collecting regular patient's feedback to evaluate their comprehension of the disease, therapeutic instructions, and health behaviours (to make the health communication truly patient-centred, participatory, and increase the patient's commitment to the intervention)

- Organising periodic training of the health care professionals and their team to imbibe effective patient-centred communication skills through and beyond the medical school (to reinforce the importance of effective communication in the context of health)

References

Ajzen, I. (1991). The theory of planned behavior. *Organizational Behavior and Human Decision Processes, 50*(2), 179–211.

Balint, M. (1957). *The Doctor, His Patient and the Illness*. London: International Universities Press.

Bandura A. (2004). Health promotion by social cognitive means. *Health Education & Behavior: The Official Publication of the Society for Public Health Education, 31*(2), 143–164. https://doi.org/10.1177/1090198104263660

Berman, A. C, & Chutka, D. S. (2016). Assessing effective physician-patient communication skills: "Are you listening to me, doc?" *Korean Journal of Medical Education, 28*(2), 243–249. https://doi.org/10.3946/kjme.2016.21

Brinkman, W. B., Geraghty, S. R., Lanphear, B. P., Khoury, J. C., Gonzalez del Rey, J. A., Dewitt, T. G., et al. (2007). Effect of multisource feedback on resident communication skills and professionalism: A randomized controlled trial. *Archives of Pediatrics & Adolescent Medicine, 161*(1), 44–49.

Centers for Disease Control and Prevention (n.d.). *Making Health Communication Programs Work Practice* (p. 2). Retrieved May 15, 2022, from https://www.cancer.gov/publications/health-communication/pink-book.pdf

Chandra, S., Mohammadnezhad, M., & Ward, P. (2018). Trust and communication in a doctor-patient relationship: A literature review. *Journal of Health Communication, 3*(36). doi: 10.4172/2472-1654.100146

Chichirez, C. M., & Purcărea, V. L. (2018). Interpersonal communication in healthcare. *Journal of Medicine and Life, 11*(2), 119.

Dellby, U. (1996). Drastically improving health care with focus on managing the patient with a disease: The macro and micro perspective. *International Journal of Health Care Quality Assurance, 9*(2), 4–8.

Disease Management Association of America: *DMAA definition of disease management* [article online, n.d.]. Retrieved March 1, 2010, from http://www.dmaa.org/dm_definition.asp

Engel, G. L. (1977) The need for a new medical model: A challenge for biomedicine. *Science, 196*(4286), 129–136.

Epstein, R. S., & Sherwood, L. M. (1996). From outcomes research to disease management: A guide for the perplexed. *Annals of Internal Medicine, 124*(9), 832–837. https://doi.org/10.7326/0003-4819-124-9-199605010-00008

Epstein, R. M., & Street, R. L. (2007). Patient-centered communication in cancer care: Promoting healing and reducing suffering. National Cancer Institute. Retrieved July 7, 2021, from https://cancercontrol.cancer.gov/sites/default/files/2020-06/pcc_monograph.pdf

Foucault, M. (1989). *The Birth of the Clinic*. London: Routledge. Ch 6 (first published as 'Naisssance de la Clinique'. France: Presses Universitaires de France, 1963).

Ghosh, S., & Kumar, M. (2019). Prevalence and associated risk factors of hypertension among persons aged 15–49 in India: A cross-sectional study. *BMJ Open, 9*, e029714. doi: https://doi.org/10.1136/bmjopen-2019-029714

Global Burden of Disease (2018). Healthcare access and quality collaborators. Measuring performance on the Healthcare Access and Quality Index for 195 countries and territories and selected subnational locations: A systematic analysis from the Global Burden of Disease Study 2016. *Lancet, 391*(10136), 2236–2271. Retrieved October 1, 2021, from https://www.thelancet.com/journals/lancet/article/PIIS0140-6736(18)30994-2/fulltext

Global Burden of Diseas Report (2019). Findings from Global Budern of Disease Study 2017. Retrieved June 7, 2021, from http://www.healthdata.org/sites/default/files/files/policy_report/2019/GBD_2017_Booklet.pdf

Ha, J. F., & Longnecker, N. (2010). Doctor-patient communication: A review. *The Ochsner Journal, 10*(1), 38–43.

Hatala, A. (2012). The status of the "biopsychosocial" model in health psychology: Towards an integrated approach and a critique of cultural conceptions,. *Open Journal of Medical Psychology, 1*(4), 51–62. https://doi.org/10.4236/ojmp.2012.14009

Herndon, J., & Pollick, K. (2002). Continuing concerns, new challenges, and next steps in physician-patient communication. *Journal of Bone & Joint Surgery, 84A*(2), 309–315.

Huntington, B., & Kuhn, N. (2003). Communication gaffes: A root cause of malpractice claims. *Proceedings (Baylor University). Medical Center), 16*(2), 157–161. https://doi.org/10.1080/08998280.2003.11927898

International Diabetes Federation (2019). *Diabetes Atlas.* Retrieved June 7, 2021, from https://www.idf.org/aboutdiabetes/type-1-diabetes.html

Irving, G., Neves, A. L., Dambha-Miller, H., et al. (2017). International variations in primary care physician consultation time: A systematic review of 67 countries. *BMJ Open, 7*, e017902. doi: 10.1136/bmjopen-2017-017902

Kasthuri A. (2018). Challenges to healthcare in India - The five A's. *Indian Journal of Community Medicine: Official Publication of Indian Association of Preventive & Social Medicine, 43*(3), 141–143. https://doi.org/10.4103/ijcm.IJCM_194_18

Kontis, V., Mathers, C. D., Rehm, J., Stevens, G. A., Shield, K. D., Bonita, R., Riley, L. M., Poznyak, V., Beaglehole, R., & Ezzati, M. (2014). Contribution of six risk factors to achieving the 25×25 non-communicable disease mortality reduction target: A modelling study. *Lancet, 384*(9941), 427–437. https://doi.org/10.1016/S0140-6736(14)60616-4

Kumar, K., & Misra, S. (2021). Sex differences in prevalence and risk factors of hypertension in India: Evidence from the National Family Health Survey-4. *PLoS ONE, 16*(4), e0247956. https://doi.org/10.1371/journal.pone.0247956

Makoul, G. (2001). Essential elements of communication in medical encounters: The Kalamazoo consensus statement. *Academic Medicine. Journal of the Association of American Medical Colleges*, 76(4), 390–393. https://doi.org/10.1097/00001888-200104000-00021

Malikhao, P. (2020). Health communication: Approaches, strategies, and ways to sustainability on health or health for all. *Handbook of Communication for Development and Social Change,* 1015–1037. https://doi.org/10.1007/978-981-15-2014-3_137

Mehta, N. (2011). Mind-body dualism: A critique from a health perspective. *Mens Sana Monographs, 9*(1), 202–209. https://doi.org/10.4103/0973-1229.77436

Mishler, E. G. (1984). *The Discourse of Medicine: Dialectics of Medical Interviews.* Norwood, NJ: Ablex.

National Health Mission, Government of India (2017). National Programme on Prevention and Control of DCCD. Retrieved June 10, 2021, from https://dghs.gov.in/content/1363_3_NationalProgrammePreventionControl.aspx

NCD Countdown 2030 Collaborators (2020). NCD Countdown 2030: Pathways to achieving Sustainable Development Goal target 3.4. *Lancet, 396*(10255), 918–934. https://doi.org/10.1016/S0140-6736(20)31761-X

NCD Risk Factor Collaboration (2021). Worldwide trends in hypertension prevalence and progress in treatment and control from 1990 to 2019: A pooled analysis of 1201 population representative studies with 104 million participants. *Lancet, 398*(10304), 957–980. Retrieved June 10, 2021, from https://www.thelancet.com/journals/lancet/article/piiS0140-6736(21)01330-1/fulltext

NPCDCS (2010). Government of India. Retrieved June 1, 2021, from https://dghs.gov.in/content/1363_3_NationalProgrammePreventionControl.aspx

Ong, L. M., de Haes, J. C., Hoos, A. M., & Lammes, F. B. (1995). Doctor-patient communication: A review of the literature. *Social Science & Medicine, 40*(7), 903–918.

Parsons, T. (1951). *The Social System*. London: Routledge.

Patel, S., Ram, U., Ram, F., & Patel, S. K. (2019). Socioeconomic and demographic predictors of high blood pressure, diabetes, asthma and heart disease among adults engaged in various occupations: Evidence from India. *Journal of Biosocial Science*, 1–21. https://doi.org/10.1017/s0021932019000671

Potnuru, B. (2017). Aggregate availability of doctors in India: 2014-2030. *Indian Journal of Public Health, 61*(3), 182–187. https://doi.org/10.4103/ijph.IJPH_143_16

Rai, R. K., Kumar, C., Singh, P. K., Singh, L., Barik, A., & Chowdhury, A. (2020). Incidence of prehypertension and hypertension in rural India, 2012–2018: A sex-stratified population-based prospective cohort study. *American Journal of Hypertension, 33*(6), 552–562. https://doi.org/10.1093/ajh/hpaa034

Ratzan, S. C., Sterans, N., Payne, J. G., Amato, P., & Madoff, M. (1994). Education for the health communication professional: A collaborative curricular partnership. *American Behavioral Scientist, 38*(2), 361–380.

Rogers, E. M. (2003). *Diffusion of Innovations* (5th ed.). New York: Free Press.

Schiavo, R. (2007). *Health Communication: From Theory to Practice*. Jossey-Bass, Wiley Publications: San Francisco.

Silverman, J. D., Kurtz, S. M., & Draper, J. (2013). *Skills for Communicating with Patients* (3rd ed). Oxford: Radcliffe Medical Press.

Singh, S., Acharya, S. D., Kamath, A., Sheetal D. U., & Rathnakar, P. U. (2018). Health literacy status and understanding of the prescription instructions in diabetic patients. *Journal of Diabetes Research*, 4517243. https://doi.org/10.1155/2018/4517243

Sriram, S., & Khan, M. M. (2020). Effect of health insurance program for the poor on out-of-pocket inpatient care cost in India: Evidence from a nationally representative cross-sectional survey. *BMC Health Services Research, 20*(839). https://doi.org/10.1186/s12913-020-05692-7

Swain, S. (2013). *Health communication between doctors and patients: Impact on patient adherence and disease prognosis* [Unpublished doctoral thesis]. Centre for Health Psychology, University of Hyderabad.

Swain, S., Hariharan, M., Rana, S., Chivukula, U., & Savio, M. (2015). Doctor-patient communication: Impact on adherence and prognosis among patients with primary hypertension. *Psychological Studies, 60*(1). doi: 10.1007/s12646-014-0291-5

Swain, S. P., Samal, S., Sahu, K. S., & Rout, S. K. (2018). Out-of-pocket expenditure and drug adherence of patients with diabetes in Odisha. *Journal of Family Medicine and Primary Care, 7*(6), 1229–1235. doi: 10.4103/jfmpc.jfmpc_24_18

Times Now Report (2017, Nov 9). Average doctor consultation time in India is just 2 minutes – How does it impact patient's well-being? https://www.timesnownews.com/health/article/average-doctor-consultation-time-in-india-is-just-2-minutes-how-does-it-impact-patients-wellbeing/121797

United Nations (2020). United Nations. Transforming our world: The 2030 agenda for sustainable development (p. 18). Retrieved May 16, 2022, from https://

sustainabledevelopment.un.org/content/documents/21252030%20Agenda%20 for%20Sustainable%20Development%20web.pdf

World Health Organization (WHO) (1948). About World Health Organization. Constitution. Retrieved September 10, 2021, from http://www.who.int/governance/eb/constitution/en/.

World Health Organization (WHO) (2015). World Health Statistics 2015. Part II: Global Health Indicators. Geneva: World Health Organization. Retrieved May 13, 2022 from https://www.who.int/docs/default-source/gho-documents/world-health-statistic-reports/world-health-statistics-2015.pdf

World Health Organization (WHO) Fact Sheet (2021). Retrieved October 1, 2021, from https://www.who.int/news-room/fact-sheets/detail/noncommunicable-diseases

Yuvraj, K., Gokul, S., Sivaranjini, K., Manikandanesan, S., Murali, S., Surendran, G., Majella, M. G., Kumar, S. (2019). Prevalence of medication adherence and its associated factors among patients with non-communicable disease in rural Puducherry, South India – A facility-based cross-sectional study. *Journal of Family Medicine and Primary Care, 8*(2), 701–705. doi: 10.4103/jfmpc.jfmpc_350_18

Zhou, B., Perel, P., Mensah, G. A., & Ezzati, M. (2021) Global epidemiology, health burden and effective interventions for elevated blood pressure and hypertension. *National Review of Cardiology.* Retrieved October 1, 2021, from https://doi.org/10.1038/s41569-021-00559-8

Zolneirek, H., Kelly, B., & DiMatteo, M. R. (2009). Physician communication and patient adherence to treatment: A meta-analysis. *Medical Care, 47*(8), 826–834.

3
HEALTH AND WELL-BEING FOR ALL
Policy Perspectives in the Indian Context

Ramya Chitrapu

Health and well-being of the individuals emerged as the topmost priority of every nation, especially in the post-COVID world. According to the World Health Organisation (WHO) (2020), "Health is a state of complete physical, mental and social well-being and not merely the absence of disease or infirmity". Following the international guidelines, many nations focus on universal health coverage (UHC) which means that "... all people receive the health services they need, including services designed to promote better health, prevent illness, and provide treatment, rehabilitation and palliative care of sufficient quality to be effective, while at the same time ensuring that the use of those services does not expose the user to financial hardship" (World Health Organisation and World Bank, 2021).

Health is a critical component of the Human Development Index (HDI), which only reiterates the correlation between healthy individuals and healthy societies. Realising the importance of health in the holistic development of societies, it has also been one of the central themes of the United Nations' goals for global development. The Sustainable Development Goals (SDGs), to be achieved by 2030, emphasise the aspect of health through SDG 3 – "Good Health and Well-Being," which focuses on "ensuring healthy lives and promoting well-being for all at all ages." The Millennium Development Goals (MDGs) of 2015 too included four goals on health – MDG 1 (poverty and hunger), MDG 4 (child mortality), MDG 5 (maternal health) and MDG 6 (communicable diseases).

In the backdrop of nations worldwide battling with the global emergency of COVID-19 and its variants, the health systems including the policies and programmes of the developed, developing and underdeveloped nations without any exception have become a central area of discussion and debate. The unprecedented global crisis also portrayed the lacuna of the health systems across the world including India. The Indian subcontinent, which is home to the second largest population in the world, is characterised by diverse social, cultural,

DOI: 10.4324/9781003360858-4

political and economic conditions in addition to a varied topography. The aspect of health and well-being continues to be a challenge India grapples with amidst these diversities.

In this context, this chapter focuses on understanding the policy perspectives of physical and mental health in India in addition to analysing the national health policies (NHPs) of India. Further, it seeks to explore the need for an evidence-based and rights-based approach to health policymaking in India. As a way forward, this chapter attempts to provide a few plausible recommendations for the improvement of the physical and mental health ecosystem in India in the post-pandemic world.

Indian Healthcare System – A glimpse

India is a federal republic with 28 states and 8 union territories (UTs) with a population of over 1210.1 million. Health is classified as a state subject (termed as public health and sanitation, hospitals and dispensaries) in the Constitution of India (Seventh Schedule, List II), which implies that state governments are majorly responsible for health policies and programmes. The central government plays a key role in the formulation of national health policies and programmes through the Centrally Sponsored Schemes (CSS) and others. In terms of spending on health, the Centre spends around 60 per cent while the remaining is borne by the states.

India has been striving to make progress to improve its performance across various health parameters in the national and international indices. NITI Aayog's Health Index 2019–20, which measures the overall progress of health outcomes including governance and information and key inputs and processes, highlights the widespread disparities in these domains across the states and UTs (NITI Aayog, 2021). India ranked 131 in the United Nations HDI 2020 and is in the category of "Medium Human Development." It scored much below the world average on three parameters relating to Quality of Health, which include Lost Health Expectancy at 14.5 per cent (2019), 8.6 physicians per 10,000 people (2010–18) and 5 hospital beds per 10,000 people (2010–19). The world average for these parameters stood at 13.2 per cent, 15.5 physicians and 27 hospital beds respectively (United Nations Development Programme, 2020).

As one of the countries with a very high out-of-pocket spending (OOPS) and a very low percentage of government spending on health, the pandemic underscored the stark realities of the health system in India. The following section throws light on some of the major aspects that shape the health ecosystem in India.

Health Policymaking in India

Effective policymaking forms the cornerstone of the welfare governance of any nation. For a country like India, which is characterised by a diverse social fabric, policymaking, especially in the area of health, continues to be an ever-evolving process even after seven decades of independence. The Indian healthcare system, from centuries ago, has its roots in the traditional forms of medicine like Ayurveda, Yoga, Unani, Siddha and Homeopathy. Notwithstanding the deep rootedness of these traditional forms of medicine in the treatment of illnesses, the Indian health system, especially through the colonial period and after, seemed to have hardly gotten its due.

Policies and programmes in healthcare in post-independent India have been implemented through the Five-Year Plans (until 2017) and the NHPs in addition to the states' efforts. The aspect of "health" was not recognised as a priority area in the Indian policymaking ecosystem for a long time. For instance, the first NHP was introduced only in the year 1983, almost four decades after India attained independence. Subsequently, the aspect of "health" became a central theme of the country's planning exercise only in the Eighth Five-Year Plan (1992–1997), which coincides with the Indian subcontinent opening up to liberalisation, privatisation and globalisation (LPG). It is interesting to note that the international covenants of WHO have been setting the tone for health policymaking in India. The Alma Ata Declaration of 1978 was the precursor to the NHP 1983 wherein India committed to "Health for all by 2000 AD" in the World Health Assembly. Similarly, the National Mental Health Policy, 2014 was introduced at a time when the World Health Assembly brought the Comprehensive Mental Health Action Plan in 2013.

If one looks at the timeline of the health policies in the post-independent era, it becomes clear that governments have attempted to bring in various policy interventions in health since the 1950s. The first few decades after independence focused largely on communicable diseases and disease control programmes such as the National Leprosy Eradication Programme (1955) and National Tuberculosis Control Programme (1962). The 1980s saw the introduction of the first NHP in 1983 followed by the National Health Policy, 2002, and the National Health Policy, 2017. The recent few decades focused on introducing policies targeting communicable diseases and other lifestyle issues and accordingly the policies included National Nutrition Policy, 1993, National Mental Health Policy, 2014 and National Policy for Rare Diseases, 2021 to name a few. It is important to note that the Indian health policies trace their roots to the Bhore Committee Report of 1946, some of the recommendations of which are relevant even to the present day.

One of the important facets of public policy is the translation of the policies into actionable goals. In the context of the health policies, it becomes evident that the goals set by some early policies like the Bhore Committee Report (Government of India, 1946) and NHP 1983 continue to be unrealised even till date owing to implementation challenges. Drawing from a preliminary analysis of the three NHPs (NHP 1983, NHP 2002 and NHP 2017), it emerges that the policies were ambitious in setting the respective goals and targets. For instance, the NHP 1983 aimed at "primary health care with special emphasis on preventive, promotive and rehabilitative aspects" through the improvement of infrastructure, human resources and policy interventions (Ministry of Health and Family Welfare, Government of India, 1983). The NHP 2002 acknowledges the lack of adequate financial resources and public health administrative capacity which hampered the achievement of the goals of NHP 1983. Accordingly, the NHP 2002, which was introduced nearly two decades after the first NHP, emphasised on "achieving an acceptable standard of good health amongst the general population of the country" through time-bound goals with a focus on infrastructure, human resources and healthcare spending (Ministry of Health and Family Welfare, Government of India, 2002). Further, the NHP 2017, while building on NHP 2002, aimed at "improving health status through concerted policy action in all sectors and expand preventive, promotive, curative, palliative and rehabilitative services provided through the public health sector with focus on quality" (Ministry of Health and Family Welfare, Government of India, 2017).

Further, it is also evident that the three policies, spanning close to four decades, do not focus enough on some critical areas like the traditional forms of medicine, mental health and holistic health.

If one looks at the NHPs and the policies and programmes and as highlighted by many studies, there is hardly any emphasis on patient centricity and biopsychosocial aspects of healthcare, which have been widely acknowledged globally as essential aspects of well-being of individuals, especially in the post-pandemic era.

Other Policies and Programmes

Realising the need to achieve universal health coverage, the government introduces various programmes, schemes and mission-mode projects with various targets. For instance, the National Health Mission (NHM), launched in 2013 and included the National Rural Health Mission (NRHM) (2005) and the National Urban Health Mission (NUHM) (2013), focused on improving health outcomes in a mission mode.

One of the major initiatives of the Indian healthcare system continues to be the insurance coverage provided to citizens, which aims at bridging the gap between government spending on health and accessibility to health services. With India being one of the nations with a very high OOPS and low government spending on health, the insurance programmes provide limited relief to the citizens. The Rashtriya Swasthya Bima Yojana (RSBY), a CSS launched in 2008, provided health insurance of Rs. 30,000 per family per annum to the Below Poverty Line (BPL) families and a few other categories of unorganised workers. It covered the hospitalisation costs in the government and empanelled private hospitals. The Government of India under the leadership of Prime Minister Narendra Modi introduced "Ayushman Bharat" in 2018 on the recommendation of the NHP 2017, which succeeded the RSBY (Government of India, 2018). It comprises two components which focus on infrastructure and insurance: – the Health and Wellness Centres (HWCs) and the Prime Minister Jan Arogya Yojana (PM-JAY). The HWCs are aimed at transforming the existing Sub-Centres and Public Health Centres (PHCs) to deliver Comprehensive Primary Health Care (CPHC) to the citizens. While HWCs took care of the infrastructural component, the PM-JAY is a health insurance scheme aimed at providing a cover of Rs. 5 lakh per annum for secondary and tertiary hospitalisation of people from low-income groups. The PM-JAY expanded the ambit of the RSBY beneficiaries from 2.75 crore households to around 12.58 crore households as of 2020.

In addition to the policies and programmes on health, the governments factored in expert consultations into the health policymaking. For instance, various committees and commissions on health such as the Mudaliar Committee (1962) and Chadha Committee (1963) provided policy recommendations for reforms in the health sector. In addition, there are also expert groups that have been making policy recommendations for improvements in the health ecosystem.

Going further, the federal nature of the Indian polity has always been a central theme of debate when it comes to policymaking, especially in the domain of health. As the responsibility of health service delivery lies with the states, they have a greater and more effective role in the implementation of health policies. Choutagunta et al. (2021) throw light on the huge centripetal tendencies of Indian federalism while highlighting the diversities of the states across various resources and their impact on health policies. Peters et al. (2003) call for "lumping" of policy issues at the central level and "splitting" of health policies at the state level to cater to the varying needs of the diverse population. Some of the other recommendations include setting up of a proper regulatory architecture, increasing the health budget (Centre and states combined) in absolute terms and as a share of the overall budget and gross domestic product (GDP), focusing attention and funds on illness prevention and health promotion rather than on expensive populist insurance schemes, prioritising the health needs and human rights of women and girls (Sen & Iyer, 2015), and culturally appropriate public health service delivery (Wasnik, 2015).

Another argument in the health policy discourse focuses on providing health as a fundamental right. The WHO in its Preamble (1948) states, "The enjoyment of the highest attainable standard of health is one of the fundamental Rights of every human being without distinction of race, religion, political belief, economic or social condition." While the Constitution includes the right to health under the right to life, there is an increasing demand for providing health as a fundamental right. However, in the existing health policy implementation scenario, providing healthcare as a fundamental right seems impossible. This has been reiterated by the NHP 2017, which is as follows:

> The policy while supporting the need for moving in the direction of a rights based approach to healthcare is conscious of the fact that threshold levels of finances and infrastructure is a precondition for an enabling environment, to ensure that the poorest of the poor stand to gain the maximum and are not embroiled in legalities. The policy therefore advocates a progressively incremental assurance-based approach, with assured funding to create an enabling environment for realizing health care as a right in the future.
>
> *Ministry of Health and Family Welfare, Government of India (2017, p. 28)*

In terms of health research, the development of robust health data infrastructure can open up avenues for high-quality policy research and analysis. Scholars suggest strengthening the theory, methodology and positionality in health policy analysis (Walt et al., 2008) and a systematic and theory-driven approach for researching health policy with inputs from political science (De Leeuw et al., 2014). Despite the emphasis on robust health statistics in the three NHPs, health-related data continues to be characterised by challenges of availability and accessibility both in terms of the public and private healthcare providers.

Despite the many interventions, Indian health system continues to be suffering from some traditional challenges like low investments, infrastructure deficit, regional disparities and an overarching policy framework to name a few. This has, in turn, led to lack of access and affordability to healthcare in the country, thus making the goal of UHC a distant dream. In this context, it also becomes pertinent to understand the status of the healthcare system in India in terms of financing, infrastructure and human resources, which are discussed in the following sections.

Health Financing

The SDG 3C emphasises on "substantially increasing health financing and the recruitment, development, training and retention of the health workforce in developing countries, especially in least developed countries and small island developing states." In India, the overall government spending includes the Centre and states spending on the health sector with the Centre spending the major share. In addition, the large private and public sector firms, which were mandated to spend 2 per cent of their net profits on corporate social responsibility (CSR) activities, have been contributing to healthcare activities.

As mentioned in the previous section, the Indian healthcare system is characterised by a high OOPS. According to the World Bank, the share of OOPS by households in India as of 2019 was 54.8 per cent of the then total health expenditure (World Bank, 2020).

Table 3.1 provides an overview of the total budgets vis-à-vis the allocations to the health sector and its percentage of the GDP in the last decade. As is widely acknowledged by researchers, healthcare experts and other stakeholders of the health ecosystem, the percentage of health expenditure as a percentage of the GDP continues to be at 2.1 per cent for 2021–22, which is a very minimal increase over the last decade. It is also important to note that this includes the pandemic-related health expenditure.

In terms of the per capita spending on health at the state level (2018–19), there exist stark variations among the states. It is interesting to note that only the state of Meghalaya has been spending 8 per cent of its annual budget on health while big states like Punjab, Telangana, Maharashtra, Haryana, Madhya Pradesh, Karnataka, Uttar Pradesh, Andhra Pradesh, Bihar and Nagaland have

TABLE 3.1 Total budgetary expenditure vis-à-vis health expenditure and percentage of gross domestic product (GDP) at the central level in India – a glimpse

Year	Total budgetary expenditure	Expenditure on health	Percentage of expenditure on health to total expenditure	Percentage of GDP
	(in Rs. lakh crore)		(%)	
2021–22 (BE)	71.61	4.72	6.60	2.1
2020–21 (RE)	65.24	3.50	5.43	1.8
2019–20	54.11	2.73	5.30	1.3
2018–19	50.41	2.66	5.28	1.4
2017–18	45.16	2.43	5.38	1.4
2016–17	42.66	2.13	4.99	1.4
2015–16	37.61	1.75	4.65	1.3
2014–15	32.85	1.49	4.54	1.2
2013–14	30.00	1.39	4.63	1.2
2012–13	26.94	1.26	4.68	1.3
2011–12	24.22	1.10	4.54	1.3
2010–11	21.45	1.00	4.66	1.3

Source: Compiled from Economic Survey 2016-17 (Government of India, 2017) and Economic Survey 2021-22 (Government of India, 2022).

Notes: BE – budget estimate, RE – revised estimate.

been spending less than 5 per cent on health, which is less than the national average of 5.18 per cent (Government of India, 2020).

One of the oft-repeated recommendations by various NHPs as well as committees and expert groups of the health sector in India is the enhancement of the public financing of health. For instance, the NHP 2002 called for an increase in health expenditure as a percentage of GDP to 2 per cent by 2010; the high-level expert group constituted by the erstwhile Planning Commission (now NITI Aayog) recommended an increase to 2.5 per cent of GDP by 2017 and the NHP 2017 also recommended enhancement to 2.5 per cent by 2025. The various Finance Commissions too recommended devolving a greater share of revenues to states by the Centre for the improvement of health parameters.

Infrastructure

The infrastructure of the Indian healthcare system is characterised by both public and private healthcare providers. The Indian public healthcare system runs through a three-tier system based on the geographic location and the population – primary, secondary and tertiary (Table 3.2). The primary tier, which is at the grassroots level, includes the Sub-Health Centres (SHCs) and the Primary Health Centres (PHCs); the secondary tier includes the Community Health Centres (CHCs) and the Sub-Divisional Hospitals; the tertiary tier includes the District Hospitals and Medical Colleges. On the other hand, the

TABLE 3.2 Health infrastructure in India – an overview (as of March 2021)

Sl. No.	Type of health centre	Rural	Urban	Total
1.	Sub-Centres	149,590	3,204	152,794
2.	Health and Wellness Centres (HWCs) – Sub-Centres (SCs)	7,821	98	7,919*
3.	Primary Health Centres (PHCs)	16,613	3,456	20,069
4.	Health and Wellness Centres (HWCs) – Primary Health Centres (PHCs)	8,242	1,734	9,976*
5.	Community Health Centres (CHCs)	5,335	350	5,685
6.	Sub-Divisional Hospitals (SDHs)	–	1,234	1,234#
7.	District Hospitals (DHs)	–	756	756#
8.	Mobile Medical Units (MMUs)		1,415	1,415#
9.	Medical Colleges		240	240#

Source: Central Bureau of Health Intelligence, 2020.

Notes: *The HWCs were the erstwhile Sub-Centres and Primary Health Centres (PHCs), which were converted under the Ayushman Bharat Mission. #Data as of March 2019.

private healthcare system operates through individual doctor-run clinics, hospitals and super-speciality hospitals. Another two important constituents of the healthcare infrastructure in India include the education infrastructure and the regulatory establishments that govern the medical institutions.

Table 3.2 provides an overview of the healthcare infrastructure in terms of the different kinds of health centres and hospitals at various levels in the country, which cater to close to over 1210.1 million population. A closer look at the government hospitals and beds in India provides interesting insights. As of 2019 and 2020, there were 8.1 lakh beds across 0.40 lakh government hospitals. The hospital beds in the urban areas were much higher than those in the rural areas with 5.2 lakh beds in 0.09 lakh government hospitals vis-à-vis 2.9 lakh beds in 0.031 lakh rural government hospitals.

When it comes to medical education, which is another constituent of the medical infrastructure, as of 2019–20, there were a total of 542 medical colleges, which include 280 government medical colleges and 262 private ones. The recent years witnessed an increase in the number of medical colleges, which led to an increase in the admissions to the MBBS course and thereby an increase in the number of doctors, although India still needs to further increase to meet the doctor-population ratio in the country. Accordingly, as of 2019–20, there were a total of 0.81 lakh MBBS seats (0.42 lakh in government medical colleges and 0.38 lakh in private medical colleges) across the 542 medical colleges. It was more than double the growth over the last decade; the admission capacity in 2009–10 stood at 0.34 lakh. A glimpse of the PG seats too offers interesting insights on the need for enhanced capacity. As of 2019, a total of only 0.48 lakh postgraduate (PG) seats were available across the Indian states and UTs, of which 0.37 lakh were constituted by Doctorate of Medicine (MD)/Masters in Surgery (MS)/Master of Chirurgiae (MCh)/Doctor of Medicine (DM)/Diploma and

0.08 lakh seats by Diplomate of the National Board (DNB) and 0.024 seats by College of Physicians and Surgeons (CPS). In terms of traditional medicine, there were 702 colleges (as of April 2018) that offered undergraduate courses in Ayurveda/Unani/Siddha/Naturopathy/Homeopathy with an admission capacity of 46,835. In terms of PG Colleges, there are 5536 seats across 203 colleges in the country. However, if one looks at the concentration of the medical colleges across the states in the country, it becomes evident that there is an unequal distribution with a large number of them concentrated in the southern and western parts of the country.

Human Resources

The significant role of the human resources that constitute the healthcare system has become even more evident globally in the wake of the pandemic. The need for enhanced health worker density and distribution has been the indicator for SDG 3C.

In India, the Human Resource for Health (HRH) include the "physicians, nursing professionals, pharmacists, midwives, dentists, allied health professionals, community health workers, social health workers and other health care providers, as well as health management and support personnel – those who may not deliver services directly but are essential for effective health system functioning, including health services managers, medical records and health information technicians, health economists, health supply chain managers, medical secretaries and others" (Central Bureau of Health Intelligence, 2020). These human resources play a very significant role in the achievement of the overall aim of universal health coverage in the country.

According to the National Health Profile 2020, as of 2019, there were 12.34 lakh doctors with a recognised medical qualification and are registered with their respective state Medical Council or the erstwhile Medical Council of India (Central Bureau of Health Intelligence, 2020). Of this, the government allopathic doctors constitute 1.41 lakh and there are around 0.08 lakh government dental surgeons. This implies that of the total number of doctors, private doctors constitute a major chunk of the health workforce in the country. Further, as of 2018, there were 7.99 lakh AYUSH Registered Practitioners in India, which includes doctors practising the traditional forms of medicine like Ayurveda, Unani, Siddha, Naturopathy and Homeopathy. Of this, Ayurveda doctors (55.5 per cent) and Homeopathy doctors (36.7 per cent) constitute the majority of the Ayush Registered Practitioners (Central Bureau of Health Intelligence, 2020).

In this context, it also becomes pertinent to look at the National Mental Health Policy 2014, which aims at achieving universal access to mental healthcare in the country (Ministry of Health and Family Welfare, Government of India, 2014). Accordingly, the human resources, which forms a critical component for mental healthcare delivery needs to be clearly chalked out. While the policy mentions psychiatrists, psychiatric nurses, psychologists, counsellors, medical psychiatric social workers and so on, there is a need to explicitly include specialised psychologists including educational psychologists, health psychologists and developmental psychologists to name a few. This becomes especially essential in the wake of the enhanced emphasis on mental healthcare in the post-COVID era and the proposed launch of a National Tele Mental Health Programme to better the access to quality mental health counselling and care services (Sitharaman, 2022).

Another important health resource in the health ecosystem includes the nurses. According to the National Health Profile 2020, nurses include the Auxiliary Nurse Midwives (ANMs), Registered Nurses and Registered Midwives and Lady Health Visitors. As of 2018, there were a total of 8.79 lakh ANMs, 21.17 lakh Registered Nurses and Registered Midwives and 0.56 lakh Lady Health Visitors across the country. The ANMs are a critical component of the system as they work at the grassroots levels in the rural areas. In addition, the Accredited Social Health Activist (ASHA) workers, who constitute around 9.29 lakh across the states and UTs in India, are also an important human resource who work at the ground level in the rural and urban areas (Central Bureau of Health Intelligence, 2020).

When it comes to medical education, there are a total of 1411 medical courses which include MBBS, postgraduate diploma, DM, PDF, MCh, MD/MS/MSc courses and super-speciality courses. In terms of the seats, as of 2019, there were a total of 1.22 lakh medical seats across the country with the majority constituted by MBBS (0.80 lakh) followed by MD/MS/MSc (0.36 lakh). In terms of the research, there are only 138 seats – PDF (100), MPhil (9) and PhD (29) – across the country, that too only in the states of Karnataka and Puducherry (Central Bureau of Health Intelligence, 2020).

The overview of the policies, finance, infrastructure and human resources reiterates the various challenges the health ecosystem grapples with. It becomes evident that the success of various national health policies falls short of effective implementation due to a lack of synergy between the Centre and the states, as is widely acknowledged by policymakers and researchers in the health domain. Considering the National Mental Health Policy of India as an example, there is emerging research that suggests the need for concerted efforts from various stakeholders for better policy outcomes. With the pandemic exposing the significance of mental health of individuals of different age groups and the increase of the burden of mental disorders across the Indian states (Sagar et al., 2020), implementation of interventions in mental health becomes an issue of immediate concern at every level.

Discussion

Health and education form the major domains of public service delivery in any developing society and India is no exception. Drawing from the overview of the health ecosystem, it is evident that it is rife with many challenges owing to many factors. This section discusses some of the major aspects and plausible recommendations.

Based on a preliminary analysis of the NHPs of 1983, 2002 and 2017, it emerges that the basic framework of the policies continues to be similar, which follows an incremental approach to a large extent. The NHP 2017 calls for advocating a progressively incremental assurance-based approach. However, taking into consideration the various challenges in terms of resources, the SDG goals and the outbreaks of different waves of the pandemic, it becomes imperative to reconsider the incremental approach to policymaking. Further, it is high time that the Indian health policies align their focus on the holistic and patient-centric approach to health while adopting biopsychosocial approaches to curing illnesses.

As highlighted in the previous section, there is a need for the Centre and states to focus on health policies that address the specific needs of the citizens. Accordingly, in addition to national health policies, the states and the UTs need to develop specific and timely health policies at the sub-national level. While the states dovetail their existing policies and programmes into the national health policies and programmes, they need to prioritise health both in letter and spirit. It is also essential for the policies to be regularly updated in accordance with the changing needs through actionable and achievable goals.

Despite the health policies emphasising on inclusivity, there is an immediate need for the policies to specify provisions for the minority groups including the disabled and the third gender or the non-binary groups. This may be achieved through the active involvement of the members of these communities right from the stage of policymaking for more informed policies on health and well-being.

In terms of innovations in the health sector, although telemedicine has been a successful practice in some states, the pandemic has opened up avenues for online/digital consultations. Drawing from this practice, it is essential that the state governments innovate and scale up telemedicine practices to create greater access and affordability, especially in the rural communities. This may be especially helpful in the domain of mental health and counselling so that the awareness of and attitude towards mental well-being is developed in the people.

In the wake of the varied access to various media and misinformation, health communication has assumed greater significance across the world, especially in the COVID era. Drawing from the experiences, the governments, at the union and the state/UT level, may devise robust communication strategies to effectively communicate aboutdiseases, precautions and treatments and guidance for well-being on a regular basis to the citizens. It is in this context that data becomes a critical resource for evidence-based and well-informed policies.

Further, with the nations turning into data-driven societies, there is a need for better collection, documentation and collation of the physical and mental health data across the country. This calls for robust Health Management Information Systems (HMIS) that could be one-stop platforms for health data. With the emphasis high on evidence-based policymaking in the healthcare sector (Rao, 2016; Ivaturi & Chitrapu, 2019), there is a greater need for authentic data which is accessible to all the stakeholders including the citizens. Further, this data can be a crucial input for enhancing the analytical capacities to predict trends in healthcare and align the policies and programmes accordingly.

Way Forward

This chapter attempted to understand the policy perspectives on physical and mental health in India. Based on the policy perspectives and other health-related programmes, it explored the need for an evidence-based and rights-based approach to health policymaking in India which focuses on bridging the gap between policy and implementation. Drawing from the discussion, it emerges that "health and well-being of all" in India can be realised only through plausible, progressive and patient-centric policymaking to cater to the needs of a post-pandemic world.

References

Central Bureau of Health Intelligence (2020). *National Health Profile 2020* (15th issue). Directorate General of Health Services, Ministry of Health and Family Welfare, Government of India.

Choutagunta, A., Manish, G. P., & Rajagopalan, S. (2021). Battling COVID-19 with dysfunctional federalism: lessons from India. *Southern Economic Journal, 87*(4), 1267–1299.

De Leeuw, E., Clavier, C., & Breton, E. (2014). Health policy–why research it and how: health political science. *Health Research Policy and Systems, 12*(1), 1–11.

Government of India. (1946). *Report of the Health Survey and Development Committee*. New Delhi: Government of India Press.

Government of India. (2017). *Social infrastructure, employment and human development*. In Economic Survey 2016–17. Retrieved March 1, 2022, from https://www.indiabudget.gov.in/budget2017-2018/es2016-17/echap10_vol2.pdf

Government of India. (2020). Finance Commission in Covid Times. Report for 2021–2026. Retrieved March 1, 2022, from http://finance.cg.gov.in/15%20Finance%20Commission/Report/XVFC-Complete_Report-E.pdf. https://www.indiabudget.gov.in/economicsurvey/doc/eschapter/echap10.pdf

Government of India. (2022). *Social infrastructure and employment*. In Economic Survey 2021–22. Retrieved March 1, 2022, from https://www.indiabudget.gov.in/economicsurvey/doc/eschapter/echap10.pdf

Ivaturi, R. and Chitrapu, R. (2019). An overview of health policy in India. *Journal of Health Studies, 1*(2).

Ministry of Health and Family Welfare, Government of India. (1983). *National health policy 2017*. Retrieved November 3, 2021, from https://www.nhp.gov.in/sites/default/files/pdf/nhp_1983.pdf

Ministry of Health and Family Welfare, Government of India. (2002). *National health policy 2002*. Retrieved February 22, 2022, from https://nhm.gov.in/images/pdf/guidelines/nrhm guidelines/national_health_policy_2002.pdf

Ministry of Health and Family Welfare, Government of India. (2014). *New Pathways New Hope National Mental Health Policy of India*. Retrieved February 22nd 2022 https://nhm.gov.in/images/pdf/National_Health_Mental_Policy.pdf

Ministry of Health and Family Welfare, Government of India. (2017). *National health policy 2017.* Retrieved February 22, 2022, from http://cdsco.nic.in/writereaddata/national-health-policy.pdf

NITI Aayog. (2021). *Healthy states progressive India. Report on the ranks of states and union territories.* Health Index Fourth Round 2019-20. Retrieved February 22, 2022, from https://www.niti.gov.in/sites/default/files/2021-12/NITI-WB_Health_Index_Report_24-12-21.pdf

Peters, D. H., Rao, K. S., & Fryatt, R. (2003). Lumping and splitting: the health policy agenda in India. *Health Policy and Planning, 18*(3), 249–260.

Rao, K. S. (2016). *Do We Care?: India's Health System.* New Delhi: Oxford University Press.

Sagar, R., Dandona, R., Gururaj, G., Dhaliwal, R. S., Singh, A., Ferrari, A., Dua, T., Ganguli, A., Varghese, M., Chakma, J. K., Kumar, G. A., Shaji, K. S., Ambekar, A., Rangaswamy, T., Vijayakumar, L., Agarwal, V., Krishnankutty, R. P., Bhatia, R., Charlson, F., ... & Dandona, L. (2020). The burden of mental disorders across the states of India: The Global Burden of Disease Study 1990–2017. *The Lancet Psychiatry, 7*(2), 148–161.

Sen, G., & Iyer, A. (2015). Health policy in India: some critical concerns. *In The Palgrave International Handbook of Healthcare Policy and Governance* (pp. 154–170). London: Palgrave Macmillan.

Sitharaman, N. (2022). Budget 2022-2023 Speech of Nirmala Sitharaman, Minister of Finance [Transcript]. Retrieved April 17, 2022, from https://www.indiabudget.gov.in/doc/budget_speech.pdf

United Nations Development Programme. (2020). *Human development report 2020.* Retrieved April 17, 2022, from http://hdr.undp.org/sites/default/files/hdr2020.pdf

Walt, G., Shiffman, J., Schneider, H., Murray, S. F., Brugha, R., & Gilson, L. (2008). 'Doing' health policy analysis: methodological and conceptual reflections and challenges. *Health Policy and Planning, 23*(5), 308–317.

Wasnik, J. (2015). Health care service delivery in India: obstacles and outcomes. In Basu, R., Alam, M. B., & Ahmad, F. (Eds.). *Democracy and Good Governance* (pp. 187–198). New Delhi: Bloomsbury India.

World Bank, (2020). *Country profiles.* Retrieved October 4, 2021, from https://apps.who.int/nha/database/country_profile/Index/en

World Health Organisation (WHO). (2020). *Basic documents forty-ninth edition 2020.* Retrieved October 4, 2021, from https://apps.who.int/gb/bd/pdf_files/BD_49th-en.pdf

World Health Organization, & World Bank. (2021). Tracking Universal Health Coverage: 2021 Global Monitoring Report. World Health Organization and World Bank. January 18, 2022. https://openknowledge.worldbank.org/handle/10986/36724

4
IMPLEMENTATION RESEARCH FOR PUBLIC HEALTH AND PREVENTIVE HEALTH CARE IN INDIA

B. R. Shamanna

The latest report of the Global Burden of Diseases, Injuries, and Risk Factors Study (GBD, 2019) shows a mixed picture. The global life expectancy at birth has increased from 67.2 years in 2000 to 73.5 years in 2019 and health indicators globally have shown an upward trend. Two hundred two countries of the 204 countries have shown an increase in life expectancy between 10 and 20 years in this period. The last three decades have demonstrated a significant fall in the mortality and age-adjusted disability-adjusted life years. This has been most pronounced for communicable, maternal, neonatal, and nutritional diseases. The last decade has seen the largest drop and progress. It is also evident from this report that health depends on the larger social determinants of health factors that include the health systems and the transitional issues that are associated with population, disease, and lifestyle. Many countries face the triple burden of disease with stretched health systems and reduced health care investments. This is exacerbated in low-middle-income countries (LMICs).

The India State-Level Disease Burden Initiative (n.d.) in collaboration with the Indian Council of Medical Research (ICMR), the Public Health Foundation of India (PHFI), Institute for Health Metrics and Evaluation (IHME) (PHF1, 2018) reports a more than one-third (36%) drop in the disability-adjusted life year (DALY) rate in the country between 1990 and 2016. The health status across states is still very unequal varying to a twofold difference sometimes in better off to worse-off states. The report provides the details of the transition from communicable which include infectious and childhood diseases to non-communicable diseases and injuries as the major disease burden in each state of the country. There is a great variation between the developed states and the poorer states in the transition over the last three decades. Communicable and nutrition-related diseases like respiratory infections and diarrhoeal diseases, anaemia, diseases of the early newborn period, and tuberculosis continue

DOI: 10.4324/9781003360858-5

to be major public health problems in many poorer north Indian states. The non-communicable disease has been the major contributor to the total disease burden and this has happened over the last 30 years. They include diabetes, cardiovascular diseases, cancers, chronic respiratory diseases, mental health and neurological disorders, musculoskeletal disorders, and chronic kidney disease. The contribution of injuries to the total disease burden has also increased in most states since 1990, with the leading ones being road injuries, suicides, and falls.

The report also highlighted undernutrition, air pollution, and a group of risks causing cardiovascular disease and diabetes as the major risk factors contributing to health loss in the country. The single largest risk factor in India responsible for 15% of the total disease burden in 2016 is still child and maternal undernutrition. In addition, air pollution, unhealthy diet, high blood pressure, high fasting plasma glucose, high cholesterol, and overweight together now contribute to a third of the total disease burden in the country.

Concerted efforts on facilitating policy prescriptions, development of robust surveillance mechanisms, intersectoral and interdepartmental collaborations, integration of national programmes, and the enhanced role of education and awareness should be made and need to be effectively scaled up, particularly to reach the services in primary care. The overall encompassing feature is to strengthen health systems. It is in this context that implementation research assumes a larger dimension both in its scope and scale.

The WHO in its preface to the report (WHO toolkit, 3) strongly argues that unless we take proven health interventions and implement them in the real world, the challenges that confront us cannot be met. In the report Knowledge to Action Framework of the WHO (WHO Report 4), the first step requires the identification of problems in the local context where translation into practice through the generation of appropriate research questions is needed. These questions are then answered using scientific methods. It is possible that for some problems, there is no need to invent the wheel as some problems have readily available solutions in the current knowledge domain (published research literature, guidelines, etc.), while for others new solutions will need to be found through appropriate contextualized research.

In the context of health care, the ecosystem is very complex when it comes to the implementation of research-based knowledge in real life, and at the same time systems and researchers are confronted with a lot of barriers. Therefore, there is a need to synthesize research data that is made available and the resulting knowledge contextualized before implementation. This highly intricate and complex process is typified by Graham's Knowledge to Action Framework (Straus et al., 2013). Hence, implementation research especially in the area of health systems and operations research is not only crucial but also critical to meeting that challenge. It provides the basis for the context-specific, evidence-informed decision-making that would be needed to make what is possible in theory a reality in practice.

```
KNOWLEDGE  ——————▶  PRACTICE
                ▲
                │
      IMPLEMENTATION RESEARCH
```

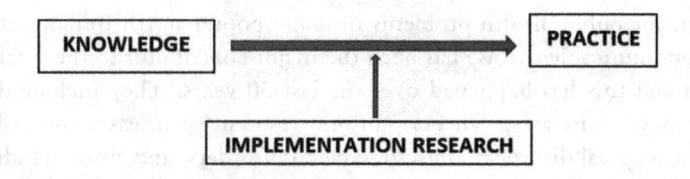

FIGURE 4.1 What Is Implementation Research?

Affordable, life-saving interventions exist but there is little understanding of how best to deliver those interventions in diverse settings and across health systems. Implementing proven interventions in real-world situations (Clark et al., 2017) is not only a challenge across the globe but is more pronounced due to the complexities of determinants of health associated with LMICs and emerging economies.

In Figure 4.1, it is seen that implementation research acts as a bridge between knowledge and practice wherein it uses all tools and an interdisciplinary approach involving the broader social determinants of health to implement solutions in real-life situations. Implementation research is more of health systems research that includes context-specific, evidence-informed decisions and interventions that are planned to be converted from theory into practice in real-life situations. It is problem-focused, action-oriented, and based on the needs of the health systems and takes into consideration issues in implementation which are very closely associated with existing contextual factors.

Implementation research looks at understanding the interface between what is expounded in theory and what reality happens in practice. This form of research has to be multidisciplinary through a collective and collaborative endeavour with engaging as many stakeholders and a range of interventions. These interventions include policies, programs, practices, and services and use a range of approaches that extend quantitative, qualitative, and mixed methods approaches. The bottom line is it is complex reflecting the realities of the context.

The core component of any implementation research is asking the right question and as the adage goes "Question? Is the king" in its evolution and delivery. The implementation research is biased towards practitioners than academic researchers. The word evidence when it comes to implementation research although very important depends on the complex situation in which a question is generated and solutions found. Implementation research provides lessons learned and cannot be a prescription as it is context-dependent. The adage that "one size fits all" does not apply in implementation research and every solution is both unique has its own merit.

The end points or deliverables of implementation research are the framework established for scaling up and health systems strengthening. The findings derived are warranted and methods being transparent allows the adaptation in complex situations reflecting real-world scenarios.

It is also a dynamic approach and a work in progress most times and needs continuous adaptation by implementers with anticipation of unpredictable effects.

Nilsen (2020) explains the theoretical approaches used in implementation science through a framework wherein:

- There is a description and/or guidance for processing the translation of research using process models into practice.
- Using frameworks and theories that are deterministic, classic, and implemented respectively and the outcomes can be influenced.
- Using methods and initiatives in evaluating implementation.

This framework proposed by Nilsen outlines the translation of theory into practice when it comes to implementation research. The WHO framework also very clearly outlines the steps in this translation initiative from evidence to policy or clinical decision as per the situation. It starts with generating, collating, and synthesizing evidence from research, putting together appropriate policies in the required environment, and applying these through stakeholder engagement, analysis, and needs. A good example is the reduction of maternal mortality rates through increasing institutional deliveries. The number of institutional deliveries has been increased through cash benefit transfers, providing transportation facilities, and increased access to facilities and human resources taking into consideration the local context.

Quoting Engelgau and Narayan (2009), "translational or now called implementation research transforms currently available knowledge into useful measures for everyday clinical and public health practice. It aims to assess the implementation of standards of care, understand the barriers to their implementation, and intervene throughout all levels of health care delivery and public health to improve quality of care and health outcomes, including quality of life". A very appropriate example can be evidenced by the development of a mechanism of supporting medical and health professionals in primary health care set-up in India through a decision support system for the management of non-communicable diseases (Anchala et al., 2015).

Good implementation research is collaborative research that is carried out through the identification of an idea and the appropriate research question, using a design that answers the question and involves key stakeholders in generating policy, managing of program, and research. It is also important that implementation research should be linked and included in the policy and programmatic decision-making. Implementation research also involves "speaking truth to power", thereby promoting accountability when it comes to health organizations.

The key to implementation is a thorough overview and understanding that is in the context and existing systems, and the ability and flexibility to adapt and use appropriate methodological approaches in implementation. There needs to be the understanding that outcomes and effects can be unpredictable and there needs to be a continuous adaptation by implementers. Implementation research is tailor-made to the particular situation in which it is conceptualized. The understanding that a context is critical to developing the right questions and evolving the approaches that are incubated in a particular context is key to its implementation and further success. For instance, what works in a rural set-up may not work in a remote tribal set-up. This again reinforces the fact that there is uniqueness within implementation science and research.

One of the frameworks used in implementation science is RE-AIM (Reach, Effectiveness, Adoption, Implementation, and Maintenance) framework (Glasgow et al., 2019). This was developed to address the issue of translation and implementing scientific advances into practice for larger public health impact and policy. The unique features of RE-AIM as quoted "include an explicit focus on contextual issues, prevailing dimensions, and steps in the design, dissemination, and implementation process that can either facilitate or impede success in achieving broad and equitable population-based impact".

RE-AIM pertains to health behaviour interventions. The goal of RE-AIM as alluded is to "encourage program planners, evaluators, readers of journal articles, funders, and policy-makers to pay more attention to essential program elements including external validity that can improve the sustainable adoption and implementation of effective, generalizable, evidence-based interventions". It also suggests that implementation research should be aligned with the need and the intended audience and be responsive to the subjects under study. A very good example of adapting and operationalizing the RE-AIM framework that has been implemented in low-resource countries led by a national government and multinational organizations is the clean-fuel cooking solutions at a grand scale: India's Pradhan Mantri Ujjwala Yojana program. It has been reported that it has already expanded access to LPG to 85% of the national population.

The research designs to be used should be capable of adapting and changing during the time of implementation. There are no fixed rules for a particular research method for implementation research and it should reflect methods to reflect the questions asked and have a dynamic approach.

Without implementation research, valuable resources can be wasted but it should also be noted that a core function of program implementation is implementation research. There is a need for more resourcing for implementation research, especially in LMIC economies where efficiency, effectiveness, and equity of program management are both a challenge and an opportunity. It is also a fact that it is a neglected field of study for two reasons: (i) a lack of understanding regarding what it is and what it has to offer and (ii) a lack of funding for the implementation of research activities. The reasons for this can be attributed to a lack of capacity building and inclusion in training in interdisciplinary and multidisciplinary curricula in our education system. As the coordination and implementation are complex and also time-consuming, it is also seen that investments and funding for such initiatives are lacking. This is seen more pronounced in LMIC.

The next section has examples and case studies on implementation research initiatives highlighting the connection between existing knowledge and reality in practice through demonstrations. Many of these examples are pitched in different fields of health disciplines extending public health dimensions and preventive health care. Points to be noted in these examples for the reader is to get an understanding of how the ideation is pursued in practice in real-life situations.

Initiatives and Case Studies of Implementation Research in the Recent Past in LMIC

Initiative 1

The Key Informant Method (KIM) (Marshall, 1996) is an ethnographic research method that evolved in anthropology and sociology disciplines. Its application has extended to the health care field recently (Pandey & Gautam, 2020). Key informant interviews are qualitative in-depth interviews (IDIs) with people who are opinion leaders and who know what is going on in the community. The purpose of key informant interviews is to triangulate information collected from a wide range of people, especially opinion leaders in different spheres where research is conducted. These usually include community leaders, professionals, or residents – who have invaluable knowledge about the community and can provide more insights into the understanding of a problem as well as evolved an implementation plan.

The KIM is a previously validated approach to identify and treat children with specific impairments or health conditions using trained volunteers from the community. It is an approach that is community-based, participatory, develops local capacity, and raises awareness. It has been used in many conditions related to disability and epilepsy in LMICs. The steps to establish the KIM include the following:

- Identifying and mapping societal networks
- Sensitization of the identified networks
- Bringing together the consenting group of key informants
- Key informant training
- Providing the communication and case-finding strategies
- Supportive supervision of these activities
- Planning and organizing the clinical examination day
- Carrying out clinical examination
- Appropriate documentation
- Referral as needed

The KIM is found to be cost-effective and sustainable to identify disabled children in communities to help in planning services for persons with disabilities (PWD) especially children (Bedford et al., 2013) in developing countries as well as identifying those who suffer have episodes of epilepsy in adults (Pal et al., 1998). This has the utility to be used in other public health-related areas like identifying blinding eye conditions in the elderly, impaired glucose tolerance, and possible diabetes mellitus as well as difficult-to-reach populations in the community setting with a targeted approach.

Initiative 2: Directly Observed Treatment, Short-Course (DOTS) – Tuberculosis (TB)

The World Health Organization (WHO, 1999) opined that the best method to stop the community's spread of TB is to cure it using the DOTS – TB strategy.

In the 1970s and 1980s, the Union previously called International Union Against TB and Lung Disease (IULTD) developed the technical strategy for DOTS in Tanzania, Malawi, Nicaragua, and Mozambique. By the year 1993, the WHO declared TB as a global emergency, and had validated and devised the directly observed treatment, short-course (DOTS) strategy, and recommended that it be followed by all countries. DOT means that a trained health care worker or other designated individual provides the prescribed TB drugs and supervises the intake of the medicine ensuring compliance. The Government of India adopted this as part of the Revised National TB Control Program (RNTCP) in the same year and scaled it to the whole country by the end of 2005.

The main components of DOTS-TB as quoted under the program include:

- Government commitment (including political will at all levels, and establishment of a centralized and prioritized system of TB monitoring, recording, and training). Case detection by sputum smear microscopy.
- Standardized treatment regimen directly of six to nine months observed by a healthcare worker or community health worker for at least the first two months.
- Drug supply.
- A standardized recording and reporting system that allows assessment of treatment results.

In the Indian context, the Revised National Tuberculosis Control Program has now been rechristened as National TB Elimination Program (NTEP) through updated recommendations. The program now brings in the private sector and service organizations including the voluntary sector, in addition to the public sector since 2016, and has been sustaining a huge impact in reducing new TB cases but is looking at drug-resistant TB more in this program and addressing it.

Initiative 3 – Health Systems Strengthening Through District Health Societies (National Health Mission, Government of India, 2013)

Before the launch of the National Rural Health Mission (NRHM) in 2005 in India, there existed a plethora of health system deficiencies. These ranged from a lack of holistic approach, negligible or absence of linkages with social determinants of health, no or shortage of infrastructure and human resources, lack of accountability and community ownership, lack of convergence in vertical disease control programs, poor resourcing for the delivery of affordable and quality health care, and its responsiveness to needs most times.

A watershed moment in India's health programs was the conceptualization and implementation of the NRHM in the year 2005. In response to the National Health Policy 2002, the goal was to provide available, accessible, affordable, and quality health care to the rural population, especially the vulnerable groups. In order to achieve this, it conceptualized the mission for making the public health delivery system fully functional and accountable to the community through:

- Developing and managing human resources management
- Mobilizing and increasing community involvement
- Program planning and implementation through decentralization
- Ensuring monitoring and evaluation against standards through a rigorous process
- Fostering health and development programs convergence from the village level upwards
- Implementing innovations and flexible financing
- Carrying out interventions for improving the health indicators

The districts will have an integrated District Health Society (DHS) and will act as the integrator and support for all the existing societies for different national and state health programs that will be merged here. The functions of the DHS will be planning and managing all health and family welfare programs in the district, both in the rural and more recently urban areas. This gives districts autonomy in access to funds, convergence for delivery of health care, and jurisdictional leverage. The common review missions and evaluation reports have proven that the DHS is a great idea and has had an impact on health care delivery across the districts in the country and scaled up similarly for the Urban Health Mission over the last 7 years in the country. Following the experience of the NRHM and its achievements, currently the rural and urban missions have been merged into the National Health Mission and now the urban underserved and vulnerable populace are also served with affordable and quality health care services.

This has proven to be a great idea for decentralization and implementation of health programs in the country and providing the direction to the mission of universal health coverage in the country.

Initiative 4 – Community-Directed Interventions for Public Health

Community-directed intervention (CDI) is a novel approach in implementation research where the community participates in discussing health problems and developing consensus interventions based on their personal experiences, and knowledge gained from health personnel and basing it on available resources. Using this approach, community members themselves gather sufficient information and then they decide, organize, mobilize, and use available resources to tackle their problems.

The CDI strategy requires the foundation of the Primary Health Care strategy for an effective and efficient model for integrated delivery of appropriate health interventions at the community level in contexts like India. The unique selling point of any CDI is that the communities themselves direct the planning and implementation of intervention delivery. The best and touted success story comes from the West African countries under the Mectizan Donation Program (Katabarwa et al., 2016) for the elimination of river blindness or onchocerciasis where the community through its leaders and key informants has distributed Ivermectin tablets across the villages and communities to save on critical costs and human resources for delivery.

The key step is through the community processes which include:

- Engaging communities
- Empowering communities
- Engaging CDI implementers

In the Indian situation, one of the most successful programs has been the "Deworm the World" (Hodges, 2019), where school-based deworming has worked through periodic distribution and treatment of school children through the school establishment for worm infestations. This has freed children from worm infection, improving their health and enabling them to attend school regularly through no sickness absenteeism. This has proved to be a key strategy in adolescent growth and development and has had far-reaching health impacts on LMICs.

Initiative 5 – Community-Based Health Insurance (CBHI)

CBHI is basically a type of health insurance that is targeted at low-income people to offset out-of-pocket expenses in these communities that did not have access to private health insurance or social security & financial protection of state governments The specific feature of CBHIs is the community drives the set-up and its management primarily and the agency mechanism is by people themselves.

CBHI is small in the incorporation and the design features include:

- Pooling of funds for community health risks within a community
- Token contributions are the same for all
- Entitlements are linked to contributions almost always
- Voluntary affiliation
- Non-profit operations

The most noteworthy happened to be the farmers' cooperative in Karnataka and SEWA in Gujarat. As per the website, Yeshasvini a "unique Cooperative Health

Care Scheme launched for the first time in the world is meant for farmers who are members of the Cooperative Societies". It aims to ensure good health for farmer cooperators of Karnataka and has merged with the state health and the national health insurance schemes now. This was launched on 1st June 2003 and has revolutionized rural health care and healing, and from the year 2014–15 it has also been extended to urban cooperatives. Preventing catastrophic health expenditure and providing wage support to the breadwinner of the family are unique features.

A very innovative Community Assisted & Financed Eyecare (Pyda et al., 2011) was carried out by the author under the aegis of the L. V. Prasad Eye Institute, Hyderabad. With the state-sponsored insurance and the move towards central health security measures, these schemes were further subsumed in themselves.

Undermentioned are a few other initiatives under the domain of implementation research as possible examples that readers can derive ideas from in their situations.

- More recently, with the onset of the pandemic and to cater to the non-COVID-19 health needs and consultations of the population, telehealth initiatives have been rolled out with scale and scope to reach larger populations.
- The initiatives to make available generic drugs to drive efforts towards universal health coverage is another aspect of strengthening the health systems approach for affordable health care delivery and ensuring equity in health care.
- Communication strategies like a child to parent and child to a child have emerged as effective implementation research tools to identify and treat ailments and disabilities. A novel method of using schoolchildren to identify impaired glucose tolerance has been used in the Prakasam district of Andhra Pradesh using the Indian Diabetes Risk Score (Sheeladevi et al., 2014).

Samastha (USAID, 2011) in Andhra Pradesh was a very successful implementation research project for HIV/AIDS. It looked at improving access to quality clinical care in facilities, instituting a system of self-assessment and continuous monitoring to prevent infection and improve quality including setting up a digital management information system (MIS) that could track individuals to support program planning and monitoring. The core design included consolidating community outreach services through micro-planning and support groups.

Another area of work is in the field of organ donation where promoting organ donation has involved a lot of innovative strategies and has helped in increasing organ donation and hence more organ transplantations. Strategies to promote this have ranged from grief counselling to hospital organ retrieval programs using innovative communication ideas.

To help the readers also get a deep dive into the implementation research projects, the author describes a few personal experiences as case studies.

Case Study 1 – Framework to Understand the Reasons for High Cesarean Section Rates in Telangana State

Births delivered by caesarean section (CS, %) as per the NFHS 5 (2019–20) rounds were 64.3% in urban and 58.4% in rural areas with a total of 60.7% across the state (NFHS 5, 2021). This is an increase from 57.7% since NFHS 4 (2015–16) to the current round.

The author was commissioned to look at developing a framework for addressing high CS rates in Telangana state, India in the year 2019 by the area office of UNICEF with the specific objectives:

- To gather evidence by undertaking a mixed-method study in units/facilities across the spectrum of rates of C-sections in the state and their beneficiaries in the community
- To develop a framework for proposing interventions to reduce the rates of C-section using the information from the data collected for the above objective

A mixed methods study approach comprising IDI, focus group discussions (FGD), and stakeholder engagement for primary data collection with observation and record linkage was carried out in Karimnagar, Nalgonda as well as Suryapet, Warangal, Hyderabad, Medak, Nirmal, and Wanaparthy districts, which had high, medium, and low rates of CS.

The determinants for CS rates based on data were as follows:

- Personal and family determinants – Elders and peers experience and counselling; plan for second pregnancy; lack of financial resources
- System determinants – PHC medical officers and ANMs/SN availability at the facility; transition management and availability of labour room staff; non-availability of surgical facilities in the vicinity (especially private); distance from referral facility
- Policy determinants – Commission of Health and Family Welfare efforts and responsiveness and the recent introduction of a tracking system

Broadly, the recommendations emerging from the data were as follows:

- To urgently address "acute staff shortages" at key positions within the care provision
- To consider and invest in capacity building of staff in existing locations through continuous education programs and about newer developments in the area
- Development and adherence to guidelines and best practice protocols for managing pregnancy and childbirth at all institutional levels
- To allay apprehensions and provide a supportive environment at community and institutional levels to prevent violence and medico-legal issues

- To develop mechanisms of feedback to referral institutions and facilities
- To look at how care can be "personalized" and continuity maintained

From the analysis of the data, the following recommendations emerged:

1. To urgently address "acute staff shortages" at key positions within the care provision
2. To consider and invest in capacity building of staff in existing locations through continuous education programs and about newer developments in the area
3. To develop and adhere to guidelines and best practice protocols for managing pregnancy and childbirth at all institutional levels
4. To allay apprehensions and provide a supportive environment at community and institutional levels to prevent violence and medico-legal issues
5. To provide a feedback system from the referral institution to the referring facility and provider to maintain continuity and personalized care
6. To study the impact of the DBT- KCR kit on institutional deliveries and its consequent CS rates. The implementation action has also been suggested to the state government for consideration in terms of the following:

- Training and posting midwives may be an option in high volume settings.
- Redistribution or creation of positions for staff nurses at PHCs and Area Hospitals.
- Need for dedicated patient counsellors to address the information needs of would-be mothers and families.
- Health care provision staff at community and primary levels need training and empowerment to manage pregnant mothers and family expectations.
- Staff nurse needs a career path as it is felt that over a period of time they lose motivation to work.
- Doctors and specialists need training and support to undertake VBAC in previous CS cases.
- Doctors and specialists need soft skills training and also negotiation skills to address legal and violence-related issues.
- Decision support system guidelines and protocols at each level of care of a pregnant woman are needed.
- The guidelines and protocols need to be followed to prevent unnecessary CS and offered where it is absolutely needed.
- Creating a system or mechanism within the workplace especially in high volume settings to prevent medico-legal and violence against health care personnel.
- Documentation and communication systems are to be put in place as per the need and context. There is a need to employ social media or mobile platforms to provide feedback mechanisms within the system to build confidence among providers and the community about care modality.

- A research study is to be undertaken to find out whether institutional deliveries promoted by Direct Benefit Transfer (KCR kit) have also resulted in the proportionate increase in CS rates.

Following the earlier research, it culminated in a funded project called "ReJudge Study: Reducing rates of non-medically indicated CS through an Open Access multi-media evidence and behavioural change program for lawyers and judges". This is supported by the Bill & Melinda Gates Foundation the University as part of the larger consortium headed by the University of Central Lancashire UK.

The project aims to re-orientate maternity malpractice litigation from a normative assumption that intervention is always beneficial for mother and baby, to one based on human rights, evidence, and amelioration.

Currently, the work includes scoping reviews, formative work, and a toolkit development by consensus, feasibility/acceptability testing with before and after measures, and finalizing the toolkit.

Case Study 2: A Micro-Needle Transdermal Patch for Supplementing Critical Micronutrients for Prevention and Control of Anemia (DBT project 2019) – Health Technology Assessment

An important facet of implementation research in health technology assessment is that apart from the availability, accessibility, affordability, and acceptability of the novel technology being assured, the accountability and quality including acceptance by the stakeholders become paramount. In that direction, we are looking at a needed aspect of health technology assessment which is to understand the perceptions of service providers and end-users of a novel way of supplementing critical micronutrients using a micro-needle transdermal patch. The micro-needle technology is novel and has not been tried to supplement micronutrients earlier. The micronutrient is fabricated as nano-needles and applied across the skin and they release the nutrients in a sustained manner.

Currently, there are no nutrient-containing micro-needles (MNs) in use in the Indian context and even worldwide there are few iron-containing patches for daily application that are available and hence this was considered a novel way to supplement much-needed nutrients to the body. It should also be understood that routine administration modalities like oral or injectable have their shortcomings when it comes to micronutrients. Also, there are no long-term sustained release MNs developed. This research in collaboration with Dr. Reddy's Institute of Life Sciences as the patch developer has the following objectives:

- Development of an optimal polymeric matrix with various iron content
- Design and fabrication of MNs
- In vitro and in vivo characterization of the MNs
- Survey primary and secondary stakeholders to identify the key acceptance criteria

The technology developed for manufacturing MNs at a small scale is simple and does not require sophisticated instrumentation and at the same time, the formulation for the patch fabrication is also achieved. It is now being patented. The proof of concept is ready and in vitro experiments have provided the evidence that it can be used as a viable option in human populations.

The implementation question that is being asked and pursued is whether the target population to which it is directed will accept the patch and further utilize it.

Hence, an acceptance and utilization survey was planned and integrated as part of the technology development proposal as the perceptions of the major stakeholders for this health technology is as important as its acceptance among the end-users. The results will provide insights into better development of the health technology for public health use, taking into consideration the views of the end-users or beneficiaries. This has the potential to be used.

Case Study 3: Tribal Health in Telangana State (Tribal Welfare Commissioner, 2020)

The Tribal Welfare Department had commissioned the Department of Anthropology of the University of Hyderabad to develop reports on the profile of the tribal population in the state of Telangana based on surveys and exploratory research. The reports include the following:

- Health status of Particularly Vulnerable Tribal Groups (PTVGs) in the state of Telangana.
- Study of health and illness behaviour in PTVGs in the state of Telangana.
- A baseline for pilot project for home-based neonatal care in tribal dominated mandals is currently ready and generates important research questions for possible implementation research ideas to the implementation portfolio. These reports provide an important baseline to develop suitable implementation research questions to develop a comprehensive tribal health plan for the state.

Case Study 4: Active Bleeding Control

A collaboration pilot program called Active Bleeding Control (ABC) between government and non-governmental agencies in Telangana spearheaded by the Emergency Medical and Research Institute (EMRI) was launched with the intention of attending to the road traffic injuries on the outskirts of Hyderabad city covering a 2.5 million population and 50 km corridor (Ramachandra et al., 2021). Volunteers mostly lay people and commoners were trained and provided with a low-cost "stop the bleed kit" to attend to injuries and provide first responder care and stop bleeding. The initial results are very encouraging with an opportunity to scale it up. This is an example of an innovative implementation research project in a much targeted area of need.

In conclusion, the multidisciplinary nature of implementation research with the problem identification, analysing the determinants, developing solutions, implementing solutions, and evaluating outcomes is the sequence of activities.

The inter- and multidisciplinary nature of implementation research with community-based participatory research, use of qualitative methods including behavioural science research, biostatistics, outcomes research and evaluations, health economics, management, leveraging information and communication technology makes it quite a complex approach but at the same time worthwhile in answering and addressing health problems in LMICs and economies.

It is important to note that as much as raising key questions is important (Rapport et al., 2018), taking them to the key points in conceptualizing and then implementing projects including scaling them up and sustaining them is critical.

Despite the importance of implementation research, it continues to be a neglected field of study because of the lack of understanding of what it is and what it entails. There is also a lack of investment in the implementation of research activities (Vedanthan, 2011). A lot of time is purportedly spent on innovations but very little time on how best to use them.

It is hoped that the readers will be sensitized to the concepts of implementation research and thus would provide an approach to address health care issues confronting public health and primary care in developing and emerging country economies.

References

Anchala, R., Kaptoge, S., Pant, H., Di Angelantonio, E., Franco, O. H., & Prabhakaran, D. (2015). Evaluation of effectiveness and cost-effectiveness of a clinical decision support system in managing hypertension in resource constrained primary health care settings: Results from a cluster randomized trial. *Journal of the American Heart Association, 4*(1), e001213. https://doi.org/10.1161/JAHA.114.001213

Bedford, J., Mackey, S., Parvin, A., Muhit, M., & Murthy, G. V. S. (2013). Reasons for non-uptake of referral: Children with disabilities identified through the Key Informant Method in Bangladesh. *Disability and Rehabilitation, 35*(25), 2164–2170. https://doi.org/10.3109/09638288.2013.770927

Clark, K. D., Miller, B. F., Green, L. A., de Gruy, F. V. III, Davis, M., & Cohen, D. J. 2017). Implementation of behavioral health interventions in real world scenarios: Managing complex change. *Families, Systems, & Health, 35*(1), 36–45. https://doi.org/10.1037/fsh0000239

Community Based Health Insurance (2020, March 7). World Health Organization. Retrieved February 10, 2022, from https://www.who.int/news-room/fact-sheets/detail/community-based-health-insurance-2020

Engelgau, M. M., & Narayan, K. V. (2009). Getting advances in science to make a difference: Translational research for improving diabetes care. *Discovery Medicine, 4*(22), 163–165.

Glasgow, R. E., Harden, S. M., Gaglio, B., Rabin, B., Smith, M. L., Porter, G. C., Ory, M. G., & Estabrooks, P. A. (2019). RE-AIM planning and evaluation framework: Adapting to new science and practice with a 20-year review. *Frontiers in Public Health, 7*, 64. https://doi.org/10.3389/fpubh.2019.00064

Global Burden of Diseases (GBD) (2019). In Lancet, T. (2020). Global health: time for radical change? [Editorial]. *Lancet, 396*(10258), 1129. https://doi.org/10.1016/S0140-6736(20)32131-0. https://www.healthdata.org/gbd/2019

Hodges, L. C. (2019, May 14). *Deworming India.* Evidence Action. Retrieved February 12, 2022, from https://www.evidenceaction.org/deworming-india/

Katabarwa, M. N., Habomugisha, P., Eyamba, A., Byamukama, E., Nwane, P., Arinaitwe, A., Musigire, J., Tushemereirwe, R., & Khainza, A. (2016). Community-directed interventions are practical and effective in low-resource communities: Experience of ivermectin treatment for onchocerciasis control in Cameroon and Uganda, 2004-2010. *International Health, 8*(2), 116–123. https://doi.org/10.1093/inthealth/ihv038

Marshall, M. N. (1996). The key informant technique. *Family Practice, 13*, 92–97. https://citeseerx.ist.psu.edu/viewdoc/download?doi=10.1.1.554.5499&rep=rep1&type=pdf

National Family Health Survey (NFHS-5) (2021). NFHS. Retrieved February 12, 2022, from http://rchiips.org/nfhs/factsheet_NFHS-5.shtml

National Health Mission, Government of India (2013). Program document. Retrieved April 18, 2022, from https://main.mohfw.gov.in/sites/default/files/56987532145632566578.pdf

Nilsen, P. (2020). Making sense of implementation theories, models, and frameworks. In: Albers B., Shlonsky A., Mildon R. (Eds), *Implementation Science 3.0*. Springer. https://doi.org/10.1007/978-3-030-03874-8_3

Pal, D. K., Das, T., & Sengupta, S. (1998). Comparison of key informant and survey methods for ascertainment of childhood epilepsy in West Bengal, India. *International Journal of Epidemiology, 27*(4), 672–676. https://doi.org/10.1093/ije/27.4.672

Pandey, A., & Gautam, P. (2020). Key informant methods: An innovative social mobilization strategy to enable community-based diagnosis, treatment, and rehabilitation for people with disability. *Journal of Nepal Health Research Council, 18*(1), 147–149. https://doi.org/10.33314/jnhrc.v18i1.1826

Public Health Foundation of India (2018). Retrieved May 24, 2022, from https://www.healthdata.org/disease-burden-india; https://phfi.org/india-health-of-the-nations-states/

Pyda, G., Shamanna, B. R., Murthy, R., & Khanna, R. C. (2011). Financing eye care in India - community-assisted and financed eye care project (CAFE). *Indian Journal of Ophthalmology, 59*(4), 331. https://doi.org/10.4103/0301-4738.82014

Ramachandra, G., Ramana Rao, G., Tetali, S., Karabu, D., Kanagala, M., Puppala, S., Janumpally, R., Rajanarsing Rao, H., Carr, B., Brooks, S. C., & Nadkarni, V. (2021). Active bleeding control pilot program in India: Simulation training of the community to stop the bleed and save lives from road traffic Injuries. *Clinical Epidemiology and Global Health, 11*, 100729. https://doi.org/10.1016/j.cegh.2021.100729

Rapport, F., Clay-Williams, R., Churruca, K., Shih, P., Hogden, A., & Braithwaite, J. (2018). The struggle of translating science into action: Foundational concepts of implementation science. *Journal of Evaluation in Clinical Practice, 24*(1), 117–126. https://doi.org/10.1111/jep.12741

Sheeladevi, S., Sagar, J., Pujari, S., & Rani, P. K. (2014). Impact of a district-wide diabetes prevention programme involving health education for children and the community. *Health Education Journal, 73*(4), 363–369.

Straus, S., Tetroe, J., & Graham, I. D. (Eds). (2013). *Knowledge Translation in health care: Moving from evidence to practice, 2nd Edition.* ISBN: 978-1-118-41354-8 August 2013 BMJ Books.

The India State-Level Disease Burden Initiative (n.d.). Up to date. Retrieved February 12, 2022, from https://phfi.org/the-work/research/the-india-state-level-disease-burden-initiative/

USAID. (2011). USAID/INDIA, Final evaluation. Samastha Project. Retrieved April 24, 2022, from http://pdf.usaid.gov/pdf_docs/ PDACR514.pdf

Vedanthan, R. (2011). Global health delivery and implementation research: A new frontier for global health. *The Mount Sinai Journal of Medicine*, 78(3), 303–305.

World Health Organization (1999). *What is DOTS?: a guide to understanding the WHO-recommended TB control strategy known as DOTS* (No. WHO/CDS/CPC/TB/99.270). World Health Organization. Retrieved April 24, 2022, from https://apps.who.int/iris/handle/10665/65979

Yeshaswin. (2011). SAHAKARA SINDHU Department of Cooperation, Government of Karnataka. Retrieved February 10, 2022, from http://sahakara.kar.gov.in/yashasivini.html

PART II
Health and Well-Being of Individuals in Society

PART II

5
RESIDENTIAL CROWDING AND SUBJECTIVE WELL-BEING

Mediating Role of Helplessness

Surendra Kumar Sia and P. S. Neethu

More than just a shelter housing provides a sense of security, privacy and comfort to the inhabitants (Suglia, Duarte & Sandel, 2011), and hence inadequate housing condition is found to be an important predictor of physical and mental illness (Suglia, Duarte & Sandel, 2011; Waterston et al., 2015). The structural features of the home (such as multiunit dwelling, housing type, etc.), structural deterioration and the other housing features such as overcrowding and lack of control over housing have been associated with distress symptoms, depression and poor mental health (Sullivan & Chang, 2011). Availability of space is found to be an important dimension of housing quality (OECD, 2021). Several researchers identified the negative effects of overcrowded houses on the health and well-being of the individual (Eurofound, 2012; Solari & Mare, 2012). According to Evans (2003), residential crowding occurs when the number of occupants exceeds the capacity of the available space in the house. A direct association between crowding and adverse health outcomes such as mental health problems and infectious diseases is reported in several studies (Goux & Maurin, 2005). Crowding in one's residential setting has been found to be stressful to the health and well-being of the inhabitants across different cultures (Memmott, Birdsall-Jones & Greenop, 2012).

Nagar and Paulus (1997) identified four components of crowding experience, namely positive relationship, space satisfaction, uncontrolled disturbance and negative relationship. Space satisfaction characterized by the extent of spatial satisfaction in a residential environment can be a major determining factor in perceived crowding (Montana & Adamopoulos, 1984; Torshizian & Grimes, 2014). A positive relationship indicates a supportive relationship, whereas a negative relationship indicates a disruptive and non-supportive relationship with the other residents in the house. Uncontrolled disturbance can arise in residential settings like disturbance from stereos, light, noise and ignored requests. These components are consistent with the contemporary approaches to crowding. Crowding,

DOI: 10.4324/9781003360858-7

owing to lack of privacy or space, can impact behaviour, sleep patterns and parent-child interactions (Evans, Ricciuti & Hope, 2010). Hence, the present study made an attempt to analyse the impact of the components of residential crowding on well-being and helplessness. Also, the study attempts to identify the mediating role of helplessness.

Crowding and Subjective Well-Being

The lack of privacy and felt demands experienced in crowded residence has a significant effect on health and well-being (Edwards, Fuller, Vorakitphokatorn & Sermsri, 2019). Chronic residential crowding leads to negative affect, anxiety, depression and other indications of psychological distress (Dunn & Hayes, 2000; Rollings & Evans, 2019).

Very few studies have been carried out on residential crowding in the Indian context. Previous and recent studies state that space satisfaction and a negative relationship in the house predict emotional health and psychological well-being (Jain, 1997; Nagar & Paulus, 1997; Neethu, Ikal & Sia, 2018). Perceived crowding has a significant negative effect on the positive affect, subjective and general well-being of the residents (Sunita, 2002).

H1: Crowding will have a significant negative relationship with subjective well-being

Crowding and Helplessness

Seligman in his helplessness theory postulated that individuals who perceive a lack of control over the environment experience learned helplessness. Feelings of helplessness mainly emerge from suboptimal environmental conditions (Evans & Marcynyszyn, 2004; Lieder, Goodman & Huys, 2013; Rollings & Evans, 2019). Previous literature suggested that high density situations lead to loss of control over the situation. Chronic environmental stressors, like accommodation in dormitories, can induce helplessness (Evans & Stecker, 2004). In another study, Tao, Wu and Wang (2016) observed a positive relationship between residential density and anxiety among college students staying in dormitories. The helplessness behaviour experienced by the individuals in crowd living settings is an indication of their powerlessness to regulate social interaction (Evans & Marcynyszyn, 2004).

H2: Crowding will have a significant positive relationship with helplessness

Helplessness and Subjective Well-Being

Helplessness is found to be associated with physical illness, anxiety and depression (Peterson, Maier & Seligman, 1993; Sparr & Sonnentag, 2008). According to Seligman (1975), helplessness is a psychological state which occurs when events are uncontrollable. As the individuals experience the situation as uncontrollable, they experience heightened negative emotions such as frustration, fear, depression, anxiety and other psychological ill effects. Studies on the direct effect of helplessness on well-being are very few and especially in the Indian context it is clearly absent.

H3: Helplessness will have a significant negative relationship with subjective well-being

Mediating Role of Helplessness

Few researchers found that a crowded living environment relates to learned helplessness (Neethu, 2018). Feeling of helplessness can impair well-being (Ramachandran & George, 2021) and influence self-concept including behavioural adjustment, freedom from anxiety and happiness (Sia & Kaur, 2015). A study by the authors indicated a negative relationship between crowding and subjective well-being. Further, perceived behavioural control mediated partially between crowding and well-being (Neethu, Ikal & Sia, 2018).

H4: Helplessness will mediate the relationship between crowding and subjective well-being

Need and Significance of the Study

Sharing a very small house with other members of the family causes a lack of sufficient space, lack of privacy and negative relationship with the family members. The average number of persons per room in urban Indian families is 2.6 and in rural families it is 2.8 (Government of India, Ministry of Housing and Urban Poverty Alleviation, 2013). So, for an average family with four members, a double bedroom house is required. In Kerala, which is one of the smallest south Indian states, there are 83,843 houses without any exclusive bedrooms amounting to approximately 2% of the total houses in Kerala, where people are exposed to crowding for a longer period of time. Most of the previous studies on crowding focus on dormitory settings, prisons and other secondary environments. But crowding research has to focus more on these populations where a significant number of people from various age groups are exposed to chronic crowding. The present study is one of the first Indian studies to focus on this particular population.

Studies on residential crowding are very few and most of them are carried out on children, primarily focusing on their health and well-being (Evans & Lepore, 1993), academic problems and vulnerability to learned helplessness (Rollings & Evans, 2019). There are few studies that report the behavioural consequences of residential crowding on adults. Mostly the crowding research focused on the direct effect of crowding on the well-being and mental health of the individuals. Most of the Indian studies on crowding also addressed these issues (Jain, 1999; Neethu & Sia, 2017), but systematic studies on mediators and moderators with the application of appropriate statistics are very rare in the Indian context. A few studies carried out in other countries have shown greater interest in revealing the mediating and moderating role of variables (Sun & Budruk, 2017; Rollings & Evans, 2019). The present study made an attempt to reveal the mediating role of learned helplessness in the relationship between crowding and subjective well-being.

Method

Sample

Among the 14 districts in Kerala, Wayanad and Kozhikode districts were selected for the study following purposive sampling. These two districts consisted of a total of 10,005 households (Wayanad – 2440, Kozhikode – 7565) with no exclusive rooms (Census Authority of India, 2011). The researcher randomly selected 150 houses without any exclusive bedrooms. Data were collected from both parents in a house. Out of the 300 questionnaires distributed, 296 completed questionnaires were collected back. After removing the missing data, the final sample consisted of 286 parents. The response rate was 95%. All the participants were within the age group of 25–45 years with an average age of 35 years.

Measures

> *Residential crowding experience Scale (Nagar & Paulus, 1997):* This is a 26 items scale with five-point Likert-type response patterns ranging from very much to very less. Space satisfaction (SS), uncontrolled disturbances (UD), negative relationship (NR) and positive relationship (PR) are the four dimensions of this scale. The reliability coefficients for the subscales are .83, .86, .73 and .73 for space satisfaction, positive relationship, negative relationship and uncontrolled disturbance, respectively.
>
> *Subjective well-being inventory (Diener, Emmons, Larsen & Griffin, 1985):* The scale is focused clearly and solely on life satisfaction as a cognitive judgmental evaluation of one's life as a whole. The items were measured on a seven-point Likert scale ranging from very strongly agree to very strongly disagree. The test-retest reliability was .83 and internal consistency ranged from .74 to .93.
>
> *Learned helplessness scale (Quinless & Nelson, 1988):* This is a 20 items measure on a four-point Likert scale. This scale comprises five factors. Factor 1 is labelled as internality-externality, which consists of five items. Factor 2 is globality-specific, which also comprises five items. Factor 3 is named as stability-instability, containing six items. Factor 4 is the ability-inability to control and factor 5 is the individual's choice of situations, consisting of two items each. Cronbach's alpha of the total scale was .95.

```
            Helplessness
           /            \
          /              \
    Crowding ──────────> Well-being
```

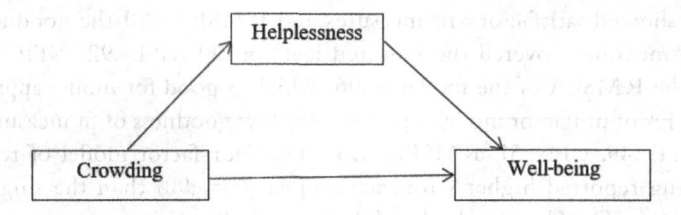

FIGURE 5.1 Proposed Model for the Mediating Role of Helplessness on the Relationship Between Crowding and Well-Being.

Data Collection

All the questionnaires were translated into the local language of Malayalam with the help of language experts through the method of forward and backward translation (Brislin, 1970). Approval was obtained for the study from the Institute Ethical Committee (Human Studies), Pondicherry University. Informed consents were obtained from participants.

Data Analysis

The Pearson product-moment correlation was carried out to find out the degree and magnitude of the relationship between the study variables. The present study analysed the proposed model (Figure 5.1) by using Anderson and Gerbing's (1988) two-step procedures. The first step in the procedure is to develop a measurement model with an acceptable model fit using confirmatory factor analysis (CFA). The maximum-likelihood method in the AMOS version 20 was used to test the measurement model. After performing the CFA, the reliability and validity of the constructs were computed. The internal consistency reliability of all the six constructs was calculated by using SPSS Version 20. The second step was to analyse the structural model by using the developed measurement models. Model fit indices were tested to check the appropriateness of the model. The significance of the indirect effect was tested by using bootstrapping in AMOS (Muthén & Muthén, 2005).

Results

Confirmatory factor analysis using AMOS version 20 was used to check all three measurement models, namely residential crowding, subjective well-being and helplessness. The single factor as well as multi factor models of all the constructs were tested to check the model fit.

Measurement Model Analysis for Residential Crowding

CFA of both four-dimensional and uni-dimensional models were done and fit measures were checked. After removing low factor loading items in model 1 and applying modification indices model 2 (19 items/4 factors) was run. This model showed satisfactory fit measures and RMSEA. All the goodness of fit (GOF) measures covered the required level of .90 (GFI: .92, NFI: .91, CFI: .92). The RMSEA of the model is .06, which is good for model appropriateness. CFA of unifactor model reported very low goodness of fit measures (GFI: .61, NFI: .49, CFI: .51, RMSEA: .15). The four-factor model of residential crowding reported higher Cronbach's alpha (α = .90) than the single factor model (α = .72). The Cronbach's alpha for each dimension, namely space satisfaction (with four retained items having factor loadings .44, .43, .44 and .57), positive relationship (with five retained items having factor loadings .84, .57, .82, .58 and .56), negative relationship (with six retained items having factor loadings .65, .77, .72, .73, .71 and .82) and uncontrolled disturbance (with four retained items having factor loadings .78, .87, .86 and .47) are .71, .77, .89, and .81, respectively.

Measurement Model Analysis for Subjective Well-Being

The CFA of five-item subjective well-being scale was carried out to check the model fitness. The results indicate that all the items in the subjective well-being scale reported higher factor loadings (SWB1 = .77, SWB2 = .67, SWB3 = .78, SWB4 = .62, SWB5 = .66), and the five-item measurement model showed satisfactory model fit indices with GFI = .99, NFI = .99, CFI = .97 and RMSEA = .07. The internal consistency reliability of the model was .92.

Measurement Model for Learned Helplessness

The confirmatory factor analysis was carried out to check whether the five-factor (internality-externality, globality-specificity, stability-instability, ability-inability, choice of situations) 20-item measurement model of learned helplessness were fit in the observed data and then a five-factor model with 16 items. Both failed the goodness of fit test. Then, the fit measures of the one-factor model were checked after removing the items with low factor loading, SI1 (β = .28) and SI5 (.09). The unifactor model with 18 items (Figure 5.2) reported satisfactory factor loadings (GFI = .92, NFI = .89, CFI = .91, RMSEA = .07). Two out of 20 items were removed from the final questionnaire due to low factor loadings. The internal consistency of the one-factor model is .91.

Correlation: The correlation analysis shows a significant positive relationship between space satisfaction dimensions of crowding and subjective well-being (r = .49**). The other two dimensions of crowding, that is, negative relationship with other residents and uncontrolled disturbances in the house, are negatively correlated with subjective well-being having r = −.48** and r = −.51**. respectively. However, both these dimensions have significant positive relationship with learned helplessness with r = 22** and r = .29**, respectively. Learned helplessness reported a significant negative relationship with subjective well-being (r = −.24**) as reported in Table 5.1.

Residential Crowding and Subjective Well-Being 79

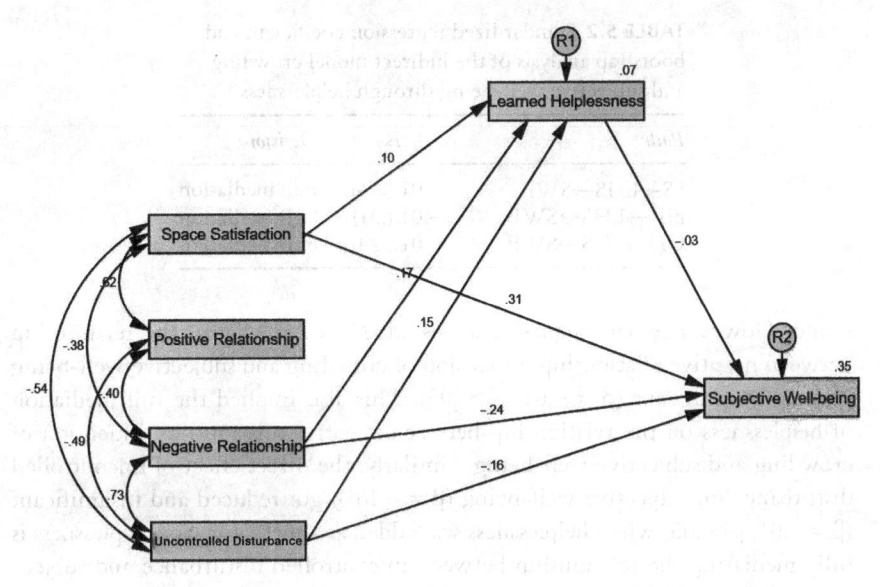

FIGURE 5.2 Structural Model for Crowding and Subjective Well-Being Mediated by Learned Helplessness.

Structural Model

The direct effect of space satisfaction on subjective well-being was significant and positive ($\beta = .31^{**}$); when helplessness was added as a mediator, the relationship became insignificant ($\beta = .01$). Hence, the result implies that helplessness is fully mediating the relationship between space satisfaction and subjective well-being. While testing the direct effect of the negative relationship dimension of crowding on subjective well-being, a significant negative relationship ($\beta = -.27^{**}$) was

TABLE 5.1 Descriptive statistics, validity measures and correlation coefficients of the constructs

Variables	Mean	SD	AVE	CR	SS	PR	NR	UD	CR	SWB	LHS
SS	2.77	.81	.52	.73	(.72)						
PR	3.29	.93	.57	.81	.62**	(.75)					
NR	2.36	1.07	.54	.88	−.38**	−.40**	(.73)				
UD	2.61	1.29	.58	.84	−.54**	−.49**	.73**	(.76)			
CR	2.76	.47	.55	.82	.15**	.20**	.71**	.63**	(.74)		
SWB	2.61	1.16	.54	.70	.49**	.08	−.48**	−.51**	−.22**	(.73)	
LHS	3.02	.22	.54	.79	−.24**	−.09	.29**	.22**	.22**	−.24**	(.73)

Notes: *p < .05 level of significance; **p < .01 level of significance.

SS – space satisfaction, PR – positive relationship, NR – negative relationship, UD – uncontrolled disturbance, CR – crowding, SWB – subjective well-being, LHS – learned helplessness, SD – standard deviation, AVE – average variance extracted (convergent validity), CR – composite reliability.

Values inside the diagonal parentheses are divergent validity measures ($\sqrt{AVE}$).

TABLE 5.2 Standardized regression coefficient and bootstrap analysis of the indirect model crowding and subjective well-being through helplessness

Path	B	Decision
SS→LHS→SWB	.01 (.24)	Full mediation
NR→LHS→SWB	−.01 (.31)	Full mediation
UD→LHS→SWB	−.01 (.24)	Full mediation

found. However, when helplessness was added as a mediator, the relationship between negative relationship dimension of crowding and subjective well-being became insignificant ($\beta = -.01$, $p > .05$). This also implied the full mediation of helplessness on the relationship between negative relationship dimension of crowding and subjective well-being. Similarly, the direct effect of uncontrolled disturbance on subjective well-being ($\beta = -.16^{**}$) got reduced and insignificant ($\beta = -.01$, $p > .05$) when helplessness was added as a mediator. So, helplessness is fully mediating the relationship between uncontrolled disturbance and subjective well-being. Table 5.2 and Figure 5.2 present the results.

The estimated structural model for the full mediation of helplessness on the relationship between crowding and subjective well-being is presented in Figure 5.2. The model reported good fit measures with GFI = .99, CFI = .99, NFI = .99 and RMSEA = .01.

Discussion

The first major finding of the present study is that the space satisfaction dimension of crowding is positively related to subjective well-being, whereas the negative relationship and uncontrolled disturbance dimensions of crowding are negatively related to subjective well-being. The findings are in line with the previous studies (Neethu, Ikal & Sia, 2018). It has been reported by other researchers that lack of available space and felt demands experienced in crowded residence can have a significant effect on health and well-being (Arku, Luginaah, Mkandawire, Baiden & Asiedu, 2011).

Lack of quiet or comfortable space in the house affects the life significantly. The physical characteristics of the housing unit and the extent of crowding in the home reduce the well-being (Solari & Mare, 2012). When an individual feels that the amount of space available in the home is insufficient, which interferes with his/her daily activities and invades the privacy, that leads to lowered well-being. Some researchers identified the relationship between space and well-being (Van Praag, Frijters & Ferrer-i-Carbonell, 2003). In a similar study, researchers observed that cramped living conditions lead to lower psychological well-being (Hu & Coulter, 2017).

Other components which are negatively related to subjective well-being are negative relationship and uncontrolled disturbance in the house. If the parents in the crowded houses feel that other members in the house are making unwanted demands on them or that they are being ignored and criticized by others, and are subjected to hostility, it can lead to the development of a negative relationship with the residents. This negative relationship in turn can reduce the subjective well-being (Asiyanbola, 2012). Excessive noise and distraction caused by others in the house lead to frustration and irritability negatively contributing to well-being. Diener's (1994) model of well-being identifies three environmental factors predicting well-being. These are an individual's feeling, perception about environmental settings and economic consequences. Of the three factors, feelings and perceptions about the environment are well reflected in the present study.

The second finding indicates a negative relationship between the space satisfaction dimension of crowding and learned helplessness whereas positive relationship between uncontrolled disturbance and helplessness. People feel better when they feel that they can control their environment (Taylor & Brown, 1988). Uncontrollability is the major factor which leads to helplessness (Winterflood & Climie, 2020). Learned helplessness, which is an individual's reaction to an uncontrollable situation, leads to low subjective well-being (Shaw, 2020; Winterflood & Climie, 2020). The findings of the present study substantiate the findings of the previous researcher which suggest that lack of privacy and felt demands in the crowded residence lead to uncontrollability over the environment (Riedel et al., 2018).

When an individual experiences campiness due to insufficiency of space, it more likely leads to learned helplessness. This finding is in line with the previous researcher who has also observed that crowding causes learned helplessness in people (Rollings & Evans, 2019). Usually, the initial response to uncontrollable situations like crowding is to adapt or cope. Failure in attempts to cope leads to realisation of a lack of control over the situation (Seligman & Maier, 1967) culminating in learned helplessness behaviour (Evans & Marcynyszyn, 2004).

Learned helplessness is found to be negatively related to subjective well-being. Parents who experience helplessness due to chronic exposure crowding measured low in subjective well-being (Shaw, 2020; Ramachandran & George, 2021).

The findings related to the second objective indicate that learned helplessness is fully mediating the relationship between the space satisfaction dimension of crowding and subjective well-being. The relationship between space inadequacy and low well-being was observed to occur through learned helplessness. Moreover, helplessness also fully mediates the relationship between the uncontrolled disturbance dimension of crowding and subjective well-being. The disruptive and non-supportive relationship as well as uncontrolled disturbances in the residential settings lowers the subjective well-being of the residents (Neethu, 2018). As per the authors' knowledge, no study has been conducted on the mediating role of helplessness in the relationship between crowding and well-being. Few researchers found that a crowded living environment relates to learned helplessness (Evan & Marcynyszyn, 2004) and feeling of helplessness will impair well-being (Winterflood & Climie, 2020). A study conducted by

Nicassio, Schuman, Radojevic & Weisman (1999) found that an individual's feeling of helplessness acts as a cognitive mediator between pain-related outcomes and well-being. Similarly, it was found to mediate the impact of stressors on cognitive distortion, disease severity (Smith, Peck & Ward, 1990) and emotional instability (Van der Werf, Evers, Jongen & Bleijenberg, 2003).

Limitations

Since the study was restricted to parents living in houses without any exclusive bedroom, the result cannot be generalized to individuals who are exposed to other crowded settings such as prisons, refugee camps, slums and flats. Another limitation of the present study is that the research design is cross-sectional, which may not portray the exact picture of causality. Further crowding research with a longitudinal design is recommended.

Conclusion

Based upon the findings of the present study, the authors came up with some useful implications with respect to both theory and practice. Findings of the study state that space satisfaction and positive relationship in the house display more subjective well-being, whereas the negative relationship and uncontrolled disturbances in the household lead to low subjective well-being. This is one of the major theoretical importance of the present study and it is a matter of concern for environmental psychologists, designers, government and policymakers. Importantly, residential crowding is also found to be an important risk factor for the transmission of major categories of close-contact infectious diseases (Pelissari & Diaz-Quijano, 2017; Weber et al., 2017) and non-infectious health disorders (Kohen, Bougie & Guèvremont, 2015; Waters, Boyce, Eskenazi & Alkon, 2016). Von Seidlein, Alabaster, Deen and Knudsen (2020) reported that crowding has the potential for exposure and transmission of COVID-19. To reduce the experience of crowding and its negative impacts, some architectural variations in the houses leave scope for more sunlight and higher ceiling reduces crowding.

The findings show that learned helplessness is an important mediator which influences the effect of crowding on subjective well-being. The necessity to reduce learned helplessness is implied through this finding. Interventions like cognitive behaviour therapy as well as other architectural changes help to reduce learned helplessness and enhance the subjective well-being of the residents. Design interventions in a built environment reduce uncontrollability as well as helplessness (Rollings & Evans, 2019).

References

Anderson, J. C., & Gerbing, D. W. (1988). Structural equation modeling in practice: A review and recommended two-step approach. *Psychological Bulletin, 103*(3), 411.

Arku, G., Luginaah, I., Mkandawire, P., Baiden, P., & Asiedu, A. B. (2011). Housing and health in three contrasting neighbourhoods in Accra, Ghana. *Social Science & Medicine*, 72(11), 1864–1872.

Asiyanbola, R. A. (2012). Psychological wellbeing, urban household crowding and gender in developing countries: Nigeria. *Developing Country Studies*, 2(11), 127–134.

Brislin, R. W. (1970). Back-translation for cross-cultural research. *Journal of Cross-Cultural Psychology*, 1(3), 185–216.

Census Authority of India (2011). Census 2011 - Household Schedule. Retrieved December 13, 2013, from http://censusindia.gov.in/ Footer_Menus/Right_to_Information/Right_to_Information_List.html

Diener, E. (1994). Assessing subjective well-being: Progress and opportunities. *Social Indicators Research*, 31(2), 103–157.

Diener, E. D., Emmons, R. A., Larsen, R. J., & Griffin, S. (1985). The satisfaction with life scale. *Journal of Personality Assessment*, 49(1), 71–75.

Dunn, J. R., & Hayes, M. V. (2000). Social inequality, population health, and housing: A study of two Vancouver neighbourhoods. *Social Science &Medicine*, 51(4), 563–587.

Edwards, J. N., Fuller, T. D., Vorakitphokatorn, S., & Sermsri, S. (2019). *Household crowding and its consequences*. Routledge, New York.

Eurofound (2012). *Inadequate housing in Europe: Costs and consequences*. Publications Office of the European Union, Luxembourg.

Evans, G. (2003). The built environment and mental health. *Journal of Urban Health*, 80(4), 536–55.

Evans, G. W., & Lepore, S. J. (1993). Household crowding and social support: A quasi-experimental analysis. *Journal of Personality and Social Psychology*, 65(2), 308–316.

Evans, G. W., & Marcynyszyn, L. A. (2004). Environmental justice, cumulative environmental risk, and health among low-and middle-income children in upstate New York. *American Journal of Public Health*, 94(11), 1942–1944.

Evans, G. W., Ricciuti, H. N., & Hope, S. (2010). Crowding and cognitive development: The mediating role of maternal responsiveness among 36-month-old children. *Environmental Behaviour*, 42(1), 135–148.

Evans, G. W., & Stecker, R. (2004). Motivational consequences of environmental stress. *Journal of Environmental Psychology*, 24(2), 143–165.

Goux, D., & Maurin, E. (2005). The effect of overcrowded housing on children's performance at school. *Journal of Public Economics*, 89, 797–819

Government of India, Ministry of Housing and Urban Poverty Alleviation (2013). *State of housing in India: A statistical compendium*. Retrieved April 28, 2022, http://www.nbo.nic.in/Images/PDF/ Housing_in_India _Compendium_English_Version.pdf

Hu, Y., & Coulter, R. (2017). Living space and psychological well-being in urban China: Differentiated relationships across socio-economic gradients. *Environment and Planning A*, 49(4), 911–929.

Jain, S. (1999). Symbiosis vs. crowding-out: The interaction of formal and informal credit markets in developing countries. *Journal of Development Economics*, 59(2), 419–444.

Jain, U. (1997). *The feeling of crowding and its psychological consequences*. Har-Anand Publications, New Delhi.

Kohen, D. E., Bougie, E., & Guèvremont, A. (2015). *Housing and health among Inuit children*. Statistics Canada. Retrieved from https://www150.statcan.gc.ca/n1/pub/82-003-x/2015011/article/14223-eng.htm on 3rd October, 2022.

Lieder, F., Goodman, N. D., & Huys, Q. J. (2013). *Learned helplessness and generalization*. In Proceedings of the Annual Meeting of the Cognitive Science Society, Volume 35, 900–905.

Memmott, P., Birdsall-Jones, C., & Greenop, K. (2012). *Australian indigenous house crowding*. Australian Housing and Urban Research Institute Melbourne, Australia.

Montana, D., & Adamopoulos, J. (1984). The perception of crowding in interpersonal situation: Affective and behavioural responses. *Environment and Behaviour, 16*, 643–666.

Muthén, L. K., & Muthén, B. O. (2005). *Mplus: Statistical analysis with latent variables: User's guide* (pp. 1998–2012). Los Angeles, CA.

Nagar, D., & Paulus, P. B. (1997). Residential crowding experience scale—assessment and validation. *Journal of Community & Applied Social Psychology, 7*(4), 303–319.

Neethu, P. S. (2018). *Impact of residential crowding on parent's wellbeing and parent-child relationship: Mediating role of social support, locus of control and helplessness* (Doctoral dissertation, Department of Applied Psychology, Pondicherry University).

Neethu, P. S, Ikal, R. & Sia, S. K. (2018). Residential crowding, perceived control and subjective well-being among students staying in hostel dormitory. *Journal of the Indian Academy of Applied Psychology, 44*(1), 4252.

Neethu, P. S., & Sia, S.K. (2017). Residential crowding, psychological distress and the mediating role of social support among dormitory residents. *Indian Journal of Health and Wellbeing, 8*(5), 410–416.

Nicassio, P. M., Schuman, C., Radojevic, V., & Weisman, M. H. (1999). Helplessness as a mediator of health status in fibromyalgia. *Cognitive Therapy and Research, 23*(2), 181–196.

OECD (2021). OECD Affordable Housing Database: December 2021 indicators. Retrieved April 28, 2022, from http://www.oecd.org/social/affordable-housing-database.htm

Pelissari, D. M., & Diaz-Quijano, F. A. (2017). Household crowding as a potential mediator of socioeconomic determinants of tuberculosis incidence in Brazil. *PLoS One, 12*(4), e0176116.

Peterson, C., Maier, S. F., & Seligman, M. E. (1993). *Learned helplessness: A theory for the age of personal control*. Oxford University Press, New York.

Quinless, F. W., & Nelson, M. A. M. (1988). Development of a measure of learned helplessness. *Nursing Research, 37*(1), 11–15.

Ramachandran, M., & George, S. (2021). Learned helplessness, psychological wellbeing, and proenvironment care behaviour among victims of frequent floods in Kerala. *Journal of Neurosciences in Rural Practice, 12*(01), 137–144.

Riedel, N., Köckler, H., Scheiner, J., van Kamp, I., Erbel, R., Loerbroks, A., Claßen, T., & Bolte, G. (2018). Home as a place of noise control for the elderly? A cross-sectional study on potential mediating effects and associations between road traffic noise exposure, access to a quiet side, dwelling-related green and noise annoyance. *International Journal of Environmental Research and Public Health, 15*(5), 1036. https://doi.org/10.3390/ijerph15051036

Rollings, K. A., & Evans, G. W. (2019). Design moderators of perceived residential crowding and chronic physiological stress among children. *Environment and Behaviour, 51*(5), 590–621.

Seligman, M. E. (1975). *Helplessness: On depression, development, and death*. WH Freeman/Times Books/Henry Holt & Co, New York.

Seligman, M. E., & Maier, S. F. (1967). Failure to escape traumatic shock. *Journal of Experimental Psychology, 74*(1), 1.

Shaw, S. C. (2020). Hopelessness, helplessness and resilience: The importance of safeguarding our trainees' mental wellbeing during the COVID-19 pandemic. *Nurse Education in Practice, 44*, 102780.

Sia, S. K., & Kaur, M. (2015). Self-concept of helpless and mastery oriented children. *Journal of Psychosocial Research, 10*(2).

Smith, T. W., Peck, J. R., & Ward, J. R. (1990). Helplessness and depression in rheumatoid arthritis. *Health Psychology, 9*(4), 377.
Solari, S. D., & Mare, R. D. (2012). Housing crowding effects on children's wellbeing. *Social Science Research, 41,* 464–476.
Sparr, J. L., & Sonnentag, S. (2008). Feedback environment and well-being at work: The mediating role of personal control and feelings of helplessness. *European Journal of Work and Organizational Psychology, 17*(3), 388–412.
Suglia, S. F., Duarte, C. S., & Sandel, M. T. (2011). Housing quality, housing instability, and maternal mental health. *Journal of Urban Health, 88*(6), 1105–1116.
Sullivan, W. C., & Chang, C. Y. (2011). *Mental health and the built environment.* In *Making healthy places.* Island Press, Washington, DC.
Sun, Y. Y., & Budruk, M. (2017). The moderating effect of nationality on crowding perception, its antecedents, and coping behaviours: A study of an urban heritage site in Taiwan. *Current Issues in Tourism, 20*(12), 1246–1264.
Sunita (2002). *Crowding and wellbeing* [Unpublished doctoral dissertation]. Maharshi Dayanand University, Rohtak.
Tao, Z., Wu, G., & Wang, Z. (2016). The relationship between high residential density in student dormitories and anxiety, binge eating and Internet addiction: A study of Chinese college students. *Springerplus, 5*(1), 1–8.
Taylor, S. E., & Brown, J. D. (1988). Illusion and well-being: A social psychological perspective on mental health. *Psychological Bulletin, 103*(2), 193.
Torshizian, E., & Grimes, A. (2014). *Residential satisfaction, crowding and density: Evidence over different geographic scales in Auckland.* New Zealand Association of Economists 2014 Conference. Retrieved from https://www.nzae.org.nz/wp-content/uploads/2015/01/Residential_Satisfaction_Crowding_and_Density_ET.pdf on 3rd Oct, 2022
Van der Werf, S. P., Evers, A., Jongen, P. J., &Bleijenberg, G. (2003). The role of helplessness as mediator between neurological disability, emotional instability, experienced fatigue and depression in patients with multiple sclerosis. *Multiple sclerosis, 9*(1), 89–94. https://doi.org/10.1191/1352458503ms854oa
Van Praag, B. M., Frijters, P., & Ferrer-i-Carbonell, A. (2003). The anatomy of subjective well-being. *Journal of Economic Behaviour & Organization, 51*(1), 29–49.
von Seidlein, L., Alabaster, G., Deen, J., & Knudsen, J. (2021). Crowding has consequences: Prevention and management of COVID-19 in informal urban settlements. *Building and Environment, 188,* 107472. https://doi.org/10.1016/j.buildenv.2020.107472
Waters, S. F., Boyce, W. T., Eskenazi, B., & Alkon, A. (2016). The impact of maternal depression and overcrowded housing on associations between autonomic nervous system reactivity and externalizing behaviour problems in vulnerable Latino children. *Psychophysiology, 53*(1), 97–104.
Waterston, S., Grueger, B., Samson, L., & Canadian Paediatric Society, & Community Paediatrics Committee (2015). Housing need in Canada: Healthy lives start at home. *Paediatrics & Child Health, 20*(7), 403–407.
Weber, A., Fuchs, N., Kutzora, S., Hendrowarsito, L., Nennstiel-Ratzel, U., von Mutius, E., Herr, C., Heinze, S., & GME Study Group (2017). Exploring the associations between parent-reported biological indoor environment and airway-related symptoms and allergic diseases in children. *International Journal of Hygiene and Environmental Health, 220*(8), 1333–1339. https://doi.org/10.1016/j.ijheh.2017.09.002
Winterflood, H., & Climie, E. A. (2020). Learned helplessness. The Wiley encyclopedia of personality and individual differences: *Personality Processes and Individual Differences,* 269–274.

6
HEALTH IN THE CULTURALLY CHANGING UNDERDEVELOPED ADIVASI COMMUNITIES

Purnima Awasthi, Madhurima Mukherjee, and R. C. Mishra

The Adivasi Context of India

The Indian society represents a culturally plural society formed by the amalgamation of different religious, linguistic, and ethnic groups, each group having its unique sociocultural features. The Adivasi represent one such group with a distinct language, physical features, mode of subsistence, habitat, development, stratification, and traditions making them greatly different from the mainstream society. Different terms such as Adivasi, Tribal, First Peoples, Native People, Aboriginals, and Indigenous Peoples have been used to describe the people who are indigenous to the soil, although each term has its historical and sociopolitical significance. India is home to 705 distinct tribes that contribute to the ethnocultural diversity of the country and account for 8.6% of the country's population (Registrar General & Census Commissioner of India, 2011). Article 342 of the Constitution of India recognizes these groups as 'anusoochit janjati' or Scheduled Tribes (ST) who are tribal communities or groups within these communities which have been declared as such by the President through a public notification. However, this list is not exhaustive as it does not include all those who identify themselves as tribals. Therefore, the term 'Adivasi' seems to be more appropriate to describe people who value their tribal lineage and still practise a relatively traditional lifestyle. The Gond, Bhil, Santhal, Great Andamanese, Khasi, Munda, and Bhutia are some of the major Adivasi groups in India.

For centuries, the Adivasi people have clustered and settled in geographically inaccessible areas such as forests and hilly regions and have primarily depended on hunting-gathering, agriculture, and forest resources for their survival. The Adivasi do not represent a homogeneous community. Based on their economic activities, Mishra et al. (1996) classified them into four distinct groups, namely

DOI: 10.4324/9781003360858-8

the hunting-gathering group, rudimentary agricultural group, irrigation agricultural group, and urban, industrial wage-earning group. Over time under the influence of developmental programmes, some Adivasi people, mostly agriculturalists, have shifted to business or daily-wage employment and in this process have adopted some of the cultural and psychological qualities of the members of other groups. Contact and interaction with the members of other groups have led to alterations in lifestyles. While many groups and mostly the youth have adapted to the lifestyle offered by the mainstream society, there are some groups such as hunter-gatherers or rudimentary agriculturalists who retain their traditional lifestyle.

This chapter concerns the role of cultural change on the major health issues of Adivasi people. Before discussing the research findings, we briefly describe the process of culture change and acculturation. We then discuss the prevalent physical and mental health problems of Adivasi undergoing cultural change. Through these studies, we intend to identify how the problems of Adivasi people are different from the members of other communities. Towards the end, we discuss the implications of these findings and the importance of considering cultural factors during policymaking.

Increased Intercultural Contact and Acculturation

For centuries the Adivasi have remained in isolation. Since colonial times, contact has been established with them for various purposes such as exploiting their natural resources and changing their traditional values and customs. After independence, different government and non-governmental organizations have attempted to uplift their educational, health, and socio-economic status and integrate them with mainstream society. These efforts at contact have resulted in noteworthy sociocultural changes. Psychological studies on Adivasi communities undergoing sociocultural change have taken different approaches. The first approach explains the modernization tradition which views changes as a linear movement from less desirable (traditional) to more desirable (modern) states. It is essentially the inculcation of the western way of life. This approach considers 'modernity' as a valued goal and thus focuses on the removal of 'unhealthy cultural practices' and the development of 'health modernity' in Adivasi people through intervention programmes (Inkeles & Smith, 1974).

A second approach comes from the industrialization and urbanization of the Adivasi belts. For instance, industrialization and bans on the free use of forest resources have led to the displacement and relocation of Adivasi groups forcing them to look for alternate jobs. A transition from subsistence mode to daily wage-earning jobs, gradual replacement of indigenous languages by majority language, increasing urbanization, and increased emphasis on modern education and healthcare system have brought about new opportunities as well as unforeseen challenges. Mishra (2017) notes that the introduction to a foreign way of life and dissonance between traditional culture and modern life have resulted in increased stressors, greater mental health problems, and a loss of happiness for the Adivasi groups in India.

A third approach, which forms the base of this chapter, is that of 'ethnic group relations'. According to this approach, sociocultural changes are viewed as resulting from contact with the members of other cultural groups. This process of culture change resulting from continuous first-hand contact of two independent cultural groups over a period of time is termed 'acculturation' (Redfield et al., 1936). This approach considers the multidirectional changes taking place in the cultural and psychological domains of both the individual and the group as adaptations to the demands of the new situation.

A direct consequence of intercultural contact is acculturation. Acculturation is a form of cultural transmission that results from contact with or influence of another cultural group and its members (Sam & Berry, 2010). Changes during the process of acculturation occur at both subjective and objective levels. Objective changes refer to the visible changes in lifestyle such as changes in clothing, language, diet, housing, and so on. Subjective changes are more latent as they take place inside the minds of people. Identifying the subjective changes is tricky and may be done through culturally sensitive instruments. Such measures tap the various changes in attitudes, values, and perceptions, giving an indirect idea as to the influence of acculturation experiences. Adivasi people may choose one of the four acculturation strategies during the process of acculturation. They can hold onto their own culture and avoid contact with the majority culture (traditional or separated), can have a strong identification with the majority culture while discarding their own culture (acculturated or assimilated), and can accept and interact with both cultures (bicultural or integrated) or neither culture (marginalized). Mishra et al. (1996) have added a fifth strategy of 'coexistence' to this model based on their studies on Adivasi groups in India. Coexistence acknowledges the differences between groups and lets the groups exist together without any comparison or compromise.

The Need to Study Adivasi Health

Cross-cultural health psychology attempts to understand the consequences of intercultural contact on health. Health is not a mere reflection of the health status of individuals but rather the development of society in educational, socio-economic, cultural, and political domains. While the most endorsed definition of health as 'a state of physical, mental, social, and spiritual wellbeing of individuals, not merely the absence of disease and infirmity' (World Health Organization, 2008) is accepted by medical practitioners, research suggests that the meaning of health and illness is culturally construed (Radley, 2004). Health status is intimately associated with cultural values and traditions as well as a socio-economic and political organization. The health problems of Adivasis are distinct from the majority of society as their lifestyles as well as diseases are governed by their habitat, ecology, diet, and genetics. Hence, presenting a universally acceptable picture of health becomes a challenging task.

Research on acculturation and health has been carried out worldwide on immigrants, refugees, indigenous groups, and minority groups. Studies have also made comparisons based on education and urban-rural contexts, but these studies often miss the cultural perspectives. The generalization of those findings on Adivasi groups may be erroneous. Therefore, in Adivasi health research, it becomes important to focus on local ecological and cultural concepts and how contact with other cultures affects their health status.

Influence of Acculturation on Physical Health

A perusal of health conditions and disease profiles of Adivasi communities across the country reveals that diseases affecting these populations differ by region, depending on environmental conditions, and sociocultural practices. A thematic analysis of various researches conducted in Adivasi areas of Rajasthan, Madhya Pradesh, Gujarat, and Orissa revealed that certain diseases like anemia, respiratory infections, diarrhea, nutrient deficiency, skin diseases, intestinal infections, goiter, yaws, malaria, guinea worm, sicklecell diseases, and sexually transmitted diseases are endemic in these areas (Basu, 2000; Indian Council of Medical Research, 2002). In Godam Line village in Darjeeling, West Bengal, a high prevalence of diarrhea, cough and cold, dysentery, hypertension, vision problems, and arthritis was found in women (Sarkar, 2016). Similarly, high mortality in the Karbi, Khasi, Jaintia and Rabha tribes in Northeast India was found due to malaria, anemia, malnourishment, tuberculosis, injuries, and accidents (Singh, 2014). Most people in these communities believe that the wrath of goddesses such as *Badi Mata, Sitla Mata*, and *Tejajee* is responsible for diseases like typhoid, measles, chickenpox, anemia, and snake bites, and thus, for treatment, they rely on traditional health practitioners and herbalists (Zou, 2016). Given that according to the 2011 census 40.6% of Adivasi were below the poverty line, their dismal health status is not surprising.

In an account of the health status of remote rural Kharwar Adivasi groups of the Indian society, culture has been found to play an important role in the health beliefs and behaviours of a variety of health problems such as diarrhea, jaundice, malaria, pneumonia, and eczema, which affect the life of a large number of the Kharwar people (Awasthi & Mishra, 2017; Mishra, 2009). These studies focus on the analysis of beliefs about causality, control, and consequences of these health problems. Findings reveal that Kharwars attributed causes of health problems either to themselves (e.g., careless attitude, bad habits) or to external factors (e.g., environmental hazards, god's wish). Often a coexistence of both sets of factors has been reported. In most cases, for treatment, they rely on local healers. It is their trust in the folk-healing systems and poor accessibility to modern healthcare facilities that lead them to seek treatment from the family, neighbourhood, and *ojha* (exorcist) even today. In the Indian cultural context, concepts of God, spirits, *karma*, and fate are transmitted to children as indispensable lessons, both informal (e.g., school) and informal (e.g., family, neighbourhood) settings. With this kind of socialization, people consider external factors accountable not only for the causation but also for the control of health problems.

Some of our studies (e.g., Awasthi et al., 2006, 2018; Awasthi & Mishra, 2011, 2013) carried out with women suffering from cancer of the cervix and diabetes in the outdoor clinics of hospital settings assessed their illness beliefs and health-seeking behaviour. The role of support systems and coping strategies in perceived controllability and consequences of chronic illness was also studied. The findings broadly suggested that internal (individual, psychosocial) and external (supernatural, environmental) causes of illness coexisted in the belief system of patients. The degree of social support received from families and friends was positively related to the physiological and psychological well-being of the patients. A high level of social support tended to reduce the severity of the negative consequence of illness. Those indicating a high level of social support also strongly believed that the illness was either in their control or in the doctor's control. A high level of social support reduced the experience of pain associated with the disease and promoted hope for better outcomes. In the case of cancer, it was noted that the patients who believed that a doctor can control their health problem (called 'doctor-control') reported lesser psychological and interpersonal consequences, lesser pain of illness, and greater hope for positive outcomes of illness than those who believed that they could control the disease (called 'self-control'). In the case of diabetes, belief in 'self-control' was found to be related to less physiological and psychological consequences, less pain of illness, and greater hope for positive outcomes. On the other hand, belief in 'doctor-control' was found to be related to fewer psychological consequences and greater hope for positive outcomes. These findings allow us to posit a similar pattern of relationship between control beliefs and the well-being of people representing weaker sections of societies by bringing out the cultural and social aspects of health. Right from the perception of health problems to their treatment, people's cultural context seems to play an important role.

Social and cultural changes taking place in several underprivileged communities add further complexity to health issues. Adivasi people are strong believers in supernatural healing, which is closely associated with cultural aspects of their life connected to nature and harmony with the environment. The concepts of etiology of disease in 'modern' society are attributed to natural phenomena that involve physiological malfunctioning of the body and poor lifestyle choices. On the other hand, in Adivasi communities, the greater emphasis lies on supernatural factors such as the evil eye, the rage of local deities, and the relationship with nature and the supernatural world. Even today, most Adivasi societies rely more on folkhealing in comparison to modern treatment facilities and less than 50% of the Adivasi from most Indian states utilize the public health system (Malakar, 2020). Boro and Saikia (2020) interviewed 60 men and women of the Bodo and Rabha tribes of Assam to identify the barriers to healthcare services among them.

They found a high reliance on traditional medicine prescribed by local healers known as 'Kabiraj' or 'Ojha' due to their innate faith in traditional medicines and their suitability for their bodies. A few excerpts of the interview were 'I am relieved when I use traditional medicine since I am accustomed to it. I have more faith in traditional medicines' and 'We have been using traditional medicines since birth, and we are used to it. Moreover, sometimes they are more helpful than modern ones'.

Nevertheless, it is important to note that under the impact of modernization, there have been gradual changes in the traditional modes of diagnosis and treatment. A changing outlook in health beliefs and behaviours has been demonstrated by age differences in findings as younger men and women to some extent considered themselves responsible for health problems, whereas the elderly largely attributed health problems to supernatural forces (Sonowal & Praharaj, 2007). Consequently, the younger generation preferred to consult a doctor, while the older generations preferred to consult a healer. However, it is their trust in the folk-healing systems and poor accessibility to modern healthcare facilities that lead them to seek treatment from the family, neighbourhood, and *ojha* (exorcist) even nowadays (Awasthi & Mishra, 2017; Mishra, 2009, 2015). A 31-year-old woman reported, 'Due to the doctor's unavailability at the required time, people in our villages go to the Ojha or Kabiraj, who are always available' (Boro & Saikia, 2020). Such findings raise the question about the sociodemographic factors that influence a tilt towards traditional or modern medicine.

Sociocultural transformation following intercultural contact may lead to changes in living conditions, modification of diet, the transmission of diseases, and finally increased stress that impairs the health of Adivasis. For instance, the Mullukurumba of Kerala has been victim of displacement and relocation resulting in alterations in their means of subsistence and food availability. Consequently, they resorted to purchasing manufactured or processed food, the side effects of which are increased prevalence of malnutrition, dental decay, lowered immunity as well as various other diseases such as anaemia, sicklecell disease, scabies, kwashiorkor, marasmus, gastroenteritis, ulcer, tuberculosis, and venereal diseases (Sathianathan, 1993). This indicates that utilization of 'modern' facilities may not essentially lead to better health outcomes.

During the last decade, under the influence of developmental policies, considerable sociocultural changes have taken place. Consequently, contact with other groups has increased and acculturation has emerged as a possible cause for the increased prevalence of hypertension. Kandpal et al. (2016) observed that more than 40% of Rang Bhotias in the Pithoragarh District of Uttarakhand were affected by hypertension. In a community-based cross-sectional study on the 4193 Adivasis of Kerala, Meshram et al. (2012) found a 40% prevalence of hypertension. Hypertension also affected 23% of the adult Adivasi population of Maharashtra (Meshram et al., 2014). An analysis of findings reveals that factors like age, gender, education, socio-economic status, obesity, and substance use (tobacco and alcohol) affect the prevalence of hypertension.

Two other conditions that have reached epidemic proportions in Adivasi communities are diabetes and obesity. India is emerging as the diabetes capital in the world with an estimated 40 million affected and the numbers are expected to reach 80 million by 2030. A meta-analytic report based on seven studies conducted from 2000 to 2011 revealed a 5.9% diabetes prevalence in Adivasi communities (Upadhyay et al., 2013). Among the nomadic group residing in the Jhunjhunu, Sikar, and Churu districts of Rajasthan, the prevalence of obesity was 15.8% (Bandana, 2012). It is surprising to note a high prevalence of obesity in a physically active community like the Adivasi. Kapoor et al. (2014) studied the Gaddi community of Himachal Pradesh and found an increased prevalence of central (abdominal) obesity, hypertension, and diabetes mellitus in urban Adivasis as compared to their traditional counterparts. The urban environment introduces a changing lifestyle reflecting an association between urbanization and the development of lifestyle-related risk factors (fat consumption, physical inactivity, substance use) and the development of chronic conditions such as diabetes, obesity, and hypertension (Awasthi et al., 2018).

These epidemiological trends over the last decade point to a possible link between increased urban contact or acculturation experiences and the development of chronic conditions. The association between acculturation and the development of chronic conditions may be explained by the notion that when the Adivasi move towards a bicultural orientation, a pattern of stress and response develops. The benefits of the majority culture depicted by advertisements and other forms of media set new aspirations for them. Assimilating or integrating with the majority culture requires major lifestyle changes which may be restrained by the person's socio-economic resources. This leads to a severe incongruence in present conditions, aspirations, and opportunities which may be the possible risk factors for high blood pressure and glucose levels. There is comparatively less research on the underlying relationship of acculturation with hypertension and diabetes among the Adivasi although it is highly desirable and essential.

Acculturative Stress and Influence on Mental Health

In scholarly writings, terms such as 'primitive' and 'backward' have been used to describe the Adivasi which indicates the negative outlook people hold towards this population. For a long, it has been believed that the Adivasi are inferior in terms of their culture, traditions, behaviour, and lifestyle although no research evidence is present to support such claims. Additionally, the 'modern' approaches to development consider Adivasi cultures as backward, primitive, and uncivilized and actively attempt to replace their cultural ways of living. Collective trauma from such loss has resulted in endemic conflicts related to several health problems in many Adivasi communities.

Despite the global magnitude of mental illness and its impact on socio-economic development, and human behaviour being reiterated by many studies, mental health is yet to become a priority in many communities. Although the mental health burden is greater in developed countries, developing countries are showing an increasing trend in terms of both disease burden and treatment gap. Prolonged contact with foreign cultures has subjected the Adivasi in developing countries to a wide range of sociocultural changes that give rise to social tensions making people vulnerable to role confusion, lowered self-esteem, and emotional disorders. Mukherjee and Awasthi (2021) have discussed the relationship between the level and strategies of acculturation and the risks of developing psychological problems. Although the results are equivocal, in general it appears that low acculturation (separation and marginalization) is related to more stressful relationships and maladjustment while high acculturation (assimilation and integration) is related to healthy family and peer relationships.

During the process of acculturation, people react differently to the change. While some experience 'behavioural shifts' due to the pressures of acculturation, others may experience 'acculturative stress' due to the turmoil. Acculturative stress involves a set of stress behaviours such as lowered mental health status reflected by confusion, anxiety, and depression, accompanied by feelings of marginality, alienation, and identity confusion, increased psychosomatic complaints, family violence, substance use, homicide, and suicide (Berry & Sam, 2016; Sam & Berry, 2010). Although acculturative stress has been largely studied among immigrants, the scenario with Adivasis is different primarily because, for immigrants, acculturation is voluntary. Involuntary acculturation experienced by the Adivasis may lead to greater acculturative stress.

In India, extensive research has been carried out on the acculturation and health of the Adivasi keeping in mind their ecological and sociocultural context. In their research with the Birhor, Asur, and Oraon groups of Bihar, Mishra et al. (1996) developed several culturally appropriate measures to assess acculturation strategies, feelings of marginality, and health of the local Adivasis. In this study, it was found that in all the three groups, 'coexistence' and 'integration' were the most preferred acculturation strategies, both for the high acculturated and low acculturated group. Individuals who opted for the 'marginalization' strategy had greater psychological and psychosomatic symptoms compared to those having 'integration' or 'coexistence' strategies. Further, the less acculturated members of all the three groups exhibited greater feelings of marginality, that is, a state of cultural loss and exclusion from the dominant society. Individuals with greater feelings of marginality also reported greater health problems leading to the conclusion that marginalization from the dominant society gives rise to both physical and mental health problems. The findings of this study and the subsequent studies with Kharwar and Agaria in Uttar Pradesh (Mishra & Chaubey, 2002) and Parhaiya, Birjia, and Oraon in Jharkhand (Kumar, 2019) reveal that in the course of acculturation, individuals who opt for 'coexistence' and 'integration' strategies have better psychological well-being and lesser health problems.

Although the Adivasi reside in relatively remote locations, their habitat may also be shared by non-Adivasi people. The developmental programmes affect both groups but their disparities stem from the degree to which interaction with the outside world disrupts their lives. To study this effect, Mishra and Vajpayee (1996) investigated the lives of Kharwar and non-tribal (Yadav) women living in the same environment. Based on observation and interviews of 60 women aged 24–58 years, it emerged that their stressors were largely related to 'financial' and 'familial' constraints, although some problems were more pronounced for Kharwar women as compared to Yadav women. Again, the two groups did not differ significantly in terms of physical health but Kharwar women reported higher psychological and psycho-physiological health problems than Yadav women. In addition, they reported more psychological symptoms than physical symptoms. For curing their problems, the Kharwar women resorted to the traditional system of healthcare (consulting the *Vaidya* or traditional healer) more often than a modern (allopathic) doctor.

Although substantial research has been carried out exploring the relationship between acculturation and mental health, the relationship remains to vary. The variations in results may be due to the variations in operational definitions and tools used to measure the constructs. However, a more plausible explanation may be that neither tribal communities nor majority groups are homogeneous. Therefore, the impact of acculturative experiences on mental health may be understood through dynamics between minority and majority groups. Researchers may identify risk factors, factors associated with traditional lifestyle, and those brought about by modernization and plan policies and interventions accordingly.

The Way Forward

The prime contribution of this chapter lies in the understanding that mere exposure to another culture may not cause distress. Acculturative stress and health problems arise in the due course of acculturation; involuntary changes are imposed upon the Adivasi people. When people are compelled to make alterations in their lifestyle, traditions, dietary habits, and mode of subsistence are result of intercultural contact, physiological, psychological, and psychosomatic symptoms begin to appear.

Each culture has unique healthcare needs, beliefs, and practices. Although the Adivasi share certain commonalities, they are very different groups based on social, geographical, economic, and cultural environments. Therefore, instead of implementing generic developmental programmes, any programme aimed at the development of the Adivasi may take into consideration their realities, values and aspirations, existing viewpoints, and priorities. The principle may be to follow area-specific, culture-sensitive planning and development.

Previous findings have indicated that a lack of awareness about diseases hampers their health-seeking behaviours and adherence to the treatment regimen. Therefore, promoting health literacy as well as providing accessible and affordable healthcare facilities may be of prime importance. One of the beneficial effects of sociocultural change has been accessing technological advancements. Technology such as folk media, mass media, and mobile applications may be developed in local dialects to spread health education in remote locations. Further, social and community support systems and availability and accessibility of resources (such as hospitals or community mental health services) may be assessed for academic research as well as practical utility. The modern medicinal approach discards the role of traditional healers, shamans, priests, and dais in Adivasi healthcare and considers them unscientific. However, these traditional healers and methods have helped the Adivasi people survive in isolation for centuries. Therefore, the problem of the non-representation of Adivasi people in the health policymaking bodies may be given utmost attention. The above discussion also finds a gradually increasing preference of the Adivasi people towards modern medicinal facilities, and thus a sensitive way of policy building may be to include both traditional and modern systems in healthcare.

Concluding Remarks

Over the past few decades, under the influence of urbanization, industrialization, and government-led developmental policies, the lives of many Adivasi groups have undergone substantial changes. These changes have altered the structure of traditional communities, in turn affecting their personal and collective identities as well as their health. In this chapter, we tried to comprehend the impact of such sociocultural changes due to acculturation on the physical and mental health of the Adivasi people.

The Adivasi groups are still in a state of transition and their health is a reflection of their acculturative experiences, challenges, and coping. On the one hand, they suffer from diseases related to underdevelopment (e.g., malaria, malnutrition, jaundice, and poor maternal and child health) and on the other hand, they suffer from diseases due to modernity (e.g., hypertension, obesity, and diabetes). Prevalence of mental health problems and substance use is on the rise as well although they need to be understood from their specific cultural contexts. Through an overview of the literature, it seems that during the process of acculturation, those having lower acculturation or opting for separation or marginalization strategies have greater feelings of marginality and poorer health. While exposure to mainstream 'modern' society has negative impacts such as displacement, relocation, and forced lifestyle alterations, the Adivasi people are also aware of the tangible benefits such as better infrastructure, education, health, and technology. As a result, bicultural orientation becomes a preferred choice as they are willing to accept the mainstream culture's modern amenities while maintaining their traditional culture.

Understanding the interrelationships between intercultural contact, sociocultural changes, and health is a pressing issue in cross-cultural health research. It, therefore, becomes the responsibility of health professionals to promote health literacy among Adivasi communities and also ensure that any change at the policy or intervention level involves the members of the Adivasi groups, their sentiments, and concerns. Efforts may be made such that while uplifting their status, we do not erode their cultural heritage.

References

AwasthiP., Mishra, R. C., & Shahi, U. P. (2006). Health beliefs and behavior of cervix cancer patients. *Psychology and Developing Societies, 18*(1), 37–58.

Awasthi, P. & Mishra, R. C. (2011). Illness beliefs and coping strategies of diabetic women. *Psychological Studies, 56*(2), 176–184.

Awasthi, P. & Mishra, R. C. (2013). Can social support and control agency change illness consequences? Evidence from cervix cancer patients. *Open Journal of Medical Psychology, 2*(3), 115–123.

Awasthi, P. & Mishra, R. C. (2017). *Understanding and management of some critical health problems in an underdeveloped Kharwar community* [Unpublished research report]. New Delhi: Indian Council of Social Science Research, Ministry of Human Resource Development.

Awasthi, P., Mishra, R. C., & Singh, S. K. (2018). Health-promoting lifestyle, illlness control beliefs and well-being of the obese diabetic women. *Psychology and Developing Societies, 30*(2), 175–198.

Bandana, S. (2012). Diet and lifestyle: Its association with cholesterol levels among Nomad tribal populations of Rajasthan. *International Journal of Medicine and Biomedical Research, 1*(2), 124–130.

Basu, S. (2000). Dimensions of tribal health in India. *Health and Population Perspectives and Issues, 23*(2), 61–70.

Berry, J. W. & Sam, D. L. (Eds). (2016). *The Cambridge handbook of acculturation psychology.* New York: Cambridge University Press.

Boro, B. & Saikia, N. (2020). A qualitative study of the barriers to utilizing healthcare services among the tribal population in Assam. *PLoS One, 15*(10), e0240096.

Indian Council of Medical Research (2002). Health status of primitive tribes of Orissa. *ICMR Bulletin, 33*(10), 1–8.

Inkeles, A. & Smith, D. (1974). *Becoming modern: Individual change in six developing countries.* Harvard University Press. https://doi.org/10.4159/harvard.9780674499348

Kandpal, V., Sachdeva, M. P., & Saraswathy, K. N. (2016). An assessment study of CVD related risk factors in a tribal population of India. *BMC Public Health, 16*(1), 434. https://doi.org/10.1186/s12889-016-3106-x

Kapoor, D., Bhardwaj, A. K., Kumar, D., & Raina, S. K. (2014). Prevalence of diabetes mellitus and its risk factors among permanently settled tribal individuals in tribal and urban areas in northern state of sub-Himalayan region of India. *International Journal of Chronic Diseases.* https://doi.org/10.1155/2014/380597

Kumar, D. (2019). Social identity and acculturation attitudes among different tribal groups of Jharkhand, India. In A. Shukla, A. Dubey, & N. S. Thagunna (Eds.), *Psyche of Asian Society* (pp. 169–180). New Delhi: Concept Publishing Company Pvt Ltd.

Malakar, K. D. (2020). Distribution of schedule tribes health configuration in India: A case study. *Science, Technology, and Development Journal (IT Publications), 9*(2), 181–203.

Meshram, I. I., Arlappa, N., Balkrishna, N., Rao, K. M., Laxmaiah, A., & Brahmam, G. N. V. (2012). Prevalence of hypertension, its correlates and awareness among adult tribal population of Kerala state, India. *Journal of Postgraduate Medicine, 58*(4), 255.

Meshram, I. I., Laxmaiah, A., Mallikharjun, R. K., Arlappa, N., Balkrishna, N., & Reddy, C. G. (2014). Prevalence of hypertension and its correlates among adult tribal population (≥ 20 years) of Maharashtra State, India. *International Journal of Health Sciences & Research, 4*(1), 130–139.

Mishra, R. C. (2009). Health cognition and practices. In A. Shukla (Ed.), *Culture, cognition and behavior* (pp. 264–276). New Delhi: Concept.

Mishra, R. C. (2015). Socio-cultural and psychological adaptations in a culturally changing tribal community. *Psychological Studies, 3*(1), 7–13.

Mishra, R. C. (2017). Meaning of happy life for the Kharwars in India in their journey towards development. *Psychology and Developing Societies, 29*(2), 221–245.

Mishra, R. C. & Chaubey, A. C. (2002). Acculturation attitudes of Kharwar and Agaria tribal groups of Sonebhadra. *Psychology and Developing Societies, 14*(2), 201–220.

Mishra, R. C., Sinha, D., & Berry, J. W. (1996). *Ecology, acculturation and psychological adaptation: A study of Adivasis in Bihar*. New Delhi: Sage Publications, Inc.

Mishra, R. C. & Vajpayee, A. (1996). Mental health problems of women in a culturally changing community. *Indian Journal of Mental Health and Disabilities, 1*(2), 8–15.

Mukherjee, M. & Awasthi, P. (2021). Involuntary cultural change and mental health status among indigenous groups: A synthesis of existing literature. *Community Mental Health Journal, 58*(2), 222–230.

Radley, A. (2004). *Making sense of illness: The social psychology of health and disease*. London: SAGE Publications Ltd.

Redfield, R., Linton, R., & Herskovits, M. J. (1936). Memorandum for the study of acculturation. *American Anthropologist, 38*(1), 149–152.

Registrar General & Census Commissioner of India (2011). *Census of India 2011. Provisional population totals*. New Delhi: Ministry of Home Affairs, Government of India.

Sam, D. L. & Berry, J. W. (2010). Acculturation: When individuals and groups of different cultural backgrounds meet. *Perspectives on Psychological Science, 5*(4), 472–481.

Sarkar, R. (2016). A study on the health and nutritional status of tribal women in Godam line village of Phansidewa block in Darjeeling district. *IOSR Journal of Humanities and Social Science, 21*(11), 15–18.

Sathianathan, S. (1993). *Tribes, politics and social change in India: A case study of the Mullukurumbas of the Nilgiri Hills* [Doctoral dissertation]. University of Hull, England. Retrieved March 27, 2022, from https://hydra.hull.ac.uk/assets/hull:10769a/content

Singh, U. P. (2014). *Tribal health in North East India: A study of socio-cultural dimensions of health care practices*. New Delhi: Serials Publications.

Sonowal, C. J. & Praharaj, P. (2007). Tradition vs transition: Acceptance of health care systems among the Santhals of Orissa. *Studies on Ethno-medicine, 1*(2), 135–146.

Upadhyay, R. P., Misra, P., Chellaiyan, V. G., Das, T. K., Adhikary, M., Chinnakali, P., & Sinha, S. (2013). Burden of diabetes mellitus and prediabetes in tribal population of India: A systematic review. *Diabetes Research and Clinical Practice, 102*(1), 1–7.

World Health Organization (2008). *The World Health Report 2008: Primary Health Care (Now More Than Ever)*. Geneva: WHO.

Zou, D. V. (2016). Peoples, power, and belief in north-east India. In M. Radhakrishna (Ed.), *Citizens first: Studies on Adivasis, tribals, and indigenous peoples in India*. Oxford: Oxford University Press.

7
SMOKING AND ALCOHOL CONSUMPTION AMONG TYPE 2 DIABETICS

Health Behaviour Models-Based Investigation

Eslavath Rajkumar, J. Romate, R. Lakshmi, and G. T. Kruthika

Diabetes mellitus (DM), also termed 'sugar', was the ninth leading cause of death in 2019 globally, with approximately 1.5 million deaths directly attributed to diabetes. According to the reports of the International Diabetes Federation, at the country level, India has witnessed 647,831 deaths due to diabetes in the year 2021. The mortality rate from DM is increasing year by year, and statistics show that between 2000 and 2016, 5% of premature deaths from DM increased significantly (World Health Organization, 2021). Further researchers estimate the prevalence of DM will be much more likely to increase and opine that DM will be a major global public health burden, with an estimated 200 million worldwide prevalence by 2040 (Zheng et al., 2018). In India, the prevalence rate is expected to reach 80 million people by 2030 (Bansode & Jungari, 2019).

The consequences of this life-long condition are so dangerous that, along with major attribution to mortality and premature deaths, it accounts for impacting an individual's overall well-being (physical, psychological, and social well-being). It further aggravates a person's physical health. It increases the likelihood of developing life-threatening diseases such as cardiovascular disease, kidney disease, neuropathy, blindness, and amputation of the lower extremities. These are significant causes of increased morbidity and mortality in people with diabetes (Deshpande et al., 2008). Along with physical comorbidities, there are also psychological comorbidities. Compared to the general population, diabetic patients are more likely to experience feelings of stress, worry, depression, anxiety, burnout, and poor quality of life (Balhara, 2011; Penckofer et al., 2007). Moreover, the suffering caused by this chronic disease is not limited to individuals, but also to their loved ones. Evidence shows the impaired quality of life and higher burden in caregivers of families with diabetes patients (Costa et al., 2020; Kristianingrum et al., 2021).

Further, the consequences of diabetes also include the economic burden. In India, a recent systematic review has indicated a high economic burden on

DOI: 10.4324/9781003360858-9

households, where the average direct cost (diagnosis, treatment, care, and prevention) of diabetes for one person is Rs. 10,585/- p.a. Similarly, indirect cost (cost for absenteeism, loss of productivity, and disability) was Rs. 18,707/- p.a. for the south zone (Oberoi & Kansra, 2020). The cost of diabetes-related healthcare treatment in India in 2021 was USD 8485.8 million and is expected to increase to USD 10,305.5 million by 2030 (International Diabetes Federation, 2021).

Type 1 diabetes, type 2 DM (T2DM), and gestational diabetes are the three types of DM classified based on aetiology and clinical features, and the others include monogenic and secondary diabetes. T2DM is a chronic disease caused by the body's inability to use insulin, a hormone that regulates blood sugar levels. Statistics have shown that it accounts for about 90% of all diabetes cases (Goyal & Jialal, 2021). Evidence supports the principle that genetic susceptibility is a significant risk factor for common T2DM. Descendants of parents with T2DM have a 40% lifetime risk of developing T2DM, which is increased to 70% if both parents have T2DM (Meigs et al., 2000). Overweight and obesity are also significant physiological risk factors for T2DM (Barik et al., 2016). Along with these physiological aspects of causation, the aetiology of T2DM could be seen at other two levels, namely, psychological and behavioural levels.

Longitudinal epidemiologic studies have found that depression and anxiety, as well as general emotional stress, sleep problems, anger, low-stress tolerance and hostility, are associated with an increased risk of developing T2DM (Knol et al., 2006; Pouwer et al., 2010; Mezuk et al., 2008). Lastly, behavioural contributions to the pathogenesis of prediabetes and T2DM include diet, exercise, sedentariness, sleep, and lifestyle, including stress (Spruijt et al., 2014). Health-risk behaviours like smoking and alcohol use are major behavioural risk factors for T2DM. A 2014 Surgeon General report found that smoking increases the risk of T2DM in active smokers by 30–40% compared to nonsmokers, suggesting that quitting smoking should be considered an important public health strategy to combat the global diabetes epidemic (Warren et al., 2014). Quitting smoking is regarded as an essential step in preventing the development of complications of diabetes such as cardiovascular diseases, macro vascular complications, impairing endothelial functions, and enhancing adherence to self-care behaviours (Chang, 2012; Solberg et al., 2004). Chronic alcohol consumption is considered a potential risk factor for the development of T2DM, which leads to insulin resistance and pancreatic β-cell dysfunction, which are prerequisites for the development of diabetes (Kim & Kim, 2012). Regular consumption of moderate amounts of alcohol by patients with T2D is associated with an increased risk of impotence, peripheral neuropathy, and retinopathy (Emanuele et al., 1998).

These behavioural risk factors are modifiable risk factors where altering health-risk behaviours makes patients more likely to cope with the severity and reduces the likelihood of developing health complications from diabetes (Engler et al., 2013; Pan et al., 2015). A unique method to alter health-risk behaviour is to identify the multiple-level associated factors that influence patients to smoke and use alcohol.

The health belief model (HBM) is one of the oldest and most popular empirically adopted health behaviour models for various cultural and topical contexts. HBM posits that a combination of the following factors drives the likelihood of exhibited health behaviour: demographic details such as age, gender, socio-economic status, ethnicity, and cultural differences; psychosocial factors such as personality, health knowledge, past experiences, etc. [Modifying factors]; perceived risk susceptibility, severity, benefits, barriers, self-efficacy [Individual perceptions], and cues to action [Likelihood of action] (Becker, 1974; Champion & Skinner, 2008; Hariharan, 2020; Rosenstock, 1974).

HBM is applied to three broad areas of health behaviours: (a) preventive health behaviours including health-promoting behaviours (such as diet and exercise), health-risking behaviours (such as smoking and drinking), immunisation practices, and contraception; (b) sick-role behaviours, which refer to adherence to recommended medical regimens, usually after a professional diagnosis of the disease; and (c) visit clinics, which includes consulting doctors for various reasons. HBM is useful for explaining self-care activities such as recommending diabetes management and emphasising behaviour related to disease prevention (Adejoh, 2014).

The theory of planned behaviour (TPB) assumes that behavioural beliefs (individual attitude towards the behaviour in question) and normative beliefs (beliefs about a significant other's attitude towards a behaviour) influence behaviour intentions. Along with behavioural and normative beliefs, the construct influenced by one's control beliefs, namely, perceived behavioural control, also predicts behavioural intentions. These perceived behavioural intentions and perceived behavioural control are fundamental factors in TPB that predict actual behaviours (Ajzen, 1991; Fishbein & Ajzen, 2010; Hariharan, 2020). TPB is one of the most widely tested health behaviours. There are many studies in which TPB has been used to describe behavioural processes occurring in various domains. This theory also showed good efficacy in explaining behavioural processes in T2DM (Akbar et al., 2015; Dilekler et al., 2021).

Socio-ecological theory (SET) broadly conceptualises health and focuses on the multiple factors affecting health. Factors that interact and determine health are intrapersonal (knowledge, attitudes, behaviour, self-concept, etc.), interpersonal processes and primary groups (family, workgroup, friendship networks, etc.), institutional factors (social institutions), community factors (organisations, institutions), and public policy (local, state, and national laws and policies) (McLeroy et al.,1988). Evidence has shown the effective role of this theory to tackle the multifaceted issues among T2DM patients (Chan et al., 2019; Hill et al., 2013).

The HBM, TPB, and SET are the most widely applied health behaviour theories (Breslow, 1996; Glanz & Bishop, 2010; Steinmetz et al., 2016). Considering the severity of T2DM and the devastating negative impacts of engaging in health-risk behaviours, there is a need to modify the health-risk behaviours. An essential step in prevention is determining why a diabetic person is engaging in risky behaviour. Hence, the present study – utilising the prominent theories that explain why behaviour occurs – is aimed to understand the factors influencing smoking and alcohol use in T2DM patients.

Method

The present study used a cross-sectional design to study the associated factors of smoking and alcohol use behaviours among T2DM based on the prominent health behaviour models – the HBM, TPB, and SET. The predictor variables for the present study include the domains of the HBM, TPB, and SET, with the criterion variables being smoking and alcohol use behaviours.

Participants

The sample for the present study was patients with type 2 diabetes. The purposive sampling technique was used to collect the data from 266 men and women. Individuals above 18 years and who have type 2 diabetes were included in the study. The data were gathered from the state of Karnataka and mainly from its northern districts. The researcher interacted with the patients at various avenues like hospitals, diagnostic centres, and homes. Of these, 53 (19.92%) participants belonged to the age group of 18–45 years, while the remaining 213 participants (80.08%) were aged >45 years. Moreover, 70 (26.32%) were females, and 196 (73.68%) were males. Nine (3.38%) participants had received no education, 144 (54.1%) had primary education, 50 (18.80%) had studied high school, and the remaining 63 (23.68%) participants had received intermediate and above levels of education. Overall, 198 (74.43%) were from urban areas, while 68 (25.56%) were from rural backgrounds. It was noted that 51.87% and 56.01% of participants showed smoking and alcohol use behaviour, respectively.

Tools

Health Belief Model Scale

To measure the HBM constructs, namely, perceived severity, perceived benefits, cues to action, and self-efficacy, a modified version of the scales validated by Champion and colleagues (Champion & Skinner, 2008) was used. The tool contained 25 items, all of which had to be rated on a five-point rating scale with response options ranging from 'strongly disagree' to 'strongly agree'. The Cronbach's alpha for perceived severity, perceived benefits, cues to action, and self-efficacy was .7, .75, .69, and .78, respectively.

Multidimensional Scale of Perceived Social Support

The perceived social support construct was measured using the multidimensional scale of perceived social support developed by Zimet et al. (1988). This self-report rating scale ranges from 1 to 7, where 1 indicates 'very strongly disagree' and 7 indicates 'very strongly agree', with a total of 12 items. The reliability of the scale was .88.

Health Beliefs Questionnaire (1)

The construct of health value was measured from the health beliefs questionnaire (based on the HBM) developed by Norman and Fitter (1991). There are four items in the health value questionnaire. All four items are answered on a scale of 1–4, ranging from 'very negative' to 'very positive'. The Cronbach's alpha coefficient was .69.

Health Beliefs Questionnaire (2)

The construct of perceived susceptibility was measured according to a health beliefs questionnaire (based on the HBM) developed by Norman and Fitter (1991). It has six items based on a five-point Likert scale, with responses ranging from 'most unlikely' to 'most likely'. The Cronbach's alpha coefficient value was .94.

Theory of Planned Behaviour Questionnaire

The three constructs of the TPB were measured using the TPB questionnaire developed by Claude (2011). The questionnaire has three subdomains measuring each theoretical domain of planned behaviour: attitudes, subjective norms, and perceived behavioural control. The questionnaire has 60 items, and each item is scored from 1 to 7.

Chronic Disease Resource Survey

To measure the subdomains of SET constructs, the chronic disease resource survey was adopted. This 64-item, five-point rating scale was developed by Glasgow et al. (2000). Internal consistency for the scale was $\alpha = .82$.

WHO STEP Tools

WHO STEPS tool (World Health Organization. Noncommunicable Diseases and Mental Health Cluster, 2005) was used to measure smoking and alcohol use behaviour.

Procedure

Permission was requested from hospitals, diagnostic centres, and primary healthcare centres before data collection. After obtaining consent from the concerned authorities, type 2 diabetes patients over 18 years of age were approached and their informed consents were obtained before enrolment. Before data collection, participants were assured of confidentiality and anonymity. Upon determining the basic demographic details, all the questionnaires were administered. Clear instructions were given for each questionnaire, and doubts were clarified. Researchers ensured that participants filled out all the items on the questionnaires, after which their participation was acknowledged. The collected data were analysed using descriptive and inferential statistics.

Results

Data were analysed using the SPSS package (version 20). Binary logistic regression was performed to assess the impact of HBM, TPB, and SET domains on smoking and alcohol-consumption behaviours among T2DM patients.

Table 7.1a presents the binary logistic regression analysis findings for the association of the HBM domains with smoking behaviour. Among the domains of

TABLE 7.1 Association of the HBM, TPB, and SET domains with smoking behaviour

Predictors	B	SE	p	OR	95% CI Lower	95% CI Upper
7.1a. Association of the health belief model domains with smoking behaviour						
Social Support	−.036	.019	.068	.965	.929	1.003
Health Value	.028	.051	.579	1.029	.930	1.138
Perceived Susceptibility	.029	.029	.310	1.029	.973	1.089
Perceived Severity	−.047	.022	.029	.954	.915	.995
Perceived Benefits	.125	.036	.001	1.133	1.055	1.217
Perceived Barriers	.011	.033	.745	1.011	.947	1.078
Cues to Action	.055	.043	.201	1.057	.971	1.151
Self-Efficacy	.030	.033	.059	1.031	.967	1.099
Omnibus test: x^2 = 30.570, df = 8, $p \leq .001$						
Model summary: Nagelkerke R^2 = .145						
7.1b. Association of the theory of planned behaviour domains with smoking behaviour						
Attitudes	.003	.008	.688	1.003	.988	1.019
Subjective Norms	−.011	.004	.002	.989	.982	.996
Perceived Behavioural Control	−.002	.008	.809	.998	.983	1.014
Omnibus test: x^2 = 10.634, df = 8, $p \leq .05$						
Model summary: Nagelkerke R^2 = .052						
7.1c. Association of the socio-ecological model domains with smoking behaviour						
Doctor and Healthcare Team	−.046	.029	.120	.955	.902	1.012
Family and Friends	.040	.030	.178	1.041	.982	1.104
Personal	−.030	.030	.322	.971	.916	1.029
Interpersonal	.058	.031	.066	1.059	.996	1.126
Community	−.064	.031	.038	.938	.883	.996
Media and Policy	.053	.022	.018	1.054	1.009	1.101
Community Organisations	−.066	.021	.002	.936	.898	.975
Omnibus test: x^2 = 36.712, df = 8, $p \leq .001$						
Model summary: Nagelkerke R^2 = .175						

Notes: B – coefficient for the constant, S.E. – Standard error around the coefficient for the constant, p – significant level, OR – odds ratio, CI – confidence interval for the odds ratio with its upper and lower limits.

the HBM, the statistically significant predictor variables were perceived severity and perceived benefits. From the omnibus test (p ≤ .001), the model exhibited a good data fit. The Cox and Snell R^2 and Nagelkerke R^2 values indicated that the explained variation in the dependent variable for this model ranged from 10.9% to 14.5%. Furthermore, the analysis showed that for every unit of increase in perceived severity, the odds of smoking tobacco decreased by 4.6% (B = .954, CI = .915–.995, p = .029) while for every unit increase in perceived benefits, the odds of smoking tobacco increased by 13.3% (B = 1.133, CI = 1.055–1.217, p = .001).

Table 7.1b presents the binary logistic regression analysis findings for the association of the TPB domains with smoking behaviour. Among the domains of the TPB, the statistically significant predictor variable was subjective norms, which refers to the individual's motivation to comply with the individual/group's opinion. From the omnibus test (p ≤ .05), the model exhibited a good fit of the data. The Cox and Snell R^2 and Nagelkerke R^2 values indicated that the explained variation in the dependent variable for this model ranged from 3.9% to 5.2%. Furthermore, the analysis indicated that for every unit of increase in subjective norms, the odds of smoking tobacco decreased by 1.1% (B = .989, CI = .982–.996, p = .002).

Table 7.1c presents the binary logistic regression analysis findings for the association of the socio-ecological model domains with smoking behaviour. Among the domains of the SET, support from the community, media, and policy has significantly predicted smoking behaviour. From the omnibus test (p ≤ .05), the model exhibited a good data fit. The Cox and Snell R^2 and Nagelkerke R^2 values indicated that the explained variation in the dependent variable for this model ranged from 13.1% to 17.5%. Furthermore, the analysis showed that for every unit of increase in the support from the community, the odds of smoking tobacco decreased by 6.2% (B = .938, CI = .883–.996, p = .038), while for every unit of increase in media and policy, the odds of smoking tobacco increased by 5.4% (B = 1.054, CI = 1.009–1.101, p = .018); lastly, similar to community, for every unit of increase in community organisations, the odds of smoking tobacco decreased by 6.4% (B = .936, CI = .898–.975, p = .002).

Table 7.2a presents the binary logistic regression analysis findings for the association of the HBM domains with alcohol use behaviour. Among the domains of the HBM, the statistically significant predictor variables were perceived severity and cues to action. From the omnibus test (p ≤ .05), the model exhibited a good data fit. The Cox and Snell R^2 and Nagelkerke R^2 values indicated that the explained variation in the dependent variable for this model ranged from 6.9% to 9.3%. Furthermore, the analysis indicated that for every unit of increase in perceived severity, the odds of alcohol use behaviour decreased by 5.3% (B = –.054, CI = .909–.987, p = .010) while for every unit increase in cues to actions, the odds of alcohol use behaviour increased by 9.5% (B = .090, CI = 1.007–1.189, p = .033).

Table 7.2b presents the binary logistic regression analysis findings for the association of the TPB domains with alcohol use behaviour. Among the domains of the TPB, the statistically significant predictor variable was subjective norms.

TABLE 7.2 Association of the HBM, TPB, and SET domains with alcohol use behaviour

					95% CI	
Predictors	B	SE	p	OR	Lower	Upper
7.2a. Association of the health belief model domains with alcohol use behaviour						
Social Support	−.029	.019	.140	.972	.936	1.009
Health Value	.013	.050	.796	1.013	.918	1.118
Perceived Susceptibility	.014	.028	.623	1.014	.960	1.071
Perceived Severity	−.054	.021	.010	.947	.909	.987
Perceived Benefits	.054	.034	.111	1.055	.988	1.127
Perceived Barriers	.019	.032	.558	1.019	.957	1.085
Cues to Action	.090	.042	.033	1.095	1.007	1.189
Self-Efficacy	.015	.032	.636	1.015	.953	1.081
Omnibus test: $x^2 = 19.136$, $df = 8$, $p \leq .05$						
Model summary: Nagelkerke $R^2 = .093$						
7.2b. Association of the theory of planned behaviour domains with alcohol use behaviour						
Attitudes	.004	.008	.620	1.004	.988	1.020
Subjective Norms	−.011	.004	.004	.989	.982	.997
Perceived Behavioural Control	−.001	.008	.949	.999	.984	1.015
Omnibus test: $x^2 = 9.504$, $df = 8$, $p \leq .05$						
Model summary: Nagelkerke $R^2 = .047$						
7.2c. Association of the socio-ecological model domains with alcohol use behaviour						
Doctor and Healthcare Team	−.074	.030	.014	.929	.875	.985
Family and Friends	.010	.030	.739	1.010	.953	1.070
Personal	−.034	.030	.262	.976	.912	1.025
Interpersonal	.052	.031	.092	1.054	.991	1.120
Community	−.054	.031	.076	.947	.892	1.006
Media and Policy	.050	.022	.025	1.051	1.006	1.099
Community Organisations	−.067	.021	.001	.935	.898	.974
Omnibus test: $x^2 = 34.664$, $df = 18$, $p \leq .001$						
Model summary: Nagelkerke $R^2 = .167$						

Notes: B – coefficient for the constant, S.E. – standard error around the coefficient for the constant, p – significant level, OR – odds ratio, CI – confidence interval for the odds ratio with its upper and lower limits.

From the omnibus test (p ≤ .05), the model exhibited a good data fit. The Cox and Snell R^2 and Nagelkerke R^2 values indicated that the explained variation in the dependent variable for this model ranged from 3.5% to 4.7%. Furthermore, the analysis showed that for every unit of increase in subjective norms, the odds of alcohol use behaviour decreased by 1.1% (B = −.011, CI = .982–.997, p = .004).

Table 7.2c presents the findings of the binary logistic regression analysis for the association of the socio-ecological model domains with alcohol use behaviour. Among the domains of the SET, advice from doctor and healthcare team, the role of media and policy, and support from the community have significantly predicted alcohol use behaviour. From the omnibus test (p ≤ .001), the model exhibited a good data fit. The Cox and Snell R^2 and Nagelkerke R^2 values indicated that the explained variation in the dependent variable for this model ranged from 12.4% to 16.7%. Furthermore, the analysis indicated that for every unit of increase in doctor and healthcare team advice, the odds of alcohol use behaviour decreased by 7.1% (B = −.074, CI = .875−.985, p = .014), while for every unit of increase in media and policy, the odds of alcohol use behaviour increased by 5.1% (B = .050, CI = 1.005−1.099, p = .025); lastly, similar to community organisations, for every unit of increase in the support from community organisations, the odds of alcohol use behaviour decreased by 6.5% (B = −.067, CI = .898−.974, p = .001).

Discussion

The purpose of this study was to profile the factors associated with smoking and drinking in patients with T2DM from the perspective of HBM, TPB, and SET which are prominent theories of health behaviours. This study's results indicated significant associations with certain domains of the three prominent theories for this study sample.

Explanation from Health Belief Model (HBM)

HBM states that a person's behaviour can be predicted based on certain issues he/she may consider when determining certain health-related behaviours (perceived susceptibility, perceived severity, perceived benefit, and perceived barrier) (Glanz et al., 1990). Among the HBM domains, the analysis showed significant associations of perceived severity and perceived benefits of smoking. Further, perceived severity, perceived benefits, and cues to action were significantly associated with alcohol use behaviour. No significant association was observed for social support, health value, perceived susceptibility, perceived barriers, and self-efficacy with smoking and alcohol use behaviour.

Personal opinions on the magnitude and severity of a disease and its consequences (i.e., perceived severity) play an important role in an individual's intention to engage in risky health behaviour (Galvin, 1992). Consistent with those mentioned above, the results of this study show that the perceived severity construct plays a significant negative role in smoking and alcohol consumption in patients with T2DM. This indicates that the more perceived severity of adverse health effects of smoking and alcohol use, the less likely a T2DM patient is to engage in these health-risk behaviours. The results of these studies are consistent with those of Adejoh (2014), with a significant relationship between perceived severity and perceived benefits in diabetes management. Health risk perception plays a vital role in driving health behaviour change (Sheeran et al., 2014). Interventions that change perceptions of risk ultimately change health behaviours. Thus, the results of this study add to the empirical evidence that perceived severity plays a vital role in health behaviours (Ferrer & Klein, 2015).

The better a patient's perceived benefit, the more likely he/she is to engage in healthy behaviour. The analysis of the study indicated that the greater the disagreement about the benefits of adhering to health-promoting behaviours, the greater the likelihood of engaging in health-risk behaviours related to smoking and drinking. Individual health beliefs and attitudes could substantiate the disagreement or inconsistencies about a healthy lifestyle – a five-year follow-up study by Mäntyselkä et al. (2019) indicated that possible reasons for individuals to resist healthy lifestyle changes are impacted by their health beliefs and attitudes, particularly negative or denial attitudes towards health promotion. The study by Oumoukelthoum (2021) showed the difficulty of following a healthy schedule, changes in working conditions, and laziness as barriers to health behaviour change in T2DM patients.

Explanation from Theory of Planned Behaviour (TPB)

Theory assumes that behaviour can be predicted from intent. The intent is determined by a person's attitude towards behaviour, subjective norms, and perceived behavioural control (Fishbein & Ajzen, 2010). In the three TPB domains, subjective norms showed a significant negative association, while attitude and cognitive behavioural control showed no association with alcohol use behaviour. No significant association was found between TPB domains and smoking behaviour.

Normative beliefs are people's beliefs about whether they think others should engage in certain behaviours. Subjective norms are derived from normative beliefs multiplied by an individual's motivation to obey an individual/group's opinion (Ajzen, 2005). The findings of the present study indicate that the more the patient feels that his/her group thinks it is important for him/her to adhere to self-care behaviour, the higher is his/her motivation not to comply with health-risk behaviour, that is, alcohol use behaviour. The primary care team plays an essential role in the patient's behavioural change, emotional support, adherence to the treatment regimen, and overall management of this chronic condition (Ahmed & Yeasmeen, 2016). Consistent with the evidence, current findings are supported by the findings of Naik et al. (2018). They found that the primary caregiver or family played an important role in the management of diabetes and they encouraged the patient to quit tobacco and alcohol.

Explanation from Socio-Ecological Theory (SET)

Factors that influence self-care behaviours are multi-systemic. SET examines issues from multiple contexts (McLeroy et al., 1988). The SET domains, namely, doctor and healthcare team, community, media and policy, and community organisations, showed significant associations with smoking and alcohol use behaviour.

The advice of physicians and health professionals also plays a vital role in reducing risky health behaviours among T2DM patients. The results of this study evidence that doctors and healthcare teams have significantly negative predictions on alcohol consumption, which indicates higher the advice from a doctor and healthcare team, the lower the involvement of individuals in health-risk behaviours. Therefore, it can be said that primary healthcare professionals, who are the first point of contact for patients, play an important role in identifying high-risk individuals and in reducing the prevalence of risky health behaviours by providing counselling, medical prescriptions, and treatment plans (Eashwar et al., 2020; Thomas, et al., 2016). A study conducted in Kerala has demonstrated the effectiveness of brief counselling by healthcare professionals in achieving the noticeable quitting rates of smoking behaviour among T2DM patients and recommended healthcare professionals to advise diabetic patients to quit smoking (Thankappan et al., 2013).

Media, a tool that ensures reach to many people, plays an essential role in promoting health education and health interventions to change risky health behaviours. Unlike some other studies that have identified the influence of mass media campaigns such as television, social media, and radio broadcasts on health promotion (Moorhead et al., 2013), the results of this study show conflicting findings that despite greater exposure to media-based health promotion, individuals are still more likely to engage in unhealthy smoking and drinking behaviours. Despite their advantages, Gupta and Purohit (2020) discussed the uncertainty regarding the effectiveness of health promotion advertisements and interventions through social media, such as easy accessibility and acceptability. They suggested that to change people's behaviour and involvement, there is a need to determine personal and environmental factors over merely providing health-promoting information.

Empirical evidence has shown the influential role of community in individuals' health. Community characteristics like supportive community health organisations, workplace support, and educational opportunities are associated with health and health behaviours (Kaplan et al., 2000). The results of this study indicate that T2DM patients are less likely to engage in tobacco and alcohol use behaviour in the presence of a supportive community. Evidence shows significant improvements in glycaemic control, health literacy, and behaviour in diabetic patients after intervention at the sub-health centre in Kerala (Rahul et al., 2021). Another community project called MUKTI in West Bengal showed a significant increase in smoking cessation rates for diabetic patients after receiving combination interventions by community health workers and SMS-based interventions (Hejjaji et al., 2021). Implementing a community-level health programme and community-based interventions will help prevent diabetes in people in the study population.

Conclusion

The health-risk behaviours smoking and alcohol consumption aggravate T2DM patients' health conditions. Studies have shown that patients with T2DM continue to engage in risky behaviours like smoking and alcohol use behaviour despite serious health conditions. Researchers have indicated the importance of studying region-specific associated factors of health-risk behaviours (as the contributing factors vary from region to region) to implement suitable population-specific preventive measures. This study determined the factors related to smoking and alcohol consumption among T2DM patients from the perspective of three established health-behaviour theories. Therefore, the results of this study can aid primary healthcare professionals to understand the factors related to smoking and alcohol use in a given study population and formulate appropriate preventive measures.

References

Adejoh, S. O. (2014). Diabetes knowledge, health belief, and diabetes management among the Igala Nigeria. *SAGE Open, 4*(2), 1–8.

Ahmed, Z., & Yeasmeen, F. (2016). Active family participation in diabetes self-care: A commentary. *Diabetes Management, 6,* 104–107.

Ajzen, I. (1991). The theory of planned behavior. *Organizational Behavior and Human Decision Processes, 50,* 179–211. doi: 10.1016/0749-5978(91)90020-T

Ajzen, I. (2005). *Attitudes, Personality, and Behavior* (2nd ed.). Berkshire: Open University Press.

Akbar, H.; Anderson, D., & Gallegos, D. (2015). Predicting intentions and behaviours in populations with or at-risk of diabetes: A systematic review. *Preventive Medicine Reports, 2,* 270–282. https://doi.org/10.1016/j.pmedr.2015.04.006

Balhara Y. P. (2011). Diabetes and psychiatric disorders. *Indian Journal of Endocrinology and Metabolism, 15*(4), 274–283. https://doi.org/10.4103/2230-8210.85579

Bansode, B., & Jungari, D. S. (2019). Economic burden of diabetic patients in India: A review. *Diabetes & Metabolic Syndrome: Clinical Research & Reviews, 13*(4), 2469–2472. https://doi.org/10.1016/j.dsx.2019.06.020

Barik, A., Mazumdar, S., Chowdhury, A., & Rai, R. K. (2016). Physiological and behavioral risk factors of type 2 diabetes mellitus in rural India. *BMJ Open Diabetes Research & Care, 4*(1), e000255. https://doi.org/10.1136/bmjdrc-2016-000255

Becker, M. H. (1974). The Health Belief Model and personal health behavior. *Health Education Monographs.* 2:324–508.

Breslow, L. (1996). Social ecological strategies for promoting healthy lifestyles. *American Journal of Health Promotion, 10,* 253–257.

Champion, V. L., & Skinner, C. S. (2008). The health belief model. In K. Glanz, B. K. Rimer, & K. Viswanath (Eds.), *Health Behavior and Health Education: Theory, Research, and Practice* (pp. 45–65). San Francisco: Jossey-Bass.

Chan, J. C. N., Lim, L. L., Wareham, N. J., Shaw, J. E., Orchard, T. J., Zhang, P., et al. (2019). The Lancet Commission on Diabetes: using data to transform diabetes care and patient lives. *Lancet,* 396(10267):2019–82. https://doi.org/10.1016/S0140-6736(20)32374-6

Chang, S. A. (2012). Smoking and type 2 diabetes mellitus. *Diabetes & Metabolism Journal, 36*(6), 399–403. https://doi.org/10.4093/dmj.2012.36.6.399

Claude, J. J. A. (2011). *An application of health behaviour models to diabetic treatment adherence: A comparison of protection motivation theory and the theory of planned.* https://citeseerx.ist.psu.edu/viewdoc/download?doi=10.1.1.861.689&rep=rep1&type=pdf

Costa, S., Leite, Ã., Pinheiro, M., Pedras, S., & Pereira, M. (2020). Burden and quality of life in caregivers of patients with amputated diabetic foot. *PsyCh Journal, pchj.341–.* doi: 10.1002/pchj.341

Deshpande, A. D., Harris-Hayes, M., & Schootman, M. (2008). Epidemiology of diabetes and diabetes-related complications. *Physical Therapy, 88*(11), 1254–1264. https://doi.org/10.2522/ptj.20080020

Dilekler, İ., Doğulu, C., & Bozo, Ö. (2021). A test of theory of planned behavior in type II diabetes adherence: The leading role of perceived behavioral control. *Current Psychology, 40*(7), 3546–3555.

Eashwar, V., Umadevi, R., & Gopalakrishnan, S. (2020). Alcohol consumption in India- An epidemiological review. *Journal of Family Medicine and Primary Care, 9*(1), 49–55. https://doi.org/10.4103/jfmpc.jfmpc_873_19

Emanuele, N. V., Swade, T. F., & Emanuele, M. A. (1998). Consequences of alcohol use in diabetics. *Alcohol Health and Research World, 22*(3), 211–219.

Engler, P. A., Ramsey, S. E., & Smith, R. J. (2013). Alcohol use of diabetes patients: The need for assessment and intervention. *Acta Diabetologica, 50*(2), 93–99. https://doi.org/10.1007/s00592-010-0200-x

Ferrer, R., & Klein, W. M. (2015). Risk perceptions and health behavior. *Current Opinion in Psychology, 5*, 85–89. https://doi.org/10.1016/j.copsyc.2015.03.012

Fishbein, M., & Ajzen, I. (2010). *Predicting and Changing Behavior: The Reasoned Action Approach*. New York, NY: Psychology Press.

Galvin, K. T. (1992). A critical review of the health belief model in relation to cigarette smoking behaviour. *Journal of Clinical Nursing, 1*(1), 13–18. doi:10.1111/j.1365-2702.1992.tb00050.x

Glanz, K., & Bishop D. B. (2010) The role of behavioral science theory in the development and implementation of public health interventions. *Annual Review of Public Health, 21*, 299–418. doi: 10.1146/annurev.publhealth.012809.103604.

Glanz, K., Lewis, F. M., & Rimer, B. K. (1990). *Health Behavior and Health Education: Theory, Research, and Practice* (2nd ed.). San Francisco, CA: Jossey-Bass.

Glasgow, R. E., Strycker, L. A., Toobert, D. J., & Eakin, E. (2000). A social–ecologic approach to assessing support for disease self-management: The Chronic Illness Resources Survey. *Journal of Behavioral Medicine, 23*(6), 559–583. https://link.springer.com/article/10.1023/A:1005507603901

Goyal, R., & Jialal, I. (2021). Diabetes Mellitus Type 2. In: StatPearls [Internet]. Treasure Island (FL): StatPearls Publishing; 2022 Jan. https://www.ncbi.nlm.nih.gov/books/NBK513253/

Gupta, P., & Purohit, N. (2020). Promoting health behavior in young people in India: Learning for use of social media. *International Journal of Behavioral Sciences, 14*(3), 122–130. https://doi.org/10.30491/ijbs.2020.210704.1178

Hariharan, M. (2020). *Health Psychology: Theory, Practice, and Research*. New Delhi: Sage Publications.

Hejjaji, V., Khetan, A., Hughes, J. W., Gupta, P., Jones, P. G., Ahmed, A., … Josephson, R. A. (2021). A combined community health worker and text messaging-based intervention for smoking cessation in India: Project MUKTI – A mixed methods study. *Tobacco Prevention & Cessation, 7*(March), 23. https://doi.org/10.18332/tpc/132469

Hill, J., Nielsen, M., & Fox, M. H. (2013). Understanding the social factors that contribute to diabetes: A means to informing health care and social policies for the chronically ill. *Permanente Journal, 17*(2), 67–72. https://doi.org/10.7812/TPP/12-099

International Diabetes Federation (2021). *Mortality attributable to diabetes (20–79 y): Deaths attributable to diabetes*. https://www.diabetesatlas.org/data/en/indicators/7/

Kaplan, G. A., Everson, S. A., & Lynch, J. W. (2000). The contribution of social and behavioral research to an understanding of the distribution of disease in a multi-level approach. In L. F. Berkman, & I. Kawachi (Eds.), *Social Epidemiology* (pp. 32–80). Oxford, England: Oxford University Press.

Kim, S. J., & Kim, D. J. (2012). Alcoholism and diabetes mellitus. *Diabetes & Metabolism Journal*, *36*(2), 108–115. https://doi.org/10.4093/dmj.2012.36.2.108

Knol, M. J., Twisk, J. W. R., Beekman, A. T. F., et al. (2006). Depression as a risk factor for the onset of type 2 diabetes mellitus. A meta-analysis. *Diabetologia*, *49*, 837–845.

Kristianingrum, N. D., Ramadhani, D. A., Hayati, Y. S., & Setyoadi, S. (2021). Correlation between the burden of family caregivers and health status of people with diabetes mellitus. *Journal of Public Health Research*, *10*(2), 2227. https://doi.org/10.4081/jphr.2021.2227

Mäntyselkä, P., Kautiainen, H., & Miettola, J. (2019). Beliefs and attitudes towards lifestyle change and risks in primary care – A community-based study. *BMC Public Health*, *19*(1). https://doi.org/10.1186/s12889-019-7377-x

McLeroy, K. R., Steckler, A., & Bibeau, D. (Eds.) (1988). The social ecology of health promotion interventions. *Health Education Quarterly*, *15*(4), 351–377.

Meigs, J. B., Cupples, L. A., & Wilson, P. W. (2000). Parental transmission of type 2 diabetes: The Framingham Offspring Study. *Diabetes*, *49*, 2201–2207.

Mezuk, B., Eaton, W. W., Albrecht, S., & Golden, S. H. (2008). Depression and type 2 diabetes over the lifespan. *Diabetes Care*, *31*(12), 2383–2390. https://doi.org/10.2337/dc08-0985

Moorhead, S. A., Hazlett, D. E., Harrison, L., Carroll, J. K., Irwin, A., & Hoving, C. (2013). A new dimension of health care: systematic review of the uses, benefits, and limitations of social media for health communication. *Journal of Medical Internet Research*, *15*(4), e85.

Naik, B. N., Krishnamoorthy, Y., Kanungo, S., & Mahalakshmy, Kar, S. S. (2018). Primary caregiver involvement in management of type 2 diabetes mellitus: A community-based observational study from urban Puducherry. *International Journal of Noncommunicable Disease*, *8*(3), 3641.

Norman, P., & Fitter, M. (1991). Predicting attendance at health screening: Organizational factors and patients' health beliefs. *Counselling Psychology Quarterly*, *4*, 143155.

Oberoi, S., & Kansra, P. (2020). Economic menace of diabetes in India: A systematic review. *International Journal of Diabetes in Developing Countries*, *40*(4), 464–475. https://doi.org/10.1007/s13410-020-00838-z

Oumoukelthoum, M. (2021). Barriers to health behavior change in people with type 2 diabetes: Survey study. *International Journal of Diabetes and Clinical Research*, *8*(1). https://doi.org/10.23937/2377-3634/1410134

Pan, A., Wang, Y., Talaei, M., Hu, F. B., & Wu, T. (2015). Relation of active, passive, and quitting smoking with incident type 2 diabetes: A systematic review and meta-analysis. *Lancet Diabetes & Endocrinology*, *3*, 958–967.

Penckofer, S., Ferrans, C. E., Velsor-Friedrich, B., & Savoy, S. (2007). The psychological impact of living with diabetes: women's day-to-day experiences. *The Diabetes Educator*, *33*(4), 680–690. https://doi.org/10.1177/0145721707304079

Pouwer, F., Kupper, N., & Adriaanse, M. C. (2010). Does emotional stress cause type 2 diabetes mellitus? A review from the European Depression in Diabetes (EDID) Research Consortium. *Discovery Medicine*, *9*, 112–118.

Rahul, A., Chintha, S., Anish, T. S., Prajitha, K. C., & Indu, P. S. (2021) Effectiveness of a non-pharmacological intervention to control diabetes mellitus in a primary care setting in Kerala: A cluster-randomized controlled trial. *Frontiers of Public Health*, *9*, 747065. doi: 10.3389/fpubh.2021.747065

Rosenstock, I. M. (1974). Historical origins of the health belief model. *Health Education Monographs*, *2*(4), 328–335. https://doi.org/10.1177/109019817400200403

Sheeran, P., Harris, P. R., & Epton, T. (2014). Does heightening risk appraisals change people's intentions and behavior? A meta-analysis of experimental studies. *Psychological Bulletin*, *140*(2), 511.

Solberg, L. I., Desai, J. R., O'Connor, P. J., Bishop, D. B., & Devlin, H. M. (2004). Diabetic patients who smoke: Are they different? *Annals of Family Medicine, 2*(1), 26–32. https://doi.org/10.1370/afm.36

Spruijt-Metz, D., O'Reilly, G. A., Cook, L., Page, K. A., & Quinn, C. (2014). Behavioral contributions to the pathogenesis of type 2 diabetes. *Current Diabetes Reports, 14*(4), 475. https://doi.org/10.1007/s11892-014-0475-3

Steinmetz, H., Knappstein, M., Ajzen, I., Schmidt, P., &Kabst, R. (2016). How effective are behavior change interventions based on the theory of planned behavior? A three-level meta-analysis. *Zeitschrift für Psychologie, 224*, 216–233. 10.1027/2151-2604/a000255.

Thankappan, K., Mini, G., Daivadanam, M., et al. (2013). Smoking cessation among diabetes patients: Results of a pilot randomized controlled trial in Kerala, India. *BMC Public Health, 13*, 47. https://doi.org/10.1186/1471-2458-13-47

Thomas, J. J., Moring, J. C., Harvey, T., Hobbs, T., & Lindt, A. (2016). Risk of type 2 diabetes: Health care provider perceptions of prevention adherence. *Applied Nursing Research, 32*, 1–6. https://doi.org/10.1016/j.apnr.2016.03.002

Warren, G. W., Alberg, A. J., Kraft, A. S., & Cummings, K. M. (2014). The 2014 Surgeon General's report: "The health consequences of smoking-50 years of progress": A paradigm shift in cancer care. *Cancer, 120*(13), 1914–1916. https://doi.org/10.1002/cncr.28695

World Health Organization. (2021). *Diabetes*. Retrieved December 17, 2021, from https://www.who.int/news-room/fact-sheets/detail/diabetes

World Health Organization. Noncommunicable Diseases and Mental Health Cluster. (2005). WHO STEPS surveillance manual: The WHO STEPwise approach to chronic disease risk factor surveillance/Noncommunicable Diseases and Mental Health. https://apps.who.int/iris/handle/10665/43376

Zheng, Y., Ley, S. H., & Hu, F. B. (2018). Global aetiology and epidemiology of type 2 diabetes mellitus and its complications. *Nature Reviews Endocrinology, 14*(2), 88–98.

Zimet, G. D., Dahlem, N. W., Zimet, S. G, & Farley, G. K. (1988). The multidimensional scale of perceived social support. *Journal of Personality Assessment, 52*, 30–41.

PART III
Psychosocial Factors in Cardiovascular Diseases

PART III

8
PSYCHOLOGICAL NECESSITIES OF PATIENTS ELECTING CARDIAC BYPASS SURGERY

A Review and Roadmap

Marlyn Thomas Savio

Surgery is deemed an art for it requires intrusive access into the living human body to repair the damage and heal the person. Surgeons have since time immemorial conjectured that an empathetic interaction with their patients endows superior recovery and minimal need for post-operative medical attention (Williams, 1956). Particularly as being witnessed with the current predominance of chronic non-curable diseases, the fluidity between mind and body demands the departure from the biomedical surgical practice wherein the body is singled out for care needs (Kurniawati, Nursalam, & Suharto, 2017). Healthcare practice ought to be as much psychosocial as biomedical.

This chapter critically inspects the prevailing care protocol for coronary artery bypass grafting (CABG). The surgical treatment restores blood to portions of the heart muscle which received short supply due to blocked arteries as seen in coronary artery disease (CAD) (Bachar & Manna, 2021). CAD, along with stroke, contributes to greater than 80% of disability adjusted life years (DALYs) among Indians (India State-Level Disease Burden Initiative CVD Collaborators, 2018). CAD in Indians is characterised by unusual attributes such as premature age (<55 years for men and <65 years for women), late presentation of the disease, multiple vessel disease, left ventricular dysfunction, diffusion of blocks, and occlusion of smaller arteries. Complex surgery is the first line of treatment in such cases, making CABG a leading option (Kaul & Bhatia, 2010). The aim of this chapter is to draw up an evidence-based theoretical frame that situates a biopsychosocial conceptualisation of the experiences and outcomes of CABG. The focus is on the participation and contributions of Health Psychology for this purpose, specifically in the Indian setting.

Psycho-Behavioural Management as Foundation of Prognosis in CABG

Despite its finesse, CABG is not a cure in itself for CAD. It does not address the process whereby blocks are formed in the arteries (known as atherosclerosis), but merely realigns the blood circulation path. Newly grafted vessels can as well get blocked, resulting in relapse and repeat invasive treatments. Secondary prevention wherein atherosclerosis is minimised becomes the primary cornerstone of care after CABG in order to sustain the benefits of surgery (Kulik *et al.*, 2015). The long-term success of CABG is a function of the patient's adherence to the care regimen. This pursuit of adherence is especially tricky when it extends beyond medication intake and includes effortful physical activity and dietary changes.

Adherence is a psycho-behavioural process. Healthcare providers assume that providing information about self-care components fulfils their responsibility towards their patients. However, as the World Health Organization (2003) acknowledged, information is the necessary yet insufficient basis for adherence. According to a study, the intention to comply with medication was strongly associated with the actual intake if patients (after CABG) specifically planned when, how, and where they would take the medicine and identified strategies to avoid forgetting to take the medicine (Pakpour *et al.*, 2014). In a qualitative exploration of patients who underwent CABG a year before, the experience of surgery and detailed communication from health professionals were found to have urged patients to reform their lifestyles vis-à-vis the doctor's recommendation. However, the time lapse from CABG, unresponsive doctors, and emotional problems due to the trauma of illness influenced patients' non-adherence (Taebi *et al.*, 2014). Interventions aiming to increase adherence must consequently be psychoeducational and collaborative in approach, that is, informative as well as motivation-rousing so that patients plan and are supported to follow the recommendations.

Cardiac Rehabilitation: Evolution from Biomedical to Biopsychosocial

In its earliest form, cardiac rehabilitation (CR) primarily targeted increasing patients' physical activity. This was found to have a pronounced impact by reducing premature mortality in cardiac patients up to 25%, albeit without significant change in the rate of re-infarction or repeat heart attacks (Balady et al., 1994). The World Health Organization (1993) insisted that CR had to be facilitated as a holistic intervention by a multidisciplinary team for all cardiac patients to reverse the pathological influences of their physical, mental, and social conditions so as to improve their overall quality of life.

CR has been successfully prevalent in the West for over five decades, yet is nearly unheard of in India. There are around 23 CR centres, housed in urban/suburban areas, largely requiring out-of-pocket payment (Babu et al., 2020). The modules confine to exercise training and nutritional counselling, catered by physiotherapists, dieticians, and nursing professionals (Madan et al., 2014).

It is worthwhile to consider the few studies that tested the practice of CR in India. A five-day exercise-based CR programme for myocardial infarction in a rural hospital was found to normalise the heart rate and blood pressure better and faster when compared with control patients by the time of discharge (Babu et al., 2010). The study highlighted the feasibility of economically and non-invasively rehabilitating cardiac patients. Rajendran et al. (2004) reported the 'DREAM' ('Diet, Relaxation, Exercise, Attitude and Motivation') programme which provided dietary guidance, taught relaxation techniques, trained patients in graded walking and exercises, addressed attitude to smoking, worries, anger, alcoholism, short temper and anxiety or hurried nature, and extended motivational reminders and doubt clarifications every fortnight. While there was a significant improvement in outcomes (fasting blood glucose, total cholesterol, triglycerides, waist-to-hip ratio, body mass index, and functional capacity) compared with the pre-operative values, there was no exploration of psychological status. In fact, it is unclear whether a psychologist facilitated the relevant components, particularly since the authors were doctors and physiotherapists. The non-involvement of psychologists remains a major shortcoming in most CR ventures. The facilitation of psychological modules such as relaxation and counselling by non-psychologists equates to imparting pseudo-remedies.

The participation of psychologists pertinently exerts the advantage of theoretical grounding for interventions in CR. For instance, theories of Health Psychology were found to resolve the challenge of low attendance in CR. A factorial design study (Mosleh et al., 2014) involved two control groups, one that received a standard invitation for CR and the other that received the standard invitation along with a supportive leaflet providing information about what the CR schedule would include. In addition, there were two experimental groups, one which received a letter based on Ajzen's (1991) theory of planned behaviour (TPB) and the other which received this letter followed by the supportive leaflet. The TPB-based letter rather than the standard invitation significantly improved attendance to the programme, regardless of the presence of the supportive leaflet. This visibly demonstrated that the content of the theory-based letter rather than the details of the programme (given in the supportive leaflet) was responsible for increased attendance. The benefits of professionally motivating patients so that they chose to participate in CR are underlined.

The principal limitation of CR is that it commences, in general, after the event of CABG or hospitalisation. The pre-surgery and peri-operative contexts are densely challenging situations for the patient to independently cope with. Any intervention must begin before CABG or at the time of admission to exert prophylactic effects through consistent biopsychosocial support and monitoring.

Psychosocial Influences on Experiences and Outcomes of CABG

CABG, like any surgery, can be understood as entailing a psychological invasion of the patient's space and being. A number of psychosocial variables naturally come into play for a patient undergoing surgery. According to review reports (Callus et al., 2020; Salzmann et al., 2020), mood states (anxiety, depression), health behaviours, and social support exerted critical effects on cardiac health and surgery outcomes. Future investigations ought to expand these findings in terms of potential interrelationships between psychosocial factors and their combinatorial impact on surgical outcomes.

Anxiety and Depression: Psychological Reactions to CABG

State anxiety in patients with cardiac disease or those undergoing CABG may be a purely circumstantial outcome resulting from the perceived imminence of death or high-risk surgery (Hocaoglu, Yeloglu, & Polat, 2011). Even so, the impact of such anxiety reaches farther than prolonging the negative mood state and exerts effects in the long term. Poole et al. (2017) found that anxiety was predictive of pain and physical symptoms 12 months post-operatively. In another study (Rosenbloom et al., 2009), a 10-point rise in anxiety score predicted an increased risk of mortality or myocardial infarction by 24%. However, there was no significant relationship between anxiety and the progress of atherosclerosis in the grafted vessels. As the authors conceded, anxiety may have acted through alternative underlying pathological processes (e.g., hyper-activation of catecholamine production) or health risk behaviours (e.g., tobacco consumption) that can similarly trigger morbidity or death. There also seems to be a trend of low exercise adherence, overuse of medications, and less stress reduction in the presence of anxiety (Kuhl et al., 2009). Plausibly, anxiety prompts individuals to be hyper-vigilant, whereby they may consume excess drugs even when they experience mild symptoms and may avoid physical activities, being wary of aggravating the disease. In view of the association between anxiety and poor outcomes in recovery and quality of life, the potential for anxiety to inhibit well-being through its direct influence or intermittent variables merits further exploration.

Depression also emerges as an outcome of the experience of illness and surgery. Prior to CABG, the occurrence of depression tends to be relatively lower than that of anxiety, and the trend reverses soon after. In Chaudhury et al.'s (2006) report based on a sample of 30 patients, 30% experienced definite depression as against 43% who were found to have anxiety. A week after CABG, 40% of patients presented depression including those who had pre-operative depression, while a reduced 37% of the sample had anxiety. Murphy et al. (2008) detailed three observations with regard to depression and anxiety in their sample of 184 patients undergoing CABG. The majority 72% of their patients had minor pre-operative depression which was reduced within six months after surgery.

Another 14% of the sample initially had severe depression that remitted within six months after surgery. The final 14% of patients had minor depression which aggravated within six months post-operatively. A larger majority of patients (92%) had minor pre-operative anxiety which declined within six months after surgery. The remaining 8% of the sample had major pre-surgery anxiety which remitted in the post-operative assessment. The results cumulatively suggest that the occurrence of depression in patients before CABG is overshadowed by that of anxiety although the impact and longevity of depression are more severe. Higher depressive symptoms before CABG were observed to be statistically associated with lengthier post-surgery hospital stay through the mediation of the higher concentration of inflammation indicators, for example, C-reactive protein response. In comparison, having no depressive symptoms before surgery was not associated with a longer in-patient stay (Poole et al., 2014). While yet to be confirmed, the consensus seems to be that inflammation is a common cause of depressive symptoms and unfavourable cardiac outcomes.

The universal prevalence of anxiety and depression in patients has led to the recognition of the unified concept of psychological distress which signifies the combination of both emotional states. Anxiety and depression generally presented below clinical significance in a majority of patients who underwent CABG (Chaudhury et al., 2006; Poole et al., 2017). Yet, the impact on prognosis and quality of life remained sizeable (Rosenbloom et al., 2009). Assessing overall psychological distress alongside the categories of anxiety and depression may be valuable to demarcate the unique and amalgamated roles of these mood states, in the course of adherence and prognosis in patients undergoing CABG.

Perceived Social Support: A Critical Scaffold of Cardiac Health

Perceived social support functions as a protective shield in potentially pathological situations. The buffering effect has been theoretically conceptualised by means of the information-based model, the identity and self-esteem model, the social influence model, and the tangible resource model. According to the information-based model, an individual may be comforted by the perception that social support can provide relevant information to re-evaluate the situation and reduce its harmful impact. The identity and self-esteem model maintains that an individual's self-esteem and identity may be boosted by the perception that social support can help overcome the situation. In the social influence model, the individual may perceive confidence over a stressful situation because social support would influence or pressurise her or him to cope fruitfully. With regard to the tangible resource model, the individual may feel secure by the perception that social support will provide him with needed resources (e.g., finances) to cope with the situation (Cohen, 1988). In each of the models, the belief that one has help at hand mitigates the negative affect and transforms the threatening situation into a manageable one. Perceived social support can, thus, be treated as a moderator of stress and its impact.

Perceived support from significant others appears to confer the necessary emotional immunity when undergoing medical procedures. Chivukula et al. (2013) contrasted levels of perceived social support, anxiety, and depression between patients undergoing diagnostic angiography and those having CABG. The type of procedure itself bore a significant impact on psychological distress such that waiting for angiography was more anxiety-provoking and depressing than awaiting CABG. Perceived social support was significantly predictive of the variance in anxiety and depression in the whole cardiac sample and the angiography sub-sample. For the CABG sample, perceived social support was a significant predictor of anxiety, not depression. Perhaps, a multiple regression analysis inclusive of the type of procedure and perceived social support would clarify the contributions of each factor individually and collectively to psychological distress.

In the context of medical treatment, one's social support network stretches beyond family and friends. A research group (Koivula et al., 2002) considered the patients' reports of the social support (informational, emotional, and tangible) received from nurses a day prior to CABG, along with an assessment of anxiety and fear of surgery. High emotional support from nurses was associated with low fear and anxiety, while high informational support was related to low fear. The study provided evidence of the need for social support from health professionals as well, in order to foster positive emotional states and constructive health cognitions in patients for CABG. In concurrence with the earlier discussed information-based model and social influence model (Cohen, 1988), patients rely heavily on social support from familial and medical professional sources in affectively coming to terms with surgery and in cognitively making sense of CABG. Interventions must aim to foster a positive relationship between providers and patients so that the detrimental effect of low perceived social support on patients' psychological state is counterbalanced. It is imperative for doctors to offer adequate informational support to their patients and thereby uphold good quality relationships, the absence of which engenders non-adherence leading to poor health outcomes (Swain et al., 2015). In sum, perceived social support benefits the behavioural and physiological mechanisms of health.

Existing Psychological Support Provisions in Healthcare Protocols

Interventions designed by psychologists or that incorporate psychological principles have been gaining ground in healthcare given the large turnout of chronic diseases. The approaches adopted in these programmes can be broadly classified into two types—educational and therapeutic.

Diagnosis of a disease generates learning needs for the patient. Patients with CAD, for example, expressed perceived learning needs pertaining to medication, risk factors, and lifestyle (Yaacob et al., 2020). Psychoeducation in medical settings is an evidence-based strategy to exploit the teachable moment and provide informational support through the use of psychotherapeutic principles such as those of cognitive-behavioural and learning theories. The awareness generated by the intervention aids patients' adjustment to the condition and reformation of modifiable risk factors (Child et al., 2010).

The application of psychoeducational intervention around the time of CABG has yielded mixed results. A randomised controlled trial (Guo, East, & Arthur, 2012) found that psychoeducation endows positive benefits immediately after the intervention. An information leaflet containing details about admission, pre-surgery tests, preparation for surgery, ICU atmosphere and environment, communication with providers, exercises, discharge, lifestyle modification, and contact information was given to the intervention group. The reduction in anxiety and depression from baseline to post-surgery assessment was significantly higher in the intervention group relative to the control group. No significant difference was observed in terms of pain, length of ICU stay, and overall hospital stay. Qualitative data revealed positive feedback for the intervention. Participants, however, expressed discontentment over the hospital staff's minimal communication and information-sharing with them. This hints at the need to additionally engage health providers in psychoeducation. The lack of significant difference in perceived pain does not necessarily imply that psychoeducation is not effective. The follow-up period of a week may have been too short for the healing of major surgical wounds.

The impact of patient education has not always been positive. A group of patients were categorised at the point of admission as having mild anxiety, moderate anxiety, and severe anxiety. All groups received an educational intervention, facilitated by a psychologist. Anxiety significantly reduced from baseline to pre-surgery assessment only for the severe anxiety group. A reduction in the mean anxiety score, albeit non-significant, was noted for the group with moderate anxiety. Surprisingly, the mild anxiety group reported a significant rise in the mean anxiety score after the intervention. The authors inferred that education may be appropriate for severely anxious patients (Akbarzadeh et al., 2009). This presents a problematic generalisation on many counts. There was no description of the format and method of administration of the pre-surgery education which prevents analysis of its strengths and limitations. No evidence indicated that the increase in anxiety for the mild anxiety group was a negative outcome, as the authors had not investigated the impact of this rise on any other variable related to recovery or well-being. Perhaps, this group may represent patients who may have been complacent or in denial regarding their surgery. These patients plausibly came to comprehend the situation of CABG only after the intervention. Alternatively, other unexplored confounding variables may have prompted mild anxiety to rise. Moreover, the trend of a decrease in anxiety for the moderate and severe anxiety groups underscores that education was a necessary interventional aid.

Among psychological interventions that directly alleviate distress, relaxation is a common and cost-effective method. In Chandrababu et al.'s (2021) meta-analysis of randomised controlled trials using music intervention with patients having cardiac surgery, anxiety and pain decreased. The passive nature of music therapy (merely listening) seems to make it less effective in managing physiological indices such as blood pressure and heart rate (Heidari et al., 2015). Elsewhere, unspecified relaxation presented by anaesthesiologists before surgery and during ICU stay lowered the values of patients' vital signs (systolic blood pressure, body temperature, pulse rate) within 48 hours after CABG. However, there was no reduction in pain perception and use of pain relievers during ICU stay (Firoozabadi & Ebadi, 2014). The use of guided imagery across studies with patients undergoing cardiac surgery produced similar effects such that anxiety and pain decreased (Hadjibalassi et al., 2018). The usefulness of relaxation techniques has not been consistently replicated for outcomes other than those mood related.

Any technique of relaxation merits being contrasted with other types of psychological intervention so that the process and extent of its impact as a therapeutic interventional approach during surgery are made explicit. Different types of relaxation bring down the sympathetic arousal response of a negative emotional state (e.g., anxiety) by creating reciprocal states of calmness and tranquillity (Chen et al., 2012). Positive affective states have been repeatedly associated with the enhancement of health-promoting behaviours and the reduction of stress responses which in turn improve health outcomes (Pressman, Jenkins, & Moskowitz, 2019). The workings of relaxation thus differ from that of psychoeducation which essentially targets health cognition. The paradigm of comparing interventions can be enlightening with regard to the distinct efficacy of different types of psychological intervention.

Savio and Hariharan (2020) used a three-group design comprising psychoeducation (named 'Programme for Affective and Cognitive Education—PACE'), relaxation (guided imagery), and standard care for CABG in India. The two intervention groups had significantly lower psychological distress and significantly better prognosis than the control group six weeks after discharge. Interestingly, these outcomes were also significantly superior for the PACE group relative to the relaxation group. PACE was designed to psychoeducate participants about surgery and post-operative care not merely from a surgeon's standpoint but also from that of former patients who retold their CABG experience, in addition to including a health psychologist's inputs on psychosocial coping. The marriage of objective and subjective perspectives in PACE made it what patients most likely seek when faced with a traumatic medical event (CABG)—expert guidance (health cognitions) and an empathetic frame of reference/belonging (perceived social support). What nonetheless remains to be assessed is the long-term impact of such interventions.

Planning Psychosocial Intervention

The available scientific literature has facilitated key insights into the field of interest. Certainly, this review may not be exhaustive yet its discursive exploration of an assortment of methods, concepts, and findings has thrown light on

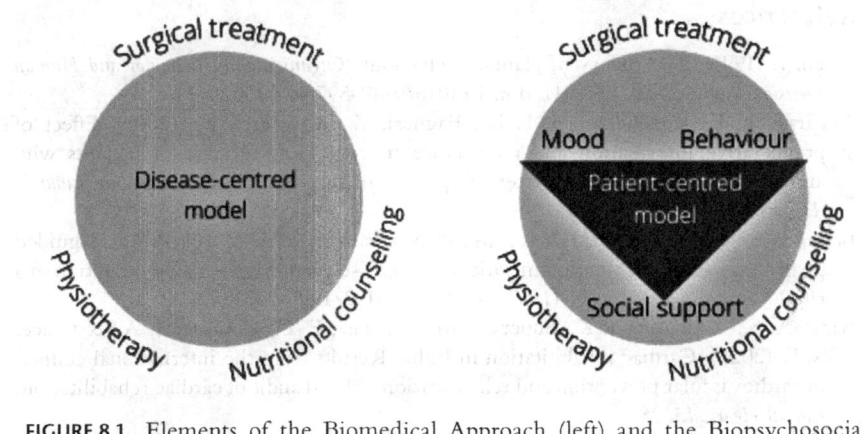

FIGURE 8.1 Elements of the Biomedical Approach (left) and the Biopsychosocial Approach (right) to CABG care.

the complementary, contradictory, and ambiguous trends related to the processes and outcomes in the nexus of CAD, CABG, and psychological distress. In so doing, this review has advocated the transformation of the exclusionist biomedical model into an inclusive biopsychosocial ecosystem of care during CABG depicted in Figure 8.1.

Psychological distress (anxiety and depression) is clearly rampant and consequential in patients being subjected to CABG. These mood states may be directly related to the apprehension or misconceptions about the procedure or may be amplified by the deficiency of perceived social support. Unless psychological distress is mitigated, the impact on patient outcomes is glaring. Good prognosis is the ultimate goal, achieving which requires addressing psychological distress and adherence behaviours.

Psychosocial intervention that is feasible and impactful in the context of CABG broadly includes psychoeducation and relaxation. The limitations of previous studies that adopted these approaches provide directions for the future. Psychoeducation must balance technical facts (from professionals) with experiential information (from peer patients). Evidence on the effectiveness of relaxation is mixed although this therapeutic approach may be particularly useful during emergency surgery wherein psychosocial intervention must share the limited time with ongoing medical protocols.

The paucity of work by psychologists with regard to psychological issues and contributions possible in the care of cardiac patients, specifically in India, was consistently observed across sections of this review. While professionals from other healthcare disciplines have commendably attempted to adapt various psychological principles for use with cardiac patients, the results were short-lived or under-explained. It is indeed time that the field of Health Psychology accomplished its role in assessment and intervention programmes, by being positioned within the mainstream Indian healthcare system.

References

Ajzen, I. (1991). The theory of planned behaviour. *Organizational Behavior and Human Decision Processes, 50,* 179–211. doi: 10.1016/0749-5978(91)90020-T

Akbarzadeh, F., Kouchaksaraei, F. R., Bagheri, Z., & Ghezel, M. (2009). Effect of preoperative information and reassurance in decreasing anxiety of patients who are candidate for Coronary Artery Bypass Graft surgery. *Journal of Cardiovascular & Thoracic Research, 1,* 25–28.

Babu, A. S., Noone, M. S., Haneef, M., & Narayanan, S. M. (2010). Protocol-guided phase-1 cardiac rehabilitation in patients with ST-elevation myocardial infarction in a rural hospital. *Heart Views, 11,* 52–56. doi: 10.4103/1995-705X.73209

Babu, A. S., Turk-Adawi, K., Supervia, M., Jimenez, F. L., Contractor, A., & Grace, S. L. (2020). Cardiac rehabilitation in India: Results from the international council of cardiovascular prevention and rehabilitation's global audit of cardiac rehabilitation. *Global Heart, 15,* 28.

Bachar, B. J., & Manna, B. (2021). Coronary Artery Bypass Graft. In Stat Pearls (Internet). Treasure Island: Stat Pearls Publishing. Retrieved March 12, 2022, from https://www.ncbi.nlm.nih.gov/books/NBK507836/

Balady, G. J., Fletcher, B. J., Froelicher, E. S., Hartley, L. H., Krauss, R. M., Oberman, A.,... Members (1994). Cardiac rehabilitation programs: A statement for healthcare professionals from the American Heart Association. *Circulation, 90,* 1602–1610. doi: 10.1161/01.CIR.90.3.1602

Callus, E., Pagliuca, S., Bertoldo, E. G., Fiolo, V., Jackson, A. C., Boeri, S.,... Menicanti, L. (2020). The monitoring of psychosocial factors during hospitalization before and after cardiac surgery until discharge from cardiac rehabilitation: A research protocol. *Frontiers in Psychology, 11,* 2202. doi: 10.3389/fpsyg.2020.02202

Chandrababu, R., Ramesh, J., Devi, E. S., Nayak, B. S., & George, A. (2021). Effectiveness of music on anxiety and pain among cardiac surgery patients: A quantitative systematic review and meta-analysis of randomized controlled trials. *International Journal of Nursing Practice, 27,* e12928. doi: 10.1111/ijn.12928

Chaudhury, S., Sharma, S., Pawar, A. A., Kumar, B. K., Srivastava, K., Sudarsanan, S., & Singh, D. (2006). Psychological correlates of outcome after Coronary Artery Bypass Graft. *Medical Journal Armed Forces India, 62,* 220–223. doi: 10.1016/S0377-1237(06)80004-3

Chen, K. W., Berger, C. C., Manheimer, E., Forde, D., Magidson, J., Dachman, L., & Lejuez, C. W. (2012). Meditative therapies for reducing anxiety: A systematic review and meta-analysis of randomized controlled trials. *Depression and Anxiety, 29,* 545–562. doi: 10.1002/da.21964

Child, A., Sanders, J., Sigel, P., & Hunter, M. S. (2010). Meeting the psychological needs of cardiac patients: An integrated stepped-care approach within a cardiac rehabilitation setting. *British Journal of Cardiology, 17,* 175–179.

Chivukula, U., Swain, S., Rana, S., & Hariharan, M. (2013). Perceived social support and type of cardiac procedures as modifiers of hospital anxiety and depression. *Psychological Studies, 58,* 242–247. doi: 10.1007/s12646-013-0199-5

Cohen, S. (1988). Psychosocial models of the role of social support in the etiology of physical disease. *Health Psychology, 7,* 269–297. doi: 10.1037/0278-6133.7.3.269

Firoozabadi, M. D., & Ebadi, A. (2014). Effect of relaxation on postoperative pain in patients after Coronary Artery Bypass Grafting (CABG) surgery. *NationalPark-Forschung in Der Schweiz (Switzerland Research Park Journal), 103,* 185–191.

Guo, P., East, L., & Arthur, A. (2012). A preoperative education intervention to reduce anxiety and improve recovery among Chinese cardiac patients: A randomized controlled trial. *International Journal of Nursing Studies, 49,* 129–137. doi: 10.1016/j.ijnurstu.2011.08.008

Hadjibalassi, M., Lambrinou, E., Papastavrou, E., & Papathanassoglou, E. (2018). The effect of guided imagery on physiological and psychological outcomes of adult ICU patients: A systematic literature review and methodological implications. *Australian Critical Care, 31,* 73–86. doi: 10.1016/j.aucc.2017.03.001

Heidari, S., Babaii, A., Abbasinia, M., Shamali, M., Abbasi, M., & Rezaei, M. (2015). The effect of music on anxiety and cardiovascular indices in patients undergoing coronary artery bypass graft: A randomized controlled trial. *Nursing & Midwifery Studies, 4,* e31157. doi: 10.17795/nmsjournal31157

Hocaoglu, C., Yeloglu, C. H., & Polat, S. (2011). Cardiac diseases and anxiety disorders. In Á. Szirami (Ed.), *Anxiety and Related Disorders* (pp. 139–150). Retrieved June 17, 2015, from http://tinyurl.com/ntm2clh

India State-Level Disease Burden Initiative CVD Collaborators. (2018). The changing patterns of cardiovascular diseases and their risk factors in the states of India: The global burden of disease study 1990–2016. *Lancet Global Health, 6,* e1339–e1351.

Kaul, U., & Bhatia, V. (2010). Perspective on coronary interventions & cardiac surgeries in India. *Indian Journal of Medical Research, 132,* 543–548.

Koivula, M., Tarkka, M., Tarkka, M., Laippala, P., & Paunonen-Ilmonen, M. (2002). Fear and in-hospital social support for Coronary Artery Bypass Grafting patients on the day before surgery. *International Journal of Nursing Studies, 39,* 415–427. doi: 10.1016/S0020-7489(01)00044-X

Kuhl, E. A., Fauerbach, J. A., Bush, D. E., & Ziegelstein, R. C. (2009). Relation of anxiety and adherence to risk-reducing recommendations following myocardial infarction. *American Journal of Cardiology, 103,* 1629–1634. doi: 10.1016/j.amjcard.2009.02.014

Kulik, A., Ruel, M., Jneid, H., Ferguson, T. B., Hiratzka, L. F., Ikonomidis, J. S.,... Zimmerman, L. (2015). Secondary prevention after Coronary Artery Bypass Graft surgery: A scientific statement from the American Heart Association. *Circulation, 131,* 927–964. doi: 10.1161/CIR.0000000000000182

Kurniawati, N. D., Nursalam, N., & Suharto, S. (2017). Mind-body-spiritual nursing care in intensive care unit. *Advances in Health Sciences Research, 3,* 223–228. doi: 10.2991/inc-17.2017.59

Madan, K., Babu, A. S., Contractor, A., Sawhney, J. P., Prabhakaran, D., & Gupta, R. (2014). Cardiac rehabilitation in India. *Progress in Cardiovascular Diseases, 56,* 543–550. doi: 10.1016/j.pcad.2013.11.001

Mosleh, S. M., Bond, C. M., Lee, A. J., Kiger, A., & Campbell, N. C. (2014). Effectiveness of theory-based invitations to improve attendance at cardiac rehabilitation: A randomized controlled trial. *European Journal of Cardiovascular Nursing, 13,* 201–210. doi: 10.1177/1474515113491348

Murphy, B. M., Elliott, P. C., Higgins, R. O., Le Grande, M. R., Worcester, M. U. C., Goble, A. J., & Tatoulis, J. (2008). Anxiety and depression after coronary artery bypass graft surgery: Most get better, some get worse. *European Journal of Preventive Cardiology, 15,* 434–440. doi: 10.1097/HJR.0b013e3282fbc945

Pakpour, A. H., Gellert, P., Asefzadeh, S., Updegraff, J. A., Molloy, G. J., & Sniehotta, F. F. (2014). Intention and planning predicting medication adherence following coronary artery bypass graft surgery. *Journal of Psychosomatic Research, 77,* 287–295. doi: 10.1016/j.jpsychores.2014.07.001

Poole, L., Kidd, T., Leigh, E., Ronaldson, A., Jahangiri, M., & Steptoe, A. (2014). Depression, C-reactive protein and length of post-operative hospital stay in coronary artery bypass graft surgery patients. *Brain, Behavior, and Immunity, 37*, 115–121. doi: 10.1016/j.bbi.2013.11.008

Poole, L., Ronaldson, A., Kidd, T., Leigh, E., Jahangiri, M., & Steptoe, A. (2017). Pre-surgical depression and anxiety and recovery following coronary artery bypass graft surgery. *Journal of Behavioral Medicine, 40*, 249–258. doi: 10.1007/s10865-016-9775-1

Pressman, S. D., Jenkins, B. N., & Moskowitz, J. T. (2019). Positive affect and health: What do we know and where next should we go? *Annual Reviews of Psychology, 70*, 627–650. doi: 10.1146/annurev-psych-010418-102955

Rajendran, A. J., Manoj, S., Karthikeyan, D., & Davis, S. (2004). Cardiac rehabilitation for CABG patients in South Indian setup: A prospective study. *Indian Journal of Physical Medicine and Rehabilitation, 15*, 23–33.

Rosenbloom, J. I., Wellenius, G. A., Mukamal, K. J., & Mittleman, M. A. (2009). Self-reported anxiety and the risk of clinical events and atherosclerotic progression among patients with coronary artery bypass grafts (CABG). *American Heart Journal, 158*, 867–873. doi: 10.1016/j.ahj.2009.08.019

Salzmann, S., Salzmann-Djufri, M., Wilhelm, M., & Euteneuer, F. (2020). Psychological preparation for cardiac surgery. *Current Cardiology Reports, 22*, 172. doi: 10.1007/s11886-020-01424-9

Savio, M. T., & Hariharan, M. (2020). Impact of psychosocial intervention on prognosis of cardiac surgery patients. *Health Psychology Research, 8*. doi: 10.4081/hpr.2020.8887

Swain, S., Hariharan, M., Rana, S., Chivukula, U., & Thomas, M. (2015). Doctor-patient communication: Impact on adherence and prognosis among patients with primary hypertension. *Psychological Studies, 60*, 25–32. doi: 10.1007/s12646-014-0291-5

Taebi, M., Abedi, H. A., Abbasszadeh, A., & Kazemi, M. (2014). Incentives for self-management after coronary artery bypass graft surgery. *Iranian Journal of Nursing and Midwifery Research, 19*, S64–S70.

Williams, C. (1956). The art of surgery. *Annals of Surgery, 143*, 561–565.

World Health Organization. (1993). *Rehabilitation after Cardiovascular Diseases, with Special Emphasis on Developing Countries.* Geneva: World Health Organization.

World Health Organization. (2003). *Adherence to Long-term Therapies: Evidence for Action.* Geneva: World Health Organization.

Yaacob, S., Zaini, N. H., Abdullah, K. L., Ahmad, N. Z., Ramoo, V., Azahar, N. M. Z. M., & Aziz, A. F. A. (2020). Perceived learning needs among coronary artery disease patients: A study in a tertiary hospital. *Malaysian Journal of Medicine and Health Sciences, 16*, 10–15.

9
ILLNESS PERCEPTION AND ADHERENCE BEHAVIOUR IN PATIENTS WITH CORONARY ARTERY DISEASE

Arti Singh and Shikha Dixit

The contribution of coronary artery disease (CAD) has increased massively from one-tenth in 1990 to a quarter of the total disease burden in India in 2016 (Indian Council of Medical Research et al., 2017). Approximately 2.8 million people died of CAD in 2016 compared to 1.3 million people in 1990 (Prabhakaran et al., 2018). This sweeping increase in cardiac disease burden requires immediate attention from healthcare practitioners and policymakers.

Literature suggests various factors contribute to the worsening of CAD and its related symptoms (American Heart Association, 2021). One such factor is non-adherence to medication, diet, and recommended lifestyle changes. Adherence behaviour can be described as "the extent to which an individual's behaviour coincides with health-related instructions or recommendations given by a healthcare provider in the context of a specific disease or disorder" (Howren, 2013). It consists of five interacting dimensions: patient-related factors, condition-related factors, therapy-related factors, healthcare team/system-related factors, and social/economic factors (World Health Organization, 2003). Studies have reported a decrease in mortality rate (Lee et al., 2018), hospital readmission rate (Al-Tamimi et al., 2021), and a lower economic burden for the community (Piña et al., 2021) when CAD patients follow adherence to recommended lifestyle.

Also known as secondary prevention practice or compliance behaviour, the recommendation for adherence behaviour for a CAD patient often includes making healthier food choices (regular intake of green and leafy vegetables, fresh fruits, less oily and fried food items, lower intake of sugar and salt), doing regular physical exercise of moderate intensity for 30 minutes, cessation of tobacco taking behaviour, control of blood pressure at or under 140/90 mmHg, achieving a triglyceride level less than 200 mg/dl, and low-density lipoprotein less than 100 mg/dl (American Heart Association, 2021). Findings indicate that 43.5% of CAD patients were non-adherent to their secondary prevention medicines (Khatib et al., 2019),

DOI: 10.4324/9781003360858-12

whereas 45.3% and 41.1% of patients were non-adherent to dietary recommendations and exercise, respectively (Ali et al., 2017). Existing literature has identified various factors of low adherence behaviour. One such factor affecting adherence behaviour is illness perception-cognitive representation of disease among patients. Leventhal proposed illness perception as consisting of eight dimensions: identity, consequences, causes, emotional perception, treatment perception, personal control, treatment control, and illness coherence (Leventhal et al., 1992).

Several studies have reported the importance of illness perception in predicting various health outcomes, including adherence behaviour. Illness perception has been studied in the literature for various diseases such as cardiovascular diseases, arthritis, hypertension, renal disease, chronic pain, contact dermatitis, and rare diseases like Huntington's disease and Addison's disease. In a study on Type 2 diabetes patients, diabetes consequences were found to affect medication adherence (Pereira et al., 2019). Illness perceptions can also predict adherence behaviour among hypertensive patients (Al-Noumani et al., 2019).

In a study, higher harmful consequences, higher illness concerns, and more emotional impairment among myocardial infarction (MI) patients were associated with post-traumatic stress (Princip et al., 2018). Illness perception has also been found to be capable of predicting misconceptions about heart disease (Figueiras et al., 2017), psychological well-being (Sawyer, Harris, & Koenig, 2019), fatigue (Bagherian-Sararoudi et al., 2019), and quality of life (QoL) (Thomson et al., 2020).

In the context of India, the issue of adherence behaviour among CAD patients becomes more complicated with certain cultural practices (Kamath et al., 2021) and lack of accessibility to appropriate healthcare facilities (Singh & Dixit, 2016). However, the literature on adherence behaviour among CAD patients has primarily focused either on Western patients or non-resident Indians. Therefore, the present study aimed to investigate adherence behaviour among Indian CAD patients. Additionally, as the literature suggests that patients' illness perceptions play a vital role in determining their adherence behaviour; it may be argued that exploring their relationship may broaden the understanding of the health behaviour of CAD patients.

Method

Research Design

A cross-sectional mixed methods study was conducted from October 2014 to August 2015. This study was conducted in two phases: in the first phase, a quantitative study was conducted. In the second phase, a qualitative study was conducted to substantiate the findings of the first phase. The study included a quantitative survey with 236 CAD patients and qualitative in-depth interviews with 22 CAD patients from the only public cardiac hospital in Uttar Pradesh (UP) – *Hriday Rog Sansthan*, Kanpur, Uttar Pradesh.

Study Sample

Only clinically stable, literate (minimum high school qualified), and middle-income patients belonging to urban or suburban areas were selected. The Prasad's scale for classification (Dudala, Reddy & Prabhu, 2014) was used to determine participants' socio-economic status. The following criteria were used to determine the clinical status of participants: (i) not faced any episode of angina or myocardial infarction (MI) in the last four months, (ii) not undergone any surgery in the last four months, and (iii) had undergone angiography test which indicated their clinical state of blockages. The ethical approval from the Institute of Ethical Committee (IEC) of the Indian Institute of Technology, Kanpur (Approval No. IITK/IEC/2015-16/1/2) was obtained. All possible measures were taken to maintain ethicality in the inquiry.

Quantitative Study

Purposive sampling was used to collect quantitative data from 249 CAD patients. Later 13 participants were excluded from the final analysis due to various reasons such as incomplete questionnaires, not fulfilling the criteria of participants' selection, or unwillingness to complete the questionnaires. Thus, the final sample of the quantitative study consisted of 236 (male = 163, female = 73) CAD patients.

Qualitative Study

Total 27 interviews were collected from CAD patients using purposive sampling. Out of these 27 participants, 12 were females and 15 were males. However, during analysis, only 22 interviews (10 were females and 12 were males) were used as the other five interviews were either not audible or participants did not complete the interview.

Reflexivity: Locating the Researcher

To maintain self-reflexivity in the research process, a reflexive log was maintained throughout the research. The self-reflective practice was started by asking questions such as, "What do I know? How do I know what I know? What shapes and has shaped my perspective? With what voice do I share my perspective? What do I do with what I have found?" (Marshall & Rossman, 2016, p. 118). The researchers used the log to acknowledge their beliefs on various aspects of heart disease such as perspective on the cause of coronary artery disease, the conceptualisation of treatment availability to patients, and its consequences. This helped in identifying their own biases and theoretical predisposition towards CAD patients. Further, this reflective log was used to jot down any relevant observation and thoughts on that observation.

Data Collection

Quantitative Inquiry

Illness perception was measured using Illness Perception Questionnaire-Revised (IPQ-R) version developed by Moss-Morris et al. (2002). To measure adherence behaviour, a scale was developed consisting of 14 items. A confirmatory factor analysis (CFA) with varimax rotation was conducted and except for one, all 13 items loaded significantly in their conceptualised dimensions. One item, which loaded weakly, was deleted from the scale. Therefore, the final version of the scale consists of 13 items and measures four dimensions of adherence behaviour: medication, diet, physical activity, and addiction restriction. Two items measured medication adherence, diet adherence behaviour was measured by six items, physical activity by two items, while three items measured behaviour for addiction restriction.

Qualitative Inquiry

A semi-structured interview schedule was used to conduct interviews. The focus of CAD patients' interview schedule was various attributes of their adherence behaviour as cardiac patients. Participants were inquired about their behaviour, attitude, and perception of their adherence behaviour. All interviews were conducted on the premises of the treatment set-up only and were audio-taped. Participants were interviewed until data saturation was achieved and no new codes emerged. Only selected interviews were transcribed and, where required, translated into English. The translation was cross-checked for accuracy by the second author.

Analysis

Quantitative Analysis

Data were analysed using Statistical Package for the Social Sciences (SPSS) version 20. Standard descriptive statistics were calculated for both variables. Multiple linear regression analysis was conducted with each of the adherence behaviour scores as dependent variables and illness perception as independent variables.

Qualitative Analysis

For analysing qualitative results, a six-step thematic analysis identified by Braun and Clarke (2006) was used. All interviews were first transcribed in the original language, that is, Hindi, and were translated into English where required. Interviews were analysed independently by the first author, and identified codes and subsequent themes were discussed with the second author. Any disagreement was discussed and resolved.

Results

Quantitative Study

In total, 236 CAD patients responded to the questionnaires. Of 236 participants, 163 were males, 73 were females, 126 were angina patients, and 110 were MI patients. The average age of the participants was 52.43 years. The majority (92.8%) of the participants were married, 63.98% were employed, and 92% had attended at least high school. Of the total sample, 39.83% of participants had taken some form of smokeless tobacco at least once in their lifetime, while 36.01% and 16.52% had taken smoking and alcohol, respectively, at least once in their lifetime. It was found that 18.22% of participants had diabetes as a co-morbidity, while 13.13% had hypertension. Table 9.1 presents the participants' characteristics.

TABLE 9.1 Demographic details of participants

Sample size	Quantitative study 236	Qualitative study 22
Mean age	52.43 years	55.43
Gender		
Male	163 (69.06%)	12 (54.54%)
Female	73 (30.93%)	10 (45.45%)
Type of CAD		
MI	110 (46.61%)	8 (36.36%)
Angina	126 (53.38%)	14 (63.63%)
Marital status		
Married	219 (92.8%)	18 (81.81%)
Unmarried	2.8 (1.2%)	03 (13.63%)
Widow	14.16 (6.0%)	01 (4.54%)
Educational status		
High school	92 (38.98%)	07 (31.81%)
Intermediate	80 (33.89%)	05 (22.72%)
Graduate	45 (19.06%)	08 (36.36%)
Postgraduate	19 (8.05%)	02 (9.09%)
Employment status		
Employed	151 (69.06%)	08 (36.36)
Unemployed (housewives, unable to work)	70 (29.66%)	10 (45.45%)
Retired	15 (6.35%)	04 (18.18%)
Addiction		
Smoking	85 (36.01%)	04 (18.18%)
Alcohol	39 (16.52%)	03 (13.63%)
Tobacco (tobacco chewing, *Paan* or *Gutka*)	94 (39.83%)	11 (50.00%)
Presence of co-morbidity		
Diabetes	43 (18.22%)	05 (22.72%)
Hypertension	31 (13.13%)	06 (27.27%)
Diabetes + Hypertension	33 (13.98%)	05 (22.72%)
Others	15 (6.35%)	03 (13.63%)

In general, participants perceived their heart condition to be more chronic in nature (M = 26.52, SD = 2.69) and having more consequences (M = 25.93, SD = 3.02). They also had high emotional representation (M = 21.72, SD = 2.67) attached to it. With respect to causal attribution, participants attributed more to risk factors. Descriptive analysis of adherence behaviour suggests that CAD patients of the present study were found to be most adherent to their diet recommendations (mean = 18.18, SD = 3.94), followed by recommendations for addiction restrictions (M = 14.27, SD = 1.68), medication (M = 8.95, SD = 1.34), and physical activity (M = 5.93, SD = 1.68).

The variables adherence behaviour and illness perception were moderately correlated (r = .47, p < .001). Personal control and treatment control and timeline cyclic dimensions of illness perception were significantly positively correlated with all four subscales of adherence behaviour. The timeline cyclic dimension of illness perception was significantly negatively related to all subscales of adherence behaviour. Interestingly, the consequence dimension was negatively associated with medication and diet adherence but was positively associated with addiction restriction. Further, attributing causes to risk factors and life stress (such as diet, smoking, my own behaviour, stress or worry, and family problem) were also correlated with medication (r = .24, p < .01) and diet adherence (r = .15, p < .05).

Multiple regression was carried out to investigate whether illness perception could predict adherence behaviour among participants. The regression results indicated that illness perception explained 22.1% of the variance, and it was a significant predictor of adherence behaviour of CAD patients, F (1234) = 66.354, p = .0001. To identify significant independent predictors of various dimensions of adherence behaviour, multiple regression was carried out. Results presented in Table 9.2 indicate that medication adherence, diet adherence, addiction restriction, and physical activity can be predicted significantly by six, two, four, and two dimensions of illness perception, respectively.

Qualitative Results

The result of in-depth interviews complemented quantitative findings. Thematic analysis suggested that various factors influenced the adherence behaviour of CAD patients. A detailed description of themes, subthemes, and codes is presented in Table 9.3.

Adherence for Physical Activity (PA)

Low Motivation

The majority of the participants were aware of the benefits of walking, but only a few of them reported regular walks. Many of these participants did not always feel like going for a walk. One participant commented:

TABLE 9.2 Multiple regression to identify predictors of various dimensions of Adherence Behaviour Scale

	Independent predictors	B	SE	p value	Adjusted R-square	F	R^2
Medication adherence					.25	8.24 $p < .00$	.29
	Identity	.13	.03	.00			
	Treatment chronic	−.10	.04	.03			
	Consequence	−.08	.03	.00			
	Treatment control	.05	.02	.01			
	Treatment cyclic	−.10	.02	.00			
	Risk factors and life stress	−.19	.05	.00			
Diet adherence					.11	3.71 $p < .00$	.13
	Treatment control	.22	.07	.00			
	Treatment cyclic	−.22	.08	.01			
Addiction restriction					.13	4.23 $p < .00$	.16
	Personal control	.08	.03	.02			
	Treatment control	.09	.02	.00			
	Coherence	.04	.01	.01			
	Emotional representation	−.09	.04	.04			
Physical activity					.13	4.31 $p > .00$	.15
	Personal control	.05	.01	.00			
	Treatment control	.06	.03	.03			

Notes: B – unstandardised regression coefficient, SE – standard error.

Yes, a morning walk is necessary. It helps in decreasing your cholesterol level.

When asked if he went for regular morning walks, the same participant replied:

No. Sometimes I do, and sometimes I don't. My children ask me to go for a morning walk, but I don't go. Even though my home is on the banks of river Yamuna, the government has made pavements and parks for walking and exercising.

When asked why he does not walk regularly, the participant responded:

To tell you the truth, it's just laziness and nothing else. I do not feel like waking up in the morning and going for a walk. I feel it is a huge task. But now I am seriously thinking of going for a walk daily.

This suggests that having awareness about the benefits of a walk or the availability of facilities that can promote healthy behaviour (like roadside pavements for pedestrians or parks) is not sufficient to motivate patients to be physically active. Many other factors can play an essential role in making a patient physically active.

TABLE 9.3 Identified themes, subthemes, and codes

A. **Physical activity**	1. Low motivation	Not interested in walking/exercise, irregular behaviour, forgets to take walk, not interested in waking up, laziness
	2. Misconception	Yoga better than walking, causes harm
	3. Replacing physical activity with everyday chores	Shortage of time, daily chores are better, daily chores involve full body exercise
B. **Diet adherence**	1. Losing taste in food	Loss of taste due to diet restrictions
	2. Misconception	Medicines can compensate for extra salt and sugar, less fried food, salt won't harm
	3. Role of family	Problems faced by other family members due to diet restrictions, cooking separate is difficult
C. **Addiction restriction**	1. Quitting SLT is more difficult	Unable to quit SLT, the substitution of SLT, a milder form of SLT
D. **Medication adherence**	1. Role of family	Supportive/non-supportive children, supportive spouse
	2. Side effects	Skipping medicines, increased fatigue due to medicines, increase in restlessness
	3. Financial constraints	Costly medicines, no financial support

Misconception

Some of the participants also reported practising Yoga to remain physically active. Interestingly, those who were practising Yoga were reported doing it as a substitute for walking. According to such participants, as walking caused breathing problems and fatigue, they prefer yoga. One such participant responded:

When I used to walk, it caused difficulty in breathing for me. Sometimes, I also felt chest pain while walking ... so, I stopped walking. I mean, I have not stopped walking altogether, but I walk only sometimes in a month, and I don't do brisk walking ... now I have started following yoga. It is more convenient as you do not need to go outside and do yoga by watching the program of Baba Ramdev. The best thing is that you do not feel fatigued or breathless after doing it.

Replacing Physical Activity with Everyday Chores

Many participants reported that they do exercise or walk but not regularly. Two factors may be attributed to their neglect of daily physical activity recommendations: (a) shortage of time due to household chores and (b) considering household chores equivalent to physical activity. One such female participant noted:

Exercise...nothing. My exercise is done in doing household chores. I have a big house, I do all cleaning and washing by myself. I have so much work to do at home ... I just do that only.

Other participants shared similar sentiments, suggesting their ignorance about the importance of engaging in physical activity in terms of suitable and adequate exercise for their disease condition.

Diet Adherence

Losing Taste in Food

Loss of taste from food has been an important factor in not adhering to the recommended dietary regime. Accepting her non-adhering behaviour to diet changes, a patient reported:

I try but I am not able to adhere ... How could I restrict my diet? There is no taste in food if I would use less oil.

Misconception

When non-adherent participants were asked if they are not worried about their behaviour, a respondent replied:

Yes ... but I don't think that it is such big deal ... because I take medicines always on time. I never forget a single tablet.

Another patient, who was hypertensive along with her condition of angina, reported:

I do not take less salt. I only take salt in food ... if there is less salt in food, I find it tasteless. Anyway, I don't eat any extra stuff like fried food items and snacks.

When further asked why she did not restrict her salt intake, she responded:

... but I am taking medicines and I am always careful about my all medicines.

Similar statements given by other patients suggest a prevalence of misconceptions regarding the effectiveness of diet adherence as well as medication adherence.

Role of Family in Diet Adherence

Patients also reported that it becomes difficult for them to adhere to the diet as other family members eat regular food. One participant responded:

It becomes difficult for you actually when other people in your family are eating regular food. It's not that you feel bad about yourself or feel jealous of others' good health. Like you can smell the food from kitchen ... then how are you supposed to control yourself? My family takes excellent care of me, they cook food according to my needs and health conditions, but when family members eat their food in front of you for which there are no restrictions, you can't control.

Another participant stated that it is not possible for any family to make food for a cardiac patient every day. He stated:

See, it's challenging to do when you are with the family. If vegetables or pulses are cooked, they would be cooked together for everyone. It's not possible to cook separately for me every time. What maximum can be done is that they (family members) will put less salt or oil, but it can't be ignored completely. It's not possible that they will prepare food for me separately every time.

Addiction Restriction

Quitting Smokeless Tobacco (SLT) is More Difficult

The majority of the participants of the present study were non-drinkers and non-smokers. Only three participants were ex-drinkers, and four were smokers, while some other participants were addicted to various forms of smokeless tobacco such as dressed *Paan* (wrapping beetle leaves with areca nut, slaked lime, and tobacco, which is optional), *Gutka* (a dried mixture of crushed areca nut, tobacco, catechu, paraffin wax, slaked lime, and sweet or savoury flavourings), or *Khaini* (a combination of tobacco and slaked lime). Those patients who were addicted to smoking or alcohol discontinued their usage after being diagnosed with CAD but those who were taking smokeless tobacco did not quit their addiction. One such participant stated:

I used to take everything: tobacco, Supaari. I stopped taking Bidi, Paan ... and I was addicted to it for last 25 years. But now I have left everything. I mean, when I feel like having such things, then I just take Supaari... but I do not take tobacco in any form.

Further, these smokeless tobacco addicted patients have been found to substitute their addiction with some milder form of addiction or some other alternative such as taking *Paan* (without any slaked lime and tobacco) or sometimes with a healthier form such as black pepper or clove.

Medication Adherence

Many patients were strict adherents of their medication regime. Such patients reported that whatever be their condition, they never forget to take medicine. One such patient commented on his medication adherence behaviour as:

No, it never happened. I take medicines regularly. I can forget about my food, but I never skip my medication because the doctor has told me that I have to take medicines regularly if I want to live.

Role of Family Members

Many patients attributed their medication adherence behaviour to their family support. A female patient mentioned:

I never forget taking my medicines. Sometimes, if I forget, my children and husband take care of it. They take very good care of me. They always take care of my needs. What I want, what I don't want ... everything.

Side Effects and Medication Adherence

Unlike patients who strictly adhered to their medication regime, many other patients reported non-adherence to medication. A majority of them talk about skipping medicines intentionally due to their perceived "side-effect." One such comment was given by a patient:

Yes, I take medicines regularly. It's another matter that I consume medicines of 15-20 days in one month. I skip medicines for a few days in between ... but whenever I come for a general check-up, everything comes out as normal ... Like if I have taken medicine for 3-4 days then I skip it for two days ... because intake of many medicines also causes problems. That's why I skip medicines for a few days.

When further probed about the problems faced due to medicines, she replied:

... sometimes I have to take 10 or 12 medicines in a day ...Due to this my throat and lips started getting dry ... sometimes I start feeling restless due to so many medicines. Whenever I feel dryness on my lips and throat, I immediately stop taking it for two days ... But I do take medicines.

Financial Constraints

Even though all participants were from financially stable families, some reported facing financial constraints due to costly medicines and treatment of their disease. A participant reported this as a cause of her inability to continue medication. Another participant mentioned:

Sometimes, if I forget to buy from the market or when I have spent all my money, only then I will not have my medicines. I never ask for any financial support from my sons and that is why sometimes I fail to take medicines on time.

Discussion

The present study sought to examine the relationship between illness perception and adherence behaviour among coronary artery disease patients of India, using a mixed methodology. In the first phase, a quantitative study was conducted followed by a qualitative study in the second phase. It was found that illness perception can significantly predict adherence behaviour among the participants.

The results suggest that medication adherence was significantly predicted by identity, treatment chronic, consequence, treatment control, timeline cyclic, and risk factor (as a causal attribution) dimensions of illness perception. Past research has also identified consequences, symptoms, and timeline dimensions of illness perception as important predictors of medication adherence (Brewer et al., 2002). Patients' emotional response to their illnesses significantly predicted their intention to adhere to medication among arthritis patients (Suh et al., 2018). Qualitative inquiry suggests that most participants who reported non-adherence to medicines reported either side effects or financial burden due to costly drugs as the cause of skipping medications. Similar findings have also been reported by other studies (Khera et al., 2019). On the contrary, family support has been reported by the participants of the present study as a facilitator of medication adherence. Existing literature also suggests the importance of the family's role in medication adherence (Rabikun & Nurachmah, 2020).

The dimensions of treatment control and timeline cyclic of illness perception were found to predict the diet adherence of our participants. Loss of taste due to the suggested limited intake of salt, sugar, and oil in their diet made some of the participants not adhere to diet-related recommendations. What family members eat in the presence of a CAD patient also affects adherence behaviour. Other studies have also reported similar concerns with regard to the role of the family in adherence behaviour (Rabikun & Nurachmah, 2020). Interestingly, some of the participants of the present study justified their intake of salty and oily food as a compromise for taking medicines on time, thus suggesting that they underestimate the effectiveness and importance of diet adherence. A previous study has also reported that diabetic patients consider adherence to medication as more important than diet and exercise (Broadbent, Donkin & Stroh, 2011).

The third dimension of adherence behaviour, namely, physical activity, was predicted only by personal control and treatment control dimensions of illness perception. Petriček et al., (2009) suggested that physically inactive patients of Type 2 diabetes have poor illness cognition and perception of poor self-control over the disease, whereas in a study on Jordanian patients of coronary heart disease (CHD), personal control, timeline, and illness coherence dimensions of illness perception were reported as significant predictors of exercise adherence (Mosleh & Almalik, 2016). The qualitative results of the study further indicated that most participants were aware of regular walking and exercise benefits for their heart ailment but were unwilling to follow due to their lower motivation, laziness, or unwillingness to take out time from their everyday chores. After reviewing numerous studies, Allen and Morey (2010) were found to have reported that patients' perceived self-efficacy and motivation could predict their adherence behaviour for physical activity. Interestingly, some participants preferred Yoga over other forms of physical exercise due to the perceived fatigue and breathing problems caused by walking and exercise. Knowledge about exercise and motivation has played an important role in long-term exercise adherence among heart failure patients (Warehime et al., 2020).

In the present study, adherence to addiction restriction was significantly predicted by personal control, treatment control, coherence, and emotional representation dimensions of illness perception. However, illness perception and smoking cessation after CAD were found not significantly related (Paryad & Balasi, 2018). Interviews from the present study indicated that those who used to smoke or drink were more willing to restrict or stop their addictions than those who were addicted to *Paan*, *Gutka*, or *Khaini*. According to Global Adult Tobacco Survey (GATS) (2017-18), only 33.2% of smokeless tobacco users made any quit attempts in the last 12 months. Further, the quit ratio among Indian smokeless tobacco users remains exceptionally low at 5.8%

among people who have ever daily used smokeless tobacco, suggesting the gravity of the issue of smokeless tobacco cessation. In a study on the Indian population, smokers were more willing to make quit attempts than smokeless tobacco users (Sarkar et al., 2013). However, the present study also suggests that patients were not aware of the adverse effects of *Paan*, *Gutka*, and *Khaini* on their heart conditions. Other studies reported similar findings (Bhaumik et al., 2019; Singh & Dixit, 2021). Further, it may be argued that as in Indian culture, smoking and alcohol are forbidden in many communities; its cessation was more socially driven and feasible in comparison to smokeless tobacco, which is more acceptable. Suggesting the importance of religious and cultural beliefs, in a study, Indonesian cardiac patients quit smoking due to their religious beliefs (Nur, 2018).

This study is not without some limitations. First, it exclusively focuses on the role of illness perception. However, in reality, there could be numerous other factors of adherence behaviour that could have affected our participants' adherence behaviour. Second, this study's sample consists of patients from only Uttar Pradesh. Thus, the findings may not be generalisable to patients from other Indian states due to different cultural norms and expectations. Lastly, as the sample consists of patients belonging to middle socio-economic strata only, it can also be considered as another limitation.

Conclusion

The results of the study suggest that (i) illness perception can significantly predict adherence behaviour among Indian CAD patients, (ii) the participants adhered most to diet-related recommendations and least to the recommendation to physical activity, (iii) misconceptions related to various recommended lifestyle changes is a significant barrier for adherence behaviour among CAD patients, and (iv) family plays a vital role in adherence behaviour.

With the rise in the number of cardiac diseases in India, it is crucial to control them and thus lower the burden on our already weak healthcare system. One such factor which could facilitate reducing CAD-related mortality and morbidity rate is adherence behaviour. Various studies have suggested its importance with respect to cardiac disease patients. However, very few studies on Indian patients have explored its role with respect to CAD patients. The present study is an attempt to fulfil this gap.

References

Ali, M. A., Yasir, J., Sherwani, R. N., Fareed, M., Arshad, F., Abid, F., Arshad, R., Ismail, S., Khan, S. A., Siddiqui, U., Muhammad, M. G., & Fatima, K. (2017). Frequency and predictors of non-adherence to lifestyle modifications and medications after coronary artery bypass grafting: A cross-sectional study. *Indian Heart Journal, 69*(4), 469–473.

Allen, K., & Morey, M. C. (2010). Physical activity and adherence. In: Bosworth, H. (eds.), *Improving Patient Treatment Adherence* (9–38). Springer, New York, NY.

Al-Noumani, H., Wu, J. R., Barksdale, D., Sherwood, G., Alkhasawneh, E., & Knafl, G. (2019). Health beliefs and medication adherence in patients with hypertension: A systematic review of quantitative studies. *Patient Education and Counseling, 102*(6), 1045–1056.

Al-Tamimi, M. A. A., Gillani, S. W., Abd Alhakam, M. E., & Sam, K. G. (2021). Factors associated with hospital readmission of heart failure patients. *Frontiers in Pharmacology, 12*, 732760. https://doi.org/10.3389/fphar.2021.732760

American Heart Association (2021). Heart disease and stroke statistics—2021 update: A report from the American Heart Association. *Circulation, 143*(8), e254–e743.

Bagherian-Sararoudi, R., Maracy, M., Sanei, H., & Shiri, M. (2019). Factors in relation with fatigue and illness perception in patients with myocardial infarction and the changes in fatigue due to intervention on illness perception: Research design, methodology, and preliminary results. *ARYA Atherosclerosis, 15*(2), 74.

Bhaumik, S. S., Placek, C., Kochumoni, R., Lekha, T. R., Prabhakaran, D., Hitsman, B., Huffman, M. D., Harikrishnan, S., & Goenka, S. (2019). Tobacco cessation among acute coronary syndrome patients in Kerala, India: Patient and provider perspectives. *Qualitative Health Research, 2*(8), 1145–1160.

Braun, V., & Clarke, V. (2006). Using thematic analysis in psychology. *Qualitative Research in Psychology, 3*(2), 77–101.

Brewer, N. T., Chapman, G. B., Brownlee, S., & Leventhal, E. A. (2002). Cholesterol control, medication adherence and illness cognition. *British Journal of Health Psychology, 7*(4), 433–447.

Broadbent, E., Donkin, L., & Stroh, J. C. (2011). Illness and treatment perceptions are associated with adherence to medications, diet, and exercise in diabetic patients. *Diabetes Care, 34*(2), 338–340.

Dudala, S. R., Reddy, K. A. K., & Prabhu, G. R. (2014). Prasad's socio-economic status classification-An update for 2014. *International Journal of Research in Health Sciences, 2*(3), 875–878. http://www.ijrhs.com/issues.php?val=Volume2&iss=Issue3

Figueiras, M. J., Maroco, J., Monteiro, R., Caeiro, R., & Dias Neto, D. (2017). Randomized controlled trial of an intervention to change cardiac misconceptions in myocardial infarction patients. *Psychology, Health & Medicine, 22*(3), 255–265.

Howren, M. B. (2013). Adherence. In: Gellman, M. D., & Turner, J. R. (eds.), *Encyclopedia of Behavioural Medicine*. Springer, New York.

Indian Council of Medical Research, the Public Health Foundation of India, & Institute for Health Metrics and Evaluation. (2017). India: Health of the Nation's States – The India State-Level Disease Burden Initiative. New Delhi, India. Retrieved April 15, 2022, from https://www.healthdata.org/sites/default/files/files/policy_report/2017/India_Health_of_the_Nation%27s_States_Report_2017.pdf

Kamath, D. Y., Bhuvana, K. B., Salazar, L. J., Varghese, K., Kamath, A., Idiculla, J., … & Xavier, D. (2021). A qualitative, grounded theory exploration of the determinants of self-care behavior among Indian patients with a lived experience of chronic heart failure. *PLoS One, 16*(1), e0245659.

Khatib, R., Marshall, K., Silcock, J., Forrest, C., & Hall, A. S. (2019). Adherence to coronary artery disease secondary prevention medicines: Exploring modifiable barriers. *Open Heart, 6*(2), e000997.

Khera, R., Valero-Elizondo, J., Das, S. R., Virani, S. S., Kash, B. A., De Lemos, J. A., Krumholz, H. M., & Nasir, K. (2019). Cost-related medication nonadherence in adults with atherosclerotic cardiovascular disease in the United States, 2013 to 2017. *Circulation, 140*(25), 2067–2075.

Lee, C. S., Bidwell, J. T., Paturzo, M., Alvaro, R., Cocchieri, A., Jaarsma, T., Strömberg, A., Riegel, B., & Vellone, E. (2018). Patterns of self-care and clinical events in a cohort of adults with heart failure: 1 year follow-up. *Heart & Lung, 47*(1), 40–46.

Leventhal, H., Diefenbach, M., & Leventhal, E. A. (1992). Illness cognition: Using common sense to understand treatment adherence and affect cognition interactions. *Cognitive Therapy and Research, 16*(2), 143–163. https://link.springer.com/content/pdf/10.1007/BF01173486.pdf

Marshall, C., & Rossman, G. B. (2016). *Designing Qualitative Research* (6th ed.). SAGE.

Mosleh, S. M., & Almalik, M. M. (2016). Illness perception and adherence to healthy behaviour in Jordanian coronary heart disease patients. *European Journal of Cardiovascular Nursing, 15*(4), 223–230.

Moss-Morris, R., Weinman, J., Petrie, K., Horne, R., Cameron, L., & Buick, D. (2002). The revised illness perception questionnaire (IPQ-R). *Psychology and Health, 17*(1), 1–16. http://dx.doi.org/10.1080/08870440290001494

Nur, K. R. M. (2018). Illness perception and cardiovascular health behaviour among persons with ischemic heart disease in Indonesia. *International Journal of Nursing Sciences, 5*(2), 174–180.

Paryad, E., & Balasi, L. R. (2018). Smoking cessation: Adherence based on patients' illness perception after coronary artery bypass grafting surgery. *Indian Heart Journal, 70*, S4–S7.

Pereira, M. D. G., Ferreira, G., Machado, J. C., & Pedras, S. (2019). Beliefs about medicines as mediators in medication adherence in type 2 diabetes. *International Journal of Nursing Practice, 25*(5), e12768.

Petriček, G., Vrcić-Keglević, M., Vuletić, G., Cerovečki, V., Ožvačić, Z., & Murgić, L. (2009). Illness perception and cardiovascular risk factors in patients with type 2 diabetes: Cross-sectional questionnaire study. *Croatian Medical Journal, 50*(6), 583–593. https://doi.org/10.3325/cmj.2009.50.583

Piña, I. L., Jimenez, S., Lewis, E. F., Morris, A. A., Onwuanyi, A., Tam, E., & Ventura, H. O. (2021). Race and ethnicity in heart failure: JACC focus seminar 8/9. *Journal of the American College of Cardiology, 78*(25), 2589–2598.

Prabhakaran, D., Jeemon, P., Sharma, M., Roth, G. A., Johnson, C., Harikrishnan, S., Gupta, R., Pandian, J. D., Naik, N., Roy, A., & Dhaliwal, R. S. (2018). The changing patterns of cardiovascular diseases and their risk factors in the states of India: The Global Burden of Disease Study 1990–2016. *The Lancet Global Health, 6*(12), e1339–1351.

Princip, M., Gattlen, C., Meister-Langraf, R. E., Schnyder, U., Znoj, H., Barth, J., Schmid, J., & von Känel, R. (2018). The role of illness perception and its association with posttraumatic stress at 3 months following acute myocardial infarction. *Frontiers in Psychology, 9*, 941.

Rabikun, R., & Nurachmah, E. (2020). Improvement of patient compliance with heart disease that gets family support. *Jurnal Keperawatan, 12*(3), 429–438.

Sarkar, B. K., Arora, M., Gupta, V. K., & Reddy, K. S. (2013). Determinants of tobacco cessation behaviour among smokers and smokeless tobacco users in the states of Gujarat and Andhra Pradesh, India. *Asian Pacific Journal of Cancer Prevention, 14*(3), 1931–1935.

Sawyer, A. T., Harris, S. L., & Koenig, H. G. (2019). Illness perception and high readmission health outcomes. *Health Psychology Open, 6*(1). https://doi.org/10.1177/2055102919844504

Singh, A., & Dixit, S. (2016). Lower socio-economic status and cardiovascular disease: Role of healthcare facility and policy in India. *Indian Journal of Community Health, 28*(3).

Singh, A., & Dixit, S. (2021). Exploring barriers of quitting smokeless tobacco among coronary artery disease patients of India: A qualitative study. *Chronic Illness*. https://doi.org/10.1177/17423953211032262

Suh, Y. S., Cheon, Y. H., Kim, H. O., Kim, R. B., Park, K. S., Kim, S. H., Lee, S. G., Park, E. K., Hur, J., & Lee, S. I. (2018). Medication nonadherence in Korean patients with rheumatoid arthritis: The importance of belief about medication and illness perception. *The Korean Journal of Internal Medicine*, *33*(1), 203.

Thomson, P., Rushworth, G. F., Andreis, F., Angus, N. J., Mohan, A. R., & Leslie, S. J. (2020). Longitudinal study of the relationship between patients' medication adherence and quality of life outcomes and illness perceptions and beliefs about cardiac rehabilitation. *BMC Cardiovascular Disorders*, *20*(1), 1–11.

Warehime, S., Dinkel, D., Alonso, W., & Pozehl, B. (2020). Long-term exercise adherence in patients with heart failure: A qualitative study. *Heart & Lung*, *49*(6), 696–701.

World Health Organization (2003). Joint WHO/FAO Expert Consultation on Diet, Nutrition and the Prevention of Chronic Diseases. Report No. 916. Retrieved April 15, 2022, from http://apps.who.int/iris/bitstream/handle/10665/42665/WHO_TRS_916.pdf;jsessionid=34AD80CBE46C9BCBCA28D62937F66BB6?sequence=1

10
OPTIMIZING HYPERTENSION MANAGEMENT
Children as Adherence Monitors for Adult Patients

Sandra Roshni Monteiro

Hypertension, or persistent elevated blood pressure (BP) recorded to be more than 140/90 mm/Hg, is one of the leading yet one of the most modifiable risk factors predicting life-threatening cardiac diseases. It has been rendered a global epidemic (Burnier & Egan, 2019) with another wave expecting to be birthed with the occurrence of COVID-19. Despite the sudden shift in focus to one's own health due to the 'new normal', the impact of non-communicable diseases is neglected. Pre-pandemic studies have noted that hypertension is present in 25–30% of urban adults and 10–20% of rural adults (Anchala et al., 2014; Gupta, Gaur, & Ram, 2019) implying debilitating daily life functions of an individual. Three major phases have been identified by a 2009 convention of healthcare professionals particularly related to patient care in the taxonomy of the medical treatment—initiation, implementation, and discontinuation (Vrijens et al., 2012). The initiation phase refers to cognizance of the disease and taking action on it. The implementation phase comprises adherence to clinical advice in terms of dosage and regularity. Here, it is important to take notice of 'drug holidays' that account for the number of missed doses that may affect mild and severe cases of hypertension differently. The discontinuation phase is preceded by lack of implementation and signifies the lapse in treatment concurrently inviting the adversities of a malfunctioning circulatory system.

It would be logical to expect that with specific advancement in medical and lifestyle solutions, there would be an effective manipulation of the highly controllable risk factor. Despite the multiple options available to enhance adherence, evidence-based studies (Tajeu et al., 2019) reported that almost half of the treatment-receiving hypertensive persons discontinue their medicines within a year of diagnosis, and the remaining 50% take about only 80% of the prescribed dosage of medicine. As a consequence, 75% of the non-compliant individuals (non-conformity to the whole regimen) are not able to achieve their

DOI: 10.4324/9781003360858-13

goal of BP management. The circumstantial data combined with unsustainable health care practices and expenses define a burning platform to develop preventive and alleviative strategies that allow patients to take better control of their illnesses. The focus of interventions to improve patients' self-management of health behaviour surpasses the need to enhance interventions for healthcare providers because unhealthy behaviour accounts for almost 40% of premature deaths as compared to 10% responsibility of healthcare deficiencies (Schroeder, 2007). The Chronic Care Model for chronic diseases (Bodenheimer, Wagner, & Grumbach, 2002), too emphasizes on a collaborative partnership between patients, families, and healthcare providers. It is essential to boost the process of self-management discerning individuals to be primary stakeholders in their healthcare decisions.

A deeper reflection of the personal triggers of non-compliance among hypertensive individuals and their participation in healthcare would highlight the causal factors. Patient-centric studies have identified 'recall barrier' (difficulty to remember doses) and 'belief barrier' (lack of confidence in the efficacy of the treatment plan) among the highest prevailing causes of non-compliance among Indians (Dennis et al., 2011). Additionally, it is also imperative to study factors that help in enhancing self-management such as illness-specific social support (Padhy et al., 2016). It challenges the oxymoronic use of the term 'self-management' which in its earlier discourse reflected only individualistic self-care but actually implies therapy 'embedded in family, community and societal conditions that shape, influence and may constrain the choices people make, or can make' (Thirsk & Clark, 2014).

Therefore, a logical and sensational change in compliance would be expected if it is aided by emotional communication and 'partnership' that matters the most behind a therapeutic pathway. Although this observation was made in the purview of rapport building and reflective listening support between a patient and a doctor, it provides exceptional insight if a similar alliance was embedded in self-management techniques. It particularly should hold true in familial contexts that naturally have an emotional affiliation with the hypertensive patient and would automatically trigger motivational health promotion.

Children as Agents of Change in Optimizing Hypertension Management

Consistent with social control models, it is suggested that a gentler guiding force will motivate positive behavioural change and inhibit deviance. A borrowed concept such as social control theory as propounded in sociology (Hirschi, 1969) may be extended to protective healthcare behaviour particular to four very relevant speculations: (i) Attachment to inner and external social circle, that is, family, friends, teachers, co-workers, and so on; (ii) commitment to dedicated and invested activities or goals; (iii) involvement in activities that strengthen the bond and leave very little time for deviance, and finally (iv) a belief in wider social values or having a strong moral core. These principles hold very strong when propagated with respect to children who would be able to guide a gentle behavioural change. Choosing children as agents of change, it is expected that their interconnectedness and family position act as an intervention and bring about attitudinal change driving them towards desirable individual transactions. This concept also gathers support from the relationship motivation theory by Deci and Ryan (2014) and the organismic integration theory by Moss (2012) which also accentuate factors of relatedness and autonomy in interpersonal relationships facilitating motivated changes in health behaviour.

Are Children Fit to Be Agents of Change?

More often than not, children are underestimated in the value of their family position and developmental phase. Children have several qualities that deem them appropriate facilitators for health behaviour change. Firstly, the attitudes developed with a strong base at an early age will transition as stable and enduring through adulthood. Secondly, it is instinctual for parents to satisfy children's demands which generate a sense of gratification in them. There has also been a progressive body of literature appreciating the mutuality of relationships between children and adults (Ambert, 2014; Bolin, 2015; Knafo & Galansky, 2008). Previously too, children have been explored as influential agents in various fields of study such as purchasing and marketing who have often been able to meet their demands even so by nagging or requesting (Henry & Borzekowski, 2011; Wingert et al., 2014). Children have also been known to dissipate informational awareness which seemed to have an affirmative impact on their parents or significant adult (McDevitt & Chaffee, 2000; Saphir & Chaffee, 2002). Children have envisaged their status as 'learners' and 'conduits of knowledge' and act as a form of 'embodied power' carrying concerns from their educational settings into other spaces of their everyday lives and influencing the practices of the people around them. Children are a dominant part of the societal structure and social actors in their own right, as opposed to dependent, sensitive, and/or passive parts of a family. Children have been undervalued as independent decision-makers and of their influence on those around them.

A similar thought is projected within the United Nations Convention on the Rights of the Child (UNCRC) which helps to shape the initiation of children and young people's participation rights (Lundy, 2007). Children also help in bridging the language barrier, as many times, older generations in rural areas are deprived of basic knowledge and understanding due to low literacy levels, especially in developing countries. Moreover, children have more exposure to the external socialization agents of unprecedented technology, the internet, and reliable material available, and their evolved skill gives them an upper hand in their relationship with their parent.

Oswell (2013) in his sociological perspective of children's agency has concisely stated that 'the health of the nation and the wellbeing of the family are seen to be dependent on the happy and talkative child.' Enabling change through children to optimize hypertension management could be the key to warding off current and future threats (Monteiro & Hariharan, 2021). Hypertension has become a common phenomenon even among young children and adolescents. Notably, working upon the risk factors of hypertension as early as possible would reap benefits by inevitably delaying the progression or onset of clinical hypertension and related cardiovascular diseases. A child as a part of the initiative to manage hypertension is not simply an alternative approach but an urgent need.

Development of Research Design to Test the Hypothesis

In order to test a hypothesis to engage a child in a sustainable healthcare practice, a method was designed to experimentally gauge the child's agency in influencing their adult family member towards hypertension adherence and achieving target BP. Inertly, it was also expected that hypertension knowledge provided to children would dissipate among their adult counterparts as well, thus also securing a logical and scientific cognitive base. To address the objectives formulated for the research, a quasi-experimental interrupted time series design as advocated by Biglan, Ary, and Wagenaar (2000) was utilized. The unique feature of this design is that while the hypertension management in adults was the dependent variable that was focused on, the target of intervention was the children in the families of the hypertensive adults. The idea was to examine the impact of knowledge intervention on children on their effective monitoring of the adults in adhering to hypertension-related medical advice.

Objectives

1. To assess the impact of the hypertension intervention module on children's hypertension-related knowledge
2. To assess the impact of the hypertension knowledge intervention module provided to the children on hypertension knowledge, hypertension compliance, and BP levels of their hypertensive adult family member

Hypotheses

1. The hypertension management intervention module provided to children will have an impact on their own hypertension knowledge level.
2. Exposures of hypertension management intervention module provided to the children will influence their hypertensive adult family members' hypertension knowledge level, their hypertension compliance level, and their BP levels.

Method

Participants

A total of 181 children studying between Class 6 and Class 9 and between the age of 11 and 14 years were recruited for the study. The demographic characteristics of the two sets of the sample are described below:

> *Hypertensive Adults:* Among the hypertensive adults, 44.7% were men ($n = 88$), whereas 55.33% were women ($n = 109$). The mean age was 48.14 years (SD = ± 11.74). The education level of this group was categorized as non-literate (11.68%), basic, that is, up to 10th and 12th standard (24.37%), and graduate and above (63.95%). The average duration of hypertension diagnosis was found to be 4.38 years (SD = ±3.07).
> *Children:* The children belonged to Class 6 (38.67%), Class 7 (29.83%), Class 8 (26.52%), and Class 9 (4.97%), and there were 121 boys (61.42%) and 76 girls (38.58%). The age range of the children was between 11 and 15 years ($M = 11.90$; SD = ± 1.14). The relationship between child and hypertensive adult consisted of one brother (.51%), mothers (31.47%), fathers (30.46%), aunts (6.6%), uncles (2.03%), grandfathers (10.15%), and grandmothers (18.78%).

Recruitment of Sample

Prior to the commencement of the study, Institutional Ethics Committee approval was secured. The study was pursued in two urban cities of India—Delhi and Kolkata. Several school heads and management were contacted using snowballing and reference. The schools which showed an interest in incorporating the study were approached and were elaborately explained the study design. After having obtained permissions from institution heads, a teacher was allotted at each of the schools to work with the investigator to help build rapport with the students and to aid fluency of the data collection. Before taking up the main study, a pilot study was conducted to test the feasibility of tools as well as the intervention module (Monteiro & Hariharan, 2021).

Psychological Tools for Both Children and Adult Family Member with Hypertension

> *Hypertension Knowledge Test:* This is a test standardized by Andrew and Hariharan (2017) to measure four dimensions of knowledge, namely, a) general awareness; b) lifestyle; c) causes, care, casualty awareness; and d) management of medication. The test has multiple choice options, out of which only one option is correct. In the development and validation of the scale, the tool had achieved high test-retest reliability overall and across sub-domains ($\alpha = .92$) and had a high significant negative

correlation with the controlled BP group, thus establishing worthy construct validity.

Hypertension Monitoring Record Booklet: A weekly record was maintained by children for 42 days (6 weeks). The children recorded whether the adult hypertensive in the family took medication, followed the prescribed diet, and did physical exercise after the child reminded and monitored them on these aspects.

Psychological Tools Administered Only on Hypertensive Family Member

Compliance Scale for Hypertensive Patients: This is a 12-item instrument (Swain et al., 2015) which has a 5-point scale and measures adherence in hypertensive patients across four dimensions of medication, diet, exercise, and self-monitoring. The total score ranged between 12 and 60, where a higher score indicated better holistic compliance towards hypertension management. In its original study, the internal consistency of this scale was reported to be .67.

BP Reading: BP was recorded using a digital sphygmomanometer.

Procedure

The study was carried out in parallel for hypertensive adults and associated children of their families. A paired sample of child and hypertensive adult from the family were studied for a period of 6 weeks to gauge the child's influence upon their adult family members towards hypertension adherence and its outcomes.

For the adults, the study was marked in two segments—one before intervention was provided to the children and the other at the end of the post-intervention follow-up session. The BP of hypertensive adults was recorded using a digital sphygmomanometer and assessed for their level of hypertension knowledge, level of hypertension compliance, and interpersonal relationship with the child. Children were assessed for their level of hypertension knowledge pre and post their intervention module. The pre-intervention assessments were followed by three sessions of intervention conducted on the 1st day, 7th day, and 21st day from pre-intervention assessment. Post assessment for children and adults was conducted on the 42nd day or the completion of 6 weeks. The intervention module consisted of an audiovisual knowledge module, informational booklet, and discussion. In order to invoke active engagement of the children during the study, they were provided with a monitoring record in which they were asked to maintain a record of regularity in monitoring the adults hypertensive in the family. This record was maintained for 42 days and three main regulating factors of antihypertensive control, that is, medicine, exercise, and diet (MED), were noted daily. The child recorded in terms of 'Yes', 'No', and 'Don't Know' contingent on their ability or failure to remind and monitor their hypertensive family member. This was submitted to the investigator every week. All the parameters assessed for adults prior to the intervention were reassessed.

Intervention for Children

The children were exposed to a 30 minutes long video clipping as a part of the intervention module where a medical professional spoke about hypertension using a slideshow with pictures and animations. The video is a window to the world of hypertension informing facts about incidence, prevalence, onset age and symptoms, consequences, risk factors, dangers of substituted or missed dosage, the holistic approach to manage the disease, and understanding the point of immediate medical attention in case of sudden shoot up of BP. The emphasis was on the need for adherence and the repercussions of non/low adherence. In addition, the children were also provided with an informational pamphlet that reinforced the discussion about hypertension.

Role of a Health Psychologist

The health psychologist moderated the educational sessions with the children. tThe importance of their role in building good health for themselves and their adult hypertensive family members by encouraging minimal but powerful involvement in daily regulations of lifestyle habits was discussed. The record booklet was observed weekly to nurture a sense of achievement in the children which helped to build upon their agency in helping maintain and condition self and others towards good health habits.

Results

In order to track the objectives, set for this study, statistical analyses were carried out using IBM SPSS v.23. Paired t tests were conducted to detect the change in hypertension knowledge for both children and adults. The results are systematically presented in the succeeding paragraphs.

Firstly, the change in knowledge levels of the children post exposure to the intervention module was observed through paired t test. Results are presented in Table 10.1.

The post-intervention scores from knowledge testing seemed to be significantly enhanced compared to pre-test scores. This increase is observed in the total score ($t = 28.58$; $p < .001$) and across all dimensions of hypertension knowledge, that is, general awareness ($t = 11.08$; $p = .000$), lifestyle ($t = 20.16$; $p \leq .001$), causes, care, and casualty ($t = 4.18$; $p < .001$), and medical management ($t = 23.85$; $p < .001$). The means of pre- and post-intervention scores of children's knowledge can be observed under *M*, variance under *SD*, along with the 95% confidence interval range mentioned under *lower* and *upper 95% CI*. Cohen's *d* was

TABLE 10.1 Mean (M), standard deviation (SD), and t values of hypertension knowledge and its subscales among children participants (N = 181)

Outcome	Pre-intervention M	Pre-intervention SD	Post-intervention M	Post-intervention SD	95% CI for mean difference Lower	95% CI for mean difference Upper	T	Cohen's d
Hypertension knowledge (total)	8.30	3.07	13.98	2.27	6.07	.89	28.58*	2.10
i. General awareness	2.62	1.28	3.72	1.07	1.29	1.58	11.08*	.93
ii. Lifestyle	1.85	1.06	3.60	1.06	1.92	.22	20.16*	1.65
iii. Causes, care, casualty awareness	1.83	1.03	2.24	1.04	.61	2.18	4.18*	.40
iv. Medical management	2.02	1.17	4.40	1.18	2.6	5.28	23.85*	2.03

Notes: *$p < .001$; CI – confidence interval.

also computed to understand the effect size of the differential score. Cohen's d for total hypertension knowledge shows that the change can be classified as a very large difference (higher than 2 standard deviations). Similarly, for general awareness about hypertension, it can be said that the strength of the change is large (close to 1 standard deviation). For knowledge about lifestyle suited for hypertension, it is indicated that the change is very large (higher than 1 standard deviation). For causes, care, and casualty related to hypertension, the change observed is medium, and for medical management for hypertension, the change again is very large (higher than 2 standard deviations). The results clearly indicate that there is a significant change in knowledge levels before and after the exposure to the module. This indicates that the module was successful in improving the knowledge levels in specific dimensions as well as the overall knowledge related to hypertension.

Secondly, though the adults were not directly exposed to the hypertension intervention module, it was expected that children would inadvertently transfer hypertension-related information to their family members. In case this happened, there should be a difference in the knowledge level of adults before and after the children were exposed to the module. In order to examine this latent dissipation, a paired t test for adults was computed.

Table 10.2 shows the results of paired t test for hypertensive adults' knowledge of hypertension. It is observed that there is a significant change in their overall hypertension knowledge scores ($t = 2.29$, $p < .05$) and their dimension of hypertension-related general awareness ($t = 2.52$, $p \leq .05$). The changes in the pre- and post-intervention in other domains of this test (lifestyle; causes, care, and casualty; and medical management) were not significant. It is derived from this observation that there was a transfer of fundamental content about hypertension from the intervention module from children to their counterparts.

The main goal of this study was to bring about a significant positive change in the compliance levels of the individual and, consequently, in their BP readings.

TABLE 10.2 Mean (M), standard deviation (SD), and t values of hypertension knowledge and its subscale among adult participants (N = 181)

Outcome	Before intervention was provided to the children M	SD	After intervention was provided to the children M	SD	95% CI for mean difference Lower	Upper	T	Cohen's d
Hypertension knowledge (total)	10.61	3.07	10.90	3.10	−.54	−.04	2.29*	.09
i. General awareness	2.81	1.07	2.99	1.14	−.33	−.04	2.52*	.16
ii. Lifestyle	2.56	1.16	2.61	1.15	−.16	.07	.76	
iii. Causes, care, casualty awareness	2.59	1.22	2.59	1.16	−.10	.11	.11	
iv. iv. Medical management	2.65	1.20	2.72	1.20	−.14	.002	1.91	

Notes: *p < .05; CI – confidence interval.

This was assessed through paired t test examining pre and post status of hypertension compliance and high BP among the adults.

In terms of overall hypertension compliance test presented in Table 10.3, the hypertensive adult showed highly significant change in their overall compliance (t = 3.66; p < .001), and specifically in their medication compliance (t = 2.35; p ≤ .05) and in the lifestyle and self-monitoring dimension (t = 2.40; p ≤ .05). The changes in the domains of exercise and diet were not significant. This suggests that the transfer of knowledge from children to adults was prominent in

TABLE 10.3 Mean (M), standard deviation (SD) and t values of hypertension compliance and its subscales among adult participants (N = 181)

Outcome	Before intervention was provided to the children M	SD	After intervention was provided to the children M	SD	95% CI for mean difference Lower	Upper	T	Cohen's d
Hypertension compliance	35.48	7.06	36.73	6.33	−1.94	−.58	3.66**	.19
i. Medication compliance	16.29	4.74	16.72	4.35	−.79	−.07	2.35*	.19
ii. Dietary compliance	7.51	2.18	7.77	1.68	−.52	.01	1.87	
iii. Exercise compliance	7.62	2.32	7.9	1.97	−.61	.07	1.57	
iv. Lifestyle and self-monitoring	4.04	1.67	4.35	1.88	−.55	−.05	2.40*	.17

Notes: *p < .05, **p < .001; CI – confidence interval.

two dimensions, namely, medication and lifestyle and self-monitoring, but the intervention module provided to the children did not make significant impact so far as change in their diet and exercise was concerned.

A change in the compliance level is expected to bring a concomitant change in hypertension management because hypertension is considered to be a lifestyle disease and a change in the lifestyle should reflect in reduced BP readings. Systolic and diastolic readings of BP were converted into mean arterial pressure (MAP) (DeMers & Wachs, 2020) by applying the following formula:

$$MAP = DP + 1/3(SP - DP)$$

where DP is diastolic pressure and SP is systolic pressure.

The value so derived has accepted use in research (Sesso et al., 2000).

A paired t test to find the difference between mean arterial pressure (MAP) of hypertensive adults before and after children's exposure to intervention module presented in Table 10.4 showed a significant positive change between the tests done at two time frames ($t = 17.10$; $p < .001$). This indicated a significant drop in the BP readings of the adult hypertensives after knowledge intervention to children followed by their monitoring.

The diary maintained by the children had three parameters of hypertension management—MED. A graphic representation of monitoring efforts classified as successful and unsuccessful was calculated in terms of percentage for each of the parameter illustrated in Figure 10.1. 'Successful' signifies the percentage of times the child reminded the hypertensive adult family member and was able to ensure compliance with the lifestyle parameter; 'Unsuccessful' is a quantified indication of the absence of effort on part of the child for whichever reason. The percentage was calculated by obtaining a mean of their successful and unsuccessful efforts over 42 days of monitoring and consequently by multiplying it with 100. The graph in the figure tells us that children were successful in monitoring 77.58%, 71.97%, and 66% of the times for antihypertensive medication compliance, exercise, and diet, respectively. On an average, they failed to monitor and record the

TABLE 10.4 Mean (M), standard deviation (SD), and t values of mean arterial pressure of adult participants ($N = 181$)

($N = 181$)	Before intervention was provided to the children		After intervention was provided to the children		95% CI for mean difference			
Outcome	M	SD	M	SD	Lower	Upper	t	Cohen's d
Mean arterial pressure	116.89	5.12	110.38	6.01	5.76	7.26	17.10*	1.17

Notes: *$p < .001$; CI – confidence interval.

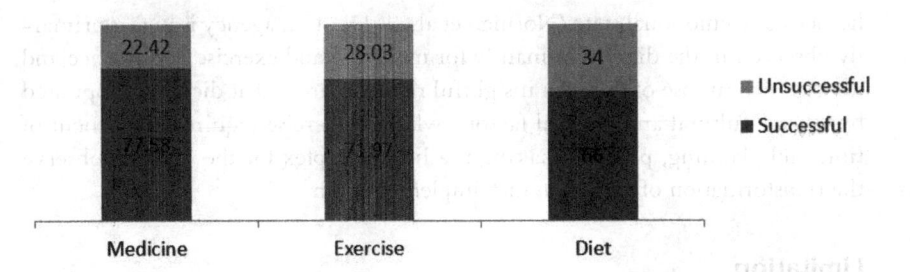

	Unsuccessful	Successful
Medicine	22.42	77.58
Exercise	28.03	71.97
Diet	34	66

FIGURE 10.1 Bar Graph Representation of Percentage of Successful and Unsuccessful Reminders of Hypertension Management Record Booklet Documented by Children for Parameters of Medicine, Exercise, and Diet.

outcome for compliance to medication, exercise, and diet 22.42%, 28.03%, and 34% of the times, respectively.

This data provides primary evidence of children's active role in influencing their adult counterparts to comply with the three major parameters of hypertension management. The percentage also infers those children were able to create an impact on the parameters of medicine more than the parameters of exercise and diet connecting the significant changes in overall compliance, predominantly in medicine intake.

Discussion

The results of this study have manifold positive findings. A sequence of behavioural initiation was expected after the exposure of the intervention module to children initiating better cognizance of the disease state. It was proposed that a dissonance would be created by the change in the knowledge status in the children. The dissonance would motivate knowledge dissipation and behavioural activation amongst adults propelled through the children's efforts in daily monitoring.

Firstly, the holistic intervention provided to children has been beneficial in establishing a strong cognitive foundation of hypertension knowledge. The partnered hypertensive adult is also seen to have an improvement in hypertension knowledge. The change in clinical compliance is expected to be preceded by a relevant change in the cognition as per the theories of Health Belief models (Prentice-Dunn & Rogers, 1986). It helps us to understand the incidental transfer of knowledge from children to adults following the intervention to the children. At this point, another noteworthy finding is that there was an increase in self-reported compliance of the hypertensive adults following the intervention to and monitoring by the children. It is established again that hypertension is reliant upon continuous self-care where the support of family members certainly cannot be overlooked. It, in fact, can buffer and even increase self-care behaviour. The behavioural agency of children to influence self-regulatory action in the adults is explained by the protection motivation drive that was triggered through a homeostatic emotional state (Norman et al., 2015). This agency is in fact primarily observed in the diary dominantly for medicine and exercise compliance and not as much in case of diet. An insightful remark here is that diet is appropriated by several cultural and familial factors, whereas exercise requires investment of time and planning, possibly making it a little complex for the child to observe the transformation of initiation into implementation.

Limitation

Managing chronic illnesses requires holistic self-care rendering it a major public health challenge till date. It is not entirely new that children have been involved in community interventions and could be effective in any concerning public health problem that needs a solution at a personal level. The evidence presented falls short to note the influence of other socialization agents, if any, and the resistant personality factors. It in fact also does not imply that capability would convert into influence.

Implications

A recent survey by the Fourth National Family Health Survey (Gupta, Gaur, & Ram, 2019) has reported the prevalence of hypertension in 207 million Indians with greater focus in urban areas. It is an 89% increase in the disease burden from 21 million in 1990 to 39 million in 2016. The increase in deaths due to hypertension is up by almost 108% since 1990. There is an urgent need to meet the challenges of higher incidences in the future. With over 200 million school going children, group education and training of children in hypertension management could prove to be a cost-effective measure of timely redressal of crisis through implementation in their own families. Enabling agency of children could be the cost-effective remedy to manoeuvre desired health changes. It is also suggested that knowledge related to lifestyle diseases be implemented in school curriculums to optimize health knowledge and practice. This area of study remains under-researched and motivates inquiry which would help to understand the influence of children on parents in depth. Likewise, the facilitators and barriers of the influential process may also be further investigated. This evidence is a powerful capital for developing countries with limited resources that could tap into children's agency to manoeuvre desired changes through education and involvement.

References

Ambert, A. M. (2014). *The effect of children on parents*. Routledge.

Anchala, R., Kannuri, N. K., Pant, H., Khan, H., Franco, O. H., Di Angelantonio, E., & Prabhakaran, D. (2014). Hypertension in India: A systematic review and meta-analysis of prevalence, awareness, and control of hypertension. *Journal of Hypertension, 32*(6), 1170.

Andrew, A., & Hariharan, M. (2017). Hypertension knowledge test: Development and validation. *International Journal of Indian Psychology, 5*(1), 44–55.

Biglan, A., Ary, D., & Wagenaar, A. C. (2000). The value of interrupted time-series experiments for community intervention research. *Prevention Science, 1*(1), 31–49.

Bodenheimer, T., Wagner, E. H., & Grumbach, K. (2002). Improving primary care for patients with chronic illness. *JAMA, 288*(14), 1775–1779.

Bolin, A. (2015). Children's agency in interprofessional collaboration. *Nordic Social Work Research, 5*(1), 50–66.

Burnier, M., & Egan, B. M. (2019). Adherence in hypertension: A review of prevalence, risk factors, impact, and management. *Circulation Research, 124*(7), 1124–1140.

Deci, E. L., & Ryan, R. M. (2014). Autonomy and need satisfaction in close relationships: relationships motivation theory. In: Weinstein, N. (eds), *Human motivation and interpersonal relationships*. Springer. https://doi.org/10.1007/978-94-017-8542-6_3

DeMers, D., & Wachs, D. (2020). Physiology, mean arterial pressure. In *StatPearls* [Internet]. StatPearls Publishing.

Dennis, T., Meera, N. K., Binny, K., Sekhar, M. S., Kishore, G., & Sasidharan, S. (2011). Medication adherence and associated barriers in hypertension management in India. *CVD Prevention and Control, 6*(1), 9–13.

Gupta, R., Gaur, K., & Ram, C. V. S. (2019). Emerging trends in hypertension epidemiology in India. *Journal of Human Hypertension, 33*(8), 575–587.

Henry, H. K., & Borzekowski, D. L. (2011). The Nag Factor: A mixed-methodology study in the US of young children's requests for advertised products. *Journal of Children and Media, 5*(3), 298–317.

Hirschi, T. (1969). Key idea: Hirschi's social bond/social control theory. In: Pratt, T. C., Gau, J. M., & Franklin, T. W. (eds), *Key ideas in criminology and criminal justice*, 55–69. Sage.

Knafo, A., & Galansky, N. (2008). The influence of children on their parents' values. *Social and Personality Psychology Compass, 2*(3), 1143–1161.

Lundy, L. (2007). 'Voice' is not enough: Conceptualising Article 12 of the United Nations Convention on the Rights of the Child. *British Educational Research Journal, 33*(6), 927–942.

McDevitt, M., & Chaffee, S. (2000). Closing gaps in political communication and knowledge: Effects of a school intervention. *Communication Research, 27*(3), 259–292.

Monteiro, S.R., & Hariharan, M. (2021). Children as adherence enhancing agents in management of primary hypertension of adult family members. *International Journal of Health and Allied Sciences, 10*(4), 280–286.

Moss, S. (2012). Organismic integration theory. https://www.sicotests.com/newpsyarticle/Organismic-integration-theory

Norman, P., Boer, H., Seydel, E. R., & Mullan, B. (2015). Protection motivation theory. In M. Conner & P. Norman (Eds.), *Predicting and Changing Health Behaviour: Research and Practice with Social Cognition Models Vol. 3 (pp 70-106)*. Open University Press: England.

Oswell, D. (2013). *The agency of children: From family to global human rights*. Cambridge University Press.

Padhy, M., Lalnuntluangi, R., Chelli, K., & Padiri, R. A. (2016). Social support and adherence among hypertensive patients. *Amity Journal of Healthcare Management, 1*(11), 33–40.

Prentice-Dunn, S., & Rogers, R. W. (1986). Protection motivation theory and preventive health: Beyond the health belief model. *Health Education Research, 1*(3), 153–161.

Saphir, M. N., & Chaffee, S. H. (2002). Adolescents' contributions to family communication patterns. *Human Communication Research, 28*(1), 86–108.

Schroeder, S. A. (2007). We can do better—improving the health of the American people. *New England Journal of Medicine, 357*(12), 1221–1228.
Sesso, H. D., Stampfer, M. J., Rosner, B., Hennekens, C. H., Gaziano, J. M., Manson, J. E., & Glynn, R. J. (2000). Systolic and diastolic blood pressure, pulse pressure, and mean arterial pressure as predictors of cardiovascular disease risk in men. *Hypertension, 36*(5), 801–807.
Swain, S., Hariharan, M., Rana, S., Chivukula, U., & Thomas, M. (2015). Doctor-patient communication: Impact on adherence and prognosis among patients with primary hypertension. *Psychological Studies, 60*(1), 25–32.
Tajeu, G. S., Kent, S. T., Huang, L., Bress, A. P., Cuffee, Y., Halpern, M. T., Kronish, I. M., Krousel-Wood, M., Mefford, M. T., Shimbo, D., & Muntner, P. (2019). Antihypertensive medication non persistence and low adherence for adults< 65 years initiating treatment in 2007–2014. *Hypertension, 74*(1), 35–46.
Thirsk, L. M., & Clark, A. M. (2014). What is the 'self' in chronic disease self-management? *International Journal of Nursing Studies, 51*(5), 691–693.
Vrijens, B., De Geest, S., Hughes, D. A., Przemyslaw, K., Demonceau, J., Ruppar, T., Dobbels, F, Fargher, E, Morrison, V, Lewek, P., Matyjaszczyk, M., & ABC Project Team (2012). A new taxonomy for describing and defining adherence to medications. *British Journal of Clinical Pharmacology, 73*(5), 691–705.
Wingert, K., Zachary, D. A., Fox, M., Gittelsohn, J., & Surkan, P. J. (2014). Child as change agent. The potential of children to increase healthy food purchasing. *Appetite, 81*, 330–336.

PART IV
Psychosocial Factors in Diabetes Management

PART IV

11

ILLNESS PERCEPTIONS AND QUALITY OF LIFE OF DIABETIC PATIENTS

Role of Perceived Control of Internal States

Meera Padhy and A. Sheila Kumari Valli

A person's health is one of the most valuable possessions he or she can own. Until the first part of the twentieth century, communicable diseases such as infectious and deficiency diseases were the leading causes of death and morbidity. Life expectancy has steadily increased in recent decades, and the shift from infectious to degenerative diseases has resulted in new lifestyle-related health issues. As a result, the situation has altered, and chronic non-communicable diseases have emerged as a serious burden in both developed and developing countries.

Over the years, the global prevalence of diabetes, one of the non-communicable diseases, increased exponentially, particularly in low- and middle-income countries. In 2019, diabetes was the ninth leading cause of 1.5 million deaths. A total of 48% of all deaths due to diabetes occurred before the age of 70 years (World Health Organization, 2021). Diabetes was found to affect 463 million individuals and is projected to affect 700 million by 2045 (International Diabetes Federation, 2019). In India, 77 million adults currently have diabetes, which is expected to be 134 million by 2045 (International Diabetes Federation, 2019). According to Luhar et al. (2021), people who live in cities and metropolitan areas in India are more likely to develop diabetes due to their lifestyle which increases a person's body mass index (BMI), identified as a diabetes risk factor. While diabetes is ranked as the ninth leading cause of death, the disease's overall burden remains unknown as the disability resulting from diabetes has many personal and socio-economic impacts. Besides the high rates of mortality and disability, the complex and chronic nature of the disease leads to severe, life-threatening, or disabling complications (complications related to eyesight, the nervous system, renal diseases, and septicaemia).

Due to the high prevalence of the disease, people with diabetes tend to develop considerable complacency to their condition leading to neglect of following the medical advice in diet, exercise, and lifestyle in general. The illness condition is

DOI: 10.4324/9781003360858-15

associated with the need for several lifestyle-related adjustments which need to be viewed with equal importance as that of taking medication. Lifestyle changes are not easy to be inculcated in the patients as they have their allegiance with motivation, emotion, the presence of social support, disease-specific health literacy, and so on. Thus, the disease condition, treatment, and sustenance have their relationship with psychosocial factors.

Psychosocial risk and protective variables are important for medical and psychological adjustment to chronic disease, as emotional or personal challenges can affect chronic disease control, affecting the disease's course and outcome (Kenowitz et al., 2020). Patients with diabetes confront increased challenges not only when they have a co-morbid disease, but also when they are dealing with other psychological concerns. To maintain quality of life (QoL), individuals diagnosed with diabetes must adjust their lifestyle significantly and radically to accommodate self-management and pharmacological treatment. Several psychosocial aspects, such as perception of the condition, health competence, and support, have a significant impact on diabetes management. People with diabetes have a relatively regimented life. The impact of these psychological aspects on diabetes patients' QoL is uncertain. In view of these, to design comprehensive diabetic self-management strategies, there is a pressing need to investigate psychosocial elements that can affect the QoL.

Quality of Life (QoL)

QoL is the individual's perceptions regarding their positions in life vis-à-vis their goals, expectations, and concerns (WHO, 1995). It is multifaceted, consisting of total well-being in social, physical, and mental functioning. QoL is now targeted as the ultimate goal of all health interventions increasingly recognized as an important marker of health (Rubin, 2000). Several factors influence an individual's health. The QoL of individuals depends on various exogenous and endogenous factors. Generally, the social, economic, and physical environment contribute to health alongside the persons' characteristics and behaviour. The individual determinants have a strong effect on a person's well-being. Acceptance of the illness and perception of control over the condition are crucial for any chronic illness to achieve good adjustment to promote the QoL.

Illness Perception

Illness perception appears to be one of the most promising psychological factors linked to varied illness outcomes in chronic patients. It refers to the patients' cognitive and emotional reactions to the illness and its treatment. It does not always reflect 'medically correct facts' and often differs significantly from conventional medical thinking. It refers to individuals' own implicit commonsense beliefs about illnesses, their symptoms, consequences, time course, controllability, and causes. Patients' perception of illness is their cognitive appraisal and personal understanding of a medical condition and its potential outcomes (Broadbent et al., 2015). Perceptions of illness serve to identify a problem and motivate action, identify control procedures, define efficiency targets, and sustain effectiveness until the problem is resolved (Leventhal et al., 2012). The self-regulation model explains the association between illness perception and self-management. The model explains the concept of illness perceptions and their association with coping behaviours and measurable outcomes such as well-being, QoL, and self-management (Cameron & Leventhal 2003). Perception of increased timeline, the seriousness of the illness, and consequences of the condition were indicative of poorer emotional health symptoms (Hudson et al., 2014).

Several studies showed that illness perceptions have an impact on illness outcomes, such as functional health and QoL, both directly and indirectly via illness behaviour (Hagger et al. 2017; Broadbent, 2015). Patients' perceptions of illness direct their response to that illness (Zhang et al., 2016). People actively try to make sense of their symptoms and form personal beliefs about their illness which determine their coping behaviour and QoL (Chen et al., 2015). Many studies have examined illness perceptions in patients with chronic diseases, finding associations between illness perceptions and adherence to treatments (French, Cooper, & Weinman, 2006), self-management behaviours (Horne & Weinman, 2002), well-being (Nagpal & Padhy, 2015), and QoL (Scharloo, et al., 2005). Research studies have shown that illness perception has an impact on disease outcomes, such as functional health and QoL, both directly and indirectly via sickness behaviour, in keeping with the assumptions of the common-sense model of self-regulation of health and illness (Fall et al., 2020). The study by Wang et al. (2021) on rheumatoid arthritis patients showed that illness perceptions influenced different dimensions of their health-related QoL (HRQoL). Patients with the worst illness perceptions had the worst HRQoL.

Perceived Control of Internal States

Recent years have seen considerable attention being paid to the concept of perceived control with chronic illness. Perceived control has been defined as the belief that one can determine one's own internal states and behaviour, influence one's environment, and/or bring about desired outcomes (Wallston et al., 1987). It is a blend of internal locus of control and self-efficacy (Padhy & Monteiro, 2020; Padhy et al., 2022). Perceived control is the extent to which individuals feel capable of bringing about a change in their health behaviour by carrying out treatment regimens and participating in several health care activities. It has been defined as the belief that one can determine one's own internal states and behaviour, influence one's environment, and/or bring about desired outcomes (Wallston et al., 1987). It refers to the individuals' cognition of their own ability to influence the situation through altering it, changing its meaning, or regulating their own behavioural and emotional reactions. People who are confident in their ability to make these changes are more likely to make and maintain them, which leads to better health outcomes.

One of the major contributors to QoL, according to Polonsky and Hessler (2013), is perceived control. The better the patients' perceived control, the higher their QoL. Individual variances exist in how people perceive and respond to different situations. Individuals with a low sense of control regard the situation as more dangerous and find it difficult to modify and cope (Pallant, 2000). According to Turiano et al. (2014), perceived control of internal states is related to better adjustment to chronic illness. A strong sense of control over one's life independently predicts better health but does not necessarily reduce the risk of mortality. Preferences for treatment options can be well understood by the measures of perceived control (Sridhar & Madhu, 2002). There is a positive association between perceived control of internal states and physical and mental dimensions of QoL (Hernandez-Tejada et al., 2012).

The Current Study

With advanced technologies, the health care profession has grown tremendously in recent years. The ability to successfully integrate these practices into one's daily routine is within the control of patients, who must cope with the increasing physical and emotional demands of chronic illness and accordingly adopt lifestyle changes. The relevance of psychosocial elements in the delivery of medical care, to help patients manage and cope with their conditions, is also emphasized by research. As mentioned, the chronic condition of diabetes is characterized by symptoms that one has to deal with every day while facing the risk of diabetes-related complications in the long run. To manage diabetes well, and reduce or delay the onset of complications, one has to adhere to a relatively strict treatment regimen and implement lifestyle changes. Such a scenario requires the patients to utilize their psychological and social resources to cope with the disease. Past research has identified that illness perception and perception of control are the two important elements contributing to treating diabetes. Persons with chronic illness can use their illness perception to assist them to stick to treatment regimens that will enhance their QoL. Patients must make rudimentary modifications in their food and physical activity, as well as be regular with their medicine and consultation visits. Therefore, perceived health control is one of the defining aspects of mastering health-related activities. Having a sense of competence makes it easier to feel confident about accomplishing relevant results that affect one's QoL.

The goal of this research is to determine the elements that primarily influence the QoL of diabetic patients. Identifying the shifting patterns of these variables will provide insight and pave the way for future therapies to help patients manage diabetes effectively and improve their QoL at various stages along their illness duration. While illness perception renders a passive role of the individuals, perception of control has the potential for subsequent behaviour. The belief that the individuals can manage the emotional consequences of the disease as well as feel equipped to cope efficiently and manage effectively assumes significance as a trigger for health behaviour. The limited research on the role of perceived control of internal states in the diabetic population leaves certain ambiguity in the way it influences individuals and their health behaviour. The present study intended to explore the relationship between illness perception, perceived control of internal states, and QoL of individuals with diabetes. It also examined the impact of various demographic variables, illness perception, and perceived control of internal state on QoL. The hypotheses were formulated along these lines.

Hypotheses

1. There will be a relationship between demographic variables (age, gender, duration of illness), illness perception, perceived control of internal states, and QoL of individuals with diabetes.
2. Demographic variables (age, gender, duration of illness), illness perception, and perceived control of internal states will predict the QoL of diabetic patients.

Method

Research Design

A correlational research design was construed with the demographic variables, illness perception, and perceived control of internal states as predictors and QoL as the criterion variable.

Participants

A purposive sampling was used. Individuals diagnosed with type 2 diabetes mellitus (T2DM) and actively seeking treatment were included. Pregnant women and individuals with other co-morbid conditions were excluded from the study. A total of 150 participants with the age range of 25–75 years (Mean = 58.75 years, SD = 11.24) were recruited for the study. The participants were divided into three groups (50 in each group) according to their duration of illness—group 1, with a diagnosis of less than one year (Mean = 51, SD = 11.04); group 2 between one and five years (Mean = 60.52, SD = 10.16); and group 3 with a diagnosis of more than five years (Mean = 64.74, SD = 7.62).

Research Instruments

Illness Perception Questionnaire-Revised (IPQ-R)

Diabetes-specific illness perception questionnaire IPQ-R (Moss-Morris et al., 2002) was used to evaluate patients' illness perception. The first part of the questionnaire consists of a set of yes/no statements regarding the patient's illness identity where they are asked if they have experienced a set of symptoms and if they believe the symptom is specifically related to their diabetes. The second part of the questionnaire consists of 38 statements corresponding to 7 domains of illness perception (timeline, consequences, personal control, emotional representation, treatment control, illness coherence, and timeline cyclical). The responses for each statement were on a 5-point Likert scale from 1 (strongly disagree) to 5 (strongly agree). The higher score in the timeline dimension indicates more chronic disease; in the cyclical timeline, subscale indicates greater variability; in the consequences, dimension indicates more serious impacts on a patient's life; in the treatment control, dimension indicates that patients are more confident of treatment; in the personal control, subscale indicates patients' perceived efficacy; in the illness coherence indicates an increased awareness of the illness; and in the emotional representation indicates a greater emotional impact of the condition. The third part consists of a list of 18 possible causes of diabetes. The reliability coefficients ranged from .70 to .92. The alpha level for Illness Perception Questionnaire-Revised for the present study was found to be .79.

Diabetes QoL Measure (DQOL)

The Diabetes QoL measure (Jacobson, 1994) consists of 46 items within four main domains—treatment satisfaction, treatment impact, worries about long-term complications, and worry about social/vocational issues. The item responses range on a 5-point Likert scale—1 (very satisfied) to 5 (very dissatisfied) for the domain 'treatment satisfaction'. The response options are in the form of frequency of behaviour—1 (never) to 5 (always) for the other three domains mentioned above. Low scores on this measure indicate higher QoL. A score of 1 indicates no impact, no worries, or always satisfied. A score of 5 represents always affected, always worried, or never satisfied. This measure has a high internal consistency with Cronbach's alpha of .92 for the entire scale.

Perceived Control of Internal States Scale (PCOISS)

PCOISS, developed by Pallant (2000), is an 18-item scale that measures the extent of control which an individual perceives to have over his/her internal states such as emotions, thoughts, and physical reactions. The response of each item is recorded on a 5-point Likert scale ranging from 1 (strongly disagree) to 5 (strongly agree). Reverse scoring is done for items according to the scoring manual of the scale. PCOISS has Cronbach's alpha of .92 (Pallant, 2000).

Procedure

Participants were recruited from five hospitals in the city of Hyderabad, India after satisfying the administrative and ethical requirements. Participants who agreed to participate in the study were asked to sign the informed consent form. The participants were then given the questionnaires and were asked to fill out their responses. All the data were later entered into SPSS 23 for analysis.

Results

The obtained quantitative data were analysed using descriptive statistics, Pearson's product-moment correlation coefficient (Pearson's *r*), and multiple hierarchical regression analysis using IBM SPSS Statistics 23.

In the analysis, the predictors were demographic variables (duration of illness, age, and gender), dimensions of illness perception (timeline, consequences, timeline cyclical, personal control, treatment control, illness coherence, emotional representation), and perceived control of internal states. The criterion was QoL and its dimensions (treatment satisfaction, treatment impact, worry about social and vocational issues, worry about long-term consequences). Prior to the hierarchical regression, Pearson's *r* was computed to find a linear relationship between the predictors and the criteria and to identify the suitable predictors to be entered into the model.

Relationship Among the Measures

The values of Pearson's 'r' along with descriptive statistics (M and SD) are presented in Table 11.1. From the table, it is found that all predictors except age and treatment control show significant correlation with total QoL ($r = .23$ to $.62$). Therefore, duration of illness, gender, timeline, consequences, timeline cyclical, personal control, illness coherence, emotional representation, and perceived control of internal states were selected for the hierarchical model to identify the predictors of QoL.

In the case of satisfaction—the first dimension of QoL— except for the duration of illness, age, and treatment control, all other predictors showed a significant correlation with satisfaction. The correlation coefficient varied between .22 and .56. Therefore, all except these three variables were selected for the hierarchical model to identify the predictors of satisfaction.

In the case of impact—the second dimension of QoL— except age and treatment control, all other predictors had a significant correlation with impact. The correlation coefficient varied between .21 and .58. Therefore, all except these two variables were selected for the hierarchical model to identify the predictors of QoL.

In the case of social and vocational worries—the third dimension of QoL— duration of illness, age, timeline, timeline cyclical, emotional representation, and perceived control of internal states, which had a significant correlation with social and vocational worries, were selected to be included as predictors in hierarchical regression. The correlation coefficient varied between .19 and .34.

TABLE 11.1 Correlation between demographic variables, dimensions of illness perception, perceived control of internal states, and dimensions of QoL (N = 150)

Predictors	M[a]	SD[a]	Treatment satisfaction QoL	Treatment impact QoL	Criterion Worry about social and vocational issues QoL	Worry about long-term consequences QoL	Total QoL
Duration of illness			−.13	−.21**	−.29**	−.28**	−.23**
Age	58.75	11.25	.03	.00	−.25**	.00	−.04
Gender			−.25**	−.30**	−.02	−.25**	−.28**
Timeline	19.61	1.690	−.22**	−.26**	−.26**	−.22**	−.27**
Consequences	17.88	4.103	.49**	.46**	.15	.44**	.51**
Timeline cyclical	12.41	4.921	.43**	.43**	.19*	.43**	.47**
Personal control	20.43	2.074	−.37**	−.32**	−.15	−.17*	−.35**
Treatment control	14.69	3.254	−.05	−.02	−.10	.13	−.02
Illness coherence	12.08	3.609	.35**	.35**	.13	.40**	.39**
Emotional representation	14.25	6.728	.54**	.58**	.34**	.52**	.62**
Perceived control	68.39	14.941	−.56**	−.52**	−.25**	−.42**	−.58**
M[b]			35.82	44.28	3.82	7.87	91.79
SD[b]			9.25	8.25	2.171	2.804	19.438

Notes: *p < .05, **p < .01.
[a]Mean and SD of predictors; [b]Mean and SD of criterions; Male = '1', Female = '2'; Low scores on QoL measure indicate higher QoL.

In the case of diabetes-related worries—the fourth dimension of QoL— except age and treatment control, all other predictors that showed a significant correlation with impact were selected for the hierarchical model to identify the predictors of QoL. The correlation coefficient varied between .22 and .52.

Predictors of QoL

Based on the above findings, five multiple hierarchical analysis models were developed for QoL and its dimensions. As the linearity assumption was tested, other essential assumptions such as normality, homoscedasticity, and absence of multicollinearity were also verified for each model. The results of these five separate models are presented in Tables 11.2–11.6.

As seen in Table 11.2, the significantly correlated predictors were entered hierarchically in three blocks—Block 1 (gender), Block 2 (dimensions of illness perception), and Block 3 (perceived control of internal states)—in respect of diabetes QoL (satisfaction).

It was found from the table that all the models were significant. After entry of perceived control at Step 3, the total variance explained by the model as

TABLE 11.2 Multiple hierarchical regression analysis for demographic variables, subscales of illness perception, and perceived control of internal states predicting QoL (satisfaction)

Model	B	SE	β	Adjusted R^2	R^2	ΔR^2
Model 1 (C = 28.92, F = 9.92***)				.06	.06**	
Gender	4.62	1.67	.25**			
Model 2 (C = 39.74, F = 18.79***)				.46	.48***	.42
Gender	1.31	1.19	.07			
Timeline	−.33	.35	−.06			
Consequences	.61	.15	.27***			
Timeline cyclical	.44	.13	.23***			
Personal control	−.98	.30	−.22***			
Illness coherence	−.09	.19	−.03			
Emotional representation	.38	.10	.28***			
Model 3 (C = 51.02, F = 19.16***)				.49	.52**	.04
Gender	1.14	1.15	.06			
Timeline	−.21	.34	−.04			
Consequences	.47	.15	.21***			
Timeline cyclical	.40	.13	.21***			
Personal control	−.89	.29	−.20***			
Illness coherence	−.09	.19	−.04			
Emotional representation	.26	.11	.19**			
Perceived control	−.16	.05	−.25***			

Notes: *p < .05, **p < .01, ***p < .001.
C – constant, B – unstandardized beta coefficient, SE – standard error, β – standardized beta coefficient, ΔR^2 – R^2 change.

TABLE 11.3 Multiple hierarchical regression analysis for demographic variables, subscales of illness perception, and perceived control of internal states predicting QoL (impact)

Model	B	SE	β	Adjusted R^2	R^2	ΔR^2
Model 1 (C = 41.10, F = 9.66***)				.10	.12***	
Duration of illness	1.73	.79	−.17*			
Gender	4.45	1.29	.27**			
Model 2 (C = 47.83, F = 16.99***)				.46	.49***	.37
Duration of illness	−.69	.65	−.07*			
Gender	1.92	1.06	.12			
Timeline	−.49	.32	−.09			
Consequences	.46	.14	.23**			
Timeline cyclical	.37	.12	.22**			
Personal control	−.60	.26	−.15*			
Illness coherence	−.15	.17	−.06			
Emotional representation	.40	.09	.33***			
Model 3 (C = 55.39, F = 16.30***)				.48	.51*	.02
Duration of illness	−.82	.64	−.08*			
Gender	1.78	1.05	.11			
Timeline	−.39	.32	−.08			
Consequences	.36	.14	.18*			
Timeline cyclical	.35	.11	.21**			
Personal control	−.55	.26	−.14*			
Illness coherence	−.15	.16	−.06			
Emotional representation	.33	.10	.27**			
Perceived control	−.10	.04	−.18*			

Notes: *p < .05, **p < .01, ***p < .001.
C − constant, B − unstandardized beta coefficient, SE − standard error, β − standardized beta coefficient, ΔR^2 − R^2 change.

a whole was 52%. The introduction of perceived control explained an additional 4% of variance in diabetes QoL (satisfaction). In the final adjusted model, five out of eight predictor variables (consequences, timeline cyclical, personal control, emotional representation, and perceived control) were statistically significant, with perceived control recording a higher beta value (β = −.25, p < .001).

As seen in Table 11.3, the significantly correlated predictors were entered hierarchically in three blocks—Block 1 (duration of illness, gender), Block 2 (dimensions of illness perception), and Block 3 (perceived control of internal states)—in respect of diabetes QoL (impact).

It was found from the table that all the models were significant. After entry of perceived control at Step 3, the total variance explained by the model as a whole was 51%. The introduction of perceived control explained an additional 2% of variance in diabetes QoL (impact). In the final adjusted model, six out of nine predictor variables (duration of illness, consequences, timeline cyclical, personal

TABLE 11.4 Multiple hierarchical regression analysis for demographic variables, subscales of illness perception, and perceived control of internal states predicting QoL (social and vocational worries)

Model	B	SE	β	Adjusted R^2	R^2	ΔR^2
Model 1 (C = 6.57, F = 8.08***)				.09	.10***	
Age	−.03	.02	−.14			
Duration of illness	−.59	.24	−.22**			
Model 2 (C = 8.97, F = 7.89***)				.19	.22***	.12
Age	−.03	.01	−.15			
Duration of illness	−.36	.24	−.14			
Timeline	−.22	.10	.17*			
Timeline cyclical	.05	.04	.11			
Emotional representation	.07	.03	.21*			
Model 3 (C = 9.52, F = 6.62***)				.19	.22	.003
Age	−.03	.02	−.15			
Duration of illness	−.37	.24	−.14			
Timeline	−.21	.10	.16*			
Timeline cyclical	.05	.04	.10			
Emotional representation	.06	.03	.18*			
Perceived control	−.009	.01	−.06			

Notes: *p < .05, **p < .01, ***p < .001.
C – constant, B – unstandardized beta coefficient, SE – standard error, β = standardized beta coefficient, $\Delta R^2 = R^2$ change.

control, emotional representation, perceived control) were statistically significant, with emotional representation recording a higher beta value (β = .27, p < .01).

As seen in Table 11.4, the significantly correlated predictors were entered hierarchically in three blocks—Block 1 (age, duration of illness), Block 2 (dimensions of illness perception), and Block 3 (perceived control of internal states)—in respect of diabetes QoL (social and vocational worries).

It was found from the table that all the models were significant. After entry of perceived control at Step 3, the total variance explained by the model did not change. In the final adjusted model, two out of six predictor variables (timeline, Emotional representation) were statistically significant, with emotional representation recording a higher beta value (β = .18, p < .05).

As seen in Table 11.5, the significantly correlated predictors were entered hierarchically in three blocks—Block 1 (duration of illness, gender), Block 2 (dimensions of illness perception), and Block 3 (perceived control of internal states)—in respect of Qol (diabetes-related worries).

It was found from the table that all the models were significant. After entry of perceived control at Step 3, the total variance explained by the model as a whole was 43%, which was not significant. The introduction of perceived control explained only an additional 1% of variance in diabetes QoL (diabetes-related worries). In the

TABLE 11.5 Multiple hierarchical regression analysis for demographic variables, subscales of illness perception, and perceived control of internal states predicting QoL (diabetes related worries)

Model	B	SE	β	Adjusted R^2	R^2	ΔR^2
Model 1 (C = 7.79, F = 10.56***)				.11	.13***	
Duration of illness	−.862	.27	−.25**			
Gender	1.20	.44	.22**			
Model 2 (C = 3.86, F = 12.97***)				.39	.42***	.29
Duration of illness	−.53	.23	−.15*			
Gender	.42	.38	.08			
Timeline	−.10	.12	−.06			
Consequences	.15	.05	.21**			
Timeline cyclical	.13	.04	.23**			
Personal control	−.003	.10	−.003			
Illness coherence	.06	.06	.08			
Emotional representation	.10	.03	.24**			
Model 3 (C = 5.25, F = 11.74***)				.39	.43NS	.01
Duration of illness	−.55	.24	−.16*			
Gender	.39	.38	.07			
Timeline	−.08	.12	−.05			
Consequences	.13	.05	.19**			
Timeline cyclical	.13	.04	.23**			
Personal control	.006	.10	−.005			
Illness coherence	.061	.06	.08			
Emotional representation	.09	.04	.21**			
Perceived control	−.02	.02	−.10			

Notes: *p < .05, **p < .01, ***p < .001.
C − constant, B − unstandardized beta coefficient, SE − standard error, β − standardized beta coefficient, ΔR^2 − R^2 change.

final adjusted model, four out of nine predictor variables (duration of illness, consequences, timeline cyclical, emotional representation) were statistically significant, with timeline cyclical recording a higher beta value (β = .23, p < .01).

As seen in Table 11.6, the significantly correlated predictors were entered hierarchically in three blocks—Block 1 (duration of illness, gender), Block 2 (dimensions of illness perception), and Block 3 (perceived control of internal states)—in respect of QoL (total).

It was found from the table that all the models were significant. After entry of perceived control at Step 3, the total variance explained by the model as a whole was 60%. The introduction of perceived control explained an additional 3% of variance in diabetes QoL (total). In the final adjusted model, five out of nine predictor variables (consequences, timeline cyclical, personal control, emotional representation, perceived control) were statistically significant, with emotional representation recording a higher beta value (β = .26, p < .001).

TABLE 11.6 Multiple hierarchical regression analysis for demographic variables, subscales of illness perception, and perceived control of internal states predicting QoL (total)

Model	B	SE	β	Adjusted R^2	R^2	ΔR^2
Model 1 (C = 86.22, F = 9.31***)				.10	.11***	
Duration of illness	−4.48	1.86	−.19*			
Gender	−3.05	3.04	.25**			
Model 2 (C = 103.08, F = 23.10***)				.54	.57***	.46
Duration of illness	−1.84	1.41	−.08			
Gender	2.94	2.31	.08			
Timeline	−1.12	.70	−.10			
Consequences	1.19	.30	.25***			
Timeline cyclical	.99	.25	.25***			
Personal control	−1.70	.57	−.18**			
Illness coherence	−.23	.36	−.04			
Emotional representation	.97	.20	.34***			
Model 3 (C = 124.75, F = 23.16***)				.57	.60**	.03
Duration of illness	−2.23	1.37	−.09			
Gender	2.55	2.24	.07			
Timeline	−.85	.68	−.07			
Consequences	.92	.30	.19**			
Timeline cyclical	.93	.24	.24***			
Personal control	−1.55	.56	−.17**			
Illness coherence	−.25	.35	−.05			
Emotional representation	.75	.21	.26***			
Perceived control	−.29	.09	−.22**			

Notes: *p < .05, **p < .01, ***p < .001.
C – constant, B – unstandarized beta coefficient, SE – standard error, β – standardized beta coefficient, ΔR^2 – R^2 change.

Discussion

From the analysis, it was noted that as the duration of illness increases, there is an improvement in QoL. This can be explained by taking into account the fact that diagnosis of diabetes at the early stage creates worry and anxiety negatively impacting the QoL. Earlier findings (Padiri, 2016) indicated a similar trend where patients diagnosed with diabetes for less than a year were found to have a low QoL on the dimension of social burden when compared to those above one year and five years of duration of illness. Diagnosis of any chronic illness initially induces stress in anticipation of problems in lifestyle (Peltzer & Pengpid, 2016). Further, the information support in terms of the need for strict compliance and the repercussions of low adherence is anxiety-inducing. This in turn is likely to create a situation of compliance anxiety and a very strict regimen to start with. Any small deviations are likely to be viewed as gross violations both by the family and by the patients concerned (Ha, Duy, & Le, 2014). This is likely to impact the QoL. However, as time progresses, the adaptation sets in, and the changed lifestyle gets integrated into the daily routine. Thus, lifestyle changes are no more the cause of worry and anxiety.

Results indicated the higher QoL among women patients. A study by Holt-Lunstad, Birmingham, and Light (2015) explained the phenomenon with the higher secretion of oxytocin as a possible pathway between social connectedness and long-term health and survival. Studies have suggested that self-care confidence and functional status were important factors affecting women's self-care behaviours (Mei et al., 2019).

One of the most difficult aspects related to lifestyle changes in diabetics is restrictions in diet. In majority of Indian families, women are at the command of the kitchens. They can plan the menu of the day in a way that caters to the dietary needs of their diabetic condition. They know and exercise the art of shortcuts in separating portions of the diet for themselves before adding the diabetic-prohibited ingredients to the menu. Thus, so far as the diet is concerned, women are facilitated with an internal locus of control, and hence there is 'voluntary' compliance than the 'imposed' compliance. When the restrictions are followed voluntarily, the affect state is not negative, which happens when the restrictions are imposed from outside. Women are more sensitive to illnesses, more able and likely to rest during an illness, and more willing to seek medical advice (Anderson, Fitzgerald, & Oh, 1993). The other reason for the voluntary adherence among women is that majority of women tend to take care of their health so that their indisposition does not cause inconvenience to the other family members.

The correlation between the dimensions of illness perception and the worries dimension of QoL is a pointer to the fact that the symptoms are associated with a higher level of perceived control and overall QoL. Higher manifestations of symptoms are indications of lower control over the disease condition and vice versa. The patients with uncontrolled diabetes have the symptoms manifesting more significantly and more frequently. Their lifestyle changes and high adherence may not bring the desirable disease management. Many such cases are termed 'uncontrolled diabetes' where the probability of adverse impact of the disease on various systems in the body is high (Delahanty et al., 2007) constituting the major reason for worry. The negative affect state due to worrying and the persistence of symptoms forms a vicious circle. Given such a situation, the QoL in those patients naturally becomes the casualty. Perceived control is associated with a positive attitude (Watkins et al., 2000) which contributes to the QoL.

The findings revealed that gender and disease duration could significantly predict QoL. Gender predicting the QoL in diabetic patients is supported by the findings of Wändell (2005) and the duration of disease by Kumar and Krishna (2015). The addition of illness perception brought a significant difference in the total variance in predicting QoL. Illness perceptions of individuals help organize information and guide the monitoring of symptoms, consequences, and subsequently their management. Hence, individuals may be less likely to engage in health-compromising behaviours that lower their QoL. Previous studies on other chronic illnesses have found that illness perception explained 27% of overall QoL at baseline assessment as well as a year later for cardiac patients (O'Donovan et al., 2015) and 17–51% in hemodialysis with T2DM patients (Pula, 2012). A self-management program was designed by van Puffelen et al. (2014) to build more adaptive illness perceptions to enhance self-management and QoL among recently diagnosed T2DM patients. Health interventions based on understanding and modifying perceptions of illness proved useful in facilitating patients' HRQoL (Dempster, Howell, & McCorry, 2015). The other significant predictor which was found in this study was perceived control. The addition of perceived control to illness perception and the other demographic variables brought about an increased percentage of variance in the prediction of QoL. From this, it can be understood that perceived control along with illness perception and other demographics (age, gender, and disease duration) could predict QoL among diabetic patients. Prior studies have found that higher perceived control was associated with less interference with personal and social functioning and lower negative feelings associated with the disease (Watkins et al., 2000). In other words, perceived control of internal states was found to be associated with a more positive attitude towards life in general. QoL is better in patients who feel in control of their condition (Harvey, 2015). Similar studies have found that patients' perceptions of illness and control were found to be the most significant predictors of health outcomes (Watkins et al., 2000). These findings indicate that by fostering appropriate illness perceptions and developing a patient's perceived control, we can enhance their overall QoL.

The study was to find out the relationship between demographics, illness perception, perceived control of internal states, and QoL and to find out the impact of demographic variables, illness perception, and perceived control on the QoL of diabetic patients. Based on the results of the present study, it was noted that illness perception and its dimensions contributed significantly to the QoL and its dimensions compared to perceived control of internal states.

Implications

The findings of this study can be useful in understanding the vital role of illness perception and perceived control of internal states in an individual's QoL. Identification of appropriate illness perceptions can bring about improvement in patients' adherence to the treatment recommendations. Illness perceptions are important potential targets to improve the QoL of people with diabetes. Illness perceptions may therefore be a useful basis for future QoL interventions. Further, the findings can help develop intervention modules to enhance QoL among the diabetic population. The intervention module should assess their perceptions of illness and perception of control. Based on this assessment, a patient education program must be designed to address the knowledge domain of the disease which should necessarily include the role of self in managing the disease. Simple and practical tips such as stimulus control in diet, mobile phone reminders for medication regulation, self-imposed incentives for adherence to physical exercise, and regular monitoring of blood glucose levels would go a long way in inculcating the control over the disease and enhancing self-efficacy. This contributes to improvement in adherence. Thus, the treatment regimen should integrate the psychological aspects influencing the initiation and sustenance of behavioural changes in disease management. By the application of such methods, health care services can be improved.

References

Anderson, R. M., Fitzgerald, J. T., & Oh, M. S. (1993). The relationship between diabetes-related attitudes and patient's self-reported adherence. Diabetes Education, 19(4): 287–292.

Broadbent, E., Wilkes, C., Koschwanez, H., Weinman, J., Norton, S., & Petrie, K. J. (2015). A systematic review and meta-analysis of the brief illness perception questionnaire. Psychology and Health, 30: 1361–1385. doi: 10.1080/08870446.2015.1070851

Cameron, L., & Leventhal, H. (2003). Self-regulation, health, & illness: An overview. In L. Cameron, & H. Leventhal (Eds.), The Self-Regulation of Health and Illness Behaviour. London: Routledge.

Chen, P., Broadbent, E., Coomarasamy, C., & Jarrett, P. (2015). Illness perception in association with psychological functioning in patients with discoid lupus erythematosus. British Journal of Dermatology, 173: 824–826.

Delahanty, L. M., Grant, R. W., Wittenberg, E., Bosch, J. L., Wexler, D. J., Cagliero, E, & Meigs, J. B. (2007). Association of diabetes-related emotional distress with diabetes treatment in primary care patients with type 2 diabetes. Diabetes Medicine, 24: 48–54.

Dempster, M., Howell, D., & McCorry, N. K. (2015). Illness perceptions and coping in physical health conditions: A meta-analysis. Journal of Psychosomatic Research, 79: 506–513.

Fall, E., Chakroun-Baggioni, N., Böhme, P., Maqdasy, S., Izaute, M., & Tauveron, I. (2020). Common Sense Model of self-regulation for understanding adherence and quality of life in type 2 diabetes with structural equation modelling Elsevier, 1–20. https://www.elsevier.com/open-access/userlicense/1.0/

French, D. P., Cooper, A., & Weinman, J. (2006). Illness perceptions predict attendance at cardiac rehabilitation following acute myocardial infarction: A systematic review with meta-analysis. Journal of Psychosomatic Research, 61(6): 757–767.

Ha, N. T., Duy, H. T., & Le, N. H. (2014). Quality of life among people living with hypertension in a rural Vietnam community. BMC Public Health, 14: 833.

Hagger, M. S., Koch, S., Chatzisarantis, N. L. D., & Orbell S. (2017). The common sense model of self-regulation: Meta-analysis and test of a process model. Psychology Bulletin, 143: 1117–1154. doi: 10.1037/bul0000118

Harvey, J. N. (2015). Psychosocial interventions for the diabetic patient. Diabetes, Metabolic Syndrome and Obesity: Targets and Therapy, 8: 29–43. doi: 10.2147/DMSO.S44352

Hernandez-Tejada, M. A., Lynch, C. P., Strom, J. L., & Egede, L. E. (2012). Effect of perceived control on QoL in indigent adults with T2DM. The Diabetes Educator, 38(2): 256–262. doi: 10.1177/0145721711436135

Holt-Lunstad, J., Birmingham, W. C., & Light, K. C. (2015). Relationship quality and oxytocin: Influence of stable and modifiable aspects of relationships. Journal of Social and Personal Relationships, 32(4): 472–490.

Horne, R., & Weinman, J. (2002). Self-regulation and self management in asthma: Exploring the role of illness perceptions and treatment beliefs in explaining non-adherence to preventer medication. Psychology and Health, 17(1): 17–32.

Hudson, J., Bundy, C., Coventry, P. A., & Dickens, C. (2014). Exploring the relationship between cognitive illness representations and poor emotional health and their combined association with diabetes self-care. A systematic review with meta-analysis. Journal of Psychosomatic Research, 76(4): 265–274. doi: 10.1016/j.jpsychores

International Diabetes Federation (2019). IDF Diabetes Atlas. 9. Brussels, Belgium.

Jacobson, A. M. (1994). The DCCT Research Group: The diabetes quality of life measure. In C. Bradley (Ed.), Handbook of Psychology and Diabetes (pp. 65–87). Chur, Switzerland: Harwood Academic Publishers.

Kenowitz, J. R., Hoogendoorn, C. J., Commissariat, P. V., and Gonzalez, J. S. (2020). Diabetes-specific self-esteem, self-care and glycaemic control among adolescents with type 1 diabetes. Diabetes Medicine, 37, 760–767. doi: 10.1111/dme.14056

Kumar, P., & Krishna, M. (2015). QoL in diabetes mellitus. Science Journal of Public Health, 3(3): 310–313. doi: 10.11648/j.sjph.20150303.12

Leventhal, H., Bodnar-Deren, S., Breland, J. Y., Hash-Converse, J., Phillips, L. A., Leventhal, E. A., & Cameron, L. D. (2012). Modeling health and illness behavior: The approach of the commonsense model. In A. Baum, T. A. Revenson, & J. Singer (Eds.), Handbook of Health Psychology (2nd ed., p. 908). New York: Erlbaum.

Luhar, S., Kondal, D., Jones, R., Anjana, R. M., Patel, S. A., Kinra, S., Clarke, L., Ali, M. K., Prabhakaran, D., Kadir, M. M., Tandon, N., Mohan, V., & Venkat Narayan, K. M. (2021). Lifetime risk of diabetes in metropolitan cities in India. Diabetologia, 64(3): 521–529. doi: 10.1007/s00125-020-05330-1

Majoor, B. C. J., Andela, C. D., Quispel, C. R., Rotman, M., Dijkstra, P. D. S., Hamdy, N. A. T., Kaptein, A. A., & Appelman-Dijkstra, N. M. (2018). Illness perceptions are associated with quality of life in patients with fibrous dysplasia. Calcified Tissue International, 102(1): 23–31.

Mei, J., Tian, Y., Chai, X., & Fan, X. (2019). Gender differences in self-care maintenance and its associations among patients with chronic heart failure. International Journal of Nursing Sciences, 6(1): 58–64.

Moss-Morris, R., Weinman, J., Petrie, K., Horne, R., Cameron, L., & Buick, D. (2002). The revised illness perception questionnaire (IPQ-R). Psychology and Health, 17(1): 1–16. doi: 10.1080/08870440290001494

Nagpal, A., & Padhy, M. (2015). Dynamics of perception of illness along time among hypertensive patients: Influence on well-being. Indian Journal of Health & Wellbeing, 6(9): 836–841.

O'Donovan, C. E., Painter, L., Lowe, B., Robinson, H., & Broadbent, E. (2015). The impact of illness perceptions and disease severity on QoL in congenital heart disease. Cardiology in the Young, 1–10. doi: 10.1016/j.hlc.2011.03.073

Padhy, M., Lalnuntluangi, R., Padri, R. A., & Chelly, K. (2022). Wellbeing of Police Personnel; Role of Perceived Social Support and Perceived Control of Internal State. The Police Journal; Theory, Practice and Principles. doi: 10.1177/0032258X221085689

Padhy, M., & Monteiro, S. R. (2020). Improving work performance: Examining the role of mindfulness and perceived control of internal states in work engagement. International Journal of Behavioural Sciences, 14(1): 27–33. doi: 10.30491/IJS.2020.203525.114523

Padiri, R. A. (2016). Adherence and Quality of Life of Patients with Type II Diabetes: Role of Psychosocial Factors [Doctoral dissertation]. Centre for Health Psychology, University of Hyderabad.

Pallant, J. F. (2000). Development and evaluation of a scale to measure perceived control of internal states. Journal of Personality Assessment, 70: 308–337. doi: 10.1207/S15327752JPA7502_1

Peltzer, K., & Pengpid, S. (2016). Anticipated stigma in chronic illness patients in Cambodia, Myanmar and Vietnam. Nagoya Journal of Medical Science, 78(4): 423–435.

Polonsky, W. H., & Hessler, D. 2013. What are the quality of life-related benefits and losses associated with real-time continuous glucose monitoring? A survey of current users. Diabetes Technology and Therapeutics, 15(4): 295–301. doi: 10.1089/dia.2012.0298.

Pula, J. L. (2012). Illness perceptions of hemodialysis patients with T2DM mellitus and their association with empowerment. Seton Hall University Dissertations and Theses (ETDs). 1802. Retrieved February 2, 2022, from https://scholarship.shu.edu/dissertations/1802

Rubin, R. R. (2000). Diabetes and quality of life. Diabetes Spectrum, 13: 21–23. Retrieved February 2, 2022, from http://journal.diabetes.org/diabetesspectrum/00v13n1/pg21.htm

Scharloo, M., Baatenburg de Jong, R. J., Langeveld, T. P. M. et al. (2005). Quality of life and illness perceptions in patients with recently diagnosed head and neck cancer. Head Neck, 27: 857–863.

Sridhar, G. R., & Madhu, K. (2002). Psychosocial and cultural issues in diabetes mellitus. Current Science, 83(12): 1556–1564. Retrieved February 2, 2022, from http://www.iisc.ernet.in/currsci/dec252002/1556.pdf

Turiano, N. A., Chapman, B. P., Agrigoroaei, S., Infurna, F. J., & Lachman, M. (2014). Perceived control reduces mortality risk at low, not high, education levels. Health Psychology, 33(8): 883–890. doi: 10.1037/hea0000022

Van Puffelen, A. L., Rijken, M., Heijmans, M. J., Nijpels, G., Rutten, G. E., & Schellevis, F. G. (2014). Living with diabetes: A group-based self-management support programme for type 2 diabetes mellitus patients in the early phases of illness and their partners, study protocol of a randomised controlled trial. BioMed Central Health Services Research, 14(1): 144. doi: 10.1186/1472-6963-14-144

Wallston, K. A., Wallston, B. S., Smith, S., & Dobbins, C. J. (1987). Perceived control and health. Current Psychological Research & Reviews, 6(1): 5–25. https://doi.org/10.1007/BF02686633

Wändell, P. E. (2005). Quality of life of patients with diabetes mellitus: An overview of research in primary health care in the Nordic countries. Scandinavian Journal of Primary Health Care, 23(2): 68–74. doi: 10.1080/02813430510015296

Wang, J., Yang, Z., Zheng, Y., Peng, Y., Wang, Q., Xia, H., Wang, Y., Ding, J., Zhu, P., Shang, L., & Zheng, Z. (2021). Effects of illness perceptions on health-related quality of life in patients with rheumatoid arthritis in China. Health and Quality of Life Outcomes, 19: 126.

Watkins, K.W., Klem, L., Connell, C. M., Hickey, T., Fitzgerald, J. T., & Ingersoll-Dayton, B. (2000). Effect of adults self-regulation of diabetes on quality of life. Diabetes Care, 23(10): 1511–1515. doi: 10.2337/diacare.23.10.1511

World Health Organization (2021). Global report on diabetes. https://www.who.int/news-room/fact-sheets/detail/diabetes

World Health Organization Quality of Life assessment (WHOQOL): position paper from the World Health Organization. (1995). Social Science & Medicine (1982), 41(10), 1403–1409. https://doi.org/10.1016/0277-9536(95)00112-k

Zhang, N., Fielding, R., Soong, I., Chan, K. K., Tsang, J., & Lee, V. (2016). Illness perceptions among cancer survivors. Support Care Cancer, 24: 1295–304.

12

ILLNESS PERCEPTIONS AND DIABETES SELF-MANAGEMENT

A Mixed-Method Approach

Chelli Kavya

Diabetes is a significant non-communicable disease accounting for the increased prevalence of morbidity and mortality among the Indian population and worldwide. As per the International Diabetes Federation (IDF) reports, nearly 415 million individuals had diabetes in 2015, and by the year 2040, this figure is likely to rise to 642 million (Ogurtsova et al., 2017). Diabetes is a growing healthcare challenge. The estimates in 2019 showed that 77 million people had diabetes in India, which is expected to rise to over 134 million by 2045 (Pradeepa & Mohan, 2021). The global expenditure on direct healthcare costs of type 2 diabetes and its related complications was estimated to be 795–1404 billion international dollars in 2015 and is expected to increase to 997–1788 billion international dollars in 2040 (International Diabetes Federation, 2015). Developing and implementing cost-effective and efficient strategies become crucial for the treatment and management of type 2 diabetes (Van Smoorenburg et al., 2019).

The role of Illness perceptions in managing chronic illnesses, including diabetes, is highlighted in the literature (Broadbent et al., 2015; Hagger et al., 2017). Illness perceptions are the organized cognitive representations or beliefs that the patients have about their illness. These perceptions were significant determinants of behaviour and are associated with several important outcomes, for instance, treatment adherence and functional recovery (Leventhal et al., 1997; Weinman & Petrie, 1997). The Common-Sense Model (CSM) of health behaviour suggests that individuals build their own cognitive and emotional representations of the illness (known as illness perceptions) in response to a perceived health threat (illness), which influence how individuals cope with their illness (Diefenbach & Leventhal, 1996; Leventhal et al., 2003). As per past research findings, illness perceptions of type 2 diabetes patients are linked to self-care behaviours (Harvey & Lawson, 2009).

A patient's cognitive representation of their illness guides the behaviour directed at managing the condition (Leventhal et al., 1984). There is growing

DOI: 10.4324/9781003360858-16

literature on how patients' illness perceptions relate to later outcomes from illness. The outcomes that researchers have examined fall into four major groups – emotional distress, recovery and disability, survival, and treatment-related behaviour, such as adherence (Petrie & Weinman, 2012). Adherence problems frequently arise because there is a poor fit between the patient's illness model and the nature of the treatment recommendation, implying that the treatment does not make sense to the patient. Heart attack patients who believed their lifestyle caused their illness, for example, were more adherent to lifestyle-change advice, whereas those who believed their condition was caused by stress or genes were much less inclined to make these changes (Weinman et al., 2000). In various acute and chronic illnesses, illness perceptions have been demonstrated to have significant associations with outcomes. There is now a need for the development of effective interventions to help patients change dysfunctional illness perceptions and, as a result, improve illness outcomes (Petrie et al., 2007). Understanding and incorporating illness perceptions into healthcare are critical to effective treatment. Inquiring patients about how they view their condition allows physicians to identify and correct any inaccurate beliefs patients may have, thus optimizing medical management (Lew & Centron, 2021).

There are seven essential self-care behaviours in individuals with diabetes that predict good outcomes. These are healthy eating, being physically active, monitoring blood sugar, compliance with medications, good problem-solving skills, healthy coping skills, and risk-reduction behaviours (American Association of Diabetes Educators, 2020). The active participation of the patients in their treatment is known as self-management (Koch et al., 2004). According to Corbin and Strauss (1988), self-management includes three distinct sets of activities – medical management (e.g., taking medication and adhering to dietary advice); behavioural management (e.g., adopting new behaviours in the context of chronic disease); and emotional management (e.g., dealing with the feelings of frustration and despair associated with chronic illness). As type 2 diabetes is a chronic illness and the patients visit health professionals a few times a year, they need to control all these aspects for the remainder of the time (Van Smoorenburg et al., 2019).

The research studies on diabetes self-management practices draw attention to various factors that take the role of facilitators or stand as barriers to disease self-management (Adhikari et al., 2021). Furthermore, knowledge of factors that influence self-management can help inform the content and design of care and support activities (Majeed-Ariss et al., 2015; Wilkinson et al., 2014). With this background, the study was conducted to examine whether illness perceptions predict disease self-management and to explore the lived experiences of type 2 diabetes patients for understanding the facilitating factors and barriers to diabetes self-management.

Method

A mixed-method design (Creswell, 2003, p. 211) was utilized in the study. A cross-sectional survey design was adopted in phase I, and in phase II, a qualitative approach was followed to explore various factors involved in diabetes self-management in individuals with type 2 diabetes. The basic objective was to give detailed examinations of personally lived experiences (Smith et al., 2009).

Participants

Phase I – The study included 286 type 2 diabetes patients (50.7% men and 49.3% women) recruited through the purposive sampling method. The age range of the sample was 27–83 years ($M = 56.09$; $SD = 11.09$). The duration of diabetes ranged from above one month to 32 years ($M = 9.24$; $SD = 7.21$). The marital status of the participants is as follows: married (60.14%), unmarried/not reported (36.36%), and widowed (3.5%). Regarding education, 219 (76.57%) participants were educated, whereas 67 (23.43%) participants had no formal education.

Based on the findings of phase I, ten participants (five with high diabetes self-management scores and five with low diabetes self-management scores) were selected (nine women and one man; age 30–73 years) and interviewed. The duration of illness of participants (type 2 diabetes) ranged from 2 to 27 years. All the participants were married, one participant was a widow, and two participants were not literate. The highest reported education was post-graduation. The following comorbid conditions were reported: high blood pressure, thyroid condition, and arthritis. Table 12.1 shows participants' demographic characteristics.

TABLE 12.1 Demographic characteristics of participants phase II

S. No.	Participants pseudonyms	Gender	Age	Education	Marital status	Duration of diabetes	Comorbid conditions	Insulin
1	Srishti	Female	69	Primary	Married	6 years	High blood pressure and thyroid condition	No
2	John	Male	68	Post-graduation	Married	2 years	None	No
3	Miriam	Female	73	Higher secondary and nursing	Married	8 years	High blood pressure	No
4	Uma	Female	54	Secondary	Married	27 years	None	Yes
5	Kumari	Female	50	Higher secondary	Married	10 years	High blood pressure, eyesight	No
6	Gurupreet	Female	53	Post-graduation	Married	8 years	Arthritis	No
7	Megha	Female	30	Middle school	Married	3 years	None	Yes
8	Seekriti	Female	33	No primary education	Married	2 years	None	No
9	Sujata	Female	45	Primary	Married	3 years	None	No
10	Honesty	Female	58	No primary education	Widow	4 years	None	No

Measures

Phase I of the study focused on assessment, whereas phase II involved semi-structured interviews. In phase I, two measures (Revised Illness Perception Questionnaire and Diabetes Self-Management Questionnaire) and a demographic form were used.

Revised Illness Perception Questionnaire (IPQ-R)

This questionnaire (Moss-Morris et al., 2002) captures participants' representations (or perceptions) regarding their diabetes. It consists of three distinct sections. The first section measures the identity aspect of illness, which comprises 14 symptoms. The participants are instructed to rate whether they have experienced the given symptoms since their diagnosis of diabetes using a 'yes/no' format. The same format was used to check if they believe that the symptom is particularly related to their diabetes. The total of yes-rated symptoms in the second column represents the identity subscale. Higher scores on this reflect participants' strong belief that the symptom experienced is associated with their diabetes.

The second section has 38 statements under following subscales: (a) timeline (acute/chronic), (b) consequences, (c) personal control, (d) treatment control, (e) illness coherence, (f) timeline cyclical, and (g) emotional representations. Each statement is given agreement or disagreement using a 5-point Likert scale and response options range from *strongly disagree* (1) to *strongly agree* (5). Some items are to be reverse scored. The third section is related to causes and comprises 18 causes, namely, stress or worry, hereditary, a germ or virus, diet or eating habits, chance or bad luck, poor medical care in past, pollution in the environment, own behaviour, mental attitude, family problems or worries, overwork, emotional state, ageing, alcohol, smoking, accident or injury, personality, and altered immunity. Each statement is rated on a 5-point Likert scale which ranges from *strongly disagree* to *strongly agree*. Towards the end of the questionnaire, the participants are requested to name the three most important factors that they believe are the causes of their diabetes in rank order.

Diabetes Self-Management Questionnaire (DSMQ)

This questionnaire (Schmitt et al., 2013) measures self-care activities associated with glycaemic control. It has 16 items under four subscales, namely, 'glucose management,' 'dietary control,' 'physical activity,' and 'health-care use.' One item (item 16) requests a total rating of the participant's self-care and it is only to be included in the 'sum scale.' Participants rate the applicability of each statement to them on a 4-point Likert scale and response options range from 'applies to me very much' (3) to 'does not apply for me (0). The participants are requested to rate the degree to which each item applies to their self-management in the previous 8 weeks. Negatively worded items are reversed as part of scoring so that higher values are reflective of effective self-care. The scores on each subscale are obtained by summing item scores and then transforming to a scale which ranges from 0 to 10 '(raw score/theoretical maximum score*10).'

Interviews

A total of five participants with the lowest scores and five with the highest scores on DSMQ constituted the subsample. Semi-structured interviews were conducted at the participants' residences and clinics based on their preferences. The average duration of each face-to-face individual interview session lasted for 25–35 minutes. The interviews were recorded and were guided by two broad questions: What are the factors that contributed to or facilitated your diabetes self-management? What are the factors that inhibited or hindered your diabetes self-management?

Procedure

The approval of the Institutional Ethics Committee was taken before conducting the study. The participants were recruited from a diabetes clinic. Written informed consent was obtained from all the participants. The questionnaires were administered individually and the average time taken to complete both questionnaires are 20–30 minutes. Interviews were conducted at the participants' residences and clinics based on their preferences. The average duration of each face-to-face individual interview session lasted for 25–35 minutes.

Results

Quantitative and qualitative analyses were conducted on the obtained data to meet the objectives of the study.

Phase I

The objective of the study was to examine whether illness perceptions predict self-management. Pearson's correlation (r) was carried out to find out the relationship between the predictors and the criterion followed by multiple regression. Both significant positive and negative relationships were observed between dimensions of illness perceptions and overall diabetes self-management.

A significant positive relationship was observed between timeline (acute/chronic) dimension and diabetes self-management ($r = .14$, $p < .05$). This implies that perceiving diabetes as a chronic condition is associated with better overall diabetes self-management. The results indicated no significant correlation between consequences and diabetes self-management. A significant positive relationship was observed between the personal control dimension and the diabetes self-management ($r = .37$, $p < .01$), implying that higher perceptions of personal control or confidence in controlling diabetes are associated with improved diabetes self-management.

Treatment control showed a similar trend as personal control. Results revealed a significant positive relationship between treatment control dimension and diabetes self-management ($r = .18$, $p < .01$). This implies that perceiving treatment as effective in controlling diabetes and delaying negative effects is associated with improved diabetes self-management. Similar to personal and treatment control, illness coherence dimension also demonstrated a significant positive relationship with diabetes self-management ($r = .22$, $p < .01$). This implies that greater understanding (coherence) of diabetes is associated with improved diabetes self-management. No significant relationship was observed between the timeline cyclical dimension and the diabetes self-management. No significant correlation was observed between emotional representations and diabetes self-management.

Simultaneous multiple regression analysis was conducted using the enter method to investigate the effect of illness perceptions on diabetes self-management for the entire sample. Table 12.2 provides the summary of simultaneous multiple regression for illness perceptions predicting diabetes self-management.

It was found from Table 12.2 that illness perceptions explained statistically significant (19%) proportion of the variance in diabetes self-management, $R^2 = .19$, adjusted $R^2 = .17$, $F(7, 278) = 9.56$, $p < .01$. In this analysis, timeline and personal control were only significant predictors of diabetes self-management, $\beta = .15$, $t = 2.77$, $p < .05$ and $\beta = .38$, $t = 6.05$, $p < .01$. This indicates that beliefs about the extent to which the illness is amenable to personal control and how long this period lasts will predict diabetes management.

TABLE 12.2 Summary of simultaneous multiple regression for illness perceptions predicting diabetes self-management

Predictors	B	SEB	β	t	p
Timeline (acute/chronic)	.05	.02	.15	2.77	<.05
Consequences	.01	.02	.04	.62	.53
Personal control	.14	.02	.38	6.05	<.01
Treatment control	−.02	.03	−.05	−.87	.384
Illness coherence	.04	.02	.11	1.83	.067
Timeline cyclical	−.02	.02	−.05	−.90	.366
Emotional representations	−.01	.01	−.07	−1.23	.218
R^2		.19			
C		2.77			
F		9.56	$p < .01$		

Notes: B – unstandardized beta coefficient, SEB – standardized error of beta, β – standardized beta coefficient, t – t values of beta, C – constant.

***$p < .01$.

The second objective of the study was to explore the lived experiences of type 2 diabetes patients for understanding the facilitating factors and barriers to diabetes self-management. The results of the quantitative analysis indicated that of all the variables only two, namely, timeline (acute/chronic) and personal control, are significant contributors to diabetes self-management. This calls for an in-depth inquiry to understand the role of these factors both in those who score highest in self-management and those who scored lowest. Interview responses of these two groups give a scope not only to understand the way these two factors contributed but also to identify those factors not covered under the illness perception scale. Thus, the combination of the quantitative results and the interview results helps in filling the gaps in either of the methods used in isolation. The qualitative analysis of phase II is discussed below.

Phase II

Themes and Sub-Themes

In the interview session, the verbatim of the participants was recorded and the non-verbal behaviours were recorded by the researcher. Subsequently, field notes were prepared and the verbatim of the audio-recorded interviews was transcribed and translated into English. Then these transcripts were read and re-read along with field notes and observation reports to obtain clarity on participants' lived experiences of factors that facilitate or inhibit their diabetes self-management. After multiple readings, codes were identified. Then similar codes were clustered together and sub-themes were identified. Similar sub-themes were grouped and were given names. Following this, similar sub-themes were put together to form a theme. The themes that emerged as facilitating factors and barriers to diabetes self-management are presented in Table 12.3. The themes were again compared to the transcripts for double verification. The themes and sub-themes with illustrative quotations are presented in Table 12.4.

TABLE 12.3 Themes and their sub-themes

	Themes	Sub-Themes
	Belief system	Belief in God
		Belief in Self
Facilitating factors	Support from family members	
	Persistent care	
	Knowledge about diabetes	
	Wish for a healthier future	
	Social constraints	Lack of financial resources
		Social obligations
Barriers	Lack of informational support from a physician	
	Poor health value	
	Presence of comorbid conditions	

TABLE 12.4 Themes and their sub-themes with illustrative quotation

Themes	Sub-themes	Illustrative quotation
Facilitating factors		
Belief system	Belief in God	'…God is the ultimate help I have. I always believe…'
	Belief in Self	'…I can control my illness…I clean my gangrene. I do all the necessary things to keep my condition in control.'
Support from family members		'My spouse and daughter help me in managing diabetes. My daughter is a nurse so she helps me manage my diabetes. My husband reads about diabetes and informs me'
		'My daughter is a doctor. She informs me about diabetes-related facts'
Persistent care		'Continuous care is required for maintaining normal blood sugar levels. I take medicines every day, control diet and go for blood testing regularly. These days my sugar levels are very normal, I don't take insulin anymore which I used to when my sugar level was high and I also lost some weight'
Knowledge about diabetes		'…And I keep reading news articles about diabetes, types of food to be taken etc.'
Wish for a healthier future		'I want to be healthy in future, so I take care of myself… I don't want to give any trouble to [my] children or other family members because of my condition…'
Barriers		
Social constraints	Lack of financial resources	'We don't have enough money to spend on medicines, blood tests, doctor fees, and travel from our village to doctor's clinic'
	Social obligations	'…Sometimes when I am attending family functions, I eat what I am not supposed to eat. I don't control my diet'
Lack of informational support from the physician		'Due to lack of information regarding diabetes, I feel tensed. I expect some more information from the doctor about my diabetes'
Poor health value		'I don't care about my diabetes. I eat whatever I want and don't exercise. I remain tension free. Whatever has to happen will happen…But I take medicines'
Presence of comorbid conditions		'I have joint pains so I can't do exercise. I just walk inside [my] house'

Discussion

The objective was to examine whether illness perceptions predict diabetes self-management among type 2 diabetes patients. The findings indicated that illness perceptions [timeline (acute/chronic) and personal control] predicted diabetes self-management in participants, whereas consequences, treatment control, illness coherence, timeline cyclical, and emotional representations did not predict diabetes management. These findings are in line with published empirical studies. For instance, greater perceptions of acute timeline, personal control, treatment control, coherence, and exercise effectiveness were found to be associated with being physically active (Broadbent et al., 2011; Searle et al., 2007; van Puffelen et al., 2015). Similarly, the results of a study indicated that illness perception predicted overall self-care practices in individuals with type 2 diabetes (Kugbey et al., 2017). Illness perceptions are the organized beliefs surrounding the time course, symptoms, consequences, causes, and controllability of an illness. Illness perceptions are shown to predict a variety of psychosocial and clinical outcomes in chronic diseases including type 2 diabetes. Illness perceptions include beliefs about the extent to which the illness is amenable to personal control and how long it will last and these two factors seem to predict diabetes management among the sample of this study.

The qualitative data supports the quantitative findings. For example, the themes of knowledge about diabetes and belief systems point to the cognitive foundation which triggers disease-appropriate behaviour or self-management. In addition to the findings of the regression analysis, the interviews could provide insight into the reasons for their efficient or inefficient self-management by identifying the facilitating and restraining factors contributing to self-management.

Facilitating Factors for Diabetes Self-Management

Various factors seemed to help the participants in managing their diabetes. *Belief in God* was a vital source of help for some. Few participants believed in prayers for better health and reported God as a 'healing' source in times of illness. This finding is supported by the research work conducted on diabetic patients where the 'divine' was reported to be the major source of hope and strength (Gupta & Anandarajah, 2014). However, relying on the belief in God without adherence to medical advice will also prove detrimental (Hariharan, 2020). Faith in divine power combined with good self-management enhances the conviction about the results of good self-management and is likely to sustain the motivation. Most of the participants believed in *'self'* and demonstrated confidence in their ability to control their illness. They were more internally oriented. Belief in oneself to carry out particular behaviour is known as self-efficacy and it is shown to directly affect self-care specific to diabetes (Devarajooh & Chinna, 2017). Beliefs are considered crucial in most health belief models as they directly influence how individuals cope with the illness.

All the participants unanimously reported support from family as one of the major sources of managing their diabetes effectively. Emotional support from spouse and tangible and informational support from children and family members who happen to be medical professionals acted as the sources of encouragement to some participants. It is a well-documented finding that family members are sources of health information (Onwudiwe et al., 2014). However, some believed in active management and sought the information independently, implying that they were proactive in seeking health information. Diabetes knowledge and diabetes education are related to better self-care activities (Jeong et al., 2014). Being aware, seeking the right information, and educating oneself about the disease and its management will help patients in better outcomes.

Diabetes management is multimodal and usually takes place in a social setting of family and friends, healthcare professionals, and the community, with each of these influencing patient's adherence (Barrera et al., 2006). Persistent care was another facilitating factor reported by participants. Few participants discussed that the desire to be healthy in the future was a motivating force. As a result, they would adopt health-promoting behaviours, which is a prerequisite for managing any chronic illness. And by adopting health-enhancing behaviours, they were also making efforts to avoid long-term diabetes complications. One of the participants reported her previous hospitalization experience and described that the incident was difficult for her close ones. Hence, the participant was making all the necessary lifestyle changes so that such situations do not repeat.

Barriers to Diabetes Self-Management

One of the significant barriers identified by some of the participants hindering their diabetes self-management was a lack of financial resources. Illness management is a lifelong process and it involves a substantial amount of expenditure towards medical care. Previous investigators documented similar findings where a lower income was related to poor adherence to diabetic medications (Rolnick et al., 2013). In a study, it was found that for diabetes treatment, about 60% of the low-income group borrowed or mortgaged their property, and about 70–80% of the high-income group spent a large part of their savings on treatment (Tharkar et al., 2010). Participants also reported the social constraints encountered during certain occasions such as marriage or a social gathering where it becomes challenging to have dietary control. A participant felt obliged to consume the food not suitable for diabetes served at the gathering. It has been demonstrated that during times of stress or social pressure dietary and exercise adherence often decreases among diabetic patients (Cramer, 2004).

One of the striking barriers identified was that participants perceived a lack of informational support from the physician. Few participants were found to assign less value to diabetes management, such as exercise and dietary recommendations. However, they reported taking regular medications. This finding is supported by a study on diabetic patients who rated medication more important than diet and exercise and indicated higher adherence to medications (Broadbent et al., 2011). The presence of comorbid conditions was one significant factor limiting effective management. The inability to perform exercise due to joint pain was one explanation given by a participant. Having comorbid conditions was observed to hinder exercise compliance, and this finding is supported by previous research (Balhara & Sagar, 2011). The demands placed on diabetic patients due to strict adherence to a complex regimen can sometimes be difficult and frustrating, which may lead to emotional distress. Diabetes self-management needs a substantial investment of the patient's time (Russell et al., 2005; Safford et al., 2005). The time and energy required for diabetes self-care could be substantially reduced when comorbid conditions are managed simultaneously.

Implications and Conclusion

The study found a relationship between illness perception [timeline (acute/chronic), personal and treatment control, and illness coherence] and diabetes management. Further, the study identified factors that facilitate an individual's diabetes self-management process and these were support from family members, belief in self and God, persistent care, knowledge about diabetes, and wish for a healthier future. This can be construed as a combination of a strong cognitive base regarding the disease condition, self-efficacy, and a good motivation to sustain future health status along with the belief in the protection of supernatural power. A good motivational level with the trust in one's own ability based on the roots of relevant knowledge is likely to contribute to a goal-oriented behaviour, which is adherence in this case. Specific barriers were also identified that were influencing participants' management of their illness negatively. The barriers are social constraints (lack of financial resources and social obligations), presence of comorbid conditions, lack of informational support from a physician, and poor health value. The list of barriers projects the lack of informational support that causes cognitive deprivation related to diabetes. In the absence of a cognitive base, it is difficult to build robust health values. Adherence behaviour is a far-fetched outcome in the absence of these two and more so when combined with comorbid conditions and inadequate financial resources. The vital task for psychological research in the area of health is to understand the factors that influence adherence to medical regimes. One of the most significant challenges for individuals diagnosed with diabetes is knowing how to acquire and maintain the necessary skills required for effective self-management. The study suggests that knowledge forms the basic foundation on which beliefs, motivation, and skill acquisition are built.

Following are a few recommendations related to psychosocial interventions to enhance adherence among the diabetic population:

- The treatment approach to diabetes should involve not just the physician but also a Health Psychologist who would make regular assessments of adherence behaviour.
- Physician treating diabetes patients should form support groups of patients and their families for knowledge exchange under the supervision of nursing staff. This enhances the cognitive base of the patients and their family members.
- The Health Psychologist should plan regular workshops with the support groups, in which skills of habit formation, exercising restraints towards

prohibited diets, inculcating intrinsic motivation to integrate exercise into the daily routine, and sessions of stress management and relaxation are alternated.
- Individual counselling by the Health Psychologist should be interwoven into the regimen so that the patients with high levels of psychological distress are helped in handling their anxiety and depression to restore the psychological equilibrium which is a necessary condition in diabetes management
- Patients with financial difficulties need to be provided with the genetic labels of the medications in their prescriptions, which are much cheaper than the commercial products.

A multidisciplinary approach to treating diabetes is the only alternative for meeting the challenge of high projections of prevalence in the next decade on the one hand and growing complacence about the disease condition on the other, both of which to a large extent are contributed by low health literacy and inadequate information exchange owing to paucity of time of the doctors and dismally low doctor-patient ratio.

Reference

Adhikari, M., Devkota, H. R., & Cesuroglu, T. (2021). Barriers to and facilitators of diabetes self-management practices in Rupandehi, Nepal-multiple stakeholders' perspective. *BMC Public Health*, *21*(1), 1–18.

American Association of Diabetes Educators (2020). An effective model of diabetes care and education: Revising the AADE7 Self-Care Behaviors®. *The Diabetes Educator*, *46*(2), 139–160.

Balhara, Y. P. S., & Sagar, R. (2011). Correlates of anxiety and depression among patients with type 2 diabetes mellitus. *Indian Journal of Endocrinology and Metabolism*, *15*(1), S50.

Barrera Jr, M., Toobert, D. J., Angell, K. L., Glasgow, R. E., & MacKinnon, D. P. (2006). Social support and social-ecological resources as mediators of lifestyle intervention effects for type 2 diabetes. *Journal of Health Psychology*, *11*(3), 483–495.

Broadbent, E., Donkin, L., & Stroh, J. C. (2011). Illness and treatment perceptions are associated with adherence to medications, diet, and exercise in diabetic patients. *Diabetes Care*, *34*(2), 338–340.

Broadbent, E., Wilkes, C., Koschwanez, H., Weinman, J., Norton, S., & Petrie, K. J. (2015). A systematic review and meta-analysis of the Brief Illness Perception Questionnaire. *Psychology & Health*, *30*(11), 1361–1385. https://doi.org/10.1080/08870446.2015.1070851

Corbin, J. M., & Strauss, A. (1988). *Unending work and care: Managing chronic illness at home*. Jossey-bass.

Cramer, J. A. (2004). A systematic review of adherence with medications for diabetes. *Diabetes Care*, *27*(5), 1218–1224.

Creswell, J. W. (2003). *Research design: Qualitative, quantitative, and mixed methods approaches*. Sage.

Devarajooh, C., & Chinna, K. (2017). Depression, distress and self-efficacy: The impact on diabetes self-care practices. *PloS One*, *12*(3), e0175096.

Diefenbach, M. A., & Leventhal, H. (1996). The common-sense model of illness representation: Theoretical and practical considerations. *Journal of Social Distress and the Homeless*, *5*(1), 11–38. https://doi.org/10.1007/BF02090456

Gupta, P. S., & Anandarajah, G. (2014). The role of spirituality in diabetes self-management in an urban, underserved population: A qualitative exploratory study. *Rhode Island Medical Journal, 97*(3), 31.

Hagger, M. S., Koch, S., Chatzisarantis, N. L. D., & Orbell, S. (2017). The common sense model of self-regulation: Meta-analysis and test of a process model. *Psychological Bulletin, 143*(11), 1117–1154. https://doi.org/10.1037/bul0000118

Hariharan, M. (2020). *Health psychology: Theory, practice and research*. India: SAGE Publication.

Harvey, J. N., & Lawson, V. L. (2009). The importance of health belief models in determining self-care behaviour in diabetes. *Diabetic Medicine, 26*, 5–13. doi: 10.1111/j.1464-5491.2008.02628.x

International Diabetes Federation (2015). *IDF diabetes atlas*, 7th edn. Brussels, Belgium: International Diabetes Federation.

Jeong, J., Park, N., & Shin, S. Y. (2014). The influence of health literacy and diabetes knowledge on diabetes self-care activities in Korean low-income elders with diabetes. *Journal of Korean Academy of Community Health Nursing, 25*(3), 217224. https://doi.org/10.12799/jkachn.2014.25.3.217

Koch, T., Jenkin, P., & Kralik, D. (2004). Chronic illness self-management: Locating the 'self'. *Journal of Advanced Nursing, 48*(5), 484–492.

Kugbey, N., Asante, K. O., & Adulai, K. (2017). Illness perception, diabetes knowledge and self-care practices among type-2 diabetes patients: A cross-sectional study. *BMC Research Notes, 10*(1), 1–7.

Leventhal, H., Benyamini, Y., Brownlee, S., Diefenbach, M., Leventhal, E. A., Patrick-Miller, L., & Robitaille, C. (1997). Illness representations: Theoretical foundations. *Perceptions of Health and Illness, 2*, 19–46.

Leventhal, H., Brissette, I., & Leventhal, E. A. (Eds.). (2003). *The self-regulation of health and illness behaviour*. Routledge.

Leventhal, H., Nerenz, D. R., & Steele, D. J. (1984). Illness representations and coping with health threats. In Baum, A., Taylor, S. E., & Singer, J. E. (Eds.), *Handbook of psychology and health: Vol. IV. Social psychological aspects of health* (pp. 219–252). Hillsdale, NJ: Lawrence Erlbaum Associates.

Lew Q. S., & Centron P. (2021). Psychiatric challenges in patients treated with peritoneal dialysis. In Cukor, D., Cohen, S. D., & Kimmel, P. L. (Eds.), *Psychosocial aspects of chronic kidney disease* (pp. 311–333). Academic Press. https://doi.org/10.1016/B978-0-12-817080-9.00015-4

Majeed-Ariss, R., Jackson, C., Knapp, P., & Cheater, F. M. (2015). A systematic review of research into black and ethnic minority patients' views on self-management of type 2 diabetes. *Health Expectations, 18*(5), 625–642.

Moss-Morris, R., Weinman, J., Petrie, K., Horne, R., Cameron, L., & Buick, D. (2002). The revised illness perception questionnaire (IPQ-R). *Psychology and Health, 17*(1), 1–16. https://doi.org/10.1080/08870440290001494

Ogurtsova, K., da Rocha Fernandes, J. D., Huang, Y., Linnenkamp, U., Guariguata, L., Cho, N. H., Cavan, D., Shaw, J. E., & Makaroff, L. E. (2017). IDF diabetes atlas: Global estimates for the prevalence of diabetes for 2015 and 2040. *Diabetes Research and Clinical Practice, 128*, 40–50. https://doi.org/10.1016/j.diabres.2017.03.024

Onwudiwe, N. C., Mullins, C. D., Shaya, A. T., Pradel, F. G., Winston, R. A., Laird, A., & Saunders, E. (2014). Barriers to self-management of diabetes: A qualitative study among low-income minority diabetics. *South African Journal of Diabetes and Vascular Disease, 11*(2), 61–65.

Petrie, K. J., Jago, L. A., & Devcich, D. A. (2007). The role of illness perceptions in patients with medical conditions. *Current Opinion in Psychiatry, 20*(2), 163–167.

Petrie, K. J., & Weinman, J. (2012). Patients' perceptions of their illness: The dynamo of volition in health care. *Current Directions in Psychological Science, 21*(1), 60–65.

Pradeepa, R., & Mohan, V. (2021). Epidemiology of type 2 diabetes in India. *Indian Journal of Ophthalmology, 69*(11), 2932.

Rolnick, S. J., Pawloski, P. A., Hedblom, B. D., Asche, S. E., & Bruzek, R. J. (2013). Patient characteristics associated with medication adherence. *Clinical Medicine & Research, 11*(2), 54–65.

Russell, L. B., Suh, D. C., & Safford, M. A. (2005). Time requirements for diabetes self-management: Too much for many. *Journal of Family Practice, 54*(1), 52–56.

Safford, M. M., Russell, L., Suh, D. C., Roman, S., & Pogach, L. (2005). How much time do patients with diabetes spend on self-care? *The Journal of the American Board of Family Practice, 18*(4), 262–270.

Schmitt, A., Gahr, A., Hermanns, N., Kulzer, B., Huber, J., & Haak, T. (2013). The diabetes self-management questionnaire (DSMQ): Development and evaluation of an instrument to assess diabetes self-care activities associated with glycaemic control. *Health and Quality of Life Outcomes, 11*(1), 138. https://doi.org/10.1186/1477-7525-11-138

Searle, A., Norman, P., Thompson, R., & Vedhara, K. (2007). A prospective examination of illness beliefs and coping in patients with type 2 diabetes. *British Journal of Health Psychology, 12*(4), 621–638.

Smith, J. A., Flowers, P., & Larkin, M. (2009). *Interpretative phenomenological analysis: Theory, method, research*. Sage.

Tharkar, S., Devarajan, A., Kumpatla, S., & Viswanathan, V. (2010). The socioeconomics of diabetes from a developing country: A population based cost of illness study. *Diabetes Research and Clinical Practice, 89*(3), 334–340.

van Puffelen, A. L., Heijmans, M. J., Rijken, M., Rutten, G. E., Nijpels, G., & Schellevis, F. G. (2015). Illness perceptions and self-care behaviours in the first years of living with type 2 diabetes; Does the presence of complications matter? *Psychology & Health, 30*(11), 1274–1287.

Van Smoorenburg, A. N., Hertroijs, D. F., Dekkers, T., Elissen, A. M., & Melles, M. (2019). Patients' perspective on self-management: Type 2 diabetes in daily life. *BMC Health Services Research, 19*(1), 1–8.

Weinman, J., & Petrie, K. J. (1997). Illness perceptions: A new paradigm for psychosomatics? *Journal of Psychosomatic Research, 42*(2), 113–116.

Weinman, J., Petrie, K. J., Sharpe, N., & Walker, S. (2000). Causal attributions in patients and spouses following a heart attack and subsequent lifestyle changes. *British Journal of Health Psychology, 5*, 263–273

Wilkinson, A., Whitehead, L., & Ritchie, L. (2014). Factors influencing the ability to self-manage diabetes for adults living with type 1 or 2 diabetes. *International Journal of Nursing Studies, 51*(1), 111–122.

PART V
Critical Care Needs and Psychological Support

PART V

13
THE INTENSIVE CARE UNIT EXPERIENCES AND REPERCUSSIONS
Need for Psychosocial Care

Usha Chivukula

Sickness is unpleasant; being seriously ill and hospitalised adds many other negative aspects to one's experience. Combating a major illness is a challenge for the patients. Illness cripples an individual physically and impedes psychological and social functioning. Hospitalisation aggravates the emotional state of the patients, inducing feelings of uncertainty, fear, anxiety, and depression. The condition demands not just comprehending the nature and symptoms of the illness but also adapting to the life changes that come along with it. The visible external indicators of illness, which are obvious and treatable, are often handled by medical professionals but the invisible indicators which are more on the psychological or social level often go untreated. These include anxiety, depression, emotional problems, social and interpersonal issues, lack of resources, and disruption in work and family life. Handling these complex issues requires extended care and support to patients and family members from the health care professionals, which include understanding their mental anguish and restoring their physical, psychological, and social functioning. This is possible only if there is a paradigm shift from the disease-centred approach of health professionals to a holistic patient-centred approach. The debate on providing holistic care in the health care field began in the early 19th century. The proposal of the biopsychosocial care model by Engel (1977) pioneered the shift from biomedical care to biopsychosocial care. According to Engel, the medical model solely looked into biological indices of the disease and failed to address the psychological and social issues attached to it. He proposed the biopsychosocial model of health which not only took into account the patients' psychological state and social context but also stressed the role of the physician and the health care system in augmenting the patients' health. The model recommended individualised treatment with emphasis on care. Illness according to this model is viewed as an interaction of the physical system, the psychological state, and the environmental interactions, thus promoting the importance of the psychosocial factors in facilitating and modifying the course of illness. According to Scholl et al. (2014), the biopsychosocial perspective of health aids in understanding the 'proximal context' of the patient which comprises the family, occupation, and the support the patient receives or perceives and the 'distal context' which comprises of the cultural or religious background and the patient's interaction with the neighbourhood and community. The biopsychosocial model not only brought in a revolution in the medical care system but also led to the emergence of other approaches like patient-centred care (Mead & Bower, 2000) and integrative medicine. The patient-centred care which got a boom in the late nineties was eventually embraced by health care organisations and brought about many changes in the policies related to medical care. Patient-centredness also stresses the uniqueness of patients, which helped in understanding patients' needs, feelings, illness beliefs, and illness experiences (Scholl et al., 2014).

The biopsychosocial perspective and its implication can be well applied to intensive care units (ICU). Intensive care is defined as an advanced level of health care, where monitoring, diagnosis, and treatment are carried out with utmost care so that the vital functions of the patients are protected and the patients move towards a meaningful life. The term 'Intensive Care' connotes that the care provided is in 'entirety' or 'holistic' and that the care would embrace the physical, psychological, social, and spiritual needs of the patient. Initiated in the 19th century, the ICUs were then rudimentary with fewer gadgets, open rooms, and natural light, where more importance was given to patient care. As technology developed, the ICUs became more sophisticated with complex equipment resulting in a shift of focus from humanised patient-centred care to dehumanised mechanical care. Thus, technology, while used as an aid, turned out to be an intrusion into patient care. The less invasive techniques and improved patient monitoring techniques have helped to reduce mortality and morbidity, but have increased the exposure to stressors. The ICU environment is thus considered overwhelming and potentially hostile and is denounced to be the cause of the unpleasant consequences on the physical and psychological functioning of the patients. Consequently, the ICU became a place where the displeasure of being sick is more immense than in the routine ward of a hospital. The ICU environment by itself is an immense source of stress for the patient. The noise from devices, the artificial lights, and the temperature (Gültekin et al., 2018) contribute to stress. Moreover, the dehumanised treatment wherein the patient is only identified with his/her bed number, disease, or the type of treatment he/she receives results in loss of one's identity including the name, family, occupation, culture, and so on (Wilson et al., 2019) The ICU stay has an adverse impact on both the physical and psychological facets of the patient. These include physical, functional, and psychological issues which have a long-term effect.

ICU Environment as a Source of Physical and Psychological Outcomes

There is a strange and eccentric niche in the ICU environment due to the different stimuli loads. The sounds and alarms from the monitoring machines and ventilators, the mourning of patients, the constant movement of doctors and nurses, and the absence of close family members interfere with the well-being of the patient (Chivukula et al., 2017). The ICU environment is unfamiliar and can induce anxiety even in a normal person. The extreme physical environment of the ICU engenders alterations in sensory inputs, namely, sensory deprivation, sensory overload, excessive noise, physical and social isolation, and restriction of movement, which are found to be some of the causes of psychological trauma. Most of these stressors are from the ICU environment and the treatment procedure, which have a short-term and a long-term impact on the patient's physical and psychological state. While physiological consequences of being in the ICU range from weakness and lack of appetite to sleeplessness which may recede after the patients have recovered from the illness, the psychological effects, namely, anxiety, depression, and trauma are long-lasting. Patients who have spent time in the ICU face physical, psychological, and social challenges.

The Impact of ICU on Patient's Physical and Functional Outcomes

Functional/physical outcomes refer to the ability of a person to complete the activities of daily living. Stay in ICU cripples a person physically. The heavy doses of medicines, lack of proper diet due to difficulty in eating and swallowing, dependency on staff for immediate needs, and one's perception of the physical changes shatter the person. The first and foremost effect seen on the critically ill patient is severe loss of weight. Loss of weight and muscle weakness are the consequences of continued ICU stay. Continuous stay in intensive care and prolonged use of ventilators can lead to muscle weakness, termed ICU acquired weakness (ICUAW), and is observed in 40% of patients across diseases (Schefold et al., 2020). ICUAW continues for a considerable amount of time after discharge. Polyneuropathy, myopathy, and muscular atrophy are the contributing factors to ICUAW (Vanhorebeek et al., 2020). Immobilisation, hyperglycaemia, sedation, delirium, and artificial nutrition are also associated with ICUAW.

Dependency as an Outcome of ICU Stay

The ICU stay leaves the patient in a state of dependency. The multiple gadgets attached to the patient's body create a feeling that they are no longer in charge of their physical condition (Almerud et al., 2007). Dependency in patients admitted to an ICU begins with their inability to perform self-care activities, which sends in feelings of powerlessness, frailty, and vulnerability. Samuelson (2011) has stated that patients in ICU have feelings of insecurity, powerlessness, and helplessness. These feelings are associated with a lack of awareness of what has happened to them, loss of information, and lack of ability to manage on their own. In a focused interview on the experiences of ICU patients, McKinley et al (2002) found that patients experienced vulnerability due to extreme physical and emotional dependency and depersonalised care The study also showed that pre-surgical information, individualised care, and the presence of family members reduced vulnerability. Almerud et al. (2007) conducted unstructured interviews with nine ICU patients to find out 'what it means to be critically ill.' Dependency was one of the constituents of patient experiences. Patients felt they were compromising on integrity and their freedom disappeared in the ICU environment. They sensed that they were monitored but at the same time felt they were invisible to the medical staff which led to feelings of insecurity and vulnerability. In a narrative study on critically ill adult patients, Lykkegaard and Delmar (2013) found that ICU patients described depending on help as unusual and embarrassing. Patients described dependency to be associated with feelings of burden and lowered dignity. Receiving help, especially for body care, was associated with shame, powerlessness, and weakness. The investigators recommended enhancing awareness in patients and improving communication from staff to reduce vulnerability in patients.

Some patients experience vulnerability not only due to the limitation of movements but also because they cannot verbally communicate due to intubation or tracheotomy. This inability to express one's thoughts verbally to ICU staff or to convey feelings to loved ones creates severe emotional distress in patients. Vulnerability can cause loss of role identity or lack of autonomy (Meunier-Beillard et al., 2017), which in turn may have serious psychological implications like depression and trauma. Thus, the research findings suggest that the medical requirements of patients in the ICUs have the potential to create a state of helplessness. Already in a vulnerable physical state, the patients easily lose orientation because of the strange surrounding in the ICU.

Stressors Triggered by the ICU Environment

Exposure to an unfamiliar physical environment has the potential to induce anxiety even in a healthy normal person because of the changes in sensory inputs. For a patient who wakes up from sedation in an ICU, it may be highly anxiety provoking. The extreme physical environment of the ICU engenders alterations in sensory inputs, namely, sensory deprivation, sensory overload, excessive noise, physical and social isolation, and restriction of movement. They are found to be some of the causes of psychological trauma. Most of these stressors are from the ICU environment and the treatment procedure. Noise levels not only cause discomfort to the patients but also disrupt sleep, impair wound healing, and cause hyperarousal.

The recommended noise levels in the ICU during the daytime are less than 35 dBA, and less than 30 dBA as per the World Health Organization

TABLE 13.1 Frequencies and percentages of stressors in the ICU

S. No.	Stressor	Frequency	Percentage
1	Hearing your heart monitor alarm go off	55	26.3
2	Being in pain	34	16.3
3	Having no privacy	33	15.8
4	Hearing the buzzers and alarms from the machinery	32	15.7
5	Being unable to fulfil family roles	28	13.4
6	Hearing other patients cry out	27	12.9

(Berglund et al., 1999) during the night. However, studies found that noise levels in intensive care units do not change during the day and night. The noise levels were measured in 1086 samples in 48 shifts in a Cardiac ICU using an Apple watch, and the average noise was 66 dBA (Scquizzato et al., 2020). The study showed that only in 2.8% of the sample the noise level was below 35 dBA. Though multiple factors contributed to the noise in ICU, namely, ventilators and monitoring devices, the main factors were found to be communication between the staff, bed occupancy, and severity of patients' conditions. A study conducted by the author of this chapter on environmental stress in ICUs in India revealed that the ICU environment and the noise from the gadgets in the ICU cause the highest level of stress for patients. Table 13.1 gives the frequencies and percentages of stressors in the ICU. The table shows that heart monitors, alarms from machines, and patients crying and moaning are the frequent stressors in the ICU.

The noise levels in ICUs lead to psychological and physiological responses. While insomnia and annoyance were the psychological responses, increased heart rate and blood pressure were found to be some of the physiological responses (Hsu et al., 2010).

The other physical environmental factor besides noise that needs to be regulated is the light. Continuous monitoring and round-the-clock medical interventions necessitate that there is constant light in the ICU. Round-the-clock light during the day and night disrupts sleep and the primary stimulus responsible for the synchronisation of the circadian rhythm is the light-dark cycle (Fan et al., 2017). Night light in the ICU also impairs melatonin secretion, which is an important immunoregulator and antioxidant (Hardeland et al., 2012; Srinivasan et al., 2010). It is recommended that the daylight in the ICU should not exceed a 30-footcandle and the night lighting should not exceed a 6.5-footcandle. In violation of this, studies have shown that the patients are exposed to the bright lights all through the night, the reason being the patient care activities taking place during the night. A study by Dunn et al. (2010) showed that patient care activities like the collection of a blood sample and patients' baths performed between 9 pm and 6 am require the use of continuous light. The prevalence of strong lighting and noise affects physiological parameters such as blood pressure, heart rate, and sleep (Korompeli et al., 2019). The artificial lighting and noise in the ICU have also been associated with delirium, which will be discussed at a later point in this chapter.

The Impact of ICU on Patient's Psychological Outcomes

Scientific advancement and medical expertise have reduced the mortality rate among ICU patients. The latest medical procedures have also helped health care providers reduce the hospitalisation period among patients, but the psychological sequel that comes along with the stay in ICU remains. Psychological effects may vary from apprehension and anxiety to more serious conditions like sensory alteration, delirium or ICU psychosis, and post-traumatic stress disorder (PTSD). Literature reveals that 29% of post-ICU patients were found to suffer from PTSD (Wintermann et al., 2016). A study on post-ICU patients after 3–12 months of discharge found a prevalence of 46%, 40%, and 22% of PTSD, anxiety, and depression, respectively (Hatch et al., 2018). Length of stay in ICU, sedation, mechanical ventilation, and intubation were the risk factors.

Sensory Alteration

Baker (2004) in a study on ICU patients found that sensory overload is caused by internal factors such as pain, anxiety, discomfort, and hallucination and external factors like constant/frequent noise (e.g., ventilators, suction, alarms, telephones, conversation), excess/constant light, frequent non-therapeutic touch (i.e., only being touched during nursing/medical interventions), and pain and discomfort and hallucinations from drugs. Similarly, sensory deprivation is also induced because of lack of communication, depersonalisation, lack of personal or uninvited therapeutic touch, invasion of personal space, lack of demarcated night/day routine, and social isolation. Depression, anxiety, confusion, and delirium are some of the responses to sensory overload and sensory deprivation. A focused group study (Wung et al., 2018) revealed that most ICU patients opined that monitors, ventilators, alarms, and intravenous pumps were the major contributors to sensory overload. The study suggested improvisations in the alarm systems and medical devices to reduce noise in the ICU.

ICU Delirium

ICU delirium is termed an 'acute state of confusion' which is found to be prevalent in 20–70% of patients admitted to ICU (McIsaac et al., 2019). ICU delirium is also found to have other negative outcomes, namely, cognitive impairment, increase in re-intubation, increased length of stay, and increased mortality (Balas et al., 2012). In an ICU setting, deep sedation, poor quality of sleep, immobility, and absence of sunlight were identified as some of the risk factors for ICU delirium (Van Rompaey et al., 2009; Xiao et al., 2020). Studies suggest some non-pharmacological strategies to reduce delirium which include maintenance of sleep wake-up cycles, reorienting the patients, family visits and interaction, early mobilisation, and use of physical barriers between beds and a window in ICU can reduce delirium (Ali & Cascella, 2020;

Arenson et al. 2013). Research has established that providing information to reduce anxiety, frequent orientation to time and place, uninterrupted sleep, less use of sedation, reduction of noise, family involvement, caring touch, and encouraging autonomy in self-care are some ways to reduce delirium (Hashemighouchani et al., 2020). Multidisciplinary rehabilitation can reduce delirium from 67% to 30% and functional status improved from 56% to 78% (Needham et al., 2010).

ICU Trauma

Experiencing treatment in a modern-day ICU is a potentially traumatic event. Amidst the life-saving machines and the noise and alarms that come from them at all times and the different gadgets which make it difficult for the patient to communicate or move (Burki, 2019), the invasive painful procedures create feelings of apprehension and anxiety in patients and send out subjective reactions of fear, helplessness, and horror that are cardinal features of psychological trauma. The ICU stay involves the experience of a serious threat to one's physical integrity, a threat to life, or an emotional experience that is overwhelming, accompanied by intense fear, shock, vulnerability, and helplessness leading to emotional numbing (Chivukula et al., 2017). Studies published in the recent past have emphasised that the psychological effects of experiences in ICU stay recur in the form of panic reactions, nightmares, flashbacks, or delusions whenever the patients revisit their experience in ICU. These experiences have an impact on the cognition and behaviour of the patient (Chivukula et al., 2017; Jackson et al., 2014). PTSD is a psychological state that develops after exposure to a traumatic event. Research findings to date suggest that PTSD-like symptoms may be associated with the ICU experience. Survivors of ICU report unpleasant and vivid memories, dreams, and nightmares (Burki, 2019). Re-experience or flashbacks, avoidance, emotional numbing, and hyperarousal (Chivukula et al., 2017) are some of the symptoms of ICU trauma that have a long-lasting effect on the patients' recovery trajectory.

Psychosocial Care and Its Implication in an Intensive Care Unit

A psychological sequel of anxiety, depression, fear, apprehension, and PTSD trails behind an ICU stay. Studies revealed that the patients and family members equally go through the painful ordeal of the procedures in the ICU. Such psychosocial outcomes can only be handled when a framework of helping which encompasses the biological, psychological, social, and spiritual aspects of care of the patients and their families is provided by the health care system. Psychosocial care is an important component of medical care that is often overlooked because the aim of the hospital is mistakenly construed as limited to the medical management of the disease. Psychosocial care is primarily intended to support such patients and family members to deal with their physical and emotional reactions post ICU stay (Chivukula et al., 2014). Psychosocial care deals with not only creating a relationship between physicians, patients, and their caregivers in emotionally charged medical environments but also extending support during crises, helping patients and their caregivers tackle the emotional reactions to critical events, and also assisting them to adapt to the ongoing situations. Psychosocial care interventions are used widely in cancer care (Weis, 2015), palliative care, HIV-AIDS, and areas of disaster management because of the severity of the diseases and the distress associated with them. However, research is not misguiding in saying that patients admitted to the intensive care unit for a surgery experience acute, multiple, recurring, and overwhelming stress (Dias et al., 2015). Intense adverse emotions, fear, anxiety, agony, loneliness, bewilderment, depersonalisation, hopelessness, and acute confusion are all the responses to ICU stay (Lusk & Lash, 2005). Since such traumatic events impose tremendous damage to the physical (health, safety), the personal/psychological (self-esteem and emotional well-being), the moral/spiritual (values and belief system), and the social (family, friends, and community health) resources, it becomes important to extend psychosocial care to patients in the ICU.

Psychosocial care can be enhanced by providing quality services in the ICU by the health care professional which can include improving the ICU quality and improving the patient-provider relationship, wherein there is a scope for the patient to express his/her needs according to the health condition and at the same time the providers understand the patients' perception of health. Enhancing the ICU environment to reduce noise and monitor the lighting conditions can prevent disorientation, sleep disruption, and delirium. Providing psychological services by appointing a health psychologist in the ICU will help patients and their family members in the assessment of psychological issues and provide the right interventions to deal with them. The trauma in patients can be mitigated by providing the family and the patient information related to the diagnosis and communicating to them the details of the procedures and the prognosis. Social support provided by the doctors and nurses, and family visits to the ICU helps in reducing the anxiety and distress in ICU patient (Chivukula et al., 2013).

Maintaining Quality of ICU to Enhance Psychosocial Outcomes

The ICU quality is measured in terms of the biomedical aspects of treatment, namely, structure and facilities in the ICU, procedures performed, medication, and hygiene, and the psychosocial outcomes of treatment, namely, physical and psychological outcomes of patients, patient satisfaction, patient respect, and patient mortality. Such quality can only be maintained by setting indicators, which can be used as instruments to supervise and monitor health care (De Vos, 2012). The national and international boards of hospitals like the National Accreditation Board for Hospitals (NABH), the Joint Commission

International (JCI), and the Society of Critical Care Medicine (SCCM) provided guidelines and set standards for hospitals to ensure holistic care to the patients. The hospitals which are accredited to these Boards are under the scrutiny of the Board and are expected to follow the set standards. The recommendation set by the Board is intended to play a major role in minimising the adverse effect of the ICU environment. An unpublished study from the doctoral thesis of the author on the quality of care in ICUs across five hospitals in Hyderabad revealed that the biomedical care provided ranged from 69% to 93%, and the environmental care and psychosocial care provided by the group of five hospitals ranged from 18% to 54% and 20% to 60%, respectively. The results showed that the hospitals place a great emphasis on biomedical care through medical intervention and emergency management and psychosocial care is often neglected. Hospitals must integrate psychosocial care into their day-to-day services. Chivukula et al. (2014) in their study suggest that just as there is a checklist or inventory about biomedical care, namely, temperature, blood pressure, and other physical parameters, the ICU staff should also maintain an inventory of each patient about orientation about the day, date and time, procedures administered to the patient, information about the patient condition to the family, and so on. Sensitising the ICU staff about the importance of psychosocial care practices in the ICU is as important as medical care. Psychosocial care if rightly practised and implemented will help reduce relapse and rehospitalisation.

Changing the ICU Environment to Reduce Stressors

Changes in ICU design and modification of some care practices can help reduce noise levels. Kol et al. (2015) found that educating ICU staff with noise-reducing strategies resulted in a quieter ICU environment and was beneficial to both patients and staff. Gupta et al. (2020) in their study stressed the need for the implementation of 'quiet-time' and 'noise reduction' strategies to reduce the noise in the ICUs. The study suggested some of the noise-reducing strategies such as designing 'patient cohorts' wherein patients who are critical are separated from non-critical patients. The patients were monitored by two different nursing stations to reduce the activity and noise. Prior to 'quiet time implementation', the nurses completed all the activities such as administering medication, clean up or sponging, and procedures like drawing blood, monitoring blood pressure, and so on, and dimming lights to provide the patients uninterrupted rest. Informing conscious patients and their family members personally about quiet time, reducing the unnecessary entry of paramedical and housekeeping staff scheduling their visits, and a display showing 'Quiet time in Progress' can help in the implementation of quiet time; using 'Alarm setting' monitoring alarms, removal of unnecessary alarms, and using visual alerts were some of the suggestions in the study. Taylor-Ford et al. (2008) advocate an educational intervention programme for nursing and other staff about the effects of noise and the importance of reduction of noise in the ICU, monitoring the noise levels during the day and night, modification of ICU staff practices can help maintain the noise levels in the ICU. The significant impact of non-pharmacological methods such as earplugs and eye masks on the improvement of the quality of sleep was advocated in a systematic review by Polat et al. (2022). As ensuring adequate sleep is an important factor effecting quality care, usage of earplugs and masks increased the amount of REM sleep and melatonin release at night (Ryu et al., 2012. A review on sleep improvement in ICU states that earplugs with sleep-inducing music help enhance sleep among ICU patients (Bion et al., 2018; Hansen et al., 2018). Nannapaneni et al. (2015) state that noise reduction in an ICU requires a multipronged effort which includes educating the nurses and paramedical staff, changes in the ICU environment, and giving the patient and the family the necessary information about the ICU environment and the procedures.

The participation of caregivers or family members in health care has been identified to be highly beneficial for the recovery of the patient. The study postulates that the presence of a caregiver or a family member not only aids the communication between the doctor and the patient but plays an important role in the recovery process (Xyrichis et al., 2019). The presence of family and their participation in the care process when the patient was in the ICU was found to enhance patient and family satisfaction by neutralising the feelings of threat, estrangement, and meaninglessness in patients (Wilson et al., 2019). Involving relatives and friends in the care process helped to maintain the patients' identity and individuality. The presence of family members in ICU provides support to patients which in turn brings down the anxiety and apprehension in the patient and the family (Olsen et al., 2009). Support, nurturance, and warmth from close family members play a vital role in the recovery process. The social and emotional support from family is an effective buffer and helps lower the anxiety in patients (Chivukula et al., 2013).

Research on the experiences of patients emphasises the need for personalised care, which is possible by providing holistic care and improving the ICU quality so that the negative effects of the ICU environment are minimised (Chivukula et al., 2017; Zamanzadeh et al., 2015). The parameters related to biomedical aspects are the most important requirements for a critical patient, but there is a need to include psychosocial care that constitutes the appropriate benchmark for the services provided in ICU. Such supportive interventions and quality care in the ICUs would distinctly bring a change in the health care perspective. Working towards providing optimal psychological care will have a positive effect on patients' psychological recovery and may also help physical recuperation after critical care. Psychosocial support can be used by the ICU team to establish therapeutic relationships. These relationships are built through psychological, social, and spiritual care. ICU care is more than just removing the disease of the patient. The health care team has to ensure that the care provided in the ICU would help the patient and their family in handling the feelings of distress and improving their well-being. In other words, what it indicates is that effective psychosocial care in ICU ensures and protects the well-being of ICU patients.

References

Ali, M., & Cascella, M. (2020). ICU delirium. *National library of medicine*. Retrieved May 04, 2022, from https://www.ncbi.nlm.nih.gov/books/NBK559280/

Almerud, S., Alapack, R. J., Fridlund, B., & Ekebergh, M. (2007). Of vigilance and invisibility – Being a patient in technologically intense environments. *Nursing in Critical Care, 12*, 151–158.

Arenson, B. G., Macdonald, L. A., Grocott H. P., Hiebert, B. M., & Arora, R. C. (2013). Effect of intensive care unit environment on in-hospital delirium after cardiac surgery. *Journal of Thoracic Cardiovascular Surgery, 146*(1), 172–178.

Baker, C. (2004). Preventing ICU syndrome in children. *Paediatric Nursing, 16*(10).

Balas, M. C., Rice, M., Chaperon, C., Smith, H., Disbot, M., & Barry, F. (2012). Management of delirium in critically ill older adults. *Critical Care Nursing, 32*, 15–26. https://doi.org/10.4037/ccn2012480

Berglund, B., Lindvall, T., Schwela, D. H., & World Health Organization. (1999). Guidelines for community noise. World Health Organisation. https://apps.who.int/iris/handle/10665/66217

Bion, V., Lowe, A. S., Puthucheary, Z., & Montgomery, H. (2018). Reducing sound and light exposure to improve sleep on the adult intensive care unit: An inclusive narrative review. *Journal of the Intensive Care Society, 19*(2), 138–146.

Burki, T. K. (2019). Post-traumatic stress in the intensive care unit. *The Lancet Respiratory Medicine, 7*(10), 843–844.

Chivukula, U. (2013). Doctoral thesis titled Psychosocial care in intensive care units: impact on trauma and well-being. Submitted to University of Hyderabad.

Chivukula, U., Hariharan, M., Rana, S., Thomas, M., & Andrew, A. (2017). Enhancing hospital well-being and minimizing intensive care unit trauma: Cushioning effects of psychosocial care. *Indian Journal of Critical Care Medicine: Peer-reviewed, Official Publication of Indian Society of Critical Care Medicine, 21*(10), 640.

Chivukula, U., Hariharan, M., Rana, S., Thomas, M., & Swain, S. (2014). Role of psychosocial care on ICU trauma. *Indian Journal of Psychological Medicine, 36*(3), 312–316.

Chivukula, U., Swain, S., Rana, S., & Hariharan, M. (2013). Perceived social support and type of cardiac procedures as modifiers of hospital anxiety and depression. *Psychological Studies, 58*(3), 242–247.

De Vos, M. L. G. (2012). *Effective use of quality indicators in intensive care*. The National Intensive Care Evaluation, Netherlands. Retrieved July 25, 2013, http://arno.uvt.nl/show.cgi?fid=128149

Dias, D. de. Sa., Resende, M. V., & Diniz, G. do. C. L. M. (2015). Patient stress in intensive care: Comparison between a coronary care unit and a general postoperative unit. *Revista Brasileira de terapia intensiva, 27*, 18–25.

Dunn, H., Anderson, M. A., & Hill, P. D. (2010). Nighttime lighting in intensive care units. *Critical Care Nursing, 30*(3), 31–37. https://doi.org/10.4037/ccn2010342

Engel, G. L. (1977). The need for a new medical model: A challenge for biomedicine. *Science New Series, 196*(4286), 129–136.

Fan, E. P., Abbott, S. M., Reid, K. J., Zee, P. C., & Maas, M. B. (2017). Abnormal environmental light exposure in the intensive care environment. *Journal of Critical Care, 40*, 11–14.

Gültekin, Y., Özçelik, Z., Akıncı, S. B., & Yorgancı, H. K. (2018). Evaluation of stressors in intensive care units. *Turkish Journal of Surgery, 34*(1), 5–8. https://doi.org/10.5152turkjsurg.2017.3736

Gupta, P., Shaji, M., Amer, A., Joseph, S., Louis, I., George, J., Al Zubi, M., McDonal, I., De Jesus, D. J. C., & El Hassan, M. (2020). *Noise reduction in an intensive care unit: Implementation of quiet time and noise-reduction strategies.* doi:10.21203/rs.3.rs-92782/v1

Hansen, I. P., Langhorn, L., & Dreyer, P. (2018). Effects of music during daytime rest in the intensive care unit. *Nursing in Critical Care, 23*(4), 207–213.

Hardeland, R., Madrid, J. A., Tan, D. X., & Reiter, R. J. (2012). Melatonin, the circadian multi oscillator system, and health: The need for detailed analyses of peripheral melatonin signaling. *Journal of Pineal Research, 52*(2), 139–166.

Hashemighouchani, H., Cupka, J., Lipari, J., Ruppert, M. M., Ingersent, E., Ozrazgat-Baslanti, T., ... & Bihorac, A. (2020). The impact of environmental risk factors on delirium and benefits of noise and slight modifications: a scoping review. *F1000Research, 9*, 1183.

Hatch, R., Young, D., Barber, V., Griffiths, J., Harrison, D. A., & Watkinson, P. (2018). Anxiety, depression, and post-traumatic stress disorder after critical illness: A UK-wide prospective cohort study. *Critical Care, 22*(1), 1–13.

Hsu, S. M., Ko, W. J., Liao, W. C., Huang, S. J., Chen, R. J., Li, C. Y., & Hwang, S. L. (2010). Associations of exposure to noise with physiological and psychological outcomes among post-cardiac surgery patients in ICUs. *Clinics, 65*(10), 985–989. https://doi.org/10.1590/S1807-59322010001000011

Jackson, J. C., Pandharipande, P. P., Girard, T. D., Brummel, N. E., Thompson, J. L., Hughes, C. G., ... & Ely, E. W. (2014). Depression, post-traumatic stress disorder, and functional disability in survivors of critical illness in the BRAIN-ICU study: A longitudinal cohort study. *The Lancet Respiratory Medicine, 2*(5), 369–379.

Kol, E., Demircan, A., Erdoğan, A., Gencer, Z., & Erengin, H. (2015). The effectiveness of measures aimed at noise reduction in an intensive care unit. *Workplace Health & Safety, 63*(12), 539–545.

Korompeli, A., Kavrochorianou, N., Molcan, L., Muurlink, O., Boutzouka, E., Myrianthefs, P., & Fildissis, G. (2019). Light affects heart rate's 24-h rhythmicity in intensive care unit patients: An observational study. *Nursing in Critical Care, 24*(5), 320–325.

Lusk, B. & Lash A. A. (2005). The stress response, psychoneuroimmunology, and stress among ICU patients. *Dimensions of Critical Care Nursing, 24*, 25–31.

Lykkegaard, K., & Delmar, C. (2013). A threat to the understanding of oneself: Intensive care patients' experiences of dependency. *International Journal of Qualitative Studies on Health Well-being, 8.* https://doi.org/10.3402/qhw.v8i0.20934

McIsaac, D. I., MacDonald, D. B., & Aucoin, S. D. (2019). Frailty for perioperative clinicians: A narrative review. *Anesthesia & Analgesia, 130*(6), 1450–1460.

McKinley, S., Nagy, S., Stein-Parbury, J., Bramwell, M., & Hudson, J. (2002). Vulnerability and security in seriously ill patients in intensive care. *Intensive Critical Care Nursing, 18*(1), 27–36.

Mead, N., & Bower, P. (2000). Patient-centeredness: A conceptual framework and review of the empirical literature. *Social Science Medicine, 51*(7), 1087–110.

Meunier-Beillard, N., Dargent, A., Ecarnot, F., Rigaud, J. P., Andreu, P., Large, A., & Quenot, J. P. (2017). Intersecting vulnerabilities in professionals and patients in intensive care. *Annals of Translational Medicine, 5*(Suppl 4).

Nannapaneni, S., Lee, S. J., Kashiouris, M., Elmer, J. L., Thakur, L. K., Nelson, S. B., ... & Ramar, K. (2015). Preliminary noise reduction efforts in a medical intensive care unit. *Hospital Practice, 43*(2), 94–100.

National Health Service. (2008). Direct quote. Retrieved October 2, 2021, from http://www.nhsdirect.Nhs.UK/Articles/Article.Aspx

Needham, D. M., Korupolu, R., Zanni, J. M., Pradhan, P., Colantuon, E., Palme, J. B., et al. (2010) Early physical medicine and rehabilitation for patients with acute respiratory failure: A quality improvement project. *Archives of Physical Medicine and Rehabilitation*, 91(4), 536–542.

Olsen, K. D., Dysvik, E., & Hansen, B. S. (2009). The meaning of family members' presence during intensive care stay: A qualitative study. *Intensive and Critical Care Nursing*, 25(4), 190–198. https://doi.org/10.1016/j.iccn.2009.04.004

Polat, E., Çavdar, İ., & Şengör, K. (2022). The effect of earplugs and eye masks usage in the intensive care unit on sleep quality: Systematic review. *Dubai Medical Journal*, 5, 133–140.

Ryu, M. J., Park, J. S., & Park, H. (2012). Effect of sleep-inducing music on sleep in persons with percutaneous transluminal coronary angiography in the cardiac care unit. *Journal of Clinical Nursing*, 21(5–6), 728–735. https://doi.org/10.1111/j.1365-2702.2011.03876.x

Samuelson, K. A. M. (2011). Unpleasant and pleasant memories of intensive care in adult mechanically ventilated patients-Findings from 250 interviews. *Intensive Critical Care Nursing*, 27(2), 76–84.

Schefold, J. C., Wollersheim, T., Grunow, J. J., Luedi, M. M., Z'Graggen, W. J., & Weber-Carstens, S. (2020). Muscular weakness and muscle wasting in the critically ill. *Journal of Cachexia, Sarcopenia and Muscle*, 11(6), 1399–1412.

Scholl, I., Zill, J. M., Härter, M., & Dirmaier, J. (2014). An integrative model of patient-centeredness—a systematic review and concept analysis. *PLoS One*, 9(9), e107828.

Scquizzato, T., Gazzato, A., Landoni, G., & Zangrillo, A. (2020). Assessment of noise levels in the intensive care unit using Apple Watch. *Critical Care*, 24(1), 1–3.

Srinivasan, V., Pandi-Perumal, S. R., Spence, D. W., Kato, H., & Cardinali, D. P. (2010). Melatonin in septic shock: Some recent concepts. *Journal of Critical Care*, 25(4), 656.

Taylor-Ford, R., Catlin, A., & LaPlante, M. (2008). Effect of a noise reduction program on a medical-surgical unit. *Clinical Nursing Research*, 17(2), 74–88.

Van Rompaey, B., Elseviers, M. M., Schuurmans, M. J., Shortridge-Baggett, L. M., Truijen, S., & Bossaert, L. (2009). Risk factors for delirium in intensive care patients: A prospective cohort study. *Critical Care*, 13(3), 1–12.

Vanhorebeek, I., Latronico, N., & Van den Berghe, G. (2020). ICU-acquired weakness. *Intensive Care Medicine*, 46(4), 637–653.

Weis J. (2015). Psychosocial care for cancer patients. *Breast care (Basel, Switzerland)*, 10(2), 84–86. https://doi.org/10.1159/000381969

Wilson, M. E., Beesley, S., Grow, A., Rubin, E., Hopkins, R. O., Hajizadeh, N., & Brown, S. M. (2019). Humanizing the intensive care unit. *Critical Care*, 23(1), 1–3.

Wintermann, G. B., Weidner, K., Strauß, B., Rosendahl, J., & Petrowski, K. (2016). Predictors of posttraumatic stress and quality of life in family members of chronically critically ill patients after intensive care. *Annals of Intensive Care*, 6(1), 1–11.

Wung, Shu-Fen, Malone, Daniel C., & Szalacha, Laura. (2018). "Sensory overload and technology in critical care." *Critical Care Nursing Clinics*, 30(2), 179–190.

Xiao, L. I., Zhang, L., Fang, G., & Yuhang, A. I. (2020). Incidence and risk factors for delirium in older patients following intensive care unit admission: A prospective observational study. *Journal of Nursing Research*, 28(4), e101.

Xyrichis, A., Fletcher, S., Brearley, S., Philippou, J., Purssell, E., Terblanche, M., ... & Reeves, S. (2019). Interventions to promote patients and families' involvement in adult intensive care settings: a protocol for a mixed-method systematic review. *Systematic Reviews*, 8(1), 1–7.

Zamanzadeh, V., Jasemi, M., Valizadeh, L., Keogh, B., & Taleghani, F. (2015). Effective factors in providing holistic care: A qualitative study. *Indian Journal of Palliative Care*, 21(2), 214.

14
AN INTERPRETATIVE PHENOMENOLOGICAL ANALYSIS

The Unmet Information and Supportive Care Needs of Cancer Patients

Mahati Chittem, Matsungshila Pongener, Sravannthi Maya, and Shweta Chawak

Recent psycho-oncology research in India revealed that patients wanted to be actively involved in their illness and treatment decisions (Datta et al., 2017), and displayed a sense of agency in assigning roles to their supportive care network (Chawak et al., 2020), yet continued to be uninvolved in their cancer/treatment decision-making (Chittem et al., 2021). This is mainly because patients' families, concerned for their mental well-being, took on the role of being primary decision-makers, often preferring cancer nondisclosure, thereby completely removing the patient from the decision-making process (Chittem et al., 2020). Physicians adhered to families' requests for not involving the patient in medical discussions, albeit unwillingly/with some discomfort (Maya et al., 2021). Hence, these aspects of cancer communication may hinder/complicate illness and treatment dialogues between the patient and their physician which, in turn, may increase the former's unmet needs.

To the best of our knowledge, there are only three empirical studies describing the unmet needs among Indian cancer patients. In a study examining the needs of advanced cancer patients receiving palliative treatment, Asthana et al. (2019) found that patients had unmet needs in a range of domains including daily living, managing physical symptoms of cancer and its treatment, financial aspects of care, treatment information, and communication with the physician. Reporting that 95% of patients with multiple myeloma who were receiving treatment for more than a year had at least one unmet need, Manuprasad et al. (2019) found that the strongest unmet need was for existential survivorship. A closer look at these findings showed that patients had unmet needs for reducing their stress (65%), addressing their worries of cancer recurrence (56%), emotional support (51%), moving on with one's life (51%), and managing one's social/work circumstances (46%). Focussing specifically on female cancer patients' unmet needs, Maurya et al. (2019) found that patients faced unaddressed issues with

DOI: 10.4324/9781003360858-19

their appearance and body image, swelling in the arm, cognitive impairments, and emotional distress (anxiety, depression, and worries).

While these studies shed much needed light on the wide range of unmet needs Indian patients encounter during the cancer continuum, they were all quantitative and thus unable to document the lived experiences of these unaddressed and, perhaps, unexpressed needs. Further, none of the studies examined the unmet needs of patients based on the length of their cancer trajectory, thus being unable to illustrate similarities and dissimilarities in patients' needs across various time-points. Hence, the current study aimed to explore the unmet needs among Indian cancer patients who were at different junctures of their cancer trajectory.

Method

Participant Information

Eleven patients (mean age = 42.82 years; range = 23–58 years) diagnosed with cancer were individually interviewed in a cancer specialty tertiary hospital in Hyderabad, India. Table 14.1 outlines patient demographic and medical details. Ethics approval for the study was obtained from the hospital where the data was collected.

Procedure

Using purposive sampling (for gender and time since diagnosis[1]), patients were recruited at the hospital by the first author, a psychologist of Indian origin trained in qualitative health research. The study objectives were explained in detail to eligible patients. The inclusion criteria were: (i) patients diagnosed with cancer, (ii) patients undergoing treatment at the time of the study, (iii) patients from any type and stage of cancer, (iv) patients who were able to communicate in Telugu (the local language) and English, and (v) patients who were not diagnosed with any psychiatric condition (self-reported). All patients who were approached provided written informed consent to participate in the study.

Interviews

Patients' demographic and medical details were first noted. Following this, the semi-structured, audio-recorded interviews commenced either in the patients' hospital room or in an empty, available consultation room on the same floor. The interview questions centred on the topics of (i) current unmet information needs regarding the illness and treatment and (ii) current unmet supportive care needs of the patients during their illness journey (see Table 14.2 for the sample interview questions). The average length of the interviews was 46.69 minutes (range = 31.31–72.2 minutes). All interviews were conducted in Telugu and transcribed into English following a forward- and back-translation process.

TABLE 14.1 Demographic and medical information

Demographic/medical detail		N/Mean	%/Range
Age (years)		42.82	23–58
Gender	Male	6	54.55
	Female	5	45.45
Marital status	Married	10	90.90
	Single	1	9.09
Number of children		2.27	0–5
Religious orientation	Christianity	1	9.09
	Hinduism	9	81.82
	Islam	1	9.09
Residence	Hyderabad	1	9.09
	Outside Hyderabad	10	90.90
Level of education	10th or below 10th grade	2	18.18
	Undergraduation	5	45.45
	Postgraduation	4	36.36
Monthly income (Rs.)	Below Rs. 20,000	2	18.18
	Below Rs. 40,000	5	45.45
	Below Rs. 60,000	4	36.36
Occupation	Employed	9	81.82
	Homemaker	1	9.09
	Retired	1	9.09
Current diagnosis	Gastrointestinal cancer	2	18.18
	Lung cancer	2	18.18
	Testicular cancer	1	9.09
	Lymphoma	2	18.18
	Leukaemia	2	18.18
	Breast cancer	2	18.18
Metastases	Yes	2	18.18
	No	8	72.73
	Relapse	1	9.09
Time since diagnosis	0–3 months	3	27.27
	4–6 months	3	27.27
	7–12 months	2	18.18
	More than a year	3	27.27
Treatment	Chemotherapy	3	27.27
	Chemotherapy and Radiation	3	27.27
	Surgery and Chemotherapy	4	36.36
	Surgery, Chemotherapy, and Radiation	1	9.09
Financial resources	Company insurance	4	36.36
	Self-financed	4	36.36
	Company insurance and self-financed	1	9.09
	Self-financed and bank loan	1	9.09
	Private insurance	1	9.09

Analysis

The interviews were analysed using Interpretative Phenomenological Analysis (IPA; Smith & Osborn, 2004). IPA is a qualitative analysis that helps assess how an individual makes sense of a phenomenon and helps examine topics that are complex, ambiguous, and emotionally laden (Smith & Osborn, 2004, 2015).

TABLE 14.2 Interview topics and sample questions

Themes	Sample questions
Unmet information needs regarding the illness and treatment	What kind of information do you want about your illness but have not received? What kind of information do you want regarding your treatment but have not received? What are your main sources of information regarding your treatment?
Unmet supportive care needs during their illness journey	Apart from information needs, what other kinds of support do you feel you require but are not receiving? What kind of unmet needs (outside of information) did you experience so far in your illness journey? Who do you wish would address (each of) these needs for you?

Owing to the in-depth nature of this inquiry and analysis, small sample sizes are often preferred to allow for a deep, rich engagement with the data (Smith & Osborn, 2004, 2015). The analysis was carried out by the first and second authors who individually read and re-read the transcripts in order to first identify any unique, independent aspects of the patient's experiences. These were then categorised into meaningful units and assigned a code (e.g., causal attributes). The authors discussed and clarified their independent interpretations of the patterns which were developing across these codes, following which they separately clustered the codes into sub-ordinate themes. Together, the authors then assembled the sub-ordinate themes so as to represent similarity in terms of the topic and content, thus developing super-ordinate themes (for a detailed process of data analysis, refer to Figures 14.1 and 14.2).

Reflexivity

Given the complex nature of the qualitative inquiry, reflexivity is considered an important and powerful tool for researchers to position their thoughtful self-awareness (Holloway & Biley, 2011). In qualitative research, the researcher is the primary figure present within and throughout the research who invariably influences participants' responses and the study's findings (Doyle, 2012; Finlay,

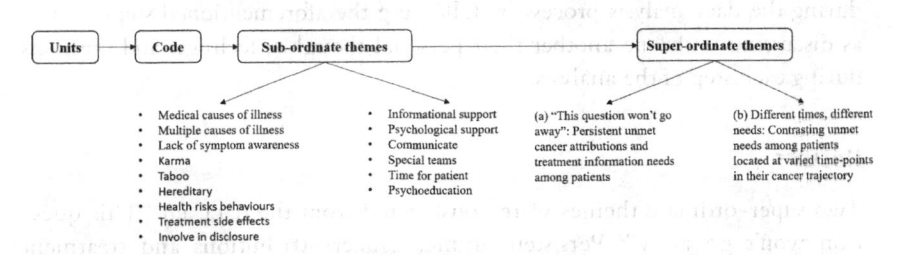

FIGURE 14.1 Interpretative Phenomenological Analysis Process.

Units → Code → Sub-ordinate themes → Super-ordinate themes

Sub-ordinate themes:
- Medical causes of illness
- Multiple causes of illness
- Lack of symptom awareness
- Karma
- Taboo
- Hereditary
- Health risks behaviours
- Treatment side effects
- Involve in disclosure

- Informational support
- Psychological support
- Communicate
- Special teams
- Time for patient
- Psychoeducation

Super-ordinate themes:
(a) "This question won't go away": Persistent unmet cancer attributions and treatment information needs among patients

(b) Different times, different needs: Contrasting unmet needs among patients located at varied time-points in their cancer trajectory

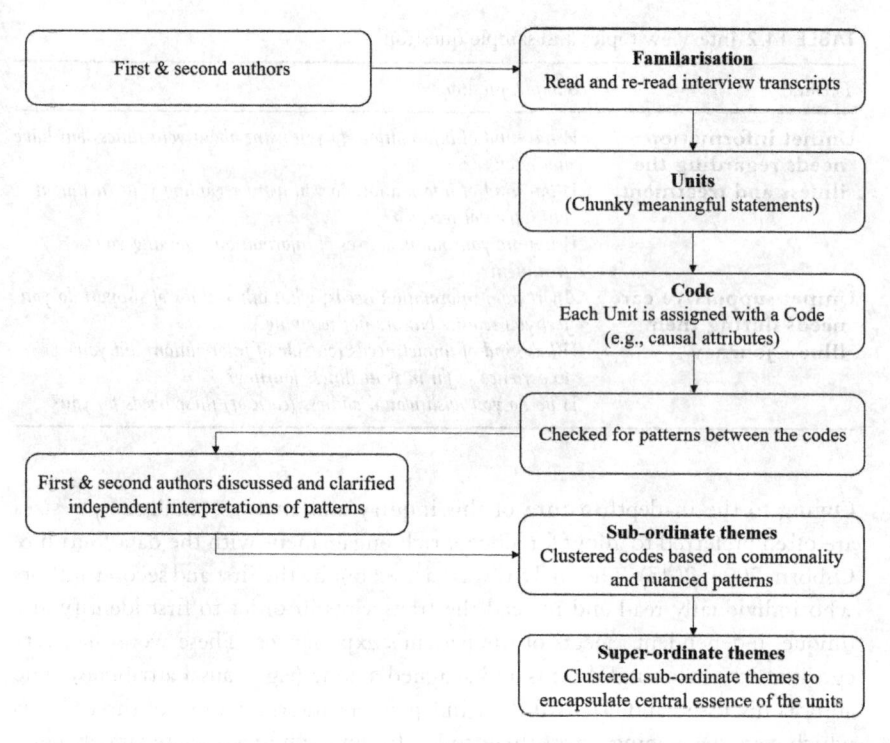

```
┌─────────────────────────────┐         ┌──────────────────────────────────────┐
│   First & second authors    │────────▶│            Familarisation            │
└─────────────────────────────┘         │  Read and re-read interview transcripts │
                                        └──────────────────────────────────────┘
                                                         │
                                                         ▼
                                        ┌──────────────────────────────────────┐
                                        │                Units                 │
                                        │   (Chunky meaningful statements)     │
                                        └──────────────────────────────────────┘
                                                         │
                                                         ▼
                                        ┌──────────────────────────────────────┐
                                        │                 Code                 │
                                        │   Each Unit is assigned with a Code  │
                                        │        (e.g., causal attributes)     │
                                        └──────────────────────────────────────┘
                                                         │
                                                         ▼
                                        ┌──────────────────────────────────────┐
                         ┌──────────────│  Checked for patterns between the codes │
                         │              └──────────────────────────────────────┘
                         ▼
┌─────────────────────────────────────┐
│ First & second authors discussed and clarified │
│   independent interpretations of patterns      │
└─────────────────────────────────────┘
                         │              ┌──────────────────────────────────────┐
                         └─────────────▶│          Sub-ordinate themes         │
                                        │  Clustered codes based on commonality │
                                        │         and nuanced patterns         │
                                        └──────────────────────────────────────┘
                                                         │
                                                         ▼
                                        ┌──────────────────────────────────────┐
                                        │         Super-ordinate themes        │
                                        │   Clustered sub-ordinate themes to   │
                                        │ encapsulate central essence of the units │
                                        └──────────────────────────────────────┘
```

FIGURE 14.2 Flow Chart of the Themes.

2002; Holloway & Biley, 2011). Reflexivity thus allows for the methodical process of engaging the researchers with its own self-aware meta-analysis to balance the collaborative nature between the researcher and the participant and pave the avenue for richer and deeper meanings surrounding "epistemological, theoretical, ethical, and personal aspects of the research question" (Beer, 1997; Finlay, 2002; Holloway & Biley, 2011; Kleinsasser, 2000). The first author engaged in reflexivity during the current study by: (i) maintaining notes about each participant's comments and their personal thoughts and feelings during the interview, (ii) maintaining a personal journal of their inner experiences soon after each interview was completed, and (iii) continuing checking and self-reflecting on their subjectivity. The first and second authors also maintained their reflexivity during the data analysis process by following the aforementioned steps as well as discussing with one another their personal thoughts, feelings, and opinions during each step of the analysis.

Results

Two super-ordinate themes were constructed from the data: (a) "This question won't go away": Persistent unmet cancer attributions and treatment information needs among patients and (b) different times, different needs:

Contrasting unmet needs among patients located at varied time-points in their cancer trajectory.

a. ***"This question won't go away": Persistent unmet cancer attributions and treatment information needs among patients***

Patients, irrespective of their time since diagnosis, revealed unmet needs for information regarding cancer causes and treatment (type and side effects). Most participants reported a strong desire to know about the causes of having cancer, especially "Why did this particular cancer happen only to me?" While some patients were able to attribute their cancer to a specific source, others were "guessing" the reasons they may have been diagnosed with cancer. Frequently, those patients who had a clear "bad" health habit were able to identify illness causation. Interestingly, a majority of the patients reported having a continued low awareness regarding the cause of their illness even though they were diagnosed for more than 3 months. Low awareness (as opposed to no awareness), in this study, was displayed in the patients' ability to proactively seek information from a variety of sources such as the internet, newspapers, leaflets/handouts, thereby contributing to an "idea" about why they may have got cancer, but not necessarily about "exactly why this cancer, in this way, and only to me".

> Hmm... For me, what I think are my habits, smoking. Yeah, I was smoking since childhood. For nearly 42 years I have smoked out of my 58 years. So, I think 90% by smoking because in my immediate family no one had any cancers.
>
> *58 years, male, lung cancer, 1 year 6 months since diagnosis*

> Many causes are there like smoking, drinking and pollution. I studied in the internet also. Paints, when we work in paint company there is a greater possibility to get cancer plus chemicals and pesticides and all..."
>
> *38 years, female, lymphoma, 6 months since diagnosis*

In some cases, patients found it difficult to derive logical causations as it did not fit their representations or beliefs about cancer. For example, a 44 years old patient with lymphoma diagnosed 11 months ago shared, "Nowadays, a boy of six or seven years of age also get cancer. So, what might be the reason for his cancer? No smoking or drinking or any other. Why does he get cancer? Similarly, in ladies." As a result, these patients engaged in cognitive distortions such as selective abstractions and arbitrary inferences. They either attributed the cause to minute details that were taken out of context (e.g., drinking cold water) or to scientifically unconfirmed information (e.g., food impacting children in the womb).

> They say hereditary is a major factor. Maybe that... I don't know about food habits because I am not a bad eater and I only used to drink

cold water, that is the only bad thing and then nothing else. We used to have very good food. My husband and myself and my children, very healthy food... We are all vegetarians and non-vegetarians. We eat a lot of meat, chicken and whatever we want. I don't know... They told me, this is one of the factors also... bad habits... I can say that I was never a bad eater. I only used to drink very cold water...

52 years, female, colon cancer, 3 months since diagnosis

When mother takes good food... children will get good resistance... when ladies carry [pregnant]... she has to take good food. Not only for her... for the carrying baby also. That could affect the baby also. Foods and everything affect the baby also. And behaviour also affects the baby.

38 years, female, lymphoma, 6 months since diagnosis

While unpacking these questions regarding causal attributions, patients recalled that they "had no idea" about cancer symptoms – considering some abnormalities (e.g., a "small" lump in the breast) to be normal – and let these changes in their bodies remain unnoticed/unchecked. Some patients noted that "nobody knows about the symptoms" or "they don't tell because they feel shy". Therefore, according to the patients, it was "only when I got the diagnosis, I came to know the symptoms of cancer", that is, the symptoms of cancer are understood retrospectively. When they were diagnosed with cancer and they asked their physician, "How come I got this?", patients were told by their physician either "not to worry" or their queries were left unanswered. This disinhibited need to bridge the gap between the lack of symptom awareness and low levels of understanding of cancer causation led patients to feel helpless, distressed, confused, and engage in fatalistic thinking.

I used to get motions regularly. I used to roam on bike for almost 150 kilometers per day. I thought that these motions are because of over heat. I have not expected that I'll get this kind of disease. After coming here [hospital for a diagnosis], I got to know that the motions were a sign of it [cancer].

41 years, male, rectal cancer, 11 months since diagnosis

I think it is karma... yes, it's my previous life deeds that resulted in it [diagnosed with cancer]. It is the result of my previous life.

43 years, female, leukaemia, 10 years since diagnosis

Similarly, a majority of the patients who suspected their susceptibility to cancer to have emerged from their "own bad choices" displayed intense feelings of distress, regret, and self-criticism. These negative feelings led some patients to consider their diagnosis as a punishment [*siksha*, Telugu word] and tended to weep profusely during the interview. In this way, patients coped with the lack of a proper understanding of a tangible, measurable, or reasonable explanation for having cancer through a host of negative cognitive mechanisms.

> I don't smoke much, only 10 cigarettes a day. God gave siksha to me. I will drink much water, eat on time... same in the evening and morning... eat at same time. I don't take much chilly and snacks from outside... I don't have any other habits except cigarette and tea.... I used to smoke more previously, now stopped and from that time I got this. My grandchildren stopped me from smoking. I didn't listen to them and now suffering. I didn't listen to the small kids that was my foolishness.
>
> *56 years, male, lung cancer, 2 months since diagnosis*

> Maybe I could have... Ah... It was getting really delayed. I mean the age gap... I mean my daughter was already eight years and we wanted to go for a second one, but I was like, you know... my weight. It was in 80 kilograms then so we couldn't wait much time. I just feel that maybe I could have reduced my weight maybe to the ideal weight or little, at least somewhere... you know, 70 kilograms, something like that. At that moment we should have gone for a second pregnancy... maybe this wouldn't have happened...
>
> *33 years, female, breast cancer, 5 months since diagnosis*

Following on from unmet needs for information on cancer causation, patients, regardless of their time since diagnosis, revealed unmet needs for treatment information. The foremost and pressing unmet need was for treatment type and side effects. Patients often recounted early instances of the treatment wherein they were "completely unprepared", leading to patients feeling "let down", shocked, and having to cope with an outcome they had "no idea about". Indeed, one patient reported that she was informed about the type of surgery she was going to receive on the very day of the operation. This left her with little to no time to come to terms with the news.

> One, they had done the surgery. So, like ah, they were I mean... not telling whether it is a mastectomy or a lumpectomy... So, I was like thinking, it might be a lumpectomy at least but on the day of the operation, they told me that they [pause] decided for a mastectomy where they remove the entire breast [pause]. So, I thought maybe if it [they] had made me prepared... I would have been a little prepared [pause]. After the operation, I was a little setback, that the complete breast was removed, but, it's okay... it's nothing greater than life...
>
> *33 years, female, breast cancer, 5 months since diagnosis*

Initial negative experiences of the treatment side effects were pervasive in that some patients "dreaded" and "feared" their treatment to the extent that it affected their psychological well-being. Often, this led patients to perceive their body as "becoming weak" through a downward spiral of negative self-talk, perpetuating a terrifying concern for their ability to withstand the treatment side effects. For some patients, the treatment severity was so intense and unpleasant that they were ridden with not only fear, depression, and despair, but also feelings of worthlessness, hopelessness, and worries of being a burden to their family members.

> Yeah, side effects [pause], sometimes I go into depression [pause]. This and that [pause]. That was also there, like, I couldn't pass toilet... then continuously I had stomach problem [pause]. That was very painful for me [pause].
>
> *52 years, female, colon cancer, 3 months since diagnosis*

> That ten days we cannot escape [pause]. Now also, you see, all these blood clots, can't eat properly, fever [pause]. Every day, I will get a fever; sometimes, it feels like I am getting used to it [laughs]. It's like that... But in 2008, I was worried [pause] because of medicines, and I am getting old. Do I have the resistance power etc.? That time, I was young, 34 years old. I had the resistance power, and my confidence level was very high... But in 2008, some [pause] like, I know something... the same dose [pause], they change the number of the dose... When I saw the protocol, I was a bit depressed [pause] this dosage, and that dosage is very much different... Can I bear it at this age or not...? Can I come out of it... or dependency...? Will I trouble others...? I felt useless... I felt it's better not to live...
>
> *44 years, male, lymphoma, 1 year 2 months since diagnosis*

b. ***Different times, different needs: Contrasting unmet needs among patients located at varied time-points in their cancer trajectory***

There were clear differences in the types of unmet needs which were linked to the time since the patients' diagnosis, such that those who were within the first 6 months of diagnosis reported strong unmet information needs for self-care during treatment while those who were diagnosed for more than a year had unmet supportive care needs for psychological support and communication. Patients who were diagnosed with cancer within a 0–6 months' time frame wanted to know more about the self-care behaviours they could engage in so as to "fight" cancer. Patients shared that cancer information, especially the "do's and don'ts", was available from such a variety of sources and was so compelling that they felt overwhelmed and confused. Dysregulation in the availability and consumption of information often from unauthenticated sources left patients feeling overstimulated which, in turn, exacerbated their fears about "cancer winning over me". Interestingly, patients reported receiving conflicting self-care information from the internet and their physician, thus challenging their trust ("what information to believe") in these sources, suggesting that patients did not differentiate between their physician and "other" sources.

> Sometimes the internet also gives information, but it also gives the wrong information. Sometimes, the internet says 100% - like I have read on the internet that says, "Don't eat any sweets, sugar items." The only things I can take is carrots and green apples. For diabetic also, it says not to take any fruits, or take any juices [pauses]. Nothing, because, cancer cells feed only on sugar, and if I take a dose of sugar, that needs a one-month extension of cancer again. That is what I had read on the internet. But doctors are telling me to take only fresh fruits and juices so, I don't know whom to believe, I will believe the doctor who is giving me the treatment but, at times, the internet also says otherwise ...
>
> *52 years, female, colon cancer, 3 months since diagnosis*

Patients who received their cancer diagnosis more than a year ago felt the strongest unmet needs in relation to getting psychological support and communication. Having spent "quite some time running around hospitals", patients in this group felt they were "losing hope" and "struggled" to stay "brave". All the patients wanted to "return to normal life" and kept asking their physician about when they would be "released" from the hospital. Patients who were diagnosed with cancer for more than a year found it particularly difficult as they were becoming unsure whether they were going to live or die – and perceived their physician to be incapable of understanding this frustration. Further complicating their feelings, the prolonged treatment timeline led some patients to feel despondent as they believed they were depleting the family's financial resources. Although their family/friends reassured them not to worry about the expenses of cancer treatment, the patients felt bereft of "someone who I can discuss my worries for my family". Indeed, patients said that they did not feel particularly satisfied or supported when they shared their feelings of despair, depression, stress, or frustration with their family/friends, clearly identifying that these aspects of their care should be met by a healthcare professional who was unrelated to their social circle.

> Stress means what I will have now at this moment. I will get stress, depression, why is it? For almost two years, I thought about this. I am stuck in the middle, I am not dying and not getting cured so whatever it may be after the treatment completes, if it cures, I would like to be stress-free. The problem is that I have no one – who can I tell now about all this stress I'm taking?
>
> *44 years, male, lymphoma, 1 year since diagnosis*

That was my feeling, but people say you should spend for yourself, but it depends. Human thought is different from each other. My father when he left us, he gave us good property or money. So, what I feel is [pause] I am melting all that I have and leave my children with nothing, and it hurts me [pause]. I spend on these medicines and all, I feel like that. If it gets cured, I will have a chance, but if not? [pause] I used to think like that, but people say, "We don't know the future, that, if you take care, you can pick-up your life again." Still, until now, I have spent around 15-20 lakhs on my treatment. If this continues and I die, what will I leave for my children? No one talks to me about that.

44 years, male, lymphoma, 1 year since diagnosis

Recognising that their treating physician may neither have the time nor "*bandwidth*" to address these needs, patients in this group believed their psychological care and communication needs could be met by allied healthcare professionals (e.g., counsellors, social workers). Interestingly, this realisation (i.e., an allied healthcare professional can help with their supportive care needs) came to patients during the course of the interview. That is, patients discovered that they felt emotionally "lighter" upon responding to the questions the first author asked as they were personal, exploring private aspects of the lived experience which so far no one had asked them. Having realised that they felt "refreshed" via the interview, patients shared their opinions on how their concerns, information needs, and doubts could be addressed in a similar way by an allied healthcare professional, thus "removing all my worries and giving me much self-confidence".

In the hospitals, yeah, I think this kind of discussion will definitely help. As for how we are now discussing, I am surprised too, you know, to know this. Such research and discussions like this, I never knew about this. I don't have the knowledge, and this will definitely help the patient — this kind of interaction with people like you. You need not be a psychiatrist, but even a counsellor, general counsellor also, would have been much helpful. Exchanging opinions, as it is… these kinds of discussions I can't do it with my family members, they won't ask me these questions. So, I don't feel like answering them [laughs]. This kind of counselling must be there in every treatment not only for cancer. Every hospital, every treatment, it would be definitely help.

58 years, male, lung cancer, 1 year 6 months since diagnosis

Since the doctor is busy he may not look after all the patients. For example, you came. Why did you come? Like you, if there are counsellors, they can explain how it is since they will have disease-related knowledge and can explain it. They can build the patients' confidence level. For example, if I have a doubt, "Why do I have this and what is happening to me...?"

44 years, male, lymphoma, 1 year since diagnosis

Discussion

The current study explored the unmet needs of Indian cancer patients across different time-points of their cancer trajectory. Patients across the cancer journey in the current study reported unmet needs for information in relation to the cause of their illness and treatment (type and side effects). Attributing a logical cause to their cancer diagnosis was paramount and a persistent need for the patients. When this need was unmet, which was frequently reported by the patients, they attempted at seeking an explanation through unauthenticated sources (e.g., the internet). Further, patients revealed that they were able to connect their physical symptoms of cancer to their diagnosis retrospectively, thereby feeling all the more helpless when their attempts to bridge the knowledge gap between illness causation and cancer symptoms were thwarted by their physician. Inaccurate or low levels of causal understanding of cancer also led patients in this study to experiencing negative cognitions such as fatalistic thinking, self-blame, and cognitive distortions. These findings suggest that (i) understanding of causal attributions of cancer is an ongoing and ubiquitous need (Barbhuiya, 2021), (ii) delays in diagnosis, mediated by poor symptoms recognition, may be linked to low awareness of cancer causes (Pati et al., 2013), and (iii) unaddressed need for authenticated causal understandings of cancer may have strong negative repercussions for the patients' mental health.

Similarities in all patients' unmet needs were also observed in terms of preparing for the treatment type and side effects, which are in line with existing research in India (Asthana et al., 2019; Maurya et al., 2019). Patients who were unprepared for a type of treatment (e.g., a radical mastectomy instead of a lumpectomy), or for negative/strong side effects, reported a myriad of psychological outcomes (e.g., negative self-talk, worthlessness, fear, depression). Research suggests that information needs throughout the treatment trajectory and beyond are important predictors of distress (Dyson et al., 2012; Wang et al., 2018). Therefore, for patients in the current study, the long-term ramifications of the unmet need for treatment-related information may be psychological morbidity, treatment abandonment, and poor quality of life.

Dissimilarities were observed mainly among patients who were diagnosed between 0 and 6 months ago and those who were diagnosed for more than a year. It is possible that those diagnosed between 7 and 12 months were able to process and settle into their treatment regimen, were hopeful, had the necessary social and financial reserves for their care, and identified adequate resources within the hospital system (e.g., Matsuyama et al., 2013). However, for patients who were early in the treatment trajectory, finding and harnessing reliable sources of information may be an active and arduous process (Chen et al., 2010; Halkett et al., 2009). This may be especially difficult in terms of self-care, as was shown in the current study since there are multiple yet unverified sources of information regarding this aspect of cancer care (Blanch-Hartigan et al., 2014; Nagler et al., 2010). A novel finding, however, was that patients in this study reported feeling confused by the discrepancies in the advice/information shared by these sources and their physicians. These findings challenge existing research in India wherein patients viewed their physicians as the expert in cancer care (Chawak et al., 2020). There may be several reasons for these conflicting findings: (i) patients in the present study may not have established a rapport yet with their physician due to the recency of the time since their diagnosis, (ii) the other information sources may be persuasive and convincing, (iii) the responses of the physician may not be to the patients' satisfaction, and (iv) the patients may have wanted to be more actively involved in their cancer care than the physician was aware of.

On the other hand, patients in the current study who were diagnosed with cancer for more than a year had unmet psychological and communication needs. Corroborating with the existing literature (Manuprasad et al. 2019; Maurya et al., 2019), patients felt isolated, despondent, and restless to be cured (i.e., for the treatment to be successfully completed) and looked to a healthcare professional to address these psychological needs. Interestingly, patients observed that their psychological distress was reduced through the interview process, thus identifying the unmet need for communication. Sentient to the strained resources available to the physician, patients were open to receiving communication support through allied healthcare professionals. Strengthening this view, psycho-oncology research has repeatedly evidenced that patients' psychological and communication needs can be addressed by allied healthcare professionals such as psycho-oncologists, patient navigators, and social workers (Natale-Pereira et al., 2011).

Implications

Taken together, these study findings underscore the need for communication skills training for both patients and their physicians. Skills for patients can include introducing and training patients to use communication aids such as the Question Prompt List (QPL; Chawak et al., 2021). A QPL is a checklist of questions a patient can refer to before attending their medical consultation, thus structuring the consult and helping patients discuss the issues which were most important/pressing for them. Skills for physicians can include empathic communication (Banerjee et al., 2021) which focuses on encouraging communication, observing patients' verbal and non-verbal cues for care needs, eliciting more discussions on these needs, and responding to these needs through constructive, informative, patient-centred dialogues.

Individual findings indicate that patients will/have a persistent lack of information regarding the causes and the treatment type and side effects. Therefore, early intervention by providing patients with ample, accessible, and verified information on these topics will be beneficial. Information can be provided in the form of pamphlets, kiosks, booklets, and the hospital website. Indeed, since these needs were the same for patients from across different timelines in the cancer journey, resources spent in this regard may not be in vain.

Patients who were diagnosed with cancer for no longer than 6 months had unmet needs for information on self-care. Physicians/hospital systems can empower these patients by referring them to allied healthcare professionals such as nutritionists, physiotherapists, and psycho-oncologists who can, in turn, equip them with more information on how to optimally self-manage during the cancer treatment. Patients who were diagnosed with cancer for more than a year had unmet supportive care needs (psychological and communication), indicating that they might experience psychological morbidity. It is important to provide targeted and tailored psychological support for these patients by training physicians on distress identification and early referrals, appointing and training psycho-oncologists who can address the psychological effects of long-term care, and introducing patient support groups in the hospital.

Limitations

This study used a qualitative methodology, and although it allowed for an in-depth and nuanced understanding of the lived experiences of the unmet needs, the small sample size did not provide a wider examination of these needs. Given the family-centred approach to cancer care (Chittem et al., 2021), more detail is required in exploring caregivers' unmet needs as this may have bearing on the patients' experiences. Finally, this study used a cross-sectional design, and a longitudinal design might help trace any changes in the patients' needs over time.

Conclusion

This study documented the unmet needs of Indian cancer patients at different time-points in the cancer trajectory. The findings revealed that patients, irrespective of where they were located in the care continuum, had unmet needs for causal attributions and treatment-related information (type and side effects). Patients who were diagnosed with cancer between 0 and 6 months reported unmet needs for self-care information whilst receiving treatment. Patients who were diagnosed for more than a year reported unmet supportive care needs (psychological and communication). These findings highlight the need to introduce communication skills training for patients and physicians alike in order to elicit and address the former's unmet needs. Additionally, providing easily accessible and authenticated informational support on causes and treatment will be beneficial to patients. Finally, the findings underscore that appointing trained allied healthcare professionals, particularly psycho-oncologists, can help alleviate and address patients' unmet self-care and supportive care needs.

Note

1 We considered the time since diagnosis to identify how far along patients were in the cancer trajectory since this forms the official beginning of this journey.

References

Asthana, S., Bhatia, S., Dhoundiyal, R., Labani, S. P., Garg, R., & Bhatnagar, S. (2019). Quality of life and needs of the Indian advanced cancer patients receiving palliative care: Assessment of the quality of life, problems, and needs of the advanced cancer patient receiving palliative care. *Cancer Research, Statistics, and Treatment*, 2(2), 138.

Banerjee, S. C., Haque, N., Bylund, C. L., Shen, M. J., Rigney, M., Hamann, H. A., ... & Ostroff, J. S. (2021). Responding empathically to patients: A communication skills training module to reduce lung cancer stigma. *Translational Behavioral Medicine*, 11(2), 613–618.

Barbhuiya, F. (2021). Causal health attributes and beliefs of tobacco-related cancer patients in Assam, India. *Journal of Psychosocial Oncology*, https://doi.org/10.1080/07347332.2021.1899354

Beer, D. W. (1997). "There's a certain slant of light": The experience of discovery in qualitative interviewing. *Occupational Therapy Journal of Research*, 17, 110–129.

Blanch-Hartigan, D., Blake, K. D., & Viswanath, K. (2014). Cancer survivors' use of numerous information sources for cancer-related information: Does more matter? *Journal of Cancer Education*, 29(3), 488–496.

Chawak, S., Chittem, M., Butow, P., & Huilgol, N. (2020). Indian cancer patients' needs, perceptions of, and expectations from their support network: A qualitative study. *Journal of Cancer Education*, 35(3), 462–469.

Chawak, S., Chittem, M., Maya, S., Dhillon, H. M., & Butow, P. N. (2021). The Question-prompt list (QPL): Why it is needed in the Indian oncology setting? *Cancer Reports*, 4(2), e1316.

Chen, S. C., Yu, W. P., Chu, T. L., Hung, H. C., Tsai, M. C., & Liao, C. T. (2010). Prevalence and correlates of supportive care needs in oral cancer patients with and without anxiety during the diagnostic period. *Cancer Nursing*, 33(4), 280–289.

Chittem, M., Maya, S., & Chawak, S. (2021). Nondisclosure of a cancer diagnosis and prognosis: Recommendations for future research and practice. *Indian Journal of Cancer*, 58(2), 158.

Chittem, M., Norman, P., & Harris, P. (2020). Primary family caregivers' reasons for disclosing versus not disclosing a cancer diagnosis in India. *Cancer Nursing*, 43(2), 126–133.

Datta, S. S., Tripathi, L., Varghese, R., Logan, J., Gessler, S., Chatterjee, S., ... & Menon, U. (2017). Pivotal role of families in doctor–patient communication in oncology: A qualitative study of patients, their relatives and cancer clinicians. *European Journal of Cancer Care*, 26(5), e12543.

Doyle, S. (2012). Reflexivity and the capacity to think. *Qualitative Health Research*, https://doi.org/10.1177/1049732312467854

Dyson, G. J., Thompson, K., Palmer, S., Thomas, D. M., & Schofield, P. (2012). The relationship between unmet needs and distress amongst young people with cancer. *Supportive Care in Cancer*, 20(1), 75–85.

Finlay, L. (2002). "Outing" the researcher: The provenance, process, and practice of reflexivity. *Qualitative Health Research*, https://doi.org/10.1177%2F104973202129120052

Halkett, G. K. B., Kristjanson, L. J., Lobb, E., O'driscoll, C., Taylor, M., & Spry, N. (2009). Meeting breast cancer patients' information needs during radiotherapy: What can we do to improve the information and support that is currently provided? *European Journal of Cancer Care*, 19(4), 538–547.

Holloway, I., & Biley, F. (2011). Being a qualitative researcher. *Qualitative Health Research*, *21*, 968–975, https://doi.org/10.1177/1049732310395607

Kleinsasser, A. M. (2000). Researchers, reflexivity, and good data: Writing to unlearn. *Theory into Practice*, https://doi.org/10.1207/s15430421tip3903_6

Manuprasad, A., Raghavan, V., Kumar, S. P. B., Raj, Z., Shenoy, P. K., & Nair, C. K. (2019). Unmet need in patients with multiple myeloma-a cross sectional study from India. *Oncology and Radiotherapy*, *1*(46), 90–94.

Matsuyama, R. K., Kuhn, L. A., Molisani, A., & Wilson-Genderson, M. C. (2013). Cancer patients' information needs the first nine months after diagnosis. *Patient Education and Counseling*, *90*(1), 96–102.

Maurya, P. B., Sadanandan, A., Aal, M., Ravi, S., & Bapsy, P. P. P. (2019). 427P - Sahai: A restorative support to address unmet needs of women with cancer–impact on quality of life. *Annals of Oncology*, *30*, ix142.

Maya, S., Banerjee, S. C., Chawak, S., Parker, P. A., Kandikattu, S., & Chittem, M. (2021). Oncologists' experience with discussing cancer prognosis with patients and families: perspectives from India. *Translational Behavioral Medicine*, ibab070, https://doi.org/10.1093/tbm/ibab070

Nagler, R. H., Romantan, A., Kelly, B. J., Stevens, R. S., Gray, S. W., Hull, S. J., ... & Hornik, R. C. (2010). How do cancer patients navigate the public information environment? Understanding patterns and motivations for movement among information sources. *Journal of Cancer Education*, *25*(3), 360–370.

Natale-Pereira, A., Enard, K. R., Nevarez, L., & Jones, L. A. (2011). The role of patient navigators in eliminating health disparities. *Cancer*, *117*(S15), 3541–3550.

Pati, S., Hussain, M. A., Chauhan, A. S., Mallick, D., & Nayak, S. (2013). Patient navigation pathway and barriers to treatment seeking in cancer in India: A qualitative inquiry. *Cancer Epidemiology*, *37*(6), 973–978.

Smith, J. A., & Osborn, M. (2015). Interpretative phenomenological analysis as a useful methodology for research on the lived experience of pain. *British Journal of Pain*, *9*(1), 41–42.

Smith, J. A., & Osborn, M. (2004). Interpretative phenomenological analysis. In: Breakwell, G. M. (Ed.), *Doing Social Psychology Research* (pp. 229–254). Blackwell Publishing, England.

Wang, T., Molassiotis, A., Chung, B. P. M., & Tan, J. Y. (2018). Unmet care needs of advanced cancer patients and their informal caregivers: a systematic review. *BMC Palliative Care*, *17*(1), 1–29.

INDEX

Note: Locators in *italics* represent figures and **bold** indicate tables in the text.

ABC *see* active bleeding control (ABC)
Aboriginals 86
Abraham, A. M. 13
Accredited Social Health Activists (ASHAs) 34, 50
acculturation strategies: coexistence 88; ethnic group relations 88; increased intercultural contact 88; industrialization and urbanization 87–88; influence on physical health *see* physical health; modernization tradition 87; stress and influence on mental health *see* mental health
active bleeding control (ABC) 67–68
addiction restriction **134**, 136
Adejoh, S. O. 106
adherence behaviour 127; Adherence Behaviour Scale **133**; dimensions of 127, 138; factors of low adherence behaviour 128; issue of 128; for PA 132–135, **134**; secondary prevention practice or compliance behaviour 127; *see also* coronary artery disease (CAD)
Adivasi communities: acculturation *see* acculturation strategies; groups 86; health problems 88–89; hunting-gathering group 87; irrigation agricultural group 87; promoting health literacy 94–95; rudimentary agricultural group 87; urban, industrial wage-earning group 87

affect 6, 8–9, 17–18, 74, 172
Agarwal, R. P. 17
Ahlawat, R. 16
air pollution 55
Ajzen, I. 117
Alabaster, G. 82
Allen, K. 138
Alma Ata Declaration of 1978 43
Almerud, S. 196
AMOS version 20 77
ancient health care practice 3
Anderson, J. C. 77
Andrew, A. 10, 147
'anusoochitjanjati' *see* Scheduled Tribes (ST)
anxiety 9, 11, 16, 98, 118, 193; CABG experienced 12, 118–122; in cancer patients 17–18; CBT 14; epidemiologic studies 99; helplessness 74–75; in ICU patients 195–196, 198–200, 202; management 4; role of perceived social support 12; yoga 7
arthritis: medication adherence 137; psychosocial factors 14–15; rheumatoid arthritis 14, 161; symptoms 14; in women 89
Ary, D. 146
Asthana, S. 206
asthma: demographic factors 15; and depression 16; National Survey Sample (NSS) 15–16; parents of children 7; psychosocial factors 15–16

atherosclerosis 116, 118
Auxiliary Nurse Midwives (ANMs) 50
Awasthi, P. 93
Ayurveda 3, 43, 49
"Ayushman Bharat" 44
Ayush Registered Practitioners in India 49

Baker, C. 198
Behavioural Cardiology 4, 9
behavioural change 8–9, 11, 66, 107, 144–145, 174
Behavioural Diabetology 4
Below Poverty Line (BPL) families 44
Bhore Committee Report of 1946 43
Biglan, A. 146
Bill & Melinda Gates Foundation 66
Biopsychosocial Model (BPS) 26–27, 193–194
Birmingham, W. C. 172
blood pressure (BP) readings 10, 27–28, 55, 92, 117, 122, 127, 143, 179, 197, 201
Boro, B. 90
BP see blood pressure (BP) readings
BPS see Biopsychosocial Model (BPS)
Braun, V. 130
Briani, R. V. 15

CABG see cardiac bypass surgery (CABG)
CAD see coronary artery disease (CAD)
cancer 7; anxiety in 17–18; attributions and treatment information 210–214; caregiver burden 17–18; of cervix 90; nondisclosure 206; palliative treatment 206; PBCR among children 6; psychosocial interventions 17–18, 200; recurrence 206; unmet information needs for self-care 214–217, 219
cardiac bypass surgery (CABG): anxiety and depression 118–119; biopsychosocial ecosystem of care 123, **123**; cardiac rehabilitation 116–117; educational intervention 121; existing psychological support provisions 120–122; music therapy 122; perceived social support 119–120; planning psychosocial intervention 122–123; psycho-behavioural management 116; psychosocial influences on experiences and outcomes 118–120; randomised controlled trial 121; technique of relaxation 122; use of guided imagery 122
cardiac rehabilitation (CR): DREAM 117; MCT 12; patients' physical activity 116; prevalence 116–117; principal limitation 117; TPB-based letter 117
cardiovascular diseases (CVD): illness perception 128; psychological factors 9; psychosocial factors 8–12; risk factors 55; stress 9
caregiver burden 17–18
CBT see cognitive behaviour therapy (CBT)
Census Report 2011 7
Centers for Disease Control and Prevention 29
Centrally Sponsored Schemes (CSS) 42, 44
Centre for Health Psychology 6
cesarean section (CS) rates in Telangana 64–66
Chadha Committee 45
Champion, V. L. 101
Chandrababu, R. 121
Chaudhury, S. 118
Chavare, S. 15
CHD see coronary heart diseases (CHD)
Chelli, K. 13
Chivukula, U. 12, 120, 201
Choutagunta, A. 45
chronic diseases 6–7, 19, 120, 144, 161, 185
chronic kidney disease (CKD) 16, 55
chronic pain 7, 128
Chutka, D. S. 32
CKD see chronic kidney disease (CKD)
Clarke, V. 130
Claude, J. J. A. 102
Clinical Psychology 19
cognitive behaviour therapy (CBT) 7, 13–14, 18
cognitive degeneration 7
College of Physicians and Surgeons (CPS) 49
Common-Sense Model (CSM) 161, 177
communicable diseases 30, 41, 43, 54–55, 159
communication in health care: from biomedical to biopsychosocial paradigms of diseases 26–27; communal 30; defined 29; doctor-patient communication 30–32; in Indian health care system 32–35; informational 30; interpersonal health communication 30, 35; intrapersonal communication 30, 35; limitations 25–26; management of NCDs 27–29; one-to-one communication 25; organisational health

communication 30; social control 30; WHO fact sheet 27
Community Assisted & Financed Eyecare 63
Community-Based Health Insurance (CBHI) 62–63
Community-Directed Interventions (CDI) 61–62
Community health 18–19
Community Health Centres (CHCs) 33
Community Health Psychology 19
Compliance Scale for Hypertensive Patients 148
Comprehensive Health Enhancement Support System (CHESS) 18
Comprehensive Mental Health Action Plan in 2013 43
Comprehensive Primary Health Care (CPHC) 44
Confirmatory Factor Analysis (CFA) 130
Contributions of Health Psychology 19
Corbin, J. M. 178
Coronary Artery Bypass Surgery (CABG) 11–12
Coronary Artery Disease (CAD) 115; addiction restriction **134**, 136; adherence behaviour 127–128, **133**; analysis, qualitative/quantitative 130; data collection 130; diet adherence **134**, 135–136; dimensions of treatment control 138; illness perception 128; inquiry, qualitative/quantitative 130; medication adherence **134**, 136–137; method 128–130; PA, adherence for 132–135, **134**; patients' emotional response 137–138; qualitative study 129; quantitative study 129, **131**, 131–132; reflexivity 129; research design 128; results **131**, 131–137
Coronary Heart Diseases (CHD) 9
Corporate Social Responsibility (CSR) activities 46
Costa, E. 16
COVID-19 pandemic 25, 30, 63
CR *see* cardiac rehabilitation (CR)
crowding: and adverse health outcomes 73; and helplessness 74; residential *see* residential crowding; and subjective well-being *see* subjective well-being
CVD *see* cardiovascular diseases (CVD)

DALYs *see* disability-adjusted life years (DALYs)
Deci, E. L. 145
Deen, J. 82

Dellby, U. 28
Delmar, C. 196
depression 7, 17–18, 98; CABG 11–12, 118–121, 123; in cancer patients 214–215, 217; caregiver 18; in CKD patients 16; in ICU patients 193, 195–196, 198–199; management 4; psychological factors 9
"Deworm the World" 62
Diabetes Atlas (2019) report 28
Diabetes mellitus (DM) 7; age-adjusted comparative prevalence 12–13; among 10–19 years age group children 6; consequences of 98–99; death rate 98; gestational diabetes 99; HbA1c levels 13–14; life expectancy 159; life-threatening diseases 98; management 14; prevalence of 159–160; psychosocial risk and protective variables 160; QOL of *see* quality of life (QOL) of diabetic patients; research findings 13; self-efficacy 13; self-management *see* diabetes self-management; T1DM *see* type 1 diabetes mellitus (T1DM); T2DM *see* type 2 diabetes mellitus (T2DM)
Diabetes Qol measure (DQOL) 164
diabetes self-management: barriers to 186–187; facilitating factors 185–186; illness perceptions 184–185; implications 187–188; interviews 181; measures 180–181; method 178–179; multiple regression analysis (phase I) 181–183, **182**; participants 179, **179**; procedure 181; psychosocial interventions 187–188; results 181; self-care behaviours 178; themes and sub-themes (phase II) 183, **183–184**
Diabetes Self-Management Questionnaire (DSMQ) 180–181
diet adherence 130, **133–134**, 138; losing taste in food 135; misconception 135; role of family 135–136; *see also* coronary artery disease (CAD)
Diffusion of Innovation model 30
digital management information system (MIS) 63
Diplomate of the National Board (DNB) 49
Directly Observed Treatment, Short-Course (DOTS) – TB strategy 60
Disability-Adjusted Life Years (DALYs) 35, 54, 115
disease management 29
Disease Management Association of America (DMMA) 29

Index

District Health Society (DHS) 61
District Hospitals 33
DM *see* Diabetes Mellitus (DM)
Doctorate of Medicine (MD) 48, 50
'doctor-control' 90
Doctor of Medicine (DM) 48
doctor-patient communication: accuracy of diagnosis 32; challenges 34; disease prognosis 32; elements 31; health insurance 34; impact of effective communication 31; patient satisfaction 32; patient's clinical consultation participation 34; patient's trust 31–32; therapeutic adherence 32; therapeutic relationship 30–31
DQOL *see* Diabetes Qol measure (DQOL)
DREAM (Diet, Relaxation, Exercise, Attitude and Motivation) 117
DSMQ *see* Diabetes Self-Management Questionnaire (DSMQ)
Dunn, H. 197

Eighth Five-Year Plan 43
Emergency Medical and Research Institute (EMRI) 67
emotion-focused intervention 18
Engelgau, M. M. 57
Engel, G. L. 26, 193
Epstein, R. S. 28
Evans, G. 73
Everson-Rose, S. A. 9
Evidence-Based Health Care (EBHC) 4; enhancing health and well-being for individuals and society 18–19; NCD, psychosocial factors in *see* non-communicable diseases (NCDs); studies on paediatric and geriatric sample 5–7
evidence-based medicine 4, 19
evidence-based nursing 4
evidence-based psychiatry 4
evidence-based treatment model 19
existential behaviour therapy 18

First Peoples 86
Fitter, M. 102
Five-Year Plans 43

gastrointestinal system 7
Gerbing, D. W. 77
geriatric population 7
geriatric sample 5–7
gestational diabetes 99; *see also* Diabetes mellitus (DM)
Glasgow, R. E. 102

Global Adult Tobacco Survey (GATS) 138
goodness of fit (GOF) measures 78
Graham, I. D. 55
Graham's Knowledge to Action Framework 55
gross domestic product (GDP) 45, 47, **47**
Guided Imagery 11
Gupta, P. 108, 201

Hariharan, M. 3, 11, 100, 122, 147
Harris, M. L. 14
Harvey, J. N. 13
HBM *see* Health Belief Model (HBM)
Health and Wellness Centres (HWCs) 44
Health Belief Model (HBM): demographic details 100; health beliefs questionnaire 102; preventive health behaviours 100, 106–107; scale 101; sick-role behaviours 100; visit clinics 100
health care, defined 3
health care economics, defined 28
healthcare system 42; and disease management 32–35; primary tier 47; secondary tier 47; tertiary tier 47
health communication 29
Health Management Information Systems (HMIS) 51
health policymaking 42–51; health financing 46–47; "Health for all by 2000 AD" 43; human resources 49–50; infrastructure 47–49, **48**; other policies and programmes 44–46; traditional forms 42–43
Health Psychology 4, 19, 115
Health-Related QoL (HRQoL) 161
Hessler, D. 162
high blood pressure *see* hypertension
HMIS *see* Health Management Information Systems (HMIS)
Holt-Lunstad, J. 172
Homeopathy 43, 49
HRQoL *see* Health-Related QoL (HRQoL)
Human Development Index (HDI) 41
Human Resource for Health (HRH) 49
hypertension: blood pressure (BP) readings 10, 143; face-to-face knowledge intervention 10–11; form and frequency of exposure 10; high prevalence and asymptomatic nature 11; patient comprehension of doctor's communication 10; in school-going children, India 6; statistics, India 9
Hypertension Knowledge Test 147–148

hypertension management: belief barrier 144; BP Reading 148; children as agents of change in 144–146; Compliance Scale for Hypertensive Patients 148; development of research design 146; discussion 153–154; Hypertension Knowledge Test 147–148; Hypertension Monitoring Record Booklet 148; hypotheses 146; implications 154; intervention for children 149; limitation 154; method 147; notice of 'drug holidays' 143; objectives 146; participants 147; procedure 148–149; psychological tools 147–148; recall barrier 144; recruitment of sample 147; results 149–153, **150–151,152,***153*; role of health psychologist 149

Hypertension Monitoring Record Booklet 148
Hypothalamic Pituitary Axis (HPA) 8

ICU *see* Intensive Care Unit (ICU)
ICU acquired weakness (ICUAW) 195
illness cognition 13, 138
illness perception 177; CAD *see* Coronary Artery Disease (CAD); and diabetes self-management *see* diabetes self-management; health outcomes 128; and QOL of diabetic patients *see* Quality Of Life (QOL) of diabetic patients; timeline cyclic 138
Illness Perception Questionnaire-Revised (IPQ-R) version 130, 163–164
implementation research 54–59, *56*, *57*; *see also* Low-Middle-Income Countries (LMICs)
In-Depth Interviews (IDIs) 59
Indian Council of Medical Research (ICMR) 54
Indian Diabetes Risk Score 63
Indian federalism 45
India's National Rural Health Mission 25
India's Pradhan Mantri Ujjwala Yojana program 58
Indigenous Peoples 86
inflammatory bowel disease 7
insomnia 7
Institute for Health Metrics and Evaluation (IHME) 54
intellectual functioning 7
Intensive Care Unit (ICU): changing environment to reduce stressors 201–203; defined 194; dependency as outcome 195–196; distal context of patient 194; external indicators of illness 193; ICU delirium 198–199; ICU trauma 199; impact on patient 195, 198; maintaining quality 200–201; physical and psychological outcomes 195–199; proximal context of patient 194; psychosocial care and its implication 199–203; sensory alteration 198; stressors triggered 196–197, **197**

internal locus of control 15
International Diabetes Federation (IDF) reports 12, 177
International Union Against TB and Lung Disease (IULTD) 60
Interpretative Phenomenological Analysis (IPA) *209*; analysis 208–209; cancer attributions and treatment information 211–214; demographic and medical information 207, **208**; findings 217; flow chart of themes *210*; implications 218–219; interviews 207–208; interview topics and sample questions **209**; limitations 219; method 207–210; participant information 207; procedure 207; reflexivity 209–210; results 210–217; similarities and dissimilarities 217–218; types of unmet needs 214–217
IPA *see* Interpretative Phenomenological Analysis (IPA)
Ischemic Heart Disease 27

Joint Commission International (JCI) 200–201
Journal of American Heart Association 9

Kandpal, V. 91
Kapoor, D. 92
Kasthuri, A. 34
Kedia, S. K. 18
Key Informant Method (KIM) 59–60
Khan, W. A. 16
Knudsen, J. 82
Kol, E. 201
Krishna, M. 172
Kumar, P. 172

Lady Health Visitors 50
Lalnuntluangi, R. 13
Law, E. 6
learned helplessness: correlation analysis 78; and crowding 74; measurement model analysis 78; mediating role of 75; *see also* crowding; subjective well-being
Learned helplessness scale 76
Leventhal, E. A. 128

Index **227**

Leventhal, H. 128
Lewis, T. T. 9
liberalisation, privatisation and globalisation (LPG) 43
lifestyle diseases *see* non-communicable diseases (NCDs)
Light, K. C. 172
Likert-type response patterns 76
LMICs *see* Low-Middle-Income Countries (LMICs)
Low-Middle-Income Countries (LMICs): active bleeding control (case study) 67–68; Community-Based Health Insurance (initiative) 62–63; Community-Directed Interventions (initiative) 61–62; DOTS – TB (initiative) 60; implementation research 54–59, 56; Key Informant Method (initiative) 59–60; National Rural Health Mission (initiative) 60–61; nutrient-containing micro-needles (case study) 66–67; RE-AIM framework 58; reasons for high CS rates in Telangana (case study) 64–66; theoretical approaches 57; tribal health in Telangana (case study) 67
Luhar, S. 159
L. V. Prasad Eye Institute, Hyderabad 63
Lykkegaard, K. 196

MacQueen, G. 16
Makoul, G. 31
Manuprasad, A. 206
Maroko-Afek, A. 17
Master of Chirurgiae (MCh) 48
Masters in Surgery (MS) 48, 50
Maurya, P. B. 206
McKinley, S. 196
Mean Arterial Pressure (MAP) 152
measurement model analysis: for learned helplessness 78; structural model 79–80; for subjective well-being 78
Mectizan Donation Program 62
Medical Colleges and Research Institutions 33
Medical Council of India 49
medical gaze 26
medical tourism 4
medication adherence 134; financial constraints 137; role of family members 136; and side effects 137; *see also* Coronary Artery Disease (CAD)
medicine, exercise, and diet (MED) 148
meditation 7, 15
Medium Human Development 42

mental health 7, 92–94; behavioural shifts 93; coexistence and integration 93; developmental programmes 93–94; minority and majority groups 94; modern approaches 92; socio-economic development 92–93
Meshram, I. I. 91
Meta Cognition Therapy (MCT) 12
Micro-Needles (MNs) 66–67
Millennium Development Goals (MDGs) 41
Ministry of Health and Family Welfare (MoHFW) 33
Mishra, R. C. 86–88, 93–94
Morey, M. C. 138
mortality 9
Moss-Morris, R. 130
Moss, S. 145
motivational interviewing 13
MSntyselkS, P. 107
Mudaliar Committee 45
Mukherjee, M. 93
MUKTI 108
Murphy, B. M. 118
Muthukumaran, A. 16

Nagar, D. 73
Naik, B. N. 107
Nannapaneni, S. 102
Narayan, K. V. 57
National Accreditation Board for Hospitals (NABH) 200
National Cancer Institute 29
National Family Health Survey (NFHS 4) 28
National Health Mission (NHM), 2013 44
National Health Policies (NHPs) 42–43; 2017 43–45, 47, 51; 2002 43–44, 47, 51; 1983 44, 51; 2002 61
National Health Profile 2020 49–50
National Leprosy Eradication Programme 43
National Mental Health Policy 43, 49–50
National Nutrition Policy, 1993 43
National Policy for Rare Diseases, 2021 43
National Program for Prevention and Control of Cancer, Diabetes, Cardiovascular Diseases and Stroke (NPCDCS) 33
National Rural Health Mission (NRHM) 44, 60–61
National TB Elimination Program (NTEP) 60
National Tele Mental Health Programme 50

228 Index

National Tuberculosis Control Programme 43
National Urban Health Mission (NUHM) 25, 44
Native People 86
Naturopathy 49
Natu, S. 15
Negative Relationship (NR) 73–76, 78–82
NHPs see National Health Policies (NHPs)
Nicassio, P. M. 82
Nilsen, P. 57
noise reduction strategies 201
Non-Communicable Diseases (NCDs) 6; aetiology of 27; arthritis 14–15; associated with CVD 8–12; asthma 15–16; for cancer 17–18; in diabetes 12–14; and disease management see health care system; non-adherence rates 34; psychosocial factors 8–18; renal diseases 16–17
Norman, P. 102
Nursing Science 19
nutrition-related diseases 54–55

organ donation 63
Oswell, D. 146
Oumoukelthoum, M. 107
Out-Of-Pocket Spending (OOPS) 42, 46

PA see Physical Activity (PA)
paediatric studies 5, 5–7
Pallant, J. F. 164
Palmer, S. 16
Particularly Vulnerable Tribal Groups (PTVGs), Telangana 67
patient-centred medicine 27
Paulus, P. B. 73
Perceived Control Of Internal States Scale (PCOISS) 164
persons with disabilities (PWD) 59
Peters, D. H. 45
Peterson, P. N. 9
Petriček, G. 138
Physical Activity (PA): adherence for 132–135; see also Coronary Artery Disease (CAD);
low motivation 132–133; misconception 134; replacing with everyday chores 134–135
physical health: chronic conditions 92; culture 89; developmental policies 91; diabetes and obesity 92; and disease profiles 89; doctor-control 90; folk-healing systems 89–90; impact of modernization 91; self-control 90;
social and cultural changes 90–91; sociocultural transformation 91; support systems and coping strategies 90; traditional medicine 91
Polat, E. 202
Polonsky, W. H. 162
Poole, L. 118
Population-Based Cancer Registry (PBCR) 6
Positive Relationship (PR) 73–74, 76, 78–79, 81–82
Post-Traumatic Stress Disorder (PTSD) 198
Primary Health Centres (PHCs) 33, 62
Prime Minister Jan Arogya Yojana (PM-JAY) 44–45
problem-solving therapy 7, 18
Programme for Affective and Cognitive Education (PACE) 11–12, 122
Psychology 29–30
Psycho-Oncology 4
psychosocial factors: arthritis 14–15; asthma 15–16; Cardio Vascular Diseases (CVD) 8–12; NCD see Non-Communicable Diseases (NCDs); renal diseases 16–17
Public Health 19, 29
public health and sanitation, hospitals and dispensaries 42
Public Health Care System 33
Public Health Centres (PHCs) 44
Public Health Foundation of India (PHFI) 54
Purohit, N. 108

QOL see Quality Of Life (QOL) of diabetic patients
Quality Of Life (QOL) of diabetic patients: current study 162–163; diabetes-related worries, case of 167; duration of illness 171; higher secretion of oxytocin 172; illness perception 160–161, 172–173; impact, case of 166; implications 173–174; method 163–165; multiple hierarchical regression analysis **167**, 167–170, **168–171**; participants 163; perceived control of internal states 161–162; predictors of 167–171; procedure 164–165; relationship among measures 165, **166**, 167; research design 163; research instruments 163–164; restrictions in diet 172; results 165–171; satisfaction, case of 166; social and vocational worries, case of 166; worries dimension of 172; see also Diabetes Mellitus (DM)

Question Prompt List (QPL) 218
quiet time implementation 201

Radojevic, V. 82
Ragupathy, A. 9
Rajendran, A. J. 117
Rajhans, P. 15
Rashmi, R. 15
RashtriyaSwasthyaBima Yojana (RSBY) 44–45
RE-AIM framework 58
Registered Nurses and Registered Midwives 50
ReJudge Study 66
renal diseases: CKD *see* Chronic Kidney Disease (CKD); psychosocial factors 16–17
Research in Health Psychology 4
residential crowding: chronic 74; data analysis 77; data collection 77; limitations 82; measurement model analysis 77–80; measures 76–77; method 76; Negative Relationship (NR) 73–76, 78–82; Positive Relationship (PR) 73–74, 76, 78–79, 81–82; Proposed Model 77, 77; results 77; sample 76; space satisfaction (SS) 73–74, 76, 78–82; Uncontrolled Disturbances (UD) 73, 76, 78–82; *see also* crowding
Residential crowding experience Scale 76
Revised Illness Perception Questionnaire (IPQ-R) 180
Revised National TB Control Program (RNTCP) 60
Rohan, J. M. 7
Ryan, R. M. 145

Saikia, N. 90
Samuelson, K. A. M. 195
Sandhu, S. 13
Santosa, A. 9
Savio, M. T. 11, 122
Scheduled Tribes (ST) 86
Scholl, I. 194
Schuman, C. 82
SDG 3C 46, 49
secondary prevention practice or compliance behaviour 127
self-control 90
self-efficacy 185
self-management 178
Seligman, M. E. 74
sensory function degeneration 7
SET *see* Socio-Ecological Theory (SET)
Sharpe, L. 15

Sherwood, L. M. 28
Siddha 43, 49
silent killer *see* hypertension
Silverman, J. D. 31
skin diseases 7
Smokeless Tobacco (SLT) 136
Social Cognitive Theory 30
Social Psychology 30
Social Work 19
Society of Critical Care Medicine (SCCM) 201
Socio-Ecological Theory (SET): community characteristics 108; doctors and healthcare teams 107–108; factors affecting health 100, 107; health promotion education and interventions 108; MUKTI 108
Sociology 29
somatisation 7
Space Satisfaction (SS) 73–74, 76, 78–82
spirituality, religion, prayers, chanting, and meditation 7
Statistical Package for the Social Sciences (SPSS) version 20 130
Strauss, A. 178
strokes 9, 27–28, 33, 35, 115
subjective well-being: crowding and helplessness 74; and crowding, structural model for 79; descriptive statistics, validity measures and correlation coefficients **79**; and helplessness 74–75; measurement model analysis 78; mediating role of helplessness 75; need and significance of study 75–76; standardized regression coefficient **80**; *see also* crowding
Subjective well-being inventory 76
Sustainable Development Goals (SDGs) 36, 51
Swain, S. 10
Sympathetic Nervous System (SNS) activation 8
symptom perception 13

Tao, Z. 74
Taylor-Ford, R. 201
telehealth initiatives 63
terminal illness 6
Theory of Planned Behaviour (TPB) 30, 102; based letter 117; behavioural and normative beliefs 100, 107; questionnaire 102
TPB *see* Theory of Planned Behaviour (TPB)
traumatic brain injury 7

tribal: communities 86; health in Telangana 67
Turiano, N. A. 162
Type 1 Diabetes Mellitus (T1DM) 13, 99; see also Diabetes Mellitus (DM)
Type 2 Diabetes Mellitus (T2DM): binary logistic regression analysis 104–106; chronic disease resource survey 102; HBM see Health Belief Model (HBM); method 101; multidimensional scale of perceived social support 101–102; participants 101; procedure 102–103; results 103–106; SET see Socio-Ecological Theory (SET); smoking and alcohol 99, **103,105**; tools 101–102; TPB see Theory of Planned Behaviour (TPB); WHO step tools 102; see also Diabetes Mellitus (DM)

Unani 43, 49, 185
uncontrolled diabetes 172
Uncontrolled Disturbances (UD) 73, 76, 78–82
undernutrition 55
union territories (UTs) 42
United Nations Convention on the Rights of the Child (UNCRC) 145
United Nations HDI 2020 42

Universal Health Coverage (UHC) 41, 46
University of Hyderabad 6
Urban Health Mission 61

Vajpayee, A. 94
Van Lieshout, R. J. 16
Verma, T. 7

Wagenaar, A. C. 146
Wainwright, N. W. 15
Wang, J. 161
Wang, Z. 74
Weisman, M. H. 82
well-being 18; defined 18; for individuals and society 18–19; mental 41, 51; subjective see subjective well-being
Wells, A. 12
WHO see World Health Organization (WHO)
World Bank 46
World Health Organization (WHO) 26; 1999 60; 2003 116; Knowledge to Action Framework 55; step tools 102
WSndell, P. E. 172

Yoga 7, 17, 43, 134, 138

Zhang, Z. 18
Zimet, G. D. 101